THE HISTORICAL FICTION OF MORI ŌGAI

鷗外博士
可徳

THE HISTORICAL FICTION OF MORI ŌGAI

edited by
David Dilworth
J. Thomas Rimer

additional contributions by
Richard Bowring
Darcy Murray
Edmund R. Skrzypczak
William R. Wilson

 UNIVERSITY OF HAWAII PRESS · HONOLULU

PL
811
.O 7
A23
1991

UNESCO Collection of Representative Works
Japanese Series

English Translation © UNESCO 1977
Preface to the Paperback Edition
© 1991 University of Hawaii Press

95 96   5 4 3 2

Book Design by Roger J. Eggers

Library of Congress Cataloging-in-Publication Data
Mori, Ōgai, 1862–1922.
[Selections. English. 1991]
The historical fiction of Mori Ōgai / edited by David Dilworth,
J. Thomas Rimer ; additional contributions by Richard Bowring . . .
[et al.]. — [1st ed.]
p.   cm. — (UNESCO collection of representative works.
Japanese series)
ISBN 0–8248–1366–9 (pbk.)
1. Mori, Ōgai, 1862–1922—Translations, English. 2. Japan—
History—1185–1868—Fiction. I. Dilworth, David A., 1934–
II. Rimer, J. Thomas, 1933–   . III. Title. IV. Series.
V. Series: UNESCO collection of representative works. Japanese series.
PL811.O7A23   1991
895.6'342—dc20   91–2350
CIP

The "Second Version" of "Okitsu Yagoemon no isho"; "Takasebune";
"Kanzan Jittoku"; and "Suginohara Shina" were previously published in
Monumenta Nipponica 26, nos. 1 & 2, 1971, and are reprinted here by
courtesy of *Monumenta Nipponica*. "Yasui fujin" was previously published
in *Mori Ōgai zenshū* (Tokyo: Chikuma Shobō, 1971), and is reprinted here
by courtesy of the Mori Ōgai kinenkai.

The frontispiece is adapted from a drawing completed in November 1991
by Hirafuku Hyakusui.

University of Hawai'i Press books are printed on acid-free paper and meet
the guidelines for permanence and durability of the Council on Library
Resources

CONTENTS

PREFACE TO THE PAPERBACK EDITION

ALMOST FIFTEEN YEARS have passed since David Dilworth and I, sharing an enthusiasm for the kinds of literary and cultural insights we discovered in the late works of Mori Ōgai, set out to translate and edit a representative anthology of his historical and literary writings. Ōgai (1862–1922) was one of the finest writers of his period and has remained a towering intellectual presence throughout much of modern Japanese cultural and intellectual history. We were delighted that the translations were well received when they were first published, and we are grateful that the University of Hawaii Press has now decided to make them newly available in a single volume and in paperback form.

In Japan, these late writings of Ōgai have been, in general, the most consistently admired among a large corpus of writing that make up Ōgai's three decades of literary output. When we began this project, we felt that these works, even in translation, might provide a privileged point of access into Ōgai's own complex mentality, one that permitted him to place the problems of his period as he perceived them in the kind of generous intellectual and moral framework that he was able to construct.

Rereading the stories in translation, the introductions, and our own essays, I believe that we still remain committed to the insights and observations we expressed there; as a result, virtually nothing in the earlier edition has been altered.

It might be argued that Ōgai has become less of a force in the new Japan of the 1990s than he was twenty or thirty years ago. During a recent trip to Japan, I noticed that the popular paperback sections of the Tokyo and Kyoto bookstores remain filled with inexpensive editions of a variety of works by Ōgai's great contemporary, the novelist Natsume Sōseki (1867–1916), while only a few of Ōgai's most accessible stories can now be found in such formats. Nevertheless, a few shelves away, the standard multiple-volume set of Ōgai's major works can invariably be found as well. The ascendency—and with such a vengeance—of popular culture in Japan makes a writer and thinker of Ōgai's complexity all the more difficult for a younger generation; after all, his readers must not only possess wide intellectual sympathies but must seek, and respect, a deeper knowledge of cultural insights as well.

Those difficulties do not diminish Ōgai's stature. Indeed, Ōgai's vision of the moral significance of the past for the present remains as suggestive an intellectual model as ever. Ōgai's model would insist that the tension between past and present can open up a channel through which an authentic personal understanding can be forged. As a thinker, he is fully grounded in the problems of our own century. The present generation, both in his culture and in ours, would do well to attempt to repossess his thought, for his insights range far beyond any particular set of specific cultural coordinates. Young writers in Japan have sometimes begun to suggest, in one way or another, that their own cultural past has become for them a kind of foreign country. If that is true, then contemporary readers may well require of themselves an initial act of will in order to enter into the kinds of mental and spiritual worlds represented in these stories, ranging from Tokugawa Japan to ancient China, even when described by Ōgai in such a careful, precise, and as he put it, "Apollonian" fashion.

In a critical essay written about the time of Ōgai's death, the British critic and novelist Vernon Lee, herself a cosmopolitan figure who wrote on Italian art and literature, expressed her conviction that language can serve as a means of an implicit self-understanding: "the real revelation of the writer (as of the artist) comes in a far subtler way than by autobiography; and comes despite all efforts to elude it; . . . for what the writer does communicate is his temperament, his organic personality, with its preferences and aversions, its pace and rhythm and impact and balance, its swiftness of language . . . and this he does equally whether he be rehearsing veraciously his own concerns or inventing someone else's."[1]

Ōgai's own use of language as a means of self-revelation is at once so powerful and subtle that the translator must admit defeat in any attempt to bring alive this kind of particular "revelation" in the borrowed dress of modern English. It remains our hope, however, that whatever the imperfections involved in our recasting of these works, their moral integrity and often austere spirituality can still shine through to the extent that something of the accomplishment of this remarkable thinker and artist may still emerge.

J. THOMAS RIMER

---

[1] Vernon Lee, *The Handling of Words* (New York: Dodd Mead, 1923), 109.

PREFACE TO THE FIRST EDITION

PARALLELING his distinguished career as a medical officer in the Japanese army, Mori Ōgai (1862–1922) became a leading figure of the Japanese literary world in the last two decades of the Meiji period (1868–1912) and the first decade of the Taishō period (1913–1926). His total literary output encompasses a broad range of styles and genres, from diaries, medical essays, works on aesthetics and literary criticism, to biographies, plays, Japanese and Chinese poetry, short stories, and novellas. As a translator of contemporary European literature, Ōgai remains without a peer among his countrymen.

Ōgai's own creative literary works total over 120 titles (mostly short stories and novellas), beginning with *Maihime, Utakata no ki*, and *Fumizukai* written in 1890 and 1891. His final period of creative writing began in 1912 when Ōgai, after the ritual suicide of General Nogi Maresuke, turned to write almost exclusively in the genre of "historical literature." In six years he produced twenty-four works, including five novellas, eleven short stories and short biographies before 1916, and three long and five short biographies between 1916 and 1918. Japanese critics usually cite this phase of Ōgai's output as the most distinctive of his entire career. In this volume and the second of the set, we have attempted to provide the reader with a representative sampling of this material.

The term "historical literature" has been chosen to cover the variety of works Ōgai wrote between 1912 and 1918. For schematic purposes we can say these works fall into two broad classifications, the historical novella (*rekishi shōsetsu*) and the historical biography (*shiden*). But it should be emphasized that Ōgai would probably not have approved of the distinction. His own comments on his final works indicate that he was endeavoring to evolve a medium of literary expression that minimized the distinction between literary and historical elements. Japanese critics have even pointed out that it was often in the "biographical" works that Ōgai pursued an oblique literary "autobiography," and wrought new changes on the themes of his earlier fictional writings.

Recent Japanese anthologies of Ōgai's historical literature have dealt with the problem of arranging his late writings in two ways. The first has been to publish the stories and biographies in purely chronological order. The second approach has been to sort out the more literary pieces from the predominantly biographical ones. While recognizing the degree of arbitrariness this latter approach entails, we have adopted it in these present volumes of translations. But to avoid yet another kind of arbitrariness, we have retained the chronological order of the stories and biographies in each of the volumes.

Ōgai's "historical literature" was the product of a rare mentality that was able to distill aesthetic significance from the historical record. He used the same medium to articulate his final philosophical outlook. The serious student of Ōgai's career, we are convinced, will discover that the "biographical" pieces grouped in volume two are as revealing of his aesthetic and philosophical intentions as the "literary" pieces of volume one.

The editors have felt it in the spirit of Ōgai's own project to annotate his presentation of historical detail. The student of Ōgai's work will again be interested in this aspect of our volumes; but for the convenience of the general reader we have employed a method that does not clutter the pages of the translations with footnotes.

The project of preparing these volumes has been a collaborative effort from its inception, when we began to translate some of the stories together in New York City in 1971. We were joined eventually by Richard Bowring, Darcy Murray, Edmund R. Skrzypczak, and William R. Wilson. Without their timely contributions, in some cases dealing with materials of unusual difficulty, we would not have been able to complete the project in its present form.

Richard Bowring received his doctorate from Cambridge University; his dissertation on Mori Ōgai is being published by Cambridge University Press. His translations of Ōgai's earlier novellas, *Maihime* and *Utakata no ki*, have appeared in *Monumenta Nipponica*. His translation of the first version of "Okitsu Yagoemon no isho" appears here.

Darcy Murray is a graduate student in the Department of East Asian Languages and Cultures, Columbia University. Her translation of Ōgai's *Hannichi* has appeared in *Monumenta Nipponica*. She has contributed the translation of "Rekishi sono mama to rekishibanare" that appears as a commentary upon "Sanshō dayū."

Edmund R. Skrzypczak has contributed the translation of "Takasebune" in volume one, and of "Tsuge Shirōzaemon" in volume two. In addition, while editor of *Monumenta Nipponica*, he worked on the preparation of the originally published translations of "Kanzan Jittoku," the second version of "Okitsu Yagoemon no isho," and "Suginohara Shina," which appears in volume two. All translations appearing in the present volumes, however, are the product of further research and refinement.

William R. Wilson is a well-known translator, whose publications include the *Hōgen monogatari* (Tokyo: Sophia University Press, 1971). His original translation of the second version of "Okitsu Yagoemon no isho" has been reworked in accordance with the editorial policies of the present volumes; his translation of "Saiki Kōi" concludes volume two.

The chief burden of the initial checking of the translations fell upon Yoshiko Inoue Dilworth. Mr. Tetsuya Sawada of the *Monumenta Nipponica* staff collaborated with Edmund Skrzypczak in checking several of the stories. The editors also owe a debt of gratitude to Mr. Katsuhiko Takeda for his painstaking work on the translation of "Yasui fujin," which appeared in *Ōgai* (no. 11, July 1973), published by the Mori Ōgai Kinenkai. The editors, however, assume full responsibility for the accuracy of the present translations.

In addition to the above contributors, many colleagues and students have given generously of their time to read and suggest revisions of parts of the manuscript at various stages of its preparation. We should like especially to thank Professor Thomas E. Swann of Colgate University, who offered detailed suggestions for improving the literary quality of many of the initial translations; Professor Nishitani Keiji, emeritus professor of Kyoto University, who worked on the translation of "Gyogenki"; and Professor Ichirō Shirato of Columbia University for his valuable suggestions in translating key terms.

Finally, we owe a life-long debt of gratitude to Mr. Milton Rosenthal of the Division of Cultural Affairs, UNESCO, Paris, who sponsored our work, was the source of constant encouragement, and saw it through to contractual terms with The University Press of Hawaii.

THE HISTORICAL FICTION OF MORI ŌGAI

THE HISTORICAL LITERATURE OF
MORI ŌGAI: AN INTRODUCTION

DESPITE a lasting reputation in Japan, Mori Ōgai has yet to achieve any satisfactory reception in the West. Natsume Sōseki, the only writer of Ōgai's generation to share his stature, has been widely translated and admired, but Ōgai remains a shadowy figure, austere, even obscure.[1] It often happens, of course, that the work of certain writers cannot be sufficiently understood outside their own cultures. Some towering figures never earn anything like their rightful reputation through translation. One thinks of the French playwright and poet Paul Claudel, whose Catholicism and expansive style have so far prevented any effective linguistic adaptations into an English-speaking, Protestant culture.

Nevertheless, there is much in Ōgai that might well appeal to a Western reader. The nature of his mental world, unlike that of a number of his contemporaries, was overwhelmingly cosmopolitan; indeed, he spent a great deal of time throughout his career translating into Japanese such diverse writers as Goethe (Ōgai's version of *Faust* is still the standard), Ibsen, Strindberg, and Hofmannsthal. In a very real sense the stories presented in this volume can be considered "translations" by Ōgai of historical Japanese and Chinese materials into contemporary terms. Our difficulties in approaching his art may lie elsewhere.

They may originate, for example, in the relatively narrow boundaries set down around the word "literature" in the Anglo-American tradition. For the French, Pascal and Montaigne are literary figures. We might feel more comfortable calling them philosophers. The combination of personal introspection and abstract concepts found in their writings seems somehow outside the scope of our own decorums. They seem both too direct and too obscure. Men like Goethe and Voltaire were permitted sufficient scope within their literary traditions to expand easily from the world of narrative to the world of ideas in their writings. Ōgai, drawing on his own heritage in Chinese and Japanese, was able to do the same. His early training in the Confucian classics, reinforced by his later studies of German literature and culture, gave him a strong sense of the high importance of literature and of the possibility—indeed the necessity—of its use as a means to convey philosophical ideas. Ōgai's work contains little that is "popular." His seriousness of purpose provides from the first a hurdle to those readers who turn to fiction, oriental or occidental, merely for pleasant entertainment. Nevertheless, these stories, read carefully, reveal a depth and precision of observation that goes far beyond the usual kind of romantic fantasy that so often constitutes "historical fiction" in the West.

Our decision to translate a number of Mori Ōgai's historical stories was made in the hope that, by putting the works into a form accessible to the English-speaking reader, we might induce him to share our conviction that there is much to be admired in Ōgai's trenchant observations and deep understanding of human nature, even though the stories operate in a series of peculiar historical situations. Other, earlier works of Ōgai are somewhat simpler and more accessible, but surely the Japanese critics are correct when they single out the works of Ōgai's later years as the very finest and most subtle he produced.[2]

Hasegawa Izumi, a leading Japanese scholar on Ōgai, writes of these later works that

> . . . here one sees Ōgai at his best as a writer, for every phase in his develop-
> ment as an artist and a man is reflected in them: the youth growing up within
> the fatally limited confines of modern Japanese society; the young man under-
> going a thorough process of Westernization; and finally, the aging giant
> adopting a characteristically Oriental approach to life which is best described as
> the philosophy of resignation.[3]

Whether such praise is warranted the reader will ultimately have to decide for himself. Forming judgments on the basis of translated material is hazardous, of course, but if the brilliant precision and striking style of Ōgai's prose cannot be adequately reproduced in English, at least the organization of his artistic material and the general thrust of his thought can be made available.

In order to place the writing of Mori Ōgai's final years in the context of his total work, some background on his earlier years is useful.[4] Mori Ōgai's life (he was born in 1862 and died in 1922) spanned one of the most tumultuous and exciting periods in the history of Japan. With the coming of the Meiji Restoration in 1868, the country was opened to foreign influence after several centuries of enforced isolation during the Tokugawa period (1600–1868). In the literary world, as well as in the spheres of politics, economics, and military strategy, Japan was forced to respond with vigor to vast changes resulting from a fairly intense contact with Western ideas and concepts that were often totally at variance with traditional Japanese views. Ōgai was a major figure in the intellectual life of his time and was involved in some fashion in many of these confrontations.

Mori Rintarō (Ōgai became his pen name) was the son of a doctor to the lord of the Tsuwano clan in the province of Shimane, a remote area on the Japan Sea. At the age of five he began his studies in the traditional fashion and was tutored in Mencius, Confucius, and some of the Japanese classics. His generation was perhaps the last to receive as a matter of course such classical training (roughly equivalent to Greek and Latin in the West). As a result, Ōgai and his contemporaries (Sōseki among them) were cosmopolitan in terms of their knowledge of Chinese literature, and in fact both Sōseki and Ōgai were more than adequate poets in classical Chinese. (Now, as a contemporary Japanese critic remarked, young writers in Japan cannot even read poetry in Chinese, to say nothing of composing it.)

Ōgai, as a promising student, was sent by his clan to Tokyo to pursue his studies. There he lived in the house of the philosopher Nishi Amane (1829–1897). Nishi Amane was one of the first Japanese to leave his country for Europe. After studying at the University of Leyden, he had returned to Japan in 1865 and spent much of the rest of his career introducing Western ideas to Japan. Ōgai seems to have been much influenced by his contact with the older man, and he remained in the household while preparing for his entrance examinations to the medical school of Tokyo University. Later he repaid the Amane family for their kindness by writing the official biography of his host and mentor.

Ōgai was an excellent student at the university. In particular, his proficiency in the German language was increased during his study with the German professors of medicine who had come to Japan to teach modern Western techniques; when he was graduated, in 1881, his chief ambition was to go abroad. He joined the army medical corps at the age of twenty-two and shortly thereafter found himself in Germany, doing research for the Japanese government on advanced techniques of hygiene and military medicine. Ōgai's activities in Germany and his discovery of European literature is a fascinating subject in itself. Here, suffice it to say that he read much of the best in Greek, German, and other classical and modern literature. Then he began writing himself. When he returned to Japan four years later, in 1888, he found himself in the vanguard of the new literary movement. He commenced a double career that was to continue throughout almost all of his active life: military doctor and bureaucrat, and man of letters.

Ōgai's return to Japan brought him fact to face with the ambiguities, the confusions, and the disappointments of a nation undergoing a rapid and forced change of its political and social structures. Coupled with his own personal frustrations (his first marriage ended unhappily, and his battles with his army superiors fatigued him), the state of the national culture gradually led him to adopt a somewhat resigned and ironic attitude reflected in many of the works of his middle years. Ōgai's greatest professional difficulty, perhaps, was occasioned by a dispute he had with the medical profession over the introduction of advanced Western medical techniques into Japan. Although Ōgai's advanced views were vindicated, his superiors expressed their displeasure in 1899 by having him transferred away from Tokyo, where he was in the center of the cultural and intellectual life, to the town of Kokura in Kyushu, the southernmost island of Japan. He was then thirty-seven years old.

This period of "exile," as Ōgai called it, lasted for almost four years. Yet for all the dismal quality of his surroundings, he took advantage of the quiet and of the routine he had established to study, to seek out materials for future writings, and to marry again. When he was able to go back to Tokyo, in 1902, he returned as a mature artist and a committed professional doctor and military official. Shortly thereafter, he was made director of the Bureau of Medical Affairs for the War Ministry.

Back in the midst of the literary world, Ōgai composed a number of his most celebrated essays and works of fiction, climaxed in 1909 by his satire on the Japanese Naturalist writers, *Vita Sexualis*.[5] The book, which seems harmless enough today, was banned by the censors and Ōgai was reprimanded personally by the Vice-Minister of War.

Ōgai was offended at the misunderstanding shown his book by the authorities and concerned that individual freedoms would be more and more suppressed. In 1910, the year following, the increasingly conservative government authorities arrested and executed the well-known and respected socialist, Kōtoku Shūsui, for his supposed connection with a plot to murder the emperor. The impact of this celebrated incident on the intellectuals was enormous: suddenly the price of progress and order seemed to require the curtailment of the very individuality and human dignity needed to form the basis of a progressive and modern society. Ōgai's apprehensions and resentments, as well as his conflicting feelings toward the place of authority and freedom in society, are mirrored in several works he wrote at this time, notably in *Chinkoku no tō* [Tower of silence] and *Shokudō* [Dining room], both of which were written in 1910.[6]

Then came the death of the Emperor Meiji in 1912. Like others of his generation, Ōgai's adult life had been spent under the reign of this man who seemed to symbolize all the progress Japan had been able to achieve, despite internal failings and certain dangers from external threats. The emperor's death was inevitable, but as an older man himself (he was then fifty), it seemed to Ōgai that the necessary spirit of sacrifice and dedication that had been so much a part of his time was now somehow endangered. The death of the emperor was followed by the ritual suicide of General Nogi

Maresuke,[7] in fidelity to his leader. This manifestation of traditional morality was both thrilling and deeply troubling to the Japanese public; many writers tried to resolve the ambiguity of their own feelings, among them Natsume Sōseki, whose celebrated novel *Kokoro* uses Nogi's death as a central symbol. Mori Ōgai himself began almost immediately after the emperor's death to compose the story *Okitsu Yagoemon no isho* [The last testament of Okitsu Yagoemon], in which he attempted to re-create the psychology of Nogi in terms of a Tokugawa setting.

Following this work, Ōgai began the composition of a number of stories on historical themes, a task that occupied him until his death in 1922. The fact that Ōgai chose historical subjects serves as no indication that he necessarily approved of the attitudes of the feudal past (against which he fought during his whole adult life), or that he preferred the old way of doing things to the new. Rather, the writing of these works seemed to serve as a means for him to deal with contemporary moral and philosophical problems from an artistic perspective congenial to him. If the characters and settings represented a vanished age, Ōgai's choice of concerns in dealing with them was thoroughly contemporary. Indeed, during the time he was working on these stories, he was also engaged in publishing a series of highly respected translations of contemporary works by Strindberg, Ibsen, Rilke, and Schnitzler.

Ōgai's contributions to the development of intellectual life in the Japan of his time were enormous. In addition to his work as a writer, his translations introduced to the Japanese a number of important works of philosophy and literature, ranging from Heine and Goethe to Hofmannsthal. He was a noted innovator in the creation of a modern poetic style in Japan, and his early experiments in writing European-style drama helped to create a viable dramaturgy for the modern Japanese theatre. He was an extremely perceptive critic, and his writings on Japanese and foreign literature are still consulted and considered valuable. His role as a public figure, informal adviser to statesmen,[8] and as a physician and student of Western medicine must also be mentioned.

All aspects of Ōgai's intellectual and spiritual life are reflected in varying degrees in his fiction, and nowhere more so than in his late works, composed when he was in full possession of his artistic facilities and in his full maturity as a man.

Even limiting a consideration of Ōgai's work to his historical stories, the amount of material to examine is considerable. There are, first of all, three extensive chronicles that, from their length and complexity, may be classed as historical novels: *Shibue Chūsai* (1916), *Izawa Ranken* (1916), and *Hōjō Katei* (1917). The three form something of a unit. In the three books, Ōgai examines the life of Shibue Chūsai, a leading physician and Confucian scholar in the late Tokugawa period, the career of his teacher Izawa Ranken, and, in the third, he reconstructs the biography of Ranken's colleague, Hōjō Katei.

The remaining works, most of which are translated in the two volumes, are usually divided into two categories by Japanese critics, the fictional pieces (*rekishi shōsetsu*) that deal with historical themes in an artistic and psychological way (volume 1) and the biographical narratives (*shiden*) that remain more closely related to the factual information unearthed on his characters by Ōgai (volume 2). Ōgai evolved a style appropriate to both genres, but to a Western reader the divisions between them may seem somewhat arbitrary, and many stories show the use of a considerable variety of subject matter and literary technique. Despite all this diversity, however, some generalizations may be useful as an introduction to the general reader in terms of what the stories are meant to represent and what Ōgai's intentions were in writing them.

Ōgai's fidelity to history was certainly an important determinant in their composition. In "Suginohara Shina," written in 1916, Ōgai wrote that he abandoned a more elaborate treatment of the material he chose because of ". . . a lack of creative power and the habit of cherishing historical facts."[9] In "Tokō Tahei," written in 1917, he was even more explicit.

> Historians, seeing what I have written, will no doubt criticize me for my willfulness. Novelists, on the other hand, will laugh at my persistence. There is a Western proverb about sleeping between two beds. Looking at my own work, it seems that the proverb can be applied to me.[10]

In his desire to cherish the facts, was Ōgai, the trained scientific scholar, merely assembling data? Although Ōgai did not often choose to write about himself, his one essay touching on the aesthetics of his historical works, "Rekishi sono mama to rekishibanare" [History as it is and history ignored] written in 1914, does contain a number of insights into his general artistic purposes.

In the essay, Ōgai confesses that even his friends debate about whether his use of historical figures permits his works to be called fiction. Ōgai counters by saying that he looks for the "natural" in history, he respects it, and he is loathe to change it. After all, he continues, if people enjoy reading about life "as it is" in modern naturalistic fiction, then they certainly ought to like reading about it as it was. Indeed, he concludes, it is precisely because he respects history that he is all the more bound by it.

Then follows the most provocative insight he provides.

Among my friends, there are those who say that while other writers treat their materials on the basis of emotion, I treat them on the basis of the intellect. Yet I hold this to be true of all my literary work, not merely of the stories based on historical characters. In general, I would say that my works are not "Dionysian" but "Apollonian." I have never exerted the kind of effort required to make a story "Dionysian." And indeed, if I were able to expend a comparable effort, it would be in an effort to make my creation all the more contemplative.[11]

Ōgai's reference to "Apollonian" and "Dionysian" is, of course, to Friedrich Nietzsche's celebrated essay of 1872, *The Birth of Tragedy*, in which the German philosopher characterized the Dionysian spirit as intoxication and rapture, dark and emotional, while the Apollonian is ". . . a discreet limitation, a freedom from all extravagant usages . . . sapient tranquillity."[12]

Here, it seems, Ōgai provides a precise self-analysis. All the virtues of his style and thought: clarity, objectivity, intelligence, and selectivity are subsumed under his borrowed metaphor. Ōgai can be moved by history but not wish to change it, he can be what Nietzsche calls ". . . a new transfiguring light needed to catch and hold in life the stream of individual forms."[13] Coolness and objectivity characterize his attitudes in re-creating the past.

Given these attitudes toward his art, Ōgai's concerns as a thinker and a writer emerge more clearly. As was suggested above, Ōgai experienced in his own lifetime the crisis of civilization in Japan: modern man had shed his feudal sense of community and his superstitions only to find them replaced by spiritual emptiness. The end of the Meiji period seemed to mark an end to that transition period. Even the death of General Nogi seemed a final gesture of the dying past. For Ōgai, the best way to pursue the future was to examine the past; by discovering and articulating the Japanese virtues that existed in the past, the problems of the present and the limitations and possibilities for the future became clearer.

Ōgai drew his metaphysical sketches on the grandest possible scale. None of the stories deal with romantic love (although many of his earlier ones do), but rather with issues he found, at this time in his life, to be of more fundamental importance: loyalty, sincerity, intellectual honesty, independence of spirit, the nature of the spiritual temperament, and the abiding relationships between parents and children. The range of moral choice and action in the stories is perhaps limited by their historical settings, yet Ōgai's selection of events and attitudes to portray reveals his altogether striking modern attitude of mind. In fact, Ōgai's choices often lead him rather far from life "as it was." His concerns are for modern values, and indeed, it is precisely this creative gap between his material and his own mental outlook that gives the stories their remarkable moral power. Without being didactic in any way, the stories are idealistic. Ōgai has located the attitudes in history that have brought spiritual satisfaction to the men and women he portrays, and he holds them up as models for contemporary society, not as models in the conventional sense, but rather as reminders, as shadows cast across the confusions of the present.

Perhaps Ōgai's attitudes can be traced back to his early training in the Confucian classics, with their rational appeal to an ordered, restrained humanitarianism. By this definition, Ōgai can be included among the last generation of Confucian writers in Meiji Japan; yet on the other hand, his attitudes and perceptions were immeasurably broadened and rendered sophisticated through his long and intimate contact with late nineteenth-century European life and literature. As a result, the best of Ōgai's work manifests both the moral power sanctioned in the Confucian tradition and a subtlety and finesse of style derived from the West, both fused into a harmonious whole. These historical stories seem well described in the remark of Stephen Ross that ". . . there is something particularly sublime about novels that not only succeed in purely literary terms but contain and develop ideas of great philosophic worth without destruction of literary values."[14]

In order to create the kind of historical and moral context in which his concepts could exist in literary terms, Ōgai developed a number of literary techniques that constitute in many ways a new genre of writing. Again, although the variety of such techniques is considerable, a few generalizations can be made on the basis of the stories as a whole.

One of Ōgai's most important artistic principles is that of selection. The kinds of incidents about which he chose to write show the precision with which he wished to voice his concerns. Most of the stories deal with specific historical events about which at least some documentation exists. To be sure, some of the stories do draw their materials from legends: "Kanzan Jittoku," for example, is an account of Chinese Buddhist mystics, and "Sanshō dayū" relates a series of miraculous happenings in medieval Japan. Yet, in all cases, the incidents, no matter how fanciful, have been carefully documented in Ōgai's sources. The bulk of his stories deal with the Tokugawa period; within that period, Ōgai's choices of material are most revealing.

The temptation for most popular writers of historical fiction is to re-create the grand episodes and large figures of the past. Such an attitude is true in Japan as elsewhere: kabuki playwrights and novelists have usually turned to colorful and dramatic incidents for their inspiration. Ōgai, on the other hand, normally chooses as his main character an obscure person who may be close to a great man but who exhibits in his own private person some attitude or quality of mind Ōgai wishes to investigate. One may catch a glimpse of a great man of history through the more commonplace eyes of one of Ōgai's characters, but most of his protagonists have been selected precisely because they are, in the very best sense of the word, ordinary.

In the same fashion, the stories often take place in the generation before or after some great historical event. The event itself is not depicted, and the times in which the characters live are more often than not outwardly peaceful and normal. These seeming restrictions actually permit Ōgai to concentrate on his characters rather than on the historical events surrounding them. The relationships of Ōgai's protagonists to others (wife, children, lord) or to abstract ideas (courage, fidelity, learning) are illustrated always in an appropriately specific fashion rather than thrown in relief against the vast forces of history. In the context of specific relationships, Ōgai's characters bear full moral responsibility for their actions. Some Japanese critics have suggested that, because Ōgai's creative powers were limited, he shied away from depicting dramatic historical events. Nevertheless, Ōgai's desire to make his work "all the more contemplative" dictated the means he used.

In particular, Ōgai wrote a number of stories about the great feudal families in Kyushu, especially the Hosokawa family. Various generations of the family are dealt with in "Abe ichizoku," "Tokō Tahei," "Kuriyama Daizen," and "Okitsu Yagoemon no isho." Ōgai may well have collected the data for these works while living in Kokura during his "exile"; the stories are filled with a wealth of careful detail on the life and manners of the period, carefully and ingeniously presented.

If the selection of an incident is one basic artistic technique at work in these stories, then another is Ōgai's method of selection within the context of a single incident. A story like "Sahashi Jingorō," for example, is constructed by the same principles of organization that govern Japanese horizontal scrolls. Major scenes are painted in a very explicit fashion; and these scenes, as they unfold, are interspersed with bits of connecting "narrative" linking them together. In his major scenes, Ōgai provides an extraordinary amount of specific detail, subjecting his narrative to relentless documentation. Yet nothing is chosen at random, for each item Ōgai chooses to mention creates an effect contributing to his total conception. These scenes, in turn, are linked with episodes of historical background, quickly sketched.

Another important technique of Ōgai is his personal assumption of the role of narrator. Ōgai the writer and the man is never far from his reader; he constantly comments, shapes the narrative before the reader's eyes, speculates on the motives for the actions he is in the process of describing. The process may seem at first somewhat troubling, even occasionally didactic. Some of the reasons for the technique, of course, are inherent in the speculative, contemplative nature of the works Ōgai wished to create. Intellectual awareness requires objectivity, and aesthetic distance permits the reader to contemplate what he has read and generalize from it. Ōgai wants more than a personal, emotional response. Bertholt Brecht, in describing his celebrated "alienation effect," wrote that his object was ". . . not just to arouse moral objections to certain circumstances of life but to discover means for their elimination."[15] Ōgai, in his own way, is attempting a similar effort in his Apollonian meditation.

The direct presentation to the reader of the working out of the author's own mental processes was a style of writing quite new in Japan at that time. Katō Shūichi has written that in Ōgai's late stories,

> . . . the form is original, almost a new genre, namely a "biography in progress," in which the author describes not only the life of the persons concerned but also the author's own intellectual process of writing a biography—his sorrow for lost documents, his joy at others discovered, his reasoning about available materials, his imagination, his insight. . . .[16]

Ōgai's sense of objectivity is chiefly conveyed through the tone of his language, which is terse, brilliant, and precise. Ōgai's style has always received unstinted praise from Japanese critics and writers. He has been admired by such diverse talents as Nagai Kafū and Mishima Yukio. Ōgai may have developed his ability to create his kind of lucid precise Japanese because, like his brilliant predecessor, the novelist Futabatei Shimei, he took an interest in the spoken language. Futabatei, a generation before Ōgai, had virtually created the modern literary language (classical Japanese having been considered unsuited for the composition of modern works) by making translations into a precise and flexible Japanese from stories of Turgenev. Futabatei knew spoken and written Russian well. Ōgai made the same use of his German. One often has the feeling there is not a word wasted in an Ōgai text; and although unfortunately the same cannot be said about the present translations, they have been made as faithful to the general tone of his language as the translators have been able.

There are many reasons why these late stories of Ōgai may have a legitimate appeal, even in translation, to a modern reader.

First of all, in terms of literary technique, the stories show considerable distinction. Ōgai's ability to establish an effective relationship between author, reader, and the materials presented in the story provides the necessary means for him to accomplish his complex ends. These ends often concern human virtue. Writers have usually found vice more simple to portray (Chaucer said it was more exciting), but Ōgai's historical stories provide some effective counterexamples. He never preaches. We are shown not merely virtue, but the *beauty* of virtue, manifested in a particular historical setting. Ōgai often chose the Tokugawa period, considered by many Japanese writers and intellectuals as the era of greatest personal repression in the history of their country; yet the choice is less a comment on Ōgai's political beliefs than on his commitment to what he saw to be the eternal human spirit. Indeed the basic Confucian view of the world seems here vindicated: man is good and can improve himself.[17]

Secondly, the stories hold considerable interest because of the light they shed on Ōgai as a leading intellectual leader of the Meiji period. Many of the difficulties and enthusiasms of that time are mirrored in these works. A close examination of the stories shows that Ōgai, with his early Confucian training overlaid with his knowledge and experience gained in Germany, was firmly aware of the nature of the time in which he lived and of the spiritual ambiguities inherent in the modern situation. He looked back at history without regret and without romantic wistfulness. He did not call for a restoration of ancient virtues at the expense of the present. If we accept the paradigm of Roger Caillois that the traditional Asian psychology sees time as circular, the Western as linear,[18] then Ōgai seems closer to the psychology of a European intellectual in his historical outlook. There is virtue in the past, and the future may be corrupt; but the configurations of the past cannot be re-created again. The question that seems to underlie each story would seem to be: If this was so, what is possible now?

Lastly, many of Ōgai's philosophical ideas, irrespective of his cultural background, are compelling. I should merely like to call attention to the fact that his treatment of the problem of human ego, and his understanding of the close and reciprocal relationship between self and self-sacrifice are as profound as those of any modern writer in the West.

Lu Hsun, the most gifted man of letters in twentieth-century China, wrote an essay toward the end of his life in which he indicated the authors who had been influential in his own work. After listing Gogol and other Europeans he finished by saying, ". . . and of course the two Japanese, Natsume Sōseki and Mori Ōgai."[19] Thanks to the work of Edwin McClellan and others, we are in a better position to understand Lu Hsun's enthusiasm for Sōseki. If the present translations can help explain the addition of Mori Ōgai's name, our labors will have been richly repaid.

J. THOMAS RIMER

THE SIGNIFICANCE
OF ŌGAI'S HISTORICAL LITERATURE

INSTITUTIONALLY, modern Japanese history is dated from the Meiji Restoration of 1868. While the deeper currents of this phase of Japan's historical process must be traced to the Tokugawa period (1600–1867), the forty-four years named for the Meiji emperor were clearly a watershed. To be sure, the cultural dynamics of this recent chapter in Japanese history can be compared with earlier periods, for it is obvious that the Nara, Heian, Kamakura, Muromachi, and Tokugawa periods of Japanese history were each a ''modern'' age in their time. In the Meiji period, however, Japan embarked upon a course of immense consequences. Responding to external and internal pressures after centuries of virtual seclusion, she began a wholesale assimilation of Western civilization.

The thinker Fukuzawa Yukichi (1835–1901) observed at the beginning of the Meiji era that social variables were then being set in motion within Japan only comparable in scope to the large-scale importation of Chinese institutions and Buddhism in the sixth century A.D.[1] Fukuzawa was only one of many Japanese intellectuals of the day who urged their countrymen to set themselves the task of catching up with, and even surpassing, the civilization of the Western world. And these were not merely rhetorical flourishes. Many of these early Meiji figures lived to see the basic accomplishment of this national project by the time of the death of the Meiji emperor in 1912.

By whatever measure, the political, economic, and cultural transformation of Meiji Japan bids fair to consideration as one of the major chapters in Japanese history. Heidegger has spoken of a ''sense of destiny'' and ''shared co-historicizing'' of a people who resolutely shape the givenness of their existence into their own authentic project.[2] It is difficult to deny such a self-conscious effort, and accomplishment, to the people of Meiji, for read in both general and particular terms, that is precisely what the historical record tells us. The Meiji legacy continues in the powerful economic and cultural momentum of present-day Japan.

But given the subsequent evolution of Japanese history, it is now possible to go further than Fukuzawa's generation and contend that the Meiji era appears to have been one of the outstanding matrices of cultural productivity in world history. It would be instructive to compare the Meiji achievement, for example, with that of Athens of the fifth century B.C., of China of the T'ang dynasty, or of the fifteenth-century Italian Renaissance. The Meiji era has at least a special claim to attention for having been one of the first successful points of integration of contemporary world culture.

Our present two volumes, consisting of the "historical literature" of Mori Ōgai (1862–1922), present a conspicuous—perhaps paradigmatic—instance of how Japanese cultural modernization worked in bridging the civilizations of the East and the West. By Japanese standards, Mori Ōgai was one of the more important figures of the modern Japanese cultural transformation. If this is indeed true, then Ōgai can be ranked as having contributed a share to the unfolding of contemporary world culture. Our aim in providing access to his "historical literature" through translation has been to make available to a wider reading public the essential dimensions of his thought in his final, most mature phase of writing.

Heretofore Ōgai has remained one of the more neglected figures in modern Japanese cultural history. This has been due presumably to the complexity of his life and works, which defies routine analysis. The stature of his genius and his place in Japan's cultural modernization is only now slowly coming into focus as we have gained competence in viewing Japan's modern cultural dynamics in international terms. Our decision to translate a representative selection of the final works of Ōgai's literary career has been motivated by the hope of contributing to a wider appreciation of Ōgai's exemplary role in the cultural modernization of the Meiji and Taishō (1912–1926) periods.

The fact is uncontrovertible that Ōgai was a major figure in his day. As the Japanese novelist and Marxist critic, Nakano Shigeharu, has observed, the Meiji era produced many great men in various walks of public life; yet Mori Ōgai and his contemporary, Natsume Sōseki (1867–1916), towered over their own society as the truly outstanding figures of their time. Their contemporaries looked up to Ōgai and Sōseki as articulators of the important responses to the problems of their day, as well as of deep attitudes toward life in general. For this reason their major writings became classics in their own time.[3]

Confining ourselves to Ōgai, Nakano Shigeharu has written, in another context, that Ōgai remains the most important "historical symbol" in the last century of Japanese history. He contends that the basic concerns and accomplishments of Japanese society are mirrored in Ōgai's career to a greater degree than in that of any other single figure in the first one hundred years since the Meiji Restoration.[4] As extravagant as this assessment appears to be, the specialist will be hard-pressed to refute it, for by every conceivable measure—even that of Sōseki—Ōgai exerted a major impact upon his times and reflected, par excellence, the spiritual forces at work in Japan's modernization process.

I have suggested that one reason for the neglect Ōgai has heretofore received from Western scholars is probably this protean career of Ōgai itself. He was in the vanguard of Western studies in his day. He combined a medical career with distinguished government service, culminating in his elevation to the rank of Surgeon General of the Japanese army, and in his participation in the advisory council to Yamagata Aritomo, the senior statesman of the time. For all this, Ōgai also dominated the literary world. His intellectual process as a serious student of Japanese, Chinese, and Western literary traditions, and as perhaps the peerless translator of foreign literature in modern times, suggests comparison with the outstanding Renaissance Humanists of the West and the greatest literati of China. Yet Ōgai's was an essentially modern mind. His double career as army medical doctor, teacher, and bureaucrat, on the one hand, and as translator, literary critic, essayist, novelist, poet, short-story writer, and biographer, on the other, helped shape powerful cultural dynamisms at the crucial juncture of late Meiji when international values were being internalized and integrated with their own indigenous culture by the Japanese people.[5]

There is the constant danger that the specialist in one aspect of Japanese culture will underestimate Ōgai simply for the want of a broad enough measure to deal with the versatility and productivity of his accomplishments. Ōgai himself, as we shall see below, was acutely aware of the strains to which his many-sided nature subjected him. A careful study of his career will show that he used the medium of his own literary creations as the chief means to integrate these tensions, and to probe their deeper ground in his own genius.

Japanese critics usually point to the last phase of Ōgai's writing as the time in which he most creatively integrated the dimensions of his career. This was a period of exceptional intellectual vitality during which Ōgai, between 1912 and 1918, reformulated his philosophical and aesthetic ideas in the genre of "historical literature." After the death of the Meiji emperor and the *junshi* of General Nogi and his wife in 1912, Ōgai chose to write almost exclusively in this vehicle of "historical literature"—a term inclusive of fictional (*rekishi shōsetsu*) and biographical (*shiden*) pieces. Here again specialists will find it difficult to sort out the two literary forms, since Ōgai himself did not care to make the distinction. Yet Ōgai's "historical literature" as a whole remains the most praised of his total literary output, and the primary source material for the student of his philosophical ideas.

Our present task, then, is the difficult one of endeavoring to understand Ōgai as a creative figure in the context of Japanese modernization. The center point of his own creativity was his literary output, which reached its most adequate form of expression in the "historical literature" of his last phase of writing. But we then need an appropriate conceptual model for probing the intellectual and aesthetic dimensions of Ōgai's "historical literature."

In this regard I would suggest that the philosopher Watsuji Tetsurō (1889–1960) has provided us with a productive heuristic model for probing the complexities of Ōgai's life and works. In his essay, "The Synchronistic Character of Japanese Culture," Watsuji has focused attention upon a repeated pattern of Japanese civilization, which consists of vigorous assimilation of waves of foreign civilization without the displacement of indigenous elements. According to Watsuji, the coexistence of various sediments of value traditions in a variety of integrative contexts allows for a distinctive kind of cultural dynamics. To borrow a metaphor from contemporary physics, the quantum-lattice of Japanese culture provides for a complex pattern of interflow between valuational levels and their potential energies in a given matrix of integration. Thus the creative process in the Japanese case—as exemplified in representative religious, philosophical, literary, and aesthetic forms—entails an internalization of the sedimented cultural tradition, on the one hand, and its crystallization into a new historical mode of disclosure, on the other.[6]

The mix of continuous and discontinuous cultural elements in the Meiji era clearly illustrates this conceptual model. But I would argue that the exceptional symbiosis of premodern and modern, Japanese and foreign dimensions in Ōgai's "historical literature" is a specific instance of the same phenomenon.

For example, the overlapping forms of historical novel and historical biography that became the chief vehicles of Ōgai's final phase of creative writing reflect the legacy of historiography, historical fiction, and literary biography, which has been a prevailing element in Japanese and Chinese civilizations. Noteworthy in reference to Ōgai's work is the tradition of the Japanese historical chronicles such as the *Heike monogatari*, the *Taiheiki*, and the *Gikeiki*, which have gained their permanent places in the mainstream of Japanese literature and philosophy. Ōgai's "historical literature" cannot fail to impress the thoughtful reader as having repossessed this ancient genre. But the same genre was transformed under Ōgai's pen into a personal vehicle of modern literature expressive of his mature philosophical outlook.

Again, Ōgai's aesthetic intention in working with historical materials grew out of his long-standing polemic against the self-confessional genre of contemporary "realistic" and "naturalistic" literature. But while the very problematic of this debate grew out of the importation of Western forms of literature and aesthetic theory in his day, Ōgai's use of the genre of "historical literature" to illustrate his own aesthetic ideals resulted in his repossession of concepts of "reality" and "nature" deeply rooted in Oriental civilization. In such representative pieces as "Sakai jiken," "Jiisan baasan," "Tsuge Shirōzaemon," or "Saiki Kōi," for example, the reader is left with a distinct philosophical impression. In these and other such stories or biographies, Ōgai's meticulous attention to detail was guided by his aesthetic intention of creating a typology of ideal human qualities set in relief by the ineluctable working of historical and natural forces. Ōgai's characteristic touch, which takes the historical particular as expressive of the wider universal, clearly links his "historical literature" with the Buddhist and Confucian sensibilities discoverable in such works as the *Heike monogatari*, the *Taiheiki*, and the *Gikeiki* of medieval Japan, or the *Chūshingura* of the Tokugawa period.

The stylistic excellence of Ōgai's "historical literature" has been noted by Japanese novelists and critics as well.[8] Both in masterpieces of literary merit such as "Abe ichizoku" and "Sanshō dayū," and in outstanding biographical works such as "Kuriyama Daizen" and "Shibue Chūsai," Ōgai is said to have achieved a creative fusion of personal, historical, philosophical, and aesthetic dimensions through the medium of an impeccable prose narrative. However, the same kind of "synchronistic" phenomenon reappears here. After establishing himself as a leading exponent of modern Japanese prose style in his pre-1912 literary works, Ōgai combined modern colloquial Japanese with a masterful use of classical Chinese to produce the historical tone of these writings.

In a word, the significance of Ōgai's "historical literature" consists in the fact that it became the final expression of Ōgai's protean genius. At the same time, it functioned as an important vector of Japanese cultural modernization. To understand this process of conceptual and symbolic transformation that took place in Ōgai's "historical literature," and to lay the groundwork for a greater appreciation of the personal dimension in the same works, let us now consider in more detail the phenomenon of Ōgai's "double career." We will then be in a position to consider some of the leading themes of Ōgai's pre-1912 novellas and short stories. Finally we shall conclude with an analysis of the "spiritual naturalism" of Ōgai's final literary output.

Ōgai's Double Career

We have said above that the historical genre to which Ōgai turned after 1912 can be understood as the final stage of integration of the many facets of his career. Even in speaking below of his "double career"—as army medical doctor and man of letters—I am risking the danger of oversimplifying Ōgai's long struggle to hold together the many dimensions of his private and public selves. John Dower has touched upon this aspect of Ōgai's career in the following words:

> "Tsuina" is one of Ōgai's more curious, and curiously revealing, pieces—a tired composition about tiredness and the difficulties of maintaining a literary reputation when one is called upon to fulfil other obligations. As an Army medical doctor, Ōgai occupied at this time a high position in the Japanese military bureaucracy; indeed, . . . for most of his life the greater part of his time and energies were devoted to concerns other than the literary and intellectual contributions upon which his reputation now rests. The extent to which his writings were influenced by this relentless everyday fact is impossible to calculate. Certainly Ōgai himself was acutely conscious of conflicting demands, and in 1910, . . . he attempted to address (and rationalize) this dilemma in an interesting story entitled *Asobi* (Play) in which the protagonist, a clear shadow of Ōgai himself, was a minor government official who had achieved a small reputation as a writer.[9]

Ōgai's works as a whole are a record of this continuing struggle with time and circumstance to realize his literary and intellectual gifts. The sometimes rough-hewn, highly condensed, and apparently unfinished character of many of his writings undoubtedly reflect this "relentless everyday fact." On the other hand, his works have the stamp of personal authenticity which this struggle helped produce. We can go further and note that the "unfinished" and "unexpressed" qualities of his stories became an element in his own self-consciousness as an "eternal malcontent" in his middle years, and are a function of his romanticism and idealism in general. His career-long struggle to be creative in the cultural sphere can in fact be found as one symbolic motif in the late historical fiction and biographies.

Let us take note of some of the elements in Ōgai's career. Ōgai graduated from the medical school of the newly established Tokyo University in 1881 at the age of nineteen. He was among the first wave of graduates of the Meiji university system to be sent abroad, and therefore, together with such other graduates of the 1880s as Inoue Tetsujirō, Okakura Kakuzō, Uchimura Kanzō, Nitobe Inazō, Miyake Yūjirō, Tsubouchi Yuzō, and Inoue Enryō, was destined to influence the new faces who graduated from the universities in the 1890s. By the time these latter figures graduated in the 1890s—including such outstanding names as Kiyozawa Manshi, Ōnishi Hajime, Natsume Sōseki, and Nishida Kitarō—Ōgai had already sojourned four years in Germany and had begun to have an impact upon the intellectual life of the times.

Ōgai's sojourn in Germany between 1885 and 1888 was primarily devoted to advanced training in the medical field at the Universities of Leipzig, Munich, Dresden, and Berlin. Yet we have evidence of the double career he had commenced even at this demanding time. According to his "Doitsu nikki," one of the four diaries he kept during these years, Ōgai had amassed a collection of one hundred seventy volumes of Western books during the first year alone of his sojourn.[10] These included German translations of Aeschylus, Sophocles, Euripides, and Dante, as well as works of Goethe, and anthologies of German and world literatures. Concerning the influence of this reading on Ōgai's development as a man of letters, Hasegawa Izumi has observed:

> The Chinese marginalia in the books which Ōgai read in Germany often include references to passages from Takizawa Bakin and Tamenaga Shunsui as well as to Chinese classics such as the *Suikōden*. This suggests that Ōgai began to cultivate himself as a writer by reading extensively in Chinese and Japanese fiction and proceeded from there to a comparative study of Oriental and Western literatures, a method that enabled him to cover new ground while gaining fresh insights into work already done.[11]

The intriguing question here is, why was Ōgai, the advanced medical student, devoting so much of his time to European *literature* at this time? Without pursuing all aspects of this question, let me note here that Ōgai's full genius seems to have been carefully nurtured from his earliest formative years. He had received an exceptional education, which enabled him to pursue the honorable profession of his samurai forebears, who were chief doctors to the daimyo of the Tsuwano domain. Just how exceptional, according to Tokugawa standards, this education was can be surmised from Hasegawa's description:

> At a very young age, Ōgai began studying Confucianism with a private tutor and later continued his training at the Yorokan, the fief school, where he studied Confucianism, Classical Japanese Literature, and Dutch, the language of medicine. Offering courses in the Japanese Classics and studies in Dutch made the Yorokan unique for a fief school because the tendency at the time was to emphasize Confucian studies to the exclusion of everything else. The man responsible for instituting this sort of progressive curriculum in anticipa-

tion of the needs of a new Era was Kamei Koremi, the daimyo of Tsuwano fief. Kamei, who believed in special education for the intellectually gifted, sent a few outstanding students from the fief school to Tokyo each year so that they could be educated as leaders of the new age.[12]

Ōgai was sent to Tokyo and first lived in the Kamei residence, moving later to the home of a relative, Nishi Amane, one of the leading figures of the early Meiji "civilization and enlightenment" movement. Nishi had a similar background in Confucian and Dutch studies. But even during this time, when the young Ōgai was preparing in earnest for the entrance examinations at Tokyo University, he began translating into modern Japanese poems from the *Genji monogatari* and other Japanese classics. He also read extensively in Tokugawa literature. Thus, given his linguistic abilities, which in due course included German in addition to Japanese, Chinese, and Dutch, it comes as no surprise that Ōgai continued to develop his literary tastes during his sojourn in Germany as a medical student.

The oblique autobiographical dimension in most of Ōgai's writings provides the reader with a fascinating set of clues, as it were, into Ōgai's psychological development. For example, we can read *Vita Sexualis* (1909), an ostensible sexual history of Ōgai's adolescence and young manhood, in this way. This work gives us many fleeting glimpses into Ōgai's school days, his exceptional study habits, his early linguistic talents (especially in Chinese). It also documents his voracious reading of such Tokugawa writers as Bakin, Kyōden, and Shunsui during his formative years.

If these clues were not enough, eight years later (in 1917) Ōgai began his biography "Saiki Kōi" with this explicit recollection of the impact of late Tokugawa fiction upon his psychological and literary development.

When I was young I devoured the books of a lending library man who used to walk around with books stacked on his back in something like a monk's backpack. These books were mainly of three kinds: historical romances (*yomihon*), copy books (*kakihon*), and popular love stories (*ninjōbon*). The *yomihon* consisted mainly of the works of Shunsui and Kinsui; the *kakihon* were what we now call scenarios for professional storytellers. After going through all of these I asked the booklender if he had any others I hadn't read, and he recommended I try reading *zuihitsu*, or miscellaneous essays. If one can get through these too, even through the likes of the antiquarian writings of Ise Teijō, he deserves a degree in lending library literature. I got this degree.

I was first addicted to Bakin, then came to like Kyōden more; but I always preferred Shunsui to Kinsui. I developed a similar partiality later on when I read German literature, always having a greater taste for Hauptmann than Sudermann.

In this passage, I submit, we have a pregnant reminiscence by Ōgai, then fifty-five, on the development of his own literary sensibility, and perhaps on his own place in modern Japanese literature. Ōgai's literary sensibility evolved as a process of integration of his youthful absorption in Japanese classical literature and the popular romance-type literature of the late Tokugawa period, on the one hand, and his pioneer role in introducing the values of German Romanticism through translation, literary criticism, aesthetic theory, and his own creative writing, on the other. (Particularly noteworthy in this latter regard was the influence of Ōgai's long-standing project of translating Goethe's *Faust*.)[13]

This fusion of Japanese and European literary forms is an example of the multi-level character of Japanese culture discussed above. It may be thought to be an essential dimension in "Maihime," "Utakata no ki," *Gan*, and other Ōgai romances, and it formed the basis for Ōgai's further idealistic recollection of "history in itself" in his final phase of writing. The material of some of the late historical stories and biographies can even be traced to Ōgai's later researches into Bakin, Kyōden, Shunsui, and other late Tokugawa writers.[14] But Ōgai conducted these researches and wrote his historical stories while he continued to translate such modern European authors as Ibsen, Strindberg, Dostoevski, and Gorki.

When Ōgai returned to Japan in 1888, his double career as both army medical doctor and man of letters blossomed almost simultaneously. In 1889, the twenty-seven-year-old Ōgai published *Omokage*, an anthology of seventeen poems in translation from such authors as Shakespeare, Byron, Goethe, and Heine. In the same year he organized a literary group called the Shinseisha (New Voice Society), which commenced publication of a magazine, the *Shigarami-zōshi*.[15] This magazine was dominated by Ōgai's monthly translations and literary criticism, and became one of the most important literary publications in its day.

With this start, Ōgai became the medium of wholesale importation of Western, particularly German, literature into Meiji Japan. His eventual translations included works of Goethe, Lessing, Hauptmann, Rilke, Sudermann, Wedekind, Schnitzler, Bahr, von Hofmannsthal, Weid, von Kleist, Hacklaender, Stern, Holz, Dehmel, Wasserman, Strobl, Schiller, Eduard von Hartmann, Lermontov, Heyse, Karamazin, Pushkin, Gorki, Tolstoi, Turgenev, Zola, Rousseau, Racine, Corneille, Daudet, Aristotle, Shakespeare, Wilde, Shaw, Dunsany, Calderon, Ibsen, Bjornson, Hans Christian Andersen, Strindberg, Varhaeren, Maeterlinck, and d'Annunzio. It is significant that Ōgai continued to translate even after he had become surgeon general of the Japanese army and had established his own reputation as a creative writer.[16]

Ōgai also became a powerful influence on the formation of the Meiji literary consciousness through his polemics in the field of literary criticism and in the philosophy of aesthetics.[17]

Yet all this time his army medical career developed apace. He earned promotions as director of the Military Medical College and as chief of the medical staff to the Imperial Guard Division. After a three-year "demotion" to Kokura in Kyushu between 1899 and 1902, he returned to Tokyo, then achieved a brilliant record for his medical contributions in innoculation and other services at the front during the Russo-Japanese War of 1904–1905. (At this time and afterward Ōgai was a personal and professional friend of General Nogi, one of the heroes of the Russo-Japanese War.) He was elevated to the rank of surgeon general of the Japanese army in 1907 and became one of Yamagata Aritomo's personal advisors at the top of the Japanese governmental bureaucracy. Ōgai retired from the Japanese army in 1916, and became head of the Imperial Museum and chief librarian in 1917.

Ōgai's contributions to the Japanese medical profession paralleled his impact upon the development of Meiji literature. He frequently attacked the leaders of the Japanese medical world for their lack of scholarship and competence. He secured legislation against antiquarian medical practices, and fought a protracted battle to organize the Japanese Medical Association on a modern charter. Entrenched conservatives in the medical establishment at one point forced Ōgai's resignation as editor-in-chief of the *Japanese Medical Journal*; he countered by founding his own medical journal to continue his more progressive views.[18]

In all of these facets of his career, Ōgai gives the impression of prodigal talents and energy. Even after his bureaucratic "exile" to the military garrison in Kokura between 1899 and 1902—during which time he is said to have begun to formulate his philosophy of "resignation" (*teinen*)—Ōgai studied French and Sanskrit, practiced Zen meditation, lectured on Clausewitz's *Philosophy of War* to the officers of the Kokura army division, finished his *Sokkyō shijin* (a celebrated translation of Hans Christian Andersen's *Improvisatoren*), and remarried (in January 1902). From Kokura he also wrote a critique of the Tokyo-centered literary world in a work entitled "Ōgai gyōshi to wa tare zo" (in 1900).[19]

As for Ōgai's own literary works, totaling over one hundred twenty titles (mostly short stories and novellas), three general areas of development are discernible. The first was comprised of three romantic novellas written after his return from Germany, namely "Maihime" (1890), "Utakata no ki"

(1890), and "Fumizukai" (1891). It has been said that Ōgai virtually
established the Japanese tradition of the "I novel" (*Ich Roman*) in his own
way through "Maihime," although he was ultimately to reject the naturalistic assumptions on the basis of which the same genre was later exploited by
Japanese writers.[20]

The second period, which runs from the end of the Russo-Japanese War to
the death of the Meiji emperor in 1912, more directly reflects Ōgai's an-
tinaturalistic standpoint, his social criticism and philosophical musings. He
composed a prodigious number of works at this time. In 1909, he published
a novel, *Vita Sexualis*, and two short stories about his life in Kyushu,
"Niwatori" [The chicken], and "Kinka" [The gold coin], as well as three
short fictional pieces based on incidents in the difficult early days of his second marriage, "Hannichi" [Half a day], "Masui" [Anesthesia], and
"Kompira," (a story, named for a famous shrine, based on the death of one
of his children). In the same year he composed two of his most important
stage works, "Kamen" [The mask], a contemporary drama, and "Shizuka," a historical play dealing with Yoshitsune and the Gempei wars of the
late twelfth century, named for the great general's mistress.

In 1910, Ōgai finished one of his most important accomplishments, the
novel *Seinen* [Youth], an account of contemporary intellectual life in Japan,
and began another, *Kaijin* [Ashes], which, after a promising beginning, was
left unfinished and later published only in fragments. He continued to write
stories that mirrored the spiritual confusions of Meiji life. Some of these
took the form of stories with a strong autobiographical element, such as
"Asobi" [Play], "Dokushin" [Bachelorhood], or "Fushinchū" [Under re-
construction]; others were experiments with allegory, such as "Kodama"
[The echo] or "Densha no mado" [From the streetcar window]. He wrote
essays on contemporary politics, "Shokudō" [The dining room], "Chinmoku no to" [The tower of silence], and on art, "Rue Parnassus Am-
bulant." His famous story on Rodin's Japanese model, "Hanako," also
dates from 1910.

In the following year, 1911, Ōgai continued to explore the emotional relationships between men and women in such works as "Hebi" [The snake]
and "Shinjū" [Lovers' suicide], as well as in the most popular of his novels
in a modern setting, *Gan* [The wild geese]. His partially autobiographical
works of that year continued to explore spiritual loneliness in "Mōsō"
[Delusion] and "Hyaku monogatari," which might be rendered as "The
Story of a Hundred" and refers to an old-fashioned means of telling ghost
stories: the listeners light candles, and when they go out, the ghost appears.

Throughout 1912, Ōgai continued his interests in the conflicts between

Eastern and Western systems of philosophy in the novella (more an intellectual tract) "Ka no yō ni" [As if], and in several short stories that pursue the same themes. He also composed an ironic essay on the Japanese literary world, "Fushigi ga kagami" [The surprising mirror], and wrote a moving, factual account of the life of a young man who, against great odds, wanted to be a doctor but died before completing his medical exams, "Hattori Chihiro."

Finally, after the *junshi* of General Nogi in 1912, Ōgai wrote "Okitsu Yagoemon no isho" and "Abe ichizoku," two stories on the subject of *junshi* set in the Tokugawa period. With this momentum he turned to write, and no less prolifically than before, in the genre of historical literature and biography. In six years he produced twenty-four works, including five novellas, eleven short stories and short biographies before 1916, and three long and five short biographies from 1916 to 1918.[21] This body of literature, to which we shall return below, probably represents one of the outstanding feats of painstaking historical research combined with creative writing, in the twentieth century.

I have said above that Ōgai's early and middle works represent a developing literary sensibility in which conceptual and symbolic elements he discovered in German literature resonated with the stratum of Japanese literature he had internalized as a youth. At the same time, these writings produced an imaginative world that concretely embodied his literary theories and aesthetic ideals. Again, they are a testament to his deepening powers of introspection and self-discipline, on the one hand, and his sensitive reactions to the political and social world, on the other. It has even been noted that Ōgai used the medium of some of his writings to articulate an indirect comment on public policies which, because of his status within the Japanese governmental bureaucracy, he could not set forth in direct terms.[22] The works of Ōgai's middle period, in particular, are a continuing reflection on a wide spectrum of contemporary social issues ranging from the question of the mythology of the Imperial House, the problems of authority in the modern state, of socialism and anarchy, and of the right of free expression, to the tensions of domestic life in Japan's rapidly changing society.

In assessing Ōgai's late phase of "historical literature" as well, we must bear in mind that Ōgai was writing as surgeon general of the Japanese army. He wrote neither for the entertainment of his potential readers, nor for pecuniary gain, nor from the despair of the alienated artist. He wrote from the dictates of his genius, to be sure, and from what I would describe as an abiding "Meiji" sensibility—that is, from a deep humanistic concern for the quality of civilization in his own times. The "historical" material of his late writings, which so remarkably repossessed the values of the pre-Meiji past, became the medium through which Ōgai continued to react to and comment upon the "modernization" process as he experienced it in his own day.[23]

Thus in addition to understanding the fusion of Tokugawa and German literary forms in his works, it is imperative for the reader to gain some insight into the philosophical sense of personal cultivation and social order which Ōgai reflects as a creative Meiji figure. The critic Katō Shūichi has indeed suggested that the greatness of Ōgai and Sōseki is bound up with the fact that they flourished in the "transitional" time of the late Meiji period when the essential philosophical values of the Tokugawa period were still a living, though transformed, part of the spiritual landscape.[24] This opinion seems to accord with Okazaki Yoshie's assessment of Ōgai as having been always an "enlightenment scholar" who strove to interpret the impact of Westernization on the indigenous Japanese modernization process.[25] The sympathetic reaction of many Japanese intellectuals who have revered Ōgai up to the present time seems partly based on the fact that they see his life and attitudes as an objectification of their own problems and concerns for meaning as modern Japanese.

But if this is so, we should ponder the implications of this phenomenon for our own interpretation of Japanese culture. In point of fact, Ōgai's "historical literature" gives the reader a vivid sense of his appreciation of a quality of spiritual life he knew had existed in the premodern, Tokugawa culture. On the whole, these writings bear eloquent witness to the continuity of Japan's premodern civilization in his own case. Simple stories such as "Jiisan baasan," "Suginohara Shina," and "Yasui fujin" bear the imprint of this appreciation. They are able to communicate Ōgai's sense of the beauty of the lives of men and women who personified the values of love, dedication, self-sacrifice, and self-cultivation, which were social ideals in the Tokugawa culture. The significance of his longer historical biography, *Shibue Chūsai*, is usually understood in this light. It probes the public and private life of a medical doctor, scholar, and man of letters of the late Edo period with whom Ōgai came to identify as almost his own earlier incarnation. He brought this project of historical self-recollection to consummation in the sequels to this work, the biographies *Izawa Ranken* and *Hōjō Katei*.[26]

If Ōgai was such a "transitional" figure in the transmission of Tokugawa culture in the late Meiji and early Taishō years, his prowess in classical Chinese was one aspect of his literary genius. This prowess has been noted by many scholars, and constitutes an important dimension of the style of the "historical literature." We can also surmise from the two stories set in T'ang

China, "Kanzan Jittoku" and "Gyogenki," that Ōgai's historical idealism included an abiding affinity with the Chinese cultural tradition. The continuing legacy of Confucian moral and intellectual cultivation, together with the variety of Dutch studies (*Rangaku*) to which he had been exposed in his early education, remained components in Ōgai's psychology as he developed into the scholar, official, and man of letters who so remarkably bridged the traditions of East and West.

But in the final analysis, Ōgai's impact upon his contemporaries consisted in the point that he contributed to their understanding of themselves as modern Japanese. His "historical" works were written, and read, as contemporary literature, expressive of the complex psychological makeup of a prominent public figure who had already communicated his inner life to his readers in the literary works of his early and middle periods.

Basic Themes of Ōgai's Pre-1912 Stories

Let us now briefly work out some of the aspects of Ōgai's inner life as he revealed it in his pre-1912 literary works. In this way we shall be in a better position to understand what he was attempting to do in his post-1912 "historical literature," and what the serious contemporary reader of this literature must have realized was taking place in Ōgai's mature psychology.

We have already noted in passing that *Vita Sexualis* (1909) furnished one clue as to the direction of Ōgai's later writings.[27] The work, a thinly veiled account of his own adolescent sexual life, was at the same time a critique of the self-confessional "I novel" and its underlying credo of Naturalism. Ōgai had engaged in this polemic ever since first returning from Germany in 1889. *Vita Sexualis* rang various changes on the distinction between love and sexual desire. It also recapitulated many of the themes and symbols of his earlier works through vignettes of his experiences and impressions as a youth. At the same time Ōgai weaved allusions to Japanese, Chinese, and German literature into these episodes. At the end he confessed that he did not know whether to call the account fact or fiction.

Vita Sexualis is important in Ōgai's developing literary career for exemplifying his basic concern to include the self-confessional approach in a wider, and more spiritual, value orientation. This unique approach, combining a selected reminiscence of personal and historical detail with an effort at imaginative expression, and both in the service of oblique spiritual autobiography, became the essential programmatic of the historical genre to which he turned only three years later.

Ironically, however, *Vita Sexualis* was grouped with the naturalistic writings of the day and banned by the authorities in the wake of a famous political trial in 1910. The goverment's sweeping suppression of free expression, combined with other political issues of the times, drew forth a complex response on Ōgai's part.[28] Not abandoning his aesthetic intention in the face of these pressures and obstacles, Ōgai began to articulate a complex philosophy of "resignation" (*teinen, akirame*) that gave a deep coloration to his already pensive works. If we bear in mind that Ōgai was himself at this time a prominent figure in the governmental bureaucracy—and commanded a wide audience of intelligent readers—we shall be better able to surmise the nuances contained in the themes and symbols of his stories and essays written between 1909 and 1912.

If we follow Okazaki Yoshie's interpretation, the concept of "resignation" formed one side of Ōgai's earliest literary expression. His first romance, "Maihime" (1898), revolves around the tension between *giri*, that is, loyalty to the performance values of clan and family, and *ninjō*, that is, the dictates of the human heart and aesthetic emotion. In "Maihime," Ōgai wrote a self-confessional account of his student days in Germany that at the same time symbolized the irreconcilable tension between his career as a public figure in the social structure and his desire to be a writer. In this work, *giri* must conquer *ninjō*, but, as Okazaki maintains, the seed had been sown in Ōgai's writings for the eventual transcendence of the former by the latter.[29]

The tension between *giri* and *ninjō*, between *teinen* ("resignation") and romantic love, reoccurs in Ōgai's next works, "Utakata no ki" and "Fumizukai." And we have clear indications of *teinen* and Ōgai's romantic idealism in *Vita Sexualis*. But for schematic purposes we can say that Ōgai's middle-period works, written between 1906 and 1912, rang various changes on the "resignation" theme, while at the end of this period his "Ka no yō ni" (1912) signaled a transition to a "new idealism" in which the "resignation" theme was transcended.

In these terms, the conceptual key to Ōgai's middle-period works can be found in an essay entitled "Yo ga tachiba" [My standpoint], also written in 1909. In this essay, Ōgai stated that he did not care to be classified or compared with such contemporary authors as Tayama Katai, Shimazaki Tōson, Masamune Hakuchō, Nagai Kafū, and Natsume Sōseki. Here "resignation" signified that Ōgai, in his own words, was "giving up all desire" of being appreciated by the Naturalism-oriented critics, and expressed contentment in his intention of "going his own way." He wrote as follows of the "serenity" (*heiki*) which this resolve had produced in him.

. . . the word that sums up my feeling best would be that of *resignation*. My feeling is not confined to the arts; every aspect of society evokes this in me. Others may think I must surely be suffering to hold such an attitude, but I am surprisingly serene. Probably there is some suggestion of faint-heartedness in an attitude of resignation, but I do not intend to make any special defense against this accusation.[30]

Despite the typical Japanese manner of self-deprecation, however, Ōgai's continuing output and unflagging energy had nothing to do with a faint-hearted attitude. It was rather a positive spiritual resolve to follow the dictates of his own self-consciousness. Spinoza's philosophy, itself mediated through Ōgai's long interest in Goethe, played a role in the formation of this "resignation" concept.[31] Like Spinoza, Ōgai was impelled to "neither laugh nor weep," but earnestly to seek to understand the ambivalences and contradictions, and the deeper harmonies, of his own life and times. But, like Goethe, Ōgai conceived of this kind of "resignation" in terms of active pursuit of duty and destiny.

We can assume that Ōgai's contemporary readers were able to understand this fusion of Japanese and German spiritual attitudes in his works. In 1910 Ōgai drew out one implication of his "resignation" concept in a short story entitled "Asobi." "Asobi" literally means "play." The protagonist, Kimura, who is both an official and a man of letters, represents another self-reflection of Ōgai at this stage in his career. Intrinsically related to the "serenity" concept found in "Yo ga tachiba," "Asobi" reexpressed Ōgai's transcendent attitude. But symbolically the *asobi* sensibility functioned as the point of harmony between politics and art, as exemplified in Ōgai's own position in late Meiji society. Other variations on the *asobi* theme appeared in "Fushigi ga kagami" and "Dengaku tōfu," both written in 1912, and can be traced into Ōgai's historical literature and biographies as well. The same sensibility contained the seeds of the contemplative, but culture-oriented, *bōkansha* ("onlooker") theme which came to the fore in Ōgai's "Hyaku monogatari" (1912), as discussed below.

Ōgai took up the question of art in a more direct way in "Hanako" (1910), a short story based upon an account of a meeting in Paris between a Japanese entertainer of questionable artistic reputation and the sculptor Auguste Rodin.[32] Far from being Ōgai's journalistic appropriation of a contemporary French account, however, "Hanako" was a brilliant tour de force in which he expressed certain elements in his own aesthetic subjectivity. This is clear from the concluding scene in which the overseas Japanese student acting as interpreter—one autobiographical reference—browses through a copy of Baudelaire's "Metaphysics of the Toy" while Rodin sketches

Hanako. Here Ōgai enlists his "play" (*asobi*) concept in the service of his theory of the beautiful and the aesthetic imagination. He employs the symbol of Rodin, the creative genius, in another self-reference. Rodin discovers in Hanako's commonplace physique a special "beauty of strength." He observes, in reference to Baudelaire's aesthetic conception:

> The same idea pertains to the human body, that the form is not interesting simply because it is form. It is a mirror of the soul. The inner flame, showing transparently through the form, alone is interesting.

Rodin also becomes a transparent symbol of the "onlooker" endowed with extraordinary spiritual perception. As for Hanako herself, she has been immortalized by Ōgai no less than by Rodin: she is the symbolic link between Ōgai's early aesthetic theory and the theme of spiritual beauty and inner strength which runs through the "historical literature" of his late phase of writing.

It is imperative to be aware of the intricate inner dialogue in Ōgai's writings. If *asobi* was one variation on the *teinen* theme articulated in 1910, Ōgai explored another—and equally autobiographical—dimension of it in "Mōsō," written in 1911. (In this work, Ōgai imagines himself in his old age; there is an intrinsic connection between "Mōsō" and *Hōjō Katei*, a late historical biography which deals with the life in retirement of a spiritual forebear of *Shibue Chūsai*.)[33] A characteristically introspective pronouncement by Ōgai in "Mōsō" has often been cited by Japanese critics as expressive of Ōgai's self-consciousness as an "eternal malcontent" (*eiennaru fuheika*) at this time. He writes of feeling a "hunger of the soul." He continues:

> What have I been doing since I was born? Pursuing always my studies, as if whipped on by something. I keep thinking that this will perfect me, make me able to carry out some task. To some extent this purpose may be fulfilled. But there is a feeling that the things I do are no more than what an actor does, who comes upon the stage and performs a certain role. A feeling that there must exist something else behind this role I play. And there is a feeling that in only being driven on there is not enough time for this something to awaken.

We must recall that Ōgai was surgeon general of the Japanese army at this time. The passage continues:

> Studying child, studying student, studying bureaucrat, studying student abroad—they are all roles. I keep wanting to wash this face painted black and red—to step a while from this stage, calmly regard myself, peek at the face of this something behind—but at my back is the lash of the stage director and I continue to perform role upon role. I cannot believe that these roles are what

life is. I wonder if something behind them might not be real life. But just as I think this something is about to awaken, it drowses and falls asleep again. The feelings like homesickness that I experience so acutely are like a floating weed that moves with the waves and drifts to far places, and yet whose movement somehow penetrates to the root. This is not the feeling of a role acted out upon a stage. But just when such a feeling seems about to raise its head a moment, suddenly it withdraws.[34]

This confession in ''Mōsō'' can be read in connection with the theme of Ōgai's novel *Seinen* (1910), whose hero, a literary youth named Koizumi Jun'ichi, is not particularly interested in pursuing any vocation, but ''cherishes hopes of being creative.'' (*Seinen* proceeds to unveil a concept of ''altruistic individualism,'' which also formed a component in Ōgai's idealistic historical literature.)

Ōgai's self-consciousness as an ''eternal malcontent'' in ''Mōsō'' was linked to his previous concepts of *teinen* and *asobi* through this kind of idealism and romanticism. Ōgai professed he was not satisfied with the actual world, and by implication, with the actual Ōgai. He felt the call to search after and express the richer possibilities of human life, as manifested in his confessed love of learning and art and his sense of the value of culture.[35]

Another intrinsic dimension of this multipolarized sensibility Ōgai elaborated in literary form the following year in ''Hyaku monogatari'' (1912). In this work, the protagonist Setsuzō is evidently a fusion of the early and middle Ōgai. He confesses to being a ''born onlooker'' (*umarenagara no bōkansha*) to life. This was related on the one hand to the ''eternal malcontent'' theme of the previous year, and on the other to Ōgai's ''Apollonian'' attitude, which already figured prominently in his uniquely ''objective'' literary style. Now it became an explicit philosophical attitude, tied to his rejection of the natural, instinctive self. The ''onlooker'' concept thus subsumed the original ''resignation,'' ''play,'' and ''eternal malcontent'' themes into a new configuration, indicative of Ōgai's spiritual individualism and quest for more adequate self-expression in spite of the internal and external obstacles he felt.

Variations on the *bōkansha* theme appear in his ''Kompira'' (1909), ''Mōsō'' (1911), *Kaijin* (1911), *Fausto kō* (1913), and *Goethe den* (1913), *Ōshio Heihachirō* (1914), and ''Suginohara Shina'' (1916). Of these, I would turn the reader's attention to the last mentioned, as an exemplification of the transformation of Ōgai's symbolism during his final period. In this historical biography, we read of the figure of Date Tsunamune, the young daimyo placed under house arrest in Edo, who had to ''look on passively'' at the so-called Sendai disturbances which broke out back in his domain. In the following passage, Ōgai weaves together the "resignation," "play," and "onlooker" themes in a historically objective, yet highly personal, self-reflection.

> Tsunamune was no ordinary daimyo. He was a gifted poet, calligrapher, and painter. He succeeded to the head of the Date house at the age of nineteen. He was lord of the 620,000 *koku* fief for barely two years when placed under house arrest for being involved in an intrigue centering around his uncle, Date Hyobu Shoyu Munekatsu. From then until he became a monk at the age of forty-four, Tsunamune was never permitted to see his son Kamechiyo, later named Tsunamura. . . . On the scrolls he did during those lonely years under domiciliary confinement, Tsunamune often used the seal *chika hikkai*, which means when one perceives his faults, he must correct them. Tsunamune's artistic talents were not confined to calligraphy and poetry. He worked in gold-lacquer ware, made pottery, and also forged swords. I find it of particular interest that Tsunamune rechannelled politically inexpressible energies in the direction of art. It is also interesting that Tsunamune's spirits did not dampen under house arrest. In the sliding door of the Shinagawa mansion he inlaid more than four hundred glass tiles, a material still rare at that time. Does this not bear witness to his indomitable spirit? His mistress Shina, who served this magnificent personality Tsunamune into his late years, was surely no ordinary woman either.

In this passage we see a typical illustration of what Japanese critics call the "new idealism" of Ōgai's historical literature. The description of Tsunamune's exceptional qualities—and of Shina, who "was surely no ordinary mistress either"—is one of many recapitulations of the main theme of "Okitsu Yagoemon no isho" written four years earlier. And this latter work, as we shall see presently, carried forward the "spiritual pragmatism" enunciated in "Ka no yō ni" just prior to the *junshi* of General Nogi.

In all of these variations on the general "resignation" concept in Ōgai's middle period, we find the keynote to be a kind of transcendent individualism as Ōgai searched for the proper vehicle to express his sense of the true and the beautiful. The turning point in this quest came in 1912 with "Ka no yō ni," which, together with "Fujidana," "Shakkuri" (both 1912), and "Tsuchi ikka" (1913), constitutes what is known as the Hidemaro series after the name of the protagonist. These works give evidence of Ōgai already beginning to transform the *teinen* sensibility of his middle years in the direction of the explicit idealism of his post-1912 historical literature.

"Ka no yō ni" represented Ōgai's endeavor to ponder the relationship between art, morality, and religion, on the one hand, and scholarship and science, on the other. It took its point of departure from the "As if" (*als ob*) idealistic philosophy of Hans Vaihinger, a German thinker who interested Ōgai at this time. It was at the same time Ōgai's personal introspection on his own career. This literary dialogue in fact formed the last link between his middle works and the hermeneutical discovery of "history as it is" (*rekishi sono mama*) in his late writings. In "Ka no yō ni," Ōgai philosophized on the phenomenon of literary "fiction" as constituting its own horizon of the expression of life and value, apart from the domain of scientific "fact." He went on to suggest that the world of ultimate values, as reflected in philosophy and religion, requires a similar "spiritual pragmatism" in regard to the "absolutes" we must live by, even though they are not verifiable in the domain of scientific fact. In this way, "Ka no yō ni" takes up the theme of philosophical truth and ideals, and religious beliefs, as "fictions" analogous to literary "fiction."[36]

But it remained for Ōgai to explore the time-honored Oriental genre of "historical literature" as a higher form of creative "fiction" in which the dichotomy between the domains of ideal value and of historical fact could be overcome. Ōgai's career-long struggle to probe the core of his own personality took the form of this progressive integration of the tension between science, scholarship, and bureaucracy, on the one hand, and his literary and philosophical sensibilities, on the other. Thus, in "Ka no yō ni," Ōgai began to shift the center of gravity of his general "resignation" sensibility toward a more explicit idealism which recapitulated his earlier concern for the beautiful and aesthetic value and allowed for the fuller flowering of his genius. The external event of the *junshi* of General Nogi seems to have acted as a catalyst which stimulated the "spiritual pragmatism" already coming to the surface in Ōgai's psyche.

We should note in passing that while Ōgai went on to create in the genre of historical literature between 1912 and 1918, he pursued these same concerns in the modern, *gendai mono* form in such works as "Tsuchi ikka" (1913), "Tenchō" (1915), and "Futari no tomo" (1915). In "Tenchō" [Favor of heaven], for example, Ōgai's belief in *ten* (heaven), reminiscent of a similar attitude in the later Natsume Sōseki and Kōda Rohan, becomes apparent. This maturing of Ōgai's spirituality in "Tenchō" sheds important light on the moral and religious coloration of some of the historical stories—for example, in "Gojiingahara no katakiuchi," "Sanshō dayū," and "Takasebune."

Finally let us observe Ōgai at work in another direction around this time. He published his novel *Gan* [The wild geese] in serial form between 1911 and 1913, and thus it was completed only after the *junshi* of General Nogi and the appearance of Ōgai's "Okitsu Yagoemon no isho" in September 1912. *Gan* has usually been acclaimed as an outstanding work in the rich canon of modern Japanese literature.[37] Its sophisticated romanticism does not well accord with some characterizations of Ōgai as an aloof or cold writer. As is true of *Vita Sexualis*, there is something intensely personal in *Gan*, although expressed by Ōgai under the powerful discipline of his "Apollonian" standpoint.

The heroine of *Gan*, Otama, appears to be a projection of Ōgai's own feminine *anima* (in Jung's sense). (This is true of the female personages who appear in Ōgai's historical literature as well—for example, Yü Hsüan-chi in "Gyogenki," Sayo in "Yasui fujin," Anju in "Sanshō dayū," Run in "Jiisan baasan," Shina in "Suginohara Shina," and Ichi in "Saigo no ikku.") Ōgai, noted for his powerful masculine mind and Apollonian vision of life, appears to have been equally possessed of a delicate feminine sensitivity in the depths of his unconscious. His creative imagination strove to integrate the two sides of his psychological makeup through the medium of his literary expression.

Otama is a hauntingly affecting character into whom Ōgai poured his own mind and soul. She becomes in the course of the novel a transparent symbol of the "onlooker" as she waits each day for the student, Okada, to pass by her house. She is made to take on the full weight of Ōgai's attitude of "resignation" as well. She falls in love with Okada but has no way of revealing or consummating her emotion. She "saves" the situation for her aging father, for whose sake she has become the mistress of a moneylender, Suezō. Through her "resignation" she also saves the situation for Suezō himself. (The novel recollects many of the themes and symbols of Ōgai's earlier works, from "Maihime" onward, in the course of events.) *Bōkansha* and *teinen* sensibilities come together in this tragic but beautiful tale of the Meiji value system as internalized by Otama, and of the pull of historical forces that finally take Okada from her through his trip to Germany.

Okada, of course, represents another autobiographical dimension in *Gan*. He is another variation on Ōta, the protagonist of Ōgai's early romantic *Ich Roman*, "Maihime." We are given to feel that just as Okada and Ōta have their lives permanently touched by the tragedy of unfulfilled love, so Ōgai must ever be the "eternal malcontent" because of his pursuit of the beautiful. Read in the light of such works as "Mōsō" and "Ka no yō ni," *Gan* also suggests the inner longing, the still unexpressed genius, of Ōgai's own psyche.

Gan, at any rate, is a highly nuanced, personal expression. It is full of an intense but subdued emotion. It is clear that these sensibilities were carried over into the "historical literature" which Ōgai began to write in 1912. They contributed to the emergence of a school of literary idealism centering around Ōgai and Sōseki at this time.[38]

In retrospect, Okazaki Yoshie seems to be right in contending that the tension between "resignation" and "romantic love" formed the subcurrent of Ōgai's literature from his earliest work, "Maihime," onward. These were the two conflicting aspects of his "double career." But in this light we cannot fail to see that there is an intrinsic link between "Maihime" (1898) and *Gan* (1911-1913). We have now to see that Otama and Okada of *Gan* were, in turn, metamorphized by Ōgai into the various personages of his "historical literature." The essential thrust of his post-1912 writings involved Ōgai in transforming the various polarizations of his public and private, outer and inner, rational and emotional, scholarly and aesthetic, roles into one whole. Far from being merely "historical," his literary writings after 1912 represent Ōgai's final phase of self-expression, and the most adequate realization of his aesthetic conception of the beautiful.

The Spiritual Naturalism of Ōgai's Historical Literature

Let me begin to approach the aesthetic idealism of Ōgai's final writings by way of comparison with a similar sensibility found in the films of Ozu Yasujirō, who has often been cited as the greatest of the Japanese filmmakers. Like the ending of a typical Ōgai story, Ozu's films usually conclude on a quiet, almost hushed note. Through this means the serene beauty of the film story lingers on in the subjectivity of the viewer. The quiet endings of Ozu's "Late Spring," "Tokyo Story," or "An Autumn Afternoon," for example, seem to have a literary precedent in the calm dignity and affecting tone of the closing paragraphs of Ōgai's "Sakai jiken," "Jiisan baasan," "Takasebune," and other stories.

Apropos of this parallel, I refer the reader to the following description of the quality of restraint in an Ozu film.

> This traditional view is the view in repose, commanding a very limited field of vision but commanding it entirely. It is the attitude for watching, for listening; it is the position from which one sees the Noh, from which one partakes of the tea ceremony. It is the aesthetic passive attitude of the haiku master who sits in silence and with painful accuracy observes cause and effect, reaching essence through an extreme simplification.[39]

Allowing for the differences in aesthetic media, it might strike us that this description can be applied intact to Ōgai's "onlooker" attitude, both as a view of life and as an aesthetic technique. And to the reader of "Takasebune," "Gyogenki," or "Saiki Kōi," for example, the following words also seem apposite.

> The end effect of an Ozu film—and one of the reasons he is thought of as a spokesman for the Japanese tradition—is a kind of resigned sadness, a calm and knowing serenity which persists despite the uncertainty of life and the things of this world. It implies that the world will go on and that mutability, change, the evanescence of things, also yield their elegiac satisfactions. One lives with and not against time, as with environment. The Japanese call this quality . . . *mono no aware*, for which the nearest translation might be *lachrimae rerum*, Lucretius's reference to those tears caused by things as they are.[40]

Indeed, it was precisely such sensibilities which formed the undercurrents of Ōgai's middle stories, and which resurfaced in his "historical literature." It is a complex of emotions found in many Japanese aesthetic works, both ancient and modern. Ōgai was able to repossess this tradition in the genre of "historical literature," which itself constituted the modernization of an ancient literary form.

Ōgai described his own attitude here as "Apollonian." But the more we probe the nuances of this term, the more we shall discover Ōgai's repossession of fundamentally Shinto, Confucian, and Buddhist sensibilities. The questions of "love" and "self" in Ōgai's earlier writings become the themes of self-transcendence and the worth of high ideals in his later stories. Ōgai's earlier preoccupation with the question of domestic relations and the broader issues of social order and authority similarly return in the coherent spiritual humanism of his "historical literature." From "Okitsu Yagoemon no isho," which was written immediately after the *junshi* of General Nogi and his wife, Ōgai's historical stories and biographies usually depict characters who, by transcending the instinctive, natural self, establish a deeper, "ideal" self in relation to lord, or parent, or husband, or wife, or the honor of their house and ancestors, or of the Japanese nation.

Further to clarify this intrinsic thematic relationship between Ōgai's middle and late phases of creative writing, let me cite two passages from his novel *Seinen* (1910–1911), another reflection of the "resignation," "play," and "eternal malcontent" complex of sensibilities at that time. In the first, the hero of the novel speaks directly of the impact of Naturalism in Japan.

> Naturalism has real and true materials, has minutely delineated each part with an equally rich and sensitive language, and these are really the merits of naturalism. Naturalism, however, should try to put more emphasis upon the spiritual values of human beings. Miracles should not be explained in terms of sensualism. Man has two parts, body and soul, which are delicately fused into one, are rather huddled together. If possible, the novel should treat Man from these two aspects. And writers should address themselves to the reaction, struggle, and harmony of the two parts. In short, it is desirable that while the writer treads the path along which Zola has been walking, he should also build an-

other path high in the air, parallel to Zola's. . . . He should erect a spiritual naturalism. Realize it and it will be another glory, another perfection, another power.[41]

Ōgai was responding to his own challenge as early as *Vita Sexualis* (1909), as we have seen. As he realized his full literary genius in his late phase of writing, he concentrated his energies on reflecting that other glory, perfection, and power through the vehicle of his historical literature.

If the above passage is evidence of Ōgai's philosophical propensity, the second citation from *Seinen* is equally revealing. Through the character Omura he articulated one dimension of his "spiritual naturalism" in terms of the standpoint of "altruistic individualism":

We make a stout self-defense and, without flagging, we also make all life our concern. We render loyal service to our lord. This service, however, we render in our capacity as citizens, not as the slavish retainers of a former age. We endeavor to be filial towards our parents. We do this, however, in our capacity as modern children and not as previous ages when it was even possible for parents to sell or kill children. In short, loyalty and filial piety give value to the entirety of the life which we have made our concern. Thereby, daily life too attains value. It is on this basis that we can be dedicated, can sacrifice and still retain our individualism. The highest affirmation of loyalty is, similarly, to die in battle. When life in its universal aspect becomes our concern, individualism dies or, rather, is transformed into universalism. This is entirely different from the ordinary modern individualism which merely seeks death by rejecting life.[42]

The typology of ideal human qualities we find in Ōgai's late historical literature was clearly a further elaboration of these tendencies in his thought.

Among the late works, "Sahashi Jingorō" and "Gyogenki" are the hardest to classify in the above terms. The cunning Sahashi and the poetess Yü Hsüan-chi are not so much paradigms of Confucian virtue or Buddhist enlightenment as embodiments of "genius." But as such they were far removed from the "common man" depicted in the naturalistic and realistic literature which Ōgai was repudiating. Ōgai appears to have cherished a similar unique quality in the life of Saiki Kōi, a "great man of taste" who patronized the Tokugawa gay quarters. It is clear from other sources that Ōgai had little literary interest in the "common man."[43] In "Suginohara Shina," we recall, Date Tsunamune "was no ordinary daimyo" and Shina, who dedicated her life to him, "was no ordinary mistress either." In other variations on the theme, Okitsu Yagoemon did not think to serve his lord in ordinary terms; the prisoner Kisuke in "Takasebune" first draws his guard's attention as "unusual, of a type not seen before"; Ichi in "Saigo no ikku" is no ordinary young girl. Stories emphasizing heroic samurai attitudes such as "Abe ichizoku" and "Sakai jiken," and even biographies of memorable individuals such as "Tokō Tahei" and "Tsuge Shirōzaemon," similarly draw the reader's attention to Ōgai's perception of extraordinary human qualities.

Ōgai in fact endeavored to create an uncommon kind of literature in his late works, focusing in the main upon the idealized samurai spirit as the vehicle for his personal self-reflection and contemporary perception of society. As Donald Keene has written:

> . . . the suicide in 1912 of General Maresuke Nogi after the death of the emperor Meiji moved Mori so profoundly that he abandoned fiction in favor of painstakingly accurate historical works that depict samurai morality. The heroes of several of his works are warriors who, like General Nogi, commit suicide in order to follow their masters to the grave. Despite his early "confessional" writing, Mori shared with his samurai heroes a reluctance (akin to traditional Japanese impassivity) to dwell on the emotions. His detachment, in part possibly the result of his scientific training, made his later works seem cold, but their strength and integrity were strikingly close to the samurai ideals he so admired.[44]

Ōgai's uncommon vehicle of literary and philosophical expression has required of even his Japanese readers an unusual degree of concentration in order to be able to appreciate the precise degree of strength and integrity of his stories.

In this connection, of course, we should reiterate that the samurai ideals Ōgai admired were as much the creation of his own mind and art as Ōgai's mere return to the Japanese past. The paradox remains that Ōgai did not endeavor to write *realistic* historical fiction. The subject matter of his historical literature, accordingly, was not that of feudal values per se, but rather the universal spiritual qualities Ōgai endeavored to distill from the given historical context he portrayed.

The thematic of his first historical story, "Okitsu Yagoemon no isho," for example, is that of the value of the tea ceremony—itself a symbol of cultural sensibilities in general—in a military age. It was Ōgai's shrewd comment on Japan's modernization process in his day—and on ours, and every modernization process. The "spiritual pragmatism" of this work is directly relatable to the theme of "Ka no yō ni," as we have seen. Even Ōgai's response to General Nogi's *junshi* was expressed in this same universalizing intentionality—he obliquely commemorates General Nogi's deed as an act of *beauty* in the standpoint of universal humanity. (Sōseki, of course, achieved a similar effect in *Kokoro*.[45])

Ōgai's next work, "Abe ichizoku," took a typically more ambivalent attitude toward the subject of *junshi*. But it would again be a mistake to read this masterpiece in realistic terms. The main theme, as Okazaki Yoshie has pointed out, is rather the ideals of loyalty and sincerity, and the tragic consequences of their absence, as universal human values.[46] And "Gojiingahara no katakiuchi," while dealing with the subject of a feudal vendetta sanctioned by the Edo shogunate, has its primary aesthetic intention in the presentation of the sterling qualities of Kurōemon, Bunkichi, and Riyo, in contrast to the "modern" rationalistic doubts and consequent spiritual collapse of the son Uhei. But Kurōemon's manly pride, Bunkichi's unswerving loyalty, and Riyo's single-minded resolve are not so much depicted as customs of the late feudal age as universal forms of man.[47] Ōgai achieved a similar aesthetic effect in the tale of multiple *seppuku* in "Sakai jiken."

Ōgai's "spiritual naturalism," then, involved the predominant intentionality of presenting the beauty of the lives of persons who have lived and died according to a basically *ideal* conception of "self." He succeeds sublimely at times in capturing the self-transcending "will" and "pride" that are essential elements in the Japanese national character. But the final impact of his historical literature is not precisely the ethical quality of his characters, but rather the aesthetic beauty they embody as human beings. In this way Ōgai ultimately repossessed the aesthetic philosophy of his earlier debates on literary criticism.

"Yasui fujin" is one of the short stories that clearly reveals Ōgai's final aesthetic sensibility and technique of literary self-reflection. Its protagonist, the scholar Yasui Sokken, is depicted with a sympathetic identification which anticipates Ōgai's "spiritual autobiography" in *Shibue Chūsai*. But, as the title attests, the real subject of "Yasui fujin" is Sokken's wife Sayo. In an important passage after Sayo's death, Ōgai reflects as follows:

> What kind of woman was Sayo? Wearing rough clothing over her own beautiful skin, she passed her life serving Chūhei [Sokken], with his simple tastes. Another member of the Yasui family named Rimpei lived at Kofuse, about two *ri* from Aza-Hoshikura of Agata-mura in Obi. His wife Oshina, remembering the anniversary of Sayo's death, took to Chūhei's house a gift of lined kimono of striped cotton. Probably Sayo had rarely worn anything made of silk during her life.
>
> Sayo never refrained from the hard labors of serving her husband. Nor did she ever ask for anything in return. Nor was it a question of her being content merely with rough clothing. She never said that she wanted to live in an elaborate house, nor that she wanted all the proper things to use in her home, nor that she liked to eat good things or to see interesting things.
>
> She was surely not so foolish that she did not understand what luxury was, nor could she have been so selfless as to have no needs or desires for anything physical or spiritual. In fact Sayo did seem to have had one uncommon desire, before which all else was only dust and ashes to her. What was her desire? It was that the intelligent persons of society would say that she had hoped for the

distinction of her husband. I who write this cannot deny it. Yet on the other hand, I cannot crudely agree with the view that she merely gave her labors and her patience to her husband as some merchant invested capital for profit, but dying before any recompense could come.

Sayo had a dream, some image of the future. Until her death, did not the look in her beautiful eyes seem fixed on some far, far place; or was it that she had no leisure even to feel that her own death might be unfortunate? Was not the very object of her hope something which she never precisely clarified for herself?

Here Ōgai has departed from the historical narrative to recapitulate the "eternal malcontent" theme of "Mōsō," and has reiterated a similar Romantic effect of "looking off into the distance" that can be found in such works as "Fumizukai," "Shizuka," "Mōsō," *Gan*, "Sanshō dayū," and other stories. Sayo's precise psychology is left unclarified by Ōgai, and yet she seems to be closely related to Shina, the mistress of Date Tsunamune in "Suginohara Shina," and is perhaps even more a reincarnation of Otama in *Gan*. She takes us to the edge of gaining insight into Ōgai's own inner psychology.

Sayo functions as an important access to Ōgai's aesthetic intention in another passage:

Sayo did her housework without any care for her own looks. Still the earlier traces of "Ono no Komachi" remained there to see. About this time a man named Kuroki Magoemon came to call on Chūhei. He had formerly been a fisherman in Sotoura of Obi, but because of his detailed knowledge of natural history he had been summoned to Edo to serve under a shogunate Censor. After Sayo served them tea, Magoemon's eyes followed her back to the kitchen, and then with a crafty and humorous look he inquired of Chūhei:

"Sir, is she your wife?"

"Yes, she is," Chūhei answered noncommittally.

"Indeed. Has your wife been educated?"

"No, not to the degree of a formal education."

"Then your wife has insight over and above your learning."

"Oh, how so?"

"Because even though she is such a beautiful woman, she became your wife."

Ōgai's technique here is that of superb impressionism.

That Sayo was not only physically but spiritually beautiful—she is thus the reincarnation of the "Hanako" theme—and was blessed, or fated, to feel the call of some transcendent purpose which gave meaning to her obscure life, is an exemplification of the kind of Platonic sense of the Beautiful Ōgai seems to have felt in his own life. This kind of intimation of the Idea of the Beautiful, often accompanied by a sense of the sublime, is integral to the mood of several of Ōgai's historical stories.

The character of Anju, the young girl who sacrifices her life for the sake of her brother's escape from slavery in "Sanshō dayū," is another illustration of this theme. As Okazaki Yoshie has observed, Anju is the central figure of this famous, and exquisitely written in Japanese, transformation by Ōgai of an old Japanese legend.[48] ("Sanshō dayū" is perhaps the work in which Ōgai has most poignantly elicited the traditional Japanese aesthetic sense of *mono no aware*.) In the course of the story Anju takes on a "mystical" dimension that sheds important light upon a similar expression of Ōgai's symbolic imagination in other female characters—in Otama of *Gan*, for example, in the old lady Run of "Jiisan baasan," in Sayo of "Yasui fujin," in Yū Hsüan-chi of "Gyogenki," in Ichi of "Saigo no ikku," in Suginohara Shina in the biography of the same name, and in Iyo, the wife of Shibue Chūsai. Anju represents the tragic, unrequited, repressed, obscure sides of these female characters in the most extreme form. She is also a reincarnation of Elisa of "Maihime."

Ōgai wrote of his devotion to "history in itself," in contrast to giving free play to his fictional imagination, in his essay "Rekishi sono mama to rekishibanare" (1915). This essay was in fact written directly after he published "Sanshō dayū," and can be read as an exegesis on that work. At the same time, we must bear in mind that Ōgai used the historical, or in this case legendary, medium as a vehicle of his hermeneutical discovery of ontological dimensions of personal and cultural experience—and as a vehicle of his literary typology of ideal human qualities. "Sanshō dayū" was a tour de force in that Ōgai worked within a predetermined story frame to create an idealization of Anju, the central expression of his creative imagination, in his own version of the legend. But even Zushiō is a reincarnation of other male characters—of Ōta of "Maihime," Okada of *Gan*, of many of the samurai personages of the late stories and biographies.

Let us take note of only one illustration of this in "Sanshō dayū." At precisely the point when Anju has led her puzzled brother to the peak of a small mountain to announce her startling plan for his escape, Ōgai employs another variation on the central Romantic symbol that appears in such works as "Mōsō" and *Gan*, and that we cited above in our comments on "Yasui fujin":

> Anju stood there staring intently toward the south. Her eyes followed the upper reaches of the Okumo River as it passed Ishiura and flowed into the harbor of Yura; she stopped when she saw a pagoda thrusting from the dense foliage on Nakayama, a mountain about two miles from the other side of the river bank.

After persuading Zushiō of her fateful plan, Anju "stood by the spring and watched the figure of her brother grow smaller as he appeared, then disappeared behind rows of pine trees.'' With Zushiō now on his precarious way to safety and to the climax of the original legend, Ōgai swiftly completes the Romantic symbolization in regard to Anju:

> Later the search party sent out by Sanshō Dayū to catch the pair picked up a pair of small straw sandals at the edge of the swamp at the bottom of the hill. They belonged to Anju.

Anju's death, as well as her parting from Zushiō, retell the tragically beautiful endings of "Maihime," "Utakata no ki," *Gan*, and other works.

Against this background it becomes possible to gain insight into "Jiisan baasan," a brief masterpiece which expresses Ōgai's continued idealization of his female characters. Written six months after "Sanshō dayū," the story revolves around the spiritual beauty of the wife Run. It would, of course, be a gross misreading of this jewel of what the Japanese call *shibui* (understated) and *sabishii* (lonely) qualities to dwell on the swashbuckling samurai episode it contains. Run's exiled husband Iori suffers the consequences of his manly pride; but the story as a whole centers around the love and faithfulness of Run, and is essentially expressive of Ōgai's characteristic sense of the fate, and often tragedy, that is associated with beauty and the attainment of worth in human life. Undoubtedly another reflection of Ōgai's inner spirituality, this writer recommends that "Jiisan baasan" also be read as the sequel to *Gan* and "Sanshō dayū."

"Saigo no ikku" portrays another side of Ōgai's own psychology, emphasizing the power of will and pride in an idealized way. His oblique comment on bureaucratic types is apparent in this story and in "Kanzan Jittoku," which builds to its dramatic and ironic conclusion in similar fashion.

But all the above elements came together in "Takasebune," which we recall was written in the same year as "Shibue Chūsai" (1916). "Takasebune" raises ethical and social questions important in Ōgai's own life—such as euthanasia—in a symbolic way, and is evidently a medium for his own latter-day transformation of the *teinen* and *asobi* sensibilities of his middle years. But the work as a whole is enveloped in a mystically serene atmosphere that may best typify the "Apollonian" quality of Ōgai's final perception of life. It is a consummate expression of the fusion of intellect and emotion in Ōgai's mature temperament.

 From this brief sampling of the themes of some of the historical stories we can conclude that Ōgai created his "historical literature" in an imaginative horizon which transcended the domain of formal historiography. The concepts of "history in itself" and "history as nature" which Ōgai set forth in "Rekishi sono mama to rekishibanare" were primarily *aesthetic* concepts, and not a retreat by Ōgai into the domain of scientific fact. Accordingly they do not represent a conversion to literary "realism" either, but rather an innovative effort at synthesis of his classicism and romanticism.

Ōgai always wrote autobiographically, and in this, to be sure, he retained the attitude and habits of a scholar and historian (often, self-historian) to a noteworthy extent, rather than giving free rein to his "fictional imagination." This was his own confession in "Rekishi sono mama to rekishibanare." In this way Ōgai strove to remain truer to his own disposition and genius than if he had striven to follow the contemporary standards of novel-making. One purport of "Yo ga tachiba" (1909) was to assert his independence from the "Western" novel-making criterion which contemporary critics were exercising. In "Tsuina," published in the same year and one month after *Vita Sexualis*, he wrote: "I, with my 'thoughts in the night,' have concluded that what we call literary prose may be written about anything and in any style."[49] Like every authentic artist, Ōgai succeeded in finding his own inimitable material and style, that of historical literature as oblique spiritual autobiography. Even *Gan*, perhaps the most "novelistic" of Ōgai's writings, becomes wholly intelligible only in the light of the continuing inner dialogue which Ōgai's stories as a whole represent.

Because of the concentrated form of that inner dialogue, Ōgai's writings place heavy demands upon the reader. His stories are a complex system of interlocking and interresonating parts, an ever-compounding fund of conceptual and symbolic elements. One is left wondering, for example, at the precise relation between "Hannichi" and "Hebi," two stories that are clearly autobiographical in respect to the tense relationship that existed between Ōgai's second wife, Shigeko, and his own mother. A much more complex synthesis of symbolic elements obtains in the vivid snake symbols employed in "Hebi" (where the sight of a snake at her mother-in-law's funeral altar causes the wife to go mad) and in *Gan* (where the student Okada saves Otama's caged canary from being devoured by a snake). Often Ōgai spreads out his own self-reflection in several characters, both male and female, in the same story, only to reverse the symbolic variables in another, but interresonating story. As I have tried to suggest above, the reader must be aware that Ōgai continued this inner literary dialogue in his late historical stories: "Jiisan baasan" (1915) is the sequel not only to *Gan* (1911–1913) but to "Maihime" (1898). The reader who will take the trouble to explore this labyrinth of symbolic clues will be rewarded by a growing insight into an intense psychology and intricate genius of genuine "East-West" proportions.

According to all commentators, the most important, if not also most difficult, clues to Ōgai's spiritual autobiography came in *Shibue Chūsai*

(1916), a full-length work. He then continued this self-reflection for over a thousand more pages in *Izawa Ranken* (1917) and *Hōjō Katei* (1918). And it is of great interest that in these late historical biographies Ōgai pursued his imaginative identification not only with Chūsai, Ranken, and Katei, three generations of Tokugawa Confucian scholars, but that his essential humanity and intellectual energy is also revealed in his exploration of the historical record of Chūsai's wife Iyo, of their seven sons and seven daughters, and of more than fifteen of his friends and teachers. This extraordinary project of Ōgai's declining years, as Okazaki Yoshie has pointed out, did not originate from any external influence.[50] The same commentator has observed that the aestheticized elements in *Shibue Chūsai* are reminiscent of a similar effect in such historical classics of the Japanese tradition as the *Kojiki, Heike monogatari,* and the *Nihon gaishi.*[51] *Shibue Chūsai* is Ōgai's "classic."

In conclusion, there is a revealing passage in the opening pages of *Vita Sexualis* in which the protagonist, a philosopher named Shizuki Kanai, says he has a habit of reading many contemporary novels, but does not find many of real aesthetic worth. To Kanai, a work achieves real aesthetic value only if it meets a very high standard.[52] This observation was perhaps part of Ōgai's own self-reflective "eternal malcontent" theme and a confession of his own unrealized genius at that time. Ōgai clearly felt a high aesthetic demand. He seems to have come closest to satisfying it in his historical literature between 1912 and 1916.

Ōgai will perhaps always remain an elusive and difficult genius. Like the characters in his historical stories, he has already become an enigmatic reflection of a particular sense of values embedded in his time and circumstance. Of the Ōgai we can understand, however, we can say that he bore witness to a sense of "civilization and enlightenment" that had few parallels among his contemporaries. And his career remains paradigmatic of the strength, dynamism, and integrity of the indigenous process of Japanese modernization in the last century. We might ponder these high distinctions as we read Ōgai's historical literature. More importantly, perhaps, we should take cognizance of the fact that not only is Ōgai a great figure in this Japanese Renaissance, but that he has sought out problems that are also *our* problems, as co-inhabitants of the twentieth century.

DAVID A. DILWORTH

THE STORIES

OKITSU YAGOEMON NO ISHO

"THE LAST TESTAMENT OF OKITSU YAGOEMON" is the first of Ōgai's historical stories. The Meiji emperor died on July 30, 1912. Ōgai participated in the funeral ceremonies, which took place on September 13. On that day, General Nogi Maresuke (1849–1912) and his wife committed *junshi*. Ōgai's diary records that he received the news of this on the following day, while he was returning from the funeral ceremonies. The entry in his diary for that day simply records: "I half believe and half doubt it." The entry in his diary five days later (September 19) records that he accompanied the bier of General Nogi, and then submitted "The Last Testament of Okitsu Yagoemon" to *Chūō kōron* magazine for publication.

The first version of the story appeared in October 1912. In December of that year he began revising it, and, according to his diary, finished a second, expanded version between April 3 and 6, 1913. This second version was published in June 1913.

At the time of his suicide, some interpreted Nogi's action as appropriate to a warrior, while others felt considerable apprehension at this manifestation of the vitality of feudalistic morality in the twentieth century. The story represents Ōgai's first reaction to the event. He took another view of *junshi* in his story "Abe ichizoku," which he finished in the last days of November 1912, and which was published in January 1913. The two stories are thus related in subject and provide a striking contrast when read together.

Ōgai's choice of a historical personage (Yagoemon) who, in fact, did commit suicide in the manner described in the story provides an effective parallel to General Nogi. Nogi's particular feelings of devotion for the emperor centered around an incident in 1877 when, during the Satsuma Rebellion (a civil uprising in southern Japan), he lost a military flag. In Ōgai's story, Yagoemon, in trying to carry out his duty to his lord, Hosokawa Sansai Tadatoki, killed a man. He too offers to commit suicide, but as was Nogi, is told to live and continue to serve. (Later, General Nogi returned from the Russo-Japanese War as the hero of the battle of Port Arthur. Ōgai had distinguished himself in the same campaign.)

The story amplifies the nature of the act and its motivation as repayment of a debt of gratitude—Ōgai moves beyond the austerity of Nogi and his value world. Yagoemon, like Nogi, had when younger requested orders to commit suicide, but for a different reason. He had killed his associate as a climax to an argument about how to spend his lord's money. The associate had insisted that to pay a premium price for incense wood was a waste, had argued that it was better to buy a cheaper substitute, that money should only be unbegrudged for things proper to a warrior, like weapons. Yagoemon's position, however, was that the lord's command must be obeyed in literal detail; and beyond this technical argument, he defends the validity of spending money for other than a purely utilitarian purpose. He is later confirmed in this position by his lord. There is more to life than weapons and horses, and Ōgai, by this analogy, is asserting there is more to life than the trappings of technologically advanced civilization. But while he makes this point, the story's most important point is in its celebration of the continued life of venerated tradition.

The story is written in the complex and ceremonial language of the Tokugawa period, which lends it a considerable note of authenticity. In the interests of clarity and readability, however, no attempt has been made to reproduce this aspect of Ōgai's original text.

Ōgai continued to write about the influential Hosokawa family in many of his subsequent historical narratives: "Abe ichizoku" and "Kuriyama Daizen," for example, paint other portraits of the three generations portrayed here but from a different vantage point. Aesthetic and philosophical themes, touched on here, also figure in the later stories. "Okitsu Yagoemon no isho" is the striking beginning to a long series.

First Version

MY RITUAL SUICIDE today will no doubt come as a great shock and there will be those who claim that I, Yagoemon, am either senile or deranged. But this is very far from the truth.

Ever since my retirement I have been engaged in building a hut of the simplest kind here at the western foot of Mt. Funaoka.[1] The rest of my family moved from the castle town of Yatsushiro in Higo after the demise of my former master Lord Shōkōji and they are now living in the same province of Higo, but at Kumamoto. They will, as a result, be extremely shaken when they set eyes on this testament, but I request that someone nearby should send it to them at the first opportunity. I have for some years now lived the life of a Buddhist priest, but compose this last testament because at heart I am a warrior and thus deeply concerned about my posthumous reputation.

My hut is of so wretched an appearance that those who see the year is drawing to its close may even suppose that I commit suicide on account of debts. But I leave no debts. Nor do I propose to put anyone to the slightest expense on my behalf. In a box in the wall-cupboard by the side of the tokonoma are some savings, which although but a trifle, I request most earnestly be used to pay for my cremation. I should deem myself most fortunate if you would also send a little something with this note to those relatives in Kumamoto whom I have just mentioned—just a fingernail perhaps, for I have shaved my head quite bare.

The three wooden funeral tablets which are standing in the tokonoma are for three men: my former master Hosokawa Tadaoki, lord of Etchū, known in retirement as Lord Sōryū Sansai and in death as Lord Shōkōji; Hosokawa Tadatoshi, lord of Etchū, known in death as Lord Myōge Inden; and Hosokawa Mitsuhisa, lord of Higo. I request that care be taken to burn them in holy fire so that they may not be subjected to any disrespectful treatment. I end my life today, the second day of the twelfth month of the first year of Manji [1658], since it corresponds to the thirteenth anniversary of the death of Lord Shōkōji, who passed away on the second day of the twelfth month of the second year of Shōhō [1645].

TRANSLATED BY RICHARD BOWRING

As I wish that the reason for my death should be understood by my descendants, I leave the following account.

It happened full thirty years ago. In the fifth month of the first year of Kan'ei [1624], a ship from Annam arrived at Nagasaki. It was three years since Lord Shōkōji had taken the tonsure. He gave me orders to purchase a rare article that he would be able to use in the tea ceremony, and so I set out for Nagasaki with a colleague. As luck would have it a large tree of rare aloeswood had been imported. It was, however, in two parts—the bole and the upper branches—and a retainer who had been sent all the way from Sendai by Lord Date Gonchūnagon decided he must have the bole. I too had my eye on the same piece of wood and so we bid against each other and gradually forced up the price.

At this point my colleague said that even if it were our master's orders, scented wood was a useless plaything and it would be wrong to throw away a vast amount of money on it. He would prefer to let the Date have the bole and ourselves to buy the upper branches. I could not agree, I told him. My master's orders were to go and buy a rare article and the finest thing among these imported goods was the aloeswood. Since it was in two parts, it was obvious that the bole was the rarest of the rare and only by buying that would we be carrying out our master's orders. If we let the Date grow ostentatious and allowed them to take the bole, the name of the Hosokawa would be defiled.

My colleague laughed at me and said I was putting too much emphasis on the matter. If it were a case of whether we should give or take a province or a castle, then of course we should fight the Date to the bitter end. But was this not just a piece of wood to be burned in the firepot of a room designed for the tea ceremony? It was unthinkable to spend so much money on it. If our master himself were bidding for it, we should, as his retainers, try to dissuade him. Even if he had his heart set on getting the bole, to let him accomplish his desire would be an act of gross flattery.

I was not yet thirty then and took offense at what he said, but held myself in check. It all sounded very clever, I said, but my one concern was for the orders and requests of my master. If he had ordered me to capture a castle I would have taken it though it had walls of steel. If he had ordered me to behead a man I would have done so though he were a devil. Similarly, since he had ordered me to buy a rare article, I felt I must look for something unique. So long as it was my master's orders, it was not for me to meddle or criticize; providing, of course, it was not contrary to moral principles.

He laughed at me all the more. He agreed with me, he said. Had I not just said one should not do anything contrary to one's principles? If we were dealing with military equipment he would not have minded spending an enormous sum of money, but to try and pay a price out of all proportion to the value of the wood was a sign of youthful imprudence, he said.

I knew the difference between military equipment and scented wood despite my age, I retorted. When Taishō Inden[2] had been head of the family, Lord Gamō[3] had said that he had heard the Hosokawa had many excellent articles and so would come himself to see them. The appointed day arrived. When Lord Gamō appeared, Taishō Inden brought out various kinds of armor, swords, bows and spears to show him. Lord Gamō was somewhat surprised, but looked them over once and then said that he had really come to see the tea utensils. Taishō Inden laughed. As Lord Gamō had said "articles" before, he had shown him the articles that a military family was usually known for. If it was tea utensils Lord Gamō wanted to see, then he did happen to have a few of those as well. Only then did he bring them out. Could there be another such family in Japan which had devoted itself to military matters for generations and yet was also skilled in such arts as poetry and the tea ceremony? If one were to claim that the tea ceremony was a useless formality, then so were state ceremonies and festivals for one's ancestors. The order we had received this time was to buy a rare article for use in the tea ceremony—nothing more. It was our master's order and so we must carry it out even at the cost of our lives. It was because my colleague did not understand the art of tea that he obstinately considered it was unreasonable for our master to spend a great sum on scented wood, I replied.

He did not even wait for me to finish. "Of course I know nothing of the tea ceremony! Of course I am a stubborn warrior! As you are so skilled in a variety of arts, let's see your main accomplishment!" he said, jumping up. There in the inn he seized his sword from the rack in the tokonoma and swung at me out of the blue. My sword was hanging in the rack under the double shelves of the alcove, and as there was nothing else near at hand I grabbed a bronze vase in which there was a spring flower arrangement of lilies and thus parried his blow. I jumped aside, reached for my sword, and whipping it out, cut him down with one stroke.

I purchased the bole of the aloeswood without further ado and returned with it to the auxilary castle of the Hosokawa family located at Kitsuki. The retainer from the Date clan had no choice but to buy the upper branches and take them back to Sendai. Presenting the scented wood to Lord Shōkōji, I requested permission to commit *seppuku*. I had placed such great store by my master's orders that I had killed a samurai who would have been of use to him. Lord Shōkōji listened to my story. He then replied that everything I said was quite within reason, and, even if the scented wood turned out not to be valuable, there was no doubt that it was the rare article he had ordered me to go and buy. I was therefore right to have felt the matter important. If we looked at everything with an eye to its utility there would be nothing left to value in the world he said. Moreover he immediately kindled a piece of the aloeswood I had brought back. It was of rare quality and he named it Hatsune ["the first song"] from the ancient poem "Whenever one hears the cuckoo call it sounds so striking; always singing its first song." He was full of praise that I had brought back an article of such quality. But the descendants of the man I had killed must not harbor any grudge, he said. He immediately ordered my colleague's son to appear, had sake brought out before us, and we pledged together that no grudge would be held on either side.

Two years later, on the sixth day of the ninth month of the third year of Kan'ei [1626], when the emperor went in progress to the castle at Nijō, he asked Myōge Inden for some of this fine incense and it was presented to him. The emperor was well pleased and I heard that he called it Shiragiku [white chrysanthemum] from the ancient poem "Who can deny this is unique; a white chrysanthemum that still blooms after the autumn colors are gone." The scented wood that I had brought had been graciously praised by the emperor and had become the pride of the family. I wept at such unexpected happiness.

I had, however, already decided to commit *seppuku* and secretly waited for an appropriate occasion. Meanwhile I was given special favors not only by Lord Shōkōji, who was in retirement, but also by the then head of the family, Lord Myōge Inden. In the ninth year of Kan'ei [1632], on the occasion of the transfer of domains,[4] I not only became a guard at the castle at Yatsushiro where Lord Shōkōji was in residence, but was even ordered to accompany him to the capital. Thus, busy with much arduous work, I saw the days and months pass by to no purpose. Then, in the fourteenth year of Kan'ei [1637], came the campaign against Shimabara and I requested leave from Lord Shōkōji to fight as a hatamoto under Lord Myōge Inden. It was my intention to die in battle, but our military fortunes were excellent and the rebel leader, Amakusa Shirō Tokisada, was killed. Even such insignificant men as myself were rewarded. So I lived on for many years, my long-cherished desire as yet unfulfilled.

However, in the eighteenth year of Kan'ei [1641], Lord Myōge Inden unexpectedly fell ill and died before his father. The lord of Higo became head of the family. Then, in the second year of Shōhō [1645], Lord Shōkōji too passed away. Before these two deaths, in the thirteenth year of Kan'ei [1636], Lord Chūnagon of Sendai, who had prized the same scented wood we had divided, died in his castle at Wakabayashi. The incense from the upper branches he had called Shibafune ["the firewood-boat"], from the poem "See the firewood-boat loaded with the cares of the world: rowed along, love will first be scorched before it is consumed"; and he had kept it as a treasured possession.

Then, in the second year of Keian [1649], the lord of Higo suddenly passed away at the age of thirty-two. In his last hours he worried that his son, Lord Rokumaru,[5] might be unable to control so large a province as he was a mere youth. He informed the shogun that he wished to return the fief. The shogun, however, remembered the family's loyalty since the days of Taishō Inden and so ordered that the seven-year-old Lord Rokumaru be confirmed in the domains.

I then requested that I might retire. I left Kumamoto and came here. But I still felt concern for Lord Rokumaru, and although I was not with him I wished to pray for him that he might rule in peace, at least until he came of age. So, despite my intentions, I lived on for many years.

However, in the second year of Shōō [1653], Rokumaru became lord of Etchū, although he was only eleven. He was given the name Tsunatoshi and enjoyed the favor of the shogun. When I received this news I secretly jumped for joy.

Now I no longer had anything on my mind and yet I felt it would be a pity for me to die of old age. I waited for today, the thirteenth anniversary of the death of Lord Shōkōji, from whom I had received so many favors and whom I yearn to follow, despite having left it so long. I know very well that to follow one's master into death is officially prohibited, but I do not expect to incur censure. I did kill my companion and should have committed suicide many years ago in my youth.

I have no regular friends, but as I have recently been on intimate terms with the priest Seigan at the Daitokuji I earnestly request that those who live nearby should show him this letter before sending it to my home province.

I have been writing this note by the light of a candle which has just gone out. But there is no need to light another. There is sufficient reflection from the snow at the window to enable me to cut across my wrinkled stomach.

The second day of the twelfth month of the first year of Manji.

The signature of Okitsu Yagoemon.

To the reader

This fictitious testament is based on information contained in the *Okinagusa*.[6] That apart, I only consulted the *Tokugawa Jikki* and the *Yashi*,[7] which both happened to be at hand. These are all in print, the *Jikki* being part of the *Zoku Kokushi taikei*. The *Okinagusa* states that Okitsu's death took place on the third anniversary of Sansai's death, but at the same time it dates it about the Manji-Kambun period [c. 1660], so there must be a mistake here. If one works it out on the basis of Sansai's death, the third anniversary would be the first year of Keian [1648]. I therefore changed it and made it the thirteenth anniversary in the first year of Manji [1658].

I do not know when Okitsu went to Nagasaki, but the record has it that the incense called Hatsune was presented to the Emperor Go Mizunoo at the time of his progress to Nijō, and so it must have been before the third year of Kan'ei [1626] when that journey took place. But it also says that Okitsu took the scented wood back to Kumamoto. Here again the year is wrong because Hosokawa Tadatoshi became master of Kumamoto castle in the ninth year of Kan'ei [1632]. As scented wood did come in from Annam in the fifth month of the first year of Kan'ei [1624], just before the Imperial progress to Nijō, I used that date instead and changed Kumamoto to Kitsuki.

Lastly I do not know how old Okitsu was when he died, but there are over thirty years between the Imperial progress to Nijō and the first year of Manji [1658]. As Okitsu was already an official when he went to Nagasaki before the progress, he must have been about sixty at his death, even if he was only in his twenties when he went to Nagasaki. It may seem pretentious to carry out research for a work like this, but I have written down these few facts so that I will not forget them.

October 1912

Second Version

 TOMORROW, I will attain the desire I have cherished for years and with a joyful heart commit *seppuku* before the grave of Lord Hosokawa Myōgein Tadatoshi.[1]

As I wish to write down and leave behind an account of the circumstances of my death for my descendants, I am composing this document in the house of my younger brother Matajirō in Kyoto.

My grandfather was Okitsu Uhyōe Kagemichi. He was born at Okitsu in the province of Suruga in Eishō eleven [1514]; he served Lord Imagawa Jibu Taifu[2] and lived at Kiyomigaseki in the same province. When Lord Imagawa died in battle on the twentieth day of the fifth month of Eiroku three [1560], Kagemichi died with him. He was forty-one years old. His posthumous Buddhist name was Senzan Sōkyū Koji.

My father Saihachi was born in Eiroku one [1558]; since he lost his father at the age of three, he was raised to manhood by his mother. As an adult he took the name of Yagoemon Kagekazu and was taken temporarily into service by Sano Kanjūrō, a relative of his mother's family living in the province of Harima. Through this means he eventually came to serve Lord Akamatsu Sahyōe no kami Hirohisa,[3] and in Tenshō nine [1581] he was given a stipend of one thousand *koku*. Four years later, Lord Akamatsu annexed the province of Awa and established his rule over it; Kagekazu became his intendant for Awa, had his stipend increased by three hundred *koku*, and continued to serve in that function until the first year of Keichō [1596]. During this time he lived in Inotsu. In the seventh month of Keichō five [1600], Lord Akamatsu, with support from Ishida Kazushige,[4] and accompanied by Onogi Nuinosuke[5] of Tamba province, set out to attack the castle of Tanabe in Tango.[6] At that time, Hosokawa Sansai Tadaoki[7] had been defending himself in the castle, but when Tokugawa Ieyasu mounted his attack on Uesugi Kagekatsu,[8] Sansai moved in Ieyasu's support. Behind him in the castle he left his father Hosokawa Yūsai Fujitaka as caretaker.

When Kagekazu had been living in the Akamatsu family mansion in Kyoto, he had become intimate with a certain nobleman, Karasumaru Mitsuhiro.[9] Mitsuhiro studied poetry with Lord Yūsai Fujitaka, and because of this connection, was granted the favor of giving in marriage his son Mitsu-

TRANSLATED BY WILLIAM R. WILSON

kata to Manhime,[10] the daughter of Sansai Tadaoki. Kagekazu, through the good offices of Mitsuhiro, was thus on close terms with both father and son of the Hosokawa family. At the time of the attack on Tanabe, Lord Sansai Tadaoki, who was in Edo, sent as a messenger to the castle a certain Mori Mitsuemon, a cousin of Kagekazu on his mother's side. Mori arrived at Tanabe, talked with Kagekazu and gave him the message; Kagekazu then consulted Ikadō Kamēmon, a unit commander of the Akamatsu family, who fired an arrow with a letter into the Myōan Maru tower of the castle. The next morning Kagekazu had Mori mingle with the scouts and sent him beyond the siege lines. Mori managed to get into the castle without incident, obtained a letter written by Lord Yūsai Fujitaka himself, and then left that night for the Kantō.[11] The house of Akamatsu was destroyed during this year; with the help of Mori, Kagekazu went to Buzen province and in the year following, Keichō six [1601], he was taken into service as retainer of the Hosokawa. In Genna five [1619], a son was born to Mitsuhisa,[12] the next lord of the Hosokawa family, and given the infant name of Rokumaru. Kagekazu was made the boy's personal attendant. In Genna seven [1621], when Lord Sansai Tadaoki retired from public life, Kagekazu also became a monk and took the name of Sōya. On the ninth day of the twelfth month of Kan'ei nine [1632], when Hosokawa Myōgein Tadatoshi arrived in Higo province as daimyo, Kagekazu accompanied him. On the seventeenth day of the third month of Kan'ei eighteen [1641], Tadatoshi died, and on the second day of the ninth month of the same year, Kagekazu also fell ill and passed away. He was eighty-four.

My older brother Kurobē Kazutomo[13] was Kagekazu's heir and came to Buzen with my father; he was summoned by Sansai Tadaoki in Keichō seventeen [1612] to serve as bodyguard and then later, because of illness, was given duties in the border guard. While Myōgein Tadatoshi was head of the Hosokawa family, Kazutomo accompanied him to the attack on Shimabara in the winter of Kan'ei fourteen [1637].[14] On the twenty-seventh day of the second month of the year following, he and Kaneta Yaichiemon were given the title of "First Attackers" in the vanguard of the Hosokawa forces; he died in battle on top of the castle wall facing the sea. His posthumous name is Gishin Eiryū Koji.

I was the second son of Kagekazu and was born in Bunroku four [1595]; my infant name was Saisuke. At seven, I came with my father to Kokura in the province of Buzen, and in Keichō seventeen [1612], I was called into service by Lord Sansai Tadaoki. In Genna seven [1621], when Lord Sansai Tadaoki retired and my father went with him, I accompanied Lord Sansai to Okitsu in Buzen; I was twenty-eight at the time and used my adult name, Yagoemon Kageyoshi.

Three years after Lord Sansai became a monk, in the fifth month of Kan'ei one [1624], a ship from Annam arrived in the port of Nagasaki; I was sent to Nagasaki, along with an associate, Yokota Seibē, to purchase some rare items for use in the tea ceremony. By a happy chance, the cargo included some remarkable, large pieces of aloeswood. There were two sorts of wood, some from the base of the tree and outer wood from the tips of the branches. Another official, representing the Acting Middle Councillor, Lord Date Masamune,[15] had been sent all the way from Sendai; he was trying every way he knew to get the base wood, but as I had my hopes set on the same wood our competition gradually drove up the price.

Yokota's opinion was that, although we were under orders from Lord Sansai, incense wood was a useless plaything and thus we should not throw away any excessive amount of money on it. He much preferred to give up the base wood to the representative of the Date family and buy the outer wood. I told him, however, that I did not agree at all; I had been ordered by my lord to "buy precious things," and since this aloeswood was the most valuable item in the ship's cargo, then the wood from the base was unquestionably the prize of prizes. We should get that wood; only thus could we fulfil our lord's command. I even punned that to let the Date family have the base wood would be to puff up its showy bombast [*date*] and thus soil the stream of the house of Hosokawa [slender river].

Yokota sneered. "It depends on where you put your muscle. If it were a question of taking or giving away a province or a castle, it would be all right to go the limit in setting up against the Date house; but that little bit of wood wouldn't even heat a room three yards square. For that, to throw away a huge price is unthinkable. If our lord himself were here and got into a bidding competition, it would be our duty as his retainers to remonstrate with him and stop him. Even though he insisted that he wanted to get the base wood, to let him go through with it would be the act of servile flatterers."

I listened to these words; I was thirty-one years old at the time. I was furious, but I endured them, and replied, "Your counsel is worthy of a sage. Be that as it may, however, for me, my lord's command is the all important thing. If he ordered me to bring down a castle, I would have to ride over and take even walls of iron; if he ordered me to take an adversary's head, I would have to strike to the finish, even if my opponent were a devil-god; in the same way, if he orders me to obtain precious goods, it is for me to find the most splendid things I can. Since this is, in fact, my lord's command, then unless I shirk my duty, it is useless for me to take a critical attitude."

Yokota smiled more and more derisively. "You don't possibly mean to say that in that way you will not be shirking your bounden duty! If this were military equipment, then no one would begrudge giving a really big sum for it. But to pay such a sum of money for incense wood is the kind of blunder a greenhorn would make."

"Greenhorn I may be," I said, "but I certainly know the difference between weapons and incense wood. In the time of Lord Yūsai Fujitaka, Lord Gamō[16] once asked, 'I have heard that the House of Hosokawa has a great quantity of splendid implements. May I come and view them?' On the appointed day Lord Gamō came, and Lord Yūsai Fujitaka ranged all kinds of helmets, armor, swords, bows, and spears to show him. Lord Gamō, thinking this peculiar, had a look at them, then said, 'Actually I wanted to see the implements for the tea ceremony.' Lord Yūsai Fujitaka smiled. 'As you originally said implements, I showed you implements of the art one naturally expects in a military house. If it is tea implements you want to see, then I happen to have a few of those also.' And with this he brought them out for the first time. The House of Hosokawa has been deeply concerned with the military arts for generations; but they have also been profoundly versed in the arts of poetry and the tea ceremony; indeed, this is a matchless combination. If you think the tea ceremony is merely a useless, empty formality, then all the great ceremonies of the nation, all the shrine festivals for our ancestors must be empty formalities as well. We have now received a command to obtain precious things useful for the tea ceremony. Since this is my lord's command, I will carry it out if my life depends on it. Your thought, sir, that spending a large sum of money for fragrant wood is improper is bull-headed; you think this way because you have no comprehension of the art."

Yokota did not wait to hear me out. "That's right. I have no comprehension of the tea ceremony. I'm just a bull-headed, simple warrior. Let me see how good you are at your proper trade, you who are so accomplished in the arts." As he said this, he rose abruptly and threw his short sword at me. I dodged. My sword was on a sword-stand at the bottom of some step-shelves; jumping back, I took it and drew. With only one blow, I finished off Yokota.

Thus I soon secured the base wood and brought it back to Okitsu. The official sent by the house of Date had to be satisfied with the outer wood, which he bought and took back to Sendai. I had the incense wood taken to Prince Sansai. Then I made the request: "Although I held my lord's command as all important, since I nevertheless have killed a warrior useful in your service, and am overwhelmed with shame, I wish to be permitted to commit *seppuku*."

Prince Sansai listened, then said to me, "What you did was correct in every respect. Even if incense wood were not so highly esteemed, because it is precisely the rare article I asked you to obtain, it was perfectly proper that you considered it important. If one looked at everything from only a utilitarian viewpoint, all the things most esteemed in this world would go out of existence. What is more, when I quickly burned some of the wood you brought as a trial, it proved to be a rare and marvelous wood. There is an old poem,

> *Kiku tabi ni*
> *Mezurashikereba*
> *Hototogisu*
> *Itsumo hatsune no*
> *Kokochi koso sure*
>
> Since it is marvelous
> Whenever one hears
> The cuckoo,
> Always one feels
> It is its first song of the year

and, with the idea of the poem in mind, I have called this wood 'First Song.' Bringing me back such a fine article is truly an outstanding service. "However, it will never do for the family of that Yokota Seibē you killed to hold a grudge against you." He immediately called Seibē's heir, and, as we exchanged sake cups in our lord's presence, we swore to bear no ill-will against each other. However—perhaps the people of the Yokota family hinted that they might have other ideas—they eventually went over to live in the province of Chikuzen. As for me, Prince Sansai granted me the use of the character "oki" from his name Tadaoki and accordingly made an official disposition to change the character with which I write my name, Okitsu.

Two years later, on the sixth day of the ninth month of Kan'ei three [1626], the emperor[17] visited Nijō castle in Kyoto. He expressed a wish for some of that famous incense of Sansai, which my lord presented to him. The emperor was highly pleased, and in the spirit of the old poem

> *Tagui ari to*
> *Tare ka wa iwamu*
> *Sue niou*
> *Aki yori nochi no*
> *Shiragiku no hana*
>
> Who shall say
> There is their equal:
> Fragrant to the last
> Lingering after autumn,
> White chrysanthemum blooms

he bestowed on the wood the name "White Chrysanthemum." The fact that this wood which I had bought received the praise of the emperor and became the glory of the house of Hosokawa was something I could never have hoped for; I was moved to tears.

After this occasion, I received special favors from Lord Sansai and when the Hosokawa family was transferred to a new fief [Kumamoto] in Kan'ei nine [1632], I was given duties in the castle of Prince Sansai at Yatsushiro. In addition, I was even sent along as an attendant when my lord went to the capital. It was at this time that the Shimabara Rebellion was put down, in Kan'ei fourteen [1637]. I was included in the bodyguard of the younger brother of Lord Tadatoshi, Lord Tatsutaka,[18] and I was entrusted with his banner. On the twenty-second day of the second month of the following year, when I placed the banner first at the point of attack of the Hosokawa forces, I was hit in the left thigh by a musket ball and barely managed to escape. At that time I was forty-five years old. After I recovered from my wound I was ordered to duty in Edo in Kan'ei sixteen [1639].

In Kan'ei eighteen [1641], Myōgein Tadatoshi passed away from a sudden and unexpected illness, dying before his father. The head of the Hosokawa family now became the present lord of Higo, Lord Mitsuhisa. My father Yagoemon Kagekazu died on the second day of the ninth month of the same year. Four years later, in Shōhō two [1645], Prince Sansai also died. Some years before, in Kan'ei thirteen [1636], the lord of the Date house in Sendai who had so highly valued that incense wood, and who had received the outer wood had passed away in his castle at Wakabayashi. It was said that he gave the name "Brush-boat" to the incense made from his outer wood, in the spirit of the poem,

> Yo no naka no
> Uki wo mi ni tsumu
> Shibabune ya
> Takanu saki yori
> Kogareyukuramu

> That brush boat
> Like my heart aflame with love
> In which one loads on me
> The bitterness of this world!
> Before one uses all one's strength
> It will be rowed away
> Before, like incense, one burns the brush—
> Like it my heart will char away

He evidently cherished it as a precious thing.

When I carefully considered everything that happened since my late father came to serve the house of Hosokawa, it is quite clear that both my father and my elder brother received special favors in all matters. As far as I myself was concerned, Lord Sansai saved my life when I finished off my colleague Yokota Seibē in Nagasaki. After the death of the master to whom I had this double obligation, I made up my mind: how could I live on?

When Lord Myōgein Tadatoshi died several years previously, nineteen men committed suicide to follow him,[19] and two years ago, when Lord Sansai died, four men—Minota Heishichi Masamoto, Ono Dembē Tomotsugu, Kuno Yoemon Munenao, Hōsen'in Shōen Gyōja[20]—also followed him in death. Minota's great-grandfather, a man named Izumi, was a Han Elder who served Sagara, the lord of Tōtōmi, and died in battle with his lord; his grandfather Wakasa and his father Ushinosuke were wanderers, but Heishichi was taken into the service of Prince Sansai with a stipend of five hundred *koku*. Heishichi committed *seppuku* at the age of twenty-three; the page Isobe Chōgorō acted as his second. Ono was taken in service in place of his grandfather Imayasu Tarōzaemon in Tango province. At the time his father, Tanaka Jinzaemon, had disobeyed his lord and absconded from his Edo mansion, Dembē, who was serving as a page, was commanded, "Search out your father and bring him back. If you come back without finding him, I will execute you in your father's place." Dembē came back with the story that although he had traveled through a number of provinces, he had not come across him. Prince Sansai then pardoned him, making the judgment that he should be praised for returning without regard for the death sentence. Dembē, bearing in mind this obligation, committed *seppuku*. His second was Isoda Jūrō. Kuno was taken into service in Tango province by Prince Fujitaka Yūsai; he was a man who had been granted a new stipend of one hundred and fifty *koku* for distinguished service at the siege of Tanabe castle. Yano Matasaburō was his second. Hōsen'in was a *yamabushi*[21] who blew a battle conch; he was the son of Ishii Bingo no kami Yoshimura, the younger brother of Tsutsui Junkei.[22] I hear that his second was a *yamabushi* friend of his.

Seeing and hearing reports of such things, I felt envious and was impatient to demonstrate my own feelings; but having been left in Edo on caretaker duty, it was impossible to make any arrangements through outsiders, and so I resigned myself to the empty passage of the days and months. After the remains of Lord Sansai were cremated in the temple Taishōin in Yatsushiro, the priest Sen'yo, in accordance with Sansai's will, escorted his bones to Kyoto on the eleventh day of the first month of last year. Six persons set out with him as attendants: Nagaoka Kawachi Kagenori, Kaku Sakuzaemon

Ietsugu, Yamada San'emon, Sakata Genzaemon Hidenobu, and Yoshida Ken'an. On the twenty-fourth, the party arrived in Kyoto and deposited the bones in the Kōtōin, in the precincts of the Daitokuji temple in the Murasakino district. This procedure was in accordance with an agreement made during Sansai's lifetime with the Abbot Seigan[23] of that temple.

When my official duties were finished this year, I stated my cherished wish to my present lord, Mitsuhisa, who acceded to my inflexible determination. On the twenty-ninth day of the tenth month, in the morning, I went to take my leave of him; he entertained me, giving me tea prepared with his own hands. As a mark of special favor he gave me two padded silk robes marked with the nine-star crest of the Hosokawa family, and lined in red. After I withdrew, he sent two gentlemen as messengers, Hayashi Geki and Fujisaki Sakuzaemon. Through them he informed me that I need have no anxiety for my family after my death; he also sent me a poem and kindly told me that when I went to Kyoto, I should make all arrangements in consultation with Furuhashi Kozaemon. Two lords, Hotta Kaga no kami and Inaba Noto no kami,[24] also sent poems. On the second day of the eleventh month, as I left Edo, Tanaka Sahyōe came along as emissary of my present lord to see me off as far as Shinagawa.

Since arriving here, I am indebted to the master of this house, my younger brother Matajirō, for his hospitality. Thus I will him my dagger as a keepsake after my death.

The men who have sent poems in Chinese or Japanese as farewell gifts are: Karasumaru Dainagon Sukeyoshi, Uramatsu Saishō Sukekiyo,[25] the Abbot Seigan of Daitokuji, and the elder monks of Nanzenji, Myōshinji, Tenryūji, Shōkokuji, Kenninji, Tōfukuji, and the Kōfukuji in Nara.

Through arrangements made by Furuhashi, I understand that a temporary building has been put up at the foot of Mount Funaoka as the place for my *seppuku* tomorrow. In the length of eighteen *chō* that runs from the front of the gate of Daitokuji to this temporary building, they have spread thirty-eight hundred straw mats; inside the temporary building they have laid one tatami mat and covered it with white cloth. All of this suggests a spectacle, and makes me feel uneasy; but if this is my lord's will, there is nothing to be done about it. As witnesses, Tani Kuranosuke, the Han Elder Nagaoka Yohachirō, and Hanzaemon of his family have come as representatives of Lord Mitsuhisa; the Abbot Seigan Jitsudō of Daitokuji will also be present. My son Saiemon also should come. I have already requested Nomi Ichirobē Katsuyoshi to serve as second.

For my posthumous name I have selected Kohō Fuhaku. Unworthy though my station may be, I do not feel I will make an ignoble end. As to this last testament, I leave it addressed to my son Saiemon: son after son, grandson after grandson should pass it down, succeeding in their turns to my aim; they must excel in loyal devotion in service to our noble house.

Shōhō four [1647], first day of the twelfth month

Okitsu Yagoemon Kageyoshi

To: Okitsu Saiemon

On the second of the twelfth month, Shōhō four, Okitsu Yagoemon Kageyoshi made a ceremonial visit to the graves in Kōtōin, then entered the temporary building set up at the foot of Mt. Funaoka. Advancing onto the tatami, he took the short sword in his hands. Turning his head toward Nomi Ichirobē standing behind, he addressed him, "I make my request." From above his white clothes he cut his belly in three parallel lines. Nomi cut the nape of the neck with one stroke, but was a little short of cutting through. Yagoemon said, "Stab my windpipe." However, Yagoemon stopped breathing before Nomi brought down his hands.

Around the temporary building, residents of Kyoto, of all ages, were crowded like a wall. Among the extemporaneous anonymous poems composed on the occasion, one put it:

> To the cloud-well (Imperial Court)
> He raised a name
> Without a peer,
> Okitsu Yagoe, hailing the sky
> Cut his belly, following his lord.[26]

The genealogical table of the house of Okitsu is in summary as follows:

[omitted]

Yagoemon Kageyoshi's heir, Saiemon Kazusada, was granted a stipend of two hundred *koku* and served until he was chief of thirty muskets; in Hōei one [1704], he died of illness. He was the fourth generation from Uhyōe Kagemichi. The fifth-generation Yagoemon served until he was chief of ten muskets, and died of illness in Gembun four [1739]. The sixth-generation Yachūta served as a provost guard and retired in Hōreki six [1756]. The seventh-generation Kurōji served as a provost guard and retired in An'ei five [1776]. The eighth-generation Kurobē was an adopted son; he served as pro-

vost guard, and died of illness in Bunka one [1804]. The ninth-generation
Eiki was an adopted son; he served as provost guard, and died of illness in
Bunsei nine [1826]. The tenth-generation Yachūta was Eiki's heir; later he
changed his name to Saiemon. He served as provost guard, and died of illness in Man'en one [1860]. The eleventh-generation Yagoemon was Saiemon's second son; later he changed his name to Sōya. He was skilled at the
exercise of shooting dogs from horseback with bow and arrow. In Meiji three
[1870] he was made *banshi* [member of a Guard unit].

   Yagoemon Kageyoshi's father Kagekazu had six sons, his eldest being
Kurobē Kazutomo, and his second being Kageyoshi. The third son, Han-
zaburō, later changed his name to Sakudaifu Kageyuki; he died of illness in
Keian five [1652]. His child Yagodaifu died of illness in Kambun eleven
[1671] and his house came to an end. Kagekazu's fourth son Chūta later
changed his name to Shirōemon Kagetoki. In Genna one [1615], in the
Osaka Summer Campaign, he followed Lord Sansai and rendered distinguished military service, but because at the time of distribution of rewards
he declined, saying he had some reservations, he was discharged from service. After that he changed his family name to Teramoto and, going to
Kameyama in the province of Ise, took service with Honda Shimōsa no kami
Toshitsugu.[27] Next, he was made commissioner of the posting towns of Sakanoshita, Seki, and Kameyama.[28] In the winter of Kan'ei fourteen [1637],
the various lords of the western provinces hurriedly departed Edo to deal
with the Shimabara uprising. Hosokawa Etchū no kami Tadatoshi[29] and
Kuroda Uemon no suke Tadayuki[30] set out from Edo on the Tōkaidō high-
way on the same day. They were hampered by a shortage of men and horses.
Tadayuki got a day's ride ahead, but Teramoto Shirōemon borrowed seven
hundred *ryō* from his younger brother, Matajirō, in Kyoto, and bought up
the men and horses available in the posting towns of Sakanoshita, Seki, and
Kameyama. These he hid in the mountains while awaiting the arrival of
Tadatoshi. Bolstered by the men and horses supplied for him by Shirōemon,
Tadatoshi passed Tadayuki at the Tsuchiyama-Minaguchi stations. Tadatoshi was happy about this, and later took Shirōemon's second son Shirobē,
who was in Edo, into his service as a salaried retainer. Shirobē's heir,
Sakuemon, was granted a five-man stipend of twenty *koku* and was taken into the Middle Page Unit; he died of illness in Genroku four [1691].
Sakuemon's child, Noboru, was appointed to duties by Etchū no kami Nobunori[31] and was granted stipends of seven hundred *koku*; he served as a
house functionary in the generation of Etchū no kami Munetaka,[32] and in
Gembun three [1738] he retired. Because Noboru's son, Shirōemon did
something against orders while serving as a unit commander in Kan'en three

[1750], his stipend and perquisites were taken from him. His son, Uheita, at first served as steward to Etchū no kami Shigekata;[33] later, becoming a close personal attendant to Nakatsukasa Taifu Harutoshi,[34] he was granted the equivalent of one hundred fifty *koku*. He was next advanced to unit commander and attached to the entourage of the Lady Tsunahime.[35] He retired in Bunka two [1805]. Uheita's heir, Junji, was a master of military science and archery; he died of illness in Bunka five [1808]. Junji's adopted son, Kumaki, was actually the third son of Yamano Kanzaemon; he received twenty *koku* as an allowance, served as a Middle Page, and died of illness in Tempō eight [1837]. Kumaki's heir, Eiichirō, later changed his name to Shirōemon, served as intendant in Tamana, and was ranked as unit commander. In Meiji three [1870], he became a ranking civil official in Kiku jail, and changed his name to Noboru. Kagekazu's fifth son, Hachisuke, injured his foot at the age of three, and walking was difficult for him. He changed his name to Muneharu, and died of illness in Kambun twelve [1672]. Kagakazu's sixth son, Matajirō, lived in Kyoto, and took Ichirōzaemon, the grandson of Sano Kanjūrō of Harima, as his adopted son.

June 1913

ABE ICHIZOKU

"ABE ICHIZOKU," or "The Abe Family," is perhaps the most grisly tour-de-force in the whole canon of these late stories. Ōgai's earlier treatment of *junshi* in the story "Okitsu Yagoemon no isho" represents his first reactions to the suicide of General Nogi at the death of the Emperor Meiji. "Abe ichizoku," however, published a few months later, provides a more ambivalent view of the custom and the mentality that produced it. Ōgai's comment that the destruction of the entire Abe family in their mansion resembles ". . . a swarm of bugs in a dish devouring each other," suggests the atmosphere of a Jacobean tragedy, which the story in many ways resembles.

There is much to admire in this overwhelming work: the meticulous attention to detail, the peculiar psychological atmosphere in the opening scenes that gives rise to the first macabre suicides, then the lucid presentation of the tangled web of relationships that eventually pulled so many into the final melee.

Ōgai's account is based on a real historical incident, but as in so many of the other stories, his selection of detail gives focus and philosophic import beyond a simple account. In particular, Ōgai sustains his mordant and penetrating irony through his delineation of the psychology of those who die for reputation in this world rather than in devotion to their former master. Understatement provides the basis for his style.

 IN THE SPRING of the Year of the Snake, the eighteenth year of Kan'ei [1641], Lord Hosokawa Tadatoshi,[1] Junior Fourth Rank, Lower Grade, Minor Captain in the Left Division of the Inner Palace Guards, and governor of the province of Etchū, cast a farewell glance at the blossoms of his domain, the province of Higo, where the cherry trees blossom earlier than elsewhere. Along with the spring that was advancing across Japan from south to north, he was about to set off for Edo to perform his annual fealty[2] to the Tokugawa shogun, with a full retinue as befits a daimyo of five hundred and forty thousand *koku*,[3] when he suddenly fell prey to illness. As the prescriptions of his court physician proved of no avail and his condition worsened day by day, a courier was dispatched to Edo with the message that Lord Tadatoshi's departure would be delayed. The Tokugawa shogun, Ieyasu's renowned grandson Iemitsu,[4] became apprehensive over the fate of Tadatoshi who at the time of the Shimabara Rebellion had defeated the insurgent leader Amakusa Shirō Tokisada.[5] Therefore on the twentieth day of the third month, he ordered a document drawn up and cosigned by Matsudaira Izu no kami, Abe Bungo no kami, and Abe Tsushima no kami,[6] directing the acupuncture physician Isaku to be sent down from Kyoto. On the twenty-second, Iemitsu dispatched an envoy, the samurai Soga Matazaemon, bearing instructions similarly signatured by the three lords. The policy of the shogun's house toward the Hosokawa daimyo was on this level of utmost courtesy. As the Tokugawa had already gone to great lengths to reward Lord Tadatoshi after the suppression of the Shimabara Rebellion three years earlier—granting him an additional plot of land for an Edo mansion and hunting grounds where cranes could be obtained— it was only natural that the shogun, on hearing of Tadatoshi's grave illness, should now be as solicitous as precedent would permit.

Before the shogun could carry out these steps, however, Tadatoshi's condition quickly deteriorated, and finally, around four o'clock in the afternoon of the seventeenth day of the third month, he passed away at the age of fifty-six at his Hanabatake villa in Kumamoto. His wife, a daughter of Ogasawara Hyōbu Taifu Hidemasa[7] whom the shogun had adopted and given in marriage to Tadatoshi, was now forty-five. She was called O-sen no kata.[8] Tadatoshi's heir, Rokumaru,[9] had come of age six years before and had been bestowed the use of the character "Mitsu" by the shogun's house; he was thereupon called Mitsusada and promoted to Junior Fourth Rank, Lower Grade. He was also granted the offices of chamberlain and lord of

TRANSLATED BY DAVID DILWORTH

Higo. Mitsusada was now seventeen years old.[10] He had been in Edo fulfilling his annual residence obligation and had returned home as far as Hamamatsu in the province of Totomi, but when word of his father's death came
he returned to Edo. Mitsusada at this time amended his name to Mitsuhisa.
Tadatoshi's second son, Tsuruchiyo,[11] had been sent as a child to a Buddhist
temple, the Taishōji in Tatsutayama. There he took the name of Sōgen and
became the disciple of the Abbot Taien,[12] who had received his training at
the Myōshinji in Kyoto. His third son, Matsunosuke,[13] had been adopted by
the Nagaoka clan, which had long-standing ties with the Hosokawa house.
His fourth son, Katsuchiyo,[14] became the adopted son of his retainer, Nanjō
Daizen. Tadatoshi had two daughters. The elder was Fujihime,[15] the wife of
Matsudaira Suho no kami Tadahiro.[16] The younger, Takehime,[17] later
became the wife of Ariyoshi Tanomo Hidenaga, a high retainer of the Hosokawa family. Tadatoshi was the third son of Hosokawa Sansai[18] and therefore had as his three younger brothers Naka-tsukasa Taifu Tatsutaka,[19]
Gyōbu Okitaka,[20] and Nagaoka Shikibu Yoriyuki.[21] His younger sisters were
Tarahime,[22] who was married to Inaba Kazumichi,[23] and Manhime,[24] the
wife of Karasumaru Chūnagon Mitsukata. Nenehime,[25] daughter of this
Manhime, was to become the spouse of Tadatoshi's heir, Mitsuhisa. Tadatoshi had two older brothers, both of the Nagaoka clan, and two elder sisters
who were married into the Maeno and Nagaoka families. His father, Sansai
Sōryū, was still alive in retirement and was seventy-nine years old. Of those
relatives, some were in Edo, like the heir, Mitsuhisa, and others were in
Kyoto or in distant provinces; but the grief of those present in the Kumamoto villa was far greater than the sorrow of those who heard of it later.
Mutsuhima Shōkichi and Tsuda Rokuzaemon set out to notify Edo of their
lord's death.

On the twenty-fourth day of the third month, the Ceremony of the First
Seventh Day following Tadatoshi's demise was performed. On the twenty-
eighth, the casket, which had been placed in the ground by opening up the
floor boards of the villa's sitting room, was unearthed. Following instructions from Edo, the corpse was cremated at the Shuunin temple in the
village of Kasuga of the district of Akita, and the ashes were interred in the
mountains outside of Kōrai gate of Kumamoto castle.[26] In the winter of the
following year, the Myōgenji was erected on the hill below Tadatoshi's
mausoleum and designated as a guardian temple of the realm. The priest
Keishitsu,[27] who was once a fellow monk of the famous Zen master
Takuan,[28] came from the Tōkaiji of the Shinagawa district of Edo to become
its abbot. After Keishitsu retired in a hermitage called the Rinryuan within
the temple grounds, Tadatoshi's second son Sōgen took the name of Tengan

and succeeded Keishitsu. Tadatoshi was given the name in Buddhahood of Myōgein-den Taiunsō Godaikoji.

Tadatoshi's remains were cremated at the Shuunin in accordance with his last will and testament. Tadatoshi had once gone on a hunt for moor hens and had stopped at the Shuunin for rest and tea. On that occasion, Tadatoshi suddenly noticed that his whiskers had grown out and asked the abbot if he could borrow a razor. The abbot fetched some water in a basin and placed a razor next to it. While one of his pages shaved him, Tadatoshi remarked good-humoredly to the abbot, "Well now, you've probably shaved a good many heads of the dead with this razor, haven't you?" Having no idea how he should answer, the abbot became quite embarrassed. From this time on, Tadatoshi and the abbot came to be good friends, and, as a result, Tadatoshi decided on this temple as the place where his remains should be cremated.

It was in the very midst of Tadatoshi's cremation that the thing happened. From among the retainers who had come to attend the casket, a voice cried out, "Look! The falcons! The falcons!" Beneath the dull blue sky outlined by the stand of cedar trees of the temple compound, and above the foliage of a cherry tree drooping like an umbrella over the circular stone wall of the well, two falcons were circling in the air. While the crowd watched in wonder, the two birds came together, one so close behind the other that beak and tail seemed to be touching, then plunged headlong into the well beneath the cherry blossoms. From the midst of a small crowd who had been arguing in front of the temple gate, two men dashed to the edge of the well, and, placing their hands on the stone wall, peered inside. The falcons by then had disappeared into the depths of the water, and the surface was once again as smooth as before, sparkling like a mirror amidst the thick growth of ferns. The two men were falconers. The birds that had plunged to the bottom of the well and drowned were Tadatoshi's beloved falcons. They had been given the names Ariake and Akashi. Once the crowd realized this, some people whispered: "So, even our lord's falcons have followed him in death!" In fact, since Tadatoshi's demise and up until the two days preceding the present one, more than ten of his retainers had committed *junshi*. Eight committed *seppuku* at one time just two days before and one more the following day. There was thus not a soul in Tadatoshi's household who did not have *junshi* on his mind. No one knew how the two falcons had been able to elude the falconers or why they had plunged into the well, as if in pursuit of some invisible prey. Neither was there anyone who attempted to probe into these things. These falcons had been Tadatoshi's favorites, and they had on the day of his cremation plunged to their death in the well at Shuunin, his place of cremation—these facts alone sufficed to make it clear that the falcons had indeed committed *junshi*. There was no room for doubt about this, nor for seeking any explanation elsewhere.

The forty-nine days of formal mourning after Tadatoshi's death ended on the fifth day of the fifth month. Until that time, Tadatoshi's second son, Sōgen, then the other Zen priests Kiseidō, Konryōdō, Tenjuan, Chōshōin, and Fujian had performed memorial services. Now the sixth day came, but incidents of *junshi* continued to be reported. Not only those contemplating *junshi* and their families and relatives, but even persons having no blood relation whatsoever to the family, had nothing else on their minds but *junshi*. While lost in their thoughts, they went about their duties, which included preparations for receiving the acupuncture physician from Kyoto, the shogun's envoy from Edo. They did not, as was customary at this time of year, pick iris to decorate the eaves of their houses for the Boys' Festival; even families whose sons were about to celebrate their first Boys' Festival were sunk in silence, as if they had forgotten their sons had been born.

The code governing *junshi* had arisen naturally, rather than having been established by someone for a specific reason at some point in time. No matter how much a retainer may esteem his lord, he could not commit *junshi* at will. The law was the same for retainers performing their annual fealty to the shogun in the peaceful world of Edo as it was for warriors setting out for battle in time of war: to accompany one's lord to the Mountain of Death and the River of the Three Crossings, one must by all means have the permission of his lord. To die without such permission was to die in vain, to no purpose. Since a samurai's honor was of the utmost importance, he should not die purposelessly. To die by rushing headlong into enemy ranks was commendable, but to die after stealing into an enemy camp ahead of one's comrades in disobedience to orders should achieve no merit at all. The same disgrace obtained in committing *junshi* without authorization. On rare occasions when this kind of death did not become a disgrace, there was usually tacit agreement between the lord and the retainer who had received his favors, and although no formal permission had been granted, the same situation existed as if permission had been given. The teachings of Mahayana Buddhism, which developed after Buddha entered Nirvana, did not have his express sanction; yet it is said that the Buddha, whose omniscience extends through the three worlds of past, present, and future, foresaw that the teaching of the Mahayana would eventually appear and in effect permitted it. Those who could commit *junshi* without the permission of the lord would therefore seem to be like those who preach the teaching of the Mahayana just as if it were expounded by Sakyamuni himself.

Such being the case, how did one receive his lord's permission? One good example would be the method used by Naitō Chōjurō Mototsugu,[29] who was one of these who committed *junshi* at this time. As Chōjurō ordinarily served at Tadatoshi's writing table and was the recipient of especially kind treatment by his lord, he was permitted to kneel by his master's sickbed to the end. When Tadatoshi realized that his recovery was uncertain, he instructed Chōjurō, "Should my death draw near, I ask you to hang near my pillow the scroll with the words, 'All is One,' written in bold characters." On the seventeenth day of the third month, as his condition gradually worsened, he commanded Chōjurō to hang the scroll. Tadatoshi glanced at the scroll and briefly closed his eyes. He then said, "My legs feel heavy." Chōjurō gently rolled back Tadatoshi's sleeved coverlet, and, while lightly rubbing his legs, fixed his eyes upon Tadatoshi's face. Tadatoshi stared back.

"Your servant Chōjurō has a request, my Lord."

"What is it?"

"Your illness seems to have taken a turn for the worse, but I pray that through the protection of the gods and buddhas and your excellent medicines you will regain your health as quickly as possible. However, there is one chance in ten thousand that your condition will not improve. Should such a thing come to pass, I beg you to allow your humble servant, Chōjurō, to follow you in attendance."

As he spoke Chōjurō gently raised Tadatoshi's foot and placed it against his forehead. Tears welled up into his eyes.

"You may not!" So saying, Tadatoshi, who until then had gazed intensely at Chōjurō half turned away.

"I beseech you not to speak so." Chōjurō again placed Tadatoshi's foot upon his brow.

"You may not! You may not!" Tadatoshi answered, his face still averted.

Among those sitting in attendance on Tadatoshi, someone said: "It might be more discreet for one so young to refrain from such obtrusive behavior." Chōjurō was seventeen years old that year.

"I beseech you!" Chōjurō said in a voice that caught in his throat, as he held Tadatoshi's foot to his forehead for the third time.

"A stubborn rascal he is!" the voice now angrily scolded. But at the same instant Tadatoshi twice nodded his approval.

Chōjurō uttered a smothered cry filled with emotion as he prostrated himself at the foot of the sickbed, all the while holding Tadatoshi's legs in his embrace. At that moment, Chōjurō felt in his heart as if he passed through the most dangerous strait and had reached the goal he knew he had to reach. Except for the slackening of tension in his body and a calmness that now filled his mind, nothing rose into his consciousness, not even the spilling of his tears upon the elegant straw matting from Bingo.

Chōjurō was still young and had performed not one single deed of conspicuous merit, but Tadatoshi had continually been solicitous of his welfare and employed him close at hand. Although Chōjurō was fond of sake and had once blundered in such fashion that had it been someone else he would have been found guilty of an indiscretion, Tadatoshi had just remarked with a laugh, "Chōjurō didn't do that. The sake did." Obsessed thereafter with the thought that he must requite his lord's favor and make up for his mistake, Chōjurō, after Tadatoshi's illness worsened, became firmly convinced that there was no other way of expressing his gratitude and making restitution than through *junshi*. If we were to probe more deeply into his motives, however, it would seem that besides his compulsion to commit *junshi* at his own request, he felt with almost identical intensity that others expected him to commit *junshi*; therefore, he was left with no other recourse but to do so, all the while seeking their approval. The reverse of the same motive was his fear that if he did not commit *junshi*, he would certainly be despised. Chōjurō was a man of such weakness, yet he had not the slightest fear of death. This is why his aspiration to gain permission from his lord dominated his entire will, brooking no obstacle.

After a while, Chōjurō thought he felt some strength return to his lord's legs, which he still embraced; it seemed as if they were becoming rigid. Chōjurō interpreted this to indicate his master's legs had again become heavy and so he resumed massaging them gently as he had done before. This time, images of his aged mother and wife floated into his mind. Thinking of how kindly the surviving relatives of one who has commited *junshi* are treated by the family of their former lord, he felt he could die serenely, having left his family in a secure position. With these thoughts, Chōjurō's face brightened.

On the morning of the seventeenth day of the fourth month, Chōjurō, dressed in formal attire, went before his mother to reveal his intention to commit *junshi* and to bid her farewell. His mother was not in the least surprised; even she, although no words had been exchanged between them, had anticipated for some time that her son would commit *seppuku* on this day. She would probably have registered genuine surprise had he reported he was not going to commit *junshi*.

Chōjurō's mother summoned Chōjurō's new bride from the kitchen, and asked her simply if the preparations were ready. The young woman immediately rose and brought the saucer-cups and tray for their farewell drink together, which had been made ready. She, like his mother, had known for some time that her husband would commit *seppuku* today. She had neatly arranged her hair and changed into one of her better garments. The formal, serious expressions of both mother and bride were the same, but since the corners of the bride's eyes were red, it was apparent that she had been crying in the kitchen. When the saucer-cups and tray were brought out, Chōjurō summoned his younger brother, Saheiji.

The four of them silently exchanged a sake cup. When the cup had gone one round, his mother spoke.

"Chōjurō. This is your favorite sake. Why don't you have a little more?"

"Yes, it is my favorite," he answered, and with a smile cheerfully drank up one cup after another.

After a while, Chōjurō addressed his mother. "The wine has really relaxed me. Perhaps because of the matters on my mind these past few days, the sake seems to have affected me more than it usually does. If you will excuse me, I'll take a short nap."

So saying, Chōjurō rose and went into the sitting room; he stretched out in the center of the room and soon began to snore. When his wife softly entered the room and placed a pillow under his head, he only groaned a little, rolled over, and continued to snore. His bride's eyes drank briefly of her husband's face, but suddenly, as if overwhelmed with emotion, she rose and went to her room. She thought she should not cry.

The house was hushed. The servants and maids were as aware as his mother and wife of their master's unspoken resolve to commit *junshi*, so neither from the kitchen nor from the stables could anything like laughter be heard.

His mother, bride, and younger brother, in their separate rooms, were sunk in thought. The head of the house snored away in the sitting room. At the open window of the sitting room was suspended a hanging fern to which a wind chime had been attached. The wind chime tinkled from time to time, as if remembering what was going to happen. Beneath it, there was a hand basin hollowed out of the crown of a tall rock. A dragonfly had alighted on the wooden ladle resting on the basin, its motionless wings forming the shape of a mountain.

One hour passed. Then a second. It was already past noon. Instructions for the preparation of the noonday meal had been left with the maids, but Chōjurō's bride hesitated to inquire about lunch as she was not sure her mother-in-law would eat at all; and because she did not want to appear to be the only one thinking about food.

At that moment, Seki Koheiji, who had been asked to act as Chōjurō's second, arrived. Chōjurō's mother summoned her daughter-in-law. The bride silently thrust out her hands before herself and bowed; when she inquired routinely about the old lady's health, her mother-in-law interrupted:

"Chōjurō said he was going to take a short nap, but he's been asleep for a long time. Besides, Seki has arrived. You should wake him now, I think."

"Yes, he has been sleeping for a long time. It would be best if it didn't get too late," the younger woman replied, and immediately rose to wake her husband.

Once inside the sitting room, the young woman again looked deeply into her husband's face as she had done when placing the pillow under his head. Since she realized she was waking him from his last sleep, she could not bring herself to stir him for some time.

It seemed that the sunlight streaming in from the garden would be dazzling to his eyes despite his sound sleep, but Chōjurō had his back to the window.

"Dear?" she called to him.

Chōjurō did not stir.

She went up to him and placed her hand on his shoulder. Chōjurō mumbled briefly, stretched his arms, and sprang to his feet with both eyes open.

"You slept quite well. Your mother inquired if it wasn't getting late, so I came to wake you. Seki Koheiji has arrived, too."

"Of course. Well, it looks as if it's noon already. I thought I would take a brief nap, but between the sake and being overtired I must have just slept on. Well, I feel much much better in any case. Let's have some rice mixed with tea or anything light, then I must proceed in due course to our temple, the Tōkōin. Tell mother this too."

A samurai does not stuff himself with food before some critical action. Neither does he set out to perform an important act on an empty stomach. Chōjurō had in fact thought to take a short nap, but since he had unintentionally had a good long sleep and now heard that it was noon, he just naturally spoke about eating lunch. The five of them went through the formality of sitting at the table and eating lunch as if it were some ordinary occasion.

Then, Chōjurō calmly got ready and proceeded with Seki to the Tōkōin to commit *seppuku*.

As he had requested at Tadatoshi's death bed, Chōjurō became one of eighteen retainers, all recipients of their lord's special favors, who had earnestly begged for and were granted permission to commit *junshi*. Each was a man whom Tadatoshi had deeply trusted. Therefore, Tadatoshi would very much have liked to leave them behind to guard the fortunes of his son,

Mitsuhisa. Indeed, he fully felt the barbarism of allowing them all to die with him. In each case, however, he had granted his permission, even while his own words pierced him like a sword, out of the sheer necessity of the relationship.

Tadatoshi knew that these, his most trusted vassals, were loyal to the point of not begrudging him their very lives. Consequently he understood that none of them would feel anguish over his own *junshi*. But what would it be like for them if they lived on, after he had refused them the permission to commit *junshi*? Their entire families might regard them as men who did not die at the appropriate time, as ingrates and cowards, and might even break off relations with them. If that were all, these retainers might endure the situation and await the time they could offer their lives to Mitsuhisa. But if someone suggested that their former master had employed ingrates and cowards without realizing it, it might be unendurable for them. They would no doubt be deeply resentful. With these considerations in mind, Tadatoshi could not but grant their requests. This is why he had done so even though it brought him mental anguish greater even than his physical illness.

When the number of retainers reached eighteen, Tadatoshi, who had lived through fifty years of peace and war and well understood the human heart and the ways of the world, constantly brooded over his own and their impending deaths even in the midst of his painful illness. The living inevitably perish, he thought, but new seedlings spring up and flourish beside an old withering tree. From the point of view of the younger men who will serve his son, Mitsuhisa, the older retainers who serve him are replaceable. They would even be in the way. Tadatoshi wanted to have his own men live on and serve Mitsuhisa as well, yet there were a number of men already serving Mitsuhisa who were waiting for the opportunity to advance themselves. Perhaps the men Tadatoshi had employed had come to be resented by some during the years of their service to him. They had at the least become objects of envy. In this light, it might not be prudent to insist that they live on. It might even be compassionate to allow them to commit *junshi*. Tadatoshi consoled himself somewhat with these thoughts.

The eighteen retainers whose requests had been granted were the following: Teramoto Hachizaemon Naotsugu, Otsuka Kinhē Tanetsugu, Naitō Chōjurō Mototsugu, Ōta Kojūrō Masanobu, Harada Jōjirō Yukinao, Munakata Kahē Kagesada and his brother Kichidayū Kageyoshi, Hashitani Ichizō Shigetsugu, Ihara Jūzaburō Yoshimasa, Tanaka Itoku, Honjō Kisuke Shigemasa, Itō Tazaemon Masataka, Migita Inaba Muneyasu, Noda Kihei Shigetsuna, Tsuzaki Gosuke Nagasue, Kobayashi Riemon Yukihide, Hayashi Yozaemon Masasada, and Miyanaga Katsuzaemon Munesuke.

Teramoto was descended from Teramoto Tarō who lived in Teramoto, in the province of Owari. Tarō's son, Naizennoshō, served the Imagawa house. Naizennoshō's son was Sahē, Sahē's son Uemonnosuke; Uemonnosuke's son Yozaemon distinguished himself under Katō Yoshitake[30] at the time of the invasion of Korea. Yozaemon's son Hachizaemon served under Gōtō Mototsugu[31] during the siege of Osaka castle. After being employed by the Hosokawa house, he received a stipend of one thousand *koku* and a command over fifty riflemen. Hachizaemon committed *seppuku* at the age of fifty-three at the An'yōji temple on the twenty-ninth of the fourth month of 1641. Fujimoto Izaemon acted as his second.

Otsuka was a subordinate inspector with a stipend of one hundred fifty *koku*. He committed *seppuku* on the twenty-sixth day of the same month. His second was Ikeda Hachizaemon.

The third of the eighteen was Chōjurō.

Ōta's grandfather, Denzaemon, served under Katō Kiyomasa.[32] At the time Katō's eldest son Tadahiro[33] was deprived of his fief in 1611, Denzaemon and his son, Gonzaemon, became *rōnin*. Gonzaemon's second son Shōjurō was a young page in Tadatoshi's service with a stipend of one hundred fifty *koku*. He was the first to commit *junshi*, committing *seppuku* at the Kasuga temple on the seventeenth day of the third month, at the age of eighteen. His second was Moji Gembē.

Harada was one of Tadatoshi's personal attendants with a stipend of one hundred fifty *koku*. He committed *seppuku* on the twenty-sixth day of the fourth month, seconded by Kamada Gendayū.

The brothers Munakata Kahē and Kichidayū were descendents of Munakata Chūnagon Ujisada; they followed their father Seihē Kagenobu in Tadatoshi's service. Each received a stipend of two hundred *koku*. Kahē committed *seppuku* at the temple of Ryūchōin, Kichidayū at the Renshōji, on the second day of the fifth month. Kahē's second was Takata Jūbē; his brother's was Murakami Ichiemon.

Hashitani was a native of Izumo province and a descendent of the Amako house. Summoned by Tadatoshi at the age of fourteen, he served as a personal attendant with a stipend of one hundred *koku* and pretasted his lord's food as a precaution against poisoning. After his illness worsened, Tadatoshi had occasionally rested using Hashitani's lap as a pillow. Hashitani committed *seppuku* at the Seiganji on the twenty-sixth day of the fourth month. Just as he was about to insert the knife into his lower abdomen, the castle drum sounded faintly in the distance. Hashitani asked one of his accompanying retainers to go out and listen to what time it was. The retainer came back to say, "I only heard the last four beats, and couldn't count the others." Hashitani and the rest of his attendants smiled at this remark. "How kind of you to make me smile one last time," Hashitani said, then handed his *haori* to the retainer and committed *seppuku*. Yoshimura Jindayū acted as second.

Ihara received a stipend of ten *koku*, which included a rice allowance for three retainers. When he committed *seppuku*, Abe Yaichiemon's retainer, Hayashi Sahē, served as second.

Tanaka was the grandchild of O-Kiku, the authoress of the *O-Kiku monogatari*.[34] He had been a childhood friend of Tadatoshi since the time they attended school together in the temple complex at Atago in Kyoto. At that time Tanaka had privately dissuaded Tadatoshi from becoming a Buddhist monk. He later became one of Tadatoshi's personal attendants with a stipend of two hundred *koku*; he was of help to Tadatoshi because of his expertise in mathematics. When he reached old age, he was permitted to sit cross-legged before Tadatoshi without removing his hood. Since his request to commit *junshi* was originally refused, he stabbed himself in the stomach with a dagger and wrote out another request on the nineteenth day of the sixth month, when permission was finally granted. Katō Yasudayū seconded.

Honjō, a native of the province of Tango, had led a wandering life before being employed by Honjō Kyūemon, a personal attendant of Lord Hosokawa Sansai. He once put down a rioter at Nakatsu and was granted a stipend of fifteen *koku*, which included a rice allowance for five retainers. He also assumed the name Honjō from this time. He committed *seppuku* on the twenty-sixth day of the fourth month.

Itō was the recipient of a small rice allowance since he served as a custodian of clothing and furnishings in Tadatoshi's living quarters. He committed *seppuku* on the twenty-sixth day of the fourth month, seconded by Kawakita Hachisuke.

Migita was a *rōnin* from the Ōtomo house who had been employed by Tadatoshi at a stipend of one hundred *koku*. He committed *seppuku* at his own residence on the twenty-seventh day of the fourth month. Katsuno Ukyō's retainer, Tawara Kambē, seconded.

Noda, the son of Noda Mino, who had been a high retainer of Amakusa Izu no kami Tanemoto, was employed by Tadatoshi for a small rice allowance. He committed *seppuku* at the Genkakuji on the twenty-sixth day of the fourth month. His second was Era Han'emon.

I will deal below with Tsuzaki.

Kobayashi received a stipend of ten *koku*, which included an allowance for two retainers. When he committed *seppuku*, Takano Kan'emon seconded.

Hayashi had been a peasant in the village of Shimoda in Nangō; he was employed with a stipend of fifteen *koku*, which included a rice allowance for ten retainers as the head gardener at Tadatoshi's Hanabatake mansion. He committed *seppuku* at the Butsuganji temple on the twenty-sixth day of the fourth month. His second was Nakamitsu Hansuke.

Miyanaga was employed at kitchen duties for a salary of ten *koku*, which included a rice allowance for two retainers; he was the first man to request permission from Tadatoshi. He too committed *seppuku* on the twenty-sixth day of the fourth month, at the Jōshōji temple. His second was Yoshimura Kaemon.

Some of these men were buried at their respective family temples, while others were buried near their lord's mausoleum in the mountains outside the Kōrai gate. A relatively large number of them received only small stipends. Among these, I have singled out the case of Tsuzaki Gosuke as particularly interesting.

Gosuke was Tadatoshi's dog handler with a stipend of six *koku* and a rice allowance for two retainers. He always accompanied Tadatoshi's hawking excursions as well, and it was in the fields that he had attracted his lord's notice. He received permission to commit *junshi* after several urgent requests, but Tadatoshi's elder statesmen told him, "While the others have high incomes and have lived in splendor, you are only our lord's dog handler. Your aspiration is commendable, and our lord's permission is the highest honor. There is no need to go through with it. We urge you to turn your aspirations for *junshi* into a desire to be of service to his heir."

Gosuke would not listen. He left his house on the seventh day of the fifth month for the Kōrinji temple at Oimawashi-tahata, accompanied by the dog he had always taken when he attended his lord on hawking excursions. His wife said good-bye to him with the words: "Gosuke, you too are a man. Show that you are not inferior to those who are prominent retainers."

The Ōjōin was the Tsuzaki family temple, but since it was connected with personages more important than he, Tsuzaki shunned it in favor of the Kōrinji as his place to die. As Gosuke entered the graveyard, he saw that Matsuno Nuinosuke, whom he had requested to be his second, was already waiting. Gosuke took off the pale blue pouch hanging from his shoulder, and produced a wicker food basket from inside it. He opened the lid. Inside were two rice balls, which he took out and set in front of the dog. The dog did not immediately go to them; he wagged his tail and looked Gosuke in the face. Gosuke then spoke to the dog as he would to a human being.

"Since you're a dog you may not understand, but our lord, who used to pat you on the head, has now passed away. That's why the high retainers who have enjoyed his favors will all commit *seppuku* today. My own status is lowly, but I am no different than them in owing my life's sustenance to his favor. I too have been honored by his personal affection. So I am going to commit *seppuku* today. After I am gone, you will be free to roam. I feel sorry for you. Our lord's falcons have plunged into the well at the Shuunin and killed themselves. How about you? Maybe you prefer to go with me. If you prefer to live as a stray, then eat these rice balls. If you prefer to die, don't eat them.''

Gosuke studied the dog's face. The dog looked back, without going near the rice balls.

"So you too wish to die, then?'' Gosuke said, his eyes still intent upon the dog.

The dog barked and wagged his tail.

"Very well, then. I hate to do it, but I will grant your request.'' Gosuke lifted the dog up, drew his short sword, and killed him with a single stroke.

Gosuke laid the dog's corpse aside. Then he pulled out a sheet of rice paper from inside his kimono, spread it out before him on the ground, and kept it flat by placing small stones at the corners. On this paper that had been folded in half was a poem, written in ordinary meter, the way he remembered having seen it at a poetry reading at someone's mansion:

> Karō shū wa
> Tomare tomare to
> Ōse aredo
> Tomete Tomaranu
> Kono Gosuke kana

> The Elders
> Urge me to stop
> Yet even so
> I cannot,
> Not this Gosuke!

There was no signature. He had simply thought that his name appearing in the poem would suffice, and his idea, in fact, accorded naturally with ancient practice.

Thinking that everything was now in order, Gosuke said, "Matsuno. Do your part,'' as he sat cross-legged, and exposed his stomach. He pointed his short sword, the dog's blood still upon it, downward, crying out, "You falconers! What about you? Our lord's dog handler is now departing,'' and opened his stomach crosswise while laughing heartily. Matsuno struck his neck from behind.

Though Gosuke's status was low, his widow later received an allowance comparable to that received by the high-ranking families of those who committed *junshi*. This was because his son had entered the priesthood as a child. She received a rice allowance for five retainers and a new home, and lived on to the thirty-third anniversary of Tadatoshi's death. A nephew took the name Gosuke and thereafter his house served in the capacity of surrogate for various *han* offices for many generations.

In addition to the above eighteen who committed *junshi* with permission, there is one additional man to be mentioned, Abe Yaichiemon Michinobu. He was originally a member of the Akashi clan; his name as a boy was Inosuke. He served near Tadatoshi's side from an early age and reached a status of more than one thousand *koku*. At the time of the Shimabara Rebellion, three of his five sons received new stipends of two hundred *koku* apiece for their military valor. The members of Tadatoshi's household knew that Yaichiemon was expected to commit *junshi*, and he himself asked for permission each time it was his turn to stand night watch by Tadatoshi's sickbed. But Tadatoshi refused him to the end. "Your aspiration pleases me, but I prefer you to live on and serve Mitsuhisa," Tadatoshi replied to each entreaty Yaichiemon made.

In fact, Tadatoshi was in the habit of not agreeing with any request of Yaichiemon. Even when Yaichiemon was still called Inosuke and served him as a page, Tadatoshi would reply to his "Shall I present your tray?" with "I'm not hungry." When other pages made the same inquiry, Tadatoshi would reply, "Very well, do so." Whenever he saw Yaichiemon's face, Tadatoshi felt a spirit of contrariness in this way. You might think that Yaichiemon would have been reprimanded, but he never was, for no man served Tadatoshi more punctiliously than he, attentive to every detail and never blundering. Tadatoshi never had cause for reprimanding him even though he might have wanted to.

Yaichiemon did unbidden what others might be ordered to do. He did in silence what others announced they would do first. Everything he did was always correct and impeccable. Yaichiemon came to serve Tadatoshi simply out of obstinance. Tadatoshi had at first resented him somewhat unconsciously, but he later came to hate him when he realized that Yaichiemon was serving him out of sheer pertinaciousness. Yet while detesting him, the shrewd Tadatoshi remembered why Yaichiemon had become that way, and understood that he had caused the situation himself. And hence although Tadatoshi intended to correct his contrary inclinations, his aversion gradually hardened with the passing months and years.

Every man has natural likes and dislikes. If he tries to understand them, he often cannot tell exactly why he feels as he does. This was the case in Tadatoshi's aversion to Yaichiemon. Somewhere in Yaichiemon, however, there must have been something which made it difficult for him to relate to others, as evidenced by the fact that he had few close friends. Everyone respected him as a worthy samurai. But no one found it easy to approach him. It was rare for someone to be curious enough to try to establish a friendship with him, yet when the effort was made Yaichiemon would not reciprocate, and the man would eventually withdraw from the attempt. When Yaichiemon was known as Inosuke and still retained his forelocks, older persons who sometimes engaged him in conversation or lent him a hand would give up, saying, "Somehow—Abe is completely locked inside himself." No wonder, then, that Tadatoshi could not bring himself to correct his attitude toward Yaichiemon even though he wished to do so.

At any rate, Tadatoshi passed away before Yaichiemon had received his permission, despite his repeated entreaties. Just before his lord died, Yaichiemon had faced Tadatoshi squarely and pleaded with him, "I have never asked for anything else. This is the one desire of my life." Tadatoshi returned his look and replied flatly, "No, I want you to serve Mitsuhisa."

Yaichiemon made his decision after a long inner debate. For a man of his status to continue living without committing *junshi* and have to face the members of his lord's household was something not one man in a hundred would believe to be possible. There was no alternative but to commit *seppuku* in dishonor or to leave Kumamoto as a *rōnin*. But I am what I am, he thought, and a samurai is not the same as a prostitute. I shall not surrender my honor even though it doesn't accord with my lord's will. He continued his duties day after day as usual while pondering his dilemma.

Meanwhile the days passed until the sixth day of the fifth month, and the eighteenth man had committed *junshi*. *Junshi* was the only topic throughout Kumamoto. "What did this one say as he died?" or "That one died more splendidly than anyone else!" Before this talk of *junshi* came to fill the air, Yaichiemon had rarely been spoken to, except on business matters; from the seventh day of the fifth month as he went to his station in Tadatoshi's residence his desolation mounted. His associates, who all along had pretended to ignore him, now took to watching him. He would feel their eyes upon him when his back was turned or he would catch their surreptitious glances out of the corner of his eye. He raged within. It was not that he was still among them because he was afraid to die; no matter how much they hate me, he reflected, they can't think me a coward; if I could, I would die right now to show them! He insulated himself with these thoughts as he took his place among them.

Two or three days later, a piece of malicious gossip reached his ears. He had no idea who started it. "Abe seems to be taking to heart our lord's refusal to let him commit *junshi*. But it doesn't mean he can't kill himself without the permission. The skin of his stomach seems to differ from everybody else's. It's so soft it can probably be pierced even by a gourd that had oil rubbed on it." Yaichiemon's rage boiled over at this. If someone wants to be malicious, he thought, let him say what he wants; but no matter how he looks at me I am no coward! So that's what they pretend to believe. In that case I will show them by cutting my belly open with an oiled gourd!

That day after returning from his duties, Yaichiemon urgently summoned the two sons who lived separately to his residence in Yamazaki. He had the panels dividing the sitting and drawing rooms removed, and sitting his heir Gombē, his second son Yagobē, and his fifth son Shichinojō, who still possessed his forelocks, at his side, solemnly awaited the arrival of the others. Gombē, whose childhood name had been Gonjurō, had been granted a stipend of two hundred *koku* for his valor during the Shimabara Rebellion. He was a young man not inferior to his father. About the recent events of *junshi*, he only once inquired of him, "Your request was not granted?" and his father had answered, "It was denied." There was no further exchange. Each understood in his heart that there was nothing more to be said.

Presently, two paper lanterns appeared at the gate. Yaichiemon's third and fourth sons, Ichidayū and Godayū, arrived at the entrance-way at almost the same moment, took off their rain gear, and entered the drawing room. The rainy season had arrived on the day following the end of the seven-week mourning period for Tadatoshi, and the sky of the fifth month had been continuously clouded over.

Even though the shoji were open, the air was hot and still. Nevertheless, the flame from the candle stand was flickering. A solitary firefly wove its way through the trees in the garden and disappeared into the night.

Yaichiemon looked at each of those present and then spoke. "I have inconvenienced you by summoning you late at night, but you have all kindly come. Since the rumor is everywhere in our lord's house, you yourselves have undoubtedly heard it. That my belly is so soft it can be opened with an oiled gourd. I have resolved to kill myself in exactly that manner. I want you all to witness it to the end."

Ichidayū and Godayū had each been granted new stipends of two hundred *koku* for their meritorious service during the Shimabara Rebellion, and each had his own residence. Of the two, it was Ichidayū who had quickly risen to become a personal attendant of the young Mitsuhisa and thus was one of those envied at the time of Mitsuhisa's succession. Ichidayū approached closer on his knees. "Now I understand. There were nuances in the remarks of my colleagues when they said that it is so fortunate for Yaichiemon and his family to have been able, by virtue of Lord Tadatoshi's will, to continue serving the Hosokawa house. I felt the innuendo in their words." His father laughed. "Probably there was. Don't associate with those near-sighted persons who only see what's in front of their noses. Now, when I have died, contrary to expectations, others will probably ridicule you as the sons of one whose suicide was unsanctioned. It is your fate to be my children. Nothing can be done about it. When disgrace comes, face it together. Do not fight among yourselves. Now mark well how one cuts himself open with a gourd."

So saying, Yaichiemon cut into his stomach in front of his sons, and died by piercing the nape of his neck from left to right by his own hand. His five sons, who had not been able to fathom their father's mind, were grief-stricken, but at the same time they felt themselves one step beyond the previous anxiety that had gripped them, as if a heavy load had been removed from their backs.

"Gombē!" Yagobē, the second son, addressed his elder brother. "Father has enjoined us not to fight among ourselves. We all agree to that. Since my post was bad at Shimabara and I did not receive any stipend, I will probably become a burden for you after this. But whatever happens, I will be one spear you can count on. You can rely upon me."

"I know I can count on you. Whatever the outcome, my stipend is also yours," Gombē replied, as he folded his arms across his chest and frowned.

"That's right. The outcome is uncertain. Someone will surely say our father's suicide wasn't the same as authorized *junshi*." It was Yaichiemon's fourth son, Godayū, who said this.

"That is obvious enough. No matter what happens . . ." Ichidayū, the third son, said and paused, while watching Gombē's face, "No matter what happens, we must stick together."

Gombē nodded in approval, his serious expression unchanged. While Gombē was considerate of his younger brothers, he was not one to mince his words. Moreover, he usually thought things out alone and did things his own way. He rarely consulted with anyone. Therefore Yagobē and Ichidayū probed for a sign of his agreement.

"Since you, my older brothers, are here together, no one will easily slander father." This had come from the mouth of Shichinojō, still pos-

sessed of his forelocks. His voice was like a girl's but it registered such strong
conviction that it brightened their hearts like a light illumining the dark
road ahead of them.

"Well, shall we inform mother of father's death and have the women
take their formal leave of him?" Gombē said, and rose from his seat.

The succession ceremonies of Mitsuhisa, Junior Fourth Rank, Lower
Grade, Chamberlain, and Governor of the province of Higo, were completed. Now stipends, increments, and changes of duties were allocated to
all retainers. The heirs of the households of the eighteen men who committed *junshi* were allowed to succeed their fathers without complication. No
heir, however young, was bypassed. The widows and elderly parents of the
eighteen were granted stipends. Residences were conferred upon them, even
when in some cases this meant building new quarters. These were households whose deceased heads had been particularly favored by Tadatoshi, and
who had even gone to attend their lord on his journey to the next life; therefore even if these families were envied by the other retainers, it was not malicious envy.

However, the one family whose succession was treated exceptionally was
that of Yaichiemon. Gombē, the heir, was unable to inherit the family's
rights and property in the manner they had been held by Yaichiemon.
Yaichiemon's fifteen hundred *koku* stipend was divided up and apportioned to include his younger sons. The total family's stipend remained intact, but Gombē, who inherited the family's main branch, had been reduced to lower status. Gombē's prestige was considerably lessened, of
course. Although the younger brothers gained individually in stipend, they
now felt a difference, for while they formerly stood under the protection of a
more than one-thousand-*koku* main-branch house as under some large,
sheltering tree, they now stood equally in stipend but the sheltering tree was
gone. Thus their newly felt gratitude was mixed with consternation.

As long as a government is consistent, no one will fault its decisions. But
when consistency is violated, questions of partiality arise. The Head Surveillant of Vassal Conduct was a man named Hayashi Geki who enjoyed the
confidence of Lord Mitsuhisa and served in close attendance on him. A man
of mediocre talent, he had been suitable as an attendant for Mitsuhisa while
Tadatoshi was still alive, but he was lacking in breadth of vision and prone
to lose himself in minute details. He reasoned that since Yaichiemon had
died without Tadatoshi's permission, he had to draw a distinction between
those who had committed authentic *junshi* and Yaichiemon. He therefore
recommended the strategy of breaking up the Abe family allotment. Mitsu-

hisa himself was a considerate ruler, but since he was still inexperienced, as well as unfamiliar with either Yaichiemon or his heir, Gombē, he was unsympathetic; he adopted Geki's policy because it entailed an increase in stipend for the younger brother Ichidayū who had been his close attendant. When the eighteen samurai committed *junshi*, members of the Hosokawa house were scornful of Yaichiemon because he had been a close attendant of Tadatoshi but had not committed *junshi*. Then, scarcely two or three days after the eighteenth had died, Yaichiemon committed *seppuku* in splendid fashion. Yet without considering the legitimacy of his act, a disgrace once incurred is not easily erased; not one person commended Yaichiemon. Since the authorities had granted that Yaichiemon's remains be interred at the side of Tadatoshi's mausoleum, it would have been wiser if they had been consistent in the matter of the succession of Gombē. If they had done this, the dignity of the Abe family would have been upheld and all its members would have given devoted service to the Hosokawa house. But since the treatment of the Abe family was a step inferior to that accorded the others, the contempt held by those in the Hosokawa household for the Abe family had now been given official sanction. Gombē and his brothers were gradually shunned by their fellow samurai and passed their days in a state of despondency.

The first anniversary of Tadatoshi's death fell on the seventeenth day of the third month in the nineteenth year of Kan'ei [1642]. The Myōgenji next to Tadatoshi's mausoleum was not completed until the following year, but a temple named Kōyōin had been erected, and in it was housed the memorial tablet of Tadatoshi. The priest in charge was named Kyōshuza. Prior to the anniversary date, Abbot Ten'yū[35] came down from the Daitokuji in the district of Murasakino in Kyoto. The anniversary was to be observed on a large scale; for a full month before, the castle town of Kumamoto was busy with preparations.

Finally, the day came. The weather was glorious, and the mausoleum was enveloped in cherry blossoms. A curtain had been strung up around Kōyōin, which was guarded by samurai. Lord Mitsuhisa himself presided, and was the first to burn incense before the tablet of his father, then before the tablets of the nineteen who had committed *junshi*. Next the families of those nineteen were permitted to burn incense. At the same time, they were presented with ceremonial garments emblazoned with the Hosokawa crest and with garments for the spring season. Those samurai of the rank of Mounted Escort and above were given sleeveless cloaks and skirt-style trousers whose legs extended into a small train. Those of the rank of Foot Soldier were given sleeveless cloaks and short, skirt-style trousers whose legs extended into a small train. Those of lesser rank received money to take care of private services for the deceased.

The ceremony would have finished smoothly except for one unusual occurrence. When Abe Gombē, as representative of one of the bereaved families, advanced in his turn before Tadatoshi's memorial tablet, he burned incense, but before withdrawing he drew the small knife attached to the sheath of his short sword, cut off his topknot, and laid it before the memorial tablet. The samurai in attendance, shocked by this unexpected action, gazed on dumbfounded while Gombē calmly withdrew as if nothing were out of the ordinary. He had withdrawn several paces when one samurai, who had finally regained his composure, called out, "Gombē! Wait," and took hold of him from behind. Then two or three others rose and helped usher Gombē off to another room.

When interrogated by Lord Mitsuhisa's attendants, Gombē answered in the following way. "You may think I have gone mad, but that is not the case at all. Because my father, Yaichiemon, devoted his life to selfless service of his lord, he has been included in the ranks of the men who committed *junshi* even though he had not obtained our late lord's permission; and I, his surviving son, have been able to offer incense before his memorial tablet in advance of some of the others. However, as I am unworthy of my father's duties in my superiors' eyes, the family stipend has been apportioned equally among his five sons. I have been disgraced before our late lord, our present lord, my late father, the members of my family, and my fellow samurai. Overwhelmed by this disgrace as I was offering incense before our late lord's memorial tablet, I resolved in a burst of emotion that I would forsake the life of a samurai. I willingly accept reprimand for my untoward behavior on this occasion. But I am in complete possession of my senses."

Lord Mitsuhisa was not pleased at the report of Gombē's interrogation. In the first place, he was displeased with Gombē for having conducted himself in a manner discourteous to his superiors. Secondly he was displeased with himself for having unthinkingly consented to Geki's strategy of dealing with the Abe family's succession. Mitsuhisa was yet an impetuous young lord of twenty-four, still lacking in self-discipline. He was deficient in that magnanimity which counters resentment with kindness. He immediately had Gombē imprisoned. When apprised of this order, Yagobē and his brothers decided to close their gate and to wait for further instructions; after night fell, the whole family deliberated in secrecy over their future course.

The Abe family decided they would appeal to the Abbot Ten'yū who had not yet returned to Kyoto. Ichidayū went to Ten'yū's lodgings, told him the whole story, and inquired if he would intercede to reduce Gombē's punishment. Ten'yū pondered Ichidayū's story. "I am overwhelmed with sympathy for your family's plight," he said. "However, I cannot comment upon the government of Lord Mitsuhisa. If Gombē be granted a death penalty, I shall certainly request that his life be spared. Especially considering that Gombē has already cut his topknot off and is, in effect, no different than a priest, I shall somehow ask that he be spared." Ichidayū returned home relieved. When they heard his report, the rest of the family felt as if they had found a way out of the crisis. Meanwhile, the days passed, and the time for Ten'yū's return to Kyoto gradually approached. Each time he met with Mitsuhisa, Ten'yū intended to bring up the subject of sparing Gombē's life, if only an opportunity presented itself. No such opportunity arose. This was not without a reason. Mitsuhisa had concluded that if Gombē was sentenced to die while Ten'yū was still in Kumamoto, Ten'yū would undoubtedly petition that his life be spared. And Mitsuhisa could not easily disregard the request of an eminent priest from an important temple. He therefore decided to postpone the sentencing until after Ten'yū's departure. In due course Ten'yū left Kumamoto without being able to intercede.

No sooner had Ten'yū left Kumamoto than Mitsuhisa ordered Abe Gombē brought to Ide no kuchi and decapitated while kneeling with his hands tied behind his back. He was executed on the sentence of having acted irreverently before Tadatoshi's memorial tablet and of having performed an act disrespectful to his superiors.

Yagobē and his brothers assembled together to deliberate. Gombē had certainly been guilty of misconduct; nevertheless their late father, Yaichiemon, had been counted among those who had committed *junshi*. As Gombē was his successor, it was inevitable that he should be awarded death. Had he been accorded the samurai's honor of committing *seppuku*, however, they would have had no objection. Yet he was beheaded in broad daylight as if he were some common thief. In these circumstances, his family could not take the matter with composure. Even if the authorities went no further, how could the family of a beheaded samurai keep face among the other retainers while continuing to serve the Hosokawa house? There was no possibility of compromise. Out of prescience of this situation, their late father had enjoined them to stay together. To a man, they resolved that they had no alternative but to die together while resisting a punitive force which would be sent by the authorities.

The Abe family assembled its women and children and secluded them in Gombē's Yamazaki residence.

The family's defiant attitude became known to the authorities. Surveillants were dispatched to confirm the facts. The gate of the Yamazaki mansion was bolted shut and no one stirred within. The residences of Ichidayū and Godayū were empty.

The punitive force was organized. The force assigned to the main gate was commanded by Takenouchi Kazuma Nagamasa, a captain of the Bodyguards; his lieutenants were Soejima Kuhē and Nomura Shobē. Kazuma drew a stipend of eleven hundred fifty *koku* and commanded a force of thirty riflemen. He was attended by his hereditary retainer, Shima Tokuemon. Soejima and Nomura received stipends of one hundred *koku* each at the time. The commander of the force for the rear gate was Takami Gon'emon Shigemasa, a captain of the Bodyguards with a stipend of five hundred *koku*. He, too, commanded a force of thirty guns. Under his command were the surveillant Hata Judayū, and Chiba Sakubē, a lieutenant of Kazuma with a stipend of one hundred *koku* at the time.

The attack was planned for the twenty-first day of the fourth month. Sentries were placed around the Yamazaki mansion on the eve of the attack. In the middle of the night, a masked samurai scaled the surrounding wall from the Abe side, but he was killed by Maruyama Sannojō, a foot soldier in Saburi Kazaemon's squad charged with sentry duty. There were no further incidents from then until dawn.

The authorities had issued orders to the houses adjacent to the Yamazaki mansion. All persons were to stay home and watch for fires, even if ordinarily one had duty in the castle at that time. And as the neighboring families were not part of the punitive force, they were strictly forbidden to enter the Abe mansion to participate; but they were free to kill deserters.

Apprised of the impending attack the day before, the Abe family first cleaned their residence thoroughly, and burned all unsightly objects. Then old and young alike gathered at a banquet. After that, the elderly and the women committed suicide, and the children were each stabbed to death. The corpses were buried in a large hole dug in the garden. Only the able-bodied remained. The four Abe brothers ordered their retainers to assemble in the main hall from which shoji and *fusuma* had been cleared away, where they chanted the name of Amida Buddha to the accompaniment of gong and drum until dawn. The Abe clan said this action was taken to mourn the elders and the women and children, but it was actually a precaution against their lower retainers losing heart.

This Yamazaki mansion was later occupied by Saitō Kansuke; it faced the residence of Yamanaka Matazaemon, and was flanked by the residences of Tsukamoto Matashichirō and Hirayama Saburō.

Of these, Tsukamoto was one of the three families of Tsukamoto, Amakusa, and Shiki that had originally shared a tripartite rule over the district of Amakusa. During the time Konishi Yukinaga controlled half of Higo province,[36] the Amakusa and Shiki clans were destroyed for having committed crimes against his rule, leaving only the Tsukamoto in the service of the Hosokawa house.

Matashichirō had been on familiar terms with the Abe family, and not only the masters of each house, but their wives as well, had frequent contact with one another. This was also true of Yaichiemon's second son, Yagobē, and Matashichirō. Yagobē took special pride in his skill with the spear, and after Matashichirō also took up the same art, they would trade boasts with one another among friends. They would say, "You may be quick, but you're no match for me," or "Never! How could I lose to you!"

For this reason, Matashichirō, upon hearing that Yaichiemon had been refused *junshi* during Tadatoshi's illness, felt deep sympathy for Yaichiemon's plight. This situation was followed in turn by Yaichiemon's suicide, the misconduct of his heir at the Kōyōin and Gombē's execution for that misconduct, and now the seclusion of Yagobē and the family at the Yamazaki mansion. As Matashichirō watched the declining fortunes of the Abe family, his grief was no less than that of the members of the family themselves.

One day during the period of seclusion, Matashichirō gave instructions to his wife to go late at night to the Abe mansion and inquire after the family. Since the Abe family had entrenched themselves in their mansion in defiance of the authorities, he could not communicate with them personally. However, since he had known the circumstances of their plight from the very beginning, neither could he repudiate them as criminals, still less in view of their warm relationship over the years. He sent his wife on the assumption that a woman's private inquiry after someone's health was not an inexcusable act, should it later be brought to light. Matashichirō's wife was pleased; she thoughtfully prepared some things to take with her and went next door after night fell. Being a person of firm character as well, she had resolved to take responsibility for her own action to save her husband from any trouble, if the visit later became known to the authorities.

The Abe family was buoyed up by her arrival. While the cherry trees are blossoming and the birds singing in the springtime air, they said, we are unfortunately abandoned by the gods, buddhas, and men, and are thus sequestered from the world. They were deeply grateful for the kind concern of Matashichirō and for her visit at his request. As tears streamed down her cheeks, they beseeched her to remember to conduct services for them, since there would be no one to pray for them after they died. Since the Abe children could not step outside the gate, when they saw their gentle neighbor, they clung to her on both sides and would not let her go home.

It was now the evening prior to the attack upon the Abe mansion. Tsukamoto Matashichirō pondered deeply. The Abe family members were his intimate friends. For this reason he had taken the risk of sending his wife to inquire after them. In the morning, however, the attack against them was finally coming. There was no difference between this force and one sent to suppress rebels. Official orders had been issued to stand by in case of fires and stay clear of the affair, but a samurai was not one to sit by as an idle spectator in this case. Feeling is one thing, duty is another. I have my own role, he thought. So when night fell, he stole out of the rear of his own house into the darkened garden and cut all the ropes which bound together the bamboo fence separating his property from the Abe's. He then returned indoors and made himself ready for the morrow; he took down his short spear from the wall beam where it was hung, removed the sheath on which a crest of falcon's feathers was affixed, and awaited the coming of dawn.

Takenouchi Kazuma, commander of the attacking party on the Abe mansion front gate, had been born into a distinguished warrior family. The founder of his family line, a vassal of Hosokawa Tadakuni,[37] was a famous bowman named Shimamura Danjō Takanori.[38] When Takanori was defeated at Amagasaki in the province of Settsu in 1531, Danjō died by leaping into the sea with an enemy soldier pinned under each arm. His son Ichibē served the Yasumi house of Kawachi province; he was for a time called Yasumi, but when the mountain pass at Take no uchi came under his jurisdiction, his name was amended to Takenouchi. Ichibē's son, Kichibē, served Konishi Yukinaga; for his valor at the time the Ōta castle in Kii province was besieged by flooding in 1585, he received from Toyotomi Hideyoshi a sleeveless overgarment for field use made of white, glossed silk, decorated with a vermilion representation of the sun. When Hideyoshi's forces invaded Korea, Kichibē was captured and confined for three years in the palace of the Yi king as a hostage of the Konishi house. After the Konishi house was dissolved in 1600, Kichibē was employed by Katō Kiyomasa at a stipend of one thousand *koku*. However, after a quarrel between him and his lord, he left the castle town of Kumamoto. He took his departure after having his retainers load their guns and ignite their firing punk to forewarn Kiyomasa against contemplating a punitive attack. Tadatoshi's father, Hosokawa Sansai, took Kichibē into service in Buzen province at a stipend of one thousand *koku*. Kichibē had five sons. The eldest, also named Kichibē, later became the monk Yasumi Kenzan. His second son was

Shichirōemon; the third, Jirōdayū; the fourth, Hachibē; and the fifth was the Kazuma of our story.

Kazuma served Tadatoshi as a page, and was at his side at the time of the Shimabara Rebellion. When the Hosokawa forces attempted to overrun the castle on the twenty-fifth day of the second month of the fifteenth year of Kan'ei [1638], Kazuma had implored Tadatoshi, "Let me fight on the front line." Tadatoshi refused. Kazuma persisted until Tadatoshi yelled angrily at him, "Idiot! Go get yourself killed, if that's what you want!" Kazuma was sixteen years old at the time. As Kazuma started off in a state of exhilaration, Tadatoshi shouted after him, "Take care of yourself." Kazuma's chief retainer Shima Tokuemon, a sandal bearer, and a spear bearer followed behind him, making a little company of four. Gunfire from the castle was so intense that Shima grabbed hold of the skirt of Kazuma's scarlet sleeveless field tunic and pulled him back. Kazuma broke free and climbed up the stone castle wall. Shima had no choice but to follow after him. When they finally worked their way up into the castle, Kazuma was already wounded. A seventy-two-year-old seasoned warrior, Tachibana Hida no kami Muneshige[39] of Yanagigawa, who had entered the castle from the same point, observed the fighting and was impressed by three men, Watanabe Shinya, Nakamitsu Naizen, and Kazuma, to whom he later sent letters of commendation. After the castle fell, Tadatoshi presented Kazuma with a short sword made by Seki Kanemitsu,[40] and increased his stipend to a thousand fifty koku. The sword was one foot eight inches long; its blade had been tempered to produce the grain instantaneously but bore no inscription; it was etched with horizontal file markings, and the ornamental plug which secured the hilt to the blade was faced with three nine-star crests in a line and made of silver; the pommel was made of a gold-copper alloy, other fittings of gold. There were two holes in the tang for an ornamental plug. One of the holes was filled with lead. Since Tadatoshi cherished this sword, even after he gave it to Kazuma, he often borrowed it to wear on such occasions as his attendance at the shogun's castle.

At the time that Kazuma was entrusted by Mitsuhisa to lead the attack on the Abe, he elatedly went down to his place of duty, where a samurai whispered to him:

"Even a scoundrel has some good points. Lord Hayashi must be commended for having chosen you to command the attack."

Kazuma pricked up his ears. "So my appointment to lead the attack was initiated by Geki?"

"Yes, Lord Geki suggested it to Lord Mitsuhisa. He said that you had been accorded exceptional favors by our late Lord Tadatoshi. He suggested this mission would be an opportunity for you to repay your debt of gratitude. A perfect opportunity for you, it seems."

"So?" Kazuma said, as the furrows on his brow deepened.

"I am still pleased. Even if I die on the mission . . ." he replied, then rose abruptly and departed the mansion.

When Lord Mitsuhisa heard of Kazuma's reaction on this occasion, he sent a messenger to Takenouchi Kazuma's residence with a message to Kazuma: "It is my wish that the mission be successfully completed without injury to yourself."

"Please inform His Lordship that I deeply appreciate his solicitude," Kazuma instructed the messenger in reply.

No sooner had Kazuma heard from his comrade that Geki had recommended his command against the Abe family than he resigned himself to die. This resignation was absolutely unshakable. Geki had spoken of giving him the opportunity to repay his lord's kindness. Kazuma had heard about this by chance, but even if he hadn't heard it, the fact remained that he had been appointed on Geki's recommendation. This realization sufficed to completely unsettle Kazuma. He was indeed in debt to Lord Tadatoshi's kindness to him. However, after he came of age he had been only one among many close retainers and had not been especially favored by Lord Tadatoshi. Everyone enjoyed the privilege of Lord Tadatoshi's patronage. What hidden nuance, then, was there in Geki's recommendation that he alone be given the opportunity to repay Lord Tadatoshi's kindness? He may well have committed *junshi*, but since he did not, he had been singled out for this perilous mission. He would willingly give his life any time, but he had no taste for dying simply because he had not pressed his opportunity to request *junshi* from Lord Tadatoshi in that earlier time. As he now was resolved to die, why did he hesitate on the ninth day after Lord Tadatoshi's death? It was inconsistent. In the end, there is no clear line between those especially favored retainers who should commit *junshi* and those who should not. Since none of the young samurai who had been personal attendants of Lord Tadatoshi had been directed to commit *junshi*, he had not attempted to be an exception. If it had been appropriate to do so, he would have been the first to commit *junshi*. He thought that much was clear to everyone. And yet he continuously lamented the fact that he was marked as a man who might long ago have committed *junshi*. He was irreparably disgraced. Only Geki could expose the disgrace so blatantly. This viciousness was only normal for Geki. But why had Lord Mitsuhisa followed Geki's recommendation? He could endure Geki's blow, but he could not endure being abandoned by his lord. When he had wanted to enter the fray in the attack on the Shimabara castle, Lord Tadatoshi had called for him to stop. He had done so because Kazuma was one of his mounted escorts, and as such should have had no thoughts of joining the front line of attack. But that was different from Lord Mitsuhisa's concern that he avoid injury this time. He was telling him, in effect, to take care of his cowardly life. His solicitude was too ambiguous. It was like flailing an old wound with a whip. I want to die now, right now. My disgrace cannot be washed away by dying, but I want to die— die even like a dog.

Kazuma was now completely beside himself. He informed his wife and children that he had been ordered to direct the attack on the Abe, and then feverishly hurried with his preparations by himself. Whereas those who had committed *junshi* had done so with serenity, Kazuma was pursuing death to escape the anguish in his heart. Aside from his chief retainer, Shima Tokuemon, who sensed Kazuma's inner turmoil and resolved to die like his master, no one in his household fathomed the suffering in the depth of Kazuma's mind. His wife, still a young girl who only last year had married Kazuma (himself only twenty), stood by holding their newborn daughter in her arms.

On the night of the twentieth, the eve of the attack, Kazuma bathed and shaved the pate of his head, and burned in the shaven hair a renowned incense named "The Nightingale's First Cry of Spring," which Tadatoshi had bestowed upon him. He fastened the sleeves of his white kimono with a white cord, and placed a white headband around his head. On his shoulder he pinned a folded paper which was to serve as the identifying emblem of the Hosokawa attacking force. The sword belted to his side was a Masamori[41] two feet five-and-a-half inches long, a momento which had been sent back to his native village after his ancestor Shimamura Danjō died in battle at Amagasaki. Alongside hung the Kanemitsu short sword bestowed on him at the time of his first battle. Kazuma's horse neighed at the front gate.

After grabbing his short spear and stepping down into the garden, he tied the cord of his straw sandals in a firm knot, and cut away the excess cord with a knife.

Takami Gon'emon, who was to command the attack on the Abe rear gate, was originally a member of the Wada clan and a descendent of Wada Tajima no kami who lived in Wada of Ōmi province. At first his ancestors had served Gamō Katahide,[42] but in the generation of Wada Shōgorō, the family became retainers of the Hosokawa house. Shōgorō distinguished himself at the battles of Gifu and Sekigahara, where he served under Tadatoshi's elder brother, Yoichirō Tadataka.[43] Tadataka incurred his father's wrath because his wife from the Maeda clan had quickly deserted him in Osaka at the time of the battle of Sekigahara [1600]; thereafter he became a wandering lay monk and took the name of Kyūmu. Shōgorō then accompanied him as far as Mt. Kōya and Kyoto. Tadatoshi's father, Sansai, then summoned Shōgorō to Kokura, granted him the Takami clan name, and made him head of the palace guards with a stipend of five hundred *koku*. Gon'emon was Shōgorō's son. He had served meritoriously at the battle at Shimabara, but because of a breach of orders, he had been temporarily relieved of his duties. Some time later, he returned and became a captain of the Bodyguards. In readying himself for the attack, he dressed in emblazoned black silk and wore his prized sword manufactured in Osafune village in the province of Bizen. He went forth carrying a three-pronged pike.

Just as Takenouchi Kazuma was attended by Shima Tokuemon, Takami Gon'emon was escorted by his own page. One summer day about two or three years prior to this incident, this page was sleeping in his room while off duty. Another page, returning there from his own duties, stripped himself naked and, taking a small wooden tub in hand, started off toward the well to draw some water when suddenly he eyed the first page sleeping. "Here I come back exhausted and have to draw the water myself while he just sleeps," he exclaimed, and kicked the page's pillow out from under him. The page jumped to his feet.

"If I had been awake, I would have gotten the water for you. So why kick my pillow out from under me? The next move will be mine!" he raged, drew out his sword and cut down his colleague.

The page calmly straddled his victim's chest and delivered the final blow, then went to his superior's quarters and reported the incident in detail. "I should have taken my own life right there, but I felt you may have some insight into my motive," he said, as he stripped to the waist and was on the verge of committing *seppuku*. "First, wait a moment," the superior ordered, and reported the incident to Gon'emon. Gon'emon, just returned from his own duties, had not yet changed his clothes, so he went off directly to the Hosokawa mansion to inform Lord Tadatoshi. Tadatoshi made the judgment. "His reaction was natural enough. There is no cause for suicide." From that time on, the page dedicated his life to Gon'emon's service.

The page, bearing a quiver and small bow, followed alongside his master.

On the twenty-first day of the fourth month of the nineteenth year of Kan'ei [1642], the sky was thin and overcast as it often is at the season of the wheat harvest.

At dawn, Takenouchi Kazuma's men arrived before the front gate of the Yamazaki mansion of the Abe family. The mansion, which had resounded with the sounds of drum and gong throughout the night, now lay so hushed it seemed to be empty. The gate was bolted. A spider's web dangled on the sweet oleander branches a few feet above the wooden fence, and the morning dew glistened on the blossoms like pearls. A swallow flew by and darted inside the wall.

Kazuma got down from his horse and slowly surveyed the scene. "Open the gate!" he ordered. Two foot soldiers climbed over the fence into the compound. As there were no Abe men in the vicinity of the gate, they broke the lock and removed the wooden bar.

When from his adjacent residence Tsukamoto Matashichirō heard the sounds of Kazuma's men opening the gate, he kicked down the bamboo fence whose binding cord he had cut the night before and dashed inside the Abe residence. He knew the arrangements of the rooms intimately from his almost daily visitations in the past. Short spear in hand, he ran through the kitchen door. Of the Abe group who were waiting behind the closed doors of the drawing room to pick off the invading force one by one, the first to feel the presence of someone at the rear entrance was Yagobē. He raised his short spear and went to check the kitchen.

The two men squared off, their spear points touching. "So . . . Matashichirō, is it?" Yagobē called out.

"That's right. You used to boast how quick you are. I've come to test your skill."

"It's about time! Come ahead!"

The two men backed off a step and crossed spears. They parried each other's thrusts for a while, but since Matashichirō's technique was superior, he pierced Yagobē's breast plate with a mighty thrust. Yagobē dropped his spear to the floor with a clatter and started to withdraw in the direction of the drawing room.

"Coward! Stay and fight!" Matashichirō yelled after him.

"I'm not running away! I'm going to commit *seppuku*," he called back and passed into the drawing room.

In that instant young Shichinojō, still with his forelocks, darted into the room like a flash of lightning: "Uncle! Try me!" he shouted and stuck Matashichirō in the thigh. Since Matashichirō had relaxed his guard after seriously wounding his close friend Yagobē, he fell at the less experienced hand of the youngster. Matashichirō let go of his spear and collapsed on the spot.

Kazuma entered the front gate and dispatched parties of men to different points of the mansion. As Kazuma's own party proceeded to the front entranceway directly forward of them, they found the wooden front door slightly ajar. Kazuma was about to lay a hand on the door when Shima Tokuemon interposed himself and interjected in a whisper:

"Wait, my Lord! Today you are commander-in-chief. Let me go first."

Tokuemon shoved open the door and rushed inside. He ran right into Ichidayū's spear, which pierced Tokuemon's right eye and sent him staggering backward to crumble at Kazuma's feet.

"Out of my way!" Kazuma cried, pushing him aside. He charged forward into the poised spears of Ichidayū and Godayū, who ripped him open on both sides.

Next Soejima Kuhē and Nomura Shobē dashed forward, only to draw back with Tokuemon, who still struggled despite his mortal wound.

Takami Gon'emon, who had meanwhile broken in the rear gate, entered the drawing room, brandishing his three-pronged pike and thrusting at Abe retainers left and right. Chiba Sakubē followed on his heels.

Now both front and rear attacking parties broke in, yelling and thrusting their weapons as they came. Even with the shoji and *fusuma* cleared away, the drawing room was smaller than thirty mats. Just as street fighting is far uglier than fighting in the field, the situation here was even more ghastly: a swarm of bugs in a dish devouring one another.

Ichidayū and Godayū were crossing spears with everyone they encountered and they sustained innumerable wounds over their entire bodies. Yet they stood firm, and abandoned their spears for their swords. Meanwhile Shichinojō had fallen.

Tsukamoto Matashichirō, whose thigh had been pierced, lay prostrate in the kitchen when one of Takami's men spotted him, and shouted "So you've been wounded. Good fighting! Get yourself out of here!" and kept on running toward the rear of the mansion.

"Can't walk . . . ," Matashichirō groaned in reply and clenched his teeth. One of his own retainers who had followed after him into the house ran up, placed Matashichirō's arm across his own shoulders, and half carried him into retreat.

Another of the Tsukamoto family personal retainers, Amakusa Heikurō, tried to protect Matashichirō's path of retreat by firing at any enemy within range, but he was killed right on the spot.

Among Takenouchi Kazuma's men, Shima Tokuemon died first, then his lieutenant, Soejima Kuhē.

While Takami Gon'emon was engaged in battle with his three-pronged pike, his page with the small bow stood fast to his flank, discharging arrows at the enemy. He later switched to his sword. An Abe retainer suddenly aimed his rifle at Gon'emon.

"I'll stop that bullet," the page cried as he jumped in front of Gon'emon, and was hit. He fell over dead. Lieutenant Chiba Sakubē, who had been withdrawn from Takenouchi's force and attached to Takami's, went into the kitchen, badly wounded, and was gulping water from a jug when he sank to the floor.

Of the Abe family, Yagobē died first by committing *seppuku*; he was followed by Ichidayū, Godayū, Shichinojō, each of whom succumbed to heavy wounds. Most of their retainers died fighting.

Takami Gon'emon assembled the men from the front and rear parties, and ordered a rear storage shed knocked down and set on fire. As there was no wind that day, the smoke from the fire rose straight up into the thinly overcast sky and was visible from a great distance. They then stamped out the fire, wet down the ashes, and withdrew from the premises. Chiba Sakubē, who had fallen in the kitchen, and the others who were badly wounded, followed behind, supported on the shoulders of their retainers or fellow samurai. It was now two in the afternoon.

Lord Mitsuhisa frequently paid visits to the homes of the distinguished members of his family. On the twenty-first, the day of the attack on the Abe family, he set out at dawn for the residence of Matsuno Sakyō.

Since Yamazaki lay directly opposite Lord Mitsuhisa's Hanabatake mansion, he could hear sounds of the fray in the direction of the Abe mansion when he came out of his house that morning.

"So the attack has begun . . . ," he said, as he climbed into his palanquin. He had only gone a short distance when an urgent message arrived. Lord Mitsuhisa was informed that Takenouchi Kazuma had been killed in action.

Takami Gon'emon, who led the surviving force of the attacking party to the front of the Matsuno residence, reported that the entire Abe clan had been killed. Mitsuhisa said he would meet personally with Gon'emon and had him escorted to the garden opposite the drawing room.

Gon'emon opened a small wicker door in the fence where the verbena were just then opening into pure white blossoms; he entered the garden and crouched respectfully on the grass. Mitsuhisa looked at Gon'emon and said: "You've been wounded . . . It was fierce work, I see." Gon'emon's black silk clothing was smeared with blood and spattered further by pieces of charcoal and ash, which had adhered to him when they had stamped out the fire of the shed before their withdrawal.

"It is nothing, my Lord. I was just grazed." Gon'emon had been struck hard in the pit of the stomach, but the spearhead had been deflected by a mirror tucked away inside his clothing. The wound had barely stained some tissue paper with blood.

When Gon'emon detailed the exploits of each individual during the attack, he accorded the highest praise to the Abe's neighbor, Tsukamoto Matashichirō, who single-handedly dealt the mortal wound to Yagobē.

"What about Kazuma?"

"Since he charged in through the front gate before me, I did not witness what happened to him."

"I see. Tell the others to come into the garden."

Gon'emon summoned the company of men inside. The entire company, except those who because of their wounds had been taken to their own homes, prostrated themselves on the grass. Those who had fought were soiled with blood. Those who had only assisted with the burning of the shed were covered with ashes. Among the latter was Hata Jūdayū.

"Jūdayū. Give me your report."

"My Lord!" Jūdayū replied, and continued to lie prostrated in silence. Jūdayū was a stalwart coward. He had lingered outside the Abe mansion, and only cautiously entered when fire was set to the shed prior to their withdrawal. When the order for the attack was first given, the sword master Shimmen Musashi[44] had met Jūdayū leaving Mitsuhisa's chambers, and slapped him on the back while exclaiming "You have been blessed by the gods and buddhas! You shall achieve great distinction!" It is said that Jūdayū turned pale, and fumbled with the cord of his skirt-style trousers which had become loosened, but his hands shook so badly that he could not do it.

Mitsuhisa rose from his seat and addressed the men. "You have all exhausted yourselves. Go home and rest."

Takenouchi Kazuma's baby daughter was given an adopted husband and permitted to succeed to the family's inheritance, but this house later died out. Takami Gon'emon's stipend was raised by three hundred *koku*, while Chiba Sakubē and Nomura Shobē each received an increase of fifty *koku*. The Han Elder Komeda Kemmotsu received instructions and despatched Squad Leader Tani Kuranosuke to commend Tsukamoto Matashichirō. When his friends and relatives came to congratulate him, Matashichirō would laugh and reply: "It was as simple as eating morning and evening meals while in the field, or while laying siege to a castle in the days of Nobunaga and Hideyoshi. Storming the Abe was just a little task before morning tea." Two years later, in the summer of the first year of the Shōhō era [1644], Matashichirō, his wound healed, was granted an audience with Mitsuhisa. Mitsuhisa put him in charge of ten riflemen, and commented: "You should take medicinal baths to heal your wounds; and look for some

site outside the castle town for a villa that I shall be conferring upon you."
Matashichirō received land for the villa in the village of Koike in the district
of Mashiki. In its background stood a mountain covered with bamboo.
"Shall I give you the mountain, too?" Mitsuhisa had asked. Matashichirō
declined, replying, "Bamboo is of use to my lord even under ordinary circumstances; in time of war, bundles of bamboo are needed in large quan-
tities. Should you confer this on me, I would not feel right about it." The
result was that the mountain was entrusted to his care in perpetuity.

Hata Jūdayū was discharged from service. Takenouchi Kazuma's elder
brother Hachibē, although he had joined the attack on his own, had not
been with Kazuma when he died, and for this reason he was ordered under
domiciliary confinement. Another retainer, Yamanaka Matabē, son of a
Mounted Escort who served as an attendant, resided near the Abe mansion
and thus had been exempted from participating in the attack because of the
order to watch for fires; he and his father had climbed upon the roofs and
put out the sparks. Later this man felt that he had acted contrary to the spirit
of the exemption and asked to be released from service. Mitsuhisa declined,
saying: "It was not cowardice; but hereafter you must be a little more attentive to orders." This attendant committed *junshi* when Mitsuhisa passed
away.

The corpses of the Abe family were taken to Ide no kuchi and examined.
When each man's wounds had been washed in the Shirakawa River, Yagobē's wound, sustained when Tsukamoto Matashichirō's spear penetrated his
breast plate, was judged to be more technically perfect than that sustained
by any other person, and so Matashichirō's reputation increased all the
more.

January 1913

GOJIINGAHARA NO KATAKIUCHI

"GOJIINGAHARA NO KATAKIUCHI," or "The Vendetta at Gojiingahara," is Ōgai's version of a celebrated incident carried out in 1835.* During the Tokugawa period, vendetta was permitted under certain circumstances prescribed by the Tokugawa government.† Such incidents often provided the plots for popular novels and kabuki plays in which all the drama and excitement inherent in such lurid situations could be exploited. The most famous of these is the celebrated drama *Chūshingura*, popularly known as "The Forty-Seven *Rōnin*."

Ōgai, however, was not interested in colorful spectacle. His account gives an impression of restraint and psychological realism. To be sure, the dramatic events of the story are not glossed over. The opening scene of the story, the Edo fire, and the final act of vengeance are powerfully presented. Connecting these moments of high drama are long narrative sections that reveal in great detail the growing fatigue and discouragement of those who search for justice, without result, on the basis of an abstract code that, to the son Uhei at least, seemed to be destructive. The reactions to the vendetta of the three major protagonists in the story vary with their own characters. Kurōemon, the middle-aged, wise younger brother of the murdered man, is calm and confident. Uhei, the son, is young and unsure of his own personality. Riyo, the daughter, is deeply emotional and committed to an act of justice. The ultimate fascination of the story lies in the interactions between the three as they face their long and dispiriting task. Riyo proves herself in the end to be of a more resolute character than her brother. In this she resembles Ichi in "Saigo no ikku." Ōgai has created in these young women two ardent personalities, forceful yet completely feminine, who are able to triumph spiritually over any obstacles placed in their paths. Despite the bizarre happenings and outlandish details of "Gojiingahara no katakiuchi," Ōgai's vision of Riyo makes this a surprisingly effective tale, powerful and altogether unsentimental.

(TR)

THE MAIN EDO MISSION of Sakai Uta no kami Tadamitsu,[1] lord of the castle of Himeji in the district of Shikito of the province of Harima, faced the left corner of the front gate of Edo castle. There were usually two samurai on duty in the treasury there. However on this occasion, around dawn of the twenty-sixth day of the twelfth month of the fourth year of Tempō [1833], the treasurer Yamamoto Sanzaemon, a retainer who was then fifty-five years old, was on duty alone. As the assistant treasurer, who normally shared the night watch with him, had been excused because of illness, Sanzaemon had endured the cold and lonely night by himself. He sat next to a thick and sturdy candle whose orange flame, now beginning to waver as the wick swam in the melting wax, illuminated the room about equally with the dawning light coming in the window. His bedding was already placed in the wicker trunk used for storing the night quilts.

Suddenly a voice called outside the screen.

"Excuse me, sir. I have an urgent message from your home."

"Who are you?"

"I am the messenger boy from the inner office of our lord's residence."

Sanzaemon opened the screen from within. Carrying a letter was a messenger of about twenty whom Sanzaemon knew by face but not by name.

Taking the envelope and squatting before the candle, Sanzaemon first adjusted the wick of the candle to burn more brightly. He then reached into his bosom for his eyeglass cases and took out his glasses. He inspected the envelope; the handwriting was neither that of his son, Uhei, nor of his wife. He held it in his hand somewhat hesitantly, but since it was definitely addressed to him, he cut the envelope open. As he spread out the letter, Sanzaemon's eyes registered bewilderment. The paper was blank!

As Sanzaemon's mind sprang to attention he felt a strong blow upon his head. And before this shock could fully register, he saw drops of blood upon the paper. He had been struck from behind.

As Sanzaemon groped for his swords lying in front of the wicker basket, his assailant struck again. Sanzaemon raised his right hand out of pure reflex to stop the blow. His hand, slashed off at the wrist, fell to the floor. He started to get up, grasping his chest with his left hand.

The assailant ripped Sanzaemon's hand away from his chest, stabbed him there with a dagger, and fled to the veranda.

Without pausing to think, Sanzaemon started after him. He got as far as

TRANSLATED BY DAVID DILWORTH

the inner gate only to find that his assailant had vanished into thin air. The wounded old man's legs were no match for those of the young assailant. Sanzaemon began to feel the burning wounds in his head and hand, and grew faint. Still he summoned every ounce of his ebbing strength to return to the treasury office, and before doing anything else he inspected the lock of the safe. It was untouched. "At least that's secure," he thought, but his brain began to blacken; he pulled over the wicker trunk with his left hand and leaned on it. His breath was now deep and slow as he slipped into unconsciousness.

The first one to hear a noise and come running was an Assistant Censor. Then a Censor and Censor General. They were followed by the Chief Accountant of the *han*. The doctor was summoned. A messenger ran to the secondary mansion of the *han* in Kakigara-chō where Sanzaemon's wife was staying.

Sanzaemon regained consciousness and replied clearly to the official's questions. He had no recollection of any grudge held against him. The person who brought the letter and cut him down was a messenger from the mansion whom he recognized by face only. He had probably been after the money. He requested that they kindly see to the matter of succession to the head of the house of Yamamoto. And he enjoined his son Uhei to seek to avenge the attack upon his father. All the while as he spoke, Sanzaemon kept repeating, "Why did this have to happen? Why? Why? . . ."

The weapon dropped at the scene was a sword stolen from the guard house where it was left two or three days before by a certain Gose who served in the maintenance office. When the guards at the gate were questioned, it turned out that the messenger named Kamezō had gone out through the gate at dawn, saying he had an urgent message to deliver. Kamezō was a young man of twenty who had been referred by Fujiya Jisaburō, an employment agent for servants in the Kanda Kyūzaemon-chō Daichi area. His sponsor was Wakasaya Kamekichi. When they searched Kamezō's room, they found envelopes addressed to four treasury officials besides Yamamoto, each with a blank paper inside.

It was apparent that Kamezō had worked out a definite plan to kill one of the treasury officials and steal the money. Since the markets of Edo were suffering a sharp inflation due to the bad crops in Ōu and other regions, it was said that people were being driven to crime. The fourth year of Tempō was the worst famine year since the Temmei period when retail rice selling at a hundred *mon* rose to five *go* five *shaku*.[2]

The doctor came and dressed Sanzaemon's wounds. His retainers came running. From the mansion in Kakigara-chō came Sanzaemon's wife and his son Uhei. Uhei was nineteen years old. Since Uhei's older sister Riyo was serving in the ladies' quarters of Hosokawa Nagato no kami Okitake,[3] she came from the Hosokawa mansion at Toshima-chō. Riyo was twenty-two. Sanzaemon's wife was his second wife, and thus the step-mother of Riyo and Uhei. Sanzaemon's younger sister, the wife of a certain Harada, who was a vassal of Ogasawara Bingo no kami Sadayoshi,[4] lord of the castle of Shinden in Kokura, was in the Ogasawara mansion in Higakubo in Azabu; because of the distance, she could not come to the Sakai mansion.

Sanzaemon, not heeding the doctor's advice to speak as little as possible, repeated again and again to his wife and children what he had said to the officials.

As the Kakigara-chō residence was too small to allow him proper care, it was ordered that Sanzaemon be taken in by a certain Kambē of a residence adjacent to Hama-chō. He was a distant relative of the Yamamoto house. Sanzaemon's wife went to attend him there. In the meanwhile, his younger sister, the wife of Harada, also arrived.

Sanzaemon breathed his last at Kambē's residence during the predawn hours of the twenty-seventh.

Toward evening of the same day, some officials of the rank of Assistant Censor, accompanied by accountants, came from the main mansion to make a report. These officials received an affidavit signed by Sanzaemon's wife, his son Uhei, and his daughter Riyo.

On recommendation of these officials an order was sent down from the Sakai house noting that Sanzaemon, although mortally wounded, had pursued his attacker as far as the inner door; it directed "that he be buried with due honor in view of his loyal service." The sword found at the scene of the attack was returned by an official to its former owner, Gose.

On the twenty-eighth, Sanzaemon's corpse was interred in the Henryūji before the Asakusa temple, where the Yamamoto family had a grave plot. Prior to the service, Kambē disposed of the things Sanzaemon had with him at the time of the attack. His two swords should have gone to the son Uhei, but at Riyo's urgent entreaty she received Sanzaemon's small sword. When Uhei had agreed to this, her tearful eyes had suddenly glistened with joy.

A samurai was expected to perform a vendetta to avenge the death of a slain parent. All the more so in this case when such had been Sanzaemon's own last wish to his relatives before he died. And thus the family and relatives convened, and after several deliberations made a formal request in the middle of the first month of the fifth year of Tempō [1834] to carry out a vendetta.

At these deliberations the one who talked most heatedly and impatiently about performing the vendetta was Uhei. He was a pale, rawboned, slightly built youth, but not sickly. Riyo said nothing throughout the discussions, but insisted upon signing her own name to the petition. Riyo was also lean in figure and of average looks. Sanzaemon's widow only rarely attended these discussions because of her chronic headaches, and when she did come she only expressed her fear that their attempt to perform the vendetta might lead to further misfortune; she kept repeating the one tedious refrain, "How did this terrible thing ever happen?" The wife of Harada from Higakubo and Sakurai Sumazaemon, the brother of her dead husband, always took pains to console her.

However, there was one man whom the whole group had in mind to help them execute the vendetta. He was in Himeji at the time and unable to participate in the deliberations, but as soon as he had received the report of Sanzaemon's demise, he had sent a letter of condolence and pledged his service in the vendetta. In Himeji he served the Han Elder, Honda Ikiri. He was Yamamoto Kurōemon, age forty-five, the younger brother of Sanzaemon by nine years.

When Kurōemon received the report about his brother, he immediately submitted a request to Lord Ikiri, saying that because his nephew and neice were involved in a vendetta, he wished to leave his affairs to his son Kenzō and set out to join them. As his lord was a grandson of the Honda Ikiri who had been made a retainer of the Sakai house by Tokugawa Ieyasu, and was therefore steeped in the code of the samurai, he immediately consented to Kurōemon's request. At the time, the family was submitting its petition to avenge Sanzaemon's death, but before it had been formally approved by the *bakufu* in Edo, Kurōemon left Himeji in possession of a finely wrought sword and an allowance of twenty *ryō* which he received from Ikiri. This was on the twenty-third day of the first month.

On the fifth day of the second month, Kurōemon arrived at the quarters of Yamamoto Uhei, at the subordinate Sakai mansion at Kakigara-chō in Edo. Uhei and Riyo, who had requested a leave of absence from the Hosokawa family, were in a state of despondency. Just seeing the figure of their uncle, so calm, quiet, yet powerfully built, gave them a sense of reassurance.

"Has the permission come yet?" Kurōemon inquired of Uhei.

"No, not yet. We have inquired of the officials, who said that perhaps it is because we are still within the period of mourning."

Kurōemon wrinkled his brows. After a pause he replied, "Big wheels turn slowly."

Kurōemon then asked whether they had completed preparations for their journey. "We shall do so as soon as the permission arrives," Uhei replied.

His uncle's eyebrows again furrowed, but this time he said nothing for a long time. After passing to other matters, he returned to the same thread of conversation: "Concerning the preparations, you don't have to wait."

On the sixth, Kurōemon visited his brother's grave. On the seventh, he went to Hama-chō to pay his respects to Kambē who had taken care of San-zaemon in his last hours. There was a strong northwest wind that day, and just as Kurōemon was in Kambē's house, a fire broke out in the Kanda area. It has come down in the history books as the Great Fire of the Year of the Horse.[5] The fire started around two P.M. in the house of a koto and samisen teacher at Sakuma-chō 2-chome, spread in the direction of Nihonbashi and burned until dawn of the next morning. Later a satirical poem was written with the line, "Sparks from the samisen house become a great fire." As Hama-chō and Kakigara-chō were downwind, Kurōemon, when he saw that the fire was advancing along three fronts, raced back to Kakigara-chō, saying that Kambē's house already had plenty of helping hands.

At the Yamamoto house, Kurōemon directed that all their luggage for the journey be taken away; by four P.M., the whole Kakigara-chō residence was on fire, the Yamamoto house included.

When the fire broke out, Riyo had run off to the Hosokawa mansion, the residence of her lord, but Toshima-chō was already ablaze. "It's danger-ous!" "Don't rush into the fire!" people cried. Finally as Riyo was caught in the crush of persons fleeing the flames and the onlookers, she could move no longer. Cinders were showering down upon the crowd. In tears, Riyo turned away from Kameichi-chō. Her uncle had already returned from Hama-chō, and had put away the luggage.

Most of Hama-chō on the side adjacent to Yanokura was burned out, but fortunately the auxiliary mansion of the Sakai family was still standing. Since it would have been too much to depend again upon the Kambē fami-ly, Uhei's family fled from the fire around eight the next morning to the residence of Yamamoto Heisaku, who was a distant relative.

The bereft family of Sanzaemon borrowed a room from Yamamoto Hei-saku, where they sat in shock, feeling as if they were experiencing one bad dream within another. The widow became bedridden with her headaches. Uhei sat with folded arms, sunk deeply in thought. Only Riyo, though she felt constrained by the new surroundings of the Heisaku house, kept her spirits up; and as soon as information came around noon concerning the residence to which the wife of the Hosokawa family had fled, she went there forthwith to attend her.

When Riyo returned that evening, Kurōemon said to her: "Well, we won't be needing a house any longer anyway. But you had better make preparations, so that our young lord won't catch a cold on the trip.'' Her uncle always referred to Uhei as ''our young lord.''

''Yes,'' Riyo answered, and that evening began work on clothing for Uhei.

On the ninth, Riyo went out to buy the things needed to complete preparations for their journey. Kuroemon had made a list of their needs. That day the wind became southerly, and when it turned unusually warm, a fire again broke out from Himono-chō at about six P.M. The house at Asama-chō, which had burned the day before, was hit again by fire.

On the tenth, as the cold northwest wind began to blow strongly again, a fire broke out at noon from the main mansion at Daimyō-koji of Matsudaira Hoki no kami Muneakira,[6] and swept forward from Kyōbashi to Shibaguchi.

There were more fires on the eleventh and twelfth. With prices soaring and fires continuing to erupt, the people of Edo were in a panic. There were unimaginable complications even in getting the few goods ordered by Kuroemon from the merchants; Riyo, despite every stratagem, was having a hard time completing the preparations.

On one of the following days, Kuroemon was smoking his pipe when he noticed Riyo knitting something; he put down his pipe with a puzzled look. ''What's that little thing for? It'll be useless because our young lord is so tall,'' he said.

Riyo blushed. ''This is for me,'' she replied. She had been knitting leggings and mittens for a woman.

''What?'' Her uncle stared wide-eyed at her. ''So you too are going to train in the arts of the warrior?''

''Yes,'' Riyo replied, without stopping her knitting.

''Is that so?'' her uncle grunted, and kept eyeing his niece for quite some time. Then he continued, ''That's nonsense. It's impossible to set out on a journey which will end no one knows where with a tender girl like you. We have no idea of where we might find our enemy, or how many years it will take. Uhei and I must hunt him down alone. It will be better to let you know after we find him.''

''It's true that you don't know where you will find him, but how will you let me know when you do if I'm in Edo? And how will you wait until I come from Edo to kill him?'' Riyo rejoined with a smile, her big brown eyes, so innocent yet clever, piercing her uncle's face.

Her uncle was by now rather astonished. ''It is true that I cannot say definitely, since it is a question of time and circumstances. If at all possible we will summon you to join us. There is always the possibility of never finding him, and since it is your misfortune to be a girl, you will just have to resign yourself.''

''But, you see, I want to ensure that I am there. If you say that a woman cannot go along, I will go as a nun.''

''Well, a nun is also a woman,'' Kurōemon countered.

Riyo grew silent, her tears now falling on her knitting. On the one hand her uncle had tried to console her as diplomatically as possible, but just the same he had firmly put an end to her hopes of going along. Riyo wiped the tears from her eyes and quietly bundled the knitting in a *furoshiki* by her side.

Sakai Tadamitsu, after submitting a notice to the Minister of State Ōkubo Kaga no kami Tadazane[7] and the three City Magistrates,[8] handed down a document cosigned by the Senior Censor addressed to Uhei, Riyo, and Kurōemon, which permitted the vendetta from that date, the twenty-sixth of the second month. The directive read: ''You should return as soon as possible after achieving your intention; if you kill your enemy, you should bring back some definite proof.'' He granted an allowance to them. A stipend was also given to the family in their absence. Although Riyo was included in the permission, she was not allowed to join in the manhunt. Kurōemon and Uhei set out as soon as living arrangements were made in Edo for Riyo and Sanzaemon's widow.

It was decided at this time that Riyo would stay with the Harada family in their residence at Ogasawara. At her own request, the sick widow was to convalesce at the house of Sakurai Sumazaemon, who was her dead husband's brother.

At long length, Kurōemon and Uhei were ready to set out, but neither one had ever seen their enemy's face. Their task was almost hopeless, having only a general description to go on; therefore they went to Fujiya Jisaburō and the Wakasaya Kanekichi, who had referred Kamezō, and asked them various questions about him. But they came away with no definite suggestions. Neither of these men had a clear recollection of what Kamezō looked like; they said he was supposed to be from Kishū, but would not vouch for that either. The only definite fact was that Kamezō had been in Takasaki in Jōshū prior to serving at the Sakai residence.

At this time a man suddenly called upon Yamamoto Heisaku. He said that he was born in Asaigōri in the province of Ōmi, had gone to Edo when a youth, and while working as a servant had served as a messenger of the Sakai house at the same time as Kamezō; he had once also served Sanzaemon, and wished to be of further service now to his family. Fortunately since he was now on leave from the Sakai residence, he could volunteer to go along as one who could identify their enemy if he saw him. His name was Bunkichi, and he was forty-two years old. To Yamamoto Heisaku he seemed to be healthy, and sincere to a rare degree for a man who lived as a temporary servant.

An interview was arranged with Kurōemon, who then and there invited Bunkichi to become Uhei's vassal.

Having determined to set out on the twenty-ninth day from the family grave at the Henryūji, Kurōemon, Uhei, and Bunkichi took their leave of Yamamoto Heisaku of Hama-chō on the twenty-eighth, and proceeded to the temple. With the exception of the widow who was still ill, Riyo and all of the relatives assembled; after first paying their respects to Sanzaemon's grave, they drank to the departure of the three. The chief priest of the temple served them with noodles and said jokingly, intending a double meaning: "It is something I chopped up myself." The relatives laughed and took turns trying to cheer up Riyo, who alone remained despondent, before returning home.

After passing the night in the temple, the three men set out on the morning of the twenty-ninth. Bunkichi walked behind Kurōemon and Uhei, carrying the baggage. On the basis of the information they had about Kamezō's residence prior to his recent job, they headed first in the direction of Takasaki in the province of Kōzuke.

Although they made Takasaki their first destination, none of them had the feeling that they would find Kamezō there. They simply started with Takasaki because they had no idea where to go. Tracking down this irresponsible drifter Kamezō somewhere in the provinces of Japan was comparable to finding a grain of rice in a granary; it was entirely arbitrary which rice bag they sifted through first. Yet however uncertain the road before them, they had to make a start somewhere. And so they decided to untie the first rice bag in Takasaki.

Since there was no trace of Kamezō in Takasaki, they proceeded to Maebashi, where there was a grave of an ancestor of the Yamamoto house in the Seijunji temple in Enokimachi. They visited this site and prayed for success. They then moved on to Fujioka, where they stayed five or six days. From Fujioka they crossed through Sakai in the province of Musashi, and stayed three days in the village of Odama. After ascending Mt. Mitsumine they made a vow to the god of the mountain, Mitsumine Gongen.[9] They journeyed through Hachiōji to the province of Kai, searched two days in Gunnai and Kōfu, then visited the shrine at Mt. Minobu. In the province of Shinano they crossed Wada pass from Kamisuwa, and visited the Kenkōji temple at Ueda. In the province of Echigo, they continued the search for three days in Takata, two days in Imamachi, one day in Kashihazaki and Nagaoka, and four days in Sanjō and Niigata. They then veered their course to the Kaga highway, entered the province of Etchū, and stayed three days in Toyama. This region had been hard hit by bad harvests; the three travelers lived on a mixture of barley and potatoes, and slept on straw mats laid out on the dirt floors of peasants' houses. They spent two days in Takayama in the province of Hida, then one day in Kanayama in the province of Mino before taking the Kiso road to Ōda. In the province of Owari they searched one day in Inuyama, four days in Nagoya, then traveled along the Tōkaidō to Miya, entered the province of Ise through Saga, took their search to Kuwana, Yokkaichi, Tsu, and spent the last three days in Matsuzaka.

When they stayed at a place for more than two days, occasionally it was to rest themselves, but generally it was because they were tracing out some special lead they thought they had. At Donomachi in Matsuzaka there was a certain official of Censor rank named Iwahashi who listened very attentively to the party's story, and made a careful check of certain leads. When he reported his findings, Kurōemon, Uhei, and Bunkichi felt as if a lantern had suddenly been lighted in the darkness.

There was a rich merchant in Matsuzaka named Fukanoya Sahē. A certain fisherman named Sadazaemon of Sotomachi of Uranage Island in Kumano in the province of Kii had fish delivered to this merchant every day. For this reason Fukanoya was on good terms with the family of Sadazaemon. However, since Sadazaemon's first son, Kamezō, had left home for Edo as a youth and had never written, Fukanoya relied upon Sadazaemon's second son, Sadasuke. But on the twenty-first day of this year, Kamezō, dressed in rags, had returned and called upon him, Fukanoya reported. Fukanoya told him: "I cannot take in such an unfilial son as you without informing your father." As Kamezō dejectedly left Fukanoya's shop, someone there had remarked: "That is Kamezō of Kishū—he looks as if he has fled Edo after doing something wrong."

On the basis of what he later told Fukanoya, Kamezō then went on the twenty-fourth of that month to the house of his maternal uncle Rinsuke in the village of Ningo in Kumano, and asked if he could be put up there; his uncle told him that he was too poor to take him in, and urged him to return to the house of his own father, Sadazaemon. So Kamezō seems finally to have returned to his father's house after finding that he was rejected by an outside acquaintance as well as by a relative. He returned to the house of Sadazaemon on the twenty-eighth.

In the middle of the second month, Sadazaemon got wind of a rumor from Matsuzaka that Kamezō had returned after getting into some trouble in Edo. When questioned by his father, Kamezō admitted to having wounded a samurai. Thereupon Sadazaemon and Rinsuke arranged for Kamezō to become a monk and climb Mt. Kōya. His father and uncle accompanied the newly shaven Kamezō as far as Miurazaka and took leave of him on the nineteenth day of that month. At the time, Kamezō was dressed in a brown-checkered, double-cotton robe, a cotton obi, dark blue pants, and leggings. He was carrying one *ryō* in his purse.

Kamezō stopped at the house of a certain Matabe of Kiyomizu village in the vicinity of Mt. Kōya on the twenty-second, and ended up staying there through the twenty-third because of rain. He climbed Mt. Kōya on the twenty-fourth. He found that there were persons there who knew him. During the night of the twenty-sixth, he descended the mountain and was seen by someone in Hashimoto. After that his trail becomes blurred. He may have crossed over into Shikoku.

When they heard these details from Inspector Iwahashi in Matsuzaka, there was not a shadow of a doubt in their minds that this new monk Kamezō, the son of Sadazaemon, was their enemy. Uhei said that they should cross immediately to Shikoku. But Kurōemon rejected the idea, saying that Kamezō's crossing over to Shikoku was a groundless conjecture on their part; he suggested that they first continue the search closer at hand, with the possibility of later going on to Shikoku if nothing turned up.

Kurōemon, Uhei, and Bunkichi left Matsuzaka and went to the Ise shrine to pray for the successful completion of their mission. Thence they went through Seki along the Tōkaidō to Osaka in the province of Settsu, where they conducted their search for twenty-three days. During this time a report came from Matsuzaka that Sadazaemon had fallen into a depression and died of worry over the fate of his son. They then moved on to the province of Harima by way of Nishinomiya and Hyōgo, went from Akashi to Himeji, and stayed three days at an inn in Uomachi. Although his son's house was located there, Kurōemon had made up his mind not to stop until their mission was accomplished. From there they entered the province of Bizen, passed through Okayama, and finally crossed from Shimoyama to Shikoku by boat on the sixteenth day of the sixth month. Uhei, while seeming a bit dissatisfied at Kurōemon's choice of itinerary for the search ever since Matsuzaka, nevertheless had followed along under the dominance of his strong-willed, steady-minded uncle. Now his spirits suddenly rose and he talked continuously on the boat during the night until dawn.

The boat reached Marugame of the province of Sanuki on the morning of the sixteenth. Bunkichi was sent to check out Matsuo, while the two others climbed Mt. Sōzu to pray to the god of the mountain. A pilgrim to the shrine informed them that he had seen a suspicious-looking priest in Marugame who was from another region. Uhei descended the mountain in the middle of the night, feeling that they had finally found their enemy. When he returned to Marugame he called Bunkichi back from Matsuo to take a look at the suspected monk's face, but it turned out to be another man.

Hearing that Dōzan in the province of Iyo was a haunt of criminals from the provinces, the group directed their search for two days into the mountains there. Then, they probed Saijō for two days, and spent two days in Koharu and Imabari, before traveling from Matsuyama to the hot spring at Dōgo. Uhei, however, who had been traveling with a fever, began to suffer from stomach cramps, and Bunkichi from diarrhea, so they convalesced for fifty days at Yumachi. Somewhat recovered, they searched through Nakaōsu for two days and went on to Yahatahama where Uhei, who had resumed traveling while still suffering from the aftereffects of his illness, lost his strength and became sick again. They had to stop for five more days before taking a boat to Kyushu. The trip to Shikoku had been in vain.

The boat landed at the toll barrier of Saga in the province of Bungo. They entered the province of Higo by the way of Tsuisaki, went to pray to the gods of the shrine on Mt. Aso and to the ancestral tomb of Katō Kiyomasa in Kumamoto,[10] searched three days each in Kumamoto and Takahashi, and then crossed by boat to Shimabara in the province of Hizen. After two days there they moved on to Nagasaki. On the third day in Nagasaki they heard that a monk matching the description of Kamezō was seen in Shimabara, so they retraced their steps and spent five more days searching through Shimabara. They then went back for three days of search in Kumamoto, two days in Udo, a day in Yatsushiro, and two days in Nankujuku, before taking another boat to the harbor below Unzendake in the providence of Hizen. A man traveling from Nagasaki told of a monk whose description fitted that of their enemy. Among the Ikkō temples in Chikugomachi in Nagasaki, there is the Kanzenji; there a young monk of about twenty had arrived and was teaching the art of the lance, their informant said. So they sailed back to Nagasaki.

They reached Nagasaki on the morning of the eighth day of the eleventh month, took their lodgings at a place called Kamiya near the pier, and inquired of a certain Fukada, the City Supervisor, concerning the man they were seeking. What they heard here tended to confirm their suspicions about the visiting monk at the Kanzenji. This was that the monk was born in Kishū, and to avoid being seen for some reason, had kept himself entirely within the temple. The kind Fukada assigned them the services of two policemen to make sure that the hunted monk would not slip from their grasp. A certain Ogawa who taught swordsmanship at the temple, upon hearing the supervisor's account, volunteered to go as a witness, and if necessary, to help in the vendetta.

Kurōemon and Uhei then submitted a request to the Kanzenji to become students of the monk, identifying themselves as samurai of the house of Ōmura who wished to learn the art of lancing. The monk agreed and directed them to come to meet him the next morning. Kurōemon and Uhei, bursting with expectations, went with Bunkichi to the temple, followed by Ogawa and the two policemen. Bunkichi was to give them a signal when he identified their enemy, but the monk turned out to bear no resemblance to Kamezō at all. When they finally found a pretext for getting themselves out of this awkward situation, they all felt frustrated, but Uhei was particularly discouraged.

After thanking Fukada, Ogawa, and the policemen, the party took leave of Nagasaki, spent one day in Ōmura, and repaired to Saga. At this time, Kurōemon was suffering from sore feet, and had to walk with a crutch. They searched five days in Kurume in the province of Okugo. In the province of Chikuzen, they first made a pilgrimage to the Tenmangu shrine in Dazaifu to pray to the god Sugawara Michizane, spent two days in Hakata and Fukuoka, and left Kyushu by ship from Kokura in the province of Buzen.

Their boat reached Shimonoseki in the province of Nagato on the sixth day of the twelfth month. Snow was falling. Kurōemon's foot sores had gradually worsened. Finally, at the urging of Uhei and Bunkichi, it was decided that he should return for a time to Himeji. Reluctantly Kurōemon booked ship's passage from Shimonoseki, and arrived at Muranotsu in the province of Harima on the morning of the twelfth day of the twelfth month. He lodged during those days at the Inadaya house in the town of Hira under the walls of Himeji castle. Until the vendetta was accomplished, he would not return to the house of his own son.

After seeing Kurōemon off, Uhei and Bunkichi themselves left Shimonoseki on the tenth of the twelfth month. They spent two days in Miyaichi in the province of Suhō, and moved on via Murozumi to Kintaibashi in Iwakuni. They searched Kintaibashi for three days before sailing over to Miyajima in the province of Aki. After eight days in Hiroshima, they entered the province of Bingo, where they continued the manhunt for seventeen days in Onomichi and Tomo, and for two days in Fukuyama. From there they passed through Okayama in the province of Bizen and returned to Himeji and Kurōemon.

Uhei and Bunkichi were reunited with Kurōemon on the twentieth day of the first month of Tempō six [1835]. Precisely at this time, a certain Taniguchi, a Shinto priest from Mt. Kōgen, informed them of a suspicious-looking beggar. Kurōemon sent Bunkichi to see if he recognized him. The beggar was said to be from Iwami. He had aroused suspicion because he was in possession of two swords. But he too turned out to be the wrong man.

Since Kurōemon's feet were still hurting him, Uhei and Bunkichi left Himeji on the second day of the second month, and reached Osaka three days later. Their lodging was the Tsunokuniya of Owaza-okuhi-machi. However, after seeing them off, Kurōemon's feet improved, and on the fourteenth he left Himeji, sailed from Akashi, and caught up with them in Osaka.

While the three were using the Tsunokuniya as a base from which to continue their search, their money ran out. With the help of the manager of their lodging, Kurōemon became a masseur, Bunkichi a "priest of Awashima." Kurōemon thought that he could have the aptitude to be a masseur as he was skilled in judo. A "priest of Awashima" did not mean serving the god in the shrine. Such a person was a beggar who wandered about tinkling a little bell, with a miniature of the shrine and other dangling objects, such as a monkey doll dressed in red silk, hanging from his neck.

At this time Kurōemon and Uhei felt that they could involve Bunkichi no further in their fruitless search. "Up to this point," they said, "we have only been able to share our bedding and food with you, without paying you for your kind services. You have been a retainer in name only and have persevered and served us well. We have already traversed almost the whole of Japan, but our enemy eludes us. At the rate we are going we do not know if we shall ever complete our mission. We may end up dying like dogs along the road without destroying our enemy. Words cannot suffice to praise your devotion, but we cannot impose upon you any longer. We find ourselves unable to ask you to accompany us any further. Although we have never seen our enemy's face and will be at a loss without you, we shall have to manage somehow. We can only trust our fate to heaven and wait for our day to come. You are a man of peerless loyalty, and will be able to realize your potential hereafter if you enter into the service of some daimyo. Please take your leave of us now."

Bunkichi listened with head bowed as tears streamed down his cheeks.

Then he raised his head and faced Kurōemon with wide eyes that were
strangely shining. "That would be impossible for me," Bunkichi said in one
breath. Then, with deep emotion that almost overwhelmed his power of
speech, he managed the following answer. "I do not consider this just another kind of employment. When one joins in a vendetta, his life is no
longer his own. Someday you two may accomplish your mission, but if by
some small chance your enemy is protected by a large number of his kind
and they try to kill you in return, I must either die fighting with you, or I
shall escape to organize a second vendetta in your name. As long as I can
stand, even if you dismiss me, I shall follow in your shadow."

Even Kurōemon was at a loss for words now. Uhei was greatly encouraged.
After this, the three men left the Tsunokuniya to take up cheaper lodgings.
As they had no idea where to turn next, they wandered about the city every
day praying for the help of the gods and buddhas, since this was at least better than doing nothing.

Meanwhile an epidemic had broken out in Osaka, and the cheap inn
where they were staying was filled with coughing invalids. In the beginning
of the third month, Uhei and Bunkichi became infected and took to their
beds with fever. With the little money Kurōemon received, the three were
reduced to sharing a small bowl of gruel once a day. Just as Uhei and
Bunkichi began to recover in the beginning of the fourth month, Kurōemon
came down with the fever. Though strong of body he was hit harder than
the other two because of his age. They summoned a good doctor who said
that he was suffering from the chills. He then was running a high fever and
kept shouting deliriously, "Stop! I've got you!"

While Bunkichi attempted to placate their angry innkeeper and attend
the patient, Kurōemon, because of his strong body, made a recovery. In a
comparatively short time, considering the seriousness of his fever, he was
well again.

After Kurōemon's recovery, Bunkichi, once more a member of the group,
had another cause for anxiety. Uhei, whose moods used to change so easily,
began to show signs of severe nervous strain after his illness.

Uhei was quiet by nature. Because he somehow did not give the impression of experience or keenness of mind, Kurōemon had dubbed him *waka-
dono*, "our young lord." However, this young lord now began to react
strongly to everything, like some slender blade of grass in the breeze; at such
times his usually pale face would flush crimson, and he would talk forcibly
like a different person altogether. When that mood passed, his emotions
would swing in the opposite direction, sinking him into a state of gloom—
his head lowered, his arms folded, his lips shut.

Kurōemon and Bunkichi had adjusted to this change in character, but now Uhei went through a more radical metamorphosis. He became jumpy and irritable the whole day through. He fretted and paced about constantly. Once in a while he used to talk on and on when in the mood, but that never happened anymore. He was now rather inclined to stony silence. But because of his newly acquired irritability, he became angry at the slightest thing. Even without provocation, he would deliberately jump at some slip of the tongue to vent his inner rage. Once his hostility built up, he would complain and sulk, without bringing his true feelings out into the open.

When this condition continued for two or three days, Bunkichi said to Kurōemon: "The young master seems to be so different, doesn't he?" Bunkichi always called Uhei "the young master."

Kurōemon, seemingly unconcerned, brushed it aside with a laugh: "Our young lord? One good meal will bring back his good humor."

Kurōemon's diagnosis was not implausible. Being together everyday, the three men had not noticed to what extent their meagre diet, illness, and wandering about had etched exhaustion into their faces, making them almost unrecognizable as the persons who had set out from Edo some time back.

The morning after this conversation, when the other lodgers at the inn had gone off to their respective jobs, Uhei came up and knelt before Kurōemon. He seemed to want to say something, but remained silent.

"What's on your mind?" his uncle inquired.

"I have been thinking a little."

"Well, no need to keep it a secret."

"Uncle, do you think we will ever find our enemy?"

"That is something neither you nor I can predict for certain."

"Maybe so. The spider spins its web and waits for some insect to fall into it. Since any insect will do, it just waits patiently. The web is useless if the spider is trying to trap a particular insect. I can't stand it anymore—just waiting for one chance in a million like this."

"But we're not just waiting, are we? We're hunting for him everywhere."

"We certainly have been searching everywhere . . . ," Uhei began, only to sink back into silence.

"Yes, we have indeed. But what's bothering you? Whatever it is, never mind; just say it."

Uhei continued to gaze silently into his uncle's eyes; after a long pause he answered: "Uncle, we have searched and searched. But we could go on forever without finding him. He might not walk into the spider's web, he might not show up no matter how much we search. I feel strange when I think of this prospect. It's driving me insane." Uhei moved even closer. "Uncle, how can you keep so composed?"

Kurōemon concentrated his whole being as he listened to this confession. "So, doubts are beginning to haunt your mind? Listen carefully. It might be as you say if fate is against us, or the gods and buddhas desert us. But we shall search as long as our legs will hold us up. When we get sick we shall convalesce and wait. If the gods and buddhas are on our side, we shall someday find him. We may take him by hunting him down; or he might come to us while we are sick."

A faintly scornful smile flashed on Uhei's face as he said: "Uncle. Do you believe that the gods and buddhas will really help us?"

Although Kurōemon was a samurai of steady mind, he experienced an uneasy feeling when he heard this. "That's something nobody knows," he answered. "Only the gods and buddhas."

Uhei's reaction was strangely oblique, and quite different from his usual attitude of irritation. "Maybe so. The gods and buddhas are inscrutable. To tell the truth, I think I won't be continuing. I'm going to follow my own light."

Kurōemon stared back with eyebrows raised; the blood rose in his sallow face, his fists clenched.

"So! Then you are abandoning the revenge of your father?"

Uhei smiled faintly. He seemed to register some satisfaction at having aroused his always placid uncle to anger. "No, I am not abandoning it. Kamezō is my hated enemy. If I run into him, I shall destroy him. But, since both searching and waiting are stupid, I shall forget about it until I meet up with him. Since I cannot continue a formal vendetta, I will not need your participation. If I am fated to know the enemy, he will eventually become known to me. I will not need someone to identify him. From now on please take Bunkichi as your own vassal. I intend to take my leave in the near future."

Kurōemon's anger dissolved as soon as it arose; he returned to his usual mild manner while listening to his nephew. But this uncle who was skilled in making light of any matter, now sank into a somber mood.

As Uhei arose from his place and was descending the veranda of the lodging, his uncle called out: "Wait! Wait!" But Uhei was already gone. Kurōemon did not realize that Uhei had just walked away forever.

When Bunkichi returned that evening Kurōemon asked him to find Uhei in the neighborhood. He went to the usual places where Uhei used to play *shogi* with the young men. At first Uhei had visited these places to see if he could get some information about the enemy; afterward he just went there to talk away the hours. Bunkichi made the rounds of these hangouts. But there was no Uhei. That night Kurōemon kept a late vigil for Uhei's return, but he never came back. In the course of searching for Uhei, Bunkichi heard of a fortune-teller at the Tamatsukuri Hōkū Inari shrine. The young men of the neighborhood told stories of her curing someone's sick parent and of her being able to tell the whereabouts of someone's lost child. Bunkichi related this information to Kurōemon, and the next day they took baths, cleaned up, and set out for Tamatsukuri. They planned to inquire about both the whereabouts of the enemy and the direction of Uhei.

As they reached the front of the Inari shrine they saw a large throng going in and out. Inside the gate the throng was milling back and forth within a tunnel formed by a seemingly endless row of torii. Around the shrine were teashops, sweet bean shops, and sweet sake stands. On the two sides of the row of torii stood toy stands and tents where brief plays could be seen. They edged their way under the torii to the shrine proper. A Shinto priest was calling out for donations, and receiving coin offerings in exchange for numbered cards. He called in visitors who wanted to make special requests in the order of these cards.

Bunkichi made an offering of all the coins he had in his purse. However, his number never came up, although he waited his turn until nightfall. He neither ate all day nor even realized that his stomach was empty. As the night fell, the priest appeared and announced: "Those whose numbers have not been called must return tomorrow morning."

The next morning Bunkichi returned to the shrine before dawn. Although there were other numbers before Bunkichi's, they had not come as yet and he was called earlier than expected. As Bunkichi was waiting for the reply while praying with his forehead bent to the sand, the priest—again, more quickly than expected—reappeared with this message: "Concerning the first person you seek, he has been living since spring of this year in the flourishing city of the eastern provinces; concerning the second, there is no answer."

Bunkichi raced back from Tamatsukuri to relate the message from the shrine to Kurōemon.

Kurōemon heard Bunkichi out and said: "So? The flourishing city of the eastern province must be Edo; but no matter how lazy Kamezō is I don't think he would be so foolish as to return to Edo. He may indeed have got wind of our being on his track, but since our other relatives also have an eye out for him, it is somehow implausible that he would return to Edo. You may have been deceived by the priest of the shrine. And when he said that the whereabouts of the second person was unknown, he may have been looking for another donation.''

Bunkichi, who took the message of the shrine very seriously, interrupted Kurōemon, requesting that he must not entertain such suspicions but should believe the message. Kurōemon replied: "I do not disbelieve Inari-sama. But somehow I feel Kamezō wouldn't return to Edo."

As they were talking the innkeeper arrived. He had just been called to his master's residence to pick up a letter from Edo addressed to Yamamoto. Kurōemon took the letter. It was addressed: "To Yamamoto Uhei-dono, Yamamoto Kurōemon-dono, from Sakurai Sumazaemon." The innkeeper and Bunkichi, the latter while trying to observe etiquette as Kurōemon's vassal, could not help looking over Kurōemon's shoulder as he spread before him the letter paper from Sumazaemon. Kurōemon anxiously searched the letter for a report of some emergency.

After the party had set out on their journey of revenge, the widow of San-zaemon convalesced in the home of her husband's brother, Sakurai Suma-zaemon. The immediate shock of Sanzaemon's misfortune had worn off and in the quiet atmosphere of her new residence her headaches had lessened to a considerable extent. Sumazaemon treated her very kindly, but since she was reduced to complete dependence on his generosity, she made inquiries about some employment that would not tax her strength, and finally entered into the service of the wife of the Master of Ceremonies, Ōsawa Ukyō Tayū Motoaki, on the Manaitabashi side of Ogawamachi.

Uhei's older sister Riyo, after going to live with her aunt's son-in-law Harada, used to gossip with the old ladies selling aniseed when she went to visit her father's grave, in the hopes of obtaining some piece of information about the enemy's whereabouts. In this way she passed her year of mourning. Thinking that if she served for two months each in several places, she would naturally come across some lead, she first took employment in a certain residence in Honjō. The residence being that of a distant relative, she contributed her services in a variety of capacities while enjoying a status somewhere between servant and guest of the family. Then because her great aunt was serving the wife of the Hori family in Akasaka, she went there to assist her. Later she served a certain family in Azabu. From there she went to assist a distant relative among the retainers of Honda Tatewaki, who was a retired direct retainer to the shogun living at Yumichō in Hongo. Changing her place of employment in such fashion, she finally entered into the service

of the wife of the retired Sakai Kamenoshin, another direct liege vassal of
the Tokugawa family, of Ochanomizu in the spring of 1835. This wife was
the daughter of Sakai Iwa no kami Tadamichi of Asakusa.

Both the widow and Riyo kept their ears open for some word about the
enemy. Riyo went especially out of her way from morning until night to un-
cover some clue, but their efforts proved entirely fruitless. There was no report from Kurōemon and Uhei, and as there was no news at their end either,
their feeling of helplessness as they remained in Edo was extreme.

The days and months passed by until the beginning of the fifth month of
1835. One day Sakurai Sumazaemon had gone to pray to the Kannon in
Asakusa and was taking tea in a teashop. The rain, which had stopped for
awhile, began to come down in buckets. Two men who looked like gamblers
sought cover under the eaves of the teahouse to avoid getting soaked. While
they were waiting for the cloudburst to pass, they started a conversation.

"I meant to tell you, but I forgot. Last night to get out of the rain, like tonight, I was squatting outside of the locked door of the wholesale sake shop
in Kanda when some fellow came running for cover. I couldn't believe my
eyes. He seemed to be that Kame who worked in the Sakai family. Wondering whether he'd dare to come back, I called out, 'Kame!' He turned immediately toward me, but then answered, 'You're thinking of someone
else, my name is Tora,' and went running off, even though it was still rain-
ing hard."

"So the rat has come back to Edo, has he?" the second man said.

Overhearing this, Sumazaemon interrogated the two men about the
Kame they were talking about. They became nervous at being interrogated
by a samurai, but the man went on to identify Kame as the servant Kamezō
who had committed a crime in the Sakai house and then fled at the end of
last year. Finally, however, the informant began to speak evasively, saying
"Since I had only a glimpse, it may have actually been someone named
Tora." Reckoning then that it would be useless to press him further now
that he had switched his story, and fearing to bring the suspicions into the
open thereby alerting Kamezō to flee from Edo again, Sumazaemon non-
chalantly dismissed the two without showing his hand.

The letter which Kurōemon received in Osaka brought this information
from Sakurai that Kamezō had been seen in Edo.

Bunkichi went immediately to Tamatsukuri to thank the god of the
shrine. Kurōemon waited for Bunkichi's return, then they separated to
make inquiries at all the gates leading out of Osaka. They searched for some

clue concerning Uhei at the palanquin resting stations on the highways and with the shipping agencies at the harbor. But they came up with nothing. Kurōemon resolved to abandon the search for Uhei and made preparations to leave for Edo. Although their travel money was completely exhausted, he had not touched their emergency food, or clothing, or his swords. Kurōemon dressed himself in unlined, light-blue cotton tied with a brown Kokura obi, donned a coat of blue linen with white dots, and wore two swords. Concealed under his clothes were a purse of auburn camlet, a bag for tissue of grey cotton, and a pair of handcuffs. Bunkichi also carried handcuffs under an unlined garment of light blue that was tied with a sky-blue Kokura obi.

After settling up with their innkeeper and stopping to say farewell to the Tsunokuniya, Kurōemon and Bunkichi sailed at night from Fushimi to Tsu on the twenty-eighth of the sixth month. Except for being detained for half a day at Sakanoshita by a howling wind on the thirtieth, they reached Shinagawa without further incident on the eleventh day of the seventh month.

The two men left their inn in Shinagawa before dawn of the next day and proceeded to the Henryūji temple in Asakusa, where they prayed at the grave of Sanzaemon. They then met with the head priest of the temple, and rested their travel-weary bodies the whole night.

The next day was the Bon festival, the day on which their relatives would be coming to visit the grave. Kurōemon forbade the priest to reveal that they had returned, and then hid with Bunkichi in the priest's living quarters. When the priest inquired why, Kurōemon only answered, ''It is essential that our plan be secret,'' and then turned the conversation to another topic. Those who came to the grave were the wives of Harada and Sakai; neither Sanzaemon's widow nor Riyo, who were busy serving in samurai residences at this time, was free to come.

Late that day Kurōemon announced to Bunkichi: ''All right then, let's begin. We will search for him till our legs fall off.''

Dressed in their same traveling garments, the two left the Henryūji and proceeded in the direction of the Kannon of Asakusa. As they approached the Kaminari gate, Kurōemon said to Bunkichi: ''He seems not to have become a monk, but whatever his disguise, don't let him escape your eye. I don't imagine he has assumed the identity of any superior status.''

After checking throughout the temple compound, they prayed before the Kannon, offering thanks that Sumazaemon's path had been fated to cross that of the man who had identified Kamezō. Then they went from Kuramae to Ryōgoku. Despite the heat and humidity, since it was a day for fireworks, crowds of people were out to cool off and were milling about the streets. As the lanterns were lit toward evening, Kurōemon and Bunkichi rested awhile in a teahouse; after their sweat had dried a bit, they continued the search. They could see neither the river nor the boats from which the fireworks were being launched. As someone yelled out "Tamaya" or "Kagiya," identifying the type of firework display, the crowd would turn their necks this way and that to watch the constellations flower above them.

Around eleven P.M., Bunkichi pulled at Kurōemon's sleeve from behind. Kurōemon followed the line of Bunkichi's sight to a tall man one step ahead on his left. He was wearing a worn, light-blue striped Hakata obi over an old, unlined garment of medium-sized pattern.

They followed behind the man in silence. The moon was bright. After turning on to Yokoyamachō, they stalked their prey from Shiochō to Odenmachō. Crossing Honchō they went along the water's edge from Kokuchōgashi to Ryūkanbashi, and Kamakuragashi. As the crowds were gradually thinning out, Kurōemon covered his head with a hand towel and began to stagger in a drunken fashion. Bunkichi walked beside him as if propping him up.

It was just about midnight when they came to Motogojiin-Nibanhara outside Kandabashi. There were now no passersby in sight. Kurōemon gave the signal. As if they were one body the two flew upon their target and, without a word, pinned his arms behind him.

"Hey! What's this?" the man cried as he struggled to release himself.

Still without a single word, while holding his arms in a vicelike grip, they dragged his struggling body into the darkness under a stand of trees by the roadside.

Kurōemon now spoke in a voice so deep-throated that it was closer to a growl. "I am Kurōemon, brother of Yamamoto Sanzaemon whom you killed last year. Identify yourself and prepare to die!"

"You are mistaken, sir. I am Torazō from Senshū. I have no idea of what you've talked about."

Bunkichi now glowered over him. "Hey! Kame! Don't pretend. I recognize you right up to the mole under your eye."

When he recognized Bunkichi, the man wilted like a blade of grass in the frost. He lowered his head, saying "So, it's you, Bunkichi."

This was all Kurōemon had to hear; he brought out the handcuffs to secure Kamezō. Then he said to Bunkichi: "This will hold him for now. Run to Sakai Kamenoshin's residence in Ochanomizu. Give them the message that I've just come from the home of Riyo who is serving the wife of this

honorable house. Tell them that her mother is deathly sick and may not last
the night. Beg of their kind consideration to give her leave to visit her
mother's death bed. Go quickly!"

"I understand," Bunkichi cried, as he raced off in the direction of
Nishikichō.

In the residence of Sakai Kamenoshin that evening, Riyo was dismissed
from attendance later than usual. She had just returned to her room and was
about to change into her night dress when an old servant lady came to call.

Not bothering to change back again, Riyo immediately rose, put on slip-
pers, and went to the old lady's room along the veranda. The old lady delivered this message: "A servant has come from your home, saying that your
mother is very sick. It is the Bon festival and your presence here is needed,
but you had better return home in view of the emergency. After you've seen
your mother, you must return here directly. Tomorrow morning you may
ask for leave again."

Riyo thanked the old lady, and slipped out of her room.

Riyo had decided to go straight home when she remembered the waiting
messenger and went to the back entrance to see who it was. She was in the
simple cotton robe of medium pattern tied with a black silk obi that she
wore while serving her lord. At the back entrance, Riyo recognized Bunkichi
dressed in his traveling clothes. Her eyes flashed in understanding as Bunkichi spoke the pretext that her mother was sick.

Three attendants who had accompanied Riyo to the back gathered on the
veranda out of curiosity to see the servant whom Riyo went to meet.

"Wait a moment. There is something I forgot," Riyo said as if to herself,
and hurried back to her room.

Locking the door from the inside, Riyo opened the lid of her wicker trunk.
She first took out a hemp garment for summer wear. Next she reached down
to her elbow and drew up a short sword. It was the sword her father Sanzaemon had been wearing on that fateful night. She quickly wrapped both
items in a *furoshiki* and went out.

Bunkichi was still relating the details of the capture along the way when
they reached Gojiingahara.

Riyo greeted Kurōemon; since there was no time to change into the summer garment, she took only the short sword from her bundle.

Kurōemon addressed the enemy. "The girl who has come is the daughter
of Sanzaemon. Confess to her that you are her father's murderer, and state
your name and origin."

The enemy raised his gaze toward Riyo, "This is my end. I will tell you the truth. I was the one who wounded Yamamoto, but I did not murder him. Desperate for money because of a gambling debt, I did that stupid, blundering thing. I am Torazō, son of Kichibē, of the village of Uenohara in the district of Ikuta of Senshū. When I went to work as a messenger boy for the Sakai residence, I just happened to assume the name of Kamezō of Kishū from one of my gambling friends. Aside from this, there is nothing to say. Do with me whatever you want.''

"Just what we wanted to hear," Kurōemon answered. He then signaled to Bunkichi and Riyo, and released Torazō's bonds. All three inched closer to him.

His bonds loosened, Torazō stood there forlornly for a second or two; then suddenly stiffening like an animal poised to pounce on some prey, he dove in the direction of Riyo and tried to shove his way past her.

In the same instant Riyo jumped back and slashed at Torazō with the short sword she had been holding. A wound opened from the right shoulder down to his chest. Torazō tottered. Riyo struck a second and a third time. Torazō fell.

"Superb! Let me finish him off!" Kurōemon shouted as he fell upon him and cut his throat.

Kurōemon wiped the blood from his sword on Torazō's sleeve. He then wiped Riyo's blade as well. Both of them were weeping.

Riyo spoke the only words: "Uhei was not here . . .''

The three went to the guardhouse in Kashi under the authority of Honda Iyo no kami Tadataka.[11] Their story was heard by the guardsman Tamaki Katsuzaburō, a retainer of Udono Kichinojō, who was an Attendant in the Western Enceinte of Edo castle and the ranking officer for that month. A report was forwarded from Honda to a shogunal Censor. The ranking officer for that year at the guardhouse, Endō Tajima no kami Tanenori,[12] forwarded a report to the chief retainer of the Edo mansion of Sakai Tadanori.[13] A new lord had been installed in the Sakai domain in the fourth month of that year.

Messengers bearing an affidavit signed by Kurōemon, Riyo, and Bunkichi were despatched from the Sakai mansion to report the incident to Tadanori.

On the morning of the following day, the fourteenth, Gojiingahara was filled with curiosity seekers. Relatives gradually came running to the side of the three who had succeeded in bringing revenge upon their father's murderer. *Sushi* and cakes were sent to them from the house of the Udono family.

Around seven P.M., at the order of the Nishimaru[14] Censor and chief po-

lice official Mizuno Uneme, the Nishimaru Assistant Censors Nagai Kameji-
rō and Kubota Eijirō, the Nishimaru Censors of Commoners Hiraoka Tada-
hachirō and Inoue Matahachi, the *han* representatives Shimoya Rinzaemon
and Itami Chōjirō, and four *han* messengers were despatched to conduct a
formal investigation. They were joined by overseers from the Honda, Endo,
Hiraoka, and Udono residences. They first examined the three—their personal condition, garments, possessions, injuries. None of them bore any
wound. They next took the affidavit addressed to Kubota. They then conducted an examination of the corpse. Torazō's wounds, recorded in the report under his assumed name of Kamezō, were as follows: "One sword gash
about an inch deep on the right side of the back, too swollen to ascertain the
exact depth; a gash at the neck, three inches long, two inches deep; another
neck wound running down one-and-a-half inches, and six-tenths of an inch
deep; a gash on the side of the left ear, one inch long, six-tenths of an inch
deep; a gash running one foot long and four inches deep from the right
shoulder to the chest; another wound under the shoulder, two inches long,
one inch deep; the throat cut three inches across; total of seven wounds."
The victim was wearing an unlined cotton garment and Hakata obi; he had a
light blue handkerchief with him. The corpse was assigned to the custody of
Tamaki Katsuzaburō. Next subpoenaed were Fujiya Jisaburō of Kanda
Kyūsaemon-chō Daichi, who had referred Kamezō for employment at the
Sakai mansion, the *goningumi*[15] of the same locality, and Wakasaya Kanekichi, Kamezō's sponsor at the time. Finally the guardsman who had first
heard Kurōemon's claim of the accomplished vendetta was subpoenaed.

   The investigating team retired at eight P.M. The investigation completed,
Udono Kichinojō reported back to the Censor Matsumoto Sukenojō of the
Western Enceinte of Edo castle. Shōno Jifuzaemon, proxy of the Sakai lord
in Edo, reported back to the Sakai mansion's Censor; and the Sakai mansion
filed a report with the Shogunate Senior Councillor, Ōkubo Kaga no kami
Tadazane.

   At the order of Mizuno Uneme, Kurōemon, Riyo, and Bunkichi were
handed over to Shōno about seven the next morning. From about six the
previous evening, two palanquins despatched from the Sakai mansion for
the sake of transporting Kurōemon and Riyo were waiting at the guardhouse. Kurōemon and Bunkichi were assigned to the custody of a certain
Honda, while Riyo was put under the custody of Kambē.

   Around seven P.M. of the same day, the Edo City Magistrate Tsutsui Iga
no kami Masanori[16] summoned the three of them. The Sakai mansion
assigned a company of foot soldiers led by a Censor, Assistant Censor, and a

lower samurai official, to escort Kurōemon and Riyo, who rode in palanquins, and Bunkichi, who walked behind them. They returned around eight P.M. after being personally interrogated by Tsutsui Masanori. On the sixteenth day, they were again summoned to Tsutsui's residence. About seven P.M. they were interrogated by Tsutsui's police official Nisugi Hachizaemon; they then signed an affidavit.

On this same day, Riyo was granted her request to be released from service in the residence of Sakai Kamenoshin, and Sanzaemon's widow was similarly discharged from the Ozawa residence. Riyo received formal congratulations for accomplishing the vendetta from her former employers, at the Hosokawa residence.

On the nineteenth, a third summons came from Tsutsui. The three listened to the draft of a document, and were taken back about seven P.M.

On the twenty-third, a fourth summons came from Tsutsui. A legal seal and thumb seal were impressed on a final draft of the document.

On the twenty-eighth, they were called to Tsutsui's residence for the fifth time. At the request of the Shogunate Senior Councillor Mizuno Etchizen no kami Tadakuni,[17] Kurōemon and Riyo were declared "extremely commendable and innocent without any crime," while Bunkichi received a formal notification of "innocent without any question." They then received the praise of Tsutsui and returned to their quarters about seven P.M.

Following the conclusion of the Edo mayor's investigation, Kurōemon, Riyo, and Bunkichi received an announcement from the Censor General's office of the Sakai house that "You are free to act as you please." Kurōemon and Riyo gave back to the same office the license granted them to perform the vendetta issued in the second month of Tempō five [1834].

On the first day of the seventh lunar month, Riyo was employed by the Sakai house. At nine o'clock in the forenoon, the relatives Yamamoto Heisaku and Sakurai Sumazaemon, dressed in ceremonial linen, accompanied them to an audience in the office of the highest *han* retainers. The Censor General, who sat next to the Han Elder Kawai Kotarō, made the announcement to Riyo: "Since you are a woman, you have especially merited our lord's praise, and therefore will succeed to the head of Sanzaemon's household; by our lord's order, you are granted a stipend of fourteen persons; he wishes that later you will find a suitable husband, and in the near future grants you an audience in his Edo mansion."

On the eleventh day, Riyo received an audience with Lord Sakai; she was presented with "one roll of crested black silk crepe, one roll of undercloth of red silk with cotton underlining, and one roll of double lined white silk."

On the same day from the Lady of Hamachō,[18] she received one roll of striped crepe silk, and from Senjuin, wife of the late Sakai Tadataka, a dyed Takasago striped crepe silk wrapper, two fans, and a purse.

Concerning Kurōemon, a document from Sakai Tadanori to the Han Elder Honda Ikiri read: "Kurōemon is free of all blame and free to act as he did before; he should be praised for his discretion, and out of special consideration for his deed, I grant him a linen outer coat with the seal of the Sakai house." Honda conferred one hundred *koku* of rice upon Kurōemon and made him an upper rank Personal Attendant. Riyo also received from Honda "one thousand *biku* [four hundred *ryō*] to buy kimono material," and from Honda's mother she received a present of one roll of striped crepe silk, and a box of dried fish.

Bunkichi was summoned to the office of the Inspector of the Sakai house, and formally made the servant and vassal of Yamamoto Kurōemon, and "concerning his extraordinary service, received the rank of Lesser Official, four *ryō* of gold, and stipend of two persons." Thereafter his name became Fukanaka, and he served as a forest warden at the Sakai family's mansion at Kisugamo.

Yashiro Tarō Hirokata,[19] who was seventy at the time of this vendetta, wrote this poem in praise of Kurōemon and Riyo:

Mata araji
Tama matsuruteu
Ori ni aite
Fuke no atauchi
Shitagui wa

How rare
Performed at the time
Of the feast of the dead
A vendetta
For father and elder brother!

Fortunately, twelve years had gone by since the death of Ōta Shichizaburō, and so there was no one who wrote a parody to poke fun at Yashiro's verse.[20]

October 1913

SAKAI JIKEN

"THE INCIDENT AT SAKAI" refers to an important event at the very beginning of the Meiji period. The Japanese government, in order to avoid involvement in a war with any foreign power during the difficult period of national consolidation after the fall of the shogunate, acceded to somewhat exorbitant French demands for reparations over the death of a group of French soldiers during a scuffle at the port of Sakai, near Osaka. Ōgai used this incident for the creation, at least by implication, of a moral and historical commentary of some profundity.

The narrative spares the reader any reflections on the politics of the situation but focuses rather on the Japanese soldiers who will die. Japan's feudal morality was to undergo a shift with the coming of the West, and indeed the twenty condemned to commit ritual suicide in the story are split between those who succeed in their fidelity to the old morality and those who, involved at least indirectly (via the French ambassador) in Western attitudes toward responsibility and death, remain alive. These men feel stripped of their honor; as they go off into exile in a country village, they seem to bear in their fragile and weary persons the whole weight of a system of dignity and loyalty that could no longer be sustained.

Ōgai presents the incident in considerable detail; but in doing so, he is not merely serving as an apologist for the past. Indeed, the strongest impression the reader carries away from the story is a sense of the relentlessness of history. Ōgai's sense of cumulative detail does, in fact, give psychological credibility to the whole train of events he records.

Incidentally, the French ambassador's queasiness at watching ritual suicide (a feeling shared, to be sure, by all modern readers, Japanese or foreign) is chronicled in contemporary European sources as well. A number of foreign diplomats witnessed similar spectacles in the early years of the Meiji period. The most celebrated firsthand account of such a ceremony by a European is that included as an appendix to Mitford's *Tales of Old Japan*.

 IN THE FIRST MONTH of the year of the Dragon, the first year of Meiji [1868], the army of Tokugawa Yoshinobu was defeated at Fushimi and Tosa, and Osaka castle could not be defended.[1] As the shogunate officials in Osaka, Hyōgo, and Sakai had abandoned their offices and gone into hiding in the wake of Yoshinobu's retreat by ship to Edo, these three cities had sunk temporarily into anarchy.[2] Therefore an Imperial order directed the three to be put under the supervision of the domains of Satsuma, Nagato, and Tosa, respectively. The Sixth Infantry Division of Tosa first entered Sakai in the second month, followed thereafter by the Eighth Division. They set up their garrisons at the police headquarters and the Dōshin mansion in Itoyamachi. Meanwhile, the Tosa *han* was also assigned the function of administering the city government, and therefore the Censor General Sugi Kiheita and the Censor Ikoma Seiji[3] came to Sakai and set up a military headquarters on the former assembly grounds at Odori-Kushiyamachi. Their agents succeeded in rounding up seventy-three former Tokugawa functionaries who had gone into hiding in Kawachi and Yamato, and ordered them back to their offices. Order was soon restored to the city, and even the doors of the theatre reopened after a temporary interruption.

On the fifteenth of the second month, the town elders reported to the military headquarters that some French soldiers were marching on Sakai from Osaka. Among the sixteen foreign ships previously anchored at Yokohama that now had moved offshore of Tempōzan in Settsu were English, American, and French vessels. Sugi Kiheita called the two Tosa infantry leaders and ordered them to despatch their troops to Yamato bridge. If the French soldiers had had official permission to pass through, he would have been informed by means of an official procedure instituted by Date Iyo no kami Munenari, the former lord of Uwajima;[4] but he had not been so informed. Thus, he thought, even if the order were late in coming, the French must have permission to travel to the interior. Without it, they could not pass. Sugi and Ikoma followed after the two divisions of Tosa troops to take command of Yamato bridge.

The French soldiers came up to the bridge. When asked through an interpreter who accompanied them about the permission, they revealed that they had not obtained it. As the French soldiers were greatly outnumbered, their way was blocked by the Tosa soldiers and they returned to Osaka.

TRANSLATED BY DAVID DILWORTH

The evening of the same day, Sakai townsmen came running to the garrison of the soldiers who had returned from Yamato bridge and reported that French sailors were coming ashore from the harbor. The French warships had anchored only a league from the harbor, and they were sending twenty dories of sailors ashore. As the leaders of the two Tosa divisions were making preparations to deploy their men, they received the official command from Sugi. They immediately despatched their men. It seemed that the sailors were not attempting to do any particular act of violence. However, the French sailors irreverently entered the Shinto shrines and Buddhist temples. They began to go into private homes. They were grabbing girls and flirting with them. As Sakai was not one of the open ports,[5] the townsmen were unaccustomed to foreigners, and many of them were in a panic; they barricaded their doors and refused to come out. The two division leaders thought they could admonish the French to return to their ships, but there was no interpreter. They resorted to waving them back with various gestures, but the sailors did not heed them. Therefore the leaders ordered the French sailors to be taken off to the garrison. As the Tosa troops started to seize the closest sailors and tie them up with ropes, the French sailors took off in a run for the harbor. One of them snatched a Tosa division flag which had been leaning against the door of a nearby house.

The two division leaders led their men in the chase after them, but they could not catch up with the long-legged French, who were more accustomed to running. The first sailors were just about to get into their dories.

In those days four or five firemen were attached to each Tosa division; they accompanied it even when it made its rounds through the city. Carrying the division's flag was one function of these firemen, and among them the head fireman, named Umekichi, was the flag-bearer. When responding to fires in Edo, he was so fast on his feet that he could almost keep up with a horse on the run. This Umekichi raced out ahead of the other Tosa soldiers in hot pursuit of the sailor who had snatched the company's flag. He lunged forward with the fire axe he was carrying and split the sailor's skull. The sailor let out a cry and toppled forward. Umekichi retrieved the flag.

Upon seeing this the sailors who were waiting in the dories suddenly fired their pistols. Quick as a flash the Tosa leaders shouted out the order, "Fire!" Their soldiers, who were anxiously waiting for the order, lined up their rifles and fired point-blank at the dories into which the sailors were jumping. About six Frenchmen fell. Some of the wounded fell into the water. Those who were not wounded dove into the water. Holding the sides of the dories with their hands, they kicked with their feet to get the boats moving away from the shore. When the Tosa rifles rang out they dove down under the water, spitting out saltwater as they surfaced again. By the time the dories finally were gotten out of range, there were sixteen dead, one of them a petty officer.

Sugi Kiheita came running down to the shore. He ordered the troops to stop firing and return to their garrison. When the two companies got back, their leaders were called to the military command headquarters. Sugi questioned them as to why they had actually fired without waiting for the order from him; they explained that they could not wait in such an emergency situation. It was true the sailors on the dories had fired first and they were simply answering the French pistol attack. But the Tosa soldiers had from the beginning harbored a grievance against the French, for a report had been received that recently while some Tosa clansmen were escorting a gold brocade Imperial flag back to Tosa to be used in an attack upon the Matsuyama domain,[6] their party had been stopped in Kobe by the French, who through an interpreter managed to take away the flag under the pretext of working out a reconciliation between the Imperial court and the shogunate.

Sugi replied to the two leaders that it was at any rate too late to undo the incident. The warships might attack, and so they must "man the defense installations." He despatched Ikoma to report the incident to the Foreign Office, and to the Representative of the Censor to the *han* mansion in Kyoto.

The two division leaders felt it improbable that with their two small companies they could make any defense against the battleships, but they sent out reconnaissance teams along the shore and ordered alternating teams of their men to mount the cannon installations in the harbor. At this time several tens of defeated shogunate soldiers who had been in their custody since Tosa took over Sakai came up and volunteered.

"If the French battleships attack, please use us. In the harbor there are thirty-six cannon which were set up during the Tokugawa regime; they are now under the charge of Okabe Chikuzen no kami Nagashiro, the lord of Kishiwada. Let us mount the cannon; you defend the shore against any barbarian landing."

The two leaders sent these volunteers to mount the cannon. Meanwhile troops from the Kishiwada domain already had been sent to mount the cannon, and their telescopes were sweeping the direction of Hyōgo.

During the night a report came in that French dories were making for the mouth of the harbor. But there were only five or six of them, and they returned without attempting to land. They were undoubtedly searching for the corpses of the sixteen sailors. There were also persons who reported that the dories seemed to have picked up some corpses and returned with them to the battleships.

At dawn on the sixteenth, an order from the Foreign Office dissolved Tosa's command in Sakai and the troops were withdrawn. When transmitting this message, Tosa's military headquarters in Sakai ordered the two division leaders to return to the *han*'s treasury building in Osaka. The two made immediate preparations and left Sakai. Traveling the Sumiyoshi highway they reached their destination at Miike-dōri roku-chōme about two o'clock in the afternoon.

The report of Ikoma Seiji, who had traveled from the Sakai military command to the Foreign Office to make his report, was received without comment. Then the Foreign Office ordered the Censor official among the military command and division leaders to appear. When Sugi Kiheita presented himself, the report of the Sakai incident already submitted by Ishikawa Ishinosuke[7] of the Tosa *han*'s mansion in Osaka was filed, and Sugi was ordered to make a more detailed report. Sugi returned to Sakai, submitted a report cosigned by the two division leaders, and added he would present himself again to the proper authorities if there were any additional questions.

On the seventeenth, as a result of the consultation the day before, the Han Elder Yamanouchi Haito, the Censor General Hayashi Kanekichi, the Censor Tani Tomo, several Censor's Representatives, and a division of soldiers stationed at Kyoto under the command of Nagao Tarobē were despatched from the Tosa *han* residence in Kyoto to Osaka. This party reached Osaka during the night, and immediately Hayashi ordered Ikoma and the two division leaders involved in the Sakai incident transferred to the Tosa *han*'s residence at Nagabori.

On the eighteenth, an order came through Nagao Tarobē to hold the two division leaders in custody, and all of their subordinates were also prohibited from leaving their barracks. The two leaders told Nagao that they were personally responsible for the incident and did not want to implicate their subordinates who had acted under their orders. The two companies delegated the Lieutenants Ikegami Yasakichi[8] and Ōishi Jinkichi[9] to inquire after the health of their two leaders in confinement. Their leaders gave them the gist of their report to Nagao.

Meanwhile three small companies of troops of the Tosa *han* arrived from Kyoto, formed a guard around the *han* residence at Nagabori, and exercised strict control over persons entering and leaving the premises.

Next the Han Elder Fukao Shigemoto Kanae,[10] accompanied by the Censor Kominami Gorozaemon, arrived as a deputy for Yamanouchi Tosa no kami Toyoshige,[11] the former lord of the Tosa domain. The reason for his visit concerned the fact that the French ambassador Leon Roche[12] had come aboard the *Venus*, the French warship, anchored in Osaka, to press negotiations for reparation with the Foreign Office. Roche's demands were immediately accepted by the Japanese government. The first demand was that the lord of Tosa personally apologize aboard the *Venus*. The second demand was that the officers who directed the Tosa domain's troops in Sakai and twenty of the soldiers who participated in the volleys upon the French sailors be executed near the spot where the Sakai incident had taken place. Thirdly, as reparation to the families of the French dead and wounded, the lord of Tosa was to pay an indemnity of one hundred fifty thousand American dollars. To complete these negotiations the lord of Tosa was to have come personally to Osaka, but because of illness, he instead despatched the Han Elder Fukao Shigemoto Kanae as his deputy.

The Censor's Representative attached to Fukao's party interrogated each of the seventy-three soldiers of the Sixth and Eighth divisions, asking whether or not he had fired his rifle during the Sakai incident. This question was tantamount to serving as a test of each soldier's bravery or cowardice. Twenty-nine men answered that they had fired on the French sailors. Those from the Sixth Division were the company leader Shinoura Inokichi,[13] his lieutenant Ikegami Yasakichi, and their soldiers Sugimoto Kogorō, Katsugase Sanroku, Yamamoto Tetsusuke, Morimoto Mokichi, Kitashiro Kensuke, Inada Kanojō, Yanase Tsuneshichi, Hashizume Aihei, Okazaki Eiheie, Kawatani Gintarō, Okazaki Tajirō, Mizuno Manosuke, Kishida Kambē, Kadota Takatarō, Kususe Yasujirō; and from the Eighth Division, the company leader Nishimura Saheiji,[14] his lieutenant Ōishi Jinkichi, and their soldiers Takeuchi Tamigorō, Yokota Tatsugorō, Doi Tokutarō (Hachinosuke), Kanada Tokiji, Takenouchi Yasaburō, Sakaeda Jisaemon, Nakajō Jungorō, Yokota Seijirō, Tamaru Yurokurō. Twenty soldiers of the Sixth Division from Hamada Yutarō and twenty-one of the Eighth from Nagano Minekichi answered that they had not fired at the Frenchmen.

On the nineteenth, this latter group of forty-one were transferred during the night to the *han*'s commercial house at Miike-dōri roku-chōme, and were informed that they would be returned to Tosa as soon as preparations were completed. Those who had answered that they had fired on the sailors were ordered to hand in their rifles and gunpowder; they were taken into custody and placed under the surveillance of a cannonry division previously despatched from Osaka. The men of the Sixth Division were returned to their former barracks at the *han*'s main residence at Nagabori; those of the Eighth were moved to a residence to the west.

On the twentieth, those who had replied in the negative sailed from a mooring in front of the *han*'s Nagabori residence. They later returned to Tosa via Marugame and the Kitayama highway. They were ordered not to take any distant journeys for several days; later they would be able to resume their normal duties to the *han*. Those who had replied in the affirmative were visited by a Censor's Representative and the troops of the cannoneers' company, who took away their swords. Having already heard that a death penalty had been decreed, there were some among them who declared that they should rather die attacking the French gunboats than waiting idly for their execution. This plan was rejected as impractical by Doi Hachinosuke. Others were of the opinion that the whole group should die by killing each other. Just at that point in the debate their custodians came to take away their swords, and so several men even tried to commit suicide then and there, saying that if they did not kill themselves now it would be too late. They were finally restrained by Takeuchi Tamigorō who, as he ordered them to obey, saying that he had a plan, went through the motions of writing with his finger on the straw mat, "There are two short swords in my carrying bag." The whole group finally handed over their swords.

On the twenty-second, Censor General Kominami Gorosaemon arrived and ordered the same group to assemble immediately in a large room to receive the order of His Retired Excellence (the title taken by Yamanouchi Toyoshige after he retired and turned the control of the Tosa domain over to his son Toyonori).[15] Except for the two division leaders and their two lieutenants, all the remaining twenty-five men were seated in the large room. Kominami and several other officials entered and took their places. Then as Nagao Tarobē entered through a golden *fusuma* directly in front of them, the entire body of men bowed to the tatami.

Nagao spoke as follows:

"His Retired Excellence intended to deliver his order personally, but because of his illness I have been charged with executing his wishes as his deputy. Since the Imperial court is being pressed by the French in reference to the recent incident at Sakai, he has ordered twenty of the guilty ones to offer their lives to meet the terms of the reparation. His Retired Excellence is deeply grieved over this aspect of the French demands. He expresses the wish that, nevertheless, twenty men will offer their lives with good will."

With this Nagao rose and entered the next room.

Then Kominami transmitted the order of Yamanouchi Toyonori, the present lord of Tosa:

"We do not know whom to chose and whom to exempt for the group of twenty men required by the terms of the reparation. Therefore you should go to the Inari shrine, pray to the gods, and determine the matter by drawing lots. Those who draw white lots shall be spared. The others should be executed. Proceed forthwith to the shrine."

The twenty-five marched from the *han* mansion down to the Inari shrine. Kominami sat under the bell of the shrine with the lots. On his right stood the Censor. Two of his Representatives stood before the steps, holding a scroll with the names of the group. Twenty or thirty paces in front of the shrine were ranged the cannoneers and foot soldiers, who had been despatched from Kyoto. At Kominami's signal, the Censor's Representative opened the scroll and read the name of each person in turn. With this each man came forward, chose a lot, held it up to view, and handed it to the Censor's Representative, who made the proper notation. Some visitors to the shrine were at first puzzled about what was going on. As they gradually surmised the meaning of the lots, they were all deeply shaken; some of them burst into tears.

Ten men of the Sixth Division and six from the Eighth drew the lots signifying execution: from the former, Sugimoto, Katsugase, Yamamoto, Morimoto, Kitashiro, Inada, Yanase, Hashizume, Okazaki Eiheie, and Kawatani; from the latter, Takeuchi, Yokota Tatsugorō, Doi, Kakiuchi, Kanada, and Takenouchi. The two division leaders and their two lieutenants were added to this list, making twenty. Five of the Sixth Division and four of the Eighth had drawn white lots.

When the whole group was returned to the palace after the lots were drawn, four men from the Eighth Division who had drawn white lots co-signed a petition. They were Sakaeda Jisaemon, Nakajō, Yokota Seijirō, and Tamaru. They wrote that while they had been exempted by drawing white lots, they wanted to be given the same punishment as the others, since they were of one mind with them from the beginning. Their petition was rejected on the grounds that the number twenty had been stipulated.

The sixteen condemned men were then returned to custody in the *han*'s main residence, together with their two division leaders, Shinoura and Nishimura, and their respective lieutenants, Ikegami and Ōishi. Those who had drawn white lots were immediately discharged from their divisions, placed under the custody of Tosa troops, and removed to a separate building. Several days later, they were ordered to return to Tosa by sea from Sakai. After being escorted back to Tosa by a Censor's Representative they were placed under the custody of their own relatives and told that they would shortly receive further orders.

That night the condemned twenty all wrote letters to their loved ones, families, and friends back home; they included locks of their hair in the envelopes, and handed them over to a Censor's Representative.

When they did so, officers of the fifth company guarding the *han* mansion came with sake and fish to bid the men farewell. The division leaders, their lieutenants, and the sixteen soldiers dined separately. The latter all got drunk and fell asleep.

Only Doi Hachinosuke had drunk moderately; when he saw the rest all snoring loudly, he suddenly shouted:

"Hey! The important day is tomorrow. How can you want to die by having your heads cut off?"

One of the others answered angrily, "Be quiet. We're sleeping because tomorrow *is* the important day."

He fell back to snoring before getting his words all out.

Doi shook the shoulder of Sugimoto and woke him up.

"Sugimoto. You should know better, even if the rest do not. How do you intend to die tomorrow—by having your neck chopped in two?"

Sugimoto jumped up.

"Now I see your point. It's an important matter. Wake everyone up."

The two men called the rest to get up. They shook those who were sleeping too soundly. Finally awake, everyone listened as Doi and Sugimoto described their predicament. No one disagreed. Dying was not the issue. They had been resigned to dying since the day they left Tosa as soldiers. But they must not die in disgrace. Therefore they resolved to request permission to commit *seppuku*.

The sixteen now got into their *hakama* and *haori*. They went to the guards' quarters and requested an urgent meeting with the officials there.

The guards went into the back room and seemed to discuss the matter; after a while they answered.

"You have made a special request, but we cannot grant it. You are under custody. You cannot go in the middle of the night to meet the officials."

The sixteen were incensed.

"This is outrageous! What is this being in custody? Tomorrow we are to give our lives for the emperor! If you won't deliver our petition, we don't need you. Get out of the way. We will go ourselves."

The whole group rose from the tatami, and started for the back room.

A voice met their advance from that direction.

"You can stay where you are. The officials will meet with you."

The *fusuma* opened, and Kominami, Hayashi, and several Censor's Representatives came in.

The condemned soldiers all bowed, and Takeuchi spoke for them.

"We are giving our lives out of reverence for the Imperial command. But we fired in Sakai at the command of our superiors. We do not consider that to be a crime. Therefore we cannot accept the punishment of execution. If we must be executed, we should like to know the name of the crime for which we are to be executed."

Kominami's brow furrowed as he listened. He glared at all sixteen as he waited for Takeuchi to finish.

"Be silent! Why would our lords execute persons who have committed no crime? Your leaders gave an illegal order, and you fired illegally."

Takeuchi was not the least silenced.

"No. I do not think your words are worthy of a Censor General. It is not a question of legality when troops act under their leader's orders. We fired when our leaders ordered us to fire. It would be impossible to fight a battle if each soldier considered the propriety of each command."

Several others came up and knelt behind Takeuchi. "We all believe that our action in Sakai was meritorious, not criminal. If you think it was a crime, describe it in more detail."

"I too do not understand."

"Nor I."

The whole group now stared defiantly.

Kominami's arrogant expression softened.

"I spoke too hastily before. If you will wait briefly, I shall bring you an answer after consultation."

He rose and entered the inner room.

The men waited with eyes fixed on that room, but Kominami remained out of sight for a long time.

"What is happening?"

"Keep up your guard." The men were whispering in this way among themselves when Kominami finally reappeared.

"I have just delivered your request to our lord's deputy. Listen to his order in reply. In the first place, our two lords are deeply distressed because of this recent incident. His Excellency (referring to the present lord of Tosa, Toyonori) came to Osaka despite his illness to apologize personally aboard the French warship and then return to Tosa. Is it not said that when one's lord is disgraced his subjects should be even willing to die? You should have obeyed without hesitation as you were ordered when you received his first command. That is still the order. Now, in reference to this recent Sakai incident, since relations with foreign countries are being renewed, our lord is dealing with this question according to international law. Therefore you are ordered to commit *seppuku* tomorrow. In any case you must consider our emperor and obey willingly. Your act will be witnessed both by Japanese dignitaries and foreign ambassadors; therefore you must resolve to manifest the samurai spirit of our Imperial nation."

Kominami spoke thus as he held the written order.

The sixteen looked at each other and could not help smiling faintly.

Takeuchi spoke again for them.

"We respectfully receive our lord's gracious command. We have now only one request concerning what you have said. Normally we would submit our petition to your Censor's Representative, but since our lord's officials are present, we will personally declare our last request in this present life. Listening just now as we did to our lord's command, we also presume that he has understood our own heart's desire. Therefore we earnestly request his consent to our common last request, which is that we be accorded the honor of samurai status both now and after our death.''

Kominami replied after thinking for some time. ''Since our Lord has ordained that you commit *seppuku*, I regard your request as reasonable. A decision will be returned to you after proper consideration.''

Saying this, Kominami again rose and retired from the room.

After another long interval, a Censor's Representative now returned and announced, ''After the deliberations of the high officials, it has been ordained that you be accorded the honor of the samurai status. Therefore you are each to wear a white silk kimono.''

With this he handed them a written record of the decision.

On their way back to their quarters after receiving this document, the sixteen soldiers reported the details of the evening's negotiations to their leaders and their lieutenants. These men were also sound asleep from the evening's meal and wine. They rose immediately at the sound of their men's knocking and huddled together with them. They had not met together since they had been taken to separate quarters. Since the result of the negotiations with the Censor General now permitted *seppuku* by the soldiers, they were promoted to samurai status; no one interfered with their movements and actions within the residences, and they could now visit their leaders freely in this fashion.

Their leaders felt a mixture of joy and sadness upon hearing their men's story. Having resigned themselves to die, they were saddened to learn for the first time of the demands of the French consul and the fate of the sixteen others. But they felt joy to hear that their men had been permitted the right of *seppuku* and were promoted to samurai status. All twenty then redivided into their three groups in good spirits and went to sleep, having decided it would be good to rest a little before the dawn broke.

The sky on the morning of the twenty-third was clear. More than three hundred foot soldiers were despatched from the Kumamoto *han* of Hosokawa Etchū no kami Yoshiyuki[16] and the Hiroshima *han* of Asano Aki no kami Shigenaga[17] to escort the twenty men to Sakai; they reached the gate of the Nagabori mansion before dawn. Within the Tosa residence, they all breakfasted on fish and sake. The two division leaders and their lieutenants wore new kimono; the sixteen soldiers dressed in the white silk they had put on during the night. Their swords were not returned to them in the mansion. They were to be brought directly to the place of *seppuku*.

As the group clopped out of the gate of the mansion in high wooden clogs, twenty palanquins made ready by the Hosokawa and Asano families were brought forward. Each of the twenty men bowed and entered an individual palanquin. A procession line was formed, led by minor officials of the two *han*, followed by a contingent of soldiers. Next came the House Attendant, Baba Hikosaemon, and the Division Leader, Yamakawa Kametarō, of the Hosokawa clan, and Watanabe Kisou, a high official of the Asano clan, each wearing a headpiece and small *hakama* and sitting astride a horse led by a lance bearer. They were followed by another contingent of foot soldiers, then a group pulling two large cannon, and finally the twenty palanquins. Each palanquin was escorted by six men carrying rifles with bayonets, and the twenty palanquins were accompanied in front and behind by one hundred and twenty soldiers, also carrying rifles with bayonets. Two horsemen bearing rifles followed next. Then twenty pole bearers, ten each carrying large paper lanterns with the emblems of the Kumamoto and Hiroshima domains, and another hundred-odd foot soldiers from each of the same *han*. A small distance behind this procession followed important officials and several hundred retainers of the Tosa *han*. The procession stretched out about five blocks.

After moving forward a short distance from Nagabori, Yamakawa Kametarō bowed to the man in each palanquin, and when he reached the palanquin of Shinoura Inokichi, he said, "You must be very cramped in this narrow space. And I am afraid you will be suffocating with the curtains drawn the whole length of this journey. May I roll up the curtain?"

Shinoura replied, "I am deeply appreciative of your kindness. If it does not trouble you, I would be pleased."

Then the curtains of all the palanquins were rolled up.

After moving forward again, Yamakawa announced to each of the twenty, "I have prepared tea and cakes for anyone who wishes."

Thus the two *han* treated the twenty Tosa men with extreme respect.

Reaching the environs of Sumiyoshi Shinkeimachi, the prisoners passed by the former barracks of the Sixth and Eighth Tosa divisions. The road was lined there with people awaiting the procession to say their farewells. As they entered Sakai, there was a crush of people on both sides, some of whom were weeping. Certain of them ran out from the throng toward the palanquins, only to be shouted off by their escorts.

A temple, the Myōkokuji, had been designated as the place of *seppuku*. At the temple gate was hung a curtain with the Imperial emblem; the area inside the gate was completely enclosed by curtains bearing the emblems of the Hosokawa and Asano houses. The place of *seppuku* itself was encircled by curtains with the emblem of the Yamanouchi family of Tosa. Within a tent pitched inside the gate, new straw matting had been laid out.

When the procession reached the gate of the Myōkokuji, the palanquins were carried into the tent within the gate and lined up in rows on the straw matting. Then, escorted by retainers of the two *han*, the palanquins were carried to the inner garden where they were set down parallel to the corridor of the main hall.

The twenty men got out of their palanquins and sat on mats arranged within the main hall. Several hundred guardsmen surrounded their mats, and whenever one of the twenty had to get up, he was escorted by four soldiers. The group continued to talk cheerfully while they waited for the time to pass.

During this interval one of the retainers of the two *han* brought a writing brush, paper, and ink. He came up to Shinoura who was sitting at the head of the twenty, and asked if he would write something as a remembrance.

Shinoura Inokichi, leader of the former Sixth Tosa Infantry Division, was from a Minamoto family; his first name was Gensho, his pen name Senzan. He was born on the eleventh day of the eleventh month of 1844 in a samurai house of Attendant rank, which received a stipend of fifteen *koku* and ration for five servants in the Ushioe village of the district of Tosa in the Tosa domain. He was now twenty-five. His father was named Chūhei, his grandfather Manjirō. His mother, Ume, was from the Yoda family. He came as a student to Edo in 1857, became tutor to the lord of Yodo in Edo in 1860, and in the same year returned to Tosa where he was appointed assistant teacher in the *han* school. He then served as Attendant to the lord of Yodo for seven or eight years, when he was promoted to the rank of Mounted Escort. With this appointment he was assigned command of the infantry division of the *han* in November of 1867, scarcely three months before the Sakai incident occurred. Because of his background, Shinoura had a taste for poetry, and could write calligraphy in an excellent cursive script.

When the writing materials were placed before him, Shinoura said, "I can only manage something clumsy," and extemporized the following seven-character Chinese verses:

> I have expressed my gratitude to our country
> by expelling the foreign devils,
> What need have I to consider the words of others?
> Let my deed serve to teach loyalty to our emperor
> For a thousand generations,
> An individual death is insignificant in comparison.

Shinoura was still an adherent of the position which called for the expulsion of the barbarians.

The twenty had been waiting for some time when retainers of the Hosokawa *han* reported that the time of *seppuku* was set for much later in the day. It was therefore decided that they could visit the temple. As they went out to view the garden, they saw that the areas both within and without the temple were thronged with people. Spectators had come not only from Sakai, but even from Osaka, Sumiyoshi, Kawachi, and other places; attempts were made to keep them away from the temple, but it was impossible to do so. Several monks ascended the bell tower to observe this crowd. Catching sight of these monks, Kakiuchi of the Eighth Division climbed up after them and said, "Your reverences, make room for one who is to die this day by *seppuku*. Some of my companions have made poems to bid this world farewell, but I cannot boast of such talent. Therefore as farewell to this world let me sound this big bell. May I do so?"

So saying, he rolled up his sleeves and grabbed the wooden bell hammer. The monks seized his arms in alarm.

"Please, sir, wait! No telling what commotion will result in this crowd if the bell sounds. For that reason alone, we beg you not to do it."

"No, it is the last request of a samurai who is offering his life for the nation! I want to ring it."

Seeing Kakiuchi and the monks debating vigorously, two or three of his companions came running up to him to lend support to the monks.

"This is very childish in view of the important matter before us. What if you frightened the people by sounding the bell? Don't be so rash."

"You are right. I have started a profitless debate on an impulse. I've changed my mind." Kakiuchi let go of the bell hammer.

Then, one of the companions who had restrained Kakiuchi reached into his sash and said to the monks, "Here is a small sum of money. It will soon be useless to me. Let me give it to you to pray for us after our death."

Others of their group, drawn by the debate between Kakiuchi and the monks, now joined in:

"Here is some more."

"Here too."

They all handed over whatever money they had been carrying to the monks. One of them asked for prayers as he said, "Although I do not wish for the Buddha's heaven." The monks took the money and left the bell tower.

Descending the tower, one of the group suggested, "Shall we not look over the place of *seppuku*?" and so they began to enter the curtained area. Retainers of the Hosokawa *han* held them back, saying, "It is better for you not to go in here."

"Don't worry. We will not trouble you," they replied, and went inside together.

The place was a broad garden in front of the main hall. Within the inner area enclosed by curtains bearing the emblem of the Yamanouchi family, a roof thatched with rush matting had been set up on four bamboo poles. On the ground beneath it, two new tatami mats were placed facedown on top of two loosely woven straw mats; these were covered with white cotton cloth and finally with a rug. Many such rugs were piled up on one side to be changed with each *seppuku*. On a table on the side of the entrance were placed many sets of large and small swords. As they looked them over, they recognized their own swords taken away at the Nagabori mansion.

They left the place of *seppuku* and went next to view their own future graves in the Hōjūin cemetery. Two rows of graves had been dug there. A large urn of more than six feet in height was placed before each grave site. Their individual names were written on each urn. While reading them Yokota turned to Doi and spoke. "You and I used to share a room in this life, and as I see how our urns are lined up next to one another I think to myself that we can continue to talk to one another in the next life too."

Doi then jumped forward and climbed into the urn.

"Yokota, Yokota. It's a very nice arrangement, isn't it?" Doi replied jokingly.

Takeuchi then said, "Doi is too eager. Don't be in such a hurry. You will soon be placed inside, and you won't come out so quickly."

Doi tried to get out of the urn, but although he had entered easily he now found the edge high and the inside slippery, making it difficult for him to maneuver. Yokota and Takeuchi had to push the urn over on its side to get Doi out.

The twenty men now returned to the main hall, where they found fish and sake prepared by the Hosokawa and Asano *han*. More than a score of persons from the town served them. The group raised their cups to toast them. Then the soldiers of the two *han*, envious of the person who had previously received the poem from Shinoura, begged for poems or some other keepsakes attached to their persons. The twenty passed around a writing brush. And since they had nothing to give as keepsakes, they tore off collars and sleeves.

The *seppuku* was finally scheduled to commence at two o'clock in the afternoon.

The seconds for the *seppuku* first took their places within the tent. Each second had been personally selected the night before by the twenty in the Nagabori mansion when they were given fish and sake by their guards from the Fifth Tosa Division. The Sixth Division men selected their seconds as follows: Mabuchi (Baba) Momotarō was chosen by Shinoura; Kitakawa

Reikei by Ikegami; Ike Shichisuke by Sugimoto; Yoshimura Saikichi by Katsugase; Mori Tsunema by Yamamoto; Noguchi Kikuma by Morimoto; Ta-
keichi Sukego by Kitashiro; Ehara Gennosuke by Inada; Chikafusa Shigeno-
suke by Yanase; Yamade Yasunosuke by Hashizume; Hijikata Yogorō by
Okazaki; Takemoto Kennosuke by Kawatani. For the Eighth Division men,
Kosaka Inui became the second of Nishimura; Ochiai Genroku of Ōishi;
Kususe Ryūhei of Takeuchi; Matsuda Hachiheiji of Yokota; Ike Shichisuke
of Doi; Kumon Sahei was selected by Kakiuchi; Tanikawa Shinji by Kanada;
Kitamori Kannosuke by Takenouchi. Ike Shichisuke was to be the second of
both Sugimoto and Doi. Each second stood behind the place of *seppuku*,
his long sleeves tucked up and held by a sash made by the cord attached to
his sword handle.

The twenty palanquins had been arranged systematically outside the tent,
ready to carry each corpse to the Hōjūin cemetery. The bodies were to be
transferred to the large urns before the graves.

The official observers were seated on stools according to the following pro-
tocol. Prince Yamashina,[18] governor of Foreign Affairs, Date Munenari and
Higashikuse Michitomi,[19] two high-ranking generals of the same office, and
high retainers of the Hosokawa and Asano *han* faced from south to north.
Nagao Tarobē of the Tosa *han* faced from north to southeast. Censor
General Kominami and several Censors faced from northwest toward the
east. The French consul, backed by more than twenty French riflemen,
directly faced the place of *seppuku* from west to east. In addition, officials
from Satsuma, Nagata, Inaba, Bizen, and other *han* were also assigned
seats.

Samurai of the Hosokawa and Asano *han* came to announce that the
seating of officials had been completed. The twenty men were taken in their
palanquins from the corridor of the main hall, accompanied by the same
escorts as in the procession from the Nagabori mansion to Sakai. When the
palanquins were arranged outside the tent, an official unrolled a scroll bearing names of the twenty men and was about to call out the name of the
highest-ranking of the twenty, Shinoura Inokichi.

Just then the sky suddenly darkened and heavy rains pounded the area.
The people thronging the temple area began to run in every direction for
cover, either beneath the eaves of the temple building or under the branches
of trees. There was complete disorder.

The time for the *seppuku* ceremony was delayed as Prince Yamashina and
the other officials withdrew inside the temple building. The rain stopped at
two in the afternoon, and it took until after three to complete the arrangements for the second time.

The official finally called out the first name: "Shinoura Inokichi." The areas inside and outside the temple became hushed. Shinoura walked to the place of *seppuku* wearing a white *hakama* and a black felt *haori*. His assistant, Baba Momotarō, stood three feet behind him. After bowing to Prince Yamashina and the other officials, Shinoura took a short sword in his right hand from a box of unpainted wood held by another official. Then he cried out in a voice like thunder:

"Frenchmen! I am not dying for your sake. I am dying for my Imperial nation. Observe the *seppuku* of a Japanese soldier."

Shinoura relaxed his garment, pointed the sword downward, made a deep thrust into the right side of his stomach, lowered the blade three inches, and pulled it across the front of his stomach and upwards three inches on the left. Because of the depth of the initial thrust, the wound gaped widely. Releasing his sword, Shinoura then placed both hands within the cut and, pulling out his own guts, glared at the French consul.

Baba struck Shinoura's neck with his sword, but failed to make a deep cut.

"Baba, don't be so nervous!" Shinoura cried out.

Baba's sword flashed again, cutting the neck vertebrae.

Shinoura again cried, "I am still alive, cut again." This voice was inhumanly loud, carrying for a distance of three blocks.[20]

The French consul, his eyes riveted on Shinoura from the start, was increasingly overcome by a mixture of shock and fear. Unable to stay in his seat after hearing Shinoura's overwhelming cry during what was for him a totally new experience, he finally stood up, looking as if he were going to faint.

Baba's third stroke toppled Shinoura's head to the mat.

Nishimura, who was called next, was a gentle man. His family lineage was Minamoto, his name Ujiatsu. He had grown up in the village of Enokuchi in the district of Tosa. He was born in 1845, and was now twenty-five with the rank of Mounted Escort and an annual stipend of forty *koku*. He had been assigned to the Sixth Tosa Division in the eighth month of 1867. Nishimura took his place on the seat of *seppuku* wearing his military uniform, the buttons of which he carefully loosened one by one. He then took his short sword, thrust it into his left side and began to pull it across to the right; but, as if he thought the penetration too shallow, he drew the blade in deeper before slowly pulling it over to the right. His second Kōsaka seemed a little frightened; even before Nishimura had finished pulling the blade to the right, he struck from behind. The head flew almost six meters.

The next was Ikegami, assisted by Kitakawa. Then Ōishi, who was an especially big man. He first rubbed his bare stomach with his two hands several times. Taking the sword in his right hand he pierced the left side of his

stomach, cut downward with his left hand pushing down on the back of the
sword blade, then, joining left hand to right, cut across his stomach to the
right side, where he again used his left hand to push the blade to cut upwards. He next placed the sword down on the mat, and spreading out both
arms, cried, "Second! Quickly please!" His second, Ochiai, bungled badly,
taking seven strokes to cut off his head. Of all the *seppuku*, the smoothest
performance was that of Ōishi.

Sugimoto, Katsugase, Yamamoto, Morimoto, Kitashiro, Inada, and Yanase committed *seppuku* in sequence. Yanase drew his sword across from
left to right, then back again from right to left, and so his entrails came
gushing out of the opening.

The twelfth man to commit *seppuku* was Hashizume. As he appeared and
advanced toward the mat, it was already growing dark and lanterns were lit
in the main hall.

To this point, the French consul had been continually standing up and
sitting down again, and seemed to be almost beside himself. His nervous-
ness spread increasingly to the French soldiers who provided his escort. Their
military stance completely collapsed; they began to move their hands and
whisper among each other. Just as Hashizume reached the *seppuku* mat, the
consul gave some kind of order, and the whole contingent left their places
and surrounded the consul who, without making any apology or explanation
to Prince Yamashina or to the other dignitaries, hurriedly left the tent. Taking the shortest line across the temple garden, the soldiers who enveloped
the consul broke into a run for the harbor as soon as they were outside the
temple gate.

At the place of *seppuku*, Hashizume had already loosened his garments
and was about to thrust in his sword. At that instant an official came running in and broke Hashizume's concentration with a cry of "Wait!" The official informed him of the French consul's departure and declared that the
seppuku ceremony was being temporarily delayed. Hashizume returned to
the other eight men and communicated this information to them.

The nine men were all gripped with the desire to die as ordered and without delay. Their impatience grew so great that they began to push against
their wardens and demand an audience with their superiors. They wanted to
know why they could not proceed; when finally brought before Kominami,
Hashizume spoke for them.

"Why has there been a delay of our *seppuku* decreed by the emperor's
order? We have come here to learn the reason."

Kominami answered, "Your inquiry is reasonable, but the French consul is supposed to observe the *seppuku*. Since he has departed, it was necessary to delay the procedures. Just now the Han Elders of Satsuma, Nagato, Tosa, Inaba, Bizen, Higo, and Aki have gone to the French warship. Return to your places and await a report in a little while.''

The nine men had no recourse but to withdraw to the main hall. Samurai of the Hosokawa and Asano *han* brought trays of food. Although the nine had no interest in eating, they were ordered to take supper, then to spread out their bedding and lie down to sleep. About eleven at night, samurai of the Hosokawa and Asano *han* came to report that the Elders of the seven *han* had just returned. The nine jumped up and went to meet with them. Three of the seven Elders advanced on their knees and spoke in turn. They had gone to the French warship to inquire about the consul's departure. The French consul, they reported, had been impressed at the courage of the men of Tosa in performing their duty, but since he could no longer endure the horrible sight of the *seppuku* he was going to request the Japanese government to spare the lives of the remaining nine men. An Imperial order would be requested tomorrow morning through General Date of the Foreign Office. The nine remaining men were to wait for the official reply from the Japanese government without making any commotion.

The nine respectfully complied.

Two days later, on the twenty-fifth, samurai of the two *han* came and announced that the nine men were to be transferred to Osaka, where Hashizume, Okazaki, and Kawatani were to be placed under the custody of the Aki domain, and Takeuchi, Yokota, Doi, Kakiuchi, Kanada, and Takenouchi under the Higo domain. The nine palanquins were brought into the main garden of the temple. As they were entering the palanquins, Hashizume attempted to commit suicide by biting his tongue; he collapsed from the loss of blood. He deeply regretted the restraining order that had prevented him from committing *seppuku* when it was his turn to follow the brave deaths of his comrades. Fortunately the wound was not deep enough to endanger his life, but the escort from the Asano *han* decided to hasten the withdrawal to Osaka before any other incidents could occur, and so the retainers started to hurry the palanquins of Hashizume, Okazaki, and Kawatani along the highway. The Hosokawa escort shouted up at them to slow down, but to no avail. They too finally began running with the remaining six palanquins.

When they reached Osaka, the nine palanquins were halted in front of the Nagabori mansion of the Tosa *han*. Kominami came out before the gate and spoke to Hashizume. Then the two escorting contingents divided into two groups with their respective charges. A doctor and a guard from the Tosa *han* as well were assigned to Hashizume.

The nine were extremely well treated by the Hosokawa and Asano houses. The Hosokawa retainers said that this custodianship was the third great honor enjoined upon their clan of this nature—the first having been the *han*'s assignment to take custody of the forty-seven *rōnin* of Akō during the Genroku period,[21] the second, custody of the Mito clansmen who had assassinated Ii Kamon no kami Naosuke in 1860.[22] The Hosokawa and Asano retainers provided their charges with new sleeping clothes consisting of striped double-lined kimono. Every evening, bedding of triple *futon* were spread out by foot soldiers. Hot baths were prepared every other day. They supplied towels and fine-quality tissue paper. At all three meals they served broiled fish pretasted by their own leaders. In the afternoon they presented them with various kinds of cakes in lacquer boxes and an assortment of fruits. Two or three escorts waited in the corridor outside the privy, and supplied the men with ladles of water to wash their hands. Night sentinels stood guard while they slept. Those who came to greet them knelt and bowed to the floor. They were given books to read. When they were sick, a doctor was sent who mixed and brewed medicines right before their eyes.

On the second of the third month, an order came from the Court commuting their sentences. They were directed to return to Tosa. On the third, division leaders of the Tosa *han* and their troops received the nine men to escort them back to Tosa. The two *han* prepared a sumptuous banquet at which they bade them an emotional farewell. On the fourteenth, the nine, escorted by a representative of the Censor and two supervisors, boarded a boat at the entrance to Kizu river; they set sail from Sembonmatsu, and reached Urado harbor during the night of the sixteenth. On the seventeenth, the road to Minamikaisho west from Matsugahana as far as Obiyamachi was lined with people who had come out to see the heroes of the Sakai incident. At Minamikaisho the Censor's Representative handed over his nine charges to Tosa officials who received them and put them under the custody of their wives and children, who had thought never to see them alive again after they had received the farewell letters and locks of hair sent when the death sentence was first ordered.

On the twentieth of the fifth month, an order came from Minamikaisho. Each of the nine men was to assemble at nine o'clock and their fathers and sons, if they had either, were to assemble a half-hour later, at Minamikaisho the next morning. At the meeting in Minamikaisho, a Censor presided while his Representative read the following three orders. First, the men were to be stripped of stipends and exiled to Watarigawa Kagirinishi, but would be permitted to wear *hakama* and swords. Secondly, their first-born sons, in the cases where applicable, were to be enrolled in the ranks of the soldiers, and assigned double stipends of four *koku* of rice. Third, those who did not have heirs were to be assigned double stipends as allowance in exile, to be paid out of the warehouse of Hatanakamura. After consulting together, the nine replied, using Hashizume as their spokesman. "We were to die for our nation because of the French demands. Consequently we were to be allowed to commit *seppuku* and received the honor of samurai status. Our lives were then pardoned through the request of the French consul. Therefore we feel we should not be punished further and should continue to hold our samurai status. Thus we cannot readily comply with the orders, since we are not informed as to why we are now being exiled."

The Censor replied in an embarrassed manner that their question was understandable. However, he continued, their exile seemed to be Lord Toyonori's disposition of their case, keeping in mind the suffering of their eleven comrades; thus he requested they comply with the order. The nine wore grim smiles when they replied that they felt anguish day and night over the deaths of their eleven comrades, and so if it were a matter of being sentenced to exile as opposed to the kind of suffering undergone by those eleven, then there could be no argument on their part; therefore they all accepted the order.

The nine set out and in unprecedented fashion: as *rōnin* wearing *hakama* and swords. Weakened by their long period under confinement, they all suffered from pains in their feet. After reaching Asakuramura in Tosagōri, they were carried in palanquins from that point on. The place of exile chosen was the village of Nyūta in Hatagōri. The village headman, Uga Sukenoshin, first arranged for each of the nine to be taken into a separate peasant household; after several days he put eight of them together in a vacant house. Through some family connection, the ninth, Yokota, was taken in by the head priest at a temple of the Lotus sect, the Shinseiji, in Ariokamura three miles to the west.

The nine first performed Buddhist observances at the Shinseiji for their comrades buried in the Myōkokuji; the next day they began to teach literary and military arts to the people of the village. Takeuchi gave instructions in how to read the Confucian Classics, Doi and Takenouchi taught swordsmanship, and each of the others taught some art according to his own talents.

The village of Nyūta was stricken by a plague during that summer and fall. In August, Kawatani, Yokota, and Doi caught fevers. Doi's wife traveled all day and night from Yasumura in Kagamigōri to come to his side. His own mother sick, Yokota's son, Tsunejirō, although a lad of scarcely nine, walked over sixty miles by himself to attend his father. The two eventually recovered, but Kawatani died of the plague at the age of twenty-six on the fourth of the ninth month.

The Tosa Censor received an Imperial order for the nine men on the seventeenth of the eleventh month. The eight surviving men prayed their farewells at Kawatani's grave, left Nyūta village, and arrived in Kōchi on the twenty-seventh. They immediately went to the Censor's official quarters, where the following Imperial order was handed to each of them.

"In consideration of the ceremony of the accession of the Emperor, you are pardoned and allowed to return home; in addition, the official rank of soldier is given to each father, who will continue in his rank as before the incident." The eight men were thus pardoned on the occasion of the accession of the Emperor Meiji on the twenty-seventh day of the eighth month of 1868; the order of being promoted to samurai status was in the end nullified.

The Tosa domain built stone tablets at the eleven graves in the Hōjūin for the men who committed *seppuku* in the Myōkokuji. The tablets were arranged in a row from the plots of Shinoura to Yanase. Under the veranda at the back of the main hall of the Hōjūin, the remaining nine large urns were laid sideways on hewn rocks. They were to stand as a momento of the nine men who narrowly escaped entering them. In Sakai, there was an endless procession of visitors to the temple grounds who referred to the stone inscriptions of the eleven graves as *go-zannen-sama*[23] and to the nine urns as *ikiun-sama*.[24]

Among the eleven, Shinoura had no son, and therefore the family line was for a time terminated; but on the eighth of the third month of 1870, the head of the household was assigned to Kusukichi, the second son of Shinoura Kōzō of the same family name; he was given a samurai family rank with a stipend of seven *koku* three *to*. Then, through the request of Kōzō, Kusukichi married a daughter of Shinoura Inokichi.

Nishimura's father, Seizaemon, had passed away earlier, but his grandfather, Katsuhē, was still living; the official head of the Nishimura household was reinvested in the grandfather. Later it came to an adopted son who was a blood relative in the Kakehi family.

Even though under age, the sons of the lieutenants Ikegami and Ōishi, and of the lower-ranking men who committed *seppuku*, were enrolled as soldiers. When they came of age, they served in the Imperial army.

February 1914

SANSHŌ DAYŪ

"SANSHŌ THE STEWARD" is one of the most affecting of all Ōgai's works. The story, based on a legend mentioned in early Buddhist tales and medieval puppet plays, is given a modern psychological treatment of the most penetrating sort, yet the elements of the story tinged with the miraculous—in particular the incidents surrounding the amulet that passes from character to character throughout the story—have been retained and are combined skillfully with the main narrative to achieve a rare blend of heightened observation and idealized emotion. Ōgai's deceptively plain language, so difficult to render into satisfactory English, masks a sophisticated arrangement of plot elements and an absolute mastery of physical detail. The reader suffers through every vicissitude faced by the children because Ōgai always manages to realize the emotional nuance of the situation and place. The morning calm when the boats set out, the flickering light on Sanshō's face, the rocks where the children bid farewell—all these moments are completely real, yet sketched quickly with a few simple sentences.

Children are often a favorite subject for writers because of the special problems and possibilities involved in evoking their mentality. In "Sanshō dayū," Ōgai has attempted perhaps the most difficult thing of all: to show a child's passage into adolescence and his discernment of the meaning of love, responsibility, and suffering. But Anju and Zushiō embody many of the qualities of the main characters of Ōgai's other stories. Such seems to have been his real reason for choosing the old legend for a retelling, and in his own terms he was completely successful. The story is regarded as one of the finest in modern Japanese fiction, and the 1954 film by Mizoguchi Kenji (entitled *Sanshō the Bailiff* abroad), widely considered as one of the great masterpieces of Japanese cinema, has made Ōgai's story well known in Europe and the United States.

 AN UNUSUAL BAND of travelers walked along the little-used road that led from Kasuga in Echigo to the province of Imazu. The little group was led by a mother, barely thirty, followed by her two children. The girl was fourteen, the boy twelve. With them was a servant woman of about forty, who urged on the two weary children. "We'll soon be at the inn where we will spend the night," she told them. Of the two children, the girl showed particular fortitude: although she dragged her feet as she walked, she kept up her spirits and tried as best she could not to show her mother or brother how tired she was, and occasionally she would remind herself to maintain a more resilient step. If the four had been making a pilgrimage to some nearby temple, their appearance would not have been extraordinary, but with their walking sticks and bamboo hats, which added a certain gallant note to their appearance, the group drew every passerby's curiosity and even sympathy.

The road now skirted a group of farmers' houses and continued along beside them. The road had many stones and pebbles, but since it was dry from the crisp autumn air and mixed with clay, it formed a hard surface easy for walking, unlike the sandy roads near the sea, where travelers were always buried up to their ankles.

As they walked along, a sudden burst of the setting sun illuminated a long row of thatched huts, roofs jumbled together, surrounded by a grove of oaks.

"Look at the beautiful maple leaves!" the mother called back to her children.

The two glanced in the direction where she pointed but did not reply, so the servant woman said, "The leaves here have turned completely. No wonder that the mornings and evenings have become so cold . . ."

The girl suddenly looked at her brother, then said, "If we could only hurry to where father is waiting for us . . ."

The boy replied in the wise fashion that children adopt, "We haven't yet gone very far."

The mother spoke in an admonishing tone. "That's right. We must cross many mountains like the ones we have crossed until now, and we must also cross many rivers and seas by boat. Every day you must exert all your energies and be very good as we walk."

"Well, I want to go as fast as we can," the girl said.

Now everyone fell silent as they went along.

TRANSLATED BY J. THOMAS RIMER

From the opposite direction came a woman carrying an empty pail. She was a worker who gathered seawater for the salt farm at the beach.

The serving woman called to her. "Is there anywhere nearby where travelers can spend the night?"

The woman stopped and examined the four of them. Then she spoke. "I'm sorry for you. You've gotten yourselves in a bad place to be when the sun goes down. There's not a house here that will put up travelers. Not a one."

"How could that be?" continued the servant woman. "Why are people so inhospitable in these parts?"

Taking notice of the increasingly lively conversation, the children walked over to the woman; now the servant woman and the children seemed to surround her.

"That's not it. There are many religious[1] and kind-hearted people here. But there are the orders from the governor of the province. There is nothing we can do about it. Look over that way," she said, pointing in the direction from which she had come. "If you go as far as that bridge, you will see there is a signboard put up. All the details are written there, they say. There have been some terrible men, slave dealers, roaming around near here, and so there is a prohibition against giving shelter to travelers. Seven nearby families have been implicated, I hear."

"How difficult for us. We have the children, and I don't think we'll be able to go on much farther. Isn't there anything we can do at all?"

"If you continue on as far as the beach where I came from, it will be completely dark, and you will have no recourse but to find a good place to sleep around there. What I would do if I were you would be to sleep over there under the bridge. There are many large logs stacked up very close to the stone wall along the shore of the river. They are logs that have been floated down from higher up the Arakawa River. Children play under them during the day. There are places deep inside where it's always dark and the wind doesn't penetrate. I sleep in the quarters of the owner of the salt fields where I work every day, just over there in the midst of that grove of oaks. After night falls, I'll bring you straw and some mats."

The mother, who had been standing apart and listening to the discussion, now came over to the woman. "We have truly met with a kind person and we thank you for your suggestion. Let's go there and stay for the night. We would be most grateful if you could lend us some straw or some matting. At least enough for me to put down a bed for the children."

The woman agreed and started home toward the grove of oak trees. The four travelers hurried off in the direction of the bridge.

The little group arrived at the foot of the Ōge bridge that crossed the Arakawa. Just as the woman had told them, a new signpost had been placed there. She had been correct as well about the orders from the governor of the province.

If there were slave traders, why was no investigation made of them in the area? Why did the governor issue orders prohibiting the lodging of strangers and thus cause great hardship to travelers arriving late in the day? This order seemed to be no real solution to the problem. Yet for the people of that time, it was the governor's decree. Indeed, the mother herself did not dispute the regulation but only lamented the family's fate at having come to a place where there were such rules.

By the base of the bridge there was a road used by people who did their laundry by the river. Using this path they climbed down to the riverbed itself. They found the logs piled up against the stone fence. Following along the wall they managed to pass underneath the logs. The boy, full of curiosity, bravely made his way first.

Crawling deep inside, they found a place where the logs formed a kind of cave. Below their feet a huge log had fallen sideways, making a floor.

The boy climbed up on the log, crawled back into the farthest corner, and called to his sister to hurry up and come inside. She timidly followed him.

"Please wait a moment," said the servant woman, and, making the children stand aside, she took down a bundle she was carrying on her back, pulled out some extra clothing, and spread it out in one corner for all of them to sit on. When their mother was seated, the children clung to her, one on each side. Since leaving their home in Shinobugōri in Iwashiro, they had slept in places more exposed than this one, even when under a roof. Of necessity they had become accustomed to difficult conditions, and what they found here was by no means the worst they had experienced.

Along with the extra clothing, the servant woman took out some food that had been carefully saved. She put it down in front of the children and said, "We can't make a fire here. We must not be found by those awful men. I will go to the home of the owner of that salt beach and see if I can bring us some hot water. And perhaps I can ask for straw or mats as well."

The servant woman hurried off in her diligent fashion. The children began to eat their dried fruits and rice with great appetite.

A moment later they heard someone's footsteps entering the hollow space under the logs. The mother called out, "Ubatake!" the name of the serving woman. However she suspected that it might be someone else, since the oak forest was too far to permit a trip back and forth in such a short time.

The person who entered was a man about forty years old. He was so lean that every muscle could be seen and counted from outside his skin; he had a smile on his face like that of an ivory doll and held a Buddhist rosary in his hands. He walked over to where the children were sitting in a nonchalant manner, as if he were in his own home, then sat down on the log beside them.

The children could only look at him in astonishment. They did not find him frightening, as he did not seem at all what they expected a dangerous man to look like.

"I am a sailor named Yamaoka Tayū. There have been some slave traders around here recently, and the governor has forbidden anyone to stop over in these parts. But he doesn't seem to be able to catch the criminals. I feel sorry for travelers in these parts, and so I try to help them. Fortunately my house is a bit removed from the road. If you stay there secretly, nobody will bother you. I sometimes walk around in places where travelers might be sleeping outside, in the woods or under the bridge, and I've already taken quite a few to stay with me. I see the children are eating sweets. That won't fill them up. And it's bad for their teeth. I've nothing special at my place, but I could fix you some rice porridge with yams. Come along and let me take care of you." The man did not try to tempt them; indeed he spoke half as though to himself.

Listening carefully, the mother was moved by the laudable intentions of this man who would go so far as to break the law to help others. She told him, "I am very grateful for your kind offer. But I am concerned that we will cause great difficulties to anyone who took us in. Yet if you could somehow manage to feed the children a bit of something hot, some rice gruel perhaps, and give us a roof to sleep under, we will all be eternally grateful to you."

Yamaoka nodded. "You are a woman who knows how to make a wise decision. Let me show you the way," he said, rising to go.

The mother added, in a tone of regret, "Please wait here just a bit more. As you have already promised to take care of the three of us, I hesitate to ask anything more of you, but there is another person traveling with us."

Yamaoka scrutinized them more carefully. "You have another companion? A man or a woman?"

"A serving woman I brought with me to look after the children. She went back down the road a bit to find us some hot water. She should be back very soon."

"A serving woman. Then I'll be glad to wait." Yamaoka's impassive face relaxed, then seemed touched with a shadow of joy.

The sun was still hidden behind the mountains of Yone, and mist hung over the deep blue water on the bay of Naoe.

A boatman helped a small group into his boat and cast off from the shore. It was Yamaoka and the four travelers who had spent the night in his house.

The evening before, they had all waited for Ubatake, who finally returned with some hot water in a cracked wine jug, before going on to stay the night with Yamaoka. Ubatake herself had been quite apprehensive but had gone with them as well. Yamaoka had put up the travelers in a thatched hut in the midst of a pine grove to the south of the main road and had given them some yams and rice porridge. Then he asked them about their itinerary. After putting the exhausted children to sleep, their mother, beneath the dim lamp, told Yamaoka something of her own situation.

She said she was from Iwashiro. Her husband had gone to Tsukushi and had not returned, so now she was taking the two children there to inquire as to his whereabouts. Ubatake, she continued, had been with the family since she served as a nurse when her daughter was born; since the serving woman had no relatives, she had made her a companion for the long and doubtful journey. They had managed to come this far, she concluded, yet in relation to the distance to the western provinces, it seemed they had hardly left home. Would it be better to go from here by land? By sea? Since Yamaoka was a sailor, he must know about even the most remote areas. She asked him to advise her as best he could.

As though he considered this the simplest of questions, Yamaoka Tayū told her without any hesitation that they should go by sea. If they continued on by land, he said, they would soon reach a dangerous place on the borders of Etchū province, where rough waves dashed against sharp rocks. Travelers waited in caves for the tide to recede so they could run along a narrow path underneath the rocks. The waves fell back for such short periods of time that children and parents alike had no time to look back at each other. If, on the other hand, they went by the mountain road, they would have to cross over a path so dangerous that if they took one false step, if even one stone loosened under their feet, they would risk plunging to the bottom of the deep valley below. There was no telling how many such difficult places they would encounter before they reached the western provinces and Tsukushi. On the other hand, the sea route was quite safe. If they found a reliable sailor, he could pilot them, with no effort on their part, a hundred *ri*, even a thousand. While he could by no means go as far as Tsukushi himself, Yamaoka said, he knew sailors from various provinces, and he could arrange to take the family by boat to a place where they could locate a boatman who would be able to take them that far. Tomorrow morning, he suggested, as though it were no trouble at all, he would take them there in his own boat.

Early the next morning Yamaoka hurried the travelers out of the house. At that moment, the mother took a bit of money from a small bag, thinking to pay him for their lodgings. He stopped her and said that he would take nothing, but suggested that he guard the small bag of money for her. Such valuable things, he told her, should always be given to the landlord when they stayed in an inn, or to the master of the ship when they traveled by sea.

Ever since she first allowed Yamaoka to give them lodgings, the mother had shown a tendency to accept his word. However, although she was grateful to him for having helped them, even to the extent of breaking the law, she did not necessarily trust him in every particular. Rather she kept consenting to the certain autocratic tone in his voice to which she was able to put up no resistance. There was clearly something unsettling about this situation, yet she did not have any reason to fear Yamaoka. She had not fully comprehended her own feelings.

She boarded the boat with a certain feeling that there was nothing else that she could do. When the children themselves saw the calm water, spread out like a blue carpet before them, they joined her, full of excitement over the beauty of what they saw. Only the face of Ubatake retained a trace of the uneasiness she had felt when she had returned the evening before to meet Yamaoka for the first time.

Yamaoka cast off. As he pushed away from shore with a pole, the boat began to roll gently in the water.

For a certain interval, Yamaoka rowed south close to the bank in the direction of the border of Etchū province. The mist suddenly vanished and the waves sparkled in the sun.

The party now came to a spot hidden by rocks, away from any sign of human habitation, where the waves washed the sand and cast up seaweed. Two boats were anchored there. When the two boatmen saw Yamaoka, they called to him.

"Anything to offer?"

Yamaoka lifted his right hand and showed them his folded thumb. Then he moored his boat beside theirs. The four upright fingers was a sign that he had four persons.

One of the boatmen was named Miyazaki no Saburō, from Miyazaki in Etchū. He showed Yamaoka his open left hand. According to the signals, the right hand meant the number of items, the left meant money. His gesture indicated a price of five *kanmon*.

"Try me!" said the second boatman, and he quickly raised his arm, showed an open hand, then held up his index finger. His name was Sado no Jirō and he bid six *kanmon*.

"How dare you!" screamed out Miyazaki. "Don't try to outbid me!"

Sado braced himself for a fight. The two boats tilted, splashing water onto the decks.

Yamaoka looked calmly at the faces of the two boatmen. "You're all excited, aren't you? Neither one of you will go home empty-handed. I'll divide my guests between you, so that they won't be overcrowded. Sado's price will serve."

Yamaoka turned to the travelers. "Go in these boats, two of you in each. Both are going to the western provinces. These boats are hard to move if they're overloaded."

Yamaoka helped the two children to enter Miyazaki's boat, and the mother and Ubatake to enter Sado's. As he did so, both Miyazaki and Sado quietly pressed some money in his hand.

Ubatake pulled on her lady's sleeve and was just saying, "What about the bag that was put in Yamaoka's charge . . . ?" when Yamaoka suddenly pushed his empty boat away.

"Now I take my leave of you. I'm supposed to turn you over to another responsible person. My job is now done. Good luck to you."

They heard the sound of oars moving busily, and Yamaoka's boat was soon far away.

The mother said to Sado, "I suppose you will be rowing along the same route, for the same harbor? . . ."

Sado and Miyazaki looked at each other and laughed loudly. Then Sado replied, "I hear the Chief Priest of the Rengebuji says that any boat you board is the ship of the Buddha, bound for the same Other Shore!"

From then on the two boatmen rowed on in silence. Sado went north, Miyazaki to the south. The passengers called desperately to each other, but the boats merely drew farther apart.

The mother, mad with grief, pulled herself up as far as she could on the gunwales of the boat. She called to the children, "The worst fate has befallen us. We may never see each other again. Anju, always take care of your guardian amulet, the image of Jizō, your guardian god. Zushiō always keep with you the sword your father gave you. And always do your best to keep together!" Anju was her daughter, Zushiō the younger son.

The children could do nothing more than call hopelessly for their mother.

The boats drew farther and farther apart. The children's mouths seemed to stay open like young birds waiting for their food, but their cries no longer could traverse the widening distance.

Ubatake raised her voice to speak to Sado no Jirō, but as he did not turn to listen, she clung to his legs, brown and tough like the trunks of red pines. "What are you doing? How can I go on living without those dear children?

Their mother feels the same. She will feel her life is worthless without them. Turn around and row after the other boat, please. Please, be merciful!''

"Quiet down!" cried Sado, as he aimed a backward kick at her. Ubatake fell to the deck. Her hair came loose and spilled over the side into the water. She rose. "I cannot bear it. Forgive me, my lady," she said, and with this, she leapt into the sea head first.

The boatman cried out and tried to catch her, but he was too late.

The mother now removed her outer robe and passed it over to Sado. This garment has little value, but I want you to have it. Goodbye.'' She put her hand on the gunwale, ready to follow Ubatake.

"You fool," cried Sado, and pulled her down by her hair. "Do you think I am going to let you die? You are much too valuable for that.''

Sado dragged out the boat's hawser and tied her securely with it. He went on rowing due north.

Miyazaki rowed southward along the bank with the two children still calling for their mother.

"Are you still at it?" Miyazaki scolded them. "Maybe the fish at the bottom of the sea can hear you, but not her. Those two have probably reached Sado by now and are already chasing the birds away in the millet fields.''

The two children held tight to each other and wept. Although they had left their home village and traveled great distances, they had at least been with their mother; now, unexpectedly separated from her, they had no idea what they ought to do. Overwhelmed with grief, they were unable to grasp how this separation might affect their own destinies.

When noon came, Miyazaki took out some rice cakes and ate them. Then he gave one to Anju and one to Zushiō. They took the cakes in their hands and held them, as if they did not want to eat; then looking at each other, they burst into tears again. At night, still sobbing, they slept under rush mats with which Miyazaki covered them.

The children passed several days like this on the boat. Miyazaki made the rounds of one bay and inlet after another in Etchū, Noto, Echizen, and Wakasa, looking for a good buyer for his charge.

Although they were young, no one offered to buy them, perhaps because they seemed frail. On the few occasions when someone seemed interested, there were always difficulties in fixing on a suitable price. Eventually Miyazaki began to grow ill-tempered and would strike them, complaining about their habitual weeping.

Miyazaki traveled from one place to another and finally arrived at the harbor of Yura in the province of Tango. Here, at a place named Ishiura, lived a man named Sanshō the Steward. He had a large house and lands. His retainers planted grains in his fields, hunted in the mountains, fished the seas, raised silkworms, wove fabrics, and manufactured everything imaginable in metal goods, pottery, and wooden utensils. Sanshō would buy up any kind of person offered. When Miyazaki could not manage to sell his victims elsewhere, he always brought them here.

Sanshō's overseer came out to the harbor and quickly bought the two children, for seven *kanmon*.

Putting the money away in his purse, Miyazaki told the overseer, "Now that I've finished with the little brats, I feel much better." He went inside the wine shop on the pier.

A fire of blazing coals filled a huge middle space in one room of the gigantic residence built on pillars that were thicker than the span of a man's arms. Facing the fire sat Sanshō, leaning on an arm rest and resting on three piled cushions spread on the floor. On his right and left, like guardian statues at a temple, sat his two sons Jirō and Saburō. Sanshō once had three sons; but after Tarō, the oldest, then sixteen, had witnessed his father brand one of the captives caught after attempting to escape, he had, without a word, wandered out of the house and was never seen again. The incident took place nineteen years before.

The overseer brought Anju and Zushiō forward and commanded them to bow to Sanshō.

The children did not seem to hear but only stared in astonishment. Just sixty that year, Sanshō's face seemed painted with vermilion. He had a wide forehead and full chin, and his hair and beard glittered with silver. The children were more surprised than frightened, and they continued to stare at his face.

Sanshō finally spoke. "So these are the children you bought? They aren't like the others. I'm not quite sure what to do with them. You said they were quite unusual children, but now that you've brought them to me, I think they look sick and pale. I don't see how we can make use of them . . ."

Saburō spoke. While he was the younger of Sanshō's sons, he was nearly thirty. "From what I just saw, they refused to bow after they were told to. And they didn't even identify themselves like the others. They may look frail, but they must be a stubborn pair. Men who serve here begin by cutting firewood and women by drawing saltwater. It should be the same for them."

"That's right," the overseer seconded. "They wouldn't tell me their names either."

Sanshō laughed derisively. "Perhaps they are too stupid. I'll name them myself. I'll call the older girl Fern and her younger brother Lily. Fern, you go to the seaside and scoop up three measures of water a day. Lily, you go to the mountains and gather three loads of firewood a day. I realize that neither of you is very strong, so I won't demand that your loads be too big."

Saburō now spoke. "I think you've been too generous. Take them along," he told the overseer, "and give them the things they need for their work."

The overseer led the children to the hut where the new workers slept. He gave Anju a bucket and a scoop, and Zushiō a basket and a sickle. He also gave each of them a container for carrying their noon meal. The hut for the newer slaves was in a different place from where the other captives lived.

By the time the overseer left, it had gotten dark. There was no lamp in the hut.

It was bitter cold the next morning. The bedding the children had found in the hut the night before had been too dirty to use, so Zushiō had gone off somewhere and found some matting. They covered themselves as they had on the boat and slept together.

Zushiō now took their food containers to the kitchen to obtain their provisions, as he had been told to do the day before by the overseer. Both the roof of the kitchen building and the straw scattered on the ground were covered with frost. The kitchen had a large earthen floor, already filling up with a great many workers waiting for food. As provisions for men and women were given out in different places, Zushiō was scolded once because he tried to obtain both his own and his sister's portions, but when he promised that each would come separately the next morning, his two containers were filled and he received two portions of rice gruel in a food box and some hot water in a wooden bowl. The rice gruel was cooked with salt.

As Anju and Zushiō ate their morning meal, they bravely came to the conclusion that, subjected to such terrible misfortunes as they were, their only recourse was to bow their heads to fate. Then Anju headed toward the seashore and Zushiō toward the mountains. They went together across the frosty grounds through the three gates that encircled Sanshō's grounds, then went their separate ways, looking back at each other many times.

The hill where Zushiō was sent lay near Yura peak, a little to the south of Ishiura. The place where he was to cut brushwood was not far from the base of the mountain. Passing through an area of outcroppings of purple rock, he came to a fairly wide stretch of land where there was a thick growth of trees.

Zushiō went into the grove and looked around him. When he realized that he did not know how to cut firewood, he hesitated to begin and sat vacantly on the fallen leaves, piled like frosty cushions. Eventually he came to himself and tried to cut a branch, then another, only to hurt his finger. He sat down on the leaves again, thinking that if the mountain was this cold, his sister must be all the colder from the wind by the sea. He burst into tears. When the sun had about reached its height, another woodcutter came along, with a load of firewood on his back. He called out to Zushiō. "So you too work for Sanshō the Steward? How much wood are you supposed to cut in a day?"

"I'm supposed to bring back three bundles, but so far I've hardly cut any at all," Zushiō told him quite honestly.

"If you're supposed to cut three, then it's better to finish two of them in the morning. Let me show you the way to cut the branches." The woodcutter put down his own load and quickly cut one bundle for Zushiō.

At this, the boy's spirits rose and he cut a bundle himself by noon and another afterwards.

Anju went north along the riverbank on the way to the beach. She came to the place where saltwater was being scooped up, but she did not know how to do it herself. Gathering her courage, she finally managed to put her ladle in the water, but the waves instantly pulled it out of her hand.

Another girl ladling saltwater nearby retrieved the scoop and returned it to her. "You can't ladle the water that way," she told Anju. "Let me show you how. Put the ladle in your right hand and dip like this. And put the water in the pail; you can hold that with your left hand." She quickly filled up a pailful for Anju.

"Thank you so much," Anju told her. "I wanted to do the work, and it's thanks to you that I've got the idea. Let me try myself now." Anju had now understood the proper method.

The girl took a liking to the simple-hearted Anju. The two ate their noon meal together, told each other about themselves, and swore to treat each other as sisters. The girl told Anju her name was Ise no Kohagi and that she had been sold into slavery at Futamigaura and brought to Sanshō's estates.

So passed the children's first day: by sunset Anju brought back her three loads of saltwater, and Zushiō his three bundles of firewood, both achieved through the kindness of others.

Anju scooped her saltwater and her brother cut his wood; she passed her time thinking of her brother, and Zushiō on his mountain thought only of his sister. They would wait for evening when they could return to their little hut; then the two of them would take each other's hands and repeat to each other how they longed for their father in Tsukushi and their mother in Sado. They wept as they spoke, spoke as they wept.

Ten days passed. The time now came when they were required to leave the hut set aside for newcomers. They were to join their respective groups of male and female workers.

The children insisted they would rather die than be separated. The overseer conveyed this to Sanshō.

"What a lot of nonsense," he replied. "Take the girl to the women's quarters and the boy to the men's."

As the overseer rose to go, Jirō, sitting at the side of his father, called for him to wait. Jirō then said, "Father, as you say, it might be just as well to separate the two. Still, they did say they would rather die than be separated. Fools that they are, they might just manage to kill themselves. Even though they don't bring in much wood or saltwater, we don't want to lose any hands. If you'll permit me, I'd like to work on a scheme that I think would succeed."

"Is that so? I don't want any losses either, of course. Do whatever you think best," Sanshō said and turned away.

Jirō had a hut built by the third gate and let the two children live in it.

One evening, the two children were as usual talking about their parents when Jirō happened to come by and overhear them. Jirō always walked around the property to see that there was no quarreling, thieving, or bullying of the weaker workers by the strong.

Jirō entered the hut and spoke to the children. "Even if you miss your father and mother, Sado is far away. And Tsukushi is even farther. They are not places that children like you could ever get to. If you want to see your parents again, then the best thing to do is to wait until you're grown up." Without another word, he left them.

On another evening, sometime afterward, the two children were again speaking of their parents. This time, Saburō happened to come by and hear what they said. Saburō liked to hunt birds in their nests and so he used to walk around with a bow and arrow in his hands, looking in all the trees.

Every time the children spoke of their parents, they were so eager to see them that they would act out a fantasy together, pretending to decide what steps to take. On this evening Anju said, "I suppose we can't make a long voyage until we are grown up. We want to do something impossible. As I think about it, I realize it's no good for both of us to run away from here. Don't worry about me. You must escape and go on ahead to Tsukushi, meet father, and ask him what to do. And then you must go to Sado and find mother."

Unfortunately, Saburō heard these last words of Anju. Bow and arrow in hand, he abruptly entered the hut. "So. You two are figuring out some scheme to escape from here. Anyone who tries that is branded. That's the rule of this house. And that red iron is hot, let me tell you.''

The two children turned pale. Anju came forward and spoke to Saburō. "It was all made up, what I said, sir. Even if my younger brother could escape, how far do you think he could get? I only said such a thing because we are so anxious to see our parents. Before, we were wishing we could turn into birds, so that we could fly to them. We're just making believe.''

Zushiō added, "What my sister says is true. We always talk about things we can never do. It's only to distract ourselves because we want to see our parents so much.''

Saburō studied their faces for a certain time and said nothing. "Well. If it's make-believe, let it be make-believe. But I heard you talking together, and I know what you said.'' With these words, Saburō left them.

That evening the children went to sleep with uneasy thoughts. Then— how long did they sleep?—they could not be sure, but both were awakened by a noise. Ever since coming to the hut they were permitted a light. In its dim glow they saw Saburō standing by their beds. He suddenly came over and grasped the children's hands. He pulled them up and out the door. They were being dragged along the wide road they had followed while looking up at the pale moon the first time they were taken to meet Sanshō. They climbed three steps. They passed along a corridor. After winding around and around, they arrived in the great hall where they had been taken the day they arrived. Many people now stood there, in silence. Saburō dragged the two of them before the fire, where the coals were red with heat. They had been apologizing to him since he first dragged them from their hut, but as Saburō said nothing and continued to drag them along, the pair finally fell silent. There were three cushions piled opposite the fire, and Sanshō was sitting on them. His face, reflecting the lamps at his sides, seemed to be on fire. Saburō drew out of the fire a pair of glowing hot tongs. He stood staring at them for some time. The iron, at first so hot that it seemed almost transparent, slowly turned black. Suddenly Saburō pulled Anju to him and began to bring the hot iron to her forehead. Zushiō tried to pull at his elbow. Saburō kicked him down and held the boy still with his right knee. He finally managed to press the cross-shaped hot iron onto Anju's forehead.

Anju's screams pierced the stillness of the room. Saburō now pushed her aside, pulled up Zushiō, and pressed the hot iron into his forehead as well. Zushiō's cries now mixed with the slackening sobs of his sister. Saburō then threw down the iron and grabbed the children in the same fashion as before. After looking around the room, he dragged them from the main building as far as the third step, then threw them down on the frozen ground. The children, almost unconscious from pain and fear, somehow sustained themselves and managed without quite knowing how to make their way back to the hut. They fell down on top of their bedding and for a time remained as motionless as two corpses. Then Zushiō called to his sister, "Take out your statue of Jizō." Anju rose at once and took out the amulet case she kept inside her robe. With a trembling hand she untied the string and took out the little image, which she set up beside their beds. They prostrated themselves before it. Suddenly the unbearable pain seemed to melt away, to vanish. Rubbing their foreheads with their hands, they found no traces of the wounds. With a shock of surprise, the two children woke up.

Anju and Zushiō sat up and talked over the experience: they both had had the same dream at the same time. Anju took out her Jizō amulet, looked at it and placed it by her bedside, as she had done in her dream. After they knelt and worshiped, they looked at the forehead of the statue in the dim light. On either side of the sacred white curl of the forehead of the statue, as if carved with a chisel, was a scar in the shape of a cross.

Since the night the children were overheard by Saburō and suffered their terrible dream, Anju's whole being seemed altogether changed. Her expression became tight and drawn; her forehead was pinched and her eyes seemed always to be staring at something far away. And she said nothing. When she came home from the seaside in the evenings, she spoke very little, although before she had eagerly awaited her brother and they would talk over things for hours. Zushiō, worried, asked her what was wrong, but she turned aside his questions with an almost imperceptible smile.

Otherwise Anju did not seem changed. When she did speak it was in the same manner as before, and her behavior also remained the same. Yet Zushiō, so used to comforting his sister and being comforted by her, now watched her undergo a change that upset him beyond measure. He now had no one in whom to confide. Their world seemed even more dreary and barren than before.

The end of the year brought fitful snowfalls. The male and female workers alike stopped their outside work and were assigned to indoor tasks. Anju was to spin thread. Zushiō pounded straw, which needed no special training, but Anju found the spinning difficult. In the evenings, Ise no Kohagi came to teach and help her. Anju said no more to her friend than to her brother; indeed she was often uncivil. Yet Ise no Kohagi took no offense and continued to treat her with sympathy.

The New Year's pine decorations were placed at the gates. But this year there were no ostentatious celebrations. The woman of Sanshō's family always remained in the inner rooms of the mansion and rarely came out, so there was little activity to make things lively. There were only the quarrels that broke out in the men's quarters as they drank sake to toast the New Year. Usually any quarreling was severely punished, but at this time of year, the overseer overlooked any incidents. There were occasions when he failed to notice that blood had been spilled in a fight, and even a murder might go unnoticed.

From time to time Ise no Kohagi would come to visit the children in their lonely hut. She seemed to carry some of the warm atmosphere of the women's quarters with her, and while she chatted gaily, she seemed to bring spring into the winter's darkness, producing even the rare shadow of a smile on the face of Anju.

When the three-day holiday passed, the work of the household began again. Anju spun her thread, Zushiō beat his straw. Anju had become sufficiently accustomed to her spindle so that, even when Kohagi came in the evening to help, there was little for her to do. Although Anju had changed, this quiet, repetitive work was quite satisfactory for her; indeed it relaxed her and somehow helped disperse her one obsession. Zushiō, who could not talk with his sister as he had before, felt reassured when he saw Kohagi come and chat with Anju as she sat spinning.

The water became warmer and grass began to sprout. On the morning of the day before the outside work was to begin again, Jirō made the rounds of the whole mansion and came to the hut. "How is it going? Will you be able to go off to your duties tomorrow? There are evidently some workers who are sick. When the overseer told me, I thought I would go from hut to hut and see for myself."

Zushiō, who had been beating straw, looked up to answer; but before he could speak, Anju stopped her spinning and, in a most unaccustomed fashion, jumped up and spoke to Jirō.

"Concerning our outside work, I have a request to make, sir. I would like to work in the same place as my brother. Perhaps you could be good enough to arrange for us to work on the mountain together." There was a flush of red on her pale face, and her eyes were sparkling.

Zushiō was profoundly surprised to see again such a change come over his sister, and he found it strange that she suddenly expressed a wish to cut wood without mentioning it to him first. He could only stare at her.

Jirō said nothing but regarded Anju's manner very closely. Anju told him, "I want nothing more. This is the only thing I ask. Please let me go to the mountain with him." She repeated her request again and again.

Jirō finally spoke. "The question of who is permitted to do what kinds of work around here is very important. My father makes all the decisions himself. But it seems to me, Fern, that you have made your request after a good deal of careful thought. I'll take it on myself to arrange things for you. I'm sure you'll be able to go to the mountain. Don't worry about anything. I'm glad you two young ones got through the winter safely." With this, he left the hut.

Zushiō put down his pounding stick and came over to his sister. "What was all that about? I would be so happy if you could come with me to the mountain. But why did you ask him all of a sudden like that? Why didn't you say anything to me about it?"

Anju's face shone with happiness. "You are quite right to be surprised. But actually, until I saw his face I had no idea of asking him anything. I just thought of it, all of a sudden."

"Is that so? How strange," said Zushiō, staring at her face as if he had never seen her before.

The overseer came to the hut with a sickle and basket. "Fern," he called, "I understand you're not going to scoop seawater anymore. You're going to cut firewood. I've brought what you need and I'm going to take back the ladle and the bucket."

"I'm sorry to cause you so much trouble," said Anju, getting up quickly. She returned the pail and ladle to him.

The overseer took them but lingered on, as if his business in the hut were not yet finished. He seemed to smile, but in his expression was a trace of embarrassment. He was a man who listened to orders from the whole family of Sanshō as if from the gods themselves, and he would carry them out without hesitation, no matter how cruel and rigorous they might be. Yet by nature he was reluctant to see others suffer, or in agony. He felt things were best when they went smoothly, with nothing distasteful involved. The forced smile on his face was a habitual sign that he realized he would have to say or cause someone else trouble.

The overseer spoke to Anju. "I've still got something to do. You see, Jirō asked the Master about this business of your cutting firewood and tried to make him agree. Saburō was there too, and he said that if you wanted to go up to the mountain, you should be made to look like a boy. The Master laughed and said it was a good idea. So now I've got to cut off your hair and take it back with me."

Zushiō heard this as if he had been pierced to the heart. His eyes filled with tears as he looked at his sister.

Surprisingly, the flush of happiness did not fade from Anju's face. "Of course. If I'm going to cut firewood, I have to be a man. Cut it off with the sickle." She bared her neck to the overseer.

Her long glossy hair was quickly cut with one stroke of the sharp instrument.

The next morning the two children, with their baskets on their backs and their sickles tied to their waists, walked hand in hand out of the gate. This was their first occasion to walk together since they came to Sanshō's estates.

Zushiō could not fathom his sister's motivations; he felt lonely and sad. The day before, after the overseer left, he had tried by various means to coax an explanation from her, but she seemed lost in her own thoughts and never made them clear to him.

When they arrived at the foot of the mountain, Zushiō could bear it no longer. "I just can't believe we're walking together like this after such a long time. I should feel so happy, but I really feel sad. Even when I hold your hand, I can't bear to look at your bald head. I am sure you are thinking about something, hiding it from me. Why can't you tell me about it?"

Anju wore the same joyful expression she showed the day before, and her large eyes were sparkling. She did not answer her brother but grasped his hand all the harder.

There was a marshy spot where the path to the mountain began. Along the shore, last year's withered rushes remained, in bunched confusion, but small green shoots were now appearing in the yellowed grass at the side of the road. Moving to the right and climbing up, the children came to a crevice in the rock where a spring of clear water came gushing out. Passing the spring, they wound up a steep path with a wall of rock on the right.

Just then the morning sun shone onto the surface of the rocks. Anju found a spot where a tiny violet was blooming, its roots sunk down in a crevice weathered between the overlapping rocks. She pointed it out to Zushiō. "Look! It's spring!"

Zushiō nodded but said nothing. The girl kept her secret to herself and the boy nursed his sorrow, and so their conversation was broken and their words sifted away like water into sand.

When they arrived at the spot where Zushiō had worked the year before, he stopped. "This is where we have to cut wood," he said.

"Let's go on and climb a bit higher," Anju told him. She immediately began to continue upward. Puzzled, Zushiō followed her. After a while they reached a relatively high place that seemed the peak of the lower mountain.

Anju stood there staring intently toward the south. Her eyes followed the upper reaches of the Okumo River as it passed Ishiura and flowed into the harbor at Yura; they stopped at a pagoda thrusting from the dense foliage on Nakayama, a mountain about two miles from the other side of the river-bank. "Look Zushiō!" she called out. "I know you must think it strange that I have been thinking about things for such a long time and I haven't been talking with you the way I always have. I know it. But today, you don't have to cut any wood. And you must listen very carefully to what I tell you. Kohagi was brought here from near Ise. She explained to me the way the road runs from her home to this place. She told me that if you cross over Nakayama mountain there, then Kyoto, the capital, is very close. It's very hard to go directly to Tsukushi from here, and to go back to Sado is also too difficult. But you can certainly get to the capital. Ever since we left Iwashiro with mother, we have only fallen on terrible people, but if fortune turns for the better, there's no telling that you won't meet some kind people as well. So I want you to gather your courage and escape from this place. You must go to Kyoto. If through the protection of the gods and buddhas, you are for-tunate enough to meet some good-hearted person, you may be able to get to Tsukushi and find father. And perhaps you can find our mother in Sado, too. Throw away your sickle and basket. Take only your box of food with you."

Zushiō said nothing, but as he listened to his sister, tears ran down his cheeks. "But then Anju, what will happen to you?"

"Don't worry about me. Do what you have to do as if we were doing it together. When you find father and bring mother back from the island the way I told you, then come back and try to help me."

"But after I'm gone, I'm afraid you'll be treated in some terrible way," Zushiō said. He remembered the frightening dream in which he and his sister were branded.

"I suppose it will be hard for me, but don't worry. I'll be able to put up with it. They would never kill a slave they paid good money for. If you're not here, I suppose they'll make me do the work of two. But don't worry. I'll cut lots of firewood there where you showed me. Maybe I couldn't man-age six bundles, but I'm sure I could cut four, or even five. Let's climb down over there and leave our baskets and sickles. I'll go with you to the foot of the mountain." She started off ahead of him.

Without making any conscious decision, Zushiō followed her instinctive-ly. Anju was now fifteen, Zushiō thirteen; already adopting an adult's man-ner she seemed now as wise as if possessed by some higher power. Zushiō simply could not go against her wishes.

When they got down as far as the grove of trees, the two put down their sickles and baskets on the fallen leaves. Anju took out her amulet and pressed it in her brother's hand. "You know how much I prize this. I want you to keep it for me until we meet again. Think that the image is me and take good care of it, just like your guardian sword."

"But Anju, what will you do without it?"

"I want you to have it. You will face greater dangers than I. When you don't come back this evening, they will send a party to search you out. No matter how fast you go, if you simply run off without a plan, you're sure to be caught. Go along the upper reaches of the river we saw just now, until you get to Wae. If you are lucky enough not to be seen and can manage to get to the opposite bank, Nakayama can't be much farther. Go there, to the temple—we saw the pagoda sticking up through the trees—and ask for asylum. Stay there for awhile, until your pursuers have given up and gone away. Then run away from the temple."

"But do you think the priest in the temple will give me shelter?"

"It's all a question of chance. If your luck is good, the priest will hide you."

"I understand. What you've said seems to have come from the gods or Buddha himself. I've made up my mind. I will do exactly what you say."

"I'm so happy. You've understood everything I told you. The priest is surely a fine man. I know he will take care of you."

"Yes. I've come to believe that myself. I'll get away and go to the capital. I'll find father and mother too. And I'll come back for you." Zushiō's eyes took on the same sparkle as his sister's.

"I'll go down to the bottom with you, so let's hurry." The pair quickly clambered down the hillside. Their whole manner of walking now changed, for Anju's intensity had been transferred to Zushiō as well.

They passed the spot where the spring gushed up from the rocks. Anju took out the wooden bowl in her provision box and dipped into the cool water. "Let us drink this together to celebrate your departure," she said, as she took a draught and passed the bowl to her brother.

Zushiō emptied the bowl completely. "Goodbye then, my dear sister. Please take care of yourself. I will get to the temple at Nakayama without being seen by anyone."

Zushiō rushed down the bit of path remaining on the hillside and took the main road running along the swampy area. He hurried off in the direction of the Okumo River.

Anju stood by the spring and watched the figure of her brother grow smaller as he appeared then disappeared behind rows of pine trees. The sun was almost at its highest point, yet she made no effort to climb the mountain again. Fortunately there seemed no other woodcutters at work nearby, so no one questioned Anju, who stood idling away her time at the foot of the mountain path.

Later the search party sent out by Sanshō to catch the pair picked up a pair of small straw sandals at the edge of the swamp at the bottom of the hill. They belonged to Anju.

Shadows of pine torches threw wild reflections on the gate of the provincial temple at Nakayama. A throng of people pressed at the gate, led by Sanshō's son Saburō, who grasped a white-handled halberd in his hand.

Standing in front of the main building he called out, "I'm from the family of Sanshō the Steward, over at Ishiura. We know for sure one of our workers escaped into the mountains. There's nowhere he could be but here. Hurry up. Hand him over." Saburō's men called out in a similar fashion.

A stone pavement ran from the front of the main temple building out past the gate. Now it was crowded with Saburō's companions, pine torches in their hand, pushing and shoving. Thronging in on either side of them were almost all the monks from the cloisters. Awakened by the clamor outside the gates, they had come out from the inner sanctuaries and the kitchens alike, wondering what was happening.

When the crowd outside first shouted for the gates to be opened, most of the priests wanted them kept shut, afraid that if the men came in there would be disorder and violence. The Chief Priest, Donmyō Risshi, insisted that the gates be opened. But, the door of the main hall remained shut and silent, even after Saburō called for the return of his fugitive.

Saburō stamped his feet and repeated his demand two or three times. Several of his followers called out to the priest; laughter mixed with their shouts.

Finally the door of the main hall opened quietly. The Chief Priest opened it himself. He wore only a simple stole and took on no air of false majesty as he stood at the top of the steps. From behind him came the dim light of a taper burning in perpetual offering. The light flickered over his tall strong frame and illuminated his even face and black eyebrows, not yet touched by age. He was just over fifty.

The Chief Priest began to speak quietly. The unruly search party fell completely silent at the sight of him, and his quiet voice could be heard in every corner.

"So you are looking for some servant who escaped. In this temple, no one would conceal a person without telling me about it. Since I know nothing about it, the person is not here. However I would like to tell you something else. All of you came here in the dead of night, weapons in hand, pushing at the gate and demanding that it be opened. Thinking some insurrection had broken out, or that you were a group supporting some rebellion, I permitted the gate to be opened. Then what do I find? A search for some menial in your household! This is a temple designated by the Imperial family for prayer. The emperor himself has presented us with an inscribed tablet. And copies of the sutras in gold written by the emperor are among the treasures stored in the pagoda. If any kind of violence is caused here, the governor of the province will surely be reprimanded by the officials who oversee the shrines and temples. And if we should report this to the central temple of Tōdaiji,[2] there is no telling what kind of action will be taken by the capital. If you consider the situation, I am sure you will agree it would be best to withdraw quickly. I am not being unpleasant, but I wish to tell you this for you own good." When the Chief Priest finished speaking, he quietly shut the door.

Saburō scowled and grimaced at the closed door. But he did not have the courage to break it down and force his way in. His followers only whispered noisily together, like a wind in the leaves.

Suddenly, a voice called out to them. "Was the one who escaped a little fellow, about twelve or thirteen? If so, I know something about it."

Surprised, Saburō turned to study the speaker. He was an older man who bore more than a passing resemblance to Saburō's own father Sanshō. He was the keeper of the temple bell. The old man went on talking, "If it's that little fellow, I saw him at noon from the bell tower. He was hurrying along outside the temple wall, going south. Didn't look strong, but then he's probably that much more light of foot. He must have gotten pretty far by now."

"So that's it. I can guess how far a boy can get in half a day. Come on!" Saburō hurried away.

The line of pine torches left the temple gate and followed along the outer walls, going south. Watching this from the bell tower, the old man laughed out loud. Startled, two or three crows, asleep in a nearby grove of trees, flew up.

The next day a number of persons were sent out from the temple in all directions. Those who went to Ishiura came back to report that Anju had evidently drowned herself. Those who went south heard that Saburō and his followers went as far as Tanabe, then turned back.

Three days later, the Chief Priest himself left the temple, going in the direction of Tanabe. He took with him a begging bowl as big as a basin and a staff as thick as a man's arm. Zushiō followed him, his hair shaved and wearing a Buddhist robe.

The two walked the roads during the days and stopped in various temples along their way to pass their nights. When they arrived at Shujakuno in Yamashiro, the Chief Priest went to rest in the Gongōdo temple. Then he took his leave of Zushiō. "Always keep your amulet with you, guard it carefully, and you will surely be able to learn something about your parents," he said as a final admonition, then turned and left. Zushiō realized that the priest had told him the same thing as his dead sister.

When Zushiō reached Kyoto, still dressed as a Buddhist priest, he spent the night in Kiyomizu temple.

He slept in a special hall set aside for those who wished to retire for religious devotions. When he awoke the next morning, he saw by his bedside an elderly man, dressed in an old-style court costume. "Whose son are you?" said the old man. "If you have anything precious with you, kindly show it to me. I have been in seclusion here since yesterday evening, praying for the recovery of my daughter, who is ill. In a dream I was granted a revelation. I was told that the boy sleeping behind the lattice at my left possessed a wonderful amulet. I was to borrow it and pray to the image. When I came to look this morning, I found you. Please tell me who you are and lend me the amulet. I am Morozane, the Chief Adviser to the Emperor."[3]

"Sir, I am the son of Mutsu no jō Masauji," Zushiō told him. "Twelve years ago my father went to the temple of Anrakuji in Tsukushi and never seems to have returned. My mother took me who was born in that year and my sister, who was three, to live in Shinobugōri in the province of Iwashiro. I grew to be a big boy there, and then my mother decided that it was time to take my sister and me on a visit to western Japan to see if we could find my father. When we got as far as Echigo, we were seized by some terrible slave traders. My mother was taken to Sado, and my sister and I were sold at Ura in Tango. My sister died there. The precious amulet I carry with me is this image of Jizō." He took it out and handed it to Morozane.

Morozane took the little statue in his hand and, holding it close to his forehead, said a prayer. Next he examined the amulet front and back several times, looking at it with the utmost care. Finally, he spoke. "I have heard of this amulet before. It is a figure in gold of Jizō Bodhisattva, Ruler of Light. This statue was originally brought from Kudara[4] and was paid special reverence by Prince Takami.[5] Since you are in possession of the statue, your noble descent is clear. In the early part of the era of Eihō [1081–1083], when the Retired Emperor[6] was still on the throne, Taira no Masauji was demoted and sent to Tsukushi because he was implicated in a misdemeanor for which the governor of his province was convicted. You are his son. There is no doubt about it. If you have any desire to leave the priesthood, there is a good chance you may later be given an important rank yourself. For the mo-

ment, please come to my home as a guest. Let us return there together
now.''

The woman referred to as Morozane's daughter was actually an adopted
niece of his wife who served as an attendant to the Retired Emperor. Her
mother was a sister of the empress. Although this lady had been ill for some
time, she quickly recovered after praying with the amulet of Zushiō.

Morozane himself had Zushiō returned to secular life and with his own
hands placed on the boy's head the cap appropriate to his new rank. At the
same time he sent a messenger with a letter of pardon to Masauji's place of
exile. But when the messenger reached Tsukushi, he learned that Masauji
was already dead. Zushiō (who had now taken his adult name of Masamichi)
was so grieved by the news that he wasted away to nothing.

In the fall of the same year, Masamichi's name was included on the appointment list as governor of Tango. The appointment was an honorary one;
Masamichi was not required to go to the province and an adjutant was sent
in his place to handle the day-to-day affairs there. However, the first action
Masamichi took was to strictly forbid slavery of any kind throughout the province. Sanshō the Steward now had to free every last one of his slaves and he
began to pay them wages for their work. Sanshō and his family expected to
face a tremendous loss, yet the farmers and the artisans greatly increased the
amount of work they did, and so his family flourished and prospered more
than ever before. The Chief Priest who had helped Zushiō was greatly elevated in rank, and Kohagi, who had befriended Anju, was able to return to
her home village. A pious ceremony of mourning was held in Anju's memory, and a nunnery was built on the shore where she drowned herself.

Having done this much for the province, Masamichi asked for a leave of
absence from his duties and crossed over to Sado, disguising his real identity.

The government authorities on Sado were located at Sawata. Masamichi
went there and requested the officials to search the entire island for his
mother, but her whereabouts was not so simple to discover.

One day Masamichi, lost in his thoughts, left his lodgings and walked
through the town. At some point he found he had strayed away from the
houses and was on a path running through the fields. The sky was clear and
the sun was shining brightly. Masamichi worried to himself over the fact that
he could find no trace of his mother. Perhaps, he pondered, the buddhas
and gods would not help him because he had simply turned his duties over
to others rather than going around to make the search himself. By chance he
noticed a rather large farm house. Looking through the sparse hedge that

grew on the south side of the building, he saw an open area where the earth had been pounded flat. Straw mats were spread there on which cut grains of millet had been spread to dry. In the midst of the drying grain sat a woman dressed in rags, who carried a long pole in her hand to chase the sparrows coming to peck at the grain. She seemed to murmur what sounded like a song.

Without knowing precisely why, Masamichi was attracted to something in the woman. He stopped and looked inside the hedge. The woman's unkempt hair was clotted with dust. When he looked at her face, he saw she was blind, and a strong surge of pity for her went through him. As the moments passed, he began to understand the words of the little song she was muttering to herself. His body trembled as if he had a fever, and tears welled up in his eyes. For these were the words the woman was repeating over and over to herself:

> Anju koishiya, hōyare ho
> Zushiō koishiya, hōyare ho
> Tori mo shō aru mono nareba
> Tō tō nigeo, awazu to mo.
>
> My Anju, I yearn for you.
>   Fly away!
> My Zushiō, I yearn for you.
>   Fly away!
> Little birds, if you are living still,
>   Fly, fly far away!
> I will not chase you.

Masamichi stood transfixed, enraptured by her words. Suddenly his whole body seemed on fire: he had to grit his teeth to hold back the animal scream welling up within him. As though freed from invisible chains, Masamichi rushed through the hedge. Tramping on the millet grains, he threw himself at the feet of the woman. The amulet, which he had been holding up in his right hand, pushed against his forehead when he threw himself on the ground.

The woman realized that something bigger than a sparrow had come storming into the millet. She stopped her endless song and stared ahead of her with her blind eyes. Then, like dried seashells swelling open in water, her eyes began to moisten and to open.

"Zushiō!" she called out. They rushed into each other's arms.

January 1915

Rekishi sono mama to rekishibanare

THE ESSAY "Rekishi sono mama to rekishibanare," which might be translated as "History as It Is and History Ignored," was published less than a month after the appearance of "Sanshō dayū" in January 1915. The text is often quoted to reveal Ōgai's aesthetic intentions in his late historical writings; it is included here as a kind of postscript to "Sanshō dayū," since the story is discussed at some length in the essay.

THERE HAS BEEN considerable discussion, even among my friends, as to whether or not my recent works that make use of actual historical figures can be considered as fiction. At a time when there has been no shortage of scholars who, under the aegis of an authoritarian ethic, insist that novels should be written in some particular fashion or other, rendering a judgment becomes rather difficult. I myself recognize in the works I have written considerable differences in the degree to which I have taken an objective point of view about my own material. For example, "Kuriyama Daizen" turned out to be little more than a simple synopsis, because of my bad health and limited time. For that reason, when I submitted the story to an editor of *Taiyō* magazine, I told him I would prefer to have it put with other miscellaneous articles, rather than have it printed as fiction. He agreed. On this one occasion I did not proofread my manuscript, and when I saw the final version as it appeared in the magazine, the text was filled with *furigana*[1] and printed as fiction. I was especially distressed to find that evidently several people had been assigned to add the *furigana*; as a result, the readings changed every two or three pages.[2] Such mistakes were, of course, inevitable.

Leaving aside the problems of such errors as those found in "Kuriyama Daizen," the kind of work I am now writing does differ from the fiction of other writers. I have not in my recent historical works indulged in the free adaptation and rejection of historical fact common to this type of composition. Previously, for example, when I wrote the drama *Nichiren shōnin tsujizeppō* [The wayside sermons of Saint Nichiren],[3] I did merge together elements from Nichiren's later treatise on the security of the country[4] with others from his earlier outdoor sermons preached in Kamakura. I have, however, completely rejected this method in my recent writing.

Why? My motives are simple. In studying historical records, I came to revere the reality that was evidenced in them. Any wanton change seemed distasteful to me. This is one of my motives. Secondly, if contemporary authors can write about life "just as it is" and find it satisfactory, then they ought to appreciate a similar treatment of the past.

Questions of literary workmanship aside, my works differ in a variety of ways from those of others, but the real basis for all those differences lies, I believe, in what I have written above.

A number of my friends say that other writers choose their material and treat it on an emotional basis, while I do so on a rational one. Yet I hold this to be true of all my literary work, not merely of the stories based on historical

TRANSLATED BY DARCY MURRAY

characters. In general, I would say that my works are not "Dionysian" but "Apollonian." I have never exerted the kind of effort required to make a story "Dionysian." And indeed, if I were able to expend a comparable effort, it would be an effort to make my creation all the more contemplative.

Just as I disliked changing the reality in history, I became bound by history in spite of myself. Suffering under these bonds, I thought I must break loose from them.

While my brother Tokujirō was alive, I collected a number of brief stories of various sorts. Among them was one about a woman who chased birds from the millet, and I told my brother I might turn the story into a one-act play. He told me that when I finished, I should submit it to the Naruta troupe.[5] Danjūrō was still alive at that time.

The story of the woman chasing the birds from the millet is part of the legend of Sanshō the Steward. I now took this simple plan for a one-act play, discarded as easily as it was conceived, and decided to resurrect it in the form of a short story. The virtue of a legend like Sanshō the Steward is that there is enough of a fixed story to prevent the writer from completely losing himself as he goes along; on the other hand, one would not be bound to pursue the story in precisely the fashion that I have. Without examining the legend in too much detail, I let myself be taken by a dreamlike image of this old story that seems itself a dream.

Long ago in Mutsu there was a man called Iwaki Hangan Masauji. In the winter of the first year of Eihō [1081], he was exiled for some offense to a temple, the Anrakuji, in Tsukushi. His wife took their two children to live in the Shinobu district of Iwashiro.[6] The daughter, who was the elder, was named Anju, and the son, Zushiō. Their mother waited until they were old enough, and then all three set out in search of the father. When they came to the Bay of Naoe in Echigo and were sleeping beneath the Ōge bridge, a slave dealer named Yamaoka Tayū arrived and lured them aboard his boat. An old woman named Ubatake accompanied the mother and children. Once Yamaoka had rowed them out into the open sea, he separated them and sold them to two boat captains. One, Sado no Jirō, bought the mother and Ubatake, then headed toward Sado. The other, Miyazaki no Saburō, bought the two children and went to Yura in Tango. The mother was delivered to Sado and set to chasing away birds from the millet; Ubatake had drowned herself during the passage. After reaching Yura, Anju and Zushiō were sold to someone called Sanshō the Steward. The girl was made to draw seawater and the boy to gather brushwood. The children pined after their mother, and when they tried to run away, their foreheads were branded as punishment. The sister, who stayed behind so her brother could escape, was tortured and killed. The boy, aided by a monk from the provincial temple in Nakayama, went to Kyoto. At the temple of Kiyomizu, Zushiō met a nobleman named Umezuin. Since Umezuin was over seventy and without an heir, he had retired to the temple to pray, in the hope of being granted a son. Zushiō was adopted by Umezuin and concurrently was named governor of Mutsu and Tango. He traveled to Sado and escorted his mother back to Kyoto. He entered Tango and had Sanshō the Steward killed with a bamboo saw. Sanshō had three sons: Tarō, Jirō, and Saburō. The older two were spared for the compassion they had shown Zushiō; the youngest was killed for having joined his father in persecuting him. These are the outlines of the legend as I know it.

Following this general account, I wrote my version according to my own imagination. The basic language of my story was composed in the kind of modern colloquial style I have long been accustomed to; the conversations take place in contemporary Tokyo language, and only in the words spoken by Sanshō and Yamaoka did I add a certain archaic element. Yet accustomed to dealing with actual historical figures as I am, I could not write the story in complete disregard for the period in which it took place. In choosing names for the various objects used at the time, I employed words I found recorded in a dictionary of old Japanese[7] I had close at hand. I also used the old forms of such things as court titles. Eventually, a certain number of classical nouns were inserted into the modern colloquial structure. Not wishing to slight the particular period itself, I constructed a chronology for the story. I arranged that Masauji, exiled in 1081, should leave behind a three-year-old Anju and a newly born Zushiō; then I placed the events of the entire story during the sixth and seventh year of Kanji [1093,1094], when Anju turned fourteen and Zushiō twelve or thirteen.

I could not formulate a clear picture of Umezuin, the man who took in Zushiō; I knew of no one else having a similar name other than Fujiwara no Motozane,[8] who was called Umezu Daijin. Since Motozane died at the age of twenty-four in the second year of Eiman [1166]—making the period later and his age wrong—I produced Fujiwara Morozane[9] who became Regent for a second time in the sixth or seventh year of Kanji.

I also noted that Masauji, the father of Zushiō, was said in the original legend to be a descendant of Taira no Masakado.[10] Since I did not find this idea of interest, I made him instead a descendent of Prince Takami in the branch of the Taira family related to the Emperor Kammu. I also saw that Sanshō was said to have had three sons. Tarō and Jirō in particular had taken pity on Anju and Zushiō; Saburō had tormented them. Since I did not feel the necessity for having two compassionate brothers, I eliminated Tarō.

When I finished the story, I looked over what I had written and was struck by a slight incongruity: while Zushiō's thirteenth year may have been an appropriate age for his enslavement by Sanshō, it was not a likely one for his becoming provincial governor. Yet he certainly would not have established himself in Kyoto and simply remained there for years without thinking about his father and mother. I would have had too great a difficulty in finding him a motive to do so. Thus I ended by committing even the creation of a thirteen-year-old governor to the unbounded powers of the Fujiwara clan. After all, the ceremony of attaining manhood at age thirteen was certainly not considered untoward.

All this is a precise behind-the-scenes account of the way in which I composed "Sanshō dayū." Since the legend was related to the question of slavery, it was inevitable that I should mention such issues as emancipation in the course of writing the story. In any case, I wrote "Sanshō dayū" using history as a point of departure. When I looked over what I had written, I somehow felt that using history in this fashion was unsatisfactory. This is an honest confession on my part.

January 1915

GYOGENKI

"GYOGENKI" (the Japanese pronunciation for the name of the Chinese Taoist nun and poetess Yü Hsüan-chi) is one of several stories that reveal Ōgai's interest in Chinese history and culture. Yü Hsüan-chi and the poet Wen T'ing-yun, two major characters of the story, were among the most talented of the T'ang poets, their work eclipsed only by that of the greatest writers, Tu Fu, Li Po, and Po Chü-i.

Ōgai's narrative, to an English reader at least, may seem more of an exploration than a finished story. Using the bare historical facts known to him, Ōgai expands them in order to raise questions concerning the nature of the connections between artistic and sexual instincts (a problem closely related to the nature of Taoism as well). He does not always answer them, however.

The narrative recounts the nature of a series of friendships between Yü Hsüan-chi and a variety of persons who play differing roles with respect to her: Li I, the wealthy man who wants her for a concubine, Ts'ai-p'in, another nun with whom she has a lesbian relationship, and Ch'en-mou, who becomes her lover. None of these human relationships was successful; it was only with a fellow poet, Wen T'ing-yun, something of a wastrel himself, that she could maintain a steady and productive contact. The two had an instinctive understanding of each other from the beginning, and both, in Ōgai's view, seem to have shared qualities (fear and jealousy in her, a wildness of untrammeled spirit in him) that kept them from normal successful lives, yet, paradoxically, provided them with the wellsprings of their art.

"Gyogenki" is filled with fascinating details about human activities in China, and for the same reason, it is rather difficult to read, since a certain familiarity with Chinese history and culture on the part of the reader was assumed by the author. Nevertheless a close reading of the text is most rewarding, not only for the human interest of the various episodes presented and for the succinctness of Ōgai's speculations and observations, but for the opportunity to read Chinese poetry in a psychological setting created by a writer able to grasp both the world of T'ang China and our own.

 YÜ HSÜAN-CHI[1] was taken to prison and charged with murder. The literati of the capital at Ch'ang-an were jolted by the rapidly spread report.

The Taoist religion flourished during the T'ang dynasty [618–907] in China because the Taoists, capitalizing on the emperor's family name of Li, proclaimed Lao-tzu to be their founder and led people into believing that devotion to him was equivalent to veneration of the Imperial ancestors.[2] During the T'ien-pao era [742–756], two main Taoist complexes had been built, the T'ai-ch'ing monastery in the Western capital at Ch'ang-an and the T'ai-wei monastery in the Eastern capital at Lo-yang. Every large city also had a branch monastery called Tzu-chi-kung where solemn ceremonies were observed on fixed days. Within the T'ai-ch'ing there were many *lou-kuan*. A Taoist *kuan* was the equivalent of a Buddhist temple, and *lou-kuan* were monks' or nuns' quarters. Yü Hsüan-chi lived in one of these, the Hsien-i-kuan of T'ai-ch'ing.

Reports of Hsüan-chi's beauty circulated through Ch'ang-an for many years. She was known more for her lush body than her austere looks. One would expect that, since she was a nun, she would dislike soiling the purity of her beauty with makeup, but this was not the case. She was always gorgeously made up. She was twenty-six when imprisoned in 868 during the reign of I-tsung.[3]

Hsüan-chi was admired by the literati of Ch'ang-an as a beauty but also as an accomplished poetess. Chinese poetry, of course, reached a peak during the T'ang dynasty. After the towering geniuses of Li Po of Lung-hsi and Tu Fu of Hsiang-yang,[4] the verses of Po Chü-i of T'ai-yüan[5] captured the universal emotions of men and the lutes of Ch'ang-an still resonated to his poetic laments. Hsüan-chi was five when Po Chü-i died in 846. Extremely intelligent, she had already memorized many volumes of poems in both ancient and modern style by Po Chü-i and his contemporary equal, Yüan Wei-chih.[6] Hsüan-chi composed her first seven-character verses at age thirteen. By fifteen, her poems were already being circulated among the connoisseurs of the capital.

Small wonder, then, that the ears of society buzzed when this beautiful poetess was jailed for murder.

Yü Hsüan-chi was born in a house on one of the small crooked lanes between the main streets of Ch'ang-an. Every family in that Red Lantern dis-

TRANSLATED BY DAVID DILWORTH

trict reared their daughters to be entertainers. The Yü house was no exception, and when Hsüan-chi expressed an early desire to learn poetry, her parents gladly consented and hired a poor struggling student of the neighborhood to teach her meter and rhyme in hopes, they said, of her someday becoming a "tree blossoming with riches."

In the spring of 857, the female entertainers of the Yü house were often summoned to entertain at a certain inn. One night, the guest of the inn was Ling Hu-kao, a son of the Prime Minister Ling Hu-t'ao.[7] This son was always accompanied by a fellow aristocrat, Fei-ch'eng, but tonight they had brought a man named Wen whom they addressed by the nickname of Chung-k'uei.[8] While the two nobles were dressed in splendid robes, Wen wore rags; the female entertainers at first took him for a servant as he seemed to be at the beck and call of the young noblemen. But as the party grew warmer with wine, Wen Chung-k'uei started to glare menacingly at the two nobles, and then to shout curses at them. He next ordered the female entertainers to play their lute and flute while he sang a poem. To their further amazement, he sang an extraordinarily beautiful poem in such splendid voice and perfect melody that he could not have been an amateur. The female entertainers had seen the mean-looking Chung-k'uei being insulted by the two young aristocrats and so had ridiculed him themselves. Now they all gathered closely around him as he sang. When Wen borrowed their instruments, they found his musical talent also surpassed their own. They were on good terms with him after that.

The female entertainers often returned to the Yü house talking of Wen, and Hsüan-chi once mentioned him to her tutor, who exclaimed in surprise: "This Wen Chung-k'uei must be Wen Ch'i of T'ai-yüan; he is also named T'ing-yin, and his formal name is Fei-ch'ing.[9] He is called Wen Pa-ch'a too because he is able to compose an eight-character verse at the poetry contests after clasping his hands together eight times. The name Chung-k'uei comes from the forbidding look of his face. Among contemporary poets he has no equal except Li Shang-yin.[10] Sometimes Tuan Ch'eng-shih[11] is ranked with them, but Tuan is really inferior to either of them."

Upon learning this, Hsüan-chi used to ask about Wen every time her sisters returned from entertaining Ling Hu-kao. They in turn began speaking of Hsüan-chi each time they met Wen. His curiosity aroused by their stories of this beautiful young poetess, Wen came to call one day at the Yü house.

When they first met, Hsüan-chi seemed like a peony bud just ready to bloom. Although Wen consorted with young noblemen, he was already forty and had features worthy of his nickname Chung-k'uei. He had married young and had a son named Hsien about the age of Hsüan-chi.

Hsüan-chi smoothed her collar and bowed deeply to Wen. He had been prepared to treat her as he did the female entertainers, but immediately changed his manner. As they conversed, he quickly realized that Hsüan-chi was no ordinary girl. This flowerlike fifteen-year-old was not the least bit coquettish and coy; she spoke as frankly as a man.

"I understand you are an accomplished poetess. May I see some of your recent verse?" Wen inquired.

"I have unfortunately not had a good teacher yet; how then could I have anything worth displaying? Still, one glance from Pai-le[12] and I would speed a thousand *li*. Will you name some theme for me?" she replied.

Wen could not repress a smile—how inappropriate for this young blossom to compare herself to a charging horse!

Hsüan-chi rose and placed a writing brush and ink before Wen. Wen immediately wrote: "Willows on the banks of the Yangtze." After musing a bit, Hsüan-chi wrote the following poem.

> *Willows on the Banks of the Yangtze*
>
> Green carpets the wild banks,
> Willows shrouded in light mist stretch to the distant pavilion,
> Shadows darken the autumnal waters,
> Petals shower upon the fisherman's head.
> Fish lurk in the hollows among old roots,
> Low branches tie the traveler's boat.
> Wind and rain lash the night outside,
> Startling me from my dream, deepening my melancholy.

After one reading Wen pronounced it excellent. He had participated in the poetry contests seven times and found the imposing-looking scholars unable to extemporize a single good verse. None of them could even remotely compare with this girl.

After this, Wen called frequently upon the Yü residence. Their conversations became one continuing loom of poetry.

In 847, when he was thirty, Wen left T'ai-yüan to take the *chin-shih*[13] examinations for the first time. Completing his poems long before his candle was consumed, and observing those sitting nearby struggling over their own, he offered to help. Each subsequent time he took the examinations, he composed poems for seven or eight of them, some of whom then passed the examinations. Wen, however, never passed.

Despite these repeated failures, Wen's fame outside the examination halls spread among the literati of Ch'ang-an, and Ling Hu-t'ao, who became prime minister in 851, often invited Wen to his parties. On one occasion Ling asked Wen a question about a certain phrase in the *Chuang-tzu*.[14] Wen's immediate reply was correct, but his words were quite indiscreet: "It appears in the text and is not an obscure allusion. Your excellency should read at times in the leisure hours your gout forces upon you."

Since Emperor Hsüan-tsung[15] also admired the words of a melody called the "P'u-sa-mang," Ling Hu-t'ao presented some accompanying verses for the emperor's enjoyment. Actually he had had Wen compose them and then had sworn him to secrecy. But Wen had leaked the true source one night when drunk. Moreover, he had once remarked, "Within the library is a general who only sits and waits"—ridiculing Ling's lack of education.

In due course, Wen's poetic reputation became known even to Emperor Hsüan-tsung when he sought a second verse among the poets of the capital to link with his own first verse. In response to the emperor's verse "A hairpin of gold," Wen submitted the verse "And earrings of jade," for which he was showered with praise by the emperor. The emperor was fond of leaving the palace incognito and soon after learning Wen's name arranged to encounter him casually at an inn. Not recognizing the emperor as they conversed, Wen gradually became arrogant and insulting.

After the poet Ch'en Hsün became head of the poetry academy, Wen was given a seat apart, and the second seat was left empty. As Wen's literary fame continued to increase, both Emperor Hsüan-tsung and Prime Minister Ling had to admire his talent, although they despised him personally. Wen's older sister, the wife of Chao-chüan, and other well-placed friends made futile entreaties on behalf of Wen's situation.

Among Wen's friends was a rich man named Li I, almost ten years Wen's junior but very talented in poetry. It was now the spring of 860. Wen had just returned to Ch'ang-an after a long sojourn in Hsiang-yang and Li came to call upon him. In Hsiang-yang, Wen had served for some time as a minor offical under the provincial governor, Hsü Shang, but he finally became bored and resigned. On Wen's desk were some poems of Hsüan-chi that Li happened to notice. He was very impressed with them and asked about their author. Wen revealed the authoress was a flowerlike young girl to whom he had begun to teach poetry three years earlier. Li asked the exact location of the Yü residence and then, as if suddenly remembering a previous appointment, rose from his seat. He sped quickly to the Yü residence where he announced to Hsüan-chi's parents that he wished to take her as his concubine. Her parents were persuaded by an extremely generous sum of money.

Hsüan-chi was brought out to meet Li. Now eighteen, she was incomparably more beautiful than when Wen first discovered her. Li himself was a handsome youth. He begged her to be his concubine and, since she did not exactly refuse, the matter was agreed upon then and there. Several days later, Li welcomed Hsüan-chi into his villa in the suburbs of Ch'ang-an.

At this time, Li thought his newly aroused desires would be satisfied, but his passion was unexpectedly frustrated. Every time Li tried to embrace Hsüan-chi she would turn and flee; when he tried to force himself upon her, she would scream loudly. The villa became a place to which Li came with burning desires in the evening only to return home unsatisfied at dawn. He began to doubt that Hsüan-chi was sexually normal. But if she were not, she would surely have refused him in the first place. He could not imagine she didn't like him—why, she had sobbed so uncontrollably that she had clung to him, trembling.

His overtures constantly rebuffed, Li's nerves gave way; he sank deeper and deeper into mental vacuity wherever he was, awake or asleep. Li's legal wife, seeing her husband's behavior becoming stranger and stranger, began to spy upon his movements. Through a servant's report, she eventually learned he was keeping Hsüan-chi in the villa. After a nasty quarrel, her father showed up to reprimand Li who finally promised to release Hsüan-chi.

Li went to the villa and urged Hsüan-chi to return to her parents. But she refused, saying that even should they forgive her she could not endure the ridicule of the other girls. Li then went to an old acquaintance, a Taoist priest named Chao Lien-shih, and arranged for Hsüan-chi to be placed under his care. This was how Hsüan-chi became a Taoist nun living in the Hsien-i-kuan.

Hsüan-chi blossomed into a flower of extraordinary talent and intelligence. Her poems were now wrought with a superior elegance and precision. After beginning study under Wen, she read so diligently in the classics, and so carefully honed her poetic vocabulary, that she almost forgot to sleep and eat. At the same time an ambition to establish her own poetic fame gradually welled up in her bosom.

Prior to becoming Li's concubine, Hsüan-chi had gone one day to the Taoist monastery, the Ch'ung-chen, and seeing the names of the successful *chin-shih* examinees recorded in the Southern Pavilion, she resentfully composed the following poem.

> Great piled clouds blanket my sight,
>   shattering the brightness of spring,
> Bright silver verses spring up like flowers before my feet,
> How hateful the gauzy feminine robes
>   cloaking my talent.
> I lift my head, vainly jealous of
>   these honored names.

Hsüan-chi's feminine body and masculine mind can be seen in this poem. Being female, she naturally longed for some excellent gentleman; but this was a woman's yearning for a male to depend upon, like some vine winding around the trunk of a tree, and not a directly sexual kind of desire. Because of this, Hsüan-chi had responded to Li's request. But as her longing was not sexual, the nights in his villa had been intolerable experiences.

Hsüan-chi, now within the Hsien-i-kuan, was able to live without worry, since Li had left her enough money for her expenses when he departed. While Chao was instructing her in the Taoist classics, she fell in love with them. Hitherto the Confucian classics and histories had been her daily fare; now the words of Lao-tzu and Chuang-tzu stimulated her mind with fresh and strange ideas.

At that time the Taoist observed a practice called "the true technique of centering one's vitality."[16] Twice on the first day of each month, after fasting three days in advance, they practiced such methods of self-cultivation as "the concentration of the four eyes and four nostrils."[17] After practicing such methods under the strictest discipline for over a year, Hsüan-chi suddenly experienced enlightenment. Becoming a true woman, she found what she lacked at Li's villa. This release occurred in 861.

Hsüan-chi became intimate with another Taoist nun who had some literary taste. She shared her room and food with this girl, named Ts'ai-p'in, and also bared her soul to her. One day Hsüan-chi presented this poem to Ts'ai-p'in.

> I shy before the sun, keeping its rays with my gauze sleeves;
> Languishing in spring, I can scarely rise to make myself up.
> Far easier to gain a priceless treasure
> Than to find a man with a true heart.
> Sunk into my pillow damp with tears,
> My heart secretly breaks among the blossoms.
> Since I could have a glimpse of Sung Yü[18]
> Why should I resent Wang Ch'ang?[19]

Ts'ai-p'in was small and impetuous. At sixteen she was three years younger than Hsüan-chi and completely dominated by her solemn roommate. When the two quarreled, Ts'ai-p'in always ended the tearful loser. This happened daily, but they quickly made up again. Such intimacy the Taoist nuns whisperingly called *tui-shih*, "eating together."[20] Their whispering was mixed with envy and jealousy.

That autumn, Ts'ai-p'in suddenly disappeared. This happened while an itinerant sculptor working in Chao's quarters took his leave and also disappeared, When nuns who had previously been critical of their intimacy now spoke of Hsüan-chi's desolation to Chao, he laughed, and thinking of their nicknames Yu-wei and Hui-lan, punned: "The duckweed has flown with the wind, leaving the orchid alone again."[21]

Chao required strict discipline during observances of Taoist ceremonies, but otherwise was not particular about persons visiting the nuns' quarters. As Hsüan-chi's reputation gradually rose, she had many callers seeking specimens of her calligraphy from her. Such callers often brought presents of money or goods. Among them were also callers who came under the pretext of obtaining a letter, but who were really motivated by reports of her beauty. Whenever a scholar would arrive with wine to entice her to drink with him, it is said she would call the servants and have him escorted to the gate.

However, after Ts'ai-p'in disappeared, Hsüan-chi's attitude changed greatly. When scholars of some literary merit came to beg a specimen of her poetry, she began having them stay for tea and entertained them with pleasant conversation. Once entertained in this way, a scholar would come again with a friend. The rumor that Hsüan-chi enjoyed visitors soon spread among the literati of Ch'ang-an. There was no danger of being driven away even if one brought wine.

But whenever some illiterate fellow would appear, vainly enticed by her reputation as a beauty, Hsüan-chi would ruthlessly insult him and get rid of him. Dull princelings sometimes came with her sophisticated guests, but even if they were fortunate enough to avoid insult, once the circle began to exchange verses or songs, they would see how out of place they were and secretly retire and leave for home.

After enjoying her guests' company, Hsüan-chi would sink into gloom upon their departure and spend a sleepless night in tears. On one of those lonely nights she composed the following poem for Wen.

> Here and there insects sing upon the steps.
> Around the garden K'o trees the mist and dew are pure.
> The sound of nearby music in the moonlight.
> From the terrace the distant mountain is bright.
> Sitting on a rare bamboo seat, a cold wind comes upon me
> As I, touching my gorgeously adorned lute,
> > reproach you with its sound;
> As you neglect to write
> What will console my autumn sorrow?

Hsüan-chi waited day and night for Wen's reply. When his letter finally came, she was still unsatisfied. This was not the fault of Wen's letter; it was something Hsüan-chi felt, something she herself could not quite grasp.

One night as Hsüan-chi was frowning and brooding in the candlelight as usual, she gradually became very nervous; she rose from her seat to pace the room, picking things up from her desk and replacing them again and again. After awhile she spread out paper and wrote a poem to a musician named Ch'en. Ten days ago, Ch'en and two or three young aristocrats had visited her for the first time. He was handsome, had gentle features, and said little himself, but had smilingly riveted his attention on Hsüan-chi's every movement. He was younger than Hsüan-chi. Her poem was as follows.

> Regret settles upon my scarlet harp,
> My aching heart cannot attain its goal.
> I swiftly understood the meeting of the clouds and rain[22]
> But never welled with the essence of the orchid.[23]
> The peach and plum now luxuriantly blossom
> Freely open to visit by a great poet.
> Deep, straight, the trunks of the pine and cinnamon!
> How I envy those enjoying them.
> My garden steps are pure and clean in the moon's light,
> The sound of my song sinks into the bamboo grove,
> Before my gate red leaves have fallen,
> I do not sweep them away, but wait for a man who understands me.

When Ch'en received the poem the next morning, he came immediately to the Hsien-i-kuan. Hsüan-chi withdrew to her room with Ch'en and instructed the servants to see her guests to the gate. From her room, low voices could be faintly heard. Ch'en left the next morning and thereafter used to enter Hsüan-chi's room without announcing himself; each time he came she would dismiss her other guests.

As Ch'en's visitations increased, Hsüan-chi's other guests were asked to leave time after time. They now had to content themselves with merely paying for specimens of her calligraphy. About a month later, Hsüan-chi dismissed her servants as well, retaining only one old woman. Since this old lady, always mean and cross, rarely spoke to anyone, the situation within Hsüan-chi's quarters came more and more to resemble a closed book to society. Hsüan-chi and her lover could see each other with little fear of outside gossip.

Ch'en often had to travel. During his trips, Hsüan-chi did not entertain her past guests as before; she kept to her room and composed poetry which she sent to Wen Fei-ch'ing for his criticism. Each time Wen received some of her poems, he was puzzled at the sudden frequency of romantic allusions and the almost complete absence of the carefree Taoist spirit. He had heard from Li himself all the details of her becoming his concubine, their short-lived relationship, and her move to the Hsien-i-kuan.

Almost seven blissful years passed. Then an unforeseeable disaster befell Hsüan-chi. Towards the end of 867, Ch'en set off on a trip. Hsüan-chi passed the days anxiously awaiting his return. One of the poems she sent to Wen during this time contained these extraordinarily bitter lines:

> The leaves filling my garden
> dance in the melancholy wind,
> Gazing through my curtains,
> I lament the waning of the moon.

In the spring of the next year, before Ch'en's return, the old servant lady passed away. As the old lady, who had no relatives to rely upon, had already made all burial arrangements right down to her coffin, Hsüan-chi merely took care of last-minute matters. After the funeral, she hired an eighteen-year-old servant girl named Lu-ch'iao. Lu-ch'iao was not pretty, but she was clever and flirtatious.

Ch'en returned to Ch'ang-an in the third month of 868. Hsüan-chi embraced him as a thirsty person kneels before a stream. Soon he was visiting her almost every day again. During his visits, Hsüan-chi noticed Ch'en frequently talking with Lu-ch'iao, but at first paid no attention to it since a servant like Lu-ch'iao was a nonentity in her eyes.

Hsüan-chi was now twenty-six. Her perfect features embodied classic lines of dignified beauty so exquisite one could hardly concentrate his eyes upon her; when fresh from a bath her face glowed a luscious amber color, her splendid body seemed like flawless jade. Lu-ch'iao, by contrast, had a face like a lion, with low forehead and short chin; her hands and feet were large and rough. Her neck and elbows were always dirty. Hsüan-chi probably despised her.

The relation between the three grew more complicated. Hitherto when Hsüan-chi's moods displeased him, Ch'en said very little or nothing; now he spoke a great deal with Lu-ch'iao on such occasions, his words becoming extremely warm. Hsüan-chi felt a knife rip her heart each time she heard them conversing.

One day Hsüan-chi was summoned by the nuns to a meeting in one of the other buildings of the monastery. As she left her study she told Lu-ch'iao where she was going. When she returned that evening, Lu-ch'iao met her at the gate with a message. "During your absence Ch'en returned to his quarters. When I told him where you had gone, he decided not to wait."

Hsüan-chi paled. Ch'en had often called while she was out, but had always awaited her return in the study. He knew she had been called to a meeting in the compound today, but had decided to return home without waiting. She suspected some secret existed between Ch'en and Lu-ch'iao.

Hsüan-chi entered her study in silence and sat brooding for some time. Her suspicions slowly flamed up, her blood began to seethe with hatred. She recalled seeing a tinge of unusual contempt in Lu-ch'iao's face at the gate. She even began to hear quite clearly Ch'en's voice tenderly flirting with Lu-ch'iao.

Just then, Lu-ch'iao's casual look seemed further clear proof of her vicious treachery. Hsüan-chi suddenly rose and locked the door. She began to question her in a trembling voice. Lu-ch'iao kept repeating, "I don't know, I don't know," which only convinced Hsüan-chi even more that she was lying. As Lu-ch'iao knelt on the floor in front of her, Hsüan-chi pushed her over. The girl stared up, terrified, into Hsüan-chi's eyes. "Why don't you confess!" Hsüan-chi screamed and clutched at her throat. Lu-ch'iao struggled, thrashing her arms and legs, but when Hsüan-chi relaxed her grip she was dead.

The murder was not discovered for quite a long time. When Ch'en came the next day, Hsüan-chi anticipated some question about Lu-ch'iao, but Ch'en never mentioned her. When Hsüan-chi at length remarked "Lu-ch'iao went away last night" while searching his face for any clue, Ch'en simply said, "Is that so?" without seeming to care one way or the other. The previous night Hsüan-chi had taken the corpse and buried it in a hole she dug in the back of the *kuan* where she lived.

Several years before she had begun to dismiss her callers because of a "living secret." But now in dread of her "dead secret," she felt that if she kept all guests away, someone interested in Lu-ch'iao's whereabouts might come nosing about the *kuan*. She thus decided that if anyone urgently sought an interview, she had better not refuse.

One day around the beginning of summer, Hsüan-chi had several callers. One of them went out to the back of the *kuan* to cool off a bit and noticed a swarm of green flies on top of a freshly turned patch of soil. He was rather puzzled about it and happened to mention it to a retainer without giving it much thought himself. The retainer in turn mentioned it to his older brother, a man who served in the city garrison. Some years ago, this guardsman had observed Ch'en leaving the Hsien-i-kuan at dawn and, hoping to blackmail Hsüan-chi, had attempted to threaten her into paying him a sum of money to keep her secret. Hsüan-chi had just laughed in his face without the least concern. The guardsman hated her after this. This information his brother brought made him guess there might be some connection between the disappearance of the servant girl and the noisome odor in the garden. He and some fellow guardsmen rushed into the Hsien-i-kuan with shovels and dug up the spot. Lu-ch'iao's decaying corpse lay under less than a foot of earth.

The city magistrate, Yin Wen-chang, had Yü Hsüan-chi arrested upon receiving the guardsman's report. Hsüan-chi confessed to the crime without offering the slightest defense. The musician Ch'en was also interrogated, but released as having no complicity in the affair.

Beginning with Li I, all the literati within Ch'ang-an and in the provinces acquainted with Hsüan-chi gave unsparingly of their talents to save her. The one person who could not exhaust his efforts on her behalf was Wen Fei-ch'ing, then serving as an official in Fang-ch'eng, far removed from Ch'ang-an.

Yin Wen-chang was unable to bend the law since the case had gained such notoriety. Around the beginning of autumn, he finally reported the incident to the emperor and had Hsüan-chi beheaded.

Of all who mourned Hsüan-chi's execution, none was as heartbroken as Wen Fei-ch'ing in Fan-ch'eng. Two years prior to the execution, Wen left Ch'ang-an and traveled to Yang-chou where Ling Hu-t'ao, who had resigned as prime minister in 849, was now provincial governor. Wen became angry with Ling for not employing him though Ling knew Wen was in Yang-chou. During the time Wen was living there without having submitted his notice of residence, he got drunk one night in a pleasure house and was struck by a man named Yü-hou. Wen's face was cut and his front teeth broken; he pressed a legal suit in reprisal. While Ling presided over the confrontation between the two men, Yü-hou skillfully described Wen's drunken conduct and was pronounced innocent. The affair became known back in Ch'ang-an. Wen returned to the capital, where he rashly wrote a petition defending himself. At that time, the alternate prime ministers were Hsü Shang, who had formerly employed him, and Yang Shou. Hsü Shang sided with Wen, but Yang rejected his defense and ordered him back to the jurisdiction of the court at Yang-chou. His judgment read as follows: "The school of Confucius stresses virtuous conduct first and literary composition second; as your conduct has been lacking in virtue, how can your literary work be praised? One who harbors undisciplined talent seldom makes a suitable contribution to his times."

Wen later moved to Sui-hsien where he died. His sons Hsien and T'ing-hao were both selected to be officials in the Hsien-t'ung period, but T'ing-hao was killed at Hsü-chou during the Lung-hsün Rebellion three months after Hsüan-chi was beheaded.

July 1915

JIISAN BAASAN

THE TOUCHING TALE that follows, based on a historical incident, is one of several attempts by Ōgai to suggest in fictional terms something of the quality of affection that existed between husband and wife in Tokugawa Japan. In this instance, the elucidation of his theme is the central function of the narrative and Ōgai's ideas are clearly and movingly expressed. Run, the "old lady" of the title (which might be translated as "The Old Man and the Old Woman"), like her spiritual sister Sayo in "Yasui fujin," shows nobility in the face of difficulty, and her reward is a spiritually fitting one. The story needs no analysis: indeed to say more may spoil the reader's pleasure in experiencing the events as they unfold.

 THE SEASON was the late spring of the sixth year of Bunka [1809]. On the land adjacent to the south of what is now the headquarters of the third infantry corps of Ryūdo-machi in the Azabu district of Tokyo, the carpenters came to repair a small vacant cottage within the mansion residence of the daimyo Matsudaira Sashichirō, the Lord Mikawakuni Okudono.[1] When neighbors asked who was going to live there, they were told that a samurai of the retainers of the Matsudaira, one Miyashige Kyūemon, was preparing a place of retirement. Indeed, the vacant cottage was no more than a separate guest room for the mansion of Miyashige; only a kitchen, and a small one at that, was being added. When the neighbors inquired whether Kyūemon was going into retirement there, they were told that this was not so. It was Kyūemon's older brother from the country who was coming.

On the fifth day of the fourth month, even before the walls had dried, an old man whom they had never seen did arrive at the residence of Miyashige, carrying a small traveling bag. He immediately took up residence in the cottage. While Kyūemon had grey hair, this old gentleman's hair was pure white. Still, his hips were not bent in the slightest. Standing erect, with his two swords of good quality, he cut a fine figure. In no way did he look like a person from the country.

Three days after the old man entered the cottage, an old woman came to live with him. She, too, with her pure white hair tied in a small bun at the back of her head, had a dignified look in no way inferior to the old man's. Up to that point, trays of food had been brought from the kitchen of Kyūemon's residence, but once the old lady came, she prepared their meals just like a little girl playing house.

The tender relationship between this old couple was extraordinary. If they were a young couple, people said, it would be impossible to look on unmoved. Some of them even remarked that the two could not be married, but must be rather brother and sister. When asked the reason for this impression, they said it was because even though inseparable, the old couple observed great courtesy to one another; for a husband and wife they seemed a little too formal.

The couple did not appear to be wealthy, yet neither did they seem to be financially in need, nor did they ever seem to trouble Kyūemon. After a great piece of luggage came, the old lady's wardrobe was observed to include a number of very elegant things. Right after her luggage arrived, a rumor that she was a lady from the court spread around the neighborhood.

TRANSLATED BY DAVID DILWORTH AND J. THOMAS RIMER

In every way, the two seemed to live a life appropriate to retirement, one of unhurried leisure. The old man would put on eyeglasses and read his books. He kept a diary in a fine script. Every morning at the same time he would polish his swords. He kept in good physical condition by practicing strokes with a wooden sword. The old lady continued as if she were a little girl playing house, and in her spare moments she would come to the old man's side to cool him with her fan. The weather was already becoming gradually warmer. After she fanned him for awhile, the old man would put down the book he had been reading and begin to speak with her. Their conversations seemed always to be very pleasant.

There were times when the two would go out early in the morning. After the first time they did so, the words of a conversation between Kyūemon's wife and a neighbor got around, somewhat as follows. "They have gone to the Shōsenji, the family temple. If their son were still living, he would be thirty-nine, at the height of his manhood." The Shōsenji is the temple of Kurokuwadani in Akasaka, just in back of the present Imperial Palace of Aoyama. Hearing these words from Kyūemon's wife, the neighbors supposed that the reason for the old couple's going out from time to time was to relive the traces of some ancient bygone dream.

The summer passed and the autumn too. Surprisingly, rumors about the old man and the old woman also ceased. Then, as the year was drawing to a close (it was already the twenty-eighth of the twelfth month), and a heavy snowfall had made the roads difficult for the trip to Edo castle, a fairly large group of high and low officials began the trip there to pay their year-end respects. In the midst of all this commotion, Matsudaira Sanshichirō, lord of the mansion, summoned the old lady to him. He transmitted to her a message from the Shogun Tokugawa Ienari.[2] It read, "Having learned that you remained faithful to the memory of your husband during his long years of banishment to a distant province, we extend to you our kindest regards and grant as a token of consideration ten *mai* of silver."

Since at the end of the year there were such events as the marriage between the Great Councillor Ieyoshi,[3] who resided in the West Enceinte of Edo castle, and Rakumiya,[4] a daughter of Prince Arisugawa Yorihito,[5] the number of persons who received gifts was greater than in usual years; but the fact that the old lady living in retirement at the residence of Miyashige was given ten *mai* of silver was praised by everyone as extraordinary.

So it was that the old man and woman living in retirement at the residence of Miyashige became famous for a time in Edo. The old man, Minobe Iori, was a retainer of the former head of the Shogun's Guard, Ishikawa Awa no kami Fusatsune, and was indeed the older brother of Miyashige

Kyūemon. The old lady was Iori's wife named Run; she had held a position of high responsibility while serving in the Kuroda family of Sotosakurada. When Run received the reward, her husband Iori was seventy-two, and she herself was seventy-one.

In the third year of Meiwa [1766], when Ishikawa Awa no kami Fusatsune became head of the castle garrison, the samurai Minobe Iori was in his company. In his skill with the sword, he outstripped his colleagues, his calligraphy was highly regarded, and he had a taste for poetry. The Ishikawa mansion was outside Suidōbashi, and the house was just at the corner where the streetcar from Hakusan now meets the streetcar coming from Ochanomizu. However, Iori was living at Banchō, and he met with the senior officials only in the guardroom.

In the spring of the year after Ishikawa had become chief of the garrison, Yamanaka Fujisaemon, the husband of Iori's aunt, who also served in the garrison, sponsored Iori's marriage. Iori was thirty years old. The girl was the older sister of the wife of a certain Aritake, a relative of Yamanaka's wife and a retainer of Toda Awaji no kami Ujiyuki.[6]

Why had the younger sister married first and left the older sister behind? The older sister was in service to a feudal lord. The two girls were daughters of Uchiki Shiroemon, from the village of Makado of Aisaigōri in Awa; in 1752, the older daughter, Run, at the age of fourteen, became a servant in the inner apartments of the Middle Councillor Munekatsu of Owari,[7] at the palace outside the gate of Ichigaya. Later in 1762, the lord of the House of Owari retired and was succeeded by his son Munechika,[8] but Run went on as before in her same position, serving for fourteen more years. During her absence, her younger sister became the bride of a son of Aritake, a retainer of the Toda family, and thus came to live in the mansion of Sotosakurada.

When she left the family in Owari, Run was twenty-nine. She then came to help in the home of her sister, who was twenty-four at the time. Run told her sister that if possible she would like to be married into a suitable house with the rank of Direct Retainer. When Yamanaka heard this, he said that he might like to interest Iori in her; Aritake, on his part, was delighted and, serving as a sponsor, he held the wedding ceremony for them. So it was that Run, who was born in Awa of the Uchiki family, took the name of Aritake and came as a bride from the mansion of Toda at Sotosakurada to the residence of Minobe of Banchō.

Run's nature was not that of a beautiful woman. If a beautiful woman can be compared to some object for display in a tokonoma, then Run was something made for more practical purposes. She was healthy and had a splendid bearing. She possessed a penetrating intelligence, and there was never any question of her idling herself away, hands empty of something to do. Although it is true that her protruding cheekbones were a flaw in her face, the space around her eyes and eyebrows seemed to indicate a great flow of talent and spirit.

Iori was skillful at the martial arts and had a taste for learning as well. He was a handsome man, with a pale skin. His only weakness was a tendency toward irascibility. When they became man and wife, Run became extravagantly attached to him; she served him with great care and she was kinder to his eighty-one-year-old grandmother than would have been required toward her own flesh and blood. Therefore Iori felt well satisfied that he had obtained a fine wife. Every trace of his short temper was suppressed, and he was on the way to acquiring a sense of restraint in all things.

In the year following, 1769, the position of the head of the Shogun's Guard went to Matsudaira Iwami no kami Noriyasu, the present head of the family served by Iori's younger brother Miyashige (who then still went by his childhood name of Shichigorō), and so Miyashige entered into the same garrison. The two brothers thus came to perform similar duties.

The work of the Shogun's Guard required that the forces change back and forth between the Nijō castle in Kyoto and the castle at Osaka. After Iori had been married for four years, the assignment of Matsudaira Iwami no kami was changed to the castle at Kyoto. Although it was necessary for Miyashige Shichigorō to go to Kyoto, he was ill. At that time it was possible to despatch a substitute, and so Iori took his place and went to Kyoto in attendance on Iwami no kami. He left behind Run, in her last month of pregnancy, and arrived in Kyoto in the fourth month of 1771.

Iori served in Kyoto during the summer of that year without incident. But about the time when the autumn winds began to blow, while passing a sword shop in Teramachi, he saw a splendid old sword which was said to be an unredeemed pawn. He had previously set his heart on having a good sword and so wanted to buy this one, but the price was one hundred fifty ryō, which, for a man like Iori, was a difficult sum to obtain.

As a precaution for any emergency, Iori always kept a hundred ryō in his waistband. He did not mind parting with this at all. But he had no idea how to raise the other fifty. Although he thought that the price of one hundred fifty ryō was not too high, he bargained with the shopkeeper in various ways and finally got him to lower the price to one hundred thirty ryō, at which point Iori made a definite promise to buy the sword. He planned to borrow the other thirty.

The man from whom Iori borrowed the money was a fellow guardsman named Shimojima Kanzaemon. While they were not usually very close, Iori had heard he had plenty of money. So he borrowed thirty *ryō* from Shimo-jima, took possession of the sword, and had it reconditioned.

Before long the sword was finished. Iori was extremely pleased. On the evening of the fifteenth day of the eighth month, he called together his closest friends, Yanagibara Kohei and two or three others, and arranged a party to show them the sword. All his friends praised the weapon. But just when the drinking was in full swing, Shimojima suddenly appeared. As he was a person who rarely came to visit, Iori, thinking that he had come to demand his money, felt quite uncomfortable at first. But Iori felt his obligation to Shimojima because of the loan, and offering him a sake cup, invited him to join the party.

As they all talked along for a while, a note of sarcasm became apparent in Shimojima's voice. In fact Shimojima had not come to demand his money, but since he felt it unfair that he had not been invited with the others to see the sword, even though he had lent Iori the money, he had purposely appeared there right in the middle of the party.

Shimojima made two or three remarks to Iori and then finally said, "A sword is a very essential piece of equipment in your duties, so it is understandable that you borrowed money to obtain one. Yet to have it mounted so splendidly is a luxury. In addition, as you have borrowed money, it is an indiscretion to show off the sword and have moonlight parties."

It was Shimojima's tone of voice, tinged with sarcasm, which was so difficult to listen to, even more than his words themselves; Iori, who heard him with his eyes cast downward, felt greatly discomforted, as did everyone there.

Iori then raised his head and spoke. "You are quite right. And since in any case I have borrowed money from you, we will be speaking about this again in the future. But out of consideration for my guests, who have been especially invited, I hope that you will be leaving now."

The color of Shimojima's face darkened. "So? If you are asking me to leave, then I will!" he blurted out. He rose to his feet and kicked over the serving tray that was set before him. "What!" exclaimed Iori, as he took up the sword by his side and rose to his feet. By this time Iori's own face was livid.

As the two men squared off facing each other, Shimojima shouted, "You fool!" No sooner were the words off his tongue than Iori's sword flashed and Shimojima's forehead was gashed.

Shimojima had drawn his sword as Iori struck; but while debating in his mind whether to attack Iori, he changed his mind, and fled to the gate with his sword still in his hand.

As Iori came out in pursuit, a retainer of Shimojima with a drawn short sword blocked him. "Get out of my way," cried Iori, and the sweep of his sword drew blood in the retainer's arm and thrust him back.

During this interval Shimojima was able to gain some distance from Iori. Iori was about to charge off after him, but Yanagibara, who had followed him, grabbed Iori firmly from behind and said, "If he wants to run away, let him." He thought that if Shimojima did not die, Iori's punishment might be lighter.

Handing his sword over to Yanagibara, Iori meekly returned to his sitting mat. He stared downward in silence.

Yanagibara sat opposite Iori and said: "This evening's affair has been witnessed by all of us here. Shimojima's conduct can indeed be judged to have been intolerable. However, tell us the reason why you drew your sword first."

His eyes wet with tears, Iori did not answer for a while. He then replied in the following verse:

> Imasara ni
> Nani to ka iwan
> Kurogami no
> Midaregokoro wa
> Motosue mo nashi

> Now,
> What is there to say?
> The anguished heart
> Heeded not
> The consequences.

The wound to Shimojima's forehead was unexpectedly deep, and he died two or three days later. Iori was taken to Edo and put to trial. The judgment read: "Out of consideration for the fact that this was a crime of passion, the death sentence is mitigated; your stipend is rescinded, and you are banished on probation to Arima Saiyonosuke Masazuni."[9] In August 1772, Iori was transferred from the Arima mansion on the outskirts of Kōbashi to Maruoka in the domain of Echizen.

The members of the Minobe household who were left behind each withdrew to their own families. Iori's grandmother Teishō-in went to live in the residence of Miyashige Shichigorō. Iori's son, Heinai, who never saw his father's face, and Iori's wife, Run, went to the residence of Kasahara Shinhachirō, a branch family of the Aritake.

About two years later, Teishō-in became lonely and went to live with Run, but soon after, at the age of eighty-three, she passed away without any particular condition of ill health. This was on the twenty-eighth day of the third month of 1776.

Run served both the grandmother-in-law and her own son with all her strength, kept vigil over their death beds, and buried them in the Shōsenji. Desiring after that to serve in some samurai household, she made inquiries of Kasahara, who had been her sponsor, and of her relatives to find her a suitable position.

Eventually, word was circulated that an experienced servant was being sought by the wife of Matsudaira Chikuzen no kami Haruyuki[10] of the Kuroda family, who was the lord of Fukuoka of the domain of Chikuzen and whose mansion was adjacent to that of Toda Awaji no kami Ujiyasu,[11] a retainer of the Aritake family. After making inquiries, Kasahara presented Run for an interview. Ujiyasu had succeeded as head of the Toda family six years before.

As soon as Run was interviewed by the Kuroda family, she was taken into their employ. This was the spring of 1777.

Thereafter Run served the Kuroda family for thirty-one years until November 1808, and was promoted to a position of high responsibility. She served the wives of four successive generations: the Lords Haruyuki, Harutaka, Naritaka, and Narikiyo;[12] at her retirement, she was awarded a double stipend to the end of her life. During these years Run had never ceased donating money to the Shōsenji for the burning of incense at the grave plot of the Minobe family.

When her retirement was granted, Run first returned to the residence of Kasahara, but then shortly after went back to her native village in Awa. At that time, it was called Makado-mura of Asaigōri, the present Emimura of the district of Awa.

In the following year, her husband Iori, who had lived and taught calligraphy and swordsmanship for thirty-seven years at the garrison of Maruoka in the domain of Echizen, returned to Edo, "pardoned by the compassion of the shogun on the eighth day of the third month, in honor of the death of the former Shogun Shunmei-In, Tokugawa Ieharu."

Hearing of her husband's pardon, Run came joyously from Awa to Edo. They were reunited at the little cottage in Ryūdomachi after thirty-seven years.

September 1915

SAIGO NO IKKU

"SAIGO NO IKKU," which might be translated as "The Last Phrase," contains the sharpest ironies of any of the works in this collection. The story is concerned, as Ōgai puts it, with "the spirit of rebellion within that of self-sacrifice," and is constructed of a series of situations climaxed by an interview between Ichi, the daughter of a criminal condemned to die, and officials of the Tokugawa government.

The dramatic potential in the encounter, carefully prepared for in the earlier incidents of the story, is all the more effectively realized because of Ōgai's sense of restraint and his interjection of a certain amount of quiet humor. Ichi's pluck and charm, those of a free spirit, are juxtaposed against the personalities of the bureaucrats, who, powerful and intelligent as they may be, are, because of their very positions, cautious and suspicious. The story ends with an act of clemency that, as it occurs through mere happenstance, adds the final level of irony to the whole incident.

Some Japanese critics have attempted to link Ōgai's attitudes reflected in this story with events that took place toward the end of his own career when he had a series of disagreements with his military superiors. Be that as it may, the story is altogether successful on its own terms, without reference to the biography of its author. "Saigo no ikku" seems in some ways the precursor of the genre of story developed a few years later in Japan by Akutagawa Ryūnosuke, whose best work often mingles historical situations with the ironic and the grotesque. Ōgai's drier style and aristocratic restraint, however, give his story a depth of philosophical import at considerable variance with the evocative mysteries of Akutagawa's stories.

 IT WAS the twenty-third day of the eleventh month of the
third year of Gembun [1738]. At Osaka, a sailor named
Katsuraya Tarobē was exposed to public view for three
days at the mouth of the Kizu River, and, in addition, a
sign was written and put up beside him which said,
"Condemned to be beheaded." While rumors about
Tarobē spread all over the city, his family, who would suffer most keenly of
all from such an experience, was living in a house by the side of the bridge of
the Horie River in Minamigumi. For fully two years, they had virtually
broken off all communication with the rest of the world.

The mother of Tarobē's wife, who lived in Hirano-machi, brought this
not-unexpected news to the Katsuraya family. The whole family referred to
this white-haired old lady as Granny of Hirano. The five children in the
family had given their grandmother this name because she always brought
them nice little presents. Eventually the husband began to call her this, and
his wife as well.

The five children teased, doted on, and loved their granny. Four of them
were born during the sixteen years since her daughter had come to the Katsuraya family. The oldest daughter Ichi was sixteen, the second daughter
Matsu was fourteen. Next was a boy of twelve, named Chōtarō, who had
been taken into the family from his mother's relatives while still a baby, as
Tarobē thought to marry him to one of his daughters. Next was a girl of
eight named Toku, still another daughter born to Tarobē. The last was the
first boy born to Tarobē, Shōgorō, who was six.

The wife's family from Hirano-machi was well off, so the grandmother's
gifts were the kind which always pleased the children very much. Yet ever
since Tarobē had been put into prison a year-and-a-half before, the children
felt she was trying to disappoint them. For now she brought mostly things
which could be useful to them in their daily life, while the dolls and candy
grew scarcer and scarcer.

Yet the spirits of these growing children were now at their highest; and so
although their grandmother's presents grew skimpier and their mother grew
morose, before long they had grown used to all of this. Their busy life, filled
moment by moment with little battles and little reconciliations, continued
on its way without the appearance of any limitations. Now, instead of the
presence of their father whom, they were told, "had gone to a far, far place
and would not come back," it was their grandmother's coming which
pleased them so much.

TRANSLATED BY DAVID DILWORTH AND J. THOMAS RIMER

In contrast to this, ever since their mother, Tarobē's wife, met with this misfortune, she was no longer able to think of anything except her remorse and bitterness, and even to her mother who gave her money and who tried to console her in the kindest way, she did not manifest a decent show of gratitude. Whenever her mother might come, she would make her listen to the same complaints endlessly repeated and then send her off home again.

When this disaster first befell her, Tarobē's wife would stare vacantly; she did no more than mechanically prepare food and help the children. She ate virtually nothing herself, and because she frequently said that her throat was dry, she would keep sipping a little hot water. Although it might seem that she would fall into a deep sleep at night from sheer exhaustion, often she would lie awake with her eyes open and sigh deeply. There were times when she would even get up and do sewing and other such chores in the middle of the night.

Aware that his mother was not sleeping nearby, the four-year-old Shōgorō would wake up. Then the six-year-old Toku would wake up. Called by her children, Tarobē's wife would crawl in bed; yet when the children, reassured, would fall to sleep again, she would open her eyes wide and sigh.

Only after three or four days had passed was she finally able to repeat her complaints and cry to her mother, who had come to stay the night with her. From then on, for a period of two full years, she went about in this mechanical fashion, repeating endlessly her sad story. She seemed always to be weeping.

On the day the signboard was put up, her mother came in the afternoon and told her that Tarobē's fate had been decided. Tarobē's wife did not seem so shocked as her mother had feared she would be; she just listened and then, as always, began to bewail her tragedy. Her mother felt this lack of response to show, somehow, too much indifference. At this moment the oldest daughter Ichi was standing in the shadow of the sliding door, listening to what her grandmother was saying.

The tragedy that befell the Katsuraya family was as follows.

The husband Tarobē was a sailor, but he himself did not pilot a boat. He owned a boat which sailed back and forth from the northern provinces and managed a transport business by employing a man named Shinshichi to sail it for him. In Osaka, a man such as Tarobē was called *isen gashira*, a term meaning a ship's owner. Tarobē employed Shinshichi, who was called an *okibune gashira*, or ship's captain. In the spring of the first year of Gembun [1736], Shinshichi's boat set sail with a cargo of rice from Akita in the province of Dewa. Unfortunately, his boat encountered a storm on the open sea, and when it began to capsize, he jettisoned over half of the rice. Shin-shichi sold the remaining cargo for cash and brought back the money to Osaka.

In his report to Tarobē, Shinshichi said that the fact of the shipwreck was widely known. Therefore, he felt there was no need to return to the original rice merchant the money gained by selling the remaining cargo. He suggest-ed that this be applied to the expense of buying another boat. Tarobē had managed his business honestly up to this point. But immediately after this experience of a great loss to the business, as he calculated his actual cash, the mirror of his conscience suddenly became clouded over and he decided to take this money.

But, the rice merchant in Akita, after being informed of the shipwreck, also heard rumors about the portion of the cargo which survived and about a man who bought it. He sent someone to investigate. He received a report of all the details down to the amount of money handed over from Shinshichi to Tarobē.

The rice merchant came to Osaka and pressed a legal suit. Shinshichi ran away. Tarobē was jailed and was condemned to be executed.

On that same night that Granny of Hirano had come, Ichi had overheard the fearful story her granny had told. The wife of Katsuraya had grown ex-hausted as a result of tearfully recounting her story over and over again, and fell into a deep sleep. Shōgorō and Toku were sleeping on either side of her. Shōgorō, Chōtarō, Toku, Matsu, and Ichi were sleeping in a row. After a while, Ichi said something from under her covers. It sounded like "Ah, let's do it. We could try."

Matsu heard her. "Ichi, you're still not sleeping," she said.

"Don't speak so loudly. I have been thinking up a good idea."

Ichi first said this to quiet her, and then she whispered in her ear.

"Father is going to be killed tomorrow. I think that we can do something so that he won't. I am going to write a letter, a petition, and take it to the Magistrate. However, if I only ask that he not be killed, they won't listen. So I am going to ask that father be spared and that we children be executed in his place. If the Magistrate accepts this petition, and father is spared, it will be good. Whether all of the children will actually be killed, or whether I will be executed and the little ones spared, I don't know. But I shall petition that only Chōtarō should not be killed with us; since he is not a true son of father, it is better that he does not die. And since father has adopted him to succeed to the head of the house, it is better that he not be executed." Ichi said only this much to her younger sister.

"But I'm afraid!" Matsu said.

"Then you don't want father to be spared?"

"Yes, I do."

"Then just follow me and do exactly as I do. Let's write the petition tonight, and bring it tomorrow morning."

Ichi got up and wrote the petition in plain kana on a piece of paper of a quality used last after a calligraphy exercise. She only needed to write: "Spare father's life and put me, my younger sisters Matsu and Toku, and my younger brother Shōgorō, to death in his place, only sparing Chōtarō, who is not his real son." But she did not know how to compose the letter, and after making a number of wrong attempts, the paper which she had received for her calligraphy exercises started to run out. However, the petition was finally completed just as the cock crowed at dawn.

Since Matsu had fallen asleep while she was writing the petition, Ichi called her softly and told her to change into her clothes that were folded by her side. Ichi got ready too.

The mother and Chōtarō slept through this activity unaware, but then Chōtarō opened his eyes and said, "Ichi, it's already getting light out."

Ichi went to the side of his bed and whispered, "It's still too early. Sleep some more. Your sisters are going out by ourselves on an important errand for father."

"In that case I'm going too," said Chōtarō as he made an effort to raise himself up.

Ichi said, "Come on, get up then. Get your clothes on. Even though you're little, since we're only girls, it will be better if you come along."

Their mother, hearing this commotion around her as in a dream, began to stir a little uneasily. She turned over, but never opened her eyes.

It was about the time of the second cock crow when the three children quietly slipped out of the house. Outside the door, frost glistened in the dawn light. Ichi met an old night watchman walking his rounds who came by carrying a lantern and clapping two sticks together, and she inquired of him the way to the magistrate's residence. The old man was a kind and thoughtful person; he listened attentively to the children's story, and politely instructed them where the residence of the Western Magistrate was located. At that time the City Magistrates were, in the east, Inagaki Awaji no kami Tanenobu,[1] and in the west, Sasa Matashiro Narimune.[2] In the eleventh month, Sasa's office had active jurisdiction.

While the old man was telling them the way, Chōtarō said, "If that's it, I know the place." Thereupon, the two sisters put Chōtarō in the lead.

When they finally trailed their way to the Western Magistrate's residence, they saw that the gate was still shut. Going up under the window of the gatehouse, Ichi called out "Hello, hello" over and over again.

After a time, the peephole of the window opened, and the face of a man about forty appeared. "What's all this noise?" he said.

"A petition for the honorable Magistrate," said Ichi, bowing politely.

The man mumbled something, but his expression showed that he hadn't understood the meaning of her words.

Ichi repeated what she had said.

Seeming gradually to understand, the man answered, "Children cannot speak to the Magistrate; you should get your parents."

"No. Our father is being executed tomorrow, and we are delivering a petition concerning him."

"Executed tomorrow? Then you must be the daughter of Katsuraya Tarobē."

"I am," Ichi answered.

The man mumbled something and thought a bit. "It's terrible; it seems that even children no longer fear the authorities. The Magistrate will not speak to you. Go home, go home," he said and shut the window.

Matsu said to Ichi, "He's so mad at us—let's go back."

"Be quiet. Even if he yells at us, we won't. Just do as I do," Ichi replied as she hunched down before the gate. Matsu and Chōtarō squatted down with her.

The three children waited a long time for the gate to open. Finally the side bolt made a creaking sound, and the gate swung back. The one who opened it was the man who had earlier showed his face from the window.

Ichi got up first and started to advance within the gate; Matsu and Chōtarō followed.

Since Ichi's attitude was so entirely composed, the gatekeeper did not stop them hastily. He stood there for a moment in amazement as they continued to walk in the direction of the inner door. Then, finally returning to himself, he shouted, "Hey! Hey!"

"Yes," said Ichi, as she obediently stopped and turned around.

"Where do you think you're going? Didn't I tell you to go home before?"

"Yes, sir, but we are not going back until we have delivered our petition."

"Indeed! But you still can't go in there. Come over here."

The children retraced their steps and came to the gatehouse. At the same time, from the side inner door, three guards came out and shouted, "What's going on here?" while surrounding the three children. Ichi, who seemed almost to have been waiting for this, squatted on the spot there, took out the petition, and held it out before the leader, who stood in front of the others. Matsu and Chōtarō squatted down together and bowed.

The head guard to whom the petition was offered seemed confused over whether to take it or what to do, and merely looked silently into Ichi's eyes.

"It is a petition for the Magistrate," Ichi said.

"These youngsters are children of Katsuraya Tarobē who has been exposed to view at the mouth of the Kizu River. They've come begging for the life of their father," the gateman interjected.

The head guard turned to his two companions, and said, "Then we better take a look and get the details." No objection was raised to this suggestion by the other two.

The head guard took the petition from Ichi's hand and entered the inner door.

The Western Magistrate, Sasa, was newly appointed; it was less than a year since he came to Osaka. The affairs of his office were discharged in consultation with Inagaki, the Eastern Magistrate, and their decisions were cleared with the lord in charge of the Osaka castle. Concerning the official disposition of Katsuraya Tarobē's case, Sasa, who was merely carrying out the decision made by the previous Western Magistrate, regarded the matter as a serious one and felt that the fact the punishment procedures were finally coming to an end was a burden off his own back.

Now, however, in his morning report, the leader of the night guard duty had stated that there were some persons who had submitted a petition to spare Katsuraya's life. Sasa thus began to feel that some trouble had entered into a situation that, up until now, had gone smoothly.

"Who were they?" Sasa's voice registered annoyance. "Tarobē's two daughters and son. The eldest daughter says that they want to present a petition. I checked it over. Does your lordship want to see it?"

"Since our superiors have arranged that there be set up a box for paper of official business, I should receive it in due course. You must tell them that there are proper procedures. Nevertheless if you have it with you, I will take a look at it now."

The leader of the guard handed the petition to Sasa. As he took it and looked at it, Sasa's face became weary.

"This girl Ichi seems to be the eldest daughter; how old is she?"

"I did not investigate, but she seems to be about fourteen or fifteen."

"Is that so?" Sasa slowly read the petition. It was written in clumsy kana writing, but with a precise logic. Indeed the feeling came upon him that even an adult could not have easily said so much in so few words. The suspicion suddenly arose in his mind that some adult might have put her up to writing it. Continuing to explore this suspicion, he wondered if this were not then a deed of some arrogant person trying to deceive the officials? Finally, he resolved to get to the bottom of the situation once and for all. Tarobē was to be exposed to public view until tomorrow night. There was still time until the execution. Until then, whether he granted the petition or not, he could consult with the Eastern Magistrate and his superior. And if there was some deception involved, it would be also possible to find it out while going through the proper procedures. At any rate, the children should be sent away, Sasa thought.

Sasa then told the leader of the guard that he had inspected the petition, but since it should not be presented directly to the Magistrate, he should tell them to bring it back and present it to the elders of their ward.

The guardsman related to Sasa how the gateman had tried to send them back, and how they had adamantly refused. In that case, Sasa replied, get some candy and use it to entice them to go back. "If they still don't obey, then drag them back," he ordered.

No sooner had the guardsman risen from his place than the keeper of the Osaka castle, Ōda Bitchu no kami Sukenaru,[3] came to call on Sasa. He came not on formal business but on some private matter. When this was concluded, Sasa mentioned that a certain matter had just come up, related his own thoughts, and requested Ōda's counsel.

Having no particular thoughts on the matter, Ōda agreed with Sasa that in the afternoon the Eastern Magistrate, Inagaki, should be present, and the five elders of the ward should be summoned to accompany the children of Katsuraya Tarobē. There may be deception involved, Ōda said, and he felt that Sasa's suspicions were reasonable; therefore he advised having instruments of torture set up at the court. This would be a means of frightening the children into spelling out the truth.

Just as this conversation was ended, the former guardsman appeared; he stood in the entrance way, looking at the two and trying to read their thoughts from their faces.

"Well, then, did the children return?" Sasa asked.

"It was as your lordship thought. We tried to give them candy to get them to go home, but the girl Ichi refused to obey. Finally we made her take the petition back and dragged them home. The younger girl was screaming, but Ichi wasn't."

"Seems to be quite a stubborn one," Ōda said, looking to Sasa.

It was toward the end of the afternoon on the fourteenth day of the eleventh month. The court at the Magistrate's Office at Nishimachi presented a splendid scene. In the hall, both the Magistrates were in attendance. In a secluded spot a special chair had been set up (although it did not face forward), since the lord in charge of the castle of Osaka had come privately to watch the conduct of the investigation. On the porch, sitting behind the scribes, were the police who had been asked to assist.

Instruments of torture were lined up in the garden, which was being solemnly guarded by the lower officials, who placed there the symbolic tridents of justice. It was to this place that the wife of Tarobē and her five children were brought by the five elders of the ward.

The questioning began with the wife. When she was asked her name and her age she could barely answer, and when questioned about anything else, she did not say anything more than "I do not know," or "Please excuse me."

Next the oldest daughter Ichi was questioned. Although she was sixteen at the time, she looked a little younger. She was a thin little girl. Without any trace of cowardice, she related the full particulars. She answered clearly everything asked about her experiences since the day before: how she listened from the shadows to the story her grandmother told; how after getting into bed that evening she got the idea of making a petition; how she confided in her younger sister Matsu and persuaded her; how she herself wrote the document; how Chōtarō woke up and was permitted to come with them; how after asking where the Magistrate's Office was located they were given directions to it; how they responded to the guards when they arrived; how they asked the police of the guardhouse to relay their petition; and how they were forced by the police to return home.

The officials carrying out the investigation then asked her, "Is it then correct that, apart from Matsu, you did not discuss this with anyone?"

"I did not tell anyone. I didn't even tell Chōtarō too much about it. I only told him that we would go to petition, so that father might be spared. When we came back from the Magistrate's residence and met with the elders, we told them that we four had made a petition to save our father by offering our lives. When we did that, Chōtarō also said that he wanted to give up his life. Finally Chōtarō had me write out a petition for himself alone, and I have brought it."

When she finished speaking, Chōtarō pulled out his own petition.

At the instruction of the investigating official, one of the lower officers took the document from Chōtarō and handed it up to the veranda.

The investigator opened it and compared it with Ichi's petition. Ichi's petition had been taken from the ward elder just before the start of the investigation.

In Chōtarō's petition it said that he, together with his elder sisters and the rest of the children, would like to die in place of their father. It was written in the same handwriting as the other petition.

The investigator called out "Matsu!" Although Matsu had been called, she did not take notice of it. It was only when Ichi said "They've called you!" that Matsu timidly lifted her drooping head and looked up at the investigator on the veranda. He questioned her. "You want to die with your elder sister?"

Matsu said "Yes" and nodded.

Next the investigator called out "Chōtarō!"

Chōtarō quickly answered, "Yes, sir."

"According to what is written here, you want to die with your brothers and sisters. Do you?"

"If everyone dies, I don't want to be the only one to live," Chōtarō answered, very precisely.

"Toku!" the investigator called out. Toku realized that her elder sisters and brothers had been called in order, and that she would be called next. She only opened her eyes wide and looked up at the face of the official.

"And you too would prefer to die?"

As Toku silently looked at his face, the color drained from her lips and her eyes filled with tears.

"Shōgorō!" called out the official.

The youngest child, Shōgorō, who was barely six, also remained silent and looked at the official, but when he was asked, "How about you? Will you die?" he shook his head briskly. The various people in the hall, seeing this, smiled unwittingly.

At this point, Sasa came as far as the edge of the hall and called, "Ichi."

"Yes, sir."

"Is there anything which is not true in your statement? If you have made any mistake, even a small one, in what you have said, or if you have discussed this with anyone else, then say so at once. If you are hiding anything, you will be tortured with those instruments until you do tell the truth."

He pointed in the direction of the place where the instruments were kept.

Ichi took one look in the direction he indicated and without any hesitation declared, "No, there is no mistake in what I have said." She had a composed look and her words were softly spoken.

"If that is so, then there is still one thing which I have to ask you. If your request to replace your father is granted, all of you will quickly be put to death. You will not see your father's face. Is even this acceptable to you?"

"It is acceptable," she said, answering in the same cool fashion; but after a moment she added, as though something had just occurred to her, "Because at any rate, in the affairs of the authorities, there are no mistakes."

The face of Sasa seemed to show signs of consternation, as though he had been taken aback, but these soon disappeared, and his eyes became sharp again as he stared at Ichi's face. They might be described as eyes full of wonder tinged with malice. Still, Sasa said nothing.

Then Sasa whispered something or other to the investigating official, who shortly instructed the ward elder, "The investigation is over, so you may leave."

Watching the children withdraw from the court, Sasa turned to Ōda and Inagaki and said, "The future of these children looks very grim, it seems to me." In his heart, the image of the pitiful girl so loyal to her father had faded, and the image of the simple children being questioned by the others had faded as well: what reverberated within him, cold as ice and sharp as a sword, was that last phrase Ichi had spoken.

At this period, the officials of the Tokugawa family had no idea of the Western word "martyr," nor was the word "self-sacrifice" in the dictionaries of the time. So it is no wonder that, as no distinction in the human spirit was made between old or young, man or woman, they did not understand the kind of behavior shown by the daughter of the criminal Tarobē. Yet Sasa, who had talked with Ichi, was not the only one to be pierced by the spirit of rebellion lurking within her attitude of self-sacrifice, for it cut into the hearts of the others in the hall as well.

The lord of Osaka castle and both of the shogun's magistrates thought of Ichi as a "queer little girl," and in addition they had a superstitious feeling that she might be possessed by some evil spirit, so that they felt little sympathy for this filial child.

Yet the administration of justice, so primitive at that time, was moving along naturally, and so it was that Ichi's plea was carried out in an unexpected way. Katsuraya Tarobē's punishment was "suspended while inquiries are made in Edo." This news reached the ward elders on the day after the investigation, the twenty-fifth day of the eleventh month. Then, on the second day of the third month of the fourth year of Gembun [1739], it was announced that "because of ceremonies to be conducted in Kyoto in connection with the enthronement of the new emperor, clemency has been decreed. Tarobē's death penalty is hereby annulled, and he is to be exiled forever from his home in Miguchi, Temma, Minamigumi, Osaka."

The Katsuraya family was again called to the residence of the Western Magistrate, where they were able to say goodbye to their father.

The ceremony in question had been held for the Emperor Higashiyama[4] in 1687, but it was not until shortly before the placard concerning Katsuraya Tarobē had been set up on the twenty-third day of the eleventh month of 1738, in fact, on the nineteenth day of the same month, that the Emperor Sakuramachi[5] had the edict carried out, after an interruption of fifty-one years.

October 1915

TAKASEBUNE

"THE BOAT ON THE RIVER TAKASE" is one of the most widely admired of Ōgai's stories and has been translated into English several times. In the space of a few pages all the hallmarks of his late style are visible: pathos, a concern for human dignity, and an exemplary clarity of style. The conversation between the constable and the prisoner is so arranged that Shōbē's gradual self-questionings lead him further and further from his habitual outlook on life until that moment of his final retreat when, as in "Saigo no ikku," the reader is given another trenchant example of Ōgai's ironic sensibility.

It may be a further point of interest that "Takasebune," a story so expressive of the peculiar "serenity" and aesthetic intention evident in Ōgai's final works, was chosen by the author himself as the title for a collection of these historical stories that appeared toward the end of his life.

Ōgai's comments on the genesis of the story are contained in a short essay following. The Takase River still remains, although in greatly diminished form, in present-day Kyoto. It runs north-south one block east of Kawaramachi-dōri, and emerges to view at several spots—for example, on the north and south sides of Oike-dōri.

 THE *TAKASE* BOATS are small craft that ply the Takase River running through Kyoto. During the Tokugawa period, whenever a Kyoto criminal was banished to a distant isle his relatives were summoned to his prison and allowed a farewell visit with him. After that the criminal would be put aboard a *takase* boat and transported to Osaka. The official who escorted him was a constable under the command of the chief magistrate of Kyoto, and it was customary for the constable to allow a close kinsman of the criminal to accompany him in the boat as far as Osaka. This was not according to the law, but it was connived at—a sort of tacit abridgment of the law.

The criminals banished in those days to distant isles were people found guilty of grave offenses, of course. This by no means meant the majority of them were vicious characters, such as would commit murder or arson for the sake of robbery. Most of the criminals who rode the *takase* boats were people who had committed their offenses unintentionally, through some miscalculation. To give a common example, you had those cases where the male partner in an attempted love suicide, of the type then called "death by mutual consent," had killed the woman but he himself survived.

Setting out with such criminals aboard about the time the evening bells were gonging, the *takase* boats would speed eastward, the dark houses of Kyoto in sight on either bank, cut across the Kamo River, and descend to Osaka. In the boats, the criminals and their relatives would discuss personal affairs the whole night through. There was always the same old litany about it being too late to undo the past. The constables whose task it was to escort them would overhear it all, and could learn in detail all the wretched circumstances of house and home that had produced the criminals—circumstances of which the officials who listened to the formal affidavits in the Magistrate's Office or read the depositions at their office desks could never even dream.

Differences of temperament could be found even among constables. While some were heartless men whose only desire at such times was to stop up their ears so they did not have to listen to the "noise," still others were deeply moved by the human pathos and, though not showing it outwardly because of their official capacity, grieved inwardly and in silence. When a particularly maudlin, soft-hearted constable happened to be escorting a criminal and his kin who had been the victims of extremely miserable circumstances, the constable would be unable to check the spontaneous flow of tears.

TRANSLATED BY EDMUND R. SKRZYPCZAK

Hence it was that escort duty on the *takase* boats was heartily disliked by
the constables of the Magistrate's Office as an unpleasant assignment.

When it was, I'm not sure. It might have been in the Kansei period, when
Lord Shirakawa Rakuo[1] was head of the government in Edo. Toward dusk
one day in spring, as the cherry blossoms of Chion temple fluttered down to
the gonging of the evening bell, an unusual criminal, of a type not seen before, was put aboard a *takase* boat.

He was named Kisuke, about thirty years of age, with no fixed abode.
Since he had no relatives who might be summoned to the prison, he was
alone when he got into the boat.

Haneda Shōbē, the constable assigned to accompany him aboard the
boat, had heard only that Kisuke had killed his younger brother. From what
he had observed of the pale, slender Kisuke while he conducted him from
the prison to the dock, the man was very docile and meek, respectful to him
as a government official, compliant at every turn. What is more, his was not
that attitude one often met among criminals of feigned docility and fawning
before authority.

Shōbē thought it singularly strange. Even after they were on the boat he
kept a careful eye on Kisuke's movements—with a watchfulness that went
beyond the mere call of duty.

That day the wind had died down after sunset; a slight overcast obscured
the profile of the moon; it was a night when the heat of approaching summer seemed to be rising in vapors from the earth on both banks and even
from the soil of the riverbed. As soon as they left South Kyoto behind and
cut across the Kamo River, they were surrounded by stillness. The only
sound was the ripple of water cleft by the prow.

Prisoners were allowed to sleep during the night trip, but Kisuke showed
no interest in lying down; he gazed up in silence at the moon playing hide-
and-seek through the layers of clouds scudding across it. His countenance
glowed and there was a gleam in his eyes.

Shōbē did not look at him directly, yet he did not take his eyes off Kisuke's face. He kept thinking: "Strange . . . passing strange." For Kisuke's
face radiated nothing but happiness; it seemed as if, were it not for the
presence of an official, he would break into a whistle or start humming.

Shōbē reflected: "I don't know how many times I've been in charge of
this *takase* boat till now. The criminals we put on it have always looked so
miserable I couldn't bear to look at them. Yet this man . . . What's wrong
with him? From the expression on his face you'd think he was on an excursion boat. They say his crime was killing his brother. No matter how bad a
fellow his brother was, or the circumstances that led to killing him, if he's at

all human he shouldn't be feeling so happy. Is this thin, pale fellow such a rarity, even as no-goods go, that he completely lacks human sentiment? Not likely. Is he out of his mind, maybe? No, no. There is none of the madman's incoherence in his speech or actions. What's wrong with this fellow?'' The more Shōbē thought about Kisuke's demeanor the more he was puzzled by it.

After a while, unable to contain himself any longer, Shōbē spoke up: "Kisuke. What are you thinking about?''

"Sir?'' Kisuke replied, and glanced about him; afraid the official was finding fault with him for something, he drew himself up and studied Shōbē's face.

Shōbē felt he had to explain the sudden question and indicate his desire to talk with him in an unofficial capacity. So he said, "Not that I had any special reason in mind when I asked you . . . . To tell the truth, for a while now I've been curious to know how you feel about going into exile. I've sent a lot of men off to exile on this boat. They were men with widely assorted histories, but every one of them took going into exile pretty hard. They always wept the whole night through, together with the kin who rode along to see them off. Yet to judge from the way you look, it seems you aren't the least bit upset about going into exile. What are your feelings?''

Kisuke smiled. "Thank you for the compliment. I'm sure that going into exile must be a distressing thing for other people. I can well imagine how they'd feel. But that's because they'd been enjoying a comfortable life in society. Kyoto is a nice place, I can't deny that, but I don't think I'll ever have to endure anything like what I suffered there, no matter where I go. The authorities have been kind enough to spare my life and send me into exile. Even if the island is a rugged place, it's not going to be a den of demons. I've never in my life been in a place I've found to my liking. Now the authorities have ordered me to stay on an island. I'm almost grateful for being able to settle down in a place where I've been commanded to stay. Besides, frail as I am, I've never been sick; no matter what hard work is waiting for me on the island I don't think my health will suffer. On top of that, for being sent into exile I have even received the sum of two hundred *mon*. I have it here.'' As he said this he patted the front of his kimono. Giving the sum of two hundred copper coins to anyone sentenced to exile was the law in those days.

Kisuke went on. "I'm ashamed to confess this, but I've never before carried in my pocket such a sum of money as two hundred *mon*. I used to roam around hoping to find some work somewhere, and when I did I worked as hard as I could. The money I received always had to pass into the waiting hands of others. And the times I could buy some food for cash I considered myself well off; most of the time I paid back a loan only to borrow again. But now since being put into prison I've been fed without having to do any work. For that reason alone I feel as if I've been taking terrible advantage of the authorities. And yet when I leave the prison I get two hundred *mon*. If I go on eating food provided by the authorities like this, I can keep all of the two hundred *mon* without spending a one. Having money of my own is something new to me. Until I get to the island I can't tell what kind of work there'll be for me, but I'm looking forward to using this two hundred *mon* as capital to get me started there." At this point he fell silent.

Shōbē said, "Hmmm, I see." But since he'd been dumbfounded by everything he had heard, he too was unable to say anything for a while and remained thoughtfully silent.

Shōbē was nearly in his forties; he already had four children by his wife. In addition, his mother was still alive, so there were seven in his family. He led a frugal life for the most part—so much so that people called him miserly—and, except for what he wore when he went to work, about the only new clothes he ever had made were nightwear. However, to his misfortune he had married a girl from a wealthy merchant family. The result was that, though his wife was sincerely well-intentioned about making ends meet with just her husband's salary, she had been spoiled by her upbringing in a prosperous family and so was unable to live within their means as well as her husband would have liked. More often than not, when the end of the month rolled around, funds were short. Then she would get money on the sly from her parents' home and balance the accounts. The reason she did this was because her husband hated to borrow money. Her carryings on were not unknown to Shōbē. And, since he took it in ill humor even when she'd use one of the five sacred festivals[2] as a pretext for receiving presents from her family or the children's *shichigosan* festival[3] as a pretext for receiving clothes for the children, whenever he found out she had gotten something to cover their deficits he was none too happy. It was this that was the source of occasional storms in the otherwise placid Haneda household.

After he listened to Kisuke's story, Shōbē compared Kisuke's personal history with his own. Kisuke had said that any pay he ever earned immediately disappeared into other people's hands. Very sad and pitiful indeed. But if you took a look at his own life—what difference was there between Kisuke and him? Wasn't he also constantly handing over to others the salary he got from the government? The difference between them was only a matter of scale, really. And yet he didn't have savings on a par with the two hundred *mon* Kisuke was so pleased with. True, viewed on a different scale, it wasn't strange for Kisuke to be happy at the thought that he had a grand total of two hundred *mon* in savings. He could understand Kisuke's attitude. Still, no matter how you viewed the matter, what was strange was Kisuke's lack of avarice and the way he was content with what he had.

Kisuke had had great difficulty finding a job in the world. When he did, he worked hard, content just with keeping body and soul together. This was why from his first day in prison he'd been surprised at getting, for no toil on his part, almost like a gift from the gods, meals he couldn't get before, and why he felt a contentment he had never experienced before.

Shōbē realized that therein lay the immense gap between Kisuke and himself—it was not a matter of a difference in scale. On his salary, things generally came out about even—despite the occasional deficits. He managed to squeak by. However, he had seldom been content with that. Most of the time he passed the days conscious of neither happiness nor unhappiness. But deep down there lurked an apprehensiveness: At this rate, what would he do if he should lose his post? What would he do if a serious sickness befell him? Whenever he found out about his wife's getting money from her parents to square acounts, these misgivings rose to the threshold of his consciousness.

Why on earth did such a gap exist? From a superficial view it would be enough to say that Kisuke had no dependents, while he did. But that wasn't right. Even if he, too, were single, it was hardly likely he'd share Kisuke's frame of mind. The root of the difference seems to lie much deeper, Shōbē thought.

His thoughts then turned to such things as a man's life in general. When a man gets sick, he wishes he were well. When day after day he doesn't get a square meal, he wishes he always had plenty to eat. When he has no reserve for a rainy day, he wishes he had at least something saved up. Even when he has a little saved up, he wishes it were much more. When you come to think of it, one thing leads to another this way, and there's no telling how far a man would go before he'd draw the line. And yet, right before his eyes was a living example of one who had drawn the line—this Kisuke—Shōbē suddenly realized.

As if seeing him now in a completely new light, Shōbē looked at Kisuke with wide-eyed admiration. It now appeared to Shōbē as if a halo encircled Kisuke's head as he gazed up at the sky.

Shōbē, his eyes fixed on Kisuke's face, spoke to him again: "Kisuke-san." This time he said "*san*," but his switch to the politer form of address wasn't fully deliberate. As soon as the words were out of his mouth he realized the impropriety of addressing Kisuke that way, but it was too late to retract them.

Kisuke, who had answered "Yes?" also seemed to feel something was amiss, for he studied Shōbē uncomfortably.

Shōbē regained his composure somewhat and asked, "I may seem to be prying too much, but I understand you're being sent into exile for bringing about someone's death. I wonder if you'd tell me how it happened, as long as you've told me the rest."

Visibly confused, Kisuke replied submissively, "As you wish, sir." Then in a low voice he began to speak.

"It was sheer foolishness on my part, and I have no excuses. When I think back I find it impossible to explain how I could've done such a thing. I was completely out of my mind when I did it.

"Both my parents had died in an epidemic when I was small, leaving me and my younger brother. In our younger days, the townsfolk were kind to us, much as one might pity pups born on one's doorstep. So by doing errands and the like in the neighborhood we grew up without starving or freezing. Even when we got bigger and looked around for jobs, we tried to stick together, the two of us, as much as possible. We lived together and helped each other in our work. Then last fall he and I both got jobs in the Nishijin textile mill; we were put to work doing figured cloth. After a while my brother fell ill and had to quit work. At that time we were living in Kitayama in a place no better than a shanty; I used to cross a bridge over the Kamiya River to get to the factory. When I'd get back home after dark with groceries and things, he'd be waiting for me, and he'd keep apologizing for making me do all the breadwinning by myself. One day I went back home as usual, not suspecting anything out of the ordinary, only to find my brother lying face down, atop the bedding, blood splattered all around him. Surprised, I dropped the packages of food I had in my hands and went to his side. 'What happened? What happened?' I cried. At this he raised a ghostly white face smeared from cheeks to chin with blood and looked at me, but he was unable to speak. The only sound he made was a quiet wheeze from his neck every time he breathed. Since I had no idea whatsoever what it was all about, I said, 'What happened? Did you throw up blood?' and tried to get nearer, when with his right arm he propped himself up a little from the bed. His left hand was pressed tight against his throat, but dark gobs of blood oozed between the fingers. With his eyes he told me to stay away, and his lips started to move. He was barely able to speak. 'Sorry. Forgive me please. There was no hope of my recovery anyway. I wanted to die quick, make life a little easier for you. I thought I'd die. I figured I had to go deep, then deeper, so I pushed it in as much as I could, but it slipped to the side. The blade doesn't seem to have broken. I think if you pull it out right, I'll be able to die. It's awful painful to speak. Please help. Pull it out.' When he took his left hand away his breath once more escaped from the wound. I tried to speak, but I couldn't make a sound. Without a word I looked at the gash in his throat. It seemed he had probably held the razor in his right hand and had cut across the windpipe, but failing to die from this, he had plunged it in deeper with a slicing motion. Hardly two inches of the handle was showing. When I saw all this, I just stared at him. My mind was all a blank. His gaze transfixed me. I finally managed to say something: 'Wait, I'm going for a doctor.' He threw me a look of reproach. Once again he pressed his throat hard with his left hand and said, 'What good's a doctor . . . It hurts . . . Hurry pull it out . . . Please.' I didn't know what to do; all I did was keep looking at him. At such times—it's strange but true— eyes have tongues. My brother's eyes kept hounding me and saying 'Quick, quick!' Everything was spinning around in my head. His eyes kept up their dreadful plea. Worse, their look of reproach gradually grew sharper and finally turned into a glare of hostile hatred. Seeing this change, I finally decided I had to do as he directed. 'All right, you win,' I said, 'I'll take it out.' Immediately his eyes completely changed expression; they became serene, truly joyful. 'You have to go through with it quickly,' I thought to myself. I knelt down and leaned forward. He settled himself back onto his side; the arm that had been raised to his throat dropped onto the bed. I got a tight grip on the handle of the razor and pulled it all the way out.

"At this moment the front door, which I had closed from inside, opened, and in walked the neighbor woman whom I had asked to tend my brother while I was out. It was already pretty dark inside the house so I didn't know how much she saw, but she gasped and dashed out without shutting the door. When I pulled the razor out I had tried to jerk it straight out, but from the way it felt when I pulled, I figured it had cut some part that wasn't cut before. The blade had been facing outward, so the outer flesh may have been cut. With the razor clutched in my hand, I just sat there in a daze and watched the old woman come in and then dash out of the house. After she'd gone, I snapped out of it and looked at my brother—he'd already breathed his last. Blood was gushing from the gaping wound. Until the leaders of the neighborhood association came in afterward and ushered me off to the town hall, all I did was set the razor by my side and stare at the face of my brother, his eyes half open in death.''

Kisuke had been speaking with his head slightly bent forward and eyes turned upward at Shōbē, but when he finished his story his glance fell to his knees.

His story was very consistent. Almost too consistent. This was because he had recalled the event any number of times during the past half year and had been forced to recount each detail very carefully every time he was questioned at the town hall or examined at the Magistrate's Office.

As he listened to the tale, Shōbē felt as if the scene were actually taking place before his eyes. Halfway through it a doubt rose in his mind whether one could really call this fratricide or murder at all; even when he'd heard the whole story he couldn't dispel the doubt. Kisuke's brother thought he'd die if the razor were pulled out, so he asked him to pull it out. Yes, one could argue that by pulling it out he made him die, he killed him. But it seems his brother was doomed to die anyway, even if he'd left him alone. The reason he said he wanted to die quickly was that he couldn't stand the pain. Kisuke couldn't bear to see him suffer so. He ended his life to free him from suffering. Was that a crime? Had he killed him, it would certainly be a crime. But when one considers that he did it to free him from suffering . . . There's where the doubt came in, and he was unable to dispel it.

After mulling over all aspects of the problem, Shōbē came to the conclusion that the only thing to do was leave it to the judgment of those above; all he could do was go along with the decision of the authority. He decided to make the Magistrate's judgment his own. Despite this decision, though, something still gnawed at his peace of mind, and he couldn't help wishing he could somehow discuss it with the Magistrate.

The gloomy night slowly wore on, and the *takase* boat with its two silent occupants slid softly over the black waters.

The Origin of "Takasebune"

The Takase River in Kyoto is said to have been dug out by Suminokura Ryōi:[4] the part south of Gojō in 1587, and the part between Nijō and Gojō in 1612. The boats that ply it are tugboats. Since *takase* originally was the name of the boat, and any river where these boats ply is called a *takase* river, rivers by that name are to be found in several provinces. But the *takase* is not limited to tugboats. Thus, in the *Wamyōshō*, the character *kyō* is used for a *takase*: "A craft that is small and deep is called a *kyō*." I referred to the *Wakan sen'yō shū* in the Chikuhakuen Library and found this description:

"The bow is high, and both the stern and the sides are low and flat." The illustration shows a boat propelled by pole.

They say that during the Tokugawa period, when a criminal in Kyoto was sentenced to distant banishment, he was transported by *takase* boat to Osaka. The constables of the Kyoto Magistrate's Office who escorted these prisoners had to listen to one sad tale after another. One time, a man was put aboard the boat who had committed fratricide, yet did not look sad at all. When asked the details, he answered that he had had trouble making a living and yet, when sentenced to distant banishent, he received two hundered *mon* in copper—this was the first time he had ever had some money that he did not have to spend. Also, asked why he had committed murder, he answered that he and his brother were hired by the Nishijin textile mill and put to work doing figured cloth, but their wages were so small they could not live on them. One day his brother attempted to kill himself but was unable to finish the task. There was no hope of his brother's recovering, so his brother pleaded with him to finish him off, and . . . so he killed him.

This story appears in *Okinagusa*.[5] In the printed version revised by Ikebe Yoshikata[6] it covers a little over one page. When I read it I thought that it contained two important issues. One is the concept of property: the joy of having money experienced by one who never had money before has nothing to do with the amount of money. Man's desires know no bounds, and once a person possesses money he is never satisfied. The fact that this man rejoiced at having two hundred *mon* as his possession is interesting.

The second issue is the matter of putting to death a man who is about to die anyway but who, still unable to die, is in great pain. To help a man die is to kill him. Under no circumstances must we kill a man. In the *Okinagusa*, too, there was some criticism to the effect that this man ended up committing murder, with no malice on his part, only because he was an uneducated man. But this is by no means a simple matter that can be settled by sticking to rules. Suppose here is a sick person who is on the verge of death and is suffering pain. There is no way to save him. How would a man at his bedside, seeing him in pain, feel? Even an educated person would surely feel that, since the fellow is to die anyway, he would not like to let the man's suffering drag on for a long time but would like to let him die sooner. Here arises the question: Is it good, or bad, to give the man an anaesthetic? Even though the amount of the drug be less than a fatal dose, it might hasten the patient's death. Therefore we must not give it to him, and we have to leave him in great pain. Traditional morality bids us to let him suffer. But in the medical world there is a view that rejects this position; it holds that, when a man is on the verge of death and is in great pain, it is good for us to let him die painlessly and save him some suffering. This is called *Euthanasia*. It means to let a person die painlessly. It seems that the criminal in the *takase* boat had been placed in just such a situation. To me this is extremely interesting.

   With these things in mind, I wrote "Takasebune." This is what I published in *Chūō Kōron*.

January 1916

KANZAN JITTOKU

THE NAMES Kanzan and Jittoku may be more easily recognized when given their proper Chinese pronunciation, Han-shan and Shih-te. Both are legendary figures in Zen Buddhism and have been the subjects of a number of famous paintings and drawings in China and Japan. According to legend, a Chinese Ch'an (Zen) master named Feng Kan, who appears in Ōgai's story, found Shih-te (the name means, literally, "picked up") and turned him over to a monastery for his upbringing. There, Shih-te became friends with Han-shan, well-known in the West for his extraordinary mystic poetry.*

The story has attracted a great deal of attention in Japan and has been singled out by a number of later writers and critics, among them the novelist Mishima Yukio, who found Ōgai's version of the tale a perfect wedding of content and form: the two worlds in which the story moves are beautifully suggested, and the suspense engendered by Lü's desire to move into metaphysical realms he can sense but in which he cannot participate is perfectly resolved in the finality of the final mocking admonishment he receives.

The genesis of Ōgai's story is charmingly told in the brief essay that concludes the story.

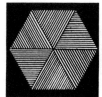THE CHEN KUAN period[1] in the T'ang dynasty was the beginning of the seventh century in the Western calendar, and in Japan, the names of the various eras were just beginning to be assigned. A government official named Lü Ch'iu-yin supposedly lived at that time. Some insist that he never existed, for although it has been said that Lü became the Keeper of Records for the province of T'ai Chou, there is no record of it in the old or new T'ang histories. This rank, Keeper of Records, was the same as that of Governor or Grand Administrator.

All of China had been divided into Circuits, and the Circuits into Provinces or Commandaries. These in turn were subdivided into Prefectures, and below them were the Districts, composed of Hamlets. In a Province, the term Governor was used, while in a Commandary, the term was Grand Administrator. Yoshida Tōgo[2] in particular has expressed his dissatisfaction with the fact that in Japan the term Commandary was generally used for an area smaller than a Prefecture. So if Lü was a Keeper of Records of T'ai Chou, then he held roughly the rank of a prefectural governor in Japan. If this was the case, then his name certainly ought to have appeared in the series of biographies in the "T'ang Histories." But if Lü never existed, this story would never have come into being, so at any rate I will presume that he did.

The story opens on the third day after Lü's arrival at his post in T'ai Chou. He had been covered with the dust of north China at the capital Ch'ang-an and had drunk its cloudy water. Now, setting his feet on the rich earth of central China and drinking its pure water, he was in excellent spirits. During the past three days, a great number of lower officials had come to pay their respects to him. Each had given a report on his respective duties in the conventional manner. Amid all this excitement, Lü tasted the extensive power a local governor held, and was in exuberant spirits.

The previous day, Lü had told his servant that this morning he would get up early and set out in the direction of the Kuo-ch'ing temple in the mountains at T'ien-t'ai. While still in Ch'ang-an, he had decided he would hurry there as soon as he arrived in T'ai Chou.

He had reason indeed for wishing to go to that particular temple. After Lü was named Keeper of Records and was planning his voyage from the capital to his new position, he unfortunately developed a headache so severe he could scarcely bear it. It was an ordinary kind of rheumatic headache, but Lü was of a somewhat nervous temperament, and so although he took the

TRANSLATED BY DAVID DILWORTH AND J. THOMAS RIMER

medicine given him by his regular physician, he did not improve very much. He had been discussing the problem with his wife, saying that he must probably delay the date of his departure, when a young servant girl came and told him: "A mendicant priest has come to the gate and says that he wishes to speak with the Master. What shall I tell him?"

"Hm . . . a priest." He thought for a moment and then instructed her: "I suppose I'll see him, so bring him here." He told his wife he would see the priest alone.

In preparing for his official examinations some years before, Lü had read the Confucian classics and had devoted a great deal of time learning to write five-character verse, but he had not read any of the Buddhist scriptures or studied Lao-tzu. For some reason or other, he still had a great sense of respect for Buddhist monks and Taoist priests. Could he, like the blind, have had respect for something he could not see? It was thus that he said he would meet the priest.

Presently the priest came in. He was a tall man and wore torn and grimy robes; he had cut off his long-flowing hair just above his eyebrows and it seemed on the verge of covering his eyes. In his hand he held a priest's iron begging bowl.

Since the priest stood there quietly, Lü questioned him: "I understand you wished to speak with me. What can I do for you?"

The priest replied: "I hear you will soon be going to T'ai Chou. I also understand that you are suffering from terrible headaches. I have come to cure you."

"Indeed, just as you say, I was thinking to delay my departure because of these headaches. But how do you plan to cure me? Do you know of some special formula?"

"The body is made of the Four Elements; any illness troubling it is illusionary. I shall only need a bowl of clear water and will cure you with a magic spell."

"Ah, so you plan to use a magic spell," Lü said, and then added, "I suppose there is no reason not to, so go ahead and cast your spell." He said this because he had never habitually considered the art of medicine carefully and had no definite view as to what treatment he should or should not follow, merely relying on his own understanding and making decisions according to each different occasion. Being this way, he had not made a careful choice of a regular physician. He had not searched out and selected one who had studied the ancient classics of medicine, but had merely chosen a doctor who lived nearby, so that there would be no difficulty in reaching him. He had thus never been given the proper medicine to take. The real reason he had decided to let the mendicant priest perform his spell was that for some reason this monk, who seemed so wise, inspired confidence in him. Secondly, he agreed because a spell involving a bowl of water, even if it went wrong, could hardly be dangerous. This is exactly the way high officials in Tokyo put their trust in Chinese folk medicine or hypnotism!

Lü called the servant girl and ordered her to fill up the begging bowl with fresh water from the well. The water arrived. The priest received it, held the bowl up to his chest, and stared fixedly at Lü. Either clear or dirty water would have served equally well, as would hot water or even tea. Indeed, the fact it was not dirty was simply a stroke of luck for Lü. During the lengthy time the priest stared at him, Lü, unaware of it, concentrated his whole attention on the water in the priest's hands.

At that point the priest took a mouthful of water from the bowl and suddenly blew it into Lü's face.

Lü was completely taken by surprise, and cold sweat broke out on his back.

"And your headache?" the priest inquired.

"Oh! It is gone." Actually, Lü's mind had been constantly fixed on the idea that his headache would not go away no matter what, but as his attention became riveted on the water spat by the priest, he forgot about his headache entirely.

The priest quietly poured the water left in his bowl on the floor. "If so, then I will take my leave." Even before he finished these words he had turned his back and walked to the doorway.

"Wait! Stop!" Lü called to him.

The priest turned around. "Is there something else I can do for you?"

"I would like to give you a small token of my appreciation."

"No. For the welfare of all sentient beings and to subdue my own arrogance, I live as a mendicant priest, but I will not accept any fee for what I have done."

"Well then, I must not insist. But where do you come from? I would be most interested to ask you . . ."

"Do you mean where have I been up until now? At the Kuo-ch'ing temple in T'ien-t'ai."

"Ah, so you were there? And your name?"

"I am called Feng-kan."

"So you are Feng-kan of the Kuo-ch'ing temple in T'ien-t'ai." Lü knitted his brows in an effort to memorize the name. "I feel all the closer to you as I myself will shortly be going to T'ai Chou. If I may, I would like to ask you something else. Can you tell me of any wise men who might be worth meeting when I reach T'ai Chou?"

"I understand. Yes, at Kuo-ch'ing temple there is a man named Shih-te.

He is actually Samantabhadra.[3] Then, to the west of the temple there is a stone cave called Cold Cliff. There you will find a man named Han-shan. Actually, he is Mañjuśrī.[4] I will take my leave now. Goodbye.'' He left immediately.

It was due to this that Lü now set out for the Kuo-ch'ing temple in the T'ien-t'ai mountains.

In general, there are three attitudes which men take toward a Way of Life or a Religion. There are men completely absorbed in their work, who pass the months and years busily and diligently, giving no particular regard to any such Way of Life. This is true of scholars also. Of course, if one reads and thinks deeply, it is impossible not to arrive at some "Way." Yet such people do not care to think so deeply, but merely wish to go along performing their everyday tasks. Such is the altogether indifferent man.

Next is the man who conscientiously seeks a Way. He concentrates on finding this Way with all his attention, and although he may abandon all things of this world, he does his daily tasks with care and never ceases to devote himself to realizing the Way. It makes no difference whether he becomes a Confucian, a Taoist, a Buddhist, or a Christian. When such a man becomes deeply involved, his daily tasks become the Way itself for him. In brief, he is a man who truly seeks the Way, whatever it may be.

Between the nonchalant man and the man who truly seeks the Way, there is another kind of person who, while objectively recognizing the existence of a Way, is neither completely indifferent nor actively interested in seeking it himself. He resigns himself to the role of one somehow distant from it, yet admires those whom he feels have an intimate connection with it. Respect can be accorded to all sorts of people. But even in terms of respect for the same goal, it seems that among those seeking the Way, the less advanced tend to honor the more advanced, and the man in the middle just mentioned tends to respect what he does not understand and cannot comprehend. This is how blind admiration is born. And in the case of blind admiration, even if the object of the admiration has drawn a correct response, it remains a superficial one lacking depth.

Lü changed his clothes and left his official residence in his palanquin with ten men in attendance.

It was the beginning of winter and a fine mist hung over the ground. The party advanced northward, skirting the left bank of the Shih-li, a branch of the Shu River. As the mist gradually lifted, pale sunlight sparkled on the wet red leaves of the maple trees on the cliff. Both old and young whom they encountered on the journey made way for the palanquin and bowed at the side of the road. Exhilaration rose in Lü's breast. It seemed to Lü he was performing an act of great merit in humbly showing his respect to the sage, despite his own exalted position of shepherd of the people, and the thought gave him great satisfaction.

It was about sixty and one-half Chinese *li* from T'ai Chou to the province of T'ien-t'ai, or about six and one-half Japanese *ri*.⁵ Since the palanquin was carried slowly, it was already past noonday when they met the servant who had come out to welcome them from the prefectural office of T'ien-t'ai. While resting and dining at the local magistrate's residence, they were informed that it was another sixty *li* to the Kuo-ch'ing temple up the mountain road. By the time they arrived it would be nightfall, so it was decided to spend the night at the magistrate's residence.

They took leave of the magistrate the next morning. The weather was exactly like the day before. Mt. T'ien-t'ai was reported to be about eighteen thousand feet high. Whether anyone had ever actually measured it or not, I do not know, but that seems too high a figure. At any rate, tigers lived on the mountain. The road up the mountain went much more slowly than previously. After stopping for lunch along the way, they reached the triple gate of the Kuo-ch'ing temple just as the sun began to set over the western ridges. This was a temple built by Emperor Yang-ti of the Sui dynasty after the death of the great founder, Chih-I.⁶

As the Keeper of Records was visiting the temple, strict formality was being observed. The priest Tao-ch'iao came out to greet them and escorted Lü to the guest quarters. After refreshments were served, Lü inquired: "Does the priest Feng-kan live at this temple?"

"He used to live in the priests' quarters behind this hall, but he went on a pilgrimage and has not returned."

"What did he do here?"

"Well, he used to pound the rice the monks eat."

"But then, were there not additional points on which he differed from the other monks?"

"Yes, there were; since he worked so hard at first, we treated Feng-kan kindly, regarding him as a member of our own family. But one day he suddenly left."

"What happened?"

"It was really strange. He returned one day riding on the back of a tiger. He kept right on going into the corridor, all the while reciting poems on the tiger's back. He liked to recite poems, and often did so at night even in the monks' quarters in the back."

"So, he is a living arhat! What is there behind the monks' quarters?"

"Now there is a vacant hut. Sometimes at night tigers prowl around there and growl."

"In that case, may I trouble you to take me there?" Lü rose from his cushion.

Tao-ch'iao, brushing away the cobwebs, led the way for Lü to the hut in which Feng-kan had lived. Since the sun had already begun to set, it looked completely bare and empty as they peered into the darkening room. Tao-ch'iao bent over and pointed out tiger prints in the dust on the stone tiles. Now and again the mountain wind whistled outside the window, swirling up the fallen leaves piling up in the garden. As the rustling sound broke the silence, Lü could feel his scalp tighten, and his skin chill with goose pimples.

Lü's pace was brisker as he walked away from the empty hut. He asked Tao-ch'iao behind him: "Does the monk Shih-te still live at this temple?"

Tao-ch'iao was puzzled. "So you know him too? Just a while ago he was warming himself by the fire with a monk named Han-shan over there in the kitchen. If you have any business with him, I'll call him."

"So. Han-shan is here too. I couldn't be more fortunate. If I may trouble you further, please take me to the kitchen."

"Of course," said Tao-ch'iao, and walked to the west along the main hall.

Lü asked from behind: "How long has Shih-te lived here?"

"For a long time now. Ever since Feng-kan found him as an abandoned child in a pine grove."

"Is that so? And what does he do here at the temple?"

"For about three years after Feng-kan brought him here, he used to have such duties as lighting the incense in front of the statue on the altar in the dining hall, lighting the night torches, and bringing the offerings to the images of Buddha. When presenting offerings of food to the statue on the altar one day, he was seen eating some of it right before the statue. He seemed unaware of how sacred is the statue of the venerable First Arhat.[7] Now he washes dishes in the kitchen."

"Is that so?" Two or three steps later, Lü added: "You also mentioned Han-shan just now; how about him?"

"Han-shan? He is living in a cave called Cold Cliff to the west of this temple. When Shih-te washes the dishes he leaves some leftover rice and vegetables in a bamboo dish which Han-shan comes and gets."

"I see," said Lü as he followed along. "If Han-shan and Shih-te, who do such things as that, are Mañjuśrī and Samantabhadra, who, then, is Feng-kan who rides on tigers?" he said to himself, feeling like some country bumpkin at the theater, totally confused about the roles and the actors.

"It's a very filthy place," Tao-ch'iao said, as he led Lü into the kitchen. The kitchen was so full of steam that they could barely make things out when they suddenly entered. Three huge black kettles were distinguishable within the greyness, along with glowing red embers beneath each. After halting a moment, they began to perceive a number of monks taking rice, vegetables, and soup from the kettles over to a table built alongside the stone wall.

Tao-ch'iao faced the back and called, "Shih-te!"

Following his line of sight to a spot in front of the farthest kettle from the entrance, Lü saw two monks squatting before the fire.

One of them had hair several inches long and wore straw sandals. The other wore a hat woven of twigs, and wooden shoes. Both were thin, shabby looking, and short, in contrast to the towering figure of Feng-kan.

When Tao-ch'iao called, the one with hair turned around and grinned, without answering. This seemed to be Shih-te. The one wearing a hat didn't move at all. He was probably Han-shan.

With these suppositions, Lü approached the two men. Then joining his sleeves together and making a deep bow, he introduced himself formally, with all his official titles: "I am Lü Ch'iu-yin, Grandee of the Fifth Imperial Rank, Governor General, Keeper of Records for T'ai Chou, and hold the Grade of Purple Silk with Fish Tally."

Han-shan and Shih-te looked up at Lü at the same instant. Then, facing each other, all of a sudden they both burst out laughing, jumped up, and tore out of the kitchen. As they fled, Han-shan cried, "Feng-kan gave us away!"

Around Lü, who was facing in the direction they had fled, the monks filling the rice, vegetable, and soup bowls shuttled back and forth. Tao-ch'iao just stood there dumbfounded.

The Origin of "Kanzan Jittoku"

In the final section of *Tsurezuregusa*, there is a story about being at a loss for an answer to explain where the first Buddha came from. We are often at a loss in answering children's questions. Religious matters tend to crop up in their questions, and to refuse an answer at all is almost tantamount to lying. Some churches in recent years have even expressed the fear that this is bad for the children.

Since Han-shan's poetry has appeared in print several times, my own children saw an advertisement about it and asked me to buy a copy for them. When I told them, "You won't be able to read it yet since it's written only in Chinese," they asked several times, "What kind of a work is it?" It may be that the children were eager to know its contents since the advertisements stress that it is a book which should be read for one's own spiritual cultivation.

But perhaps I say this too hastily. They may have been thinking of the picture which had recently been hung in the tokonoma. The picture was of two laughing children who looked Chinese, with the inscription: "Kanzan and Jittoku." I told them that the poetry of Han-shan was written by the Kanzan in the picture, and that it was very difficult.

The children looked as if they got my point and said: "The poems may be hard to understand, but what kind of a person was this Kanzan, and Jittoku who was with him?" I had no recourse but to tell them the story of Kanzan and Jittoku.

Since it happened that at that very time I had been asked to write a short story, I wrote "Kanzan Jittoku" down almost exactly as I told their story to my children. I did so without consulting my notebook, as I normally do.

I haven't sent in this "Kanzan Jittoku" story to a publisher yet, but perhaps it will go to *Shinshōsetsu* magazine.

My children were not satisfied with the story. Adult readers will perhaps be even less satisfied. In my children's case, they asked me various questions after I told them the story and I had to try to provide one answer or another, but I can't put all of them down here. I was really at a loss to answer when they asked about Mañjuśrī and Samantabhadra, for I had said that Kanzan was Mañjuśrī and Jittoku was Samantabhadra. I tried to reply somehow or other, but they declared they didn't understand how Mañjuśrī was Kanzan and Samantabhadra was Jittoku! I finally told them the story of Miyazaki Toranosuke.[8] Miyazaki claims to be the messiah, and there are even people who go to worship this messiah. I thought that if I explained it with a modern example, it would be somewhat easier for them to grasp.

However, this explanation did not do the trick. Just as the children could not understand how in ancient times Kanzan was Mañjuśrī, they didn't understand how in modern times Miyazaki could be the messiah. I felt I had escaped from one impasse only to fall into another, so I ended up saying: "Actually papa, too, is Mañjuśrī, but nobody has come to worship me yet."

January 1916

SAHASHI JINGORŌ

THE STORY, which bears the name of its main character, is set in a period chosen by Ōgai for a number of his major historical works: the generation of consolidation just after the battle of Sekigahara in 1600. In this particular story he brings the reader close to the grandest figure of the whole period, Tokugawa Ieyasu himself, but Ieyasu is shown under rather atypical circumstances, at the end of his career and after he has officially retired from his duties as head of state.

Ōgai has written also of an important, yet often neglected, aspect of the early years of the Tokugawa period, that of foreign relations. While it is true that Ieyasu's successors maintained a policy of isolation, the early seventeenth century saw considerable activity with foreign nations. The Japanese campaigns in Korea under Toyotomi Hideyoshi just before the turn of the century ended badly for the Japanese and devastated Korea; as a result communications between the two countries were not resumed until the arrival of the mission described in Ōgai's story.

Against this tense and exotic background, Ōgai sketches a series of striking vignettes, many of them sensational and violent in nature. His understated yet precise style permits him to avoid the merely colorful, and indeed, the counterplay of cunning between Ieyasu and Sahashi tie the incidents together to provide an evocative image of the realities of the period.

 ALTHOUGH TRAVEL between Japan and Korea had been discontinued since Hideyoshi had attacked the peninsula, Yoshitoshi,[1] the lord of Sōtsushima, received orders from the Tokugawa family to use his influence to negotiate a renewal of official visits. Thus toward the end of the ninth year of Keichō [1604], three priests from Korea, named Song Un-son, Nun Ik, and Kim Hyo-sun, arrived on an unofficial preliminary visit. Tokugawa Ieyasu[2] had them put up at the Daitokuji temple in Murasakino of Kyoto. Soon after the New Year ceremonies were finished, he granted them an interview when they came up to Edo in the retinue of Hidetada.[3]

The first official Korean embassy came in the fourth month of 1607. Since Ieyasu had already gone into retirement in Sumpu, the legation, which had reached Kyoto, was directed to proceed first to Edo. The members of the group reached the Honseiji in Edo several weeks later, and were granted an interview with Hidetada on the sixth day of the fifth month. The legation members left Edo on the fourteenth, and arrived at the Seikenji in Okitsu five days later. Ieyasu invited the envoys to appear for an interview at his castle in Sumpu on the twenty-first, at eleven in the morning. The envoys went first to the mansion of the Minister of State Honda Kōzukenosuke Masazumi,[4] where they changed into ceremonial robes before proceeding to the castle.

The three highest envoys on this occasion were the Grand Administrator Ryŏ Sŏk-kil, and the Grand Councillors Kyŏng-sŏm and Chŏng Ho-Kwan. They rode in palanquins decorated with Korean designs. In Ryŏ's palanquin, a doll holding an artificial flower had been placed on the right of the sitting mat. The message from Yi Yŏn, the king of Korea, was to be presented to the shogunate in Edo. The next three highest officials, Kim Ch'ŏm-chi, Pak Ch'ŏm-chi, and Kyo Ch'ŏm-chi, rode in palanquins of unpainted wood made for them in Nagasaki. They were followed by twenty-six high officials, eighty-four middle grade officials, and one hundred and forty lower officials, making a retinue of two hundred and sixty-nine persons. The whole procession consisted of one hundred and fifty saddled horses in a line, followed by more than two hundred pack horses, and over three hundred men on foot.

Before the interview at the castle took place, the official gifts from the envoys were spread out on the great veranda. There were four types of articles: sixty catties of ginseng root, thirty rolls of white hemp cloth, one hundred

TRANSLATED BY J. THOMAS RIMER

catties of honey, and a hundred catties of beeswax. Compared with the eleven articles presented to the shogun in Edo, the presentation arranged for Ieyasu was a far less formal one. In the beginning there had been no intention on the part of the envoys to divide the gifts between Edo and Sumpu, and therefore the latter arrangements were no doubt made in light of these sudden difficulties. In Edo, the list which accompanied the king's message mentioned eleven articles, but it was said that the document showed that it had undergone some revision.

On this occasion Ieyasu was dressed in green. He sat on a cushion covered with a striped brocade placed on top of two tatami mats. The three envoys advanced to the base of the dais, bowed deeply twice, and then ranged themselves from right to left. The three highest officials, Kim Ch'ŏm-chi, Pak Ch'ŏm-chi, and Kyo Ch'ŏm-chi, all stood together on the veranda and bowed. At this time there was no presentation of papers or documents. Nor were tea and sake presented by the hosts. After a while, the highest envoys again bowed deeply, and the three envoys on the veranda did the same. They then withdrew in order of rank.

Ieyasu, as he watched the six Koreans depart, unexpectedly inquired of his attendants, "the third man who was on the veranda—haven't I seen him before?"

Nearby Ieyasu stood Honda Masazumi and over ten other personal attendants; Yoshitoshi, who had escorted the envoys to Ieyasu, was also there. Sensing their lord's words to have some meaning concealed in them, no one replied for a certain time, until finally Yoshitoshi spoke out with a degree of caution.

"The third man is named Kyo Ch'ŏm-chi."

Ieyasu cut off Yoshitoshi with a cold glance, and he turned his eyes on the whole company.

"Does no one remember him? I am now sixty-six years old, but rarely do my eyes fail me. He was twenty-three when he fled from Hamamatsu in the eleventh year of Tenshō, and so he is forty-seven now. The brazen fellow! He's now posing as a Korean. That man is Sahashi Jingorō."

All those present exchanged glances, but this time no one ventured to speak for an even greater length of time. Honda's gaze probed Ieyasu's mood, waiting to ask him something.

Ieyasu looked at Honda. "That will do. I leave their entertainment in your charge."

Since the orders relaying Ieyasu's decision to retire to the castle at Sumpu had only been received on the twenty-fifth day of the first month of the year, the building was still under construction. Ieyasu had thus requested that the banquet be held in Honda's mansion.

As if to test his lord's mood, Honda said, "Shall we investigate that matter?"

"No. Everyone will say they know nothing about it. In fact, perhaps the senior officials do not know anything about it. In any case, it would be wise to send these envoys away as soon as you can. Make sure that the local people here have as little contact with them as possible."

Having received his lord's instructions, Honda withdrew hurriedly. Preparations for the banquet had already been made. The Korean envoys were to be entertained after returning to Honda's mansion and changing back into their ordinary clothes. When Honda came back from the castle, he found Ryŏ Sŏk-kil resting after his change of clothing. Through Yoshitoshi, Honda inquired in a round-about-manner whether, among those who had presented themselves that day, there might have been someone whom Ieyasu had known previously. The answer came back through the interpreter that Ryŏ knew nothing whatsoever about such a situation. Indeed, since he seemed truly surprised by the question, he gave no sign at all of holding back any information.

There was no commingling with the Koreans as they were entertained. When the trays of food were removed, Ōsawa Jijū, Nagai Ukonnoshin, and Jō Oribe came as messengers from Ieyasu. They presented gifts to the three highest officials: three sets of armor, three long swords, and three hundred pieces of silver. To the next three, Kyo Ch'ŏm-chi and others, they presented three ordinary swords and one hundred fifty pieces of silver. The next twenty-six in rank received two hundred pieces of silver, and those remaining were given five hundred *kwan* in coin.

By Honda's order, the entourage left before sundown and went as far as Fujieda. They had first arrived in Murasakino in Kyoto on the twenty-ninth day of the fifth month; they were now, on the eighth day of the sixth month, on their way back to Osaka, where they boarded their ship three days later.

On orders from Edo, one thousand three hundred forty men and women, taken prisoner in the attacks on Korea, were released and sailed home with the legation.

When the castle at Hamamatsu was finished in 1570,[5] Ieyasu, who then was the lord of Mikawa, went to live there and sent his son Nobuyasu[6] to live in the castle of Okazaki, where he, Ieyasu, had previously resided. It was then that Nobuyasu received the name of Okazaki Jirōsaburō Nobuyasu. When Lord Okazaki was about eighteen, he was served by a page two years younger named Sahashi Jingorō. Sahashi was a youth so quick-witted that he would begin to carry out a command even before the order was finished, and among his comrades of the same age he had no peer in the martial arts. In addition, he was known for his aesthetic sensibilities, and was especially accomplished in playing the flute.

Once, when Nobuyasu and his party returned from visiting a temple, they passed near the edge of the castle grounds. It was early in the spring, when the water was just beginning to grow warm. Suddenly they saw a heron standing on the other side of a wide pond, a pinch of cotton above the black earth at the edge of the water that shimmered in rows of sparkling silver. One of the pages asked if the bird were in range. Most in the group seemed finally to agree the bird was too far off. Jingorō said nothing at first; but after all the others concluded that the bird was impossible to shoot, he spoke, as if talking to himself, "I wouldn't say that it was entirely impossible . . ."

At this a page named Hachiya spoke sharply to him, "If that's what you think, let's see you do it."

"I wouldn't mind trying, but what will you give as a wager?" Jingorō replied.

"I'll bet you anything I've got with me," Hachiya countered.

"Fine! Then I'll give it a try," Jingorō agreed, and went over to Nobuyasu to ask his permission. Nobuyasu, now quite interested in the whole affair, asked for his own rifle from a foot soldier and handed it over to Jingorō.

"This is a question of pure chance. So don't laugh if I miss," Jingorō exclaimed; and then without the least hesitation, he fired. Everyone watched with bated breath; the heron seemed to start to lift its wings to fly away, but the pinch of white cotton against the black earth never moved. A spontaneous cry of praise rang out. Some foot soldiers were left behind to pick up the heron in a borrowed boat, while the rest of the party returned to the castle.

The next morning the residents of the castle were jolted by the unexpected report that the page Hachiya was dead. No sign of any wound could be found on his body. Jingorō had disappeared completely. After the heron had been shot and the company entered the castle, one of the pages overheard Jingorō say to Hachiya, "We will talk about your promise later." Those who investigated Hachiya's corpse noticed that in place of his long and short swords, which had silver inscriptions, there were swords which seemed to belong to Jingorō. Otherwise, there was no evidence whatsoever to help explain this strange event. According to some of the pages, Hachiya had claimed that his swords belonged to his ancestors and that he always took very good care of them. Others remembered that Jingorō had often admired them.

Jingorō's whereabouts went unknown for a considerable time. Eventually the first anniversary of Hachiya's death passed. Then one day a cousin of

Jingorō named Sahashi Gendayū appeared at Ieyasu's castle at Hamamatsu with a request. The cousin had learned that Jingorō was hiding not far away in the countryside, and came to ask that Jingorō's life be spared. He contended that Hachiya had made a wager to Jingorō that if he hit the heron he would be willing to forfeit anything he had with him. As Jingorō had been lucky enough to hit the heron, he claimed the swords which he had been admiring for a long time. Moreover, Jingorō did not merely propose to take them, but to trade Hachiya for his own in return. But Hachiya refused, saying that these engraved swords were important in the history of the Hachiya family. Jingorō would not accept this. "After a warrior makes an oath, he will give up his life if necessary. Even if these swords are something special to you, they are the only things on your person I claim. You must give them to me." "No, I cannot. If it were my life, I would surely give it up. But even my life is not enough to give in exchange for the treasure of our house," Hachiya replied. Jingorō rejoined with the curse, "You are a dog to go back on your own promise." Hachiya, now enraged, began to draw his sword, and Jingorō gave him a good and strong blow. Hachiya never revived. Thus, the cousin said, Jingorō, who normally accomplished what he set out to do, finally took the swords from Hachiya's body, left his own behind, and fled. Gendayū related this to Ieyasu, stressing that whatever else might be said, Jingorō was a very young man, and expressing the hope that his lord might spare him, or, if that were not possible, that Jingorō might at least be permitted to commit suicide and not be reduced to dying by the hand of another.

Ieyasu heard him out and then, after some thought, gave his reply. "Your account seems to make Jingorō's motives and actions seem reasonable, although such is really not the case. However, as you say, he is a very young man, and therefore if he will perform some outstanding service for me, I will spare his life."

Gendayū acknowledged Ieyasu's words, holding his head bent almost to the floor for several moments. Finally he lifted his tear-filled eyes and looked at Ieyasu, and asked: "This service which Jingorō should perform . . . ?"

"Jingorō is said to be a very clever young man who is skilled in the martial arts. If he can, I want him to kill Amari," Ieyasu said as he rose from his mat.

There was a full moon over the castle of Koyama in the district of Haibara in the province of Totomi, where Lord Takeda Katsuyori of Kai[7] had placed his liege vassal Amari Shirōsaburō in charge of the fortification. Preparations for a moon-viewing party had been made. Amari, a very tall and heavy-

---

bodied man, drained one large cup of sake after the other as he commanded the young warriors to display their various artistic accomplishments.

> Mikawa no mizu no
> Ikioi mo
> Koyama ga sekeba
> Tsui oreru
> Susamaji no wa
> Oto bakari

> The rush
> Of the waters of Mikawa
> Will be stopped
> By the mountains of Koyama
> Only their sound
> Is awesome!

The whole group began to sing in a boisterous fashion. After many hours had slipped by, Amari bade his guests good-night, with the exception of a newcomer among the young men there.

"Ah, what a noisy bunch they were. The moon is loveliest from this time on. Why don't you play your flute for me?" Amari asked, as he invited the young man to kneel on the pillow opposite him.

The young man played. As he was frequently called on to play at unexpected times, he always carried his flute with him. The night deepened. The wick of the candle, which now stood thin and tall where the wax had melted away, turned white on the top and cinnabar on the bottom, while the wax hung like icicles and piled up below. Its dim and muddy light was now overwhelmed by the brilliance of the moon, which bathed the whole room in its glow. The chirping of crickets nearby blended with the deep mood of the flute. Amari's eyelids grew heavy.

Suddenly the sound of the flute was cut.

"Should you be cold, my lord?"

Putting down his flute, the young man pressed softly on the left side of Amari's upturned chest, just where the family crest had been dyed into his pale blue kimono.

Amari, half dreaming, was happy to feel the young man making sure that his collar was not open. At the same instant, something as cold as ice sunk deeply into his chest from the spot where he felt the youth's warming hand. A new warmth now spread from his chest to his throat. Amari's life blood ebbed away.

Having so easily despatched Amari, a man of tremendous power and influence in Mikawa, and then having cut off his topknot as proof of the deed,

Jingorō slipped away like a weasel from the castle at Koyama. Before long, his cousin Gendayū returned to Ieyasu's mansion in Hamamatsu. Ieyasu, as he had promised, summoned Jingorō, but during the interview there was not a single word exchanged concerning Amari. Hachiya's family was by no means pleased to see Jingorō return, but they could scarcely protest against Ieyasu's wishes.

Even after Amari's death, however, the forces in the castle at Koyama did not surrender to Ieyasu. Meanwhile, a number of events took place. Uesugi Kenshin died several years after Takeda Shingen.[8] After Ieyasu was appointed commander of the Right Imperial Guards at the age of thirty-six, his family began to flourish, but in this year, when his first son Nobuyasu was twenty-one, and Ieyasu's second son Ogimaru (later Hideyasu)[9] was five, Nobuyasu was mercilessly forced to commit suicide because of a suspicion of Oda Nobunaga in regard to what became known as the "Tsukiyama Incident."[10] This very year Ieyasu's third son Nenosamaru, who later as Hidetada became the second Tokugawa shogun, was born; his younger brother Fukumatsumaru (later known as Tadayoshi)[11] was born the following year. Two years later, the forces at the castle at Koyama, an obstacle for Ieyasu for so many years, finally capitulated; indeed this event served as prelude to the tragedy which brought Takeda Katsuyori to ruin.

About the time of the destruction of the Takeda clan in 1582, the fate of the Tokugawa house hung in the balance. Akechi Mitsuhide[12] suddenly rebelled and killed Nobunaga. Hideyoshi made peace with the Mōri family in Kyushu and returned to meet Mitsuhide's challenge. Ieyasu, away from his own home base at this time as well, barely managed to escape and return to Okazaki through the combined help of Chaya Shirōjirō's money and Honda Heihachirō Tadakatsu's soldiers.[13] Ieyasu was mustering troops as far away as Narumi when a messenger from Hideyoshi arrived, announcing the death of Mitsuhide.

Just as Ieyasu was in the process of persuading the former retainers of Takeda to join with him, Hōjō Shinkurō Ujinao of Odawara fomented an uprising in Kai and mounted an attack.[14] Ieyasu, whose troops were deployed as far as Kofu, faced Hōjō's army of fifty thousand with a force of less than eight thousand men. At this time, Sahashi Jingorō, along with another young warrior, Mizuno Tōjurō Katsunari,[15] was active at Wakamiko and wounded. At the end of the year, a number of soldiers were rewarded for their valor; Jingorō was among their number, but neither Jingorō nor Tōjurō was given any special commendation.

In the eleventh year of Tenshō [1583], busy preparations were made in the Tokugawa mansion at Hamamatsu for the impending marriage of Ieyasu's second daughter, Tokuhime, into the Hōjō family in Odawara. An an-

nouncement of the marriage was sent to the family of Hideyoshi, who had
now moved to Osaka.

Jingorō, who was serving in the Hamamatsu castle, was present in the adjacent room and listening when Ishikawa Yoshichirō Kazumasa came before
Ieyasu and received his command to carry the news of the wedding to Osaka.

"Take some shrewd young man with you," said Ieyasu.

"In that case, perhaps Sahashi might do . . . ," Ishikawa suggested.

For a long time Ieyasu said nothing. Just as Jingorō was beginning to
wonder what might have happened, Ieyasu finally replied.

"I don't want to use him out of my sight. I learned recently from the people of Kōshū who have come over to my side how Amari had loved him like
his own son. And yet the cruel fellow killed Amari in his sleep."

Hearing these words, Jingorō gave an involuntary snort and nodded his
head slightly. He rose from his seat and left the room; without even returning to the house where he was living with Gendayū, he vanished into thin
air. When Gendayū questioned the others in the house, he learned that Jingorō always carried with him a money belt with about a hundred *ryō* in small
coins.

After vanishing from Hamamatsu in 1583, was it really Jingorō who came
from Korea as Kyo Ch'ŏm-chi twenty-four years later? Or was it only a mistake on Ieyasu's part? Nobody could tell for sure. When questioned, the
Sahashi family all expressed complete ignorance of the matter. However,
when it later became known that the family had come into possession of a
very large quantity of fine quality ginseng root grown in the shape of a doll,
there were persons who voiced suspicions as to where it might have come
from.

This account is based on the *Zokubuge Kanwa*.[16] According to the genea-
logies of the Sahashi family, Jingorō had already joined an Ikkō group[17] and
died in battle in 1563. In the *Koshōshi yawa*,[18] an old retainer of the
Tokugawa family who participated in the Korean embassy of 1607 is identified as a certain Kakehi Matazō.[19] In works such as Hayashi Shunsai's *Kanshirai heiki*,[20] only two officials, referred to merely as Kim and Pak, are
recorded as having had interviews with Ieyasu. If there is any one who knows
another version of the incidents surrounding the career of Sahashi Jingorō, I
would be most grateful if he would send me an outline of whatever evidence
he can produce, indicating his sources.

April 1913

YASUI FUJIN

Ah, how mighty was Lord Tokugawa, his name one to make the earth tremble!
That was as it should be. And Master Bashō was a humble man, with but one
garment to his name, and his fame has come down to us, even as that of Lord
Tokugawa. Men are known not by what they are born to, but by what they do.

Thus, says the eminent modern Japanese novelist Nagai Kafū, the Tokugawa Japanese defined a virtuous man.* Mori Ōgai's story is an attempt to
give a considered portrait of one such person. The record is drawn from life:
Ōgai's model, Yasui Chūhei, or, as he was formally known, Yasui Sokken
(1799–1876), was one of the last great scholars of Chinese learning in the
late Tokugawa period. The portrait is a friendly but by no means idealized
one: Ōgai's account is based on meticulous historical research and at least
some of Sokken's blemishes, physical and spiritual, are recorded. Yet the
man who emerges is an exceptional one.

If Ōgai has managed to portray a good man, he has also succeeded in
making him sympathetic and believable as well, thanks to the cumulative
effect of the considerable detail given about Yasui's life and career, details
that are carefully selected to help construct a reality in which Ōgai's concep-
tions are carefully imbedded; the story, rather than a didactic statement, is a
carefully poised construction.

The title "Yasui Fujin," which might be translated as "The Wife of
Yasui," indicates Ōgai's deepest concerns in composing the story, for the
loving relationship between Yasui and his lovely bride Sayo is the central incident of the narrative; in fact, all that Ōgai has written serves as an explanation in depth of the remark made by Kuroki Magoemon to Yasui that
". . . even though she is such a beautiful woman, she became your wife."

 ALONG WITH THE OPINION that "Chūhei will be a great man," whispered comments that "Chūhei is ugly" spread all over the village of Kiyotake.

Chūhei's father, Yasui Sōshū, had two *tan* and eight *se* worth of land in the village of Kiyotake in Miyazaki in the province of Hyūga, where he had built a large house for himself and now lived. For income he held some nearby rice fields, and although for some years he taught Chinese learning to students in his home, he never ceased cultivating his fields. However, when he was thirty-eight Sōshū went to study in Edo, returning home two years later; because from then on he was increasingly employed by the Obi *han*, he arranged for most of his fields to be tilled by tenant farmers.

Chūhei was Yasui Sōshū's second son. When their father had left them behind to go to Edo in 1805, Chūhei was six and his brother Bunji was nine. After their father's return, the boys, now grown tall, would tuck a book inside their clothes and go off to the fields to work each morning. While the others took a rest, Bunji and Chūhei would bury themselves in their studies.

Several years later, shortly after Sōshū had been made teacher of the Obi *han*, several unpleasant incidents occurred. When Bunji, then seventeen or eighteen, and Chūhei, who must have been fourteen or fifteen, walked along to the fields as usual, passersby on the road, as if by common consent, would stare at the differences between them; if in a group, they would whisper to each other. Indeed the two did seem in every way an ill-matched pair. Bunji was tall, with white skin and splendid features, while Chūhei was short, dark, and had only one good eye. Both brothers had caught smallpox at the same time. Bunji fell only slightly ill but Chūhei was seriously stricken. He remained pockmarked by the disease and suffered the loss of his right eye. As his father had also lost an eye from smallpox as a child, the fact that Chūhei was maimed in the same way seemed proof indeed that mere Chance itself was cruel.

Chūhei began to be self-conscious about walking with his brother. Therefore in the morning he tried to finish up his breakfast before Bunji and set out earlier, and in the evening he began staying behind to finish up something or other so as to return home later. Yet passersby on the road still did not stop whispering to their companions when they saw him. And that was not all. For now they seemed even bolder than when he had walked with Bunji; they whispered louder than ever, and among the whispers there were even those who let themselves be heard.

TRANSLATED BY DAVID DILWORTH AND J. THOMAS RIMER

"Hey! Today there's the monkey walking all by himself."

"Strange to see the monkey reading a book."

"They say the monkey can read better than his trainer!"

"Mr. Monkey. What happened to your trainer today?"

In such a little-traveled place as this, Chūhei knew most of the faces he met on the road. Walking by himself, Chūhei made two discoveries. One was the fact that, although up until now he had been going along under the protection of Bunji, he had not been aware of it. The other was real cause for surprise: both of them had been given nicknames. Not only was he called "monkey" because of his ugliness, but Bunji was the "monkey trainer." Chūhei stored these discoveries away in the back of his mind and said nothing to anyone, but he no longer tried going to and from the rice fields on a separate schedule from Bunji.

Bunji, who had a frail constitution, died in his twenties, while Chūhei was attending the school of the Confucian scholar Shinozaki Shōchiku[1] in Osaka. In the spring of his twenty-first year, in 1820, Chūhei had received the sum of ten *ryō* from his father and had left Kiyotake. He arrived in Osaka at the daimyo's treasury at Tosabōri san-chome, and rented one room in a warehouse. He did all his own cooking. For the sake of economy he used to eat a meal of rice, to which he added soy beans previously cooked with salt and soy sauce. This mixture earned the name "Chūhei Beans" at the warehouse. The others who lived there, fearing that Chūhei's body could not be sustained in such a fashion, urged him to drink sake. Chūhei humbly followed their advice and bought one tiny bottle of sake each day. When evening came, he would tie up the bottle with a paper string and hang it to warm over the candle heat of the night lantern. Then facing the light, he would read through the books he had borrowed from Shinozaki's school. Later, about midnight, when everyone had quieted down, steam would come bursting forth from the mouth of the bottle, warmed at the bottom by the lantern. Chūhei would put aside his book, drink the sake with evident relish, and go to sleep. Two years later, when Chūhei was twenty-three, word reached him of Bunji's death back in Kiyotake. Inferior to Chūhei in learning, Bunji was nevertheless a young man of keen intelligence; but frail as he was, he did not last past twenty-six. When Chūhei received the news, he immediately left Osaka for home.

Later, in 1825, when Chūhei was twenty-six, he went to Edo, where he entered the Shōheikō,[2] enrolling as a pupil of Koga Tōan.[3] Chūhei, who wished to fathom the meaning of the Confucian classics directly without depending on the commentaries made in later ages, would have preferred to study with Matsuzaki Kōdō[4] rather than with Koga, but to enter the Confucian college, it was necessary for him to study first under either Hayashi⁵ or Koga. Even here this country-boy scholar with his pockmarks, his one eye, and his short body, had to bear the jibes of his fellow students. Chūhei nonetheless remained silent, paid no attention to the unkind comments, and lost himself in his reading. When his friends came to tease him, they found the following verse written on a narrow strip of ornamental paper pasted on the pillar near his seat:

Ima wa ne o
Shinobu ga oka no
Hototogisu
Itsuka kumoi no
Yoso ni nanoran

Now concealing his song
In the depths of the forest
The nightingale
Will one day in the sky
Sing out clearly!

When his friends saw this they would say, "That's a pretty high-flying ambition!" and go off laughing, but actually they felt a bit uneasy inside. This verse was a momento of the time when, at nineteen, Chūhei had thrown himself into his Chinese studies and yet managed in addition to study something of Japanese literature; imitating the various styles of poetry, he had written the verse in retribution for the teasing of his friends.

While Chūhei was still in Edo, he was made tutor to the lord of the *han* at twenty-eight. When his lord returned to the Obi *han* in the following year of 1828, Chūhei accompanied him. At the beginning of that year, construction was started on a small school for the *han* at Aza Nakano in the village of Kiyotake, and the building was now partly finished. When completed, the new *han* school was to be the lecture hall to be used by both Chūhei's father Sōshū, now sixty-one, and Chūhei, now twenty-nine. It was at this point that Sōshū thought to find a wife for his son.

But this was by no means easily accomplished, for even the villagers who declared that "Chūhei will be a great man some day," upon hearing of his return from Edo and his training at the Confucian college, could not help whispering as well, "Chūhei is ugly," because of his pockmarks, his one eye, and his squat appearance.

Sōshū was now a man of experience who, when he was in his late thirties, had managed to go as far as Edo for his own training. Now that Chūhei's education was already completed and he was going on thirty, Sōshū felt that he must find a proper wife for his son. But he was well aware of how difficult the selection would be.

Sōshū was not as short as his son, but as he suffered also from pockmarks and the loss of an eye, he had lived through his own painful experiences with women because of such deformities. He knew that in his own case it had been impossible to arrange a formal meeting with an unknown girl in order to settle an engagement, and he knew that the same would be true for Chūhei, who, in addition to having his father's defects, was of much shorter stature. There was no solution other than to choose as soon as possible from among the girls who already knew Chūhei. Sōshū thought about another aspect of the situation in the light of his own past experience. Since even a woman considered beautiful cannot hide a lack of intelligence over a short period of contact, at some point her beautiful face will be forgotten. As she loses her youth in her thirties and forties, this lack of intelligence will appear on her face, and her former beauty will later seem to have been impossible. And on the contrary, even if a woman's face is flawed, if she is a person with any mental qualities, then as one comes to know her, her ugliness will come to be forgotten. Indeed as she grows older, these qualities of mind will make even her features beautiful. As for Chūhei, when one looked at him, his one black eye sparkling when he spoke, he was certainly a splendid man. These thoughts were not merely the favoritism of a parent. Indeed, Sōshū wanted to find Chūhei a wife who appreciated human character. This is more or less the way he looked at it.

At the gatherings of the relatives at yearly festivals and family memorial services, Sōshū would look over the marriageable girls. The most lovely girl, and the one who attracted the most attention, was named Yaeko. She was nineteen. Her father had worked for the daimyo's representative in Edo and had taken a bride from the capital, where Yaeko had been born. Yaeko wore her makeup in the Edo style, she spoke the Edo dialect, and her mother was teaching her to dance. Sōshū thought she was not yet at the proper age to marry, and that in any case, the choice would not be a good one. He thought that there must be some girl who was modest in appearance and yet refined, and who perhaps might even read books a little. Unfortunately there did not seem to be any such girl. They all were of the most ordinary sort indeed.

After wavering in his choice from one girl to another, Sōshū's selection finally fell on the daughter of the nearby Kawazoe family living in the Koaza-Oka section of the same Ōazaimaizumi section of Kiyotake. They were relatives of Sōshū's wife. There were two girl cousins of Chūhei in the Kawazoe family. The younger sister Sayo was sixteen and too young to be the bride of Chūhei, who was thirty. Besides, she was considered a very attractive girl: the young men there called her "Oka no Komachi"⁶ among themselves. She seemed quite unsuitable for Chūhei. As for the older sister Toyo, she was already twenty, old for an unmarried girl, although in this case, the differences of age did not present an insurmountable gap. She had very ordinary features. Her character was surely not extraordinary, but for a woman she was extremely cheerful and she said precisely what she felt. Her way of speaking her mind was very direct, and never involuted. Her mother used to say, "I am embarrassed at her lack of shyness," but it was precisely this quality which attracted Sōshū to her.

Setting his mind on Toyo, Sōshū carefully considered what means to take to broach his intentions. Whenever he spoke to the two girls, they always listened very respectfully. Thus he felt he could not speak directly to Toyo. After Sōshū's wife lost her father and mother, all the remaining family members were in an inferior position to Sōshū himself; if he announced his intentions to them, they would probably be put in an embarrassing position. He knew of other cases where after such a subject had been broached and found unsatisfactory, the two families had become estranged, at least for a time. In the case of relatives it was all the more necessary to be prudent.

Chūhei had an older sister whom people called "the wife of Nagakura." Sōshū decided to reveal his intentions to her.

"If the girl were to become the wife of Bunji, before he died, there would be no question or hesitation at all . . ." she first replied, in a diffident way. She had never looked at Toyo from the point of view her father Sōshū suggested. However, now that he asked her directly, she realized that while it indeed never occurred to her that Toyo would make a suitable wife for Chūhei, she did not know that Toyo would automatically refuse. Thus she eventually took on the role of envoy for Sōshū.

In the Kawazoe house, preparations were being made for the Doll Festival. Boxes with various labels indicating their contents were strewn out on the straw mats in the back room and from them Toyo was taking out the dolls representing the emperor and empress and the five court musicians. As she removed the cotton and Yoshino paper wrappings, her younger sister Sayo put her hands out eagerly to touch them. "It is fine the way it is. Just leave things to me," Toyo scolded her, "I'll take care of them myself."

Just then the wife of Nagakura opened the sliding door and looked in. She was carrying some branches of dark pink peach blossom which she had cut as a present. "Oh, I see you two are very busy," she said. Toyo was taking out the Jōuba dolls.⁷ Putting the rake and hoe in their hands, she stopped to look up at the peach blossoms. ''Are your peach trees already in full bloom like that?'' she asked. ''Ours still have very tiny buds.''

''Since I was in a hurry to come, I just had a few cut. If you want to make a flower arrangement, please send someone over to take as many as you like,'' Nagakura's wife said as she handed Toyo the branches.

Toyo took the peach branches and started for the kitchen with them, saying to her younger sister, ''Just leave everything here as it is.''

Nagakura's wife followed her.

Toyo took a wooden pail from a kitchen shelf, carried it out to the well, drew a bucket of water and put the peach branches to soak. Every motion she made was very efficient. Thinking of her reason for coming, Nagakura's wife could not help smiling as she speculated to herself how this efficient Toyo would quickly be a benefit to the Yasui house if she became Chūhei's bride. Toyo, who had slipped out of her wooden clogs and entered the kitchen, was drying her hands on a towel hanging on the wall. Nagakura's wife came over to her side.

''In the Yasui family it has been decided to arrange a wedding for Chūhei,'' she announced directly to Toyo.

''Oh, from where?'' Toyo said.

''The bride?''

''Yes, who?''

''The bride chosen,'' she said as she looked straight into Toyo's eyes, ''is yourself.''

Toyo's face registered annoyed astonishment, but she said nothing. After a while she began to smile and said: ''It must be a lie.''

''It's true. I've been sent to tell you. Then I'm going to speak with your mother.''

Toyo let the towel slip from her hands which now hung limply by her sides as she studied her guest's face. The smile faded from her lips. ''I am sure that Chūhei is an excellent person, but I would not want to be his wife,'' she said calmly.

Toyo's refusal was so frankly expressed that Nagakura's wife could not find any grounds to continue the conversation. However, remembering that she had come on such an important mission and could not return without speaking about it with the two girls' mother, she related the details of her unsuccessful attempt to speak directly with Toyo to the wife of Kawazoe. Then, after drinking some white wine poured out in a ceremonial cup, she took her leave.

Since Kawazoe's wife was herself fond of Chūhei, she was quite unhappy about Toyo's refusal. She requested that her daughter's frivolous answer not be revealed to the house of Yasui since she wanted to try to persuade Toyo herself. Nagakura's wife therefore promised to refrain temporarily from reporting Toyo's answer. Not believing that Toyo was about to change her mind, she said, as she took her leave, "Please don't attempt to force her."

Nagakura's wife had gone about two or three cho from the Kawazoe residence when Otokichi, their man servant, came running after her. He brought the message that something important had come up, and would she please be kind enough to come back to the house?

Nagakura's wife thought this strange. She could not believe that Toyo had suddenly changed her mind. "Talk about what?" she thought, as she came back to the Kawazoe house with Otokichi. Kawazoe's wife, who was waiting for her, began to speak even before she fully entered the guest room: "Please excuse me for calling you back after you were on your way home, but something unexpected has occurred."

"Yes?" Nagakura's wife said as she studied Toyo's mother's face. "It's about Chūhei's wedding, you see. I personally feel that we would be unexpectedly fortunate to have him as a son-in-law and so I spoke to Toyo myself. However, she still refuses. Toyo told her younger sister Sayo, who then came to me as if she had something on her mind. When I asked her about it, Sayo inquired if she could be Chūhei's bride in Toyo's place. I thought that she must be saying this without clearly understanding what becoming a bride really meant, but when I questioned her further, she positively said that she wants to be Chūhei's bride, if his family will accept her. It is extremely impertinent of me, of course. Not knowing how the Yasui family will react, I'd like to ask your advice." The mother chose her words very carefully.

Nagakura's wife thought this new development even more strange. When Sōshū had brought up the matter he had said "Sayo is too young," and added "She's too pretty anyway, isn't she?" However, it was plain from her daily observations that he was not unfond of Sayo. Probably he had chosen Toyo, the older and less-exceptional sister, because she was a better match with Chūhei. Yet if the younger and more beautiful Sayo came, that was all the better. Indeed Sayo, who was not known as either aggressive or outspoken, had been able to make her feelings quite clear to her mother. After Nagakura's wife speculated in this wise, she decided she would inform her father and Chūhei of this turn of events; then, if possible, Sayo might have her wish.

"Really?" she now said to Sayo's mother. "Father has chosen Toyo, but as I think about it, Sayo might also be acceptable to him. I will take your request directly to him. Still, our introspective little Sayo certainly surprised you, didn't she?

"Yes she did. I am still astonished. We mothers think we know everything going on in our children's minds, but we're so wrong. If you will speak with your father about her, then let me call Sayo now and you can talk to her yourself," she said, and then called Sayo into the room.

Sayo opened the sliding panel and entered the room very timidly.

Her mother said to her, "About what you said before . . . if Chūhei would take you for his bride, you would accept, wouldn't you?"

Blushing right up to her ears, Sayo answered "Yes, I would," and lowered her already bowed head even farther.

Sōshū was just as surprised as Nagakura's wife. But the most surprised of all was the prospective bridegroom, Chūhei! The Yasui household experienced a mixture of surprise and joy, while the young men of the neighborhood felt a mixture of surprise and envy. They circulated jokes like "Oka no Komachi is going to the house of the Monkey." As the jokes spread around Kiyotake, there was no one who was not surprised at the news. But theirs was a surprise without either joy or envy.

The marriage was sponsored by the Nagakuras, and the ceremony was held even before the peach blossoms had fallen to the ground. Now the hitherto merely attractive and doll-like Sayo, like a butterfly coming out of her cocoon, left behind her retiring and introspective manner and took over a house busy with the coming and going of young students.

The new school building, called the Meikyōdō, was completed in the tenth month, and as old friends and relatives came to the Yasui house to join in the celebration, the guests bowed spontaneously and sincerely before this young wife who was so beautiful yet so unaffected. She was entirely different from the usual kind of young bride about whom everyone usually gossips.

In the following year (1829) when Chūhei was thirty and Sayo seventeen, their first daughter Sumako was born. In the seventh month of 1831, the *han* school was moved to Obi. The next year Sōshū, now sixty-five, became head of the Obi school, which was named the Shintokudō. Chūhei, at the age of thirty-three, served under him as assistant instructor. A neighbor, a man named Yuae, moved into their former house in Kiyotake, while the Yasui family received an estate in Kamo of Obi.

At the age of thirty-five, Chūhei accompanied the lord of the *han* to Edo, returning in the following year (1835). Sayo was for the first time left in charge of the house during this somewhat long sojourn of Chūhei.

Sōshū died of paralysis at the age of sixty-nine, the year after Chūhei returned from his second sojourn in Edo.

At the age of thirty-eight, Chūhei went to Edo for the third time, while the twenty-five-year-old Sayo again remained at home in the *han*. The following year (1838) Chūhei became a teacher in the Shōheikō school, the official Confucian college in Edo. Chūhei was then also given the office of Head of the Garrison at the *han*'s Edo mansion in Sotosakurada. He returned home the next year, then went back to Edo after only a brief stay. On this occasion he promised to call Sayo to Edo as soon as their place of residence was settled. He had resolved to resign from his *han* posts in order to open a private school and teach.

About his time Chūhei's learning was gradually gaining public recognition. Among his friends there was an excellent scholar named Shionoya Tōin.[8] As they walked along together, neither of them cut a very fine figure, but still, since the tall Shionoya stood out in contrast, people used to make jokes like "Shionoya's hips are up in the clouds, while Yasui's head is somewhere down in the grass."

Even after he went to Edo, the simple Chūhei lived an extremely frugal life. On his most recent visitation there, before entering the Shōheikō school he lived at the branch mansion of the *han* in Sendagaya. Later he lived at the main mansion in Sotosakurada and also at one time in the Konjiin within the precincts of the Zōjōji temple. In each case he cooked his own meals. More and more resolved to move into his own quarters, he lived for a time in Sendagaya, but only after a fire broke out in the lower mansion did he purchase a house sold on bankrupt terms in Gobanchō for twenty-nine *mai* of silver.

After he again moved his residence from Gobanchō to Kaminibanchō he called Sayo to Edo. They called their home the Sankei Juku.[9] Downstairs there were a few three and four-and-a-half mat rooms, and upstairs there was a study in which he hung some calligraphy in a frame of elegant spotted bamboo. Chūhei had brought the roots of this special variety with him when he left his temporary house at Kariya in the Tanomura section of his native *han* at the time he moved to Edo. Chūhei was now forty-one, Sayo twenty-eight. They had two more daughters after Sumako, Mihoko and Tomeko, but Mihoko died suddenly from unexpected complications during a minor illness. Sayo came to the Sankei Juku accompanied by Sumako, who was eleven, and Tomeko, now five.

Chūhei and Sayo did not employ any servants at the time. Sayo cooked their meals and Sumako did the shopping. Because Sumako's Hyūga accent was unintelligible to the shopkeepers, she often came home in tears without having fulfilled her missions.

Sayo did her housework without any care for her own looks. Still the earlier traces of "Oka no Komachi" remained there to be seen. About this time a man named Kuroki Magoemon came to call on Chūhei. He had formerly been a fisherman in Sotoura of Obi, but because of his detailed knowledge of natural history he had been summoned to Edo to serve under a shogunate Censor. After Sayo served them tea, Magoemon's eyes followed her back to the kitchen, and then with a crafty and humorous look he inquired of Chūhei,

"Sir, is she your wife?"

"Yes, she is," Chūhei answered noncommittally.

"Indeed. Has your wife been educated?"

"No, not to the degree of a formal education."

"Then your wife has insight over and above your learning."

"Oh, how so?"

"Because even though she is such a beautiful woman, she became your wife."

Chūhei couldn't help smiling a little. Amused at this impolite flattery of Magoemon, he played a game of go with him—something Chūhei loved to do although he was not a good player—and then saw him off.

The year that Sayo came from the *han* to Edo, Chūhei moved to Ogawa-machi, and the following year he bought a house near Ushigome-mitsuke. The price was barely two *ryō*. The eight-mat room had a tokonoma and a veranda; in addition there was a four-and-a-half mat room, a two-mat room, and a small wooden corridor. Chūhei placed his desk in the eight-mat room, piling up mountains of books around him. About this time he used to borrow books from the library of Kajimaya Seibē[10] of Reiganjima. Although Chūhei was himself a learned scholar, he never developed the habit of accumulating a library. By nature always frugal, now, although he never was short of daily necessities, it was another matter when it came to buying books. He used to borrow and return the borrowed books after reading them through and copying out the important passages. Even a trip he made to the Shinozaki private school in Osaka was for the purpose, not of studying there, but of borrowing books. He also stayed once in the Konjiin in Shiba in order to hunt out old books.

In this same year, the death by sudden illness of their third born, Tome-ko, was followed by the birth of their fourth daughter, Utako.

The next year the lord of the Obi *han* became Master of Ceremonies[11] for the shogunate, and Chūhei was offered the office of Recording Secretary.[12] He declined with the excuse that his vision was bad, and indeed since he did read so much in dim light, his eyesight was not good.

The following year Chūhei moved to Nagasaka-uradori in Azabu. The house was constructed by bringing materials from the old house in Ushigome. Immediately after moving in, Chūhei made a sightseeing trip to Matsushima. He wore a slit outer coat of light-blue woven cotton, a samurai *hakama*, swords of silver design at his waist, a sedge hat on his head, and straw sandals on his feet. After his return home, Sayo now thirty-one, gave birth to their first son Yōzō. He grew into a handsome youth very much resembling his mother "Oka no Komachi," a genius of a boy who would "someday rule the empire," as it says in the twenty-ninth chapter of the *Chin-wên shang-shu*.[13] Unfortunately he died of cholera in the summer of his twenty-second year.

Two years later Chūhei and Sayo took up temporary quarters in the main mansion of the *han*, then later moved into a residence in Sodefurizaka of Banchō. That summer Sayo, aged thirty-three, gave birth to their second son, Kensuke. Unable to nurse him properly, she gave the baby over to the village headman of Zōshigaya to be cared for by a wet nurse. Kensuke grew up to be rather strange-looking, resembling his father. He took the name of Andō Ekizai and practiced medicine in Higashigane and Chiba. He also taught Chinese learning as a secondary occupation. He later committed suicide there during one of his inborn fits of anger, at the age of twenty-eight. His grave is in the Dainichi temple in Chiba.

When the American warships came to Uraga in 1846 and the whole world seemed in an uproar, Chūhei was forty-eight and Sayo was thirty-five. Chūhei had by then earned a considerable reputation and was known as the great Confucian scholar, Master Sokken. He barely managed to escape being caught up in the whirlwind of the times.

In the Obi *han*, Chūhei served as a Councillor. In 1848 he presented a plan for coastal defense. At fifty-four, in 1852, he became the friend of Fujita Tōko;[14] now Chūhei's ideas gained influence with the lord of the Mito clan.[15] The following year, in response to the threat posed by Perry's visit, he developed "A Plan to Repel the Foreigners and Defend the Harbors." Since the *han* authorities did not approve his plan, he resigned his position. Yet although he left his position of Councillor and remained only a Steward, his duties were exactly the same as before. When he was fifty-seven, he prepared "A Treatise on the Development of Hokkaidō." When he was sixty-three, he requested permission from the head of the *han* to retire. This was in the year 1860, when Ii Naosuke[16] was assassinated at the Sakurada Gate and the lord of Mito died.

The family had moved to Hayabusa-chō in 1849. The next year, because of the earthquake, they sold off what remained of their burned storehouse and various house fittings and moved to Banchō; when Chūhei was fifty-nine, he and his family moved to Zenkokujidani in Kojimachi. When they were living in Banchō, Chūhei wrote in calligraphy the phrase ''no discussion of frontier matters'' and hung it on the wall of his second-floor room.

Sayo had managed to recover from a serious illness when she was forty-five, but in the spring of her fiftieth year she took to her bed and died on the fourth day of the following New Year. Chūhei was then sixty-four.

Among their children were two boys, Yōzō, whose own life was soon to end as well, and Kensuke. Two of their daughters were still alive. Sumako had married the son of a steward of the Akimoto family, Tanaka Tetsunosuke, had been divorced, and then later, through the intermediary of Shionoya Tōin, had married Nakamura Teitarō,[17] a loyalist from Shimabara in Hizen who went by the pseudonym of Kitaarima Tarō. When Sumako's second husband died in prison in 1861, she returned home to her father's family with her two children, the girl Ito and her son Kotarō. Seven months after Sayo died, her daughter Utako followed her to the grave at twenty-three.

What kind of woman was Sayo? Wearing rough clothing over her own beautiful skin, she passed her life serving Chūhei, with his simple tastes. Another member of the Yasui family, named Rimpei, lived at Kofuse, about two ri from Aza-Hoshikura of Agata-mura in Obi. His wife Oshina, remembering the anniversary of Sayo's death, took to Chūhei's house a gift of a lined kimono of striped cotton. Probably Sayo had rarely worn anything made of silk during her life.

Sayo never refrained from the hard labors of serving her husband. Nor did she ever ask for anything in return. Nor was it a question of her being content merely with rough clothing. She never said that she wanted to live in an elaborate house, nor that she wanted all the proper things to use in her home, nor that she liked to eat good things or to see interesting things.

She was surely not so foolish that she did not understand what luxury was, nor could she have been so selfless as to have no needs or desires for anything physical or spiritual. In fact Sayo did seem to have had one uncommon desire, before which all else was only dust and ashes to her. What was her desire? It was that the intelligent persons of society would say that she had hoped for the distinction of her husband. I who write this cannot deny it. Yet on the other hand, I cannot crudely agree with the view that she merely gave her labors and her patience to her husband as some merchant invested capital for profit, but dying before any recompense could come.

Sayo surely had a dream, some image of the future. Until her death, did not the look in her beautiful eyes seem fixed on some far, far place; or was it that she had no leisure even to feel that her own death might be unfortunate? Was not the very object of her hope something which she never precisely clarified for herself?

In 1863, six months after his wife's death, Chūhei was brought to Edo castle, at the age of sixty-four. Two months later he was summoned for an interview with the shogun, Tokugawa Iemochi, and was given the position of Chamberlain. The next year he was awarded the even greater title of Keeper of Documents and was made a Head of the Pages. Chūhei now became a Liege Vassal, while his son Kensuke was given an office in the Obi *han*. Kensuke also later became a teacher at the shogun's Confucian college. As for the family line of succession in the *han*, in 1859 Nakamura chose Takahashi Keizaburō as a son-in-law for his daughter Ito born to Sumako. However, the young couple died soon afterward. Later Sumako's son Kotarō succeeded as head of the Yasui family.

At sixty-six, Chūhei was to be made Intendant of Hanawa in Mutsu, with an income of sixty-three thousand nine hundred *koku* a year. But pleading illness, he declined the honor and took a lesser position.

When he was sixty-five, Chūhei moved his home to Kachimachi in Shitaya. When he was sixty-seven, he lived in the main mansion of the *han* for a time, then bought a house near Hanzomon no Horibata in Kōjimachi 1-chome, and moved there. The Sea Cliff Tower where he viewed the moon with the conspirator Kumoi Tatsuo[18] was actually the second floor of that house.

In 1869, during the period when Edo suffered terrible confusions in the wake of the collapse of the shogunate, Chūhei, now seventy, made public his resignation. Soon afterward his Sea Cliff Tower was destroyed in a fire, and he lived for a time in the upper and the lower mansions of the Obi *han*. While the uproar in the city was at its height, he retired to the home of Masakichi, the younger brother of a farmer, Takahashi Zembē, at Ryōkei-mura in Ōji. Since Chūhei's daughter Sumako had returned to Obi three years earlier, he was now joined by Kensuke's wife Yoshiko, who came from the Amano family, along with her child Sengiku, born the summer before. Yoshiko's body had been weakened by the childbirth, and six months after she came to live with Chūhei she died at twenty-nine, without ever seeing her husband who was then away in Shimofusa.

Chūhei remained in his place of retirement until winter and then moved to the mansion of the Hikone clan in Yoyogi. He was invited to do so because he had published for the Hikone clan a commentary on the *Tso Chuan*.[19] When he was seventy-one, Chūhei moved back to the Sakurada mansion of his old *han*, and at seventy-three, he moved again to Dote san-banchō.

Chūhei died on the twenty-third day of the ninth month of his seventy-eighth year. His grandson of ten, Sengiku, born of Kensuke and Yoshiko, became the heir to the family. After Sengiku's premature death, he was succeeded by Jirō, the second son of Kotarō.

April 1914

TSUGE SHIRŌZAEMON

IN 1869, Tsuge Shirōzaemon assassinated Yokoi Shōnan, a leading thinker and political figure of the time who, in a moderate and enlightened way, hoped to open Japan to foreign influence. Conservatives of the time approved of the violent act, yet within a few years, Tsuge's name was all but buried in oblivion as the public mood shifted dramatically to espouse a philosophy of "civilization and enlightenment" during the first decade of the Meiji period. No more eloquent statement of the effect of historical change on a generation can be imagined. The transmission to the next generation of these confusions of attitude is also an integral part of the meaning of this somber rendering by Mori Ōgai of the life and death of a man now only remembered and admired by his son, a friend of Ōgai's brother. As the son searches for the meaning of his father's life, and by implication for his own, it is easy to understand why Ōgai wrote that ". . . in studying historical records, I came to revere the reality that was evidenced in them. Any wanton change seemed distasteful to me."*

Ōgai's fidelity to history plunges the reader into the midst of the details of early Meiji history, seen not from the elevation of generalization but as it was lived and suffered through, and indeed the richness of the material provides a perfect vehicle for Ōgai's characteristic reflections on the fragility and ambivalence of the values by which men live and die. In this sense, the story is a shrewd comment on the process of "modernization."

Ōgai's final appendix gives additional details, especially those concerning Nihoko, a striking figure involved in the periphery of the account. One only regrets that he had no more materials on which to draw.

TSUGE SHIRŌZAEMON was my father. But the name probably means nothing to people now. That's only natural. Were anyone to suggest that my father died without contributing a thing to society, that he merely withered away like a weed, I would have to agree.

If I were to add by way of explanation that Tsuge Shirōzaemon was the man who beheaded Yokoi Heishirō, people no doubt would exclaim: "Oh, so that's who he was!" While no one knows my father, everyone has heard of Yokoi Heishirō. Everyone has heard of "Shōnan Sensei"[1] from Kumamoto.

To my way of thinking, the Yokoi family was a respected house, favored by fortune, while the Tsuge family was a disgraced, ill-starred one. I can only lament this circumstance. What brought about such differences of good and bad fortune, with the obscurity and fame attending each? I would like to present the whole story and clear my father's name.

At the close of the Tokugawa period, the nation was divided into two views: "Revere the Emperor" and "Support the Shogunate." Those for whom moral integrity meant anything at all clung to the former view. In all the slogan spouting at that time, "Expel the Foreigners" (*jōi*) was paired with "Revere the Emperor" (*sonnō*), and "Open the Country" (*kaikoku*) with "Support the Shogunate" (*sabaku*). In each pair the two phrases were indissolubly linked. It was impossible to conceive of one without the other—that is to say, in the minds of the people.

Viewed in the context of the general trend of history, opening of the country was inevitable, expulsion of the foreigners was impossible. The men of wisdom[2] knew that. Though knowing it, they concealed it. They thought the best way to destroy the declining shogunate lay in urging the impossible policy of expelling the foreigners. Their secret did not filter down to the attention of the masses at all.

Opening of the country was inevitable for the simple reason that Europe and America, though regarded as foreign barbarians at the time, possessed a civilization superior to ours. The men of wisdom knew that. Yokoi Heishirō was one of those who knew that earlier than others. My father was among those who, to the very end of their lives, did not grasp that fact.

In 1847 Yokoi's elder brother fell ill. Yokoi had him taken care of by a doctor of Dutch medicine, a certain Fukuma. Yokoi then was consorting with such men as Motoda Eifū,[3] and he had his own school of Neo-

TRANSLATED BY EDMUND R. SKRZYPCZAK

Confucian studies; yet when it came to treating the illness of his own brother, he turned to the medical skill of Europe. Yokoi was thirty-nine then.

In 1852 Ikebe Keita opened a school of Dutch gunnery in Kumamoto, and Yokoi sent a pupil of his to study there. Ikebe was a disciple of Takashima Shūhan[4] of Nagasaki; when Takashima had fallen under suspicion and been summoned up to Edo, Ikebe had been imprisoned along with him. Yokoi knew that Europe was superior both in military weapons and in the technical use of them. He was then forty-four.

The next year, when Yokoi was forty-five, Perry came to Yokohama. Yokoi very quickly sensed the necessity of opening the country. In 1854, at forty-six, he went to Nagasaki in order to meet the Russian envoy.[5] During his absence Yoshida Shōin visited his home, where he left a letter for Yokoi.[6] The hidden thoughts of one thinker were beginning, ever so slightly, to be communicated to another. The next year, when Yokoi turned forty-seven, the pupil studying at Nagasaki became acquainted with Katsu Yoshikuni,[7] who had gone there to study naval science, and Katsu and Yokoi began to meet. This was another contact between thinkers.

In 1866, when Yokoi was fifty-eight, he sent two nephews, Saheita[8] and Tahei, to America to study naval science. The two students were both sons of Yokoi's elder brother; the older of the two was later called Ise Tarō, and the younger, Numakawa Saburō. Yokoi had earlier succeeded to the house of his elder brother, and he in turn ceded it to Ise Tarō.

There were wise individuals among both imperial loyalists and shogunate partisans. But the former took pains to conceal the light of their wisdom, for concealment was more expedient for controlling the masses. They kept their secret so well that the necessity of opening the country did not filter down to the populace. A record which dispassionately portrays the events of that period in careful detail, like a drama, is the story of Iwakura Tomomi and Tamamatsu Misao in Inoue Kowashi's *Goin zankō*.[9] Since extracts of it appear even in textbooks, there is no need to repeat it here. But if the story is true, how was the secret kept? Why did the "secret back door" of the hermitage in Iwakuramura remain unnoticed?[10] The mass of people are fools, that's why.

I hate to say this, but I must admit my father was one of them. Yes, he was a fool. But in his defense I wish to submit two facts: first, father was a young boy at the time, and secondly, his social position was a low one.

When father was born, the wise man Yokoi was forty years old. The latter had studied in Edo at thirty-one, and at thirty-two he had returned to Kumamoto. The journey from Edo in those days was equivalent to a trip across the ocean today. Yokoi was sixty-one and in the important post of Junior Councillor when father cut him down. Father was a vagrant youth of twenty-two.

Whereas Yokoi was the son of a magistrate of the Hosokawa family (albeit his stipend came to less than two hundred *koku*), father was the son of a village headman in Okayama. When Iki Wakasa[11] became Supreme Commander of Pacification Forces in Bitchū and Echizen, father tried to join the foot soldiers of Iki's Valiant Fighting Force (Yūsentai), but even in this he met many obstacles.

Wisdom develops with age. Even though father was not intelligent by birth, who knows but that he died before he had a chance to develop the little he had? Again, wisdom grows through experience. Though father was a fool, he might have been able to correct his erroneous ideas had he had opportunities for close contact with wise men. He may not have had the makings of a prophet, but wasn't his inability to join the group of *consacrés* and learn the secret of the times due entirely to his low social position? People may say that I am just prejudiced in favor of my own kin, but I find it impossible to arrive at any other conclusion.

Our family served for generations as village heads of Ukida-mura in Jōdō District, Bizen Province. Ukida-mura used to be called Numamura; it contains the ruins of Ukita Naoie's castle.[12] The Tsuge family home was located within what still remained of the castle moat. Three ri east of Okayama, it was backwoods country with not a single feature to attract attention.

My grandfather was called "Village Headman Tsuge Ichirōzaemon." In accordance with a custom widespread in old families, he took a wife from a branch house of the same family. My grandmother's personal name was Chiyo. She was said to have been related to the Marquis Ikeda family of Bizen,[13] and to have been privileged to ride to Okayama palace in a palanquin. I imagine she was probably a wet nurse. These were my father's parents.

Father was born in 1848. His childhood name was Shikata. Again in accordance with a custom in old families, his future was arranged by his parents and he had a wedding ceremony while still a child. He exchanged nuptial cups with a girl named Take, daughter of the Shiomi family. I think this probably took place in 1851, when Shikata was four and Take, a year older, was five.

Little Shikata grew up in a turbulent world, in the midst of rumors about Perry's "black ships." In the conversations of visitors to his father's house he invariably overheard such remarks as "so-and-so is a man of 'righteousness,'" "so-and-so is a man of 'irresolution.'" "Righteousness" meant re-

verence for the emperor and expulsion of the barbarians, while "irresolution" meant support of the shogunate and of opening the country. Opening
of the country should by rights have meant a bold, progressive policy, yet it
was termed "irresolution" because it was seen as capitulation to the foreign
barbarians from fear of their threats. Behind this was the subconscious influence of Chinese history, which depicts those who discuss amity with foreign
barbarians as traitorous subjects. Lurking in the background of people's
hatred for anyone who advocated opening the country lay a revulsion against
such historical figures as Ch'in Kuai.[14] Shikata longed to grow up as fast as
possible—to grow up as soon as possible and become a man of righteousness.

In 1862, at age fifteen, Shikata celebrated his coming of age and shaved
his forelocks. When the tall, well-built lad bound his hair in a long queue,
he looked a magnificent specimen of manhood. He was given the ordinary
name Shirōzaemon, and the formal name Masayoshi. I am told the former
was abbreviated in the public register to Shirō, out of deference to the
Saemon in the Ikeda family. My grandfather, Ichirōzaemon, also publicly
went by the name Ichirō.

Shortly after Shikata came of age, he and Take, whom till then he had
treated as a sister, became true man and wife. From about this time Shikata
became a resident apprentice of Abe Morie of Okayama[15] and studied
swordsmanship. Abe was at that time renowned through all of Kansai for his
swordsmanship.

I was born in the second month of 1863,[16] when father was sixteen and
mother seventeen. I inherited father's childhood name and was called
Shikata.

In the winter of 1867, long-fermenting changes in society finally reached
the boiling point; Tokugawa Yoshinobu[17] restored the reins of government
to the emperor and resigned his position as shogun. In Okayama, among the
Han Elders who served Ikeda Echizen no kami Shigemasa, was an imperial
loyalist named Iki Wakasa. This Iki had once given lodging to Kagawa Keizō
of Mito, Kawada Sakuma of Inaba, Katsura Kogorō of Nagato,[18] and other
such well-known loyalists, and this is why he was made Supreme Commander of the Pacification Forces of Bitchū and Echizen in January the next year,
1868.

Iki had a force of but three hundred foot soldiers. This was inadequate, so
acting upon the advice of Matsumoto Minosuke,[19] he first organized what
was called the Valiant Fighting Force. This he did by recruiting volunteers
from the samurai of Okayama *han*. Shirōzaemon immediately tried to
volunteer, but he was rejected because he was the son of a village headman,
hence of low social rank.

It did not take long to assemble the Valiant Fighting Force; Noro Katsunoshin[20] was put in command, and they set out for Matsuyama in Bitchū. Shortly after the force left Okayama, Noro happened to look up front and saw, just ahead of the vanguard, a man marching briskly down the middle of the road. He looked as if he might be the force's guide. A tall, well-built fellow, he was all dressed up in court apparel, with a long-sword in his belt. Noro halted the force and had the man summoned. He identified himself as one Tsuge Shirōzaemon, pupil of Abe Morie, and went on to tell Noro his story. He had long embraced the imperial cause; when the Valiant Fighting Force was being formed, he had so desperately wanted to join that he had applied at once; for being a village headman's son he had been turned down; from a distance he had witnessed the force's stirring departure, and the thought of remaining alone in Okayama had been more than he could bear; if fighting broke out he wished to be of some help, however slight, so he was marching along with them. Noro was taken by the man's attitude and manner of speaking; without further delay he appealed to Iki and had Shirōzaemon admitted into the force. Shirōzaemon was twenty-one.

Itakura Iga no kami Katsukiyo[21] of Matsuyama was a former member of the shogun's Council of Elders, yet he had no desire to oppose the trend of the times by offering resistance to the imperial forces, so Iki's army was able to carry out its objective of pacification without shedding any blood. For about half a year, till the sixth month, the army was stationed in Matsuyama, where Iki mustered a second army. This was the so-called Loyal Fighting Force (Gisentai), commanded by Fujishima Masanoshin[22] of Bitchū.

One day a trial of martial arts was scheduled for the training ground outside the castle; divided into Bizen and Bitchū teams, the men pitted their skills against one another. Since the Bitchū team had more able swordsmen, the Bizen side was taking a bad beating. Then Shirōzaemon stepped forth and defeated several of Bitchū's most formidable swordsmen. Iki was so delighted he presented Shirōzaemon with the horse he himself rode. When the contest ended and Shirōzaemon rode back on this horse, people along the route, thinking it was Iki, bowed in obeisance.

In the sixth month Iki united the Valiant and Loyal Fighting forces and withdrew to Okayama. Both forces were billeted at a temple, the Shōrinji on Mt. Misao in Kokufu-mura. In addition to his army duties Shirōzaemon became a personal attendant of Iki Takumi,[23] member of an Iki branch family, and gave instructions in swordsmanship.

While Shirōzaemon was in the Valiant Fighting Force he made friends with Ueda Tatsuo,[24] who was something like an advisor to the commander of the Loyal Fighting Force, Fujishima Masanoshin. Whenever the two men met they spoke about the imperial cause; stirred to indignation, they saw traces of "irresolution" in the Bakufu's "total reform of the nation" (*banki-isshin*)²⁵ treatment of the court, and they were unhappy about the way foreigners were being accorded undeserved respect. This all stemmed from the secret intention, held all along by the senior and junior councillors, to open the country, a purpose which finally surfaced in their operation of the government.

One day Shirōzaemon and Tatsuo decided to desert the *han* and go to Kyoto. Together they would live near the imperial residence and observe at firsthand what was being done in the government. Already a plan to ferret out the root of the maladministration and promptly eradicate all the traitors on the imperial side began to take shape in the two men's hearts.

They left for Kyoto. There they inquired about, trying to ascertain which councillors were favorably disposed to the foreign devils. The one they judged to be the chief of the traitors had become a *chōshi*²⁶ and had come up from Kumamoto in the third month, had spent some time as a judge in the Bureau of Institutions,²⁷ then had been promoted to junior councillor: Yokoi Heishirō.

Yokoi had long enjoyed the confidence of his lord, Matsudaira Echizen no kami Yoshinaga;²⁸ he had advocated the union of court and Bakufu (*kōbu-gattai*) and had submitted to Yoshinaga a plan for opening the country. Also, through Ōkubo Kaname,²⁹ steward of the warden of Osaka castle (Tsuchiya Uneme no shō Tomonao),³⁰ he wrote to Tokugawa Yoshinobu; through the good offices of Fujita Seinoshin³¹ he also wrote to Mito Nariaki.³² Popular hearsay distorted the contents of the proposed plan. "It suggests dethronement of the emperor," people said; "He is planning to make a secret agreement with the foreigners and grant official approval to Christianity," and so on.

That the *kōbugattai* advocate Yokoi should appear somewhat suspect in the eyes of pure and simple *sonnō* loyalists was completely natural; that he appeared to them absolutely guilty stems from a different cause. Yokoi was a wise man in his day, but his way of thinking was comparatively straightforward; when he expressed his views he did not take the necessary precautions to allay men's suspicions. Yokoi recognized, in the light of political history, the value of republican government; he felt that there had existed a republican form of government in China as far back as the times of Yao and Shun, several centuries before the Athenian government: "How can we say the monarch is appointed by Heaven? The monarch is said to rule the people as the representative of Heaven, but Heaven is not a human, a person of great virtue, so how can the monarch claim he is fulfilling the mandate of Heaven? Yao turned over the reins of government to Shun. This is what truly great virtue is.'' But this did not mean he was advocating republican government in Japan. Again, Yokoi saw how the Christian religion was extremely powerful in the West because of the way it united men's minds, so he deplored the stagnation of Shinto, Confucianism, and Buddhism. "The West says it has the true Teaching. This Teaching is centered around a Supreme Being. It guides people by means of commandments. It encourages good and castigates vice. Both high and low believe this Teaching. They establish their laws by it. Government and Teaching are as one. In this way the people are inspired to action.'' This does not imply he wanted to spread Christianity in Japan. At the close of the above lines he wrote: "Ah, ah! In the time of T'ang and Wu the Way was as clear as a morning sky; yet we have abandoned it, are ignorant of it, and are instead content to become slaves of the West.'' Yokoi was politically a *sonnō* partisan, ideologically a Confucian. His resentment at the Japanese people's passively becoming slaves of the West in no wise differed from the sentiment of any *jōi* partisan. But the loyalists ended up misunderstanding Yokoi since their thinking at that time was even simpler than his.

This was not the first time Yokoi had been considered a traitor by the loyalists. In 1861, six years before, while serving in Edo during his lord's absence, he was drinking in a restaurant in Gofuku-chō with Tsuzuki Shirō and Yoshida Heinosuke[33] when assailants rushed in and tried to kill him. Yoshida stood up to the attackers; he sustained a deep cut on one shoulder and died as a result. Yokoi managed to slip away and fled the scene with Tsuzuki. Yoshida's son, Shikuma, set out in revenge and slew one of the assailants in Tsurusaki in Bungo Province. On the grounds that Yokoi's action in Gofuku-chō was sheer cowardice, he was deprived of his stipend as soon as he returned to Kumamoto.

Ueda Tatsuo and Shirōzaemon made up their minds to watch for a chance to slay Yokoi. But Yokoi no longer was the simple *han* warrior he had been six years earlier. He was now a high official of the court and went about in a palanquin, surrounded by followers and attendants. If the two attacked alone they were bound to fail. Thus they quietly hunted among the *rōnin* then in Kyoto and found four allies. One was Yanagida Tokuzō from Kōriyama *han*,[34] another was Kashima Matanojō from Bishū *han*;[35] the other two were both from Totsugawa: Maeoka Rikio and Nakai Toneo.[36]

Shirōzaemon changed his name to Tsuchiya Nobuo and went into hiding in the home of Miyake Tenzen[37] in Tsutsumi-chō, to the south of Shirakawa bridge in Awata, Kyoto. From time to time the seven[38] accomplices met and discussed plans for "slaying the traitor.'' However, Yokoi suffered from an intestinal ailment and for quite some time did not go to work. Reconnaissance of his residence revealed only that a messenger from the Cabinet[39] was making frequent trips back and forth bearing a large letter box.

The accomplices were for rushing into the residence and attacking. But Ueda, who had assumed leadership of the secret band, would not hear of it. He argued that Yokoi realized full well that he was hated by the *rōnin* and was taking full precautions at his residence; if they stormed the place, even their contingent of six men would have no guarantee of success.

As the year drew to a close, Yokoi recovered and started going to work every day. The accomplices met and resolved to carry out the job very early the next year. Once arrangements were settled, Shirōzaemon set off for his home to bid farewells.

Even after Shirōzaemon had gone to Kyoto, his father kept sending him money from the family in Ukida-mura by means of a secret messenger. The accomplices' meetings were held in a geisha house in a new section of the Gion area in order to mislead prying eyes and ears; the one who usually paid the bill for their meetings was Shirōzaemon. Fair-complexioned, gentle and calm, good-mannered even when drinking, Shirōzaemon, it is said, was idolized by the geishas and maids. One of the accomplices once said of him: "I remarked that it was a shame to make only Tsuge shell out money the way we did; there were ways to raise funds for our cause; why not imitate other people and try dunning some skinflint? At this Shirōzaemon drew himself up straight, looked around the group, and said: 'Ours is an association of righteousness. Since I am to offer myself in service of the empire, I cannot lend myself to behavior no better than that of a common thief. Even if on my deathbed I cared nothing for my own dishonor, I must not sully my ancestors' name or bequeath shame to my posterity. I, at any rate, cannot agree to the idea.' "

It was a snowy night, the last day of the year. From the house of Sugimoto, a relative of the Tsuge family also living in Ukida-mura, a messenger arrived at the Tsuge home. The matter was urgent, he said, and everyone in the house was requested to come over together, but in a manner that would not draw attention. The old couple felt something was amiss, but nevertheless told Shirōzaemon's wife, Take, to hurry and get ready. Though apprehensive that it must have something to do with her husband, my mother, who was twenty-two at the time, took me (I was six) and followed on the heels of my grandparents.

My father was waiting at the Sugimoto house. Being a mere child at the time, I cannot even recall clearly how he looked. All I faintly remember is that he said, "Hi there, son!" and smiled as he patted me on the head. I heard later he told his parents and my mother that his absence would be quite long, so he had come back for a brief visit. He set out from Ukida-mura before daybreak and hastened back to Kyoto.

The attack occurred on the afternoon of the fifth day of the first month in 1869. Yokoi Heishirō was on his way from the Cabinet office, and his palanquin had just come down the Teramachi to the section south of Goryōsha.[40] Flanking both sides of the palanquin were his followers, Yokoyama Sukeno-jō and Shimotsu Shikanosuke.[41] In addition to two attendants, Ueno Yūjirō and Matsumura Kinzaburō,[42] a sandal-bearer also accompanied the party. Suddenly a pistol shot shattered the leaden air of that cloudy day; from between two tradesmen's houses a half-dozen warriors stepped out, drawing their swords in unison. It was Ueda and his band. Nakai had purposely fired the pistol into the air to frighten the palanquin bearers and retainers.

The palanquin bearers dropped the palanquin and ran. Yokoi's followers, Yokoyama and Shimotsu (he had expected some incident on the way and had picked competent swordsmen), drew their swords and faced their adversaries. Yokoyama crossed swords with Kashima; Shimotsu crossed swords with Yanagida. Maeoka and Nakai held the attendants at bay.

As Ueda and Shirōzaemon stood watching a short distance behind the others, the flap of the palanquin opened, and out stepped Yokoi. The oldest of all the *chōshi*, he wore his slightly thinning white hair in a topknot. That year he had turned sixty-one. Without the slightest sign of panic, he gripped a short-sword in his right hand and cooly surveyed the band of men. Yokoi had once spent time learning fencing. He had refused to face the assailants in Shinagawa seven years before because there had been a chance to escape. Seeing that flight was impossible here, he was determined to fight to the bitter end.

"Now!" said Ueda with a glance at Shirōzaemon. The latter, expecting it to take but a stroke, swung down upon Yokoi. But Yokoi easily parried the blow. Fighting on equal terms with Shirōzaemon, who so prided himself on his swordsmanship, Yokoi deftly caught some fifteen blows. This short-sword remains in the Yokoi family; the blade is so badly nicked it looks more like a saw.

While Yokoi was fending off Shirōzaemon's blows, Yokoyama gashed Kashima on the forehead. With the blood running into his eyes, Kashima retreated a few steps. Ueda saw Yokoyama trying to follow up the advantage and finish off his man, so he fell upon Yokoyama from the flank. The ferocity of Ueda's attack proved too much for Yokoyama and, though he managed to graze Ueda on one arm, he broke off fighting and started to run. Hot in pursuit, Ueda slashed him across the back of the head, then gave up and returned to the scene.

Met by Yokoi's unexpected resistance, Shirōzaemon's anger flared; finally under the vicious onslaught of Shirōzaemon's blade, the short-sword was knocked from Yokoi's hand. In a flash Shirōzaemon plunged his sword home; shoving Yokoi to the ground, he took hold of his topknot and cut off his head.

"Let's go!" he shouted and started running with Yokoi's head dangling from his left hand. Townsmen from Teramachi Street and passersby, who had gathered round the group of combatants and stood watching in great terror, now, when they saw Shirōzaemon coming toward them with bloody sword and dripping head, were quick to clear the way.

Meanwhile, Yokoi's follower Shimotsu, undaunted by a gash on his forehead administered earlier by Yanagida, ended a hard-fought struggle by putting a deep slice in Yanagida's shoulder. Unable to bear the pain, Yanagida crumpled to the ground. Just then Shimotsu saw Shirōzaemon take his beloved master's head and run from the scene, so he abandoned Yanagida and set off in pursuit of Shirōzaemon.

At this point Ueno, one of the attendants held at bay by Maeoka and Nakai, slipped away from the group and joined Shimotsu.

Ueno, fleeter of foot than Shimotsu, had almost caught up with Shirōzaemon when the latter whirled around and flung the head straight at him. It struck him hard on the right arm. He stumbled, and in that instant Shirōzaemon made good his escape.

After Ueno had raced off in pursuit of Shirōzaemon, the attendants kept falling back under a rain of blows from Maeoka and Nakai. When the latter saw that Shirōzaemon had taken Yokoi's head, they changed tactics and fled. Kashima, cut on the forehead by Yokoyama, and Ueda both saw their chance and also fled. The only one of the band left at the scene was the badly wounded Yanagida.

Ueno, in his hands the head hurled at him by Shirōzaemon, and Shimotsu were returning to the place of their master's corpse when Yokoyama also came back. Out of the crowd of bystanders, other attendants stepped forth and truncated corpse inside the palanquin. It was about then that a large number of police on duty in the city arrived on the scene, arrested Yanagida, and led him away.

After racing through the city and coming out onto a path through some paddyfields, Shirōzaemon washed the blood from his sword in a creek that ran beside the path, replaced it in its sheath, and then turned off the path and headed for the home of Miyake Sakon,[43] in Saga. Sakon was a swordsman whom Shirōzaemon had met at the home of Miyake Tenzen. Behind the Sakon place was a small sake shop. Shirōzaemon bought a three-pint jug of sake there and with the jug in one hand went through a back gate hidden in a bamboo thicket. After Shirōzaemon's capture and death, I am told, that jug was wrapped in a purple silk-crepe wrapper and carefully stored away in Sakon's house.

The prisoner Yanagida would not utter a word, and the judges and other officers ordered to conduct an investigation did not try to force any information out of him, so the names of the accomplices remained unknown for some time. But those who had had any dealings with Yanagida were summoned one by one, and some were clapped into prison.

Shirōzaemon went into the city every day; he made inquiries wherever he went, hoping to find out whether Yanagida was alive and who had been arrested. That Yanagida was badly wounded but still alive, that he would not reveal the names of his accomplices, and so on—these were common gossip in the city. Those who had been summoned and detained in the government office, or captured and put in prison, were for the most part people publicly known as proponents of *sonnō-jōi*. Best known among them was Naka Zuiunsai[44] of Izumi; he was imprisoned with his eldest son Katsuki, his second son Kanae, and third son Takeshi. Kanamoto Kenzō from Izumo, Masuda Jirō from Totsugawa, Koyasu Riheiji from Shimōsa, Ōkuma Kumaji from Echigo,[45] and others, were also imprisoned. Of Shirōzaemon's fellow countrymen, Kaima Jūrōzaemon[46] was summoned, but after some questioning he was immediately set free. Kaima was owner of the Yoshidaya, an inn for travelers in Kamiya-chō in Okayama and was rumored to be rendering assistance to the group.

Opinion in Kyoto was in general sympathetic to the band; indeed, it tended to censure the crimes of the slain Yokoi. Yanagida's silence was lauded. The way the little band kept their secret so well and covered up their tracks was admired. Having a lot to do with this general attitude was a document posted at all crossroads a few days after Yokoi was slain. Who the author of this document was, the band did not know; to judge from its contents, it was not written in the same jesting mood as the lampoons,[47] but seemed to be an outright attempt to defend the band. The police officials lost no time going round and ripping down the posters, but several copies of it circulated in the city. The text read as follows:

On the fifth preceding, the *chōshi* Yokoi Heishirō was slain by the sword in broad daylight in Teramachi. One of the assailants was captured; it is said that the remainder, who fled, are diligently being sought out. I do not as yet know what manner of men cut Yokoi down, but their actions would seem to be motivated by an intense concern for the welfare of their country. The wickedness

of this Heishirō was something known to all in the land. In the beginning he
played up to the Bakufu; then he advocated—I hesitate even to say it—
dethronement of the emperor, and placed in jeopardy the line of emperors un-
broken for ages eternal. In addition, he made criminals out of true patriots by
use of slander, and had them killed. Recently he secretly contacted the barbarians and agreed to propagation of the Christian religion in our empire. Also,
he tried to shunt aside the court's most urgent need, military arms. His other
evil crimes are too numerous to mention. At a time when the country is being
reformed into a land of imperial rule and has become the center of attention of
the whole world, this traitor in key position was obstructing progress, introducing irregularity in court practices, breaking down imperial authority, creating
chaos in the empire, and attempting to turn this majestic divine land of ours
into a dependency of barbarians no better than brute animals. His assailants,
finding such things intolerable, were forced to slay him by sword. The heroic
daring of their deed is comparable to that of the Mito warriors at Sakurada
gate.[48] For these reasons, there is no one with an iota of righteousness who does
not rejoice over their deed. In general, such incidents as this occur because the
opinions of ordinary citizens do not reach the ears of the statesmen. From the
beginning the Five Articles of the Imperial Oath called for free exchange of
views between high and low, but this has remained empty, insubstantial verbi-
age. A man of loyal heart, one upright and true, is cast aside as a bigot, and a
traitorous subject like Heishirō, who betrays the court, is appointed instead;
around him gather men of the very same breed; they corrupt the government
of our land, and the barbarians grow more and more powerful. Loyal men,
concerned about the situation, could tolerate it no longer and at an opportune
time made known their true views, but these were dismissed as insubstantial
and not adopted. Hence it was that they took strong action, slew the chief of
the traitors, and have caused us to reflect on past political errors in regard to the
court. The above is because views between high and low are not being exchanged. I make a heartfelt plea that the court harken to the truth in what is
said above, proclaim an imperial edict requesting the whole nation to speak up
freely, banish all traitors, appoint to office faithful and upright men, abandon
erroneous views, and let the law of justice shine bright. Also, as for the assailants who slew this Yokoi fellow with the sword, be pleased to commend their
sentiments, overlook their crime, and release them at once. If this is done, not
only can the national polity most surely be secured and the barbarians' inso-
lence be requited, but also warriors throughout the land will admire the
court's speed in admitting and rectifying its own mistakes, and such acts as the
slaying of traitorous subjects will cease entirely. But if the court hesitates to carry out the above matters, it will be filled with traitors, the emperor's grip on
the reins of administration will slacken, and one calamity will follow upon
another. There will be no difference between this government and the Bakufu
government that collapsed. When things come to such a pass, loyal patriots
will rise up in anger and sweep away all treacherous subjects without exception.
The above is not the right way to keep intact the prestige of the imperial court.
Yet the Sun Goddess, founder of the imperial family, watches from Heaven.
Whether what I say is correct or not requires no proof. Let all who agree with

my view when they read this written appeal assemble at Mt. Hiei; let us together discuss how to achieve the great task of reforming our country.

spring, first month, 1869

A son of Great Japan who laments
the present state of affairs

To this poster was appended an additional piece of paper, on which was written: "This notice should be posted for three days. Anyone removing it without cause will be cut down." This was copied from an official document by Shirōzaemon's instructor in swordsmanship, Abe Morie, who afterward worked in the Justice Department.[49]

On the fourteenth day of the first month, nine days after killing Yokoi, Shirōzaemon went to the home of a friend from Shinshū, Kondō Jūbē,[50] who at the time was an official in the Cabinet. While he was inquiring about rumors in government circles, police officials stepped in and led away both host and guest. This resulted from Ueda's capture together with Kashima at the base of Mt. Kōya, at which time the police decided that Shirōzaemon, Ueda's close friend, should also be arrested. When Kashima was first called in, the judge had questioned him about Bizen loyalists, but Kashima was evasive in his replies and kept suspicion from falling upon Ueda and his men. But when Ueda was arrested because of the sword wound on his arm, Kashima's efforts came to naught.

Yanagida died from his injury on the sixteenth, two days after Shirōzaemon was captured. Since customs from the old Bakufu times were still being observed in prisons, the corpse was packed in salt. After Ueda and Shirōzaemon were captured, the organizer of the Valiant Fighting Force in Bizen, Matsumoto Minosuke, was put into prison, and a retainer of the Han Elder Tokura Sazen, Saitō Naohiko,[51] who assisted in organizing it, also underwent questioning.

In the absence of any reliable records, and because those involved in the affair are all dead, I do not know the details of what happened in the tribunal at that time; but if the story is true that even some of the judges were sympathetic to the accomplices, this would explain why they did not take severe measures. I also heard that there was a certain woman named Niho-ko,[52] who petitioned to have Shirōzaemon released. I was a mere child at the time, and when told she tried to save father, imprisoned for acting for the sake of His Majesty, I envisioned a court lady with long hair hanging down her back and dressed in a scarlet garment. In reality, though, I do not know what her social position was. I heard that later, around 1878 or 1879, Nihoko came to Okayama, gathered some followers and spoke to them of respecting the gods and revering the emperor; she also composed poems which she sent to various people, but I was no longer in Okayama by then.

I was told that father was executed on the tenth day of the tenth month of 1870. He was buried in an unmarked grave, so as not to offend government circles. I have no parental grave where I can place incense and flowers. I do not recall clearly now, but people tell me that, when I heard the news of father's death, I asked how he died. Mother's answer was that he died by the sword. I replied that if so he must have had some enemy, and this is how I would cut that enemy down—at this I leapt out into the garden and with a wooden sword snapped a branch off a jasmine tree. Mother was so alarmed that she stopped speaking about father in my hearing from that time on.

After father died, grandfather's spirits fell; he even stopped supervision of the tenant farmers working our fields. The harvests gradually diminished, our finances declined, and afterward mother and I were left almost propertyless. We were not just an ordinary widow and orphan child. We were the wife and child of a man who had been executed as a criminal. We were people with a dark past.

To bring me up and, as I gradually grew older, to send me to school, mother worked herself to the bone. Thanks to her I eventually gained admission into Tokyo University, but on account of various problems I withdrew before finishing. I do not wish to enumerate all those problems here, to make feeble excuses over them. One thing I do want to state, however, is that, driven from childhood by a fierce desire to clear my executed father's name, I was unable to set my mind to acquiring an education.

People may say that acquiring an education, making a name for myself, and restoring the fortunes of my house would have been the way to clear father's name. But that is abstract theory. My heart ached day and night for my deceased father; I could not apply my mind to study. The power of cool reason was too feeble to calm my burning emotions.

Father killed a man. To do so was bad. But if the slain man were a bad man, if he were always regarded as bad, killing him would have been taken for granted. Unfortunately, the slain man was not a bad man. No one looking back from our present perspective would say he was bad. Did father, then, kill someone good? No, he killed someone who was, in his eyes, bad. This is not to say that father was the only one who made this judgment. At that time people in general judged Yokoi to be bad. Criteria for good and bad change with times and places. Father, living in a certain age, killed a man who, in that age, was bad. Why did father have to be executed? Why must his wife and child become social outcasts? Rambling, repetitive, vicious circles of thought such as these wrapped themselves round my mind like spider webs; they forced me to shut books and cast aside writing brushes poised in hand.

After abandoning my studies, I joined the ranks of lower-echelon public servants and received enough pay to feed mother and myself. Since the jobs I took up afterward were limited to mechanical, mentally tedious tasks, I tried to use all my strength to clear father's name. But it was an indescribably arduous undertaking.

First of all I tried to learn in as minute detail as possible the things father did. Convinced he was a good man, I felt that the more people knew about what he did, the greater his glory would be. Every time I had a vacation I went on a trip and finally I traversed every district father had. When I learned of someone who knew father, or who had heard about him, I visited the person and listened to his story, regardless of the distance. However, fifty years had passed since father's death. Though the mountains and rivers were the same as before, old roads had disappeared, new roads had been cleared, paddies and fields had been converted into residences and city streets. The same with the people. There were very few around who had even heard of father, let alone who knew him personally, and even they were so old they complained of failing memories or poor hearing.

The things I recounted earlier are what I have pieced together as I could from scraps of data collected in the manner just mentioned. There may have been errors in the telling; there may have been errors in the hearing. Again, it is not impossible that in some places my imagination unconsciously asserted itself and put in things that were not there. For the most part, however, I believe I can say the following. My expectations did not play me false. They were not biased. Father was a good man. He was a man who esteemed moral integrity. He was a loyalist. A patriot. A man who possessed something more precious than life or property. He was an idealist.

While I believe this, I also can console myself. On the other side of the picture, however, I also have to admit that father was a simpleton and a fool, unable to see the signs of the times. I have to deplore his lack of natural endowments, and lament that no one was kind enough to enlighten him.

This is my concluding judgment—the eulogy I append to father's biography. I here express my thanks to those who told me about father. One of the principal of these is the widow, Lady Kaima. Possessing a woman's natural delicate sensitivity to the slightest stimuli, she recalled things which others could not; as a result, I was given numerous details of father's personal history. Another is the son of Miyake (Sakon), Takehiko; sympathizing with father in his destitute wandering, he harbored him in his home for a long time. Next I mention the names of two men who spoke in defense of father: Niwa Hiroo and Suzuki Muin.[53] Niwa was a senior statesman in Bizen with a stipend of three thousand *koku*. He had this to say: "To criticize Shirōzaemon as a simpleton is too harsh. Japan was an isolated country at the time, and Bizen was an isolated fief within an isolated nation. People in Okayama could not set foot outside the fief boundaries. When young lads had a hankering for women, they went to Miyauchi, about one ri west of Okayama. If they were treated insultingly by anyone they could not take the fellow to task because it would betray the fact that they had gone into Bitchū territory. To blame these lads for being out of touch with trends in the world is unreasonable. When I was in Kyoto I too once tried to stab a certain individual. But circumstances prevented me from doing so and I returned to Okayama without realizing my purpose. Before long, due to my comparatively high social position, I was appointed a minor government official. After that I associated with higher authorities and gradually heard about conditions in foreign lands. I am not pretending to be wise, but between Shirōzaemon and me there was no difference whatsoever." Suzuki was a scholar versed in domestic and international law who had worked on national affairs with Arao Sei and others. He sent me the following message: "I knew Shirōzaemon. He was no fool. There were fitting reasons for his slaying Yokoi." But Suzuki died before I could meet him. I do not know what story he had to tell me, but I feel cheated.

I was not satisfied with just digging up father's past. My desire since childhood was to do something positive to clear father's name, as if I were to wash away mud smeared on his face. As a child I thought to myself: "Father acted for the sake of His Imperial Majesty. Yet somebody killed him. I must kill the man who killed him." When I grew a little older I realized it was not a man who killed father, but the law. I felt I had lost my purpose in life. I felt life had become meaningless. I remember that this discovery tortured me for days and months on end.

After I passed through this internal struggle I lived in a daze for some time; as equilibrium of mind gradually returned, the positive means of clearing father's name that I had adopted in the past rose into consciousness again in completely new guise. I resolved to have my deceased father some way or other granted a special imperial favor. Father had been among the first to rise up at the time of restoration of imperial rule and serve the court's cause. He had slain Yokoi because their political views were incompatible. Yokoi was a victim of political conflict. Now that the times had changed and both fanaticism and hate had subsided, what was there to prevent his dry bones from being bathed in imperial favor? With this idea in mind, I first consulted a senior official from my part of the country and then appealed to the proper high authorities. This was after I had abandoned my studies.

From 1886 to 1887 the pros and cons of conferring posthumous rank on Tsuge Shirōzaemon were discussed by the authorities, I was told. But in the end it was decided that conferral of posthumous rank on someone not given amnesty and executed as a criminal could not be sought from the emperor. I was dismayed; once again I felt life had become meaningless. Still, compared with the previous time I had lost my object of revenge, my suffering this time was rather slight and short-lived. Perhaps it was because I had matured; then again, it could very well be that I had grown callous.

I have given up my cause. What with one compromise after another, my ambition has gradually shrunk to the point where now my only desire is to have someone put this story in writing for future generations.

The narrative ends here. The "I" of the tale is the son of Tsuge Shirōzaemon Masayoshi, the person named Shikata. This much is already clear from the story. This is not all, though. The reader no doubt has also been able to size up to some extent Shikata's character, circumstances, and past history.

As the editor of this narrative, I feel no need to make numerous additions. I only wish to explain the events which led to its being made public at my hands. It all started when I was already out of college but still at home, and my younger brother, Tokujirō, was still going to college. I asked Tokujirō, "Tell me, are there any outstanding fellows among your schoolmates?" My brother immediately mentioned the names of two of his classmates. One was K., a big-hearted person, the other was Tsuge Masataka, an uncompromising fellow, he said. My brother later came to consider a man of talent as ideal, but his ideal then was still the outgoing type. He introduced K. and Tsuge to me. K. was as huge as a wrestler and liked judo. Unfortunately, under the influence of alcohol he did something that was interpreted as robbery and was expelled from school. Tsuge, or Shikata, is the author of this narrative.

Tsuge was a light-complexioned youth with an oval face, his brows knitted in a perpetual frown. It seems to me his family's misfortunes were, like the sign of Cain, written on his countenance. He was a reticent person, and, since I also was not much of a talker then, our first meeting almost ended up with us staring at each other. But from then till the present day, a span of thirty years, Tsuge has not been remiss in writing to me. My own negligence in replying has not bothered him. Shortly after we met he left college and started drifting from place to place. His letters have come from Hokkaido. They have even come from Korea. Still he has never completely disappeared from sight.

On 13 October 1913, Tsuge suddenly visited my house and told me the story of his father, Shirōzaemon. The narrative is almost exactly as he told it. He wanted me to revise it, but because the words have so much forcefulness, flowing as they did from the heart, I am publishing them almost verbatim. All I did was verify points regarding the times and places mentioned in his story with Sugi Magoshichirō, Aoki Umesaburō, Nakaoka Moku, Tokutomi Iichirō, Shimizu Koichirō, and Yamabe Takeo;[54] then I made two or three corrections. During the long period since we last met, Tsuge became a robust, cheerful-looking fellow; not a shadow remained of his old melancholic gloom. As I bring this postcript to a close, I sincerely wish him good health.

The story above, originally published in *Chūō kōron*, was the means of my coming to know a good many people. Among them were even some who had been friends of Shirōzaemon. Through these people's conversations, letters, documents in their possession, and so on, I made a few editorial changes in regard to the names appearing in the story. I adopted what I judged to be comparatively accurate. I was also able to learn the following several facts:

That, in appearance, Tsuge Shirōzaemon resembled the Masataka mentioned above can be surmised from the text. However, Shirōzaemon is said to have had a slightly larger physique and a somewhat rounder face.

The storehouse of the Miyake Tenzen family in Kyoto, where Shirōzaemon stayed in hiding, is said still to retain its old exterior even though the main building was later rebuilt; one can see it from the road. The woman who carried food to the storehouse and otherwise looked after Shirōzaemon is still alive and living in Hakusan Goten-machi, but she does not want her name made public.

In the text I wrote that when Ueda Tatsuo and Shirōzaemon left their fiefs and went to Kyoto they soon determined on a plot to assassinate the traitor. But this might not necessarily have been the case. After the two of them arrived in Kyoto, they took an active part for a while in the ''Imperial Bodyguards Affair.''[55] One of the court nobles left his family, recruited some lordless samurai, and laid plans for protecting the imperial family. He wanted the roster filled by lordless samurai because he feared *han* samurai would scheme for their own masters. I leave the name of that court noble unwritten here. But if some day materials on the Restoration are made public, this matter might not be able to remain a secret.

Among the *rōnin* were many samurai from Totsugawa. The rest were from various other provinces. Foremost among those samurai of note who were enrolled in the imperial bodyguards was Naka Zuiunsai.

The Naka family used to be called Urikami, and was an illustrious Kawachi family. In 1653 they moved to Gomon in Kumatori-mura, Izumi Province, and for generations were known as rural samurai. Included among the branch houses of the Naka family was the Negoro family[56] living in Honjō in Edo—direct vassals of the shogun, with an income of three thousand six hundred *koku*. Born third son of the Negoro family, Zuiunsai succeeded to the main family and himself had three sons. The eldest was Katsuki, the second Kanae, and the third Takeshi. In addition he had an adopted son, Kaoru.

Zuiunsai early passed the house on to Katsuki; he then went to Kyoto and joined the loyalists. When Shirōzaemon and the others were imprisoned, Zuiunsai was arrested along with his three sons. He was sent under guard to Aomori Prefecture, but died en route; Katsuki and Takeshi died in a Kyoto prison; Kanae was released after ten years' imprisonment. Meantime their three sisters were living in their home town of Kumatori-mura. A certain guardian looked after them; he made arrangements with Tatsunosuke, the second son of Hara Bumpei of Kotani-mura, and married him to the eldest daughter, Sumi. After his release Kanae was not kindly received by Tatsunosuke and his family, so, changing his name to Ken'ichirō, he moved to Sakai and set up in business; when he ran out of capital, he became the priest of Homuda shrine in Furuichi-mura, Minamikawachi District, Osaka. Ken'ichirō's children were Kanae, Takeo, and Yukio; Kanae is a lower-echelon official in the tax office, Takeo an assistant engineer under the Governor-General of Formosa, and Yukio a student of history in college. The eldest daughter married the grandson of Miyake Tenzen, Tetsuo. I owe this family history to Yukio.

Among the accomplices of Zuiunsai was Miya Taichū of Totsugawa.[57] At that time he was known as Ōki Mondo. Taichū was well known for his proficiency in Japanese, Chinese, and Western studies. He was put into the same prison as Shirōzaemon and the others, then banished to Miyake Island; after being pardoned he was able to return to his home. Taichū's son Taimo lives at 19 Kita Iga-chō, Yotsuya-ku.

Another Totsugawa samurai imprisoned in the same way was Kamihira Chikara (if one is careless in writing the horizontal stroke in his name, the result will be Shimohira); exiled to Nii Island, he also was able to return home.

Ichinose Tonomo[58] was another Totsugawa samurai imprisoned; exiled to Hachijō Island, he was later pardoned and returned home.

Naka and company wanted to form a band of imperial bodyguards but were unable to do so because they were thwarted by such people as Kanda Kōhei,[59] Nakai Hiroshi,[60] and Yokoi Heishirō.

At this time a document titled "On Reform of the Way of Heaven" circulated among the loyalists. According to contemporary reports, the text was composed by Yokoi Heishirō, the document was issued by the priest of Aso shrine, and it was passed around by Koga Jūrō.[61] The text runs as follows:

> Just as the human body has four limbs and a hundred bones, so there are mountains, rivers, trees, grasses, human beings, birds, and beasts. Hence, he who does not know the essence of the universe is no different from one who does not know that his body is equipped with arms and legs. Now, all countries in the world are like one body, and there is no distinction between "others" and "self." It is necessary to understand the principle of proximity and distance and grasp that interior and exterior [Japan and other lands] are one and the same. From ancient times, it has been customary for an illustrious sovereign to spread his dignity and virtue all over the world, and all countries that submit to him, without exception, find, because of the sovereign's magnanimity, entrance into his expansive heart; nothing proves impossible to grant; his heart, evolving in accord with his beneficence, is in harmony with this constantly changing world. Thus this sovereign can be lord of the world and monarch of all people. However, if through shallowness of mind he does not know the principle of the whole world being one body, one being, it would be as if the whole body were insensate and felt neither pain nor itch. A hundred generations would not suffice for such a one to gain understanding. Is this not something to be pitied? . . . Today there is a movement—indeed, since the beginning of time there has never been a greater one—toward renovation of political rule, and thus many foreign countries are striving to understand, to discover, and to attain a high level of culture on the basis of natural principles. However, Japan alone huddles to its isolated small islands . . . and so cannot achieve this. Its fall is inevitable. We must at once sweep away the great evils of narrow-mindedness and deep-rooted abuses, must, guided by the idea that we are "eternal as heaven and earth," see through distorted opinions and must be intent on our land becoming the greatest in the universe. If in this way we search for principles, shall we not in the end attain a clear insight into the principles of all things?

> Teibō, third month, at the southern window, on the spur of the moment.

> Shōnan

I have omitted some two to three hundred irrelevant words and transcribed here the remainder. However, both the style and diction can, for the most part, be gathered from this much. "Teibō" is 1867. The general idea is an elaboration of the five-character poem "Human Rulers How Divinely Appointed?" For something supposed to have been written by Yokoi, it is quite inferior.

It is said that when Shirōzaemon and the others read it they were absolutely sure it was Yokoi's writing. Convinced the situation had become critical, they abandoned the imperial bodyguards idea and laid plans to cut down Yokoi.

The spot where Shirōzaemon and the others killed Yokoi is reported to be south of the crossroads of Maruta-machi and Teramachi, beyond Goryōsha, but before one reaches the Hikaru-dō. This information is based on Minami Jun'ichi's *Fūbunroku*.[62] Jun'ichi later changed his name to Hisatoki. The incident took place on 5 January 1869. On the sixth, a government proclamation was issued.

> The killing of the *chōshi* Yokoi Heishirō was an outrageous act in complete disregard for the imperial constitution. Matters such as assassination cannot be undertaken by anyone who belongs to a *han* or who holds prefectural office. Perhaps assassination was resorted to on grounds that speech and writing are shackled, but after the Restoration of 1868 discussion has become free and there ought to be no *han* or prefecture where communication is impossible. If anybody can desert his *han* and in effect decide what is right and wrong in society, thus undermining the court's laws, how will public discipline be maintained and the empire sustained? This is the question asked by His Majesty, who is extremely distressed by what has happened. He has given orders that, especially in Kyoto but in other prefectures also, deserters from their *han* are to be tracked down relentlessly, and that at all times strict control is to be kept without relaxing of vigilance.

This text is recorded by Osatake Takeshi.[63] The Osatake family now lives in Kasumigaoka-chō, Yotsuya-ku.

Both Miyake Tenzen, at whose house Shirōzaemon stayed in hiding before the incident, and Miyake Sakon, whose house he visited afterward, were from Tsurajima in Bitchū Province. Takehiko, the heir of Tenzen, whose pen name was Gazen, speaks about Sakon in writing as follows:

> In an article about my deceased father reference is made to a wine shop and a sake jug. Come to think of it, at that time, there was an old man named Miyake Sakon, also from Tsurajima, who was a retainer at Saga palace [Daikaku-ji]. A swashbuckling type of old man, with neither wife nor children, he lived in Saga in Kyoto. There was, as a matter of fact, a thicket behind the house, and a sake shop. This Miyake Sakon used to meet with my deceased father in our house, and, because he boasted of his swordsmanship, he and my father finally held a contest; he was soundly defeated. From that time on he felt a respectful admiration for my father and became something of a pupil of his. I imagine that my father did take some sake to the Sakon house. Sakon's real name is Sahei.

I have mentioned before that the Naka family were in-laws of Takehiko. Takehiko lives in Dote Sanbanchō, Kōjimachi-ku.

The woman whom I described in the text as defending Shirōzaemon, Nihoko, was reported to be the daughter of Fushimi-no-miya Shodaibu, Wakae Shuridaibu. The letter Nihoko presented to the Bishū *han chōshi* Arakawa Jinsaku[64] ran as follows:

On what grounds was the decision made in regard to the disposition of the man who killed Yokoi Heishirō? Since it was decided by the authorities, we ought by no means question it; still, in a written document presented by the man who killed Yokoi, it is stated that: "Yokoi's close associates were scheming to spread the Roman Church throughout all of Japan." On the basis of only this one document, one might suspect the man was using a widespread rumor as a pretext to vent a personal grudge; however, since the whole country knew about Yokoi's scheme, it cannot be said the man was taking advantage of a public rumor for his own ends. To have killed a Councillor of the imperial court is a serious matter, and of course it ought to be punished severely. But in view of the fact that this man put to death someone who, as I said above, everyone knew was guilty of a crime, he is, really, a man moved by a spirit of patriotism; although he committed the serious crime of killing a man, still, by special dispensation, please commute the death penalty one degree. This is inconsistent with what I said the other day about it being a well-deserved punishment and it may strike you as suspicious; but if in these present circumstances you were to punish such men with severity, it would immediately alienate men's hearts from the government, and other incidents will, it seems quite clear, flare up everywhere. On top of this, rumor has it that there have been many with no direct part in the matter who have denounced themselves to the authorities as being of the same mind as the slayers. These people who have surrendered themselves are all known to be faultless, righteous men. I think it fitting to use special clemency and pardon them. Indeed, righteous subjects are a nation's strength and vigor; to put even one of them to death as a criminal is naturally to damage the strength and vigor of the nation. If its strength and vigor are damaged, the very life of all those entrusted to it by Heaven will perish. I beg you to give full consideration to these reasons, by special dispensation to commute the death penalty of the leader one degree, and to grant complete pardon to all those who surrendered themselves as being of like mind. Though they may be great criminals, I think they have committed no more than a minor offense when compared with that of the enemies of the emperor. By reason of my speaking thus, I suppose suspicion will fall on me: "She has something to do with this matter; that is why she is asking this . . ." If suspicion does fall upon me, I shall say nothing in my own defense, so be pleased to arrest me at once and punish me—but only me—with death; then I trust you will pardon all the rest. If you punish with severity both the young leader and his comrades as well, without distinction, I think that righteous men throughout the land will at once harbor feelings of indignation and bitterness against the court; you will unwisely arouse public opinion and the situation will get out of control. I understand that at the close of last year you ordered a religious service performed for those punished by death in the time of the tyrannical

Bakufu government; it seems to me that to enroll among the gods those already dead and then punish with death the still living is no policy for stability in government. I know Your Excellency is indisposed at present, but I trust that this matter will be handled with fitting discernment. With earnest entreaty for your kindest consideration.

First month, 21st day, Nihoko.

The recipient of this letter, Arakawa Jinsaku, resigned because of illness from his post as Junior Councillor in the third month of 1868, changed his name to Ozaki Yoshitomo, and is reported to have lived in Nagoya.

Nihoko's letter passed from Tanaka Fujimaro[65] or Niwa Juntarō (later named Masaru)[66] to the Owari *han* warrior Matsuyama Yoshine[67] of the Mighty Fighting Force (Hōhakutai); he was older brother of former Minister of the Navy Yashirō.[68] From him it passed into the possession of Kurachi Iemon of the Komaki Post Office in Owari; Kurachi then presented it, through me, to Tsuge. Kurachi believes that it is the autograph copy of Nihoko herself. Another version has it that the original manuscript of Nihoko's letter is in the possession of one Nishida Jirō, priest of Funae shrine in Funae, Shinjō-mura, Funae District, Tamba Province. This is based on Miyaki Takehiko's account of the facts.

Nihoko's letter has already been published. It appeared in the newspaper *Enkin Shimbun*, number five, published 10 April 1868 and copyrighted by Tsuji Shinji[69] and Gotō Kenkichi, who reside on the campus of Kaisei Gakkō.[70] Osatake has the paper in his possession. What I have transcribed above is the result of using the Kurachi copy as the basic text and then comparing it with the *Enkin Shimbun* copy. There were a few differences between the two texts. That the Kurachi is the autograph copy is somewhat doubtful.

According to what I heard from Mimaki Motoyoshi,[71] Nihoko was not a good-looking woman, but she was a talented one. When the Empress Shōken[72] was still residing in her Ichijō home, Nihoko gave her lectures on Chinese works. Mimaki himself had attended Nihoko's lectures. Because she spoke out about matters of state, she was told to quit her position and was placed with a Tanaka employed by the Fushimi-no-miya family. Later, because of an indiscretion, she was shunned by self-respecting folk; she then dwelt in isolated retirement in the vicinity of Akashi, in Suma, where it seems she died.

Nihoko's poems have made their way here and there into the world. Miyake Takehiko possesses a small book of them. In June of 1915, a Meiji Commemorative Exhibition was held in Manshōji temple in Nagoya. Among the items on display was a scroll with a poem by Nihoko.

The days of seclusion pass drearily. Sitting idle all the day long, I brood in sorrow and lament the times, till day reaches its close. When cool breezes fan the room where I lie dozing, I know the heat of day has passed. Seen from my window at dawn, traces of the night's rain remind me how wearily the night dragged on. The acclaims and strictures of human society are things of the distant past, the vicissitudes of life have vanished like a dream. No matter how many the reverses I have suffered, I remain as rash and senseless as ever.

Early fall; living in confinement. Nihoko.

It had one seal, and on the design was printed "Suga-shi." Wakae seems to have been a Sugawara. This was copied out by Kurachi and brought to me. Also, others have said they saw these words written by Nihoko: "There are so many thousands of men in our divine land, but is there one who grieves as I?"

I have already given supplementary material about Nihoko, the daughter of Wakae Shuridaibu, but since then I have heard from Honda Tatsujirō[73] that the Shuridaibu's personal name was Kazunaga, and that he had once been chief of the Bureau of Imperial Mausolea.[74] As a result of this bit of news I made inquiry of Shiba Katsushige,[75] from whom I received in writing the following information.

The girl Nihoko's father was the head of the household staff of Fushimi-no-miya and a man of court rank. The Wakae family originally was a Sugawara, from the stock of Arikimi, son of the Shikibu Gon-no-taifu, Sugawara no Kimisuke. The name was first Mibu Bōjō, then Nakamikado, then once again changed to Wakae. The Wakae first began serving Fushimi-no-miya in the time of Nagachika, who was the tenth generation away from Arikimi. Nagachika was born on the twenty-ninth day of the third month in 1664, and he passed away on the ninth day of the seventh month in 1720, at the age of fifty-seven. Kazunaga was the son of Kimiyoshi, who was the fifth generation from Nagachika; born on the thirteenth day of the twelfth month in 1812, he came of age on the twenty-eighth day of the third month in 1825 (at the age of fourteen), was appointed Echigo Gon-no-suke, and granted the privilege of attending the imperial court within the hall—all on the same day. Later he became vice-minister in the Imperial Police Department, and then went on to become Shuridaibu; Junior Grade Fourth Court Rank was conferred on him on the twenty-second day, twelfth month, 1842. This much can be known from the *Jige-Kaden*.[76] Besides this, according to the diary of Nonomiya Sadayoshi, on the twenty-fourth day, second month, 1864, restoration of the Bureau of Imperial Mausolea was announced, and the man appointed at the time to become its chief was this Kazunaga. However, it seems Kazunaga had no special knowledge of mountainous regions. Anything to do with mountains, apparently, he entrusted almost entirely to two subordinates, Yamato no Suke Tanimori Tanematsu[77] and Chikuzen no kami Suzuki Katsunori.[78] To come to the point, there is something of interest with regard to his daughter Nihoko. From the account given by Mimaki Motoyoshi it has already been seen that Nihoko was a talented woman and that, because she was well-versed in Japanese and Chinese studies, especially the latter, she went to give lectures on Chinese literature when Empress Shōken was still in her Ichijō home. Now a section in the annals of Toda Tadayoshi[79] contains the following account:

> From 1867 on, their lordships Nijō and Nakayama were extremely concerned about the marriage of H.M. the Empress. Both of them requested me to give the matter some thought. Just as I was at my wits' end, it was brought to my attention that Nihoko, the daughter of Wakae Shuridaibu—he had for some time been working closely with me in connection with the Imperial Mausolea—was teaching *waka* to the daughters of Lord Ichijō; I therefore visited her to seek her advice concerning a suitable prospect, but she told me that His Lordship's second daughter was already specially designated; when I reported this to their lordships Nijō and Nakayama, I was instructed to visit the Ichijō palace at once and very discreetly observe the second daughter firsthand; I accordingly discussed the matter with Nihoko and together with her did visit the palace and meet the daughters, after which I made my report on the second daughter. At this juncture, however, His Lordship Nijō was relieved of his post because of certain suspicions harbored against him; later, however, he was appointed commissioner for the wedding, everything went off well, and the wedding took place. . . .

According to this, then, Nihoko's advice seemed to play a considerable part in the selection of the Crown Princess who was destined to become Empress Shōken. In the sixth month of 1867, announcement was made of Empress Shōken's entrance into court, and shortly afterward women were chosen to serve as her upper and middle ladies-in-waiting; at this time Nihoko was again requested to come to the palace and give lessons. The entry for the ninth day of the eighth month of that year in the court record of Hashimoto Saneyoshi[80] gives the following:

> Also, since the younger sister of Wakae Shuridaibu has for many years been devoted to learning, and since she is well known for her admirable depth of wisdom, would it not be advisable to allow her to visit the palace to give lessons to the Crown Princess? I have been told that the chief of the Imperial Guards has indicated the matter should be left to my discretion; as far as I am concerned, it seems advisable to permit her attendance, and I have submitted a report to this effect.

However, the papers of the Ichijō family have, in the entry for the third day of the ninth month:

> I met with Norikata, the messenger of Fushimi-no-miya, and our discussions lasted for several days. I received answer to the effect that he had no objection to acceding to the Crown Princess' request that Wakae Shuridaibu's daughter, Ofumi, give lessons in recitation of the Chinese classics.

On the tenth day of the same month we find: "The Crown Princess said that, for the instructor on the *Book of Filial Piety* in the Palace, she wished Ofumi to be invited," while for the fifteenth day we find mention of Nihoko's going to the Palace for the lessons, entering by way of the door to the ladies-in-waiting quarters, and giving instructions on the *Book of Filial Piety*. The above-mentioned invitation was probably a formal notification renewed on the occasion of the Crown Princess' formal entrance into court; it surely was not the first time she ever gave lessons there. One thing, though: how does one explain the fact that the Saneyoshi court record gives her as the younger sister of the Shuridaibu? Also, was "Ofumi" an earlier name of Nihoko? I have not been able to find any absolute proof for Nihoko's visiting the palace after Empress Shōken's entrance into court. It could very well be that, because of her participation in political matters and the like, an invitation from the Crown Princess was never forthcoming. It is a shame, finally, that her indiscretions brought her to such an unfortunate end. Ueda Keiji's *History of Empress Shōken*[81] states that, "Even after the empress' entrance into court, Nihoko received special preferential treatment; she died peacefully in 1872 in Marugame in Sanuki, where her remains lie even today." But I have not succeeded in discovering any proof for this statement.

Since Kazunaga used to be chief of the Bureau of Imperial Mausolea, I [Shiba] tried asking Tateo, second son of the late Tanimori Tanematsu (he later changed his name to Yoshiomi), whether he had ever seen or heard anything about him. (Yoshiomi was my maternal grandfather, and Tateo my uncle.) Tateo told me this:

> There was a small shrine in Demizu in Kyoto called "Wakae Tenjin," and the Wakae family lived next to it. I think it was when I was about ten years old; one day my father took me to visit the Wakae residence. I there met two girls who were introduced to me as Wakae's daughters. The younger one was an ordinary girl and looked every bit a court nobleman's daughter, with her hair tied behind and flowing down in back; but the older one was an unusual woman: dark-complexioned, with no makeup whatever, her hair bound artlessly. I recall how, more than a match for any man, she heatedly engaged my father in argument. Even he said he could not stand up to such a woman. This

was Nihoko, probably. I also heard that later her whereabouts became unknown, but as for her having yielded to temptation because of her family's not being well off, well, maybe what happened deserves our sympathy more than anything else. It may also be true that she died in Sanuki, but I do not think it was an ordinary death. I also do not think she was the younger sister of Kazunaga. I remember her being introduced as his daughter.

April 1915

KURIYAMA DAIZEN

"KURIYAMA DAIZEN" makes use of an incident in history to define the nature and quality of loyalty. In particular Ōgai seeks to illustrate the conflict involved between allegiance to institutions and traditions (in this particular case, the great family of Kuroda) as opposed to the men who merely represent them.

The events of the story (all historically quite accurate) take place on the periphery of some of the most important moments in Japanese history: the rise of Oda Nobunaga and Toyotomi Hideyoshi, followed by the establishment of a hegemony over all of Japan by Tokugawa Ieyasu and his descendants. Yet in concentrating on the situation in the country two decades after the battle of Sekigahara, Ōgai has managed in a penetrating way to suggest the legacy of difficulties remaining to the rulers. The story provides a real sense of the quality of life (at least of moral and spiritual life) as perceived by those men of public importance who were determined to see peace and order prevail.

Ultimately the most intriguing aspect of the story remains Ōgai's mastery of the technique of understatement in order to reveal an intricate moral dilemma. There are opportunities for melodramatic and violent scenes throughout, but Ōgai never succumbs to the temptation to provide them. In particular, he refrains from any speculation on the precise nature of the attraction felt by Tadayuki for Jūdaiyū. All the formidable complications of the narrative are marshalled around the central conflict, never resolved until the moment of Toshiaki's quiet testimony to the shogun's retainers in Edo, just before the end of the story.

Toshiaki, Ōgai felt, was the kind of man to inspire the deepest admiration, and in his telling of "Kuriyama Daizen" he makes his reasons for believing so abundantly clear.

ON THE FIFTEENTH DAY of the sixth month of Kan'ei nine [1632], an agent of Kuroda Uemonnosuke Tadayuki,[1] lord of the castle at Fukuoka in the province of Chikuzen, arrested a suspicious-looking man in Dōmachi at the Hakata crossroads. When the matter was investigated, he was found carrying with him a sealed document from Kuriyama Daizen Toshiaki[2] addressed to Takenaka Unemenoshō,[3] the Public Censor of the Tokugawa shogun living at Hida in the province of Bungo. When those at the castle read the document, they found that Toshiaki had accused his lord Tadayuki of fomenting a rebellion.

At this time the relationship between Lord Tadayuki and his retainer Toshiaki had become very strained. Early that year, when Tadayuki returned home from the capital after the funeral services for the former shogun Tokugawa Hidetada, all of his principal retainers came as far as Hakozaki to meet him. Only Toshiaki, on the pretext of illness, shut himself up in his rooms in his quarters in the castle town and did not appear. When Lord Tadayuki's entourage passed by the house, he sent Yamashita Hyōbē as a messenger to inquire after Toshiaki's health, wishing him a complete recovery and requesting his attendance as soon as he was well. Afterward Lord Tadayuki often sent messengers to inquire about Toshiaki's well-being, and he also made inquiries about Toshiaki's condition from the doctor who was treating him, Takatori Chōshōan. Yet from what the doctor and the messenger reported, it seemed clear that Toshiaki was not suffering from any serious disease. Thus, on the thirteenth day of the sixth month, Lord Tadayuki sent Kuroda Ichibē and Okada Zen'emon as envoys to Toshiaki, to inform him that since he was not so ill that he could not be moved, he should appear in attendance, even if he needed help in walking. Toshiaki answered that he could not be moved and that he would come as soon as he was well. Lord Tadayuki sent both envoys back immediately to say that he ordered Toshiaki to come to the gate of the castle, riding, if necessary, in a vehicle, even though the trip might risk making him weak or dizzy. And should that prove impossible, Lord Tadayuki added, then he would come to call on Toshiaki himself. Toshiaki sent back the answer that he could by no means be seen until he was completely well. Lord Tadayuki then asked his envoys how many retainers Toshiaki had with him, and if they had noticed any weapons. They answered that there were about twenty men with Toshiaki, who had kept himself surrounded, and that some weapons were visible. Lord Tadayuki received this report in one of the large open rooms of the castle; now,

TRANSLATED BY J. THOMAS RIMER

seemingly having made up his mind, he suddenly announced that he would go and force his way into Toshiaki's residence himself. Commanding everyone to make proper preparations, he quickly withdrew. Those in attendance all sent servants home to get their arms.

Rumors soon spread throughout the castle town, and guardsmen and young samurai began to throng in front of Toshiaki's residence. At this moment, two of Lord Tadayuki's senior retainers arrived, Inoue Sohō Yukifusa (who went by the name of Dōhaku)[4] and Ogō Kuranojō. Pulling Lord Tadayuki back, they urged him to remember that such behavior on the part of Toshiaki was, after all, only a trifling thing, and that it would be embarrassing to everyone concerned if Edo learned of the matter. They offered to pledge their own honor for Toshiaki, they continued, and surely the matter could be cleared up in some fashion or other; if not, then let Toshiaki commit *seppuku* if that were Lord Tadayuki's order. Lord Tadayuki finally grew calmer. Inoue and Ogō then left to announce that no one at all would be permitted to go to Toshiaki's residence. Anyone who had already gone to the front of Toshiaki's residence was sent over to the mansion of Kuroda Mimasaku (who at that time went by the name of Suiō),[5] the husband of Toshiaki's older sister, and to the office of the *han* Councillors situated across the way from there. On the next day, the fourteenth, Inoue and Ogō conveyed to Toshiaki these decisions made at the castle. Toshiaki immediately cut off his hair and sent his wife and second son Kichijirō as hostages to the castle. There they were placed in the care of Kuroda Hyōgo, Toshiaki's father-in-law. All of these events took place the day before Lord Tadayuki obtained the letter sent by Toshiaki to the Public Censor.

Lord Tadayuki and his retainers who were on duty at the castle found it scarcely credible that Toshiaki had written such a document. Certainly Lord Tadayuki himself had no intention whatsoever of raising a rebellion against the Tokugawa shogun. At this time, however, all the feudal lords had to be on their guard against something or other being seized as a pretext to suggest their disloyalty. It was for such reasons that in the fourteenth year of Keichō [1609], Tōdō Sado no kami Takatora first took the initiative and sent his wife and children to Edo as proof of his loyalty. After the fall of Osaka castle in the first year of Genna [1615], Lord Tadayuki's father Nagamasa[6] also sent his wife Hoshina,[7] their eldest daughter Toku,[8] their second son Inuman,[9] and their third son Mankichi[10] to Edo as hostages. Hoshina was now in Edo, together with Hisamatsu, the wife of Lord Tadayuki. Such were the steps taken to convince the Tokugawa family that no secret intentions were being harbored against them.

Lord Tadayuki and his retainers were shocked to find that, although Lord

Tadayuki harbored no disloyalty against the shogunate, Toshiaki of all people had accused him of doing so. It is true that the relations between the two had become extremely strained. The quarrel between them had grown to the point where Lord Tadayuki would no doubt have ordered Toshiaki to commit *seppuku* if he had made another move of any kind. Tadayuki felt that no matter how faithful a retainer Toshiaki might be, to act in such a way toward his lord was altogether scandalous; for his part, Toshiaki was convinced that, no matter how wise his lord might be, Tadayuki was insulting an older man who had rendered faithful service to two generations of the Kuroda family. Although Tadayuki was furious, he maintained a somewhat diffident attitude, while none of his retainers could comprehend why Toshiaki, whom they respected even while they feared him, should try to ensnare Lord Tadayuki in a false crime.

Not only did the secret letter of Toshiaki surprise and shock everyone concerned, but the whole incident made them visibly full of apprehension. Not only did the letter allege that Lord Tadayuki was planning a rebellion; there was an appendix attached to the letter stating that in order to make sure that it reached proper hands two copies had been made and given to two different persons, sent off by separate routes. It might well be that even if the Kuroda family had been fortunate enough to intercept one copy, the other had probably been received without difficulty in Hida, to be sent on by Takenaka to the Tokugawa house in Edo. Even the impetuous Lord Tadayuki realized, however dimly, that if he put to death such a meritorious retainer of the Kuroda house as Toshiaki, he would surely be accused of violating the laws set down by the Tokugawa family. If the letter reached Edo, as it may well have, then Toshiaki now was the man who could not be put to death under any circumstances: for if Lord Tadayuki was interrogated by the Tokugawa family concerning the question of a possible rebellion, there would be no means to clear himself other than by a direct confrontation with the man who had dared to accuse him of the crime.

Toshiaki's father Kurimoto Toshiyasu[11] was descended from a branch of the Akamatsu family in Harima. His childhood name was Zensuke; later he took the name of Shirōemon and finally the name Bingo. He was born in the castle of Agō in Harima in the twentieth year of Tembun [1551]; when he was fifteen, he entered the service of Kuroda Kambē Yoshitaka[12] at Himeyama in the same province. After the birth of Yoshitaka's son Shōju in the eleventh year of Eiroku [1568], Toshiyasu was appointed as his young lord's personal attendant. Yoshitaka was the grandfather of Tadayuki. His father was Shōju, who later took the name of Nagamasa.

In the sixth year of Tenshō [1578], Araki Settsu no kami Murashige[13] closed himself up in the castle of Arioka at Itami in Settsu and began his rebellion against Oda Nobunaga. Yoshitaka went to the castle to remonstrate with Murashige, who promptly took him prisoner. Toshiyasu, together with Mori Tahyōe Tomonobu (who was later called Tajima) and Inoue Kurōjirō Korefusa (who was later called Suhō), took turns disguising themselves as tradesmen, and managed to loiter around the quarters where Yoshitaka was confined, in order to watch over their lord. At one point Toshiyasu disguised himself as a moneylender of Itami, and under cover of darkness, deceived the sentinels, swam across the irrigation pond behind the prison building, broke in, and managed to speak personally with Yoshitaka. On the eleventh month of the following year, when Takikawa Sakon Kazumasu[14] captured the castle of Arioka, Toshiyasu arrived just as the guards fled, broke open the locks and led Yoshitaka out of his prison. Toshiyasu took him to Arima and had him take healing baths, so that Yoshitaka finally regained the use of his arms and legs.

In the tenth year of Tenshō [1581], Oda Nobunaga was assassinated by Akechi Hyūga no kami Mitsuhide.[15] From that time on, Yoshitaka and his son served Toyotomi Hideyoshi. In Tenshō fifteen [1587], Yoshitaka was made lord over six counties in the province of Buzen. At this time Toshiyasu received a portion of the land. Two years later Yoshitaka retired, taking the name of Jōsuiken Ensei, and Nagamasa became the head of the Kuroda family. Two years after that, on the twenty-second day of the first month, Toshiyasu's wife Murao gave birth to his son Daikichi, who later took the name Daizen Toshiaki. In the first year of Bunroku [1592], Nagamasa took Toshiyasu and Tomonobu with him among the troops crossing to Korea. Yoshitaka later entered the Korean capital as an envoy for Toyotomi Hideyoshi.

In the fourth year of Keichō [1599], when Tokugawa Ieyasu went to the Kantō Plain to attack Uesugi Kagekatsu[16] of Aizu, Nagamasa accompanied him. Before he set out from his home at Temma in Osaka, Nagamasa called together Toshiyasu, Tomonobu, and Miyazaki Sukedayu Shigemasa (later known as Oribe), and left them with precise instructions. While he was gone, should the forces of Toyotomi Hideyoshi advance, they were to take his wife and mother and escape with them to the Nakatsu River before they could be taken as hostages. Since there was a chance that insurrection might not break out, however, they should not act in too great a haste. In any case they should not misjudge the situation and thereby permit the two women to be taken prisoner. He asked that Toshiyasu and Tomonobu concern themselves with any attacking enemy and that Shigemasa remain with the women; if it seemed clear that escape was impossible, Shigemasa was to kill the two women and commit suicide himself.

A short time after this, as expected, Ishida Jibushōyu Mitsunari[17] left his castle at Sameyama and assembled a group of allied daimyo in Osaka. Toshiyasu and the others immediately took the two women, Kushibashi,[18] the wife of Yoshitaka (then a lady of forty-eight), and Hoshina (who was sixteen), the wife of Nagamasa, wrapped them in straw sacks, put them in baskets, and carried them in this fashion through a hole they dug in the base of the wall of the bathing room. The baskets were passed over to Tomonobu who, disguised as a merchant, carried them away on his shoulders. Tomonobu took the baskets along the path, thick with reeds, that followed the river flowing by Nagamasa's mansion. The women were eventually concealed with Naya Kozaemon, a credit merchant in Temma. All of these efforts were made to prevent the discovery of the women by the advance scouts of the forces of Hideyoshi. Both women were hidden in the inner storehouse of Naya's shed. In addition, as a precaution against a possible house search, Naya dug a hole under the wooden floor in the bedroom and placed a mat in it, so that the space would be ready if the women should suddenly have to be moved from the storehouse. Naya's wife took food to them in such a way that even the servants were not aware of their presence. Shigemasa lived there and acted as a guard, while Tomonobu watched over the house from another building close by.

After two or three days had passed, Toshiyasu went to the home of Tōjō Kii no kami Nagayori[19] to learn the latest developments. Talking with him, Tōjō learned that soldiers were gathering to attack the Kuroda mansion. Saying he knew nothing at all about this, Toshiyasu asked Tōjō the circumstances as a means of sounding out his allegiance. Toshiyasu thought that, depending on the answer, he might take Tōjō prisoner and then return to the Kuroda mansion. Tōjō, however, said he knew nothing about it. Toshiyasu leaped on his horse and sped back to Temma. The Kuroda mansion was still quiet. Shortly a secret envoy from Kōri, Shume Muneyasu,[20] arrived with word that the attacking party was approaching. Shortly afterward, fifty samurai mounted on horses and about six hundred foot soldiers, armed with two-hundred-odd guns, surrounded the house. The leader of the party asked if the two ladies were inside. Toshiyasu affirmed the fact that they were. The soldiers withdrew leaving a guard behind. Next came an envoy from the castle asking if the two ladies could be seen, saying that acquaintances of the women were being sent who could identify them. Toshiyasu refused, saying that wives of warriors could not be subjected to such public scrutiny. The messenger said that he was sent to see the wives of other daimyo as well and urged again that the women show themselves, even if screened off from direct view. Toshiyasu, telling them that he could not foresee the reprimand that would be coming when his master returned, agreed there was nothing to be done but let them be seen in this way. The women came who were to identify the two. One had known Kushibashi as a young woman, and the other had known Hoshina when she was twelve.

In Toshiyasu's household was a lady attendant, born in Shinano, the daughter of Ogasawara Kuranosuke, who was about the same age and with roughly the same physical proportions as Kushibashi. Toshiyasu had this woman recline behind gauze mosquito netting and had her daughter, who was also an attendant, sit outside it and converse with her, while the two observers watched from an adjoining room. Fortunately the trick worked and the party withdrew.

Toshiyasu and his men now deliberated as to how to find a way for the ladies to escape. There was a man named Kajiwara Tarōzaemon from Iejima in Harima, a ship's captain who transported goods for the Kuroda family. Plans were made with him for the use of his boat. However, the forces of Hideyoshi had set up a check point to prevent the escape of the wives of the various daimyo. The guard, located below Fukushima in Osaka at the confluence of the Tenryū and Kizu rivers, consisted of a hundred armed soldiers on one large boat, and two smaller ones as well. Toshiyasu and the others waited for a proper occasion, but somehow they were never able to slip through.

It was now the seventeenth day of the seventh month. Wives of various daimyo who sided with the Tokugawa forces had been forced to stay in the citadel of the Osaka castle as hostages. The forces of Hideyoshi first despatched a number of men to the home of Hosokawa Etchū no kami Tadaoki.[21] Without even listening to the protests of the retainers of the Hosokawa family, the soldiers pushed their way right in. Akechi Gracia,[22] the wife of Hosokawa, saying that she refused to expose herself in Osaka castle and did not wish to stand in her husband's way in serving the Tokugawa cause, took her own life. The household retainers, Ogasawara Bizen, Kawakita, Iwanami, and the others, shut the gates for a final defense for the family, then set fire to the buildings and committed suicide. Chastened by this experience, the forces of Hideyoshi abandoned the attempt to hold the wives of daimyo as hostages.

Toshiyasu's men had been keeping their small boat out on the upper reaches of the Fukushima River to study the situation at the guard post. In this way they learned that when the Hosokawa mansion went up in flames, the guards had gone in small boats to the site of the fire. When he received this report, Toshiyasu immediately put the two women into a large box, which he took from the rear door of the shed, and loaded it on a boat. To-monobu was given a long spear with an immense handle; it was inlaid with pearl, more than seven feet long, and in an elaborate case. He was charged with protecting the boat, along with a group of fifteen strong attendants. When the boat reached the check point, Tomonobu grasped the spear in his hand and demanded to see the guard, an acquaintance of his, named Suga Uemon no Hachi. Tomonobu told the guard that he had business to do in his home village and demanded that the boat be searched so that he might pass. Suga Uemon no Hachi knew very well that Tomonobu was a warrior of great physical stature and tremendous strength; he cravenly replied that the boat need not be searched. So they went down the Dempō River and trans-ferred the two women to Tarōzaemon's boat, which was waiting. One of the serving maids of Hoshina, named Kiku, had escaped from the mansion and followed them. She too was put on the boat. Under Tomonobu's escort the boat arrived without difficulty at the Nakatsu River four days later. Shigema-sa went by boat past the borders of Izumi Province, where he boarded still another vessel; Toshiyasu went by land as far as Muro in Harima, then boarded a boat and returned to the Nakatsu River. Kuroda Yoshitaka (who had now taken the name of the lay priest Josui), having surmised the situa-tion in Osaka, tried to send a boat with Mori Yosabē for the two women, but could not manage to do so in time. Shinomiya Ichibē remained behind in the Temma mansion in Osaka where he made desperate excuses to the high officials of the Toyotomi forces. After this, the wife of Katō Kazoe no kami Kiyomasa,[23] led by Kajiwara Sukebē, also escaped from Osaka. The pair made their way to the Nakatsu River, where they stayed in the home of Kaji-wara Hachirō Dayū, the older brother of Katō's wife. Josui presented Katō's wife with clothing and had Kiku, who had come to the Nakatsu River ac-companying Hoshina, attend her to Kumamoto.

The year following, Keichō five [1600], Nagamasa was awarded the pro-vince of Chikuzen for his service to the Tokugawa house at the battle of Se-kigahara. At the end of that year, he entered the castle at Najima in Kasuya-gōri for the first time. A year later, after discussing the situation with Josui, who had returned from Kyoto for a brief visit, Nagamasa built a castle at Fu-kuzaki which at that time was in the village of Keiko in Nakagōri. The area is now Fukuoka in Chikushi-gun. Within the six outlying fortifications which were built at the time, Tokiyasu was put in charge of the castle at Matera in Kamizagōri, Tomonobu of the castle at Takatori in Kurategōri, and Yukifusa of Kurozaki in Ongagōri.

In November of Keichō seven [1602], Nagamasa's first son Tadayuki was

born in the east citadel of the castle at Fukuoka. His childhood name was
Mantoku. The main citadel had been built on the site of a Shinto shrine; in
order to avoid defiling this shrine, the eastern citadel, also under the charge
of Toshiyasu, was chosen as the place for the delivery of the child. Two years
later, Josui died at fifty-nine on the outer fortification of the castle. In 1606,
Nagamasa's first daughter Toku was born; his second son Inuman was born
four years later, and his third son Mankichi two years after. Inuman was later
known as Nagaoki, and Mankichi as Takamasa.

From Keichō nineteen [1614], through the first year of Genna [1615],
there were a series of disturbances by the Toyotomi forces in Osaka. In the
winter battle of 1614, Nagamasa was in charge of Edo, and the forces of Tadayuki, now thirteen, began to push north from Fukuoka, despite the fact
that he had not recovered from a severe fever. Toshiaki served under Nagamasa, while Toshiyasu came down from Edo and took Nagamasa's place in
Fukuoka. At the time of the summer battle of 1615, Nagamasa left from
Edo and Tadayuki from Fukuoka to join forces in Osaka. Toshiyasu remained behind in Chikuzen, while Toshiaki joined Tadayuki's forces. It was
immediately after the fall of Osaka castle[24] that Hoshina took Toku, Inuman, and Mankichi to Edo.

In 1616, the year when Tokugawa Ieyasu died at Sumpu, Nagamasa's
third daughter Kame[25] was born. In 1622, when the daughter of Hisamatsu
Kai no kami Tadayoshi was seventeen, the shogun Tokugawa Hidetada
adopted her as his daughter and sent her as a bride for Tadayuki. A year
later, Hidetada turned over the office of shogun to Iemitsu. When Hidetada
and Iemitsu went up to Kyoto, they sent Nagamasa on ahead from Edo. Nagamasa, then fifty-three, brought Tadayuki with him and while they were
staying at Nijō castle in Kyoto, Nagamasa suddenly died of a stomach can-
cer. His final testament was heard by Toshiaki and Ogō Kuranojō. Nagamasa's remains were taken back to his home province, and he was cremated
at Matsubara in Hakozaki. Toshiaki, now thirty-one, accompanied the coffin
in front while Tadayuki, now twenty-two, followed at the foot. When Nagamasa died, Toshiyasu was seventy-three and had taken holy orders. He took
the name Ichiyōsai Bokuan.

With such a relationship between them, why were Lord Tadayuki and
Toshiaki now embroiled in such a struggle between themselves? It was not
that Toshiaki had changed; rather, it was Tadayuki who had.

In the full vigor of his youth, Tadayuki suddenly became a daimyo of
more than 500,000 *koku*. As he was naturally intelligent, he thought to
manage his territories by his own efforts and with his own wisdom, without

the restrictions that might be placed on him by his senior retainers. For this purpose he needed a subordinate of whom he could make use in a free manner. It so happened that there was a clever young man named Jūdayū, the son of the chief of the foot soldiers, Kurahashi Choshirō, who had been employed the year before at the Nakatsu River. Tadayuki made this boy his personal attendant and used him for a variety of purposes; in a very short space of time he had added to the boy's stipend a number of times. Those who wished Tadayuki well grieved for their lord and their province; those who were timid stood in awe of Jūdayū; and those who were vulgar or depraved sought merely to use him to advance themselves.

However, according to the final wishes of Nagamasa, to which Toshiaki and Ogō were witness, three Han Elders—Toshiaki, Kazunari, and Ogō—were to consult together in any affairs of importance concerning the province, while under any exceptional circumstances, Toshiyasu (retired as Bokuan) and Yukifusa (retired as Tōhaku) were to be consulted as well before any final decision was made. Thus the year after the death of Nagamasa, the three Elders prepared a written document of allegiance and presented it to Lord Tadayuki. The document was composed of five sections. First, the three affirmed that they were concealing no treasonous thoughts of any kind against Lord Tadayuki. Second, they affirmed that if they learned that someone, no matter who it might be, was plotting against Lord Tadayuki or attempting to bring harm to their province, they would inform Lord Tadayuki and ask that such a person be properly disposed of. Third, if any party attempted to estrange one of the three from the other two, each would confide in the others so that the truth of the matter would be revealed. Fourth, the three wished to affirm a brotherly feeling between themselves. Fifth, should any of the three Elders encounter any slander concerning themselves, the three would with one heart and mind inform Lord Tadayuki of the allegations. As for Jūdayū, who had received such exceptional favors, they did not feel they understood his real feelings. They watched him night and day, wondering if the second part of their document of allegiance might apply to him.

However, there were no suspicious flaws in the conduct of Jūdayū. The first thing that Toshiaki and the others noticed was merely that decisions about which they had always been consulted were now being made without their consent. At first Lord Tadayuki and his subordinates had only taken independent action in affairs of a trifling nature that could, indeed, be handled in such a fashion; but soon relatively important matters were being handled in the same way. Later, when Toshiaki and the others would ask the subordinates involved, they would reply that no offense of any kind was intended and that it simply had not occurred to them to consult the three. These latter incidents became more frequent. Toshiaki and the others always seemed to be pursuing matters that had already been decided.

The three Elders became increasingly distressed. From time to time they complained directly to Lord Tadayuki concerning the fact that certain official procedures were not being followed with sufficient care. He too replied that he had meant no offense but simply had not thought to consult them. They could get no satisfactory answers from anyone they spoke to, either above or below their rank.

At one point Toshiaki and the others determined to try to put an end to this untenable situation. Needless to say there was a close connection between these abuses they had witnessed and the conduct of Jūdayū, who attended constantly upon Lord Tadayuki. Yet Jūdayū's conduct was impeccable and he had made no obvious blunders in his own administrative activities. It was only that Toshiaki and the others felt instinctively that, somehow or other, the whole atmosphere around them was changing.

They began to observe more sharply. Soon they began to distinguish in precisely what way the changes were becoming apparent.

They first became aware of a certain slackness in the administration of everyday affairs. There was a tendency for Lord Tadayuki to delay arriving for his hours in public attendance, while his retirement to private quarters seemed to begin earlier and earlier. Consequently officials seemed late to appear and quick to withdraw. In his visit to the shogun in Edo, Lord Tadayuki's behavior was precisely the same: he was late in attendance at the castle and he withdrew more quickly than had been his custom. Envoys from the province to Edo, and to the representatives of the Tokugawa in Bungo were always being despatched later than the scheduled date.

Next they noticed that various arrangements were being carelessly made and then changed in a hasty and confused manner. The most flagrant example of this concerned the choice of an envoy to Edo. The person first chosen was Mori Shōzaemon, then a change was made to Tsukigase Umenojō, next Mori was chosen again, finally Tsuboda Shōzaemon. There were also instances when a man who had been treated kindly and who had served Lord Tadayuki well would suddenly seem to incur great disfavor.

It also seemed that trifling things, matters for mere amusement, were given precedence over matters of serious importance, and often serious injunctions over minor matters were set up. Mere *sarugaku* actors were often called upon as special couriers, yet travelers were not permitted to cross through the hawking fields. Returning from Edo, Lord Tadayuki had sent for women entertainers while staying in an inn at Hyōgō, without regard for his own reputation.

Then again, tendencies toward luxurious living became apparent. Clothing and utensils became more splendid, and provisions and menus became more elaborate.

Next they noticed that such important events as funeral ceremonies, certain festivals, condolence calls and similiar observances began to be neglected. On the fifteenth day of the ninth month of the third year of Kan'ei [1626], when the mother of the former shogun Hidetada, Oda Tachiko, also known as Ōmi Daidokoro, died, Lord Tadayuki not only failed to observe ritual abstinence but even was seen on his hawking grounds. Nor did he observe the abstinences on the memorial days for the deaths of Tokugawa Ieyasu or his grandfather Yoshitaka. When he returned from Edo, he did not make the proper visits to the shrines of Yoshitaka and Nagamasa.

It was true that nothing more serious than this had been observed. Yet under the circumstances, there seemed at least a possibility that something serious might well develop. Toshiaki and the others thought that when the proper occasion presented itself, they would speak quite firmly to Lord Tadayuki.

Finally a man was punished for a crime he did not commit, while another was pardoned for an equally serious crime. Jūdayū was involved in both these incidents. In the first instance, a merchant from Hakata refused to give a folding screen painted by an artist named Ukiyo Matabē[26] to Jūdayū, who was anxious to have it. Jūdayū sent his retainers to take the screen by force; when the merchant tried to get it back, Jūdayū had him thrown in prison. In the second instance, a man was apprehended stealing from a farmer in Shimagōri; but when it was discovered that the thief was an elder brother of the mistress of Jūdayū, he was released.

Toshiaki at last gathered his courage, discussed the situation with Kazunari and Ogō, and then wrote out a letter of admonition to Lord Tadayuki. He divided it into various sections, and quoted appropriate examples from the Classics and Histories to buttress his criticisms. In all, he listed twenty-five items. The document was composed in a circumspect fashion: the matter of the false judgments that had prompted Toshiaki to act was placed in a section listing events concerning which neither praise nor blame could clearly be given. Nor did he give too much importance to any censuring of Jūdayū, but rather called on Lord Tadayuki to reflect sincerely on his own conduct. Toshiaki made a clean copy of the document and then asked Bokuan and Tōhaku to read it. This was the twelfth day of the eleventh month of the third year of Kan'ei [1626]. Bokuan and Tōhaku both wrote an endorse-

ment of what Toshiaki had composed. Kobayashi Takumi, Kinugasa Bokusai, and Oka Zenzaemon were entrusted with presenting the document to
Lord Tadayuki.

When Lord Tadayuki read it, he was furious. He felt sure that it was composed as the result of jealousy against Jūdayū and prompted by a desire to
find fault. When he saw the many learned quotations he realized at once
that Toshiaki had written it, and all Lord Tadayuki's rage centered on him.
Lord Tadayuki first thought to call Toshiaki and scold him severely. Then he
realized that Toshiaki was not the kind of man to sit and take a scolding
silently. Lord Tadayuki decided that rather than facing disagreeable opinions in a wearisome interview, he would simply dismiss the matter completely without making any comment whatsoever.

Toshiaki and the others waited for Lord Tadayuki to take some kind of action, but there seemed to be no reaction at all. The whole mechanism of administration went on as before. Jūdayū continued to behave in his superficial, clever way. The only difference was that Lord Tadayuki would turn his
face aside every time he met Toshiaki. The letter of admonition had no
other result whatsoever.

Lord Tadayuki carried on this treatment of Toshiaki in a stubborn fashion, and Toshiaki repaid him in kind. It was at this point that the period of
mourning was ended for the death of Kushibashi, the wife of Yoshitaka,
who died in Kan'ei four [1627].

The year following, Lord Tadayuki announced that for his annual visitations to Edo he was having a large boat constructed which he named ''Precious Jewel,'' so that he could sail the distance between his domain and
Osaka. He also announced that Jūdayū should have his own contingent of
soldiers, and without reporting the fact to Edo, he collected together three
hundred foot soldiers for the purpose. The extravagances mentioned in the
letter of admonition were no longer confined to food and clothing: the boat
was constructed in a luxurious fashion and Jūdayū now received his extraordinarily large contingent. Toshiaki no longer felt that he could remain a
bystander in such a situation, and despite the efforts of Ogō and Kazunari to
stop him, he resigned his position as Lord Tadayuki's retainer on grounds of
ill-health. Lord Tadayuki accepted the resignation immediately. Toshiaki
vacated his residence near the castle in silence and secluded himself in his
quarters at Matera.

Lord Tadayuki felt he had removed this annoying source of criticism, but
the year following, he suddenly received an official statement of advice from
the shogun, sent to him by Doi Ōi no kami Toshikatsu.[27] The statement was
a reminder that the Kuriyama family, as retainers to the Kuroda family,

were supposed to lead and guide their young lord. Toshiyasu might be excused from this duty, as he was close to eighty years old, but the fact that Daizen Toshiaki was confined to his home was most improper. A means should be found to persuade Toshiaki to resume his duties. Now, of necessity, Lord Tadayuki was forced to request Toshiaki to return to service.

Toshiaki did eventually take over his duties again, but Lord Tadayuki still continued to turn away from him. There was absolutely no change in the situation since Toshiaki had resigned. As Toshiaki's services were requested by the shogun, Lord Tadayuki could do nothing, which in turn made the secret feelings of ill-will he felt for Toshiaki grow even stronger.

While this tense situation continued, unpleasant as it was to both parties, Toshiaki's father Bokuan suddenly died in his sleep, on the fourteenth day of the eighth month of the eighth year of Kan'ei [1631]. He was eighty-one. By this time Jūdayū had finally managed to gain the rank of Han Elder and received lands valued at nine thousand *koku*. Actually the income they produced was around thirty thousand *koku*. Toshiaki, Kazunari, and Ogō all informed Lord Tadayuki that, although of course Jūdayū was a person who could render good service, it was quite inappropriate to give the status of Han Elder to a man without lineage. Lord Tadayuki did not listen to them.

At a certain point, Lord Tadayuki, declaring that there should be some valuable possessions in the home of his new Han Elder, sent Jūdayū a suit of armor given to his father Nagamasa by Tokugawa Ieyasu at the battle of Sekigahara. When Toshiaki heard this, he went out to the residence of Jūdayū and confiscated the armor himself. Yet even after Toshiaki had taken a step of these proportions, he did not notify Lord Tadayuki. Furious as he was, Lord Tadayuki allowed the incident to pass without a comment of any kind.

The retired shogun Hidetada died in 1632. Lord Tadayuki participated in the funeral procession in Edo and then returned to his domain. It was at this point that the dispute arose concerning Toshiaki's failure to attend upon Lord Tadayuki and Tadayuki's threat to go personally to Toshiaki's residence. Toshiaki was essentially a man of tremendous patience, but so was Tadayuki. On this one occasion, however, there was a particular reason why Lord Tadayuki had become so irritated that he lost his good judgment. Hidetada died on the twenty-fourth day of the first month. The funeral was held on the night of the twenty-sixth at the temple of Zōjōji in Edo. On the twenty-second day of the second month, the imperial messengers were despatched, and on the eleventh day of the third month, Lord Tadayuki took leave of the shogun and left Edo. When he arrived home in the fourth month, a serious incident had just arisen in the adjacent domain of Higo.

On the tenth day of the fourth month, an anonymous letter was brought to the home of Muroga Gen'ichirō Masatoshi[28] in Nagata-chō in Edo. The letter revealed the supposed treachery of the lord of Kumamoto castle in Higo, Katō Tadahiro.[29] Inoue Shinzaemon, the father-in-law of Masatoshi, was intimate with Lord Doi Toshikatsu and so told him about the letter. Toshikatsu ordered the man who brought the letter apprehended. When he was found four days later, at Dobashi in Kōji-machi, he was identified as Maeda Gorōhachi, a retainer of Katō Mitsumasa, the son of Katō Tadahiro. As the shogun Tokugawa Iemitsu was on a visit to Nikkō and was stopping at Utsunomiya in the province of Shimotsuge, Toshikatsu sent Masatoshi there and had him present the charges against Katō. Inaba Tango no kami Masakatsu was chosen to serve as envoy from the shogun to Kumamoto and order Katō to come to Edo. Since Masakatsu passed through Yamaga in Onga of Chikuzen Province on the way to Kumamoto, Lord Tadayuki, just returned from Edo himself, sent a party from Fukuoka to greet him. Jūdayū was chosen as Lord Tadayuki's chief envoy, and Kuroda Ichibē was to serve as his assistant. Jūdayū's party contained, in addition to two hundred of his new retainers, other foot soldiers and some troops armed with muskets, all together about three hundred and fifty men, while those accompanying Kuroda were no more than thirty-eight all together. Arriving at Yamaga, the welcoming party waited on Masakatsu at his inn. Masakatsu announced that he had never heard of the name Kurahachi Jūdayū, but he had heard that Kuroda Ichibē was of good lineage, and so he would confer with Kuroda. Even though Jūdayū was chief of the delegation, he was not granted an interview and had to retire. The townspeople of Fukuoka and Hakata despised the tyrannical ways of Jūdayū, and the whole incident made excellent gossip for everyone.

When Lord Tadayuki heard what happened, he was even more angry than when he had received the letter of admonition from Toshiaki. He ordered that those who spread rumors about the affair should be identified and arrested. Shortly afterward several townspeople were killed. Of two persons who were talking on the street of Amibachō, Sugihara Heisuke was cut down while the other escaped. At Gofuku-chō in Fukuoka, where three people were chatting together, Sakada Kazaemon was killed and the two others escaped. In Tojinchō, Hamada Tazaemon was killed and one escaped. The townspeople were terribly intimidated. The incident about the Katō family came to be interpreted as an attempt by Katō Mitsumasa to slander his father Tadahiro. Tadahiro was eventually accused of taking his two-year-old son, born of a concubine, back to his native province without informing the shogun's authorities; on the first day of the sixth month, he was stripped of his rank and all the emoluments accompanying it.

The anger that almost drove Lord Tadayuki to force his way into Toshi-aki's quarters was manifested in the same nervous excitement that caused the death of several townsmen in repayment for the insults received by his favorite retainer, Jūdayū.

On the twenty-fifth day of the eighth month of 1632 a messenger arrived from the shogun, with an order for Lord Tadayuki's attendance in Edo. For the first time Lord Tadayuki seemed to become aware of the dimensions of the situation, as if awakened from a dream. He left Fukuoka shortly after-ward, taking with him Kazunari and Ogō Kaganojō. When they were close to Edo they learned that a party of Tokugawa liege vassals, captains of ar-tillery, and some twenty or more men of lower rank were waiting for Lord Tadayuki at Shinagawaguchi, with orders to put him in quarters at the Tō-kaiji temple in Shinagawa. Lord Tadayuki felt that even if he could not escape his own ruin, he was determined to end his days in his own mansion in Edo. Ogō devised a plan, and a few retainers, armed with spears, set out about midnight from Kanagawa with Lord Tadayuki in his palanquin. The small group was able to pass quickly through Shinagawa and enter Lord Tadayuki's principal residence at Sakurada in Azabu. When dawn arrived, just as Kazunari and Ogō were preparing to arrange the Kuroda party in a proper procession and go to Shinagawaguchi, a messenger came from the guard house with instructions from Abe Tsushima no kami Shigetsugu,[30] who indicated that Lord Tadayuki was being requested to stop for a short time at the Tōkaiji. Ogō answered that Lord Tadayuki had suddenly been summoned for an emergency and had already entered the capital with a few retainers during the night.

Shortly afterward, a messenger from the shogun's highest councillors ar-rived at Lord Tadayuki's mansion at Sakurada. He came to announce that Lord Tadayuki was to be quartered in the Hase temple in Shibuya. Lord Tadayuki answered that he was unaware of how he had incurred his lord's displeasure, but should prefer to receive his punishment at his own resi-dence. At this, the messenger withdrew. Next, Lord Naruse Hayatonoshō Masatora[31] of the Owari branch of the Tokugawa family, and the lords Andō Tatewaki Naotsugu[32] and Takiguchi Bingo no kami[33] of the Kii branch of the Tokugawa family, came to request an interview. The three, who were usually on excellent terms with Lord Tadayuki, persuaded him to allow him-self to be moved to the Haseji.

Now a special message was despatched by mounted courier to Fukuoka from the mansion at Sakurada. When the messenger arrived in Chikuzen, the retainers in charge of the castle, the captains of the soldiers, and the

other samurai gathered to discuss the situation. When their deliberations
were finished, the results were reported to their subordinates in the following terms. Those samurai who wished to hand over the castle and evacuate it
were to leave immediately. Those who were determined to take a final stand
were urged to make appropriate preparations. No one spoke for evacuation.
It was decided to take the women and children into the castle and that all
would give up their lives in a final battle. Finally, plans were made to defend
the castle.[34]

In Edo, meanwhile, Lord Tadayuki was summoned by the shogun's councillors and went to the West Enceinte of Edo castle on the seventeenth day of
the eleventh month. There he was informed that the authorities regarded as
transgressions his employment of subordinates in general, and the incident
of Jūdayū's serving as chief envoy to Inaba Masakatsu in particular. He was
told that an official investigation would be carried out. That night, Andō
Naotsugu came to call on Lord Tadayuki and informed him that Naruse
Masatora had fallen ill. About eight that evening, Lord Tadayuki went to
visit Naruse. On the nineteenth day, Tadayuki was permitted to return to
his own quarters, but as he felt some apprehension about occupying the
principal mansion, he moved instead to a secondary residence where his
younger brother Takamasa had been living. Takamasa moved to the out-
buildings.

Early in the second month of 1633, Lord Tadayuki was called three times
in the course of several days to the West Enceinte and was questioned by the
shogun's councillors. He was also asked about Toshiaki's accusation that he
was fomenting a rebellion, but Lord Tadayuki defended himself in a clear
and logical manner. After this interrogation Lord Tadayuki deliberately
showed great restraint and remained within the Hase temple.

At this time, Takenaka Unemenoshō arrived in Edo, escorting Toshiaki.
On the twenty-fourth day of the second month, there was a confrontation
between Toshiaki, Jūdayū, and the others, at the mansion of Lord Doi Toshikatsu. Attending were thirteen high officials,[35] ranged around Toshikatsu
to witness the discussion. Takenaka, with Toshiaki beside him, sat on one
side about three feet from the seat of the Censor General. On the other side
sat Kazunari, then Jūdayū.

A brief inquiry was begun. Toshiaki began by asserting that the affair was
of no great import and that he would like to request that the investigation
be confined to the circumstances surrounding his letter of admonition to
Lord Tadayuki the year before and the events that followed, since it was this
incident that generated the present situation. He said nothing further.
Kazunari and Jūdayū replied that there was no evidence that their Lord Ta-

dayuki had rebellious attitudes against the Tokugawa and could not understand how Toshiaki could make the accusation he did. Following this exchange, both men were questioned by the shogun's councillors concerning the facts of the alleged misdemeanors of Tadayuki.

During the investigation, Kuroda Kenmotsu was called upon and questioned concerning the unauthorized increase in foot soldiers.

Next Ogō Kaganojō was called in. Since he appeared without having been officially summoned, his testimony was not considered admissible by the shogun's inspectors. After Ogō made his obeisances to the assembled officials, he made his usual salutation to Toshiaki. He began by declaring that Lord Tadayuki had no treasonous intentions whatsoever. Why Toshiaki had made such a complaint was a mystery to him. When Toshiaki was born, the previous lord of Chikuzen, Nagamasa, had presented to Toshiaki's father Toshiyasu a wet nurse, a short sword, baby clothing, and ceremonial rice wine and fish. Nagamasa himself had taken the gifts to the Kuroda household, and Toshiaki's father had gone himself to the gate in the most humble way to thank Nagamasa for his great favors. When Toshiaki grew up, he too received favors from Nagamasa. Thus wondering how Toshiaki could have lodged such a complaint, Ogō suddenly broke into tears. Then he continued by saying that, were there any treasonous activities being plotted by Lord Tadayuki, then surely Tōhaku (Yukifusa) would not fail to be aware of them. Getting up from his seat, Ogō left the room and returned with Tōhaku himself, whom he brought before the officials.

After Tōhaku paid his respects to all present, he suddenly moved toward Toshiaki and crouched down before him. "Please move down a little. I am sitting here," he spoke out. "Please, put yourself at ease," replied Toshiaki, without moving. "But Lord Tadayuki will be coming soon," continued Tōhaku. "Would you move down just a bit?" At that, Toshiaki moved down one space. Now Tōhaku took his seat in a position of greater honor than Toshiaki.

Actually Tōhaku, like Ogō Kaganojō, had not been summoned. However since Doi Toshikatsu was acquainted with him, he called on him to speak. Then Andō Naotsugu asked Tōhaku, "You must be the father of Awaji?"[36] Naotsugu was acquainted with the son of Tōhaku.

Tōhaku next spoke to Toshiaki. "I was a good friend of your father Bokuan. Bokuan never told a lie in his life. You are less worthy than your father." Toshiaki replied, "Sir, you have not been apprised of recent events and you are not aware of the situation."

Next Tōhaku faced the shogun's officials and spoke. The empire, he began, is gained by the military arts and protected through the arts of civil rule. Had Lord Tadayuki any treacherous intentions, he could do nothing without making his accomplices those samurai who had a great deal of experience themselves. Kazunari was the most experienced of the Kuroda family retainers. Ogō Kaganojō and Kenmotsu had also been involved two or three times in military encounters. He himself, Tōhaku continued, had to some extent the requisite experience. Certainly these two or three would have to be consulted, and as for Toshiaki, he was no man to become involved in any warlike battles. The very fact that Toshiaki seemed to be the only one who knew anything about Lord Tadayuki's supposed intentions was surely a proof that no such plans existed. If Lord Tadayuki because of his youth had been negligent in his administrative duties and was thus to be stripped of his domain, then he, Tōhaku, was resigned to obey the shogun's order. But he only wished to remove the false charge laid against Lord Tadayuki. After all, at the time of the battle of Sekigahara, had not Tokugawa Ieyasu himself taken the hand of Kuroda Nagamasa, who was then the lord of Chikuzen, and told him that the success of the Tokugawa family had been greatly aided through the efforts of the Kuroda family? Had Ieyasu not promised that the house of Kuroda would never in the future be slighted by the house of Tokugawa? Such matters, Tōhaku reminded his listeners, were surely known to some there in attendance: Lord Doi, Lord Ii, and Lord Sakai.[37]

Kazunari and Ogō expressed their agreement with what Tōhaku had said. Then the three took their leave. Toshiaki was also sent away, on orders from Naruse Masatora.

Two or three days later, Lord Tadayuki was called by the shogun's councillors to the West Enceinte, where he was given his sentence. As there were clearly evidences of misconduct, his lands in Chikuzen were to be confiscated. Nevertheless, as the military prowess of his family and his own personal loyalty were well recognized, he would be reappointed as lord over Chikuzen. That night Andō Naotsugu sent a letter to Tadayuki saying "You are now free to act as you wish." During the night Tadayuki entered his mansion in Azabu.

At the beginning of the third month, Toshiaki was called to the mansion of Naotaka. Doi Toshikatsu was in attendance, as well as many of those who had participated in the earlier meeting at Doi's residence. Toshiaki, who was without his swords, took his seat. Takenaka Unemenojō informed him of the decision that had been made. First of all, it had been agreed that the incidents mentioned in Toshiaki's original letter of admonition to Lord Tadayuki were substantially correct. Yet the charge that Lord Tadayuki was guilty of treason was certainly false. He was asked to explain precisely how he had come to make such an accusation. Toshiaki replied that he considered it a great blessing that the letter of admonition had been accepted as correct. He had accused his lord of treason, Toshiaki continued, because he wanted to stop Lord Tadayuki from putting him to death for his own personal reasons. Toshiaki was not concerned for his own life and insignificant death, but he knew that if Lord Tadayuki had continued in the same fashion he would have had his lands taken from him without an investigation and without any recourse. His accusation, he explained, was the strategy he chose to save the situation as best he could. Toshiaki's words brought a flush of emotion to the faces of the officials in attendance.

Two or three days later Toshiaki was again called to the mansion of Naotaka. The same officials were in attendance, with the addition of Nambu Yamashiro no kami Shigenao.[38] The decision rendered was conveyed to Toshiaki by Matsudaira Tadahiro, who told him that Kuroda Tadayuki would have his lands confiscated on a temporary basis, because of various improprieties in his conduct. However, in view of Lord Tadayuki's distinguished family and his personal loyalty to the Tokugawa, his lands would be returned to him. Toshiaki was to be placed under the custody of Nambu Shigenao in Morioka. Toshiaki thanked them and respectfully moved back a considerable distance, tears welling in his eyes. "This is a piece of great good fortune for me," he said. Shigenao came forward at this point and said that Toshiaki would receive a stipend of one hundred fifty *koku* from the shogun's authorities, and, until he set out for Morioka he would now be free to travel as he pleased within a space of two or three ri. Toshiaki again paid his deepest respects to all those assembled.

At about the same time, Masatora and Naotsugu came to the mansion at Azabu, where they met with Tōhaku, Kazunari, Ogō, Kenmotsu, and Jūdayū. Masatora said, "On this occasion, the affair with Lord Tadayuki has been successfully resolved. This is a matter to rejoice over. Yet, if he had been sent into exile, what would have happened to all of you?" Tōhaku, after pondering the question for a moment, spoke up. "If such a decision were made, then all of Lord Tadayuki's retainers would retire from all activities."

"All of them? Without exception?"

"Yes," they told Masatora.

As he rose, Masatora said, "Then indeed the house of Kuroda is fortunate to have retainers of such caliber." The conversation served as a commitment from Lord Tadayuki's retainers that the preparations made for a siege in Fukuoka would never become public knowledge.

Again, two or three days after this, Jūdayū was called to the home of

Andō Naotsugu. Masatora was also present, at Naotsugu's request. They suggested that Jūdayū would be well advised to take the tonsure and retire to the Buddhist temples at Mt. Kōya. Jūdayū, overwhelmed, accepted their proposal.

On the eighth day of the fifth month, Lord Tadayuki was granted an interview by the shogun Iemitsu, and good relations between the Tokugawa and the Kuroda families were restored. Five years later, Lord Tadayuki won considerable renown at the battle of Shimabara,[39] and three years after that was put in charge of coastal defense preparations at Nagasaki. From this time on, Dutch ships that formerly called at Hirado were now directed to Nagasaki.

When the Shimabara Rebellion broke out in Kan'ei fourteen [1637], Jūdayū slipped away from Mt. Kōya and joined a group of Christian converts. When the Shimabara castle fell, he was killed in the general tumult.

Toshiaki arrived in the castle town of Morioka in Iwate in the province of Mutsu at the end of the third month of Kan'ei eleven [1634]. The Nambu family welcomed him with a magnificent house prepared for him on the main thoroughfare.

Only two years before, on the fourteenth of the sixth month, Toshiaki had faced the most difficult day he had during the entire affair. He had sent his wife and his second son Kichijirō to Lord Tadayuki's castle as hostages and prepared the two copies of his accusation addressed to Takenaka Unemenoshō, sending one copy by a skilled and trustworthy man on a special route to Hida; the other he sent quite intentionally with a suspicious-looking farmer. It was this man who had been apprehended in the town. Before taking this final step, Toshiaki had gone both to his quarters near the castle and to his residence at Matera in order to put things in proper order, paying special attention to safeguarding the most valuable items he possessed. Among those was a written document dated the nineteenth day of the ninth month of Keichō five [1600], presented to Kuroda Nagamasa by Tokugawa Ieyasu. It was a letter of thanks which read, "As the peace prevailing throughout the land is indeed due to your loyalty and devotion, your descendants will never be treated with disrespect." Toshiaki handed it over to Kajiwara Heijūrō Kagenao and told him that with Lord Tadayuki and himself now called to Edo, Toshiaki felt that the fortunes of the Kuroda family were in great danger, and that it might be necessary for Kajiwara to take the document to Edo and bring it to the attention of the shogun's senior retainers—Kii, Doi, Sakai, and the others.

Kajiwara Kagenao himself was a man with a special relationship to the

Kuroda family. His legal father, Kanzō Kagetsugu, was the son of Suruga no kami Kagenori, lord of the castle of Takasago in Harima and Akaishi, the younger sister of the mother of Kuroda Yoshitaka. This Kagetsugu had married a woman named Onoe, and Kagenao was her son. Onoe's father Yasuemon, however, was himself the husband of the younger sister of Kuroda Yoshitaka. After he was killed in battle and his wife had retired from the world and become a nun, Onoe became a lady-in-waiting to Kushibashi, the wife of Kuroda Yoshitaka, and she became pregnant by Yoshitaka. Kagetsugu was married to her by the order of his lord and brought up Kagenao as his own son. Thus in reality, Kagenao was the illegitimate child of Yoshitaka, the younger brother of Nagamasa, and the uncle of Lord Tadayuki.

As it was, the document was not needed. Eventually it was returned to Lord Tadayuki's descendant, Kuroda Tsugutaka, by the Kajiwara family in Meiwa five [1768], more than a hundred years later.

At the time when Lord Tadayuki was called to Edo, Toshiaki took refuge in the official residence of Takenaka in Hida; it was Takenaka who had taken him to Edo just before the investigation of Lord Tadayuki began.

When Toshiaki left for Morioka, he took his first son, Daikichi, with him. Accompanying him were two of his own former personal retainers, Senkoku Kakuemon and Zaitsu Ōemon, as well as quite a number of other liege vassals. Toshiaki's wife and son Kichijirō, who had served in the mansion of Kuroda Hyōdo, were later given a stipend of five hundred *koku*.

Toshiaki began his service in Morioka when he was forty-four years old. He was full of strength and vigor. He took a second wife, Uchiyama, and she later gave birth to a girl.

In the winter of 1641, when Tadayuki was given his position at Nagasaki, a certain Inoue, the governor of some territories of the shogun not far from Morioka, heard of Toshiaki's extraordinary character and personal qualities and requested an interview. Toshiaki sent him the following answer. "As I am, actually speaking, without a proper master, I feel that it would be improper of me to accept your kind invitation. However, since I am leading a quiet and retired life, it would be a great pleasure if you would come and visit with me."

Inoue came to visit the mansion on the main thoroughfare. When he entered, he saw Toshiaki, wearing a loose work cap, bending over the hearth. Toshiaki lifted his head and made an informal greeting, without any usual show of deference to a man of Inoue's rank. Toshiaki was then fifty-one, but his complexion was still that of a man in his prime.

Inoue felt that, considering his position as a direct representative of the shogun, the greeting was rather inappropriate. He waited to see how Toshiaki would continue to conduct himself. Nothing else was said, however, that could be interpreted as rude. He exchanged a few words with Toshiaki and returned home.

Afterward, Inoue began to puzzle over Toshiaki's attitude. Why had he been greeted in such a negligent fashion? The problem remained on Inoue's mind even after he returned home. He could make nothing of the whole situation and so decided to go and talk to Toshiaki again in order to ascertain his real attitude.

The second time as well, Toshiaki greeted Inoue in the same way and with the same seemingly careless attitude. Inoue immediately spoke out very strongly. He had come twice, he began, because he heard that Toshiaki was no ordinary person. He had been looking forward to discussing things together, and he even thought that on certain matters he might like to ask Toshiaki for some advice. Yet from all appearances, there was nothing extraordinary about him at all. He was rather disappointed, Inoue concluded.

Toshiaki replied that, indeed, he was nothing out of the ordinary. He did feel, however, that the only proper way to judge a person's wisdom and moral sense was to engage in a serious discussion.

Then, said Inoue, he wanted to bring up a question at once. Whatever his own personal qualities, he continued, he was a direct personal representative of the shogun. Thus he was unable to understand Toshiaki's motives in greeting him in such an obviously off-handed manner.

Toshiaki replied by suggesting to Inoue that perhaps he had not thought through his own reaction with sufficient care. After all, he reminded him, when he, Toshiaki, had been in Chikuzen, he had been in charge of the castle at Matera, with a territory yielding twenty-five thousand *koku*. True enough, after the battle of Osaka, Matera, like all other outlying fortifications, had been destroyed.[40] But he still retained the domains as before. Then again, as a chief retainer of the Kuroda family, he had been privy to responsibilities to administer a territory with an income of more than five hundred thousand *koku*, and he had been in charge of more than fifty thousand soldiers. Indeed the actions of a family with the prominence of the Kuroda were closely aligned to the welfare of the entire nation. At the time of the battle of Sekigahara, the Tokugawa family had been able to unite the country because Nagamasa and Yoshitaka served Ieyasu as faithful allies. There was certainly no reason, Toshiaki finished, why he should bend his knee to an official with an income worth some three or four hundred bags of rice.

Inoue recognized immediately the truth of what Toshiaki told him, apologized for his lack of perceptivity, and began to discuss a variety of matters on a most friendly and intimate basis.

When Inoue asked Toshiaki about the virtues and failings of different types of military strategy, Toshiaki explained his ideas as follows. The art of government requires a judicious mixture of civilian and military elements. The civilian aspects suggest moderation, the military, fierceness and strength. But "military" does not mean merely the use of weapons. It is only an aggressive and vainglorious rule that consistently depends on military might. Indeed no more than one aspect of military strategy depends on the force of arms. Various contemporary theories on the military arts are useless; outside of the Seven Books,[41] there are no other works of note to study. Have strong and brave men close by you, scrutinize the enemy's movements, and you will win. The question of strategy is always to be considered. If strategy is only conceived of in terms of numbers of men and how they are outfitted, there will be little chance to gain the final victory.

Inoue asked Toshiaki about the proper function of a castle. He replied that a castle should serve as a storehouse in times of trouble, so that families, provisions, and implements might be placed there for safe keeping. In a sense, a castle resembles the storehouse of a farmer or merchant. A fine general will not place too much importance on his citadel. Loyal retainers are the most important element in a strong castle. Those who have the status of daimyo should fear no one under the emperor. The training of good subordinates must always be kept in mind. Situations must always be watched as they develop, so that a lord's holdings may be enlarged whenever the occasion presents itself.

Inoue asked Toshiaki about the aspirations that samurai should cultivate. He replied that a samurai's aspiration must be high. If one were born in China, he should dream of becoming emperor. If born in Japan, one should aspire to become the shogun. Yet in order to accomplish his ambition, a samurai must always act prudently and treat others with genuine respect. When one has gained control over the provinces, he must make use of others with discretion and good judgment. Of ten men who can be of service, he should praise six and criticize four; if he praised all ten, he could only be weak and servile. Finally, the question of timing must always be carefully considered. At the right moment, decisive action is always required. To seize is against propriety; to protect is the proper order of things. Should you become aware of some misdemeanor, make sure you will not suffer from any misstep you make yourself, then make your decision and carry it out.

Toshiaki died at the age of sixty-two, on the first day of the third month of the First year of Jōō [1652], the year after Tokugawa Iemitsu was succeeded by Ietsuna. Toshiaki's grave and a large memorial tablet still remain on a hillside near the remains of the Hōrinji on Atagoyama at the village of Yonai in Iwate prefecture of the Tōhaku region. A young man named Uchiyama Zenkichi was adopted as heir for Toshiaki's family and married his daughter. He was in the service of the Nambu family with a stipend of two hundred *koku*. Toshiaki had decided to drop his own name, Kuriyama, since he felt it might remind people of the unfortunate incident of his earlier lord's misconduct. He purposely had the family adopt the surname of their maternal relative. Toshiaki's own retainers Kakuemon and Ōemon were called into service by the Nambu family and each received a stipend of fifty *koku*. Toshiaki's first son Rishū declined a similiar invitation from the Kuroda family and ended his days as a private gentleman.

September 1915

SUGINOHARA SHINA

"SHINA OF SUGINOHARA" is a popular story in Japan, yet an English-speaking reader may be puzzled at the attraction it has sustained. The narrative is broken up by the enumeration of small details that eventually seem to overwhelm the flow of events completely. In fact, however, the historical incidents with which the story deals are among the most famous in the history of the Tokugawa period. The quarrel of the Date family in Sendai over succession rights eventually involved the shogunate and cast into question many of the political principles on which the Tokugawa hegemony was constructed.* The incident was dramatized in a 1777 kabuki play *Meiboku Sendai hagi* that dominated the repertoire for several generations and is still performed with some frequency today. A Japanese reader, in other words, comes to the story with the necessary background, and interest, to follow the details of Ōgai's arguments.

In this perspective, Ōgai's accomplishments are considerable. He penetrates the myths surrounding the story of Tsunamune (who, according to popular accounts, was merely a dissolute) in order to discover his true temperament and character. Ōgai also locates with unerring precision the area of greatest potential interest for a writer: the psychological attitude of Tsunamune in exile, forced to watch passively the events that swirled around him. Ōgai, who often described himself as a "bystander" in his own earlier work, was no doubt naturally attracted to the character and situation of Tsunamune.

In addition, Ōgai provides a trenchant example of his dictum that ". . . the relations between the sexes are inscrutable . . ." in his sketch of the relations between Hatsuko and Shina, for whom the story is named. Shina, like several other women who figure in the historical narratives, represents a complex of virtues that, for Ōgai, make her altogether exceptional.

Ōgai's account falls short of fiction. As he himself points out in the course of his narrative, his regard for the historical facts, obtained through painstaking research, required a fidelity that precluded the creation of any new set of legends. We are left then with a web of facts and conjectures; read with understanding, they can exert a considerable appeal.

 I WAS ABOUT to set off for Kyoto to participate in the succession ceremony of the emperor one day, when a magazine of a certain society of which I was a member arrived.[1] Glancing through it in the midst of more pressing business, I noticed a story claiming that the descendants of a geisha named Takao were living in Sendai. I knew some rather comprehensive and ruthless evidence by Ōtsuki Fumihiko[2] that disproved this legend. As I wondered why this mistaken view was now being circulated anew, I realized, after pondering the matter more carefully, that a good reason existed.

Every writer has entertained the same question in his mind, I suppose; namely, how many people really read his work? Once a work is published, the possibility is born of its being read. However, the number of persons who actually do read it are few indeed. And not only are there comparatively few readers among the great masses of people—even among avid and learned readers their powers of reading are limited. They cannot read all the books that come out; hence even persons interested in such history as appears in the magazine I mentioned are not necessarily aware of the painstaking research of Ōtsuki Fumihiko.

The facts of the article were based on the "Ōshūbanashi" [Tale of Ōshū],[3] written by a certain Ayako,[4] the daughter of Kudō Heisuke of Sendai who became the wife of Tadano Iga. Ayako's claim to fame was her acquaintance with Takizawa Bakin. However, Ōtsuki Fumihiko also knew of the tale and demolished its credibility.

According to Ayako, the daimyo Date Tsunamune[5] had ransomed a geisha named Takao of the Shinyoshiwara district in Edo and brought her back to Sendai, where she died at a ripe old age; she says Takao's grave is in the Butsugenji temple in Aramichi and her descendants are the Suginohara family.

This account was completely erroneous. Date Tsunamune succeeded his father, Tadamune,[6] who died in the first year of Manji [1658]. On the first day of the second month of the third year of Manji [1660], Tsunamune was ordered by the Bakufu to direct the dredging of a canal in Koishikawa in Edo. He came to Edo from Sendai in the third month and commenced operations. The project extended from Sujikaebashi, the present-day Manseibashi, to Ushigome-dobashi. Therefore Tsunamune moved his headquarters to a temporary residence within the precincts behind Kichijōji temple. Kichijōji was a temple in present-day Komagome and at that time was still at the north foot of Suidōbashi, on the east side. Tsunamune first visited the li-

TRANSLATED BY DAVID DILWORTH

censed quarters at Yoshiwara at this time. This was not unusual for daimyos then, but the fact that his conduct was exaggerated and so quickly brought to the attention of the Bakufu seems to have been due to the connivance of certain people out to disgrace him. On the ground of misconduct, Tsunamune was ordered under house confinement and moved from the mansion at Shibahama to Shinagawa. The Shibahama mansion was apparently right in the middle of present-day Shimbashi Station. On the twenty-fifth day of the eighth month, his first son, Kamechiyo,[7] succeeded to the head of the Date house. At this time Tsunamune was twenty and Kamechiyo scarcely two. The dredging project was continued under the supervision of the Date family, and was completed in the following year.

Now, the Yoshiwara personage Tsunamune visited seems to have been a certain Kaoru of the Yamamoto-ya in Kyōmachi. In proof that she could not have been the Takao of the Miura-ya, it has been established that there was no geisha named Takao in the Miura-ya between the third and seventh months of the second year of Manji [1659]. There being no Takao for Tsunamune to visit, he could not have ransomed her either. Moreover, Tsunamune never went back to Sendai after being put under house arrest in the mansion in Shinagawa. At the age of forty-four in the third year of Tenna [1683], he became a monk and took the name Kashin. He died at seventy-two on the sixth day of the sixth month of the first year of Shōtoku [1711]. Even if there were a geisha Tsunamune ransomed, he could not have taken her back to Sendai.

Ayako, wanting to refute the popular version of the story that Tsunamune had ransomed Takao and then sailed off with her and killed her at Mitsumata, had Takao accompany him to Sendai and bear him sons there. She simply replaced one erroneous version of the story with another.

Whose grave, therefore, is in the Butsugenji temple mentioned in the "Ōshūbanashi"? It is that of a mistress of Tsunamune named Shina, whose descendants have the name of Suginohara since she was originally from that family. Shina was neither a Yoshiwara geisha nor the person named Takao.

What kind of person was this Shina? I myself was planning to write a story centering around Tsunamune in Shinagawa, and worked on the historical background of the plot for quite a long time. Tsunamune was no ordinary daimyo. He was a gifted poet, calligrapher, and painter. He succeeded to the head of the Date house at the age of nineteen. He had been daimyo of the six hundred twenty thousand *koku* fief for barely two years when he was placed under house arrest for being involved in an intrigue centering around his uncle, Date Hyōbu Shōyū Munekatsu.[8] From then until he became a monk at the age of forty-four, Tsunamune was never permitted to see his son Kamechiyo, later named Tsunamura. Kamechiyo became Sōjirō Tsunamoto at the age of eleven in the ninth year of Kambun [1669]; two years later he became the nominal father-in-law of Ichi no kami Muneoki,[9] the heir of Munekatsu. Because in that year there occurred the incident in which Harada Kai cut down Date Aki in the mansion of Sakai Uta no kami Tadakiyo, patron of Munekatsu, Kamechiyo could set his mind at rest concerning the domain he thought himself about to lose.[10] In the fifth year of Empō [1677], at the age of nineteen, he changed his name to Tsunamura. Munekatsu, his secret enemy, died two years later—four years before the reunion of Tsunamune and Tsunamura. On the scrolls he did during those lonely years under domiciliary confinement, Tsunamune often used the seal *chika hikkai*, which means "When one perceives his faults, he must correct them." Tsunamune's artistic talents were not confined to calligraphy and poetry. He worked in gold-lacquer ware, made pottery, and also forged swords. I find it of particular interest that Tsunamune rechanneled politically inexpressible energies in the direction of art. It is also interesting that Tsunamune's spirits did not dampen under house arrest. In the sliding door of the Shinagawa mansion he inlaid more than four hundred glass tiles, a material still rare at that time. It is said that the larger tiles sold for seventy *ryō* each. Does this not bear witness to his indomitable spirit? His mistress Shina, who served this magnificent personality Tsunamune into his late years, was surely no ordinary woman either.

Tsunamune did not have a legal wife. The two main women who lived with him were Misawa Hatsuko,[11] the mother of Kamechiyo, and this Shina.[12] Hatsuko was born in the eleventh year of Kan'ei [1639]. She was the same age as Tsunamune, while Shina seems to have been one year older. Of the two women, Hatsuko came from a good family and was well-sponsored. When he took her in, Tsunamune went through a formal marriage ceremony, but it was never registered with the Bakufu. It was held when Tsunamune and Hatsuko were both sixteen, three years before he succeeded as the head of the family. Four years later, on the eighth day of the third month of the second year of Manji [1659], Kamechiyo was born. This was the year prior to the assignment of the canal project. Shina came to serve at the age of twenty-one in their Hama mansion in the year that Hatsuko gave birth to Kamechiyo. She apparently caught Tsunamune's eye immediately and began receiving his favors about the time of Hatsuko's delivery.

Hatsuko, who served Tsunamune before Shina, was a person of excellent lineage. Iijima Saburō Hirotada, the eighth-generation grandson of Mutsu no kami Mankai, who was in turn the fourth son of Rokusonnō Tsune-moto,[13] was lord of Misawa in Izumo; Hirotada's great-grandchild was Misawa Rokurō Tamenaga. The tenth-generation grandson of Tamenaga, one Sakyonosuke Tametora, had moved to Fuchū in Nagato, serving first under Amako Yoshihisa,[14] later under Mōri Terumoto.[15] Tametora's eldest son, Tanomonosuke Tamemoto, had a dispute with his father and fled to Ōmi. This Tamemoto had a son and a daughter. The older brother Gonnosuke Kiyonaga[16] became the adopted son of Ujiie Hirosada, lord of the castle of Ōgaki in Mino; because of the outcome of the battle of Sekigahara, he and Hirosada were placed under the custody of Hosokawa Tadaoki.[17] The younger sister, Kii, through the sponsorship of Tadaoki served in the inner court of Edo castle, and became the lady-in-waiting of Tokugawa Ieyasu's adopted daughter, Furihime.[18] Since Furihime became the wife of Date Masamune in the third year of Genna [1617] while Kii was serving her in the inner court, Kii also accompanied the bride to Sendai. During this time Kii's older brother, Kiyonaga, wandered about and ended up in Tottori in Inaba, where Hatsuko was born to him and a daughter of Kutsuki Nobutsuna. Hatsuko was taken away by her aunt Kii to serve in the ladies' quarters of the Date family.

Furihime was actually the child of Ikeda Terumasa;[19] her mother was Ieyasu's second daughter, Kōhime. Ieyasu adopted her and married her to Tadamune. Date Tsunamune was born to Kaihime,[20] a concubine of Tadamune, but was later adopted by Furihime and registered as a legitimate son. Kaihime was a daughter of Kushige Sachūjō Takamune,[21] and the younger sister of Mikushige no Tsubone, the mother of Emperor Gosai-in.[22]

Three years before his death, Tadamune became fond of the beautiful and clever little Hatsuko whom he used to see in the company of Kii. He told Kii that he wished Hatsuko to become his son's concubine. But Kii, reeling off the lineage of their own house, refused. Therefore Tsunamune and Hatsuko's marriage ceremony took place in the Hama mansion in the first month of the first year of Meireki [1655].

Hatsuko's beauty can be surmised even from a wooden image of her that survives. Specimens of her accomplished calligraphy remain in the poems written on long strips of paper, some letters, and a copy of the *Lotus Sutra* by her own hand. She was also well-versed in poetry. She seems to have been a beautiful and refined woman. Probably for these reasons Tadamune chose this niece of his wife's lady-in-waiting for his own son Tsunamune, even permitting their marriage.

The relations between the sexes are inscrutable, of course, but for Shina, who herself came only obliquely into the picture, to have gained Tsunamune's affection precisely at the time that Hatsuko was bearing him an heir, would seem to have been impossible without some special attraction in her personality. Therefore, not only for the sake of again emphasizing that Shina was not Takao—proven beyond question by Ōtsuki Fumihiko long ago—I should here like to present Shina of Suginohara on her own merits.

What was Shina's family lineage? One member of the Akamatsu family of Harima was Suginohara Iga no kami Tatamori. Later he shaved his head and became the monk Sōi. The name Suginohara was based on the name of a region in Harima. One of Katamori's descendants was a person named Shinzaemon Morinori. Tradition says Morinori became a *rōnin* at the time of the destruction of the Akamatsu clan and went off to Edo, where he died from injury in the great fire of the third year of Meireki [1657]. The time of the destruction of the Akamatsu clan seems to mean the time when Akamatsu Norifusa,[23] holding a ten thousand *koku* fief in Awa, cast his lot in with Osaka at the battle of Sekigahara, and was killed as he fled from the battlefield. If that is true, then even if Morinori was a youth of fifteen at the time, he must have been fifty-three when Shina was born in 1639. At any rate, Shina seems to have been born to Morinori in his later years after he became a *rōnin*. Also in view of the record which says that Morinori's wife, who bore Shina, was the daughter of a Nichiren priest named Nichidō of the Seitaiji temple in Azabu, we can surmise that Morinori was married while a *rōnin* in Edo. Morinori had two children, Shina and a younger son named Unenosuke who died in infancy. Thus when Morinori died, the nineteen-year-old Shina was his only descendant and was taken to live in the Seitaiji temple.

Two years later, in the second year of Manji [1659], Shina was received as a servant in the Hama mansion, and seems immediately to have become Tsunamune's mistress. An incident only obliquely reported suggests that Tsunamune bestowed great affection upon her afterward. When Tsunamune was charged with intrigue and moved to domiciliary confinement in the mansion of Shinagawa in the third year of Manji [1660], Shina, who went with him, requested a day's leave during which she hurriedly met her grandfather, Nichidō, and relatives and old friends in Edo to bid them farewell forever. This signified that she was cutting all relations with society to devote her life to Tsunamune in his adversity. Tsunamune is reported to have been very pleased with this and to have given Shina one of the emblems of the Date family, the *yukisusuki*[24] emblem.

Shina never went back on her commitment to Tsunamune. She served him loyally from the day they fell in love when Tsunamune was twenty until he was an old man of seventy-two. When Tsunamune died she became the nun Jōkyū-In and moved to Sendai. She died at seventy-eight in the first year of Kyōhō [1716].

During these years, Tsunamune shaved his head when Shina was forty-five; Hatsuko died three years later. It seems safe to say that Tsunamune, now the lay monk Kashin, lived the long stretch of the next twenty-five years together with Shina. This cannot be proven, but I cannot help seeing Shina, who gave her love to this Kashin who bore his misfortune with indomitable spirit, as not only a loyal concubine but a companion of exceptional spirit and vitality.

In her later years, Shina adopted Ishi, a daughter of Nakatsuka Jube Shigebumi, and married her to Kumagai Itsuki Naokiyo; therefore Shina's line was continued by Naokiyo's second son, Tsunenosuke. The present Suginohara family derives from this Suginohara Tsunenosuke.

After Tsunamune was moved to the Shinagawa mansion on the twenty-sixth day of the seventh month of the third year of Manji [1660], the so-called Sendai disturbances broke out over his sentence, climaxing on the twenty-seventh day of the third month in the eleventh year of Kambun [1671] when Harada Kai cut down Date Aki[25] in the mansion of Sakai Tadakiyo.[26] Tsunamune had to watch these disturbances as a passive spectator. The mansion of Minamioi-mura in Shinagawa was a residence of modest dimensions which had been built by clearing away a temple and farm houses. Tsunamune lived there with one retainer put in his service. At that time his brother-in-law, Tachibana Tadashige,[27] wrote him a secret letter politely begging him not to try anything, saying "As far as I am concerned, you may walk about the mansion, but so as not to draw attention." At a time when his youthful and exuberant nature was so cooped up that he found it difficult even to walk with due composure within the mansion, Tsunamune now had the added burden of anxiety over the safety of the young Kamechiyo and the political situation in Sendai. His retainer at that time, Ōmachi Bizen, seems to have been a person of no great merit, which left only Hatsuko—and no doubt Shina—to share his depression.

Kamechiyo, who appeared so often in Tsunamune's anxious dreams, lived in the Hama mansion from the third year of Manji [1660] until the second month of the eighth year of Kambun [1668]. In fires of that month the Hama mansion was burned down together with the main mansion in Atagoshita. In the Date house, the main mansion seems to have been used only on special occasions. In Tsunamune's day the main mansion was in Sakurada, located just at the northeast corner of present-day Hibiya Park. At such times as Tsunamune received orders from the shogun, he would come from the Hama mansion to the main mansion. At the time of the fires, Kamechiyo moved to Shirokanedai in Azabu. This was a substitute location which they received when Sakurada was confiscated by the Bakufu in the first year of Manji [1658]. Atagoshita, which to that time functioned as an intermediate residence between the Sakurada and Hama mansions, became the main mansion of the Date family. But it too was burned down together with the Hama mansion. Repairs of the main mansion in Atagoshita were completed thereafter in the twelfth month of the year of the fires, and Kamechiyo moved in there. From that time on, the Date family always lived in the main mansion.

During this time Kamechiyo succeeded to the head of the Date house when he was two, in the eighth month of the third year of Manji [1660]; he had an audience with Tokugawa Ietsuna[28] when he was six, in the sixth month of the fourth year of Kambun [1664]; and after he moved to the residence in Atagoshita, when he came of age at eleven in the second month of the ninth year of Kambun [1669], his name became Sōjirō Tsunamoto, later changed to Tsunamura in the first month of the fifth year of Empō [1677].

In the shadows of this public career, there lurked dangers which proved Tsunamune's anxieties over Kamechiyo to be well warranted. These dangers surfaced in two poisoning attempts.

The first incident occurred on the twenty-seventh day of the eleventh month of the sixth year of Kambun [1666], when Kamechiyo was eight. Prior to this there had been no untoward incidents other than Kamechiyo coming down with smallpox in the ninth month of the second year of Kambun [1662]. In his attendance there were many retainers serving as bodyguards, but as he was under ten at the time, he was probably cared for by female servants. The chief of these women seems to have been a servant named Toba.[29] She was the daughter of the Edo *rōnin* Sakakida Rokuzaemon Shigeyoshi, and had been the attendant first of Furihime, then of Hatsuko, and finally of Kamechiyo. She turned forty-seven that year.

The meals set before Kamechiyo at the time were customarily pretasted by close vassals called *oni banshū*.[30] On one occasion a few of them died, among them being Yoneyama Heizaemon and Senda Heizō. Then they gave the food to a lower vassal and two dogs, and they also died. When Kamechiyo's guardian, Date Hyōbu Shōyū, received the report, he had a man named Kumada Jihē brought to the Hama mansion and executed together with the doctor Kōno Dōen and his three sons. The report says about seven or eight of the male servants from the cook on down and about ten female servants were also killed. Since Toba had been in the presence of the food, she was sent to Sendai and put under the custody of Daijō Gemba.

Since there were such facts as Toba having been once entertained by Dōen on a boat, if Dōen had actually prepared the poison, then Toba is not beyond suspicion. But as she later received a generous fief in Sendai, we reach the end of the thread suggesting her possible participation in the crime. And if Munekatsu, who had Dōen killed, had himself ordered the poisoning, what might his motive have been? Even if Kamechiyo died, since there was a younger brother born to Hatsuko, the authority of the main family could not have been handed down to Hyōbu's son, Ichi no kami. Did Munekatsu do it, then, simply to diminish the fief of the main house and increase the stipend of his own house? This poisoning incident took place when Kamechiyo was eight years old.

The second poisoning attempt occurred in the Shirokanedai mansion in the eighth year of Kambun [1668]. It took place in the interval between the fire incident at the Hama mansion and Kamechiyo's entering the newly repaired mansion in Atagoshita. On a certain day in the eighth month, a certain Shiozawa Tanzaburō, who had become a page through the good offices of Harada Kai, poisoned a serving of sea bass and died after eating it himself. He had poisoned the fish at Harada Kai's order, but had eaten it himself when he could not bear to present it to his lord. It is reported that since Tanzaburō had revealed this plot to his mother the night before, she also killed herself by falling forward on a sword. Kamechiyo was now ten. Just as there was no one named Takao in the alleged Yoshiwara affair of Tsunamune, so too in this poisoning incident there was no woman corresponding to the Asaoka of the popular legend.

Seeing the danger surrounding Kamechiyo both Hatsuko and Shina probably wanted to act as personal guardians—Hatsuko for the sake of her own son, Shina for the sake of her lord. There are indeed hints of Hatsuko's visits to Kamechiyo's mansion, but unfortunately no visitation is actually reported.

Next, what about the political situation in Sendai which made Tsunamune so anxious? The central person on this end of the Sendai trouble was Tsunamune's uncle, Date Hyōbu Shōyū, the guardian of Kamechiyo. Since it was said that if a person were in league with Hyōbu he would be rewarded even if undistinguished, but if he opposed Hyōbu, would be punished even if he were blameless, it seems that his administration of government was totally irresponsible. The leader of the Sendai administration was Watanabe

Kimbē, who came to exercise power irresponsibly in his office of Han Censor from around the third year of Kambun [1663]; after becoming Head Page the next year he became increasingly despotic. The oppressive policies of the Watanabe faction were underlined later when Date Aki enumerated one hundred twenty persons given capital sentences by them. The most conspicuous among those punished were Date Aki and Itō Uneme.[31] Itō Uneme was the adopted son of Itō Shinzaemon,[32] who died of illness right after becoming Han Elder in the third year of Kambun [1663]. His death in domiciliary confinement started a struggle over the ranking of seats in the *han* government. When the shogunate's Censor was entertained in the seventh year of Kambun [1667], the greetings of the *han* officials were made in the order of Han Elders, Councillors, Master of Ceremonies, Head of the Garrison, Civil and Financial Commander, Head of the Pages, and Censors. When their winecups were poured, Uneme, whose office was that of Master of Ceremonies, was made to wait until after the Censors. Harada Kai instigated this at the prompting of the Watanabe Kimbē faction.

Date Aki had jurisdiction over Tōdagōri and lived in Wakuya. Toyomagōri, which bordered on the north, was ruled over by Date Shikibu[33] in Teraike. However, a border dispute arose between Osatomura on the northern border of Tōdagōri and Akōzumura of Toyomagōri. On this occasion, Aki ceded the territory in dispute to Shikibu and there was no trouble. This was the fifth year of Kambun [1665]. Two years later, another border dispute arose between a detached territory under Shikibu's jurisdiction in southwest Momogōri and Aki's adjacent territory in Tōdagōri. A year later Aki lodged a complaint with the Han Elders, but the following year the *han* investigators decreed a new boundary extremely favorable to Shikibu. Incensed, Aki decided in Kambun eleven [1671] to press a legal suit at Edo even if it cost his life. Therefore these boundary disputes, like Uneme's over recognition of his rank, were arguments over essential rights, but both Uneme and Aki took these opportunities to resist the misgovernment of the Watanabe faction. Even in so doing Aki was primarily motivated by his desire to impeach the tyrannical retainers for the sake of his lord, and only secondarily by the legality of the border questions. For this reason he succeeded. Watanabe was placed under the custody of Date Kunai Shōyū[34] and died of self-inflicted starvation.

I contemplated writing a story about Tsunamune passively watching this trouble in Sendai. My interest focused upon his psychological state as an objective spectator completely powerless to act in these matters. I wanted to depict his life's companions, the refined and gentle Hatsuko and the intelligent and firm-willed Shina, and to construct a plot of tensions underlying the composure within this triangle. However, I abandoned this plan both from a lack of creative power and a habit of cherishing historical facts.

On fifth May last year [1915] I visited the Sendai grave of Hatsuko in the Kōshōji located in Shinterakoji. This is the grave people refer to when they talk of "visiting the grave of Asaoka." Within a time-worn old fence a new granite gravestone had been placed with the inscription "The grave of Misawa Hatsuko." It struck me as the grave of some school girl who had recently died.

I refrained from going to the grave of Shina in the Butsugenji.

January 1916

TOKŌ TAHEI

TOKŌ TAHEI is a short piece illustrating the virtues of resoluteness and fidelity in the Tokugawa system of values. As in other similar accounts by Ōgai, the reader is given characters who are not famous men themselves but who are involved in some way with extraordinary figures in history, in this case, with Miyamoto Musashi, a legendary swordsman and student of Zen. The period and events described seem all the more real when related not to some unusual personage but to a plain and simple man much closer to the ordinary reader in outlook and psychology.

Ōgai charts Tokō Tahei's activities quite precisely and with enough detail to make him real and credible. For those interested in Ōgai's methods of composition, the story is especially revealing for the sections that show his methods of construction: he uses meticulous historical analysis combined with real psychological insight into the personality he is analyzing in order to construct a proper framework for his story. If the results do, as Ōgai puts it, lie somewhere between history and fiction, the end result is no less satisfying.

 TOKŌ TAHEI was a retainer of the Hosokawa family: he served both Tadatoshi, the governor of Etchū, and Mitsuhisa, the governor of Higo.[1] Tahei's uncle, a lay priest named Tokō Mikawa, first served the Ōtomo family[2] in Bungo, but when Ōtomo Yoshimune was banished, the retainers of the Tokō family became *rōnin*. Mikawa's nephew Tahei was called to serve the Hosokawa family at the time when Tadatoshi was still ruling over the province of Buzen, and was employed as an ordinary page.

When Hosokawa Tadatoshi's domains were transferred to Higo, Tahei accompanied him to Kumamoto.

At the time of the Shimabara Rebellion, Tahei served in Tadatoshi's forces.[3] For his valor in being "first to storm the citadel" during the attack on Hara castle, he was awarded a stipend of three hundred *koku*, and a company of ten riflemen was placed in his charge.

Later, while in the service of Hosokawa Mitsuhisa, Tahei was put in charge of a rifle company of thirty. However he asked that he might "respectfully decline those duties" because of his age, and instead he took a subordinate position and then retired in the first month of the second year of Empō [1647]. On the same day of the same month, his son, also named Tahei, became head of the Tokō house.

Such are the facts as officially set down in the records of the Tokō family.

Tahei had two or three extraordinary things happen to him in the course of his life, and mention of them turns up in various records. As these anecdotes seem to differ slightly from one account to another, I have been selective in what I have retained and in what I have passed over, according to my own judgment. Nevertheless I have managed to put down at least the general outlines of what happened, as a legacy for the future.

One of these anecdotes concerns the fact that Tahei's abilities were discovered by Miyamoto Musashi.[4] This anecdote has already found its way into a book about Musashi edited by a committee in Kumamoto, and so a certain number of people must by now be aware of the incident. In this volume, however, Tahei is referred to as Tokō Kimpei. A search of the Tokō family records reveals no one by that name, other than a certain Kimpei in the ninth generation, who lived at the time of the Meiji Restoration. But it is possible, I suppose, that the first-generation Tahei may have used the name Kimpei at a certain time during his life.

Indeed the book contains only the vaguest of references to the time when

TRANSLATED BY J. THOMAS RIMER

the affair took place. The entry begins, "One day, Musashi was by the side of Lord Tadatoshi," and says no more than that Musashi had an occasional audience with him and, further, that the incident took place at one of them. In one record the same event is mentioned in connection with Musashi's first interview with Tadatoshi. This possibility strikes me as likely.

However, it is by no means clear as to precisely when Musashi had his first audience with Tadatoshi. Musashi left Kyoto for Kokura in Buzen in the fourth month of Keichō seventeen [1612]. At that time, the head of the Hosokawa family was still Tadaoki [5] the father of Tadatoshi. Musashi went to Kokura hoping to test his skill against Sasaki Kojirō,[6] a swordsman in the employ of Tadaoki. The man who served as a mediator for the swordsmen was a disciple of Musashi's father, the swordsman Shimmen Munisai,[7] who now served under a retainer of Tadaoki. His name was Nagaoka Sado Okinaga. The match between Musashi and Kojirō is popularly referred to as the Match at Ganryū Island.[8]

After the match, Musashi is supposed to have left immediately for Shimonoseki. It has been suggested that he then returned a second time to Kokura, but I find no mention of any meeting with Tadaoki.

Later Musashi was patronized by Tadaoki's heir Tadatoshi in the eighth month of Kan'ei seventeen [1640]. These two events are separated by twenty-eight years. During that interval, the Osaka Winter and Summer Campaigns were waged,[9] the Shimabara Rebellion was put down, and the Hosokawa family changed its lord and its territory.

Taking this well-known period of history as a large hill standing as a marker on the road of time, I have tried to be as precise about the meeting between Musashi and Tokō Tahei as I can.

In order to understand the significance of their meeting, it is necessary to look not at the career of Musashi but at the historical facts concerning Tahei. Tahei was taken into service by Hosokawa Tadatoshi in Buzen sometime after Genna seven [1621], that is, after Sansai Tadaoki retired, but before his successor Tadatoshi was reissued lands in Higo in Kan'ei nine [1632]. Then again, Musashi must have discovered Tahei before he had risen to any position of eminence, that is to say, no later than the fall of Hara castle during the Shimabara Rebellion on the twenty-seventh day of the second month of Kan'ei fifteen [1638].

Therefore the two must have met at some time between Genna seven [1621] and Kan'ei nine [1632].

Let me again make some observations on Musashi's career. Previously I mentioned only the occasion when Musashi received a stipend from Tadatoshi, but now I wish to consider the occasion of their first meeting. It is not certain that both events occurred at the same time. Indeed it strikes me that two separate occasions were involved. This is because if Musashi's service with Tadatoshi began after the fall of Hara castle, then Tahei would not have been an unproven person whose abilities Musashi first noticed. Guessing from the known facts, it seems quite likely that Tadatoshi had an interview with Musashi before taking him into his service. Thus Tadatoshi, after receiving his new territory in 1621, saw Musashi before the swordsman was appointed to his service in 1640. It must have been on such a prior occasion that Tahei received Musashi's praise.

However the twenty-year period between 1621 and 1640 seems too long. Indeed if we look at the career of Tahei after his meeting with Musashi and subtract the three years after the fall of Hara castle in 1638, we make no significant progress in terms of an understanding of his careeer as a whole.

I would like to be as precise as possible in delineating the exact amount of time involved. My own analysis is as follows. Musashi, after he served with the Hideyoshi forces at the battle of Osaka, reportedly traveled through quite a number of provinces. However there is no record of his having been in Kyushu again until Kan'ei eleven [1634], when he came to Kokura in Buzen with his adopted child Iori as a guest of Ogasawara Ukyōdaiyū Tadazane,[10] who had been assigned the territory after the transfer of the Hosokawa family. Was it not perhaps during this visit to Kyushu that he visited Tadatoshi in Kumamoto? If so, it was within five years of the fall of Hara castle; at some point during those years, Tadatoshi probably met Musashi, and Musashi recognized Tahei's merits. At least I would like to think so. If I were writing a novel, I could merely write that it was so and not waste words in the fashion I have.

I have here exposed to view the conventional sort of mechanisms brought to bear on what is usually termed the historical novel.

Historians, seeing what I have written, will no doubt criticize me for my willfulness. Novelists, on the other hand, will laugh at my persistence. There is a Western proverb about sleeping between two beds. Looking at my own work, it seems that this proverb can be applied to me.

There is some discrepancy in the records concerning the meeting between Miyamoto Musashi and Tokō Tahei. Based on the reasoning I have outlined above, I have selected and discarded information at will, but I think the event was surely something like what follows here.

Musashi arrived at the castle town of Kokura, bringing Iori with him. This Iori was supposedly the orphan of an acquaintance Musashi knew from a family at Shōhōjigahara in the province of Dewa. I have tried to locate the place name of Shōhōji, but without success. When I made inquiries later I learned that there is reportedly such a place next to Kowakubino in the district of Senbaku in the province of Ugo. This might have been Iori's original home. After arriving in Kokura, Musashi remained a guest of Ogasawara, but Iori went into his direct employ and was given a very responsible position. His descendants still bear his name. When I myself went to Kokura I was shown at their home various objects bequeathed to the family by Musashi. One thing I still remember seeing there was a wooden sword with the luster of a mirror. And there was an unsigned picture of Bodhidharma.[11] I thought to call on the current Mr. Iori and inquired about him. According to what I was told, he is a farmer living in the country near Dairi in Fukuoka. Deterred by government business, I was unable to visit him. In any case, it is not about Iori that I now wish to write.

Musashi did not seek to serve any daimyo in an official position. Yet he seems to have selected some place in Kyushu to live out his days. Hosokawa Tadatoshi was learning swordsmanship of the Yagyū school;[12] thus he thought he would like to have a look at Musashi. It was no doubt because of the desire on the part of both men that Musashi had his audience with Tadatoshi.

It must have been some time after Musashi first arrived in Kokura, probably just before the uprisings at Shimabara—thus between Kan'ei eleven [1634] and Kan'ei fourteen [1637]. I imagine the interview took place in 1635 or 1636, during the time when Tadatoshi was in residence there.

I suppose they met at the Hanabatake mansion in Kumamoto. For the retainers who were serving at the mansion, the appearance of the matchless Shimmen Miyamoto Musashi was awaited as a sensational event.

Among them was Tokō Tahei. At that time he had worked for the Hosokawa family for no more than sixteen years and no less than four, depending on whether he joined Tadatoshi's service just after Tadatoshi assumed his position as head of the Hosokawa family, or only after the lands were transferred. Tahei held the rank of Ordinary Page and he was a man of no apparent talents. Tahei, seeing everyone so excited, knit his brows and muttered to himself, "Who is this Musashi? . . . just some nondescript retainer . . . It is quite unwarranted to summon him and give him an audience like this. There is certainly no excuse for all this pretentious preparation." When Musashi arrived and came to the mansion, Tahei sat on the steps of the entrance and watched him come and go.

When the official interview was concluded according to proper ceremony, both host and guest changed their seats and continued talking informally.

In the course of their conversation, Tadatoshi asked Musashi a question: Among Tadatoshi's own retainers, were there any whose skill and valor in the martial arts were known to Musashi? Musashi replied, "Yes, I just now saw such a man." When asked who it was, he replied that he did not know the man's name. Tadatoshi called from among those in attendance all those known for skill in military tactics, archery, and riflery and had them sit in a row. Looking them over, Musashi replied, "I regret to say the person I mentioned to you is not among these men."

"If that is the case," Tadatoshi told him, "would you be kind enough to go out, find him, and bring him back to me?" Musashi agreed and rose to go; and within the space of a moment he returned from the official's waiting room with Tokō Tahei.

When Musashi brought Tokō Tahei before Hosokawa Tadatoshi, Tadatoshi said to Musashi, "I know the man, but what was it about him that attracted your attention?"

"If you question him concerning his state of continuous enlightenment, you will surely understand," Musashi replied.

"Is that so? Well then, Tokō, give me some indication about how enlightened you are." As Tadatoshi said this, all the men there looked at Tokō's face as if for the first time.

"Indeed," Tahei replied, "I haven't the kind of enlightenment you speak of."

Musashi interrupted. "Tokō, I have reported that I had an intuition of your military discipline. You need only explain your customary habits of mind and that will serve admirably."

Tahei thought for a moment, then spoke. He was not considering what he should answer but was thinking rather how to put into words what he knew he wanted to say.

"If you speak of the Way of the Warrior, I cannot claim to have accomplished a single thing. Let me rather give my opinion concerning what you referred to as my customary habits of mind. I would say that I suddenly thought of myself as a criminal whose head can be cut off to test a new sword, and I took this realization to heart and concentrated on it. A man who is like this can be destroyed at any time. And in fact he comes to accept destruction with a light heart. At first he is unlikely to forget his insignificance, and yet precisely because this thought is always with him, he ceases to be afraid of it. Eventually as he begins to concentrate on the idea, it becomes perfectly natural for him. I am sorry to offer such a poor explanation," Tahei concluded, and he prostrated himself on the ground before them.

Before Tadatoshi could say anything, Musashi spoke. "Did you hear what he said? That is truly the essence of military valor."

Tahei withdrew, having earned a great deal of respect he had never anticipated.

I would like to think that the Shimabara uprising took place a year or two after this. In the tenth month of that year, Kan'ei fourteen [1637], when the uprising began, Masuda Shirō Tokisada[13] arrived at Hara castle at the head of the rebellious forces, on the first day of the eleventh month. The castle fell the following year, on the twenty-seventh day of the second month.

Miyamoto Musashi left Kokura with the troops of Ogasawara Tadazane in the capacity of honorary military commander. Tahei served in the Hosokawa forces that set out from Kumamoto. It was during this campaign that he distinguished himself and received the stipend of three hundred *koku*. Then, two years later, Musashi made his decision to retire in Kumamoto, and the Hosokawa family made him an honorary retainer, with the position as Head of a Reserve Command. On the seventeenth day of the third month of the year following, Tadatoshi died. Musashi followed him four years later, on the nineteenth day of the fifth month of Shōhō two [1645]. Such constitutes the story of Musashi's "discovery" of Tahei.

Another incident is that of Tahei's work as a stone thief. The records do not indicate when the incident took place. The gist of it is as follows: when the Edo castle was under renovation, various daimyo were asked to contribute large stones for the purpose. Eventually stones from various provinces began to arrive in Edo, but the ship from Higo with its cargo of stones still did not arrive. Tokō Tahei was asked how the matter might be taken care of; he evidently promised to supply the stones as soon as possible, and, by means of a most unusual procedure, he did manage to obtain them. I would like to determine as precisely as possible when this incident took place.

Tokō Tahei made a promise to take these unusual steps in order to try to cover over an unfortunate situation. When did the incident occur? As the various daimyo had received orders to send stones to Edo and were in the midst of dispatching them, it would have been almost impossible for anyone to obtain any stones while himself in Edo. To have asked this difficult task of a retainer, the Hosokawa family would surely have chosen someone of more than average ability. If this is so, the one chosen would not be the Tahei who was merely an Ordinary Page and had not yet manifested any of his abilities, but rather the Tahei who had received a stipend for his brave conduct. It seems to me that the repairs to the Edo castle must thus have taken place after the fall of Shimabara castle in 1638.

I do not have at hand any detailed materials referring to the various changes made to the Edo castle. According to Tokugawa official records, the various gates at Edo castle were ordered to be repaired on the fifteenth day of the second month of Kan'ei sixteen [1639]. On the second day of the eighth month of the same year, repairs were ordered on the enclosures of the West Enceinte. However, on the eleventh day of the same month there was a fire in the castle, and another order for major repairs was issued on the sixteenth. This work took eight full months to complete. From this date until the death of Tokō Tahei in Shōō two [1653], there is no record of any further repairs being made to the castle.

It thus seems to me that Tahei probably obtained these stones for the repairs in Kan'ei sixteen [1639]. The only worrisome thing is that I do not have the necessary documents to tell me which daimyo were asked to contribute building materials. I have heard that documents appropriate for such research are now in the process of compilation by the Hosokawa family. It would no doubt be wise to use the information in these records to verify the incident.

The unusual methods Tahei employed to obtain the stones were extremely simple. According to the records, "Taking day laborers with him, he removed the identifying marks on stones contributed by other daimyo and replaced them with marks bearing the name of his province, Higo. He finished this work in several days."

Tahei was suspected of being the guilty party and was apprehended by the Tokugawa government. When questioned, he said he knew nothing. Then he was tortured. First he was forced to carry heavy stones. Then he was given a treatment that went by the name of "bamboo massage."

In a book entitled *Miyamoto Musashi*, the following description is provided: "The small ends of hollow bamboo tubes are hollowed out very thin. These are pushed into the knee and rubbed about, so that the flesh enters the tubes. When the bamboo is then removed, there are small holes left in the knees, into which boiling soy sauce is poured as a torture."

Saying that the jailor's methods were too lax, Tahei took the bamboo in his own hands and twisted it himself, then also poured in the soy himself. From the holes, bumps of raw flesh appeared, as big as wild peaches. It is said that the Tokō family will not eat that fruit even now.

Tahei was not the sort of man who would give in to torture. The Tokugawa officials had no other resort than to try to replace torture with trickery.

One day Tahei was dragged into court. The official in charge suddenly raised his voice and pronounced the following: "Tokō Tahei, the stone thief, you are not to be punished. Rise." Tokō remained where he was, as if he had heard nothing.

Shortly, the official then declared: "Tokō Tahei. You have been cleared of the charge of stealing of the stones. Rise." Now Tahei rose slowly and withdrew from the court. His guard, flustered, followed him out. It had been decided beforehand to let him go free if the last trick didn't work.

In *Miyamoto Musashi* only the incident of Tokō's discovery by Musashi and the incident of the prison sentence for stealing the stones are recorded.

As for the next incident, in which Tokō Tahei was part of an undercover maneuver, the records are also incomplete. Nevertheless, in terms of Tahei's own career, the two most important incidents were, in a public sense, his meritorious service at the battle for Hara castle, and, in a personal sense, his efforts concerning the problem of the succession within his lord's family.

The year after Hosokawa Tadatoshi welcomed Miyamoto Musashi as a guest, the lord of Higo died in Kan'ei eighteen [1641], on the seventeenth day of the third month. On the fifth day of the fifth month of the same year, his son Mitsuhisa took over the rule of the house. On the nineteenth day of the twelfth month of Shōhō two [1645], Miyamoto Musashi himself died. On the second day of the twelfth month of the same year, Tadatoshi's father, the long-retired Sansai Tadaoki died as well. Mitsuhisa died in the third year of Keian [1649] on the twenty-seventh day of the first month.

At Mitsuhisa's death, his son Rokumaru[14] was only an infant. For the Hosokawa family, with properties of five hundred forty thousand *koku*, the assurance of Rokumaru's succession without difficulty was a question of life or death. The Han Elder Nagaoka Shikibu was placed in charge of this grave matter and dispatched to Edo, along with two retainers sent to accompany him. One was Umehara Kuhei[15] and the other was Tokō Tahei.

Umehara was on good terms with Sakai Uta no kami Tadakiyo.[16] In discussing the pending visit to Sakai's mansion at Ōtemae, Shikibu cautioned Kuhei, "If our request is not granted as a matter of course, do not simply retire but hold yourself in readiness." Shikibu also told him, "You must always discuss everything with Tokō frankly and work closely together with him for the sake of our lord." Tahei's duties were also extremely important.

Nagaoka Shikibu's mission obtained the goal desired. On the eighteenth day of the fourth month of Keian three [1650], Rokumaru was appointed without difficulty as lord of the Hosokawa domain. He later took the name Etchū no kami Tsunatoshi.

The attitude Tokō adopted throughout his life was extremely simple. In a word, it was precisely the conviction on his part to be prepared to face death. No matter what the issue, he approached it with a willingness to die if necessary. And when he could not accomplish his aim, he would not give in. No matter what means might be required, he never questioned them.

The Hosokawa family ruled over a large province, and those charged with the responsibility of the family's affairs were of course not lacking in subordinates of talent. But when any situation reached the stage where a solution seemed impossible, Tahei was sure to be called upon. I have not sketched in any detail the character of Umehara. When the problem of the succession came up, however, he was no doubt selected because of his intimacy with Sakai. Yet Tahei was sent with him. Was it not Tahei's duty to keep pressing Umehara?

To be willing to die is no doubt a straightfoward attitude of mind. Nevertheless, among samurai, those who had such a will, no matter during what period, in no matter what domain, were, it seems, not so easy to find.

Enterprise and the resolution to die are complementary virtues; in that sense there is a decisive difference between a mere adventurer and a "man of enterprise." In addition to the incidents already mentioned, there is still another anecdote that has been handed down about Tokō Tahei. But I do not think that the incident contributes much to any understanding of his significance as a human being. Indeed, as far as I am concerned, if there were any purpose served in bending the truth to protect him, then the whole affair might as well be passed over in silence.

The month and year of the incident are not recorded. Nor is the place mentioned. Surely Tahei would not have behaved in such a fashion, however, after being awarded his three hundred *koku* for his brave efforts at Shimabara. Indeed it seems unlikely that he would have become involved in such an affair after being taken on by the Hosokawa family as a mere page. The whole thing was surely a simple diversion during his early life when he was a *rōnin*.

One day Tokō Tahei was crossing a certain street. A group of people had collected in front of a house and were milling around shouting abusive language. When he asked what was going on, someone in the crowd explained that a man who looked like a *sumo* wrestler had killed someone and then run into the vacant house with his sword still drawn. Now he had locked the door from the inside.

"Isn't there anyone among you who could capture him?" Tahei asked.

"As you see, there are policemen here in front of the house, but there seems to be nothing they can do."

"Then I'll quiet him down for you. Do you have any kind of tool that will break down a wall? A big wooden pounder would do as well."

Someone or other hurried off and returned with a large pestle. Tahei took it and walked around to the back of the house. Then he began breaking through the wall of the house in an overly dramatic fashion. Eventually he knocked a hole in the wall large enough for someone to crawl through. Tahei hoisted up his clothes and went in backwards, buttocks first. As the crowd watched in astonishment, Tahei soon came back out of the hole, dragging the offender with him. It seemed easier than pulling something out of a bag.

Later Tahei was asked how he had managed to accomplish this. He laughed as he answered. "There is nothing very complicated about it. When I went in by the wall, rather than the door, and buttocks-first instead of head-first, the man inside stopped to look at me, thinking the whole affair very strange. It was his moment of negligence that let me get a hold of him. Even if he had taken a swipe at my buttocks I have a little extra to spare."

Tokō Tahei's descendants have continued on in a direct line until the present. Tahei's son died in 1696, and his grandson, who was put in charge of twenty archers, died of illness in 1715. The Tokō of the fourth generation held a high position under a shogunal administrator; he resigned in 1756. Gennosuke, in the fifth generation, was placed in charge of ten riflemen in 1780; in the sixth generation, Kōgorō was appointed an assistant chief for a group of thirty riflemen in 1803. Heya (later called Hōsuke) in the seventh generation was placed in charge of ten riflemen in 1838. In the eighth generation, Fukuma (later called Kurosuke) was placed in charge of ten riflemen and died of illness in 1853; in the ninth generation, Kimpei (later called Sahei) was put in charge of thirty riflemen and resigned in 1867. In the tenth generation, Genzō was attached to the first group of reserve forces in the Kimamoto domain. The present head of the Tokō family, Tokō Chiaki, the oldest son of Genzō, became an employee of the Yatsushiro paper mill in the village of Matsukuma in the district of Yatsushiro in Kumamoto province.

January 1917

SAIKI KŌI

―――――――――――

"EVALUATIONS of human life are so endlessly diversified and subjective," wrote Mori Ōgai toward the end of this complex account, and this phrase may well serve as the real justification for these investigations that took him into the extraordinary world, and underworld, represented in this absorbing re-creation of the last days of the Tokugawa gay quarters and its colorful inhabitants. Ōgai's curiosity over his reading of popular literature of the Edo period and the purchase by his father of a small house serve as double means to involve him in a search for those who lived in a special society that, although it existed up until a generation previous, seemed to Ōgai as remote —and as fascinating—as any novel by Saikaku. The reader too is pulled into this world and can follow with great interest the slow accumulation of detail with which Ōgai reconstructs the past.

Ōgai seldom if ever wrote on such subjects, but his detached tone and sharp sensibility are nowhere seen to better advantage than here, in an atmosphere of the theater, tea house, and drinking party. Such subject matter may be more typical of the novelist Nagai Kafū, who considered Ōgai his mentor, but the results are pure Ōgai, and worthy of comparison with his best work.

SAIKI KŌI[1] is also known under the names of Tsutō and Tsunokuniya Tōjirō.[2] It was in reference not to Kōi himself but his father Ryūchi[3] that I first came across the name of Tsutō. The name Tsunokuniya Tōjirō continued through two generations.

When I was young, I devoured the books of a lending library man who used to walk around with books stacked on his back in something like a monk's backpack. These books were mainly of three kinds: yomihon,[4] kakihon,[5] and ninjōbon, or popular love stories.[6] The yomihon consisted mainly of the works of Kyōden[7] and Bakin,[8] the ninjōbon of the works of Shunsui[9] and Kinsui;[10] the kakihon were what we now call scenarios for professional storytellers. After going through all of these I asked the booklender if he had any others I hadn't read, and he recommended that I try reading zuihitsu, or miscellaneous literary essays. If one can get through these too, even through the likes of the antiquarian writings of Ise Teijō,[11] he deserves a degree in lending library literature. I got this degree.

I was first addicted to Bakin, then came to like Kyōden more; but I always preferred Shunsui to Kinsui. I developed a similar partiality later on when I read German literature, always having a greater taste for Hauptmann[12] than Sudermann.[13]

In Shunsui's ninjōbon, a character named Tsutō-san often appears as a kind of deus ex machina. He is a good samaritan, a rich man who rescues the lovers from the jaws of fate. Usually this Tsutō-san is only mentioned in the dialogue, but does not appear in person. One exception to this is the character of Umegoyomi Chitō, also known as Chiba Tobē.[14]

At that time a certain connoisseur of letters and the arts, a member of a group which called itself the Kokurabakama, informed me: "It is said that Tsunokuniya Tōjirō was a real person." The literary term modelle had not yet been used in such a sense.

This Tsutō senior was the proprietor of a wineshop in Yamashiro-chō in Shimbashi of Edo. From this locality he acquired the name of the Master of Yamashiro Riverbank, and this was also abbreviated to simply Riverbank Master. His clan was Minamoto, his family name was Saiki, and his crest was the holly; because he had a triangular fish-scale shape dyed onto the shop curtain under the horizontal character for "one," he used the pen name of Ichirindō, meaning Hall of One Scale. He signed his calligraphy with Ryūchi, meaning Dragon Pond, and his haiku with Sen'u, meaning Wizard Castle; he sang kyōka[15] under the names of Tōkōen, Tsuru no To Hinakame, and later Minamoto no Yamahito.

TRANSLATED BY WILLIAM R. WILSON

Ryūchi's father was named Ihē. Ihē was a shopman of Ryūchi's grandfather; relying on his character, he made Ihē his adopted son. This original
Ihē had built the earthen walls around the Tsunokuniya. He also built the
first and later warehouses, increased the size of the property, and created the
wealthy house identified with the Yamashiro Riverbank.

When he was approaching seventy, Ihē turned the shop over to Ryūchi
and went into retirement, taking up residence in the inner quarters of the
second floor of the Yamashiro Riverbank. Even after he retired he continued
to be a model of industry. For example, he used to pick up discarded straw
sandals on the streets, bring them home, wash and dry them in the sun,
then chop them up himself to give to the plasterers who frequented the
shop.[16] Ihē, however, was no miser. There is a story that one year as the anniversary of the forty-seven *rōnin* of Akō was being celebrated in the Senga-
kuji of Shiba, an old man in cotton clothes visited the graves, contributed a
hundred *ryō* in gold at the offering place, and departed without leaving his
name. When a monk, thinking this strange, had him followed, the old man
returned inside the curtain of the Yamashiro Riverbank Tsunokuniya.

After Ryūchi succeeded to the household, he closed the wineshop and
made his chief business purveying to daimyo households with which the
Tsunokuniya enjoyed ancestral ties. The principal residences were those of
the Kaga Middle General in Hongō go-chōme, the Uesugi Chamberlain in
Sakuradahori-dōri, and the Matsudaira Lower General in Sakurada Kasumi-
gaseki. Maeda of Kaga was the lord of the castle in Kanazawa, Uesugi of the
castle in Yonezawa, and Asano Matsudaira of the castle in Hiroshima.

Ryūchi was married in the first year of Bunsei [1818] while his father and
mother were still living. He used to send his senior shopman Kimbē and
others to solicit business from the noble residences, and on the three ceremonial days of each month he would himself also make the rounds of the
mansions to offer his greetings. In the house of Kaga, it was just before Lord
Hizen no kami Narinori was succeeded by his son Nariyasu. In the house of
Uesugi, it was the generation of Lord Danjo-no-taihitsu Narisada; in the
house of Asano, it was that of Lord Aki no kami Narikata.

His father Ihē had probably never written a character except in account
books or on bills. Ryūchi, however, practiced calligraphy under Hata Seichi.[17] He studied *kyōka* under Hinamaro, the first generation of the house of
Yayoi'an,[18] and was given the name Hinakame; in later years he was called
Momonomoto Kakuro, and also Gensen. He also wrote *haikai*[19] under the
pen name of Sen'u.

His father Ihē had probably never set foot in a place of entertainment.

Ryūchi, however, frequented the theaters and the gay quarters. After each visit to the Nakamura, Ichimura, and Morita theater houses,[20] he would invite the famous actors to teahouses and ply them with drink. He frequented the gay quarters in Fukagawa[21] and Yoshiwara, also in Shinagawa[22] and Naitō Shinjuku.[23] His favorite in Fukagawa was an old courtesan named Yamamoto no Kampachi. In the Yoshiwara, it was a principal courtesan of the Hisakimanjiya[24] called Akashi.

When Ryūchi went to the gay quarters his boon companions were such denizens of the Fukagawa district as Sakuragawa Yoshijirō,[25] Tobaya Kosanji, Masumi Wajū, Kenkonbō Ryōsai,[26] Iwakubo Hokkei,[27] Onomaru Kokane, Chikunai, Sanchiku, Kisai, and their like. Yoshijirō later moved to the Yoshiwara, and became the second-generation Zenkō. Wajū was a master chanter of *katōbushi*;[28] Ryōsai was a *rakugo* performer; Hokkei a painter of ukiyoe who left the Kano for the Hokusai school. Chikunai was a physician,[29] Sanchiku and Kisai were masseurs.

Ryūchi used to wrap ceremonial gifts of money in thick offering-paper, put paper decorations on them, and had them piled up on great offering-stands to be given away to those he patronized.

But Ryūchi had not the capacity for even one drop of wine. Even when he took a sake cup in hand, he only pretended to drink. Also, he never spent a night in a brothel.

While the *ninjōbon* writer Tamenaga Shunsui was still called Sanro and Somabito,[30] he became acquainted with Ryūchi and was his companion in these amusements. This was the basis for Ryūchi's name coming to be enshrined in the *ninjōbon* romances.

Ryūchi was not averse to having his name broadcast about like this by Shunsui. Indeed, he himself wrote a pamphlet entitled "Famous Places of Tsunokuni," which he had printed and distributed to his friends. The pamphlet featured stories in which his own companions in amusement were likened to famous places in Japan, illustrated with Hokkei's ukiyoe drawings.

Ryūchi's wife gave birth to a boy in the fifth year of Bunsei [1822]. This boy, whom they called Nenosuke, was the heir to the Tsunokuniya. As that year was under the zodiacal sign of the horse, they followed the common custom of making a name of the seventh sign from that, called *ne*, the zodiacal sign of the rat. Kōi the Dilettante, who as the second-generation Tsutō achieved a fame verging on notoriety that exceeded that of his own father, was this Nenosuke.

I came across the name of Kōi around the time I first happened upon the name of Tsutō through those *ninjōbon*. Actually it may have been at the same time. The name came to my attention several times thereafter, but always as a fleeting impression that never sank in. Ryūchi and Kōi, father and son, were confused in my mind.

Some time afterward the name Kōi came to be constantly in my mind. This was after I moved into the house in Dangozaka[31] where I now live.

This house has a relationship to Kōi, and was discovered by my then living father. My father had been practicing medicine in Senju, but decided to give it up and live with me. So he started to walk around every day looking for a house. This house soon caught my father's eye as one commanding a fine view.

South from the top of Dangozaka there is a lane resembling a steep path which comes out at the back of the Nezu Gongen shrine.[32] They call this Yabushita Road. What are now called the Yabushita houses at that time occupied only the east side of this road, near the Nezu shrine. Contrary to this, in the area near Dangozaka, there were no houses on the east side of the road, which cut over the top of a declivity. The front part of the little house faced out over this cliff, which was separated from it by the lane. It was a little shingle-roofed house.

The top of the rise is a hill that ranges from Mukōgaoka to Ōji.[33] Separated from them by the gardens and rice fields beneath the cliff, the house faces out on the hills of Ueno across the way. If one stands in front of the house and looks out, he will see to the right a spur of the hills of Ueno; the space between this spur and Mukōgaoka opens expansively into a sea of houses reaching to the far-off horizon. The view I have from the platform on top of my present house in this direction is one of white sails off Shinagawa moving above the tops of the trees of the Hama Detached Palace.

My father set his eye on this little house and often went to the top of the cliff to look at it. In the house there was a window facing out over the cliff, and in the window there was always an old woman with her head shaven. "A pretty nun," my father used to say.

Consulting his map, my father deduced that the house of the pretty nun was located on what had originally been the compound of the Sezon-in temple.[34] This temple has now lost the greater half of its former compound, and is crowded into its western corner.

My father led me to the top of the cliff to show me the house. I had been aware of both the cliff and the house before, but had not yet looked at them with the interest that father had. The house itself was a perfect "retreat within the city's midst." And behind the bamboo grille sat the pretty nun. She seemed to be over fifty. If one can call an old woman beautiful, I should say that this nun was beautiful.

Having won my approval, my father now determined to buy the house, and so made inquiries about its owner. At that time there was a gardener named Senjuen who lived below Dangozaka. My father knew the man and asked him about the nun's house.

According to Senjuen, the little house on the rise was the property of the old woman we had seen. She was a certain Takagi Gin, and the relative of someone named Ogura.[35] Ogura was originally a pawnbroker, and after he retired had been a hanger-on of Kōi the Dilettante. He died in that house. The old woman, Senjuen concluded, would probably be amenable to an offer.

Through Senjuen's assistance the negotiations were concluded with unexpected ease. The property owned by Takagi Gin was originally a rather extensive angular piece, but since a corner of it had been sold off, the remainder, from the side on which the small house faced out over the cliff, was left in a hook shape on the side facing the street on the top of Dangozaka. There were two small houses on the parcel which faced the street. One, with both house and land owned by Takagi, was a rental shop, the other was a house built on the Takagi land by a fire chief named Ishida, who was living there. After we acquired title, Gin moved into the rental shop.

Father disposed of the big house in Senju and moved into this little house on the cliff-top. The Senju house had been the residence of a man named Okada, who said it had been used as a resting place when the Tokugawa shogun went out to the hawking fields. In it my father had enough equipment for a small hospital. As he moved into the smaller residence, he exclaimed: "I feel like I've put down a heavy load." I came from my rented house in Otanohara to join him there.

The little house had three rooms and a kitchen. The three rooms were, respectively, of six, three, and four and a half mats—the last in tearoom style. Later this tearoom came to be the place of my father's last hours.

In the three-mat room adjacent to the tearoom were two sliding door panels covered with old pieces of paper. The papers were a travel account in the *haibun* style of poetic prose, about half in characters and half in illustrations. On the first page there was a half-length portrait of Kōi the Dilettante. It was only a sketch in black brush strokes, but enough to suggest that Kōi had been a round-faced, fat man.

The little house on the cliff-top became dilapidated after father's death, and because it was difficult to repair, fell into decay. The paper screens also completely peeled away. When I think about it now, they seem to have been the rough copy of the travel account of Kōi's tour of Enoshima and Kamakura, which he made at the age of thirty-eight in the sixth year of Ansei [1859].

More than half of what is left of the little house on the cliff-top is now vacant ground. Since my mother requested that a room be built in place of her seventieth birthday celebration in Taishō four [1915], I ordered an estimate from a carpenter for a four-and-a-half mat room in accordance with her wish. Meanwhile she fell gravely ill. I hurried the work to get the room completed while she was still alive. The room was finished and the second coat of plaster added to the walls in March of 1916. Mother moved in her bed and was happy in that room, but she soon departed this world. The room is my present study; the walls have never been replastered. The room is the site of the kitchen of the little house on the cliff-top long ago.

From the time I moved in with my father and mother, I had the name of Kōi firmly in mind. I already knew that the former owner of the house, Ogura, was later called Zeami.[36] Kōi received a number of ''-ami'' pen names[37] from the Reverend Yūgyō, chief priest of the Shōjōkōji[38] in Fujisawa of Kōza county in Sagami. He styled himself Juami, but then gave this name to Kawatake Kisui[39] and became Bai'ami. He later changed to Hōami, and parceled out other Ami names to his followers. They say Zeami was one of these.

Kōi died on the tenth of September, the third year of Meiji [1870]. His relatives held the anniversary memorial service on the tenth of September of the following year. Afterward his followers gathered at the house of Ogura Zeami and held Buddhist services on the tenth of October of every year, and then visited Kōi's grave at the Gangyōji in Komagome.[40] The place of these observances was the little house on the cliff-top.

Kōi, that is, Nenosuke, in youth studied the Chinese classics with Kita Seiro[41] and calligraphy with Matsumoto Tōsai.[42] When Nenosuke was fourteen, Seiro had already reached seventy and was living in retirement in Takegawa-chō Nishiura-machi. It is said that Nenosuke had barely attained knowledge of the Chinese characters when he began to inquire into the Way of Lao Tzu and Chuang Tzu. Tōsai was a famous calligrapher who had achieved his name in the style of Tung Ch'i-ch'ang;[43] he resided in Honkoku-chō Shiogashi.

There are very few facts by which one can establish the chronology for the interval from Nenosuke's birth to his becoming a man. In Bunsei six [1823] Ryūchi's teacher, Hata Seichi, died at the age of sixty-one, when Nenosuke was two. His grandfather Ihē's wife died on the twenty-ninth day of the seventh month of 1825. Her name in the Buddha is Rinshoin Sōyo Geigetsu

Daishi. At this time Nenosuke was four. Nenosuke was seven when his father's friend So Mabito took the pen name of Kyokuntei Shunsui in 1828. In addition to Shunsui, Ryōsai, and Hokkei, his father Ryūchi's friends at this time included Katsuta Moromochi.[44] Succeeding Chikusa'an Kawaguchi Sōo,[45] the *kyōka* master of Suwa-chō,[46] Moromochi was called the second-generation Chikusa'an. His name in the Itchūbushi school of *jōruri*[47] is Miyako Ikkansai. Ikkansai later established a separate school, changed his name to Uji Shibun[48] and lived in Ikenohata.[49] At this time, Ryūchi had Hokkei do impromptu sketches at gatherings with his friends and had Moromochi make block prints of them with *kyōka*; he amused himself in the gay quarters accompanied by Shunsui, Ryōsai, and others.

From about his seventeenth year in 1838, Nenosuke began to frequent the restaurants and riverside teahouses,[50] became the intimate of geisha, and before long took his pleasures in the brothels of Naitō Shinjuku and Shinagawa.

It seems that Ryūchi and Kōi encountered one crisis after another around 1841. Ryūchi divorced his wife, the mother of Nenosuke and his elder sister, about this time. Nenosuke's older sister served in the women's quarters of the mansion of Uesugi Danjo no taihitsu Narinori[51] in Soto Sakuradahoridōri. Ryūchi took as his second wife Sumi, the elder sister of Mimura Seikichi of the Tobaya in Takekawa-chō. This was a branch family of the house of Mimura Seizaemon, a member of the Ten-Man Company of Moneychangers to the Shogunate,[52] who lived in Sanjikken-hori.[53] At the same time he established a separate house in Sannō-chō and kept a mistress.

Before very long Ryūchi was on the point of being officially punished and in fact only narrowly escaped. This was because a *Guide to Harlotry*[54] which he had written, printed, and circulated among his friends and acquaintances came to the attention of the Edo City Commissioners. Fortunately the headman in Kaga-chō, Tanaka Heishirō, got wind of it and secretly informed Ryūchi. Ryūchi quickly sent money to various functionaries to patch things up; he dismissed the mistress, sold the separate house, and stopped his own visits to places of amusement. It was at that time that he made the Uchiyama-chō house of the blind man, Middle Chanting Master Momoshima Kōtō, his place for diversion and gathered Moromochi and the others there.

Nenosuke was placed under the charge of the Tobaya, the home establishment of his stepmother, in the last days of the last month of this year. This was because he had run up debts in the appointment teahouses[55] in the Shinjuku and Shinagawa gay quarters. Nenosuke was now twenty.

However, while Ryūchi had stopped frequenting the gay quarters, Neno-

suke did not. From about the third month of 1842, Nenosuke of the stylish-
ly cropped head began to leave the Tobaya accompanied by an apprentice
named Kanekichi on visits to the calligraphy master Matsumoto, the *kyōya*
master Umeya Kakuju,⁵⁶ and the like. But on his way home he would send
Kanekichi on ahead, while he himself stopped in at the theater and brothels. Kanekichi had the nickname of Toba-picture Boy.⁵⁷ He was probably so
named because he was an apprentice boy of the Tobaya and was funny-
looking. Later he became the famous Meiji writer, Kanagaki Robun.⁵⁸

The theater was the Kawarasaki-za⁵⁹ in Kobiki-chō. The most popular ac-
tor was the eighth-generation Danjūrō.⁶⁰ He visited the playwright Katsu
Genzō in his room and made friends with him. Genzō later was the famous
Kawatake Shinshichi.⁶¹

The brothels chiefly were the Shimazaki Minatoya and the Dozō Sagami⁶²
in Shinagawa; his favorite assignation teahouse was the Ōnoya Manji. He
had his longest affair with Osome of the Minatoya.

His companions included the playwright Iwai Shigyoku⁶³ of the
Kawarasaki-za, Takedaya Umahei, the master of the teahouse attached to
that theater, the Shinagawa male geisha Tomimoto Tona Taifu and Tomimoto Noshi Taifu, and Sakuragawa Zenjibō, as well as such characters as the
haikai master Maki Otsuga and the wrestler Ikioi Tōgo. Shigyoku was later
Harufuji, the founder of the Shōdenbushi⁶⁴ school of *jōruri*; Otsuga was the
later Tōei VI.

Ryūchi's congratulatory gifts were a pretty sight with their paper decorations, but what he spent on them did not come to very much. Nenosuke, on
the other hand, racked his brain for ingenious gifts, and was indifferent to
price. He piled up huge bills for pocketbooks and tobacco pouches at bag
shops like the Maruri, Marujō, Yamadaya. Once while he was behaving like
this, the date for seasonal change of attire came around. Nenosuke had an
unlined haori and lined kimono brought to the gay quarters and changed
into them. He gave away by lot to the male and female geisha the clothes he
had thrown off—a lined haori of imported taffeta,⁶⁵ a flat silk wadded garment, underclothes of Ryūkyū pongee, a singlet of silk crepe, and so forth.

When he learned that Nenosuke's dissipation was becoming worse and
that the Mimuras left him alone and took no heed of it, Ryūchi himself
stepped in to control him. It was the middle of the sixth month. While Nenosuke was in the Minatoya in Shinagawa, Ryūchi came flying in a two-man,
open sedan-chair to the Ōnoya. Then he sent the message in to Nenosuke,
"Urgent business! Come!"

Fearing his father, Nenosuke jumped down into the garden from a lower room of the Minatoya, crossed the shallows along the shore, and tried to make his escape; but he was discovered by the messenger and caught.

Ryūchi dragged Nenosuke home and put him under the charge of Sahē, an agent he had set up on land he owned in Saiwai-chō. He was about to take steps to disinherit him. Through the mediation of the shop people, however, Nenosuke returned to the Yamashiro Riverbank and came to accept his father's supervision.

Happily, Ryūchi did not use hypocritical methods to discipline his son. He made Nenosuke attend upon his own more conservative amusements, and accomplished his purpose to teach him about these things, even though "on the mats of women and wine," with an attitude in which he never lowered his own dignity. These events were in Nenosuke's twenty-first year.

The seventh-generation Danjūrō,[66] to whom Ryūchi had given his patronage, was banished from Edo on the twenty-second of the sixth month, and Ryūchi's close friend Tamenaga Shunsui died in prison on the thirteenth of the seventh month of this same year.[67] These incidents may also have been indirectly intermediary in making the father and son of the Yamashiro Riverbank feel the displeasure of the authorities.

Few noteworthy facts are recorded for the interval from this time up to 1856. In Tempō fourteen [1843], the Kawarasaki-za moved to Saruwaka-chō to join the Nakamura-za and Ichimura-za which had moved previously; Katsu Genzō became chief playwright[68] with the name of Shiba Shinsuke after his place of residence in Udagawa-chō in Shiba. He later succeeded to the name of Kawatake Shinshichi through the recommendation of the third-generation Sakurada Jisuke.[69] Nenosuke's grandfather Ihē died at more than seventy on the twenty-seventh of the sixth month of 1848. His name in the Buddha is Kenyo Hōju Tokushō Zenshi. His grave is in the family plot by the Gangyōji temple. Ryūchi's teacher Seiro died this same year at eighty-three. Juami Donchō[70] also died at this time. Juami was most likely an acquaintance of Ryūchi and his son, but the nature of their association is not clear. However, Nenosuke later received the Juami pen name from the Shōjōkōji and therefore indirectly succeeded to the -ami pen name identified with Mashiya. In 1850, Ryūchi's friend Moromochi left the Miyako school of jōruri and styled himself Uji Shibun. In 1854, the eighth-generation Danjūrō, of whom Ryūchi and his son had been patrons, committed suicide with a sword. The next year, 1855, was the year of the great earthquake.[71] The gay quarters of Edo fell upon unprecedentedly hard times; it is said that male geisha resorted to selling tempura in street stalls, and female geisha of the town[72] sold oden stew and hot sake in rush-mat–covered shacks. Not even the beneficent patronage of the Yamashiro Riverbank seems to have been enough to bail them out.

Ryūchi was laid low by illness in the summer of 1856. He died on the twentieth of the ninth month, and was also buried at the Gangyōji. His name in the Buddha is Hakuyō Ungai Ryūchi Zenshi. The employees of the firm, concerned about its future under the young master Nenosuke, favored his elder sister's husband, Tsunokuniya Isaburō, who kept a bookstore in Osaka-chō,[73] and tried to have him succeed as head of the house. Nenosuke's elder sister had left her employment in the women's quarters of the Uesugi mansion, married this Isaburō and founded a branch house. However, Nenosuke's stepmother Mimura Sumi refused the proposal of the employees, stating that if she subjected the rightful heir Nenosuke to the misfortune of disinheritance, she would be looked upon by society in a way damaging to her own position. Nenosuke ultimately succeeded as head of the main house of Yamashiro Riverbank. He was thirty-five at this time. I note in passing that Ryūchi's *kyōka* teacher, the first Yayoi'an Hinamaro, died in the same month of the same year as Ryūchi.

Nenosuke, who became the second Tōjirō after succeeding his father, was on his best behavior for a while out of deference to his stepmother Mimura Sumi, his other relatives, and the many employees, from Kimbē, the most senior, on down. But after the completion of the distribution of presents on the forty-ninth day of mourning, he resumed his visits to the gay quarters, and once his old habits were re-established, came to take no account of the opinion of those around him. He had taken a wife in the time before he inherited the Tsunokuniya and already had two children. Her family was that of Enshūya Taemon of Kiba in Fukagawa. However, both wife and father-in-law had no course other than to look on, powerless to interfere.

Just as royalty and aristocrats often patronize literary figures and make them instruments to promote their own prestige and decorate their presence, Tōjirō associated with *haikai* masters, *kyōka* teachers, *kyōgen* playwrights, calligraphers, woodcarvers, and painters. There was almost no difference between his treatment of the majority of these persons and of male geisha. His father Ryūchi always took pleasure in *kyōka*; in contrast, Tōjirō's preference ran toward the *haikai*. The places where he assembled his companions were the Umenoya in Hasegawa-chō and the Kashiwagitei in Yorozu-chō.[74]

As Nenosuke, Tōjirō had the pen name Rikaku which he wrote in two different ways; but after he inherited the Tsunokuniya he received the formal name of Umenomoto from Seki Izan.[75] He further received the character

Shin from Shin Eiki,[76] and named himself Kōi which he wrote with various characters. Occasionally when he wrote *kyōka*, he signed himself Naninoya. In the theater, Kōi was the patron of Kawarasaki Gonjūrō, who was later the ninth-generation Danjūrō.[77] Kōi organized his company of favorites into a group he called the Araisoren[78] and had Katsuta Moromochi draw up its by-laws. The success of the ninth Danjūrō at a later time was due in large part to Kōi's patronage. Also, after the suicide of the eighth Danjūrō, Gonjūrō's real father Jukai Rōjin, who was the seventh Danjūrō, had returned to Edo, and so Kōi became his patron too. In addition to this father and son, other actors who enjoyed Kōi's patronage were Ichikawa Kodanji,[79] Nakamura Kōzō, Ichikawa Yonegorō, and Matsumoto Kunigorō.

As to brothels, Kōi first frequented the Tamaya Sansaburō in the Yoshiwara Edo-chō Itchome, later the Inamotorō in Sumi-chō.[80] In the Tamaya, his favorite was Komurasaki; in the Inamoto, it was the second-generation Koine. When he went to the Tamaya, his appointment teahouse was first the Ōmiya Hanshirō, later the Ōsakaya Chubē; when he went to the Inamoto, it was the Tsuruhiko in Nakanochō.[81]

Kōi's hangers-on were almost uncountable. Among them there were also persons to whom we should probably be doing injustice by ranking them as mere "hangers-on." However, it is not easy to draw the line, to make a distinction among them.

Among *haikai* masters, in addition to Izan and Eiki already mentioned, there were Torigoe Tōsai,[82] Harada Bainen,[83] Maki Tōei, and Nomura Shuitsu. Bainen was later the eighth-generation Setchūan. It is said the sequence in this school was Ransetsu,[84] Ritō,[85] Ryōta,[86] Kanrai, Taizan, and Bainen. The common name of Shuitsu was Shinzō; he was styled Kakuhoan.

Kōi's favorite *kyōka* masters included Katsuta Moromochi and his son Fukutarō,[87] Murota Kakuju, and Ishibashi Makuni.[88] Fukutarō had the nickname of Abura Tokuri (Oil Bottle). He later succeeded to his father's name in the Itchūbushi *jōruri* as the second-generation Shibun. Kakuju was called Umeya. His common name was Matabē; he ran an assignation teahouse in Hasegawa-chō. Makuni's common name was Shichibē.

His best friend among playwrights included Kawatake Shinshichi and Segawa Jokō.[89] Shinshichi originally was Shiba Shinsuke. Among his favorite woodcarvers there was a certain Ishiguro. As for artists, there were innumerable men among his favorites, but these included Matsumoto Kōzan,[90] Kanō Ansen,[91] Tsukioka Hōnen, Shibata Zeshin,[92] Torii Kiyomitsu ,[93] Tsuji Kasetsu, Fukushima Chikaharu,[94] and Yomo Umehiko.[95] Among copyists, there was Miyagi Gengyō.

Merchants and those retired from commercial houses in Kōi's entourage included Ogura Asaru (later Zeami), the retired pawnbroker of Dangozaka; Ashin'an Zebutsu, who was the master of the Yanaka Mikawaya,[96] and Ōtsuya Koboku, the retired master of the Funayado;[97] and Kanaya Sennosuke (Chikusen),[98] a peddlar of kimono material in Takekawa-chō. There was also a medical doctor, Ishikawa Hojun, a surgeon by profession who had the *haikai* pen name of Gango.

Among his favorite comic storytellers, there were Kenkonbō Ryōsai, Gomeirō Tamasuke,[99] Shumpūtei Ryūshi,[100] and Irifune Yonezō. Tamasuke was a later name of the *haiku* poet Bashō. Among professional storytellers, there were the second Bunsha, Momokawa Enkoku, and Matsubayashi Hakuen. Enkoku was the later Joen.

The professional male geisha of the town who at that time were frequently in the house of the Yamashiro Riverbank were Sakuragawa Zenkō, Ogie Chiyosaku, Miyako Senkoku,[101] and Sugano Nonko. Senkoku's first name was Ogie Rosuke; later he was called Senchū. He lived in Genyadana.[102] Also, those who were called when Kōi went to the Yoshiwara included Miyako Uchū, Miyako Gombē, Miyako Yonehachi, Kiyomoto Senzō, Kiyomoto Nakasuke, Sakuragawa Juroku, and Hanayagi Narusuke. Among these, Kōi particularly admired the ready wit of Uchū, and always had him at his side.

Four female geisha of the Yoshiwara were regularly engaged through the geisha business office[103] of Daikokuya Shōroku.[104] They were Kiwa, Gin, Haru, and Tsuru. Kiwa later became the wife of Hanayagi Jusuke.[105] Haru had at that time already become the wife of Miyako Gombē. Tsuru of the Surugaya soon became Kōi's mistress.

After visiting the Yoshiwara for a while, Kōi bought out the contract of Komurasaki of the Tamaya.[106] A poem-strip said to have been written by Komurasaki at that time was left in the Tamaya:

> Murasaki no
> Hatsumotoyui ni
> Yuikomeshi
> Chigiri wa chiyo no
> Katame narikeri

> The troth that Murasaki plighted
> With her first hair-paper
> Is a pledge firm
> To eternity.[107]

Kōi's original wife was sent back to Kiba on the grounds that she had made a poor adjustment to Komurasaki. Komurasaki now became his wife Kumi and then changed her name to Fusa. This was before Tsuru, his favorite of the geisha indentured to the appointment-teahouse Surugaya in Nakano-chō, was ransomed and made his mistress.

Kōi's daily life at home was not conspicuously luxurious. His food was usually ordered from the Isekan in Minaminabe-chō. He liked broiled eel, and the Owariya and Kitagawa[108] were always coming to the house. When he specially treated someone, he usually went to the Shimamura Hanshichi in Sukiya-chō. The sedan-chair firm which considered Kōi its best customer was a house called Hōkaku in Ginza Yokochō. In those days when there was no postal service, a two-man team was on duty every day at the Tsunokuniya as letter carriers.

Kōi's visits to the Yoshiwara did not stop even after Komurasaki came to live with him. One grown accustomed to the gay quarters cannot forget the charm of a seat on the mats with the lamps ranged about. His next favorite was Wakamurasaki of the same Tamaya.

On a certain day, Kōi visited Matsumoto Kōzan in the compound of the Tomigaoka Hachiman shrine in Fukagawa, where he saw Kōzan's painting of pine and bamboo on a pair of gold screens. Those screens had been ordered by someone to present to Senshu, a geisha indentured to Izumiya Heizaemon in Edo-chō Itchōme.

Kōi seized these screens and as payment sent Kōzan twenty-five *ryō* in silver in stacks like cut rice cakes, to which he added bean jam from the Tenshindō in Takekawa-chō. This was because at the time they called a packet of twenty-five *ryō* "cut rice cakes."[109] Kōzan was a nondrinker.

Kōi wrote down the story of how he lifted the screens and had it made up as a satirical print,[110] which he passed out among his friends and acquaintances. Then he sent the screens to Tamaya Sansaburō. However, he had a bond placed on Sansaburō to the effect that he must not stand these screens upon the bed of a prostitute.

In Ansei four [1857], tobacco pouches with silver chains were popular in Edo. Kōi placed an order with the Maruri company for some thirty or forty, and gave them to all his cronies. He did the same with a set of haori of imported taffeta of the same pattern at about this time.

In the spring of this year, a certain Mimura of Takekawa-chō sent Kōi a hanging scroll of a carp painted by Ōkyo. With this as a start, the thirty-six-year-old Kōi took it into his head to collect thirty-six carp scrolls by Ōkyo. Dealers in books, pictures, and curios searched as far as the Kyoto-Osaka area and assembled a number of scrolls. However, when he showed them to Kōzan and Shibata Zeshin, most of them turned out to be fakes. Enraged, Kōi proceeded to choose thirty-six living artists and commissioned each to paint a carp. Then in the eleventh month he summoned Eiki and put on a performance of linked verse about carp. For the volume of eighteen verses which he distributed at this time, Torii Kiyomitsu drew a carp cover picture, and Kōi did a preface modeled on the declamatory speech typical of *Shibaraku*.[111] The last part goes as follows:

> Ten naru gozare
> Sokuten ni,
> Suao no kaki no
> Hetanagara,
> Tachi no kireji ya
> Teniwoha wo,
> Tadashite ten wo
> Kakeeboshi,
> Waruku soshiraba
> Katappashi,
> Bō wo shiyotta
> Ageku no hate,
> Kono yo no nagori
> Shuhitsu no aragoto,
> Fude no sokkubi
> Hikkonuki,
> Suzuri no umi e
> Hafurikomu to,
> Hoho uyamatte mōsu

> If it is the mark of excellence,[112] let it be!
> On making the mark of judgment[113]
> *He*, persimmon colored like the warrior's robe,
> And like a persimmon's stem,[114]
> While I am unskilled,
> Like a sword cut, the poem's cutting word,
> Here, the case particles, *teniwoha-*
> Corrected, write the mark!
> The warrior's hat, without chin-cord tied,
> If one speaks ill of it, scathingly,
> By one end, the cudgel,
> The end when one has shouldered it,
> The last linked-verse ending,
> Like a leave-taking from this world,
> Writing it is rough,
> In writing, playing at violence,
> Grabbing and pulling back,
> On the neck of the writing brush,
> One throws it in—
> Into the sea of the ink-stone, thus,
> Hoho! I speak with all respect!

In the fall of this year, *Ami Moyō Tōro no Kikukiri* by Kawatake Shinshichi was performed at the Ichimura-za in Saruwaka-chō. The play conjoins the story of Amiuchi Shichigorō with an episode in the life of the pleasure woman Tamagiku[115] in the Kyōhō era [1716-1736]. Kōi gave Kawarasaki Gonjūrō and Ichikawa Kodanji each one draw-curtain, and donated the costumes and properties for Ichikawa Yonegorō, who played the geisha Osan, and for Nakamura Kōzō, who played Sakuragawa Zenkō. This was all in patronage of Gonjūrō.

At about this time also, Kōi had an audience with the chief priest Yūgyō[116] of the Nichirinji in Asakusa and received from him a number of -ami names. Kōi styled himself Juami, but before long yielded this to Kawatake Shinshichi, and changed to Bai'ami. Kōi was now thirty-six.

In the third month of 1858, a *kyōgen* entitled *Edozakura Kiyomizu Seigen*[117] was performed at the Ichimura-za. The scene is in front of an appointment teahouse in Nakanochō. The courtesan-maid[118] played by Gennosuke[119] is gripping the collar of the *haikai* master Tōei, played by Kichiroku. Tōei is about to have his eyebrows shaved off in accord with the law of the licensed quarter for having committed the "crime of evil nature"[120] by being unfaithful to his regular favorite, the apprentice courtesan Hanakawa. The brothel pimp played by Shigizō Takesuke backs up Tōei and he goes inside the door-curtain. Next, Kunigorō, Yonegorō, Kohanji, Santarō, and Shimazō, all samurai, come out on the *hanamichi*, and are guided by Shigizō inside the curtain. The father of the pleasure woman Agemaki, Oshiagemura Shimbē, played by Sanjūrō, comes out as a sake peddler. The samurai come out, drink sake, and enter onto the *hanamichi* without paying. Sukeroku of the Blackhand Gang, played by Kodanji, twists the arm of one of the samurai, and comes out on the *hanamichi* to chastise them. The samurai take flight up the *hanamichi*. At this point Kinokuniya Bunzaemon, played by Gonjūrō, lifts the door-curtain and makes his entrance. He wears a taffeta haori, a short sword in his girdle, and low wooden clogs. Behind him follows Tōei, holding a paper umbrella with a wide circular band. As musical accompaniment, the shamisen play Itchūbushi style. Bunzaemon calls Sukeroku over and admonishes him. When the stage turns, it is Agemaki's room. Bunzaemon buys out Agemaki's contract, and marries her to Sukeroku. Agemaki was first played by Eisaburō, later by Baikō.[121]

This character Bunzaemon was named after and represented Kōi (who was called Ima Kibun at this time in the gay quarters). Tōei was Maki Tōei. The costumes and properties of the two chief actors were entirely donated by Kōi, and Bunzaemon's silver-fitted short sword was one which Kōi always wore. The writer of this *kyōgen* was Kōi's crony, Kawatake Shinshichi. After playing Tōei, Kichiroku had the stage name of Hissei Tōri; Tō commemorated the role of Tōei, and Ri was taken from Kōi's pen name of Rikaku.

On the twenty-sixth of the eighth month of this year, Ichikawa Gonjūrō wrote out an actor's testament in which he vowed to be diligent in his art and never to turn his back on his supporters. He had his father, the old gentleman Jukai (the seventh Danjūrō), endorse it, and sent it to Kōi. The brothel which Kōi frequented at this time was the Inamoto; his partner there was the second Koine. As a follower, his ever-present "shadow" was Tōei, and his favorite male geisha was Miyako Uchū.

Uchū was originally a cloth-print dyer and was not educated, even though he was well versed in the arts of entertainment. He therefore sought knowledge in borrowed books, and took greatest pleasure in the Chinese novel, *The Romance of the Three Kingdoms*. Kōi was amused at Uchū extolling "Kōmei" every time he opened his mouth, and gave him money to celebrate a "Kōmei" festival.[122] This was like rich men nowadays putting on a Nogi Festival. After that Uchū acquired the nickname of War Drum.

Kōi was now thirty-seven. This year saw him at perhaps the height of his fame. Katsuta Moromochi, one of his followers, died this year on the twenty-second of the second month at the age of sixty-eight. He may have been afflicted with cholera,[123] the same as the scholar Shibue Chūsai,[124] the calligrapher Ichikawa Beian,[125] the kyōka master Rokudaen Arai Gachō,[126] and the third-generation master of the Kiyomoto school, Enju Taifu.[127] Moromochi was the first Uji Shibun.

It seems that Kōi's fortunes began to decline somewhat in 1859. It is said that loans to such houses as the Maeda and the Uesugi were for the most part paid off, and the silver and gold laid up for years in the Tsunokuniya were nearly all drained off. Kōi's extravagant pleasures, however, continued unabated. In this year Kōi made a sightseeing tour of Enoshima, Kamakura, and Kanazawa, accompanied by such men as Izan, Tōsai, Eiki, and Chikusen. If the travel account consisting of the words and illustrations we found pasted on the sliding panels of the tearoom of Ogura Zeami did in fact describe this frolic, then two or three women also went along. As Uchū had promised to join them but was late for the departure, he rushed on to Kanagawadai by three-man sedan-chair; as a reward he received five *koban*, and the carriers also received two.

Kōi visited the Shōjōkōji temple in Fujisawa on the way, where he received nine more -ami names from the chief priest, Yūgyō Shōnin; he gave these out to his friends.

After this tour, Kōi went back to visiting the Inamoto as of old. His lover was Koine. At this time, however, the Inamoto had a courtesan of the highest rank named Hanatori. Hanatori had a fearsome history. Once after becoming someone's mistress, she had secret meetings with another lover;

when the day came to be discharged from the former, she extorted heart-balm money from him. On other occasions she took money in down payment to become the mistress of various nobles, only to deliberately urinate in bed and thus secure her dismissal.[128] She was voluptuously beautiful.

Every time Hanatori met Kōi in the corridor, she gave him amorous looks. One evening when Kōi was suffering with boredom alone as Koine was entertaining another customer, a little maid came with a message from Hanatori. Kōi thoughtlessly fell into Hanatori's trap.

It was a few days later. The night, after the closing of the stalls in the street, was dead still. Keeping his appointment, Kōi went in behind Hanatori's screens. Suddenly someone else roughly pulled the screens away and jumped inside. It was Toyohana, the apprentice geisha of Koine.

Kōi, dragged by Toyohana, went and sat in a sitting room. Tsuruhiko of the appointment teahouse was summoned by a fast messenger. Attracted by the shrill voice of Toyohana who was raised in the Fukagawa area of Edo, crude-mannered men and women gathered in the passage, and the papered doors to the adjoining rooms were pierced here and there by moistened fingertips.

The geisha Kiwa[129] appeared at this juncture as go-between. She went into the next room with Toyohana and Tsuruhiko, arrived at a settlement whereby Kōi would give a hundred ryō each of hush money to Koine and Hanatori, and conveyed this to him. Kōi, however, did not have two hundred ryō in ready money on him.

Kiwa had Toyohana wait while she rushed out of the Inamoto, made the rounds of gay quarters to find men like Uchū, Yonehachi, and Gombē, who were indebted to Kōi, and made them dig to the bottom of their purses; but their combined resources still fell short by fifty ryō. Kiwa then borrowed the rest at high interest.

Kōi withdrew to a teahouse under cover of darkness; he thanked Kiwa effusively; then took his leave with the words, "I'll be sending the money soon from the shop," and got into a two-pole sedan-chair and sped back to the Yamashiro Riverbank.

This episode occurred in Kōi's thirty-eighth year. In this year, his favorite actor, the old gentleman Jukai (the seventh Danjūrō) died in his house on Saruwaka-chō Itchōme on the twenty-third day of the third month. Kōi made arrangements with Kakuju and distributed memorial prints. The print was a portrait by Toyokuni[130] depicting Jukai in the role of Renshōbō. Among Kōi's memorial poems was one which read:

> Kaerimiru
> Haru no sugata ya
> Ebi no kara

The form of spring
Which I look back upon!
A lobster shell.[131]

In the summer of 1861, Kōi had a temporary house in Fukagawa. Renewing old friendships, he invited Gengyo[132] and Robun to Shimamura Hanshichi's place in Sukiyachō. Uchū and Yonehachi came as entertainers. After the party they hired a boat at the Saya-chō riverbank and went to the Inamoto in Matsuichō.[133] Koine and Hanatori were no longer there. The one they called the third Koine was the apprentice Ukon of the earlier Koine. Kōi had Gengyo and Robun settle on partners, while he himself took his leave with Uchū and Yonehachi.

This year Kōi was forty. While he indulged in parties and pleasures as of old, he had finally come to know his own fate.

Toshi shiju
Tsuyu ni ki no tsuku
Hanano kana

Forty years,
Aware of transience,
The flowered plain.

The story about Mori Kien[134] scolding a man at a drinking party at the Yamashiro Riverbank seems also to date from about this time.

The Yamashiro Riverbank went bankrupt in 1862. Kōi handed the shop over to his stepmother, and after arranging to receive an allowance from the shop upon his retirement, gave his mistress Tsuru her dismissal. Kōi, accompanied by his wife Fusa and son Keijirō,[135] moved to the compound of the Sarudera temple[136] in Asakusa Umamichi. On the gate of a spare grass hut was hung the nameplate of Bai'ami.

After Kōi moved to the wretched abode in the Sarudera compound he sought to supplement his allowance from the Yamashiro Riverbank by the path of literary hack work. Through the introduction of Kawatake Shinshichi, he became a playwright of the Ichimura-za, and they listed his name of Bai'ami on the show bills. He did *haikai* wood-block prints under the seal of Umenomoto, and he did *kyōka* prints under the name of Naninoya. To order, he wrote handbills for shop openings. These activities, of course, had not begun at this time. His "*Kyōka* Twenty-Four Examples of Filial Piety in This Realm," "*Kyōka* Pitch Pipe," and the like on the listings of the Bun'endō publishing house had already been printed in Kaei six [1853]. It was only that this sort of work had now become an occupation. But it did not bring much gain.

Against this, his so-called humble abode became the pleasure haunt of his artist familiars of old. Among actors, such notables as Ichikawa Shinsha, Ichikawa Ichizō, Ichikawa Kyūzō, and Bandō Kakitsu[137] were his constant guests. Shinsha was the later Monnosuke, Kakitsu the later fifth-generation Kikugorō. Kōi, having now reached a position in life where he associated with these artists as an equal, no longer gave out "congratulatory gifts," but the trifling fees from his literary work could not cover the cost of the sake and food he served them. The time this began is unclear, but it is said that dining trays were always laid out without fail for guests in the house of Kōi—while the food did not exceed one or two side dishes of salted fish and the like to go with the rice, invariably, on one corner of the tray a small paper package was placed with two *bu* of money inside. Kōi, again pressed by debt, had to fall back further in retreat from his holding position at the Sarudera. Kōi was now forty-one.

In the spring of 1863, through the help of a certain relative, Kōi retired to Shirahata Hachimanmae in Samukawa, county of Chiba in the province of Shimofusa. Samukawa is a fishing village. No more than two or three villagers could read characters or had a knowledge of *haikai* and the like. Kōi had a banked ring made on the sandy beach, gathered the village children, and had them wrestle sumo-style. To the winners he gave prizes of one Tempō *sen*.[138]

However, boats carrying fish and shellfish plied back and forth between Samukawa and Nihonbashi in Edo. Kawatake Shinshichi, Eiki, Chikusen, and other old friends availed themselves of these to send Kōi letters of comfort. From time to time they also used available boats to visit him. It is said that at such times they were deeply moved at seeing Ofusa, the former Komurasaki, faithfully going about her work with the sleeves of her cotton kimono tucked back with a cord.

> Hari motte
> Yūjo oikeri
> Ame no tsuki

> Holding a needle
> The pleasure-woman has grown old—
> Moon in the rain.

This was a poem by Kōi about his actual circumstances.

One day when the weather was good and the sea calm, Kōi came out on the beach. A ship arrived there and from it emerged a crowd of sumo wrestlers from Edo. When Kōi out of curiosity inspected their faces, he saw some men he knew, wrestlers above the third rank. The wrestlers nodded to one another as soon as they recognized Kōi. Coming up to him and prostrating themselves on the sand, they said: "Well, well! Please come and see us on the first day of the tournament." The villagers who had come out to welcome the wrestlers all popped their eyes with astonishment. "It seems the retired master of Tsunokuniya is a famous man! See how the champion wrestlers kneel on the sand in respect," they could be heard whispering to one another. Kōi sent the sumo wrestlers a basket of various eatables, and in consequence had to economize for more than a month.

Kōi lived in Samukawa from 1863 to 1866, in all, four full years. This was from his forty-second to his forty-fifth year. In this interval Umeya Kakuju died in 1864 and Tsuji Kasetsu in 1865. Kasetsu is the man who began *kyōka* contests.

Kōi returned to the Yamashiro Riverbank in 1866. Now retired in the shop where the family business no longer prospered, few among his companions of old came there to visit him. There was at this time a resident of Shinbori named Gotō Shin'ichi; he was known in the gay quarters by the nickname of the Shinbori Lad, and took great pride in extravagant pleasures. When Gotō heard of Kōi's return to Edo, he took it into his head to entertain him as his senior, and in consultation with a certain Okada Ryūgin of Kiba, invited Kōi's old followers, such as Hōnen, Bainen, Shigyoku, and Chikusen, to a party for Kōi at a restaurant in Shimbashi. Kōi, as a "great one overthrown," took no pleasure in showing his face on this occasion, but reluctantly accepted the request of Gotō and the others.

To add to the entertainment at this party, the hosts, Gotō and his friends, had engaged Matsunoya Kazan, a male geisha popular at the time. Kazan had acquired a reputation for dancing naked. He danced stark naked without even a breechcloth. And not only that, naked as he was he also did things unfit to set down in writing. His engagement for this particular party was of course a case of being right in style. But one of the invited guests, Shigyoku, had abominated Kazan's conduct from a previous party, and was all set for him: "If he puts on his indecent performance before my eyes, I'll give him a lesson," he vowed.

Hōnen surmised Shigyoku's intention and forewarned Kazan, who applied to Chakō for help. Chakō was a so-called man of respect—a gangster type—who exercised power in the Shimbashi area, and Kazan was under his boss Chakō's patronage and protection.

Chakō accepted Kazan's petition. The location of the party is in my territory, he thought. My own protégé, Kazan, is about to go there alone and be humiliated. I can't very well fail to respond and help him out. However, how shall I help Kazan? So pondering the matter, Chakō took the simplest method of bribery. He gave congratulatory gifts to all of Gotō's guests.

Shigyoku threw his gift on the floor and cursed Chakō. Once the mood of Gotō's party was destroyed by this crude behavior, the guests dispersed.

Fearing that Gotō might possibly get into trouble as a result, Kōi called Shigyoku to his house the next day and admonished him. He tried to get Shigyoku to apologize to Chakō for his misconduct. Shigyoku, however, would not listen to him. To entertain through one's talents and art is the function of a male geisha, Shigyoku said. But to associate with one who has discarded all sense of shame for love of money is something I will never do. For Shigyoku's rejection of Kazan, the fault lay with Kazan. For Shigyoku's refusal of the gift, the fault lay with Chakō. Shigyoku held adamantly to this position, and would not listen.

Kōi, bowing to the inevitable, arranged an amicable settlement between Gotō and Chakō through an intermediary. They say the two met in a tea-shop in Kubo-chō and "patched things up." This occurred in Kōi's forty-fifth year. Gotō later changed his name to Shōkichi, and entered the rice-brokering business.

In 1867 a collection of silhouette pictures entitled *Kumanakikage* (Sha-dows without Shade) was published on the third annual memorial obser-vance of Tsuji Kasetsu, and Kōi himself wrote the preface. On the picture of Kōi inside the book there is pasted a poem-strip with the "Holding a nee-dle" verse which I have quoted above. A copy of this book which I have handled myself is in the collection of the Bun'endō publishing house.

The Yamashiro Riverbank shop was shut up in 1868. At the time, Saiki Isaburō, the husband of Kōi's elder sister, kept a bookstore in Sannō-chō. Sannō-chō is the present Sōjūrō-chō in Tokyo. Kōi, his wife Fusa, and his son Keijirō lived with this Isaburō. At the time he was forty-seven.

Kōi took to his bed in the ninth month of 1870, and died on the tenth day at the age of forty-nine. His name in Buddha is Baiyo Kōi Koji. He was laid to rest in the cemetery of his forefathers in the Gangyōji temple. Among the rough notes he left are these:

Fuyugarete ita wa
Kisama ka
Ume no hana.

Kōbai ni
Yuki mo yokeredo
Kagenmono.

Tada asobu
Ukikusa mo furu
Tsukihi kana.

Tsugomori ya
Yoshi naki keshi no
Hana akari.

Nusumaremu
Negi mo tsukurite
Nochi no tsuki.

Matsu koto no
Arige ni nokoru
Nomi ka kana.

Ne no takai
Mizu ni suna haku
Shijimi kana.

Ji ni tsukanu
Uchi zo nodokeki
Mau konoha.

Hana ni uru
Ippon mono ya
Edo gatsuo.

Kiri harete
Mina kochira muku
Yama no nari.

Ajikiri no
Nibuku mo hikaru
Samusa kana.

Wabi nureba
Fugu wo misutete
Nadaikon.

Onore ni mo
Akite no ue ka
Yarebashō.

The winter-withered—
Was it you?
Plum blossom.

On the red plum
Snow would be good, but
"How much" is the problem.

Even for the floating weed
Who only plays
The months and days pass!

Last day of the month.
Glow from the flowers
Of the trivial poppies.

Having grown onions
Probably to be stolen,
A later moon.

As if they were waiting,
They remain—
The fleas and mosquitos.

High priced,
It spews out sand into the water—
Freshwater clam.

Serene, but only while
Still floating in the air
The dancing tree-leaves.

Self-Portrait
Sold at its season's height
An item worth a hundred coins
Edo bonito.

Self-Pride
After the mist has cleared
All face this way,
The mountain shapes.

Samukawa
So cold!
A little fish-knife glitters
Though it is dull.

A Thought
When poor,
One gives up blow-fish
For greens and radishes.

Maybe it's tired
Even of itself
The tattered banana-tree.

On the tenth day of the tenth month of 1871, after intentionally delaying by one month after the first annual memorial service held by relatives, Kōi's past beneficiaries assembled at the house of Ogura Zeami on Dangozaka; they reminisced about the old days, then together paid a visit to Kōi's grave. Moromochi, Kakuju, Kasetsu, Kōzan were already long dead and the writer Tōsai had passed away in the fourth month of the same year as Kōi. Kanō Ansen, Kawatake Shinshichi, Kikakudō Eiki, Chikusen, Shigyoku, and Zenkō were among this group that visited the grave.

> Kono haka no
> Ochiba mukashi no
> Koban kana

> On this grave
> The fallen leaves are gold coins
> Of yesteryear.

> Eiki

The years rolled on, gradually swallowing up Kōi's companions in pleasure. Isan died in 1878, Gengyo in 1880, Chikaharu in 1882, Tōsai in 1890, Zeshin in 1891, Ansen and Kiyomitsu in 1892, Eiki in 1904.

For Kōi's personal history I have mainly followed Kanagaki Robun's *Sairai Kibun kakkagai*.[139] I hear it is now entitled *Ima Kibun Kuruwa no hanamichi*. Because of my bad memory I made notes from the book which Suzuki Shumpō[140] loaned me with the suggestion there might be a story idea in it. In addition I consulted Nemoto Tohō's *Daitsūjin Kōi*. However, Nemoto seems to have also relied on Robun's account. I also benefited from conversations of two artists, Matsuda Kōen and Kubota Beisen,[141] as recorded by Suzuki Shumpō, and from the book entitled *On*[142] published by Hashimoto Sokō, alias Chikusen, which was in the possession of my younger brother Junzaburō.

If you go along the wooden fence of the First Higher School in Tokyo and turn east, then on the next corner turning north is the Saikyōji temple. Passing the front gate of this temple, if you continue on looking to the right at a boarding house where paulownia flowers bloom at the side, there will be three or four shops in a row, then another temple. This is the Gangyōji.

The gate of the Gangyōji faces south at the inner end of an alleyway; across the road from the boarding house is the outer enclosure of the graveyard. This enclosure was originally a straggling hedge, over which grave stones of various shapes and sizes met the eye of passersby in the street. Now, both the Saikyōji and Gangyōji have been renovated, and the hedge has been replaced by a strong stone wall. Only the two or three old trees with dense foliage towering into the air and covering all this preserve a continuity with the past.

I decided one day to visit the grave site of Kōi's family, and entered the gate of the Gangyōji. A strapping fellow wearing a blue summer kimono with white splashes was waving iron dumbbells around in the stand of cedar trees inside the gate, and did not even glance up as I entered. I walked along looking at the grave stones arranged in a row, around by the east side of the main temple toward the north rear. The sun was already getting low, and the inscription I was looking for continued to elude me.

Suddenly I heard the voice of a baby laughing, and turned and looked. A beautiful woman was standing there holding the baby in her arms; she had been watching me as I was walking along reading the characters of the epitaphs.

I broke off my search and asked, ''Are you connected with this temple?''

''Yes, I am, sir. Whose grave are you looking for?'' Her voice as well as the color of her face was bright and cheerful, making a vivid contrast with the gloomy surroundings. ''I'm looking for Tsunokuniya. Perhaps the family name is Saiki.'' In Robun's account, the name is read both Saiki and Hosoki, but I had thought that perhaps the typesetters had accidentally made it Hosoki, although Saiki was the correct reading.

''But one writes the character 'Hosoki,' I think,'' she replied. She obviously knew Chinese characters.

''That's so? Then you know it?''

''Yes, I know it. Those at the end there are the Tsunokuniya graves.'' The baby in her arms kept watching me all the while laughing and wiggling around. I thanked her and made my way to the gravesite. I somehow had the feeling I had been talking with the wife of a Protestant minister.

At the middle of the east side of the main temple building, there is a little lane that goes along straight out toward the stone wall. The tombstone stands at the end of it, facing west with the wall at its back.

Opposite, on the left side, a stone lantern has been erected, and on it is carved ''Tsunokuniya.''

The tomb is nearly square and in the stone of its rather wide face many posthumous Buddhahood names are carved on two levels, upper and lower; beneath each a death-day is recorded.

As the posthumous names are set down in order on the Tsunokuniya stone going back to the remote ancestors of the house, I could read the names in Buddha from Kōi's grandfather to Kōi himself in the left corner of the lower row.

On my way back after paying my respects to the grave, I had to again pass by the woman with the baby in her arms.

"Do relatives of the Tsunokuniya visit the tomb?" I asked her.

"Yes. One lady who married into another family is alive and comes here on death anniversaries. I'm sure she's the wife of a man named Niihara Motosaburō;[143] they say he is a charcoal dealer in Shiba. The temple priest knows her well, but right now he is away. If you like, you can ask the flower seller who lives between here and the Saikyōji."

I thanked her again and left the temple. Then I stopped in the street and looked for the flower seller.

The shops between the Saikyōji and the Gangyōji temples are all small and newly built. Hemmed in between them there is a house, so tiny and old it is almost impossible to call it a house at all, surrounded with reed screens. As I looked at it, I remembered I had previously noticed Chinese anise branches in front of it.

I went inside the reed screens. Inside the house it was already almost pitch dark. When I became accustomed to the dim light, I saw a decrepit old man and woman crouched down. The house and its people gave me the feeling they had been somehow left untouched by the march of civilization. I also felt as if the semidarkness was permeated by the atmosphere of a fairy tale.

When I said, "Hello there," the old man stood up and came to meet me. The old woman remained crouched down.

"Perhaps you know the Tsunokuniya tomb in the Gangyōji?" I inquired. However, they both were hard of hearing, and I had to gradually raise my voice and repeat this two or three times.

The old lady in the rear was the first to make out my words. "Do you mean Hosoki-san?" she said. From this I decided at first to read Kōi's family name Hosoki, and sent it to the printer with that reading. But when I found that Chikusen, who was Kōi's intimate friend, wrote it Saiki, I again decided that Saiki was correct.

I wished to ask the name of the woman in Shiba who was Kōi's descendant, and also to assure myself of the name of her husband; but neither of them seemed to know anything about them.

The old woman only said, "They say he was a very rich man. People said then, if only they could be left some money, because only a little would be enough—they always say this."

I handed a small silver coin to the old man and asked him to offer Chinese anise branches at Kōi's grave.

"Very good, sir," he replied. "It's late now, I'll do it tomorrow morning."

Without trying to visit the temple priest of the Gangyōji after that, I finally finished this manuscript as it now stands without going into the details of Kōi's living descendent. When I recently asked Takahashi Kunitarō, he told me that the writer, Akutagawa Ryūnosuke, is a relative of Kōi. I shall be happy if Mr. Akutagawa would correct any mistakes in this manuscript.

Several years ago I wrote my *Hyaku monogatari*[144] based on an anecdote of Kajimaya Seibē.[145] For the times in my writing when there was wording which treated Kajimaya in a somewhat eulogistic manner, a critic attacked me for my "presumptuousness." I have no detailed recollection of it now; but it's easy to find a copy of the criticism, and if you take the trouble to do so, you can get to the bottom of it.

Kajimaya was a "Big Spender." The inability of a hard-up scholar like me to investigate and know his circumstances is like the inability of a pauper to divine the interior of an emperor's palace. Hence the charge of presumptuousness.

Evaluations of human existence are endlessly subjective and diverse. When my father lived in northern Senju, there was a servant woman in the house. She was plump, fair-skinned, and agreeable; her manner also was refined. However, the stories she used to tell me and my brothers and sisters shocked us.

When she was a young girl this servant served in a great establishment in the Yoshiwara and was praised for her loyalty. She returned to her family's village of Senju after she had passed the age of twenty.

This servant considered the *oiran*—the highest-ranking courtesan—to be the noblest of human beings. Members of the nobility and high government officials were all, in her eyes, uncouth customers. The high towers and great pavilions of the brothel and the serving men and women, the underlings in it, she saw only as instruments to serve and adorn the *oiran*; even the brothel master, however he might prosper through sensuality or exercise his authority, was no more than the chief among these inferior creatures.

The thoughts and sentiments of this servant woman centered entirely upon the *oiran*. In her judgment, the Yoshiwara district was civilization, outside it was wilderness; the Yoshiwara was the center of culture, outside were the barbarians. This is because the Yoshiwara is the "residence" in which the *oiran* lives.

My younger brother would say, "Yoshi, tell us a story." Yoshi was the name of the servant woman.

"All right, come here, I'll tell you a story." Yoshi would seat herself quietly on the board-floor of the kitchen and draw my younger brother onto the round mound of her knees. Her voice was clear and melodious. "Once upon a time there was an *oiran*. This *oiran* was one-eyed. A customer came to her.

This customer was pockmarked. The next morning, when the customer was going home, the *oiran* came out to see him off, and said, *Yuzukinamasue* [a pun on words, at the same time meaning 'Please come again many times,' and 'Citron-flavored fish salad']. I suppose the pockmarked face looked like a citron. Then they say the customer replied, *Mekkachi yokkachi jibun ni wa koyo yo* [another pun, meaning alternately 'I'll come around nine or ten in the evening,' and 'I'll come around the one-eyed, ten o'clock at night']." In Yoshi's fairy tales only *oiran* and their customers appeared as characters.

Evaluations of human existence are endlessly subjective and diverse. One can consider either the Buddha or the devil as a king. If Kōi and Seibē are big-spender kings, then *parvenu* with all their riches, reduced to being pennypinchers, probably repent their sins. If an *oiran* is the model for a queen, then virtuous women and heroines, sagacious wives and good mothers, reduced to being maiden ladies ignorant of the facts of life, no doubt hang their heads in shame.

Just as some great and learned priest should be the king of practitioners of religion, so also there is probably one who should be a novelist king. And just as a great scholar of encyclopedic learning should be a philosopher king, so also there is probably one who should be a critic king, and probably one who should be a publisher king, and probably one who should be a newspaper publisher king. Evaluations of human existence are endlessly subjective and diverse.

After I wrote the biographies of Izawa Ranken and Shibue Chūsai, I happened by chance to write the biography of this Saiki Kōi. When one of so little talent as I presumes to write literature, then regardless of the fact that I have not questioned the nature of the object in my chosen topic and have insofar as possible avoided crossing over into criticism, the charge of presumptuousness is something I could not escape.

September 1917

As I wrote the manuscript of the above biography of Saiki Kōi in haste, I was not able to escape some errors. I wish to correct them here.

I noted at the end of the biography that Akutagawa Ryūnosuke was Kōi's relative. Happily Akutagawa sent me a letter and also came to visit me. This was not our first meeting. It was only that we hadn't seen each other for quite some time.

According to Akutagawa, Kōi had an older sister, whose husband was the bookseller Isaburō in Sannō-chō. Kōi passed his last years in their house.

Isaburō's daughter Tomo[146] married into the Akutagawa family. Tomo was Akutagawa's mother. There is a story "Hell of Solitude" in the collection of Akutagawa's short stories entitled *Rashōmon*. It is said that the material for it is something the author heard from his mother. Kojima Seijirō had told me this prior to my meeting with Akutagawa.

In Kōi's biography I also wrote about an old woman who made visits to the grave at the Gangyōji. I said this woman was the wife of a man named Niihara Genzaburō. When I inquired of Akutagawa, he told me the woman's name is Ei. Kōi's heir is Keisaburō, and Keisaburō's daughter is this Ei. The name of her husband was correct.

I wish to add a note to the matter of Ei's visit to the grave. It concerns the old couple who sold Chinese anise branches by the Gangyōji. This old couple, of whom I once inquired about Ei, have now passed away. The other day I walked north in the vicinity of the First Higher School and by chance noticed that the Chinese anise seller's shop was closed up, so I visited a second-hand bookstore nearby and asked how the old couple was getting along. The old man, they said, died first, around April, and the old lady followed him within a hundred days. I could not help feeling deeply moved. Just as I was writing this, a postcard came from Miyazaki Toranosuke[147] with the message: "Prayerful greetings. Friend Mori! What is it that looms way over there? It is death! The wisest man acknowledges death as certain! December seventh. Prayers."

Next I wish to set down two or three miscellaneous facts I heard from Akutagawa. Kōi's family name is correctly read Saiki. But Kōi had sometimes gone under the name of Hosoki only because so many other people called him by that name.

Akutagawa made known to me the poem Kōi composed on his death bed. Following Robun's account, I had cited the poem above:

> *Last Writing*
> Maybe it's tired
> Even of itself
> The tattered banana-tree.

However, it is said that the true death-bed poem was this one:

> Ume ga ka ya
> Chotto denaosu
> Kakitonari.

> Fragrance of plum[148]
> It comes again a bit
> Hedge neighbor.

This latter poem has a feeling of freedom and ease. I think it is better.

Akutagawa has in his possession a one-volume travel account of a tour of Kamakura, Enoshima, and Kanagawa made by Kōi's father. It is a beautiful volume, fair copied before it was engraved in wood-blocks for printing; it has some tens of illustrations by Kunitomo, a disciple of Ichiyūsai Kuniyoshi.[149]

This was a five-day excursion beginning from the sixth day of the fourth month of 1855, as indicated at the beginning of the book. Also, among the *kyōka* in the Chinese seven-character, ancient verse style of Liu Shan-yin appended at the end, there are verses such as:

> Four seas, Ansei *kinoto-u* year
> Lined kimono, fourth month, every day pleasurable
> Going and coming five days, on the road, serene.

Kinoto-u was the year of the Great Winter Earthquake.

The book records the names of twelve participants in the excursion: Sharakuō, Kunitomo, Senkaku, Sōri, Senro (Seikansai), Kyōei, Kosanji (Toba), Kunitomo, Enjō, Senka, Ryōko, and Ankō (Amma Kōsuke). Sharakuō is probably Ryūchi. It is said that Isaburō was among them, but his pen name is not known. The story is that Kōi declined, saying, "When I go along with the old man I have no say, so please excuse me."

Kōi, Gango (Ishikawa Hōjun), Yohei, Ihaku, and Shūu (Gengen Mabito) came to welcome them when the group returned.

> Su e modoru
> Oya matsu niho no
> Morone kana.

> The tearful notes
> Of the little grebe who waits
> His parent returning to the nest.

The epilogue Kōi himself drafted. Other than that, *tanka, haiku,* and *kyōka* in the old and new Chinese style by several others are also appended.

It occurs to me that *kinoto-u* was the year before Ryūchi died, when Kōi was thirty-four. This is about the extent of the information Akutagawa was able to give me.

In addition to Akutagawa, there were others who had information about Kōi. One acquaintance said to me, "In the first year of Meiji there was a geisha house named the Minatoya next to Imadobashi. The master was named Kōno; he was short and fat. His wife was a daughter named Minato of the assignation-teahouse Minatoya in the Yoshiwara; she was usually called Miichan. This geisha house was named after the Minatoya in the Yo-shiwara. About February of 1871, the employees of this house were Kanro-ku, Bankichi, and Ryūhachi. I hear this Kōno was Kōi's son." I have not been able to verify this story. Moreover, I have not tried to ask Akutagawa about it. However, if Kōno were, after all, Kōi's son, would he not then be the dregs to which Keijirō had been reduced in his later years?

I also obtained two or three reports about Kōi's friends. A certain Katō, who was known as Kokai'an of the Onoe school of kabuki, told me: "In Kōi's biography you mention Kōi's friend, Shin Eiki; I don't think you were right in recording his death year as 1904. Both the father and grandfather of the present Ki'ichi were known as Eiki. Kōi's friend was probably the grand-father, and the one who died in 1904 was probably the father." Because I do not know for certain the genealogy of Kikakudō, I may have made such a mistake. So I made inquiry about it to the owner of the Bun'endō in Asaku-sa. His letter in reply was to the effect: "Kōi's friend Eiki had a close associa-tion with both Ichikawa Danjūrō IX and Onoe Kikugorō V. Danjūrō's handwriting was exactly like Eiki's. This Eiki lived in Kikakudō in the pre-cincts of the Misono shrine of Mukōjima around the first year of Meiji; later he moved to the vicinity of Maruyama in Shiba and died there. The day of his death was January 10, 1904, and his age was eighty-two. His temple is the Nihon Enoki Jōgyōji, the same as Kikaku's." If we agree with this ac-count there seems to be no mistake in my date. It should be looked into fur-ther.

My near neighbor Umemoto Takasada told me something about some of Kōi's other friends. "In the biography you say Kōi's friend Ashin'an Zebu-tsu was the master of the Yanaka Mikawaya; Zebutsu's ordinary name was Saitō Gonuemon," he informed me. From this I learned for the first time that Zebutsu was the real father of Kariya Noriyuki. Saitō Gonuemon had three sons. The eldest, Gonnosuke, was the fourth-generation Kiyomoto master named Enju. In some books his ordinary name is recorded as Genno-suke, but he may have changed to that name later. The middle son, Sabue-mon Noriyuki, was the adopted son of Kariya Sampei Yasuyuki, who was the natural son of Ekisai Mochiyuki. The youngest, Gonuemon, succeeded to his father's name; he is said to have become a master of a pawn shop.

Mr. Umemoto spoke of one more of Kōi's friends, Ogura Zeami. "Zeami was of the Takagi family; Ogura was his business name. He had a pawnbro-ker business on the top of Dangozaka, just as you say in the biography. Zea-mi's wife was named Gin, and their child was called Sahei. Sahei had a son Shintarō and a daughter Kei. However, both Sahei and the two children died, leaving the widow Gin. She was the mistress of the house on the cliff-top." Through this I learned that my father had bought my present house from Zeami's widow.

Finally, facts about two other friends of Kōi were related to me by the owner of the Bun'endō. They concern Ishibashi Makuni and Shibata Zeshin. "Ishibashi Makuni left numerous unpublished manuscripts on linguistics. They are now in the possession of Mr. Matsui Kanji.[150] Among the so-called light reading in this collection, there is one entitled *Inri no ki* [An account of the secret villages].[151] It is a study of the development of gay quarters outside of the Yoshiwara, that is, the *Oka-basho*. Makuni wrote splendidly in a T'ang-style hand. He was the master of a teashop in the area of the Edo City Commissioner's Office. Shibata Zeshin was a man with a sharp temperament. He was very friendly with Kōi, and among the things Kōi had printed there are many which include Zeshin's pictures. The following is typical of the anecdotes about him. Once Zeshin took his son and a number of his pupils to the Yoshiwara, where he entertained them with comic interludes. He had food and drink served to feast them. When he noticed, however, that one of the pupils had relaxed his formal sitting posture, he thundered and scolded at him. Zeshin had no qualms about setting foot in the gay quarter; he was no stickler, but he had a streak of sternness in him."

1917

NOTES

THE HISTORICAL LITERATURE OF MORI ŌGAI: AN INTRODUCTION

1. Edwin McClellan, *Two Japanese Novelists* (Chicago: University of Chicago Press, 1969), p. xi.

2. There are dissenters among Japanese literary historians, too, of course. As most of the stories are set in the Tokugawa period, Marxist critics, who see the period as "feudal" in the pejorative sense of the word, are impatient with the "conservatism" of Ōgai. These rather complicated issues are not recapitulated here, as they are not germane to the present discussion.

3. Hasegawa Izumi, "Mori Ōgai," *Japan Quarterly* (April 1963):244.

4. The Hasegawa Izumi article, mentioned above, is probably the most thoughtful article on Ōgai in English. Among the many excellent works on Ōgai in Japanese, perhaps Okazaki Yoshie's book *Ōgai to teinen* [Ōgai and resignation] (Tokyo: Hōbunkan, 1969), is the most compelling.

5. Mori Ōgai, *Vita Sexualis*, trans. by Kazuji Ninomiya and Sanford Goldstein (Tokyo and Rutland, Vt.: Charles Tuttle Co., 1972).

6. Other writers reacted as strongly. Nagai Kafū, for example, wrote in his essay *Fireworks* that the incident caused him to abandon any attachments to the perniciousness of the contemporary world. For a partial translation, see Edward Seidensticker's *Kafū the Scribbler* (Stanford: Stanford University Press, 1965), p. 46.

7. General Nogi (1849–1912) was one of the great generals and popular heroes of the Sino-Japanese War and the Russo-Japanese War.

8. In particular, to Yamagata Aritomo (1838–1922), a prominent military leader and Privy Councillor of the Meiji period. For a few details on their relationship, see the Hasegawa article cited in note 3 above.

9. *Mori Ōgai Zenshū* (Tokyo: Chikuma Shobō, 1971), vol. 4, p. 45.

10. Ibid., p. 233.

11. *Mori Ōgai Zenshū* (Tokyo: Chikuma Shobō, 1971), vol. 7, pp. 105–106.

12. Friedrich Nietzsche, *The Birth of Tragedy*, trans. by Francis Golffing (New York: Doubleday Anchor, 1956), p. 21.

13. Ibid., p. 145.

14. Stephen Ross, *Literature as Philosophy* (New York: Appleton, 1969), p. 12.

15. John Willett, ed., *Brecht on Theatre* (New York: Hill and Wang, 1964), p. 75.

16. Katō Shūichi, "Japanese Writers and Modernization," in *Changing Japanese Attitudes toward Modernization*, edited by Marius Jansen (Princeton: Princeton University Press, 1965), p. 435.

17. Japanese critics often comment on Ōgai's sense of resignation gained through his growing sense of disillusionment over aspects of his own life and career, as well as the shortcomings of Meiji Japan. But these last stories harbor attitudes far more penetrating in their observations of the human condition than those generated by emotional fatigue.

18. See Roger Caillois, "Circular Time, Rectilinear Time," *Diogenes* (Summer 1963):1–13.

19. An English translation of Lu Hsun's 1933 essay "How I Came to Write Stories" is included in *Selected Works of Lu Hsun*, trans. by Yang Hsien-Yi and Gladys Yang, vol. 3 (Peking: Foreign Languages Press, 1959), pp. 229–232.

THE SIGNIFICANCE OF ŌGAI'S HISTORICAL LITERATURE

1. Fukuzawa Yukichi, *Outline of a Theory of Civilization*, translated by David A. Dilworth and G. Cameron Hurst (Tokyo: Sophia University Press, 1973), p. 1.

2. Martin Heidegger, *Being and Time*, translated by John Macquarrie and Edward Robinson (New York: Harper and Row, 1962), p. 436.

3. Nakano Shigeharu, *Ōgai: sono sokumen* (Tokyo: Chikuma Shobo, 1972) pp. 209–212.

4. Ibid., pp. 263–267. Some estimate of the importance of Ōgai can be gained from the comprehensive bibliography of secondary source material on Ōgai in Japanese. A recent compilation of this scholarly literature runs to fifty pages of small print. See *Mori Ōgai zenshū*, 9 vols., (Tokyo: Chikuma Shobo, 1971), vol. 9, pp. 349–398.

5. See Katō Shūichi, "Japanese Writers and Modernization," in *Changing Japanese Attitudes toward Modernization*, edited by Marius Jansen (Princeton: Princeton University Press, 1965), pp. 425–444.

6. Watsuji's "Nihon bunka no jūsōsei" first appeared in his *Guzō saikō*, 1918; it is found in the *Watsuji Tetsurō zenshū*, 20 vols. (Tokyo: Iwanami Shoten, 1963), vol. 17.

7. See Kōsaka Masaaki, ed., *Japanese Thought in the Meiji Era*, translated by David Abosch (Tokyo: Toyo Bunko, 1958), Part 6, 1, "Natsume Sōseki, Mori Ōgai, and Naturalism," pp. 392–470; and Okazaki Yoshie, ed., *Japanese Literature in the Meiji Era*, translated and adapted by V. H. Viglielmo (Tokyo: Toyo Bunko, 1955), especially "The Idealistic Romantic School," pp. 163–178, and "The Dawning Light of Neo-Idealism and Humanism," pp. 300–316.

8. For example, see Mishima Yukio, in Tanizaki Jun'ichirō et al., ed., *Nihon no bungaku: A Treasury of Japanese Literature, 3: Mori Ōgai* (Tokyo: Chūō Kōronsha, 1967), vol. 1, pp. 532–534, and Edward Seidensticker, *Kafū the Scribbler: The Life and Writings of Nagai Kafū, 1879–1959*, (Stanford: Stanford University Press, 1965), p. 28. See also note 24 below.

9. John Dower, "Mori Ōgai: *Tsuina*, *Hebi*, and *Sakazuki*," *Monumenta Nipponica* 26 (1971):116–117.

10. Hasegawa Izumi, "Mori Ōgai," *Japan Quarterly* 12 (April-June 1965): 239. Cf. Karen Brazell, "Mori Ōgai in Germany: A Translation of *Fumizukai* and Excerpts from *Doitsu nikki*," *Monumenta Nipponica* 26(1971):77–114.

11. Hasegawa, ibid. *Suikōden* refers to *The Water Margin*, a famous Chinese novel.

12. Ibid., p. 238.

13. The early influence of Goethe's *Faust* on Ōgai's literary and philosophical sen-

sibilities has been documented by Thomas E. Swann, *"Mori Ōgai no Utakata no ki,"* in *Ōgai* 9 (June 1971):105–137.

14. For example, Ōgai's "Gojiingahara no katakiuchi," "Suginohara Shina," and "Saiki Kōi." On Takizawa Bakin(1767–1858), Santō Kyōden(1761–1816), and other late Tokugawa era writers, see Leon Zolbrod, *Takizawa Bakin.* (New York: Twayne Publishers, 1962).

15. See James Morita, "Shigarami-zōshi," *Monumenta Nipponica* 24(1969): 47–59.

16. Ōgai completed his still standard translation of Goethe's *Faust* in 1911–1912 while he was Surgeon General of the Japanese army and, as noted below, in the midst of a prolific period of creative writing. Among other things, he translated Ibsen's *Ghosts* in 1912, Ibsen's *Doll House* and Shakespeare's *Macbeth* in 1913, and Strindberg's *Storm Weather* in 1914. The full list of items translated by Ōgai between 1912 and 1917 runs to over fifty-five titles, mostly novels and short stories, including the works of Verhaeren, Schnitzler, Dostoevski, Tolstoi, and Gorki. He translated over 100 items between 1900 and 1911.

17. Okazaki Yoshie has argued that Ōgai's greatest impact upon the Meiji literary world before the Russo-Japanese War was in this area. See Okazaki, *Ōgai to teinen* (Tokyo: Hobunkan, 1969), pp. 615–616. See also Okazaki's "Ōgai to Shōyō to no ronsō," in *Mori Ōgai zenshū*, vol. 9, pp. 86–97.

18. Hasegawa Izumi, "Mori Ōgai," *Japan Quarterly* 12(April-June 1965):241.

19. Ibid., pp. 242–243.

20. See Ivan Morris, ed., *Modern Japanese Stories: An Anthology* (Tokyo and Vermont: Charles A. Tuttle, 1962), p. 15. Ōgai's *Maihime* (1890) and *Utakata no ki* (1890) gave birth to the Romantic novel in modern Japanese literature. They did so three years prior to the inaugural issue of *Bungakkai*, a literary journal published by Kitamura Tōkoku and Shimazaki Tōson in 1892, which later became the mainstay of the Romantic movement in Japan.

21. Ōgai continued to do careful research until his death by either atrophy of the kidney, or pulmonary tuberculosis, in July 1922. He published *Hyōjun Nihon otogi bumpō* [Standard Japanese Fairy Tales] in 1920, and *Teishi kō* [A Study of Imperial Posthumous Names] and *Gengo kō* [A Study of Reign Names] in 1921.

22. Examples of this are "Ka no yō ni," "Chinmoku no tō," "Shokudō," "Fujidana," and *Ōshio Heihachirō*. See Katō Shūichi, "Japanese Writers and Modernization," p. 428, and note 5 above.

23. Ibid., pp. 433–444. See also John Dower, "Mori Ōgai: Meiji Japan's Eminent Bystander," *Harvard Papers on Japan*, vol. 2, 1963.

24. Katō Shūichi distinguishes the Meiji "compromise" literature of such writers as Ōgai and Sōseki from the "contemporary" postwar scene. In this context he writes: "The influence exerted on the Impressionists by the ukiyoe of Edo period Japan was a triumph for the Impressionists, not for Japanese art. The influence of German literature on Mori Ōgai was a result of Ōgai's own greatness rather than the grace of German literature. The level of traditional Japanese culture, however—as Nagai Kafū, among others, pointed out—has declined steadily ever since Meiji times. It is for precisely this reason that literature since Mori Ōgai and Natsume Sōseki has never been able to attain the heights of that Meiji 'compromise' achieved in those artists." See Katō Shūichi, *Form, Style, Tradition: Reflections on Japanese*

Art and Society, translated by John Bester (Berkeley: University of California Press, 1971), p. 176. In another context, in reference to literary style, Katō observes: "The second approach, which resists the general tendency for the literary and colloquial languages to come close together, was first evolved by Mori Ōgai. However, the lowering of the public's ability to appreciate literary classics since Ogai's time has been so marked, that there is little hope of a contemporary writer producing work of Ōgai's standard. Ōgai could write in *kambun*. . . . His public could at least read it, if not write it. Today, even the writer cannot write *kambun*, and can only read it with the greatest difficulty. As for his public, the majority cannot even read it." (Ibid., pp. 190–191)

25. Okazaki, *Ōgai to teinen*, pp. 624, 632, 638.

26. See Ōoka Shōhei, in Tanizaki Jun'ichirō et al., ed., *Nihon no bungaku: A Treasury of Japanese Literature, 3: Mori Ōgai*, (Tokyo: Chūō Kōronsha, 1967), vol. 2, p. 549.

27. Mori Ōgai, *Vita Sexualis*, translated by Kazuji Ninomiya and Sanford Goldstein (Tokyo and Vermont: Charles A. Tuttle, 1972). See also Hasegawa Izumi, *Mori Ōgai: Vita Sexualis kō* (Tokyo: Meiji Shoin, 1967).

28. Two decisive events in the development of modern Japanese literature were the Treason Trial of Kōtoku Shūsui and other alleged anarchists in 1910, and the death of the Emperor Meiji and the *junshi* of General Nogi and his wife in 1912. In both cases, the Japanese literary world seems to have followed the lead of Ōgai's initial reactions. For example, as noted by Fred Notehelfer in *Kōtoku Shūsui: Portrait of a Japanese Radical* (Cambridge: Cambridge University Press, 1971, pp. 1–2, 203), such literary figures as Tokutomi Rōka, Nagai Kafū, and Ishikawa Takuboku reacted to the 1910 incident. But Tokutomi's often-quoted speech on Kōtoku Shūsui delivered at the First Higher School in Tokyo was made in February 1911. Ōgai's "Shokudō" and "Chinmoku no to" had already appeared in the November and December issues of *Mita Bungaku* in 1910, and the trial did not take place until December 10 of that year. Kafū's "Hanabi," which dealt with the same events, was written in 1919. (Notehelfer, incidentally, does not even mention Ōgai.) As another example, Sōseki's *Kokoro*, which concludes with an important reference to the *junshi* of General Nogi, came out in 1914, and hence followed Ōgai's immediate reaction to the same *junshi* in "Okitsu Yagoemon no isho" (completed in the five-day interval between General Nogi's death and funeral in 1912), and in "Abe ichizoku," written in 1913.

29. Okazaki Yoshie, *Ōgai to teinen*, p. 5.

30. *Mori Ōgai zenshū*, vol. 7, p. 99.

31. Okazaki, *Ōgai to teinen*, pp. 297–298; Kōsaka, ed., *Japanese Thought in the Meiji Era*, p. 455.

32. For background to "Hanako," see Donald Keene, *Landscapes and Portraits: Appreciation of Japanese Culture* (Tokyo: Kodansha, 1971), pp. 250–258.

33. Okazaki, *Ōgai to teinen*, p. 338.

34. *Mōsō*, translated by John Dower, *Monumenta Nipponica* 25(1970):418.

35. Dower writes: "The bystander [in *Mōsō*] presents himself also as the 'eternal malcontent' and it becomes apparent that his dilemma transcends the Meiji scene. It is rooted in larger philosophical and existential questions relating to life and death,

art and science, genius and mediocrity, and the meaning of progress." (Ibid., pp. 415–416)

36. Mori Ōgai, "As If," translated by Gregg M. Sinclair and Kazo Suita, in *Tokyo People*, edited by R. McKinnon (Tokyo: Hokuseido, 1957), pp. 61–115.

37. Ōgai's *Gan* is translated as *The Wild Geese* by Kingo Ochiai and Sanford Goldstein (Tokyo and Vermont: Charles A. Tuttle, 1959).

38. See Okazaki Yoshie, ed., *Japanese Literature in the Meiji Era*, "Romanticism and Idealism around Sōseki," pp. 268–284, and "The Dawning Light of Neo-Idealism and Humanism," pp. 300–316. The *Shirakaba* (White Birch) group of writers were heirs to this tradition from the Taisho period on. See also Katō Shūichi, *Form, Style, Tradition: Reflections on Japanese Art and Society*, p. 186.

39. Donald Richie, *Japanese Cinema* (New York: Doubleday, 1971), p. 64.

40. Ibid., p. 69.

41. Cited in *Vita Sexualis*, "Introduction," p. 15.

42. Cited in Kōsaka, ed., *Japanese Thought in the Meiji Era*, p. 463.

43. Okazaki, *Ōgai to teinen*, p. 476.

44. Donald Keene, "Mori Ōgai," in *Encyclopaedia Britannica*, vol. 15, p. 841 (Chicago: Encyclopaedia Britannica, Inc., 1973).

45. See Natsume Sōseki, *Kokoro*, translated by Edwin McClellan (Tokyo: Charles A. Tuttle, 1971).

46. Okazaki, *Ōgai to teinen*, pp. 484, 486, 488.

47. Ibid., p. 494.

48. Ibid., pp. 514–515.

49. Mori Ōgai, *Hebi-Tsuina-Sakazuki*, translated by John Dower, *Monumenta Nipponica* 26(1971):134.

50. Okazaki, *Ōgai to teinen*, pp. 563–564.

51. Ibid., p. 569.

52. *Vita Sexualis*, p. 24.

OKITSU YAGOEMON NO ISHO (*First Version*)

1. Mt. Funaoka was in the province of Yamashiro, the present-day Kyoto.

2. Taishō Inden was Hosokawa Fujitaka, the father of Lord Shōkōji (Hosokawa Tadaoki).

3. Gamō Ujisato (1557–1596). The Meiji novelist Kōda Rohan wrote a loosely constructed biography of this man in 1925.

4. The Hosokawa were moved in this year from Buzen-Bungo (residence Kokura: 370,000 *koku*) to Higo (residence Kumamoto: 540,000 *koku*).

5. Care must be taken to distinguish between this Lord Rokumaru and the man of the same name who appears in the revised version, who is his father Mitsuhisa. Both father and son had the same *yōmyō* ("infant name").

6. A collection of *zuihitsu* ("miscellaneous essays") by Kamizawa Teikan (1710–1795).

7. The *Dai Nihon yashi* written in 1851 by Iida Tadahiko.

OKITSU YAGOEMON NO ISHO (*Second Version*)

1. Hosokawa Tadatoshi (1586–1641), whose posthumous name was Myōgein, was head of the Hosokawa domain in the province of Higo; he succeeded his father Tadaoki in 1619. For further information, see note 7 below, and the opening paragraphs of "Abe ichizoku." This last testament of Okitsu Yagoemon Kageyoshi is addressed to his son, Saiemon. Kageyoshi (1594–1647) was a retainer of Hosokawa Tadatoshi with a stipend of two hundred *koku*; he was fifty-four at the time of this story.

2. Imagawa Yoshimoto (1519–1560), a warlord of the early sixteenth century.

3. Akamatsu Hirohisa (dates uncertain) was lord of the castle of Koshio.

4. Ishida Kazushige (1560–1600) was a close retainer of Toyotomi Hideyoshi; he was defeated by the forces of Tokugawa Ieyasu in the Battle of Sekigahara in 1600.

5. Onogi Nuinosuke (?–1600), lord of the castle at Fukuchiyama in the province of Tamba; he was also defeated by Ieyasu in 1600.

6. The castle at Tanabe was held at this time by Hosokawa Fujitaka (1535–1610), whose name as a monk was Yūsai. He was the father of Tadaoki and grandfather of Tadatoshi. After Nobunaga's death in 1582, Fujitaka supported Toyotomi Hideyoshi, but also held Tanabe castle in Tango, which his son had taken in 1584. Fujitaka was famous as a scholar of poetry and as a literary figure, and was the repository of secret knowledge held in certain schools about the *Kokinshū* and *Genji monogatari*. He refused to join the Ishida faction against Ieyasu. When Tanabe was beseiged by the forces of Ishida Mitsunari (Kazushige) in 1600, the Emperor Go Yōzei interceded out of fear for the loss of his poetic secrets.

7. Hosokawa Tadaoki (1563–1645), son of Fujitaka, was originally lord of the castle at Miyazu in Tango. Like his father, he had been loyal first to Nobunaga, then Hideyoshi, but with Hideyoshi's death his allegiance swung to Tokugawa Ieyasu. In 1600, his wife, the Lady Gracia, a convert to Christianity, was killed by his order rather than become a hostage to Ishida. After the battle of Sekigahara, he was given the fief of Buzen in north Kyushu at Kokura in 1600. He was charged with watching the Shimazu, and was with Ieyasu at the siege of Osaka castle in 1615. In 1619, he yielded the domain to his son Tadatoshi, and took the tonsure with the name of Sansai. He had wide aesthetic interests, including the tea ceremony, in which he was a disciple of the famous master Rikyū, and on whose death he received certain famous implements; Tadaoki (Sansai) was himself noted as a master of secrets of the tea ceremony. Tadatoshi was Tadaoki's son by Lady Gracia. A hostage in Edo at the time of Sekigahara, he had received the "Tada" in his name from Ieyasu's son, Hidetada. He accompanied Hidetada in the force which moved to chastise the Uesugi clan. In 1609 he married Hidetada's adopted daughter. In 1632, he took over the fief of Higo (Kumamoto), valued at 540,000 *koku* annually; Tadatoshi's forces were distinguished in the pacification of the Shimabara Rebellion in 1637/38.

8. Uesugi Kagekatsu (1555–1622) was an adopted son of the famous warlord Uesugi Kenshin (1530–1578). He served under Toyotomi Hideyoshi and became lord of the castle at Wakamatsu in Aizu province in 1597. He was at this time an ally of Ishida Kazushige against the forces of Ieyasu.

9. Karasumaru Mitsuhiro (1577–1638), a member of the Northern House of the Fujiwara, held several court titles and contributed to the revival of literature in the

early Tokugawa period as a poet and writer of *kana zōshi* (story books in Japanese letters).

10. Manhime (1598-1664), the fourth daughter of Hosokawa Tadaoki.

11. The Kantō plain is the region in which Edo (now Tokyo) was located.

12. Mitsuhisa (1619-1649), the oldest son of Hosokawa Tadatoshi. He inherited the domain in 1641, as we read in Ōgai's "Abe ichizoku."

13. Kurobē Kazutomo (?-1637).

14. The Hosokawa daimyo gained in prestige when his forces took the head of Amakusa Shirō Tokisada (?-1638), the insurgent leader of the Shimabara Rebellion, in 1638. The victory 'brought to a climax the persecution of Christians in Japan when, in 1637, the long-Christianized peasantry of the Shimabara region near Nagasaki rebelled in desperation at the economic and religious oppression. More than twenty thousand people, basing themselves in the abandoned Hara castle, withstood for almost three months the combined assault of the Tokugawa forces, supported by the firepower of Dutch ships. The Christian rebels were eventually slaughtered almost to a man.

15. Date Masamune (1567-1636), an ally of Tokugawa Ieyasu in the battle of Sekigahara; he later became lord of Sendai and Mutsu in 1607, and gained the Court office of Middle Councillor in 1617. He was a connoisseur of poetry and the tea ceremony.

16. Gamō Ujisato (1556-1595), a warlord of the Azuchi-Momoyama period, served Nobunaga and Hideyoshi, and was enfeoffed with the territories in the province of Aizu. He was known as a master of *renga* (linked verse) and the tea ceremony, and was a Christian convert.

17. Emperor Gomizuno-o (r. 1611-1629).

18. Hosokawa Tatsutaka (1615-1645), the fifth son of Tadaoki, and younger brother of Tadatoshi.

19. Ōgai takes up the story of these nineteen earlier *junshi* in "Abe ichizoku."

20. Minota Masamoto (1623-1645), Ono Tomotsugu (1621-1645), Kuno Munenao (?-1645), Hōsen'in Gyōja (?-1645).

21. *Yamabushi* were wandering Buddhist priests who lived in the mountains; they were popularly considered to be exorcists.

22. Tsutsui Junkei (1549-1584), a warlord of the Sengoku period.

23. Seigan Jitsudō (1588-1661).

24. Hotta Masamori (1608-1651), lord of the Kaga domain; Inaba Nobumichi (1608-1673), lord of the Bungo domain.

25. Karasumaru Sukeyoshi (1623-1669) and Karasumaru Sukekiyo (dates uncertain), both sons of a daughter of Hosokawa Tadaoki, were accomplished poets of the time.

26. The text of this kyōka style poem is as follows:

> *Hirui naki*
> *Na wo ba kumoi ni*
> *Ageokitsu*
> *Yagoe wo kakete*
> *Oibara wo kiru.*

The pivot words (-*okitsu Yagoe*) play on his name as well as have the meaning of a "hail he raised." *Oibara* specifically refers to *junshi*. The reference here to *kumoi*, cloud well, a euphemism in classical poetry for the Imperial Court, may be intended as a reference by Ōgai to General Nogi's ritual suicide.

27. Honda Toshitsugu (1595–1668) became lord of the domain in 1636; he received larger territories in Ōmi province in 1651.

28. These were posting towns along the Tōkaidō highway.

29. Ōgai's text at this point has Hosokawa Tsunatoshi, but this is apparently a mistake for Tadatoshi (see note 1), who was lord of the domain at this time (1637). Tsunatoshi, born in 1643, was Tadatoshi's grandson.

30. Kuroda Tadayuki (1602–1654) inherited the domain of Fukuoka in Echizen province in 1623, and received the order from the shogunate to participate in the pacification of the Shimabara Rebellion at this time (1637). Ōgai's text reads Mitsuyuki, but Mitsuyuki (1628–1707) was Tadayuki's son.

31. Hosokawa Nobunori (1676–1732), who inherited the domain in 1712.

32. Hosokawa Munetaka (1718–1747), son of Nobunori; he inherited the domain in 1732.

33. Hosokawa Shigetaka (1720–1785), son of Munetaka; he inherited the domain in 1747.

34. Nakatsukasa Harutoshi (1759–1787), the eldest son of Shigetaka; he inherited the domain in 1785.

35. Tsunahime (1785–1861), daughter of Hitotsubashi Dainagon Haruzumi; she was the wife of the heir to the Hosokawa domain.

ABE ICHIZOKU

1. Hosokawa Tadatoshi (1586–1641) was fifty-six at this time. See also the opening pages of Ōgai's *Tokō Tahei*.

2. Reference to the *sankin kōtai* system established by the Tokugawa shogunate in 1615.

3. Of the approximately two hundred seventy feudal lords at this time, only seven daimyo ruled territories evaluated at over 500,000 *koku* annually.

4. Tokugawa Iemitsu (1604–1651), the third shogun.

5. Amakusa Shirō Tokisada (?–1638), insurgent leader of over twenty thousand Christians in the winter of 1837. When Hara castle at Shimabara in the province of Hizen fell in the second month of 1638, Hosokawa Tadatoshi's forces were in the vanguard of the attack and took Amakusa's head. Since this victory removed the last obstacle to its hegemony throughout Japan, the Tokugawa house held the Hosokawa house in the highest esteem, as indicated in the story.

6. Matsudaira Izu no kami Nobutsuna (1596–1662), Abe Bungo no kami Tadaaki (1602–1675), and Abe Tsushima no kami Shigetsugu (1598–1615) were the highest councillors (*rōjū*) of the shogunate at this time.

7. Ogasawara Hidemasa (1569–1615).

8. O-sen no kata (1597–1649).

9. Rokumaru, later the daimyo Mitsuhisa (1619–1649).

10. Actually, Mitsusada must have been twenty-three at the time.

11. Tsuruchiyo (1635–1685).

12. Taien (1588–1653), the thirty-ninth abbot of the Myōshinji.

13. Matsunosuke (1637–1680).

14. Katsuchiyo (1641–1703).

15. Fujihime (1634–1698).

16. Matsudaira Tadahiro (1631–1700).

17. Takehime (1637–1694).

18. Sansai Sōryū was the Buddhist name of Hosokawa Tadaoki in retirement. Tadaoki (1563–1645) appears in Ōgai's "Tokō Tahei."

19. Tatsutaka (1615–1645).

20. Gyōbu Okitaka (1617–1679).

21. Nagaoka Shikibu Yoriyuki (1617–1666).

22. Tarahime (1588–1614).

23. Inaba Kazumichi (1587–1641).

24. Manhime (1598–1665).

25. Nenehime (1620–1636).

26. The outer gate of the southwest corner of Kumamoto castle.

27. Keishitsu (1597–1666).

28. Takuan (1573–1645).

29. Naitō Chōjurō Mototsugu (1625–1641).

30. Katō Yoshitake (1563–1631), a famous general of Toyotomi Hideyoshi; he later served Tokugawa Ieyasu.

31. Gōtō Mototsugu (1560–1615) formerly served the Kuroda house, then became a rōnin and fought on the side of Toyotomi Hideyoshi at the siege of Osaka castle in 1615, where he died in battle.

32. Katō Kiyomasa (1559–1611), a retainer of Toyotomi Hideyoshi; he was later appointed lord of the castle at Kumamoto.

33. Katō Tadahiro (1598–1653), son of Kiyomasa, an ally of Toyotomi Hideyoshi. Kiyomasa was made lord of Kumano castle in 1600. Tadahiro took over his father's estates while still young and allowed a series of quarrels to develop among his retainers. He was officially reprimanded by the shogun, later called to Edo and exiled. He figures in Ōgai's Kuriyama Daizen."

34. The O-Kiku monogatari, written in 1615, was a story describing the life of the twenty-year-old girl within the fortification at the time of the siege of Osaka castle. It was later conjoined with the O-An monogatari and published in 1637.

35. Ten'yū (?–1666).

36. Konishi Yukinaga (?–1600), son of a merchant who rose to become one of Toyotomi Hideyoshi's highest generals. Together with Katō Kiyomasa he put down the Higo Rebellion in 1587, and as a reward was appointed lord over half of Higo province. He was later defeated and beheaded at the battle of Sekigahara in 1600.

37. Hosokawa Tadakuni (1484–1531).

38. Shimamura Danjō Takanori (?–1531).

39. Tachibana Muneshige (1569–1642), a warrior who had first served under Hideyoshi, later under Ieyasu at the siege of Osaka castle in 1615, and finally under Iemitsu at the siege of Hara castle at Shimabara in 1638, as reported in the story.

40. Seki Kanemitsu: Ōgai seems to have mistaken this name for Kanemoto, the sixth-generation master of the Seki family, a famous sword-making family of Akasaka in Mino during the Muromachi period. But several of the texts Ōgai used have the name Kanemitsu.

41. Masamori, a famous line of swords produced in Higo province around 1510–1520.

42. Gamō Katahide (1524–1584), a valiant warrior who served under Oda Nobunaga.

43. Yoichirō Tadataka (1580–1646).

44. Shimmen Miyamoto Musashi (1584–1645), the legendary swordsman who appears in Ōgai's "Tokō Tahei." He was called into the service of Hosokawa Tadatoshi in 1640.

GOJIINGAHARA NO KATAKIUCHI

*This story is based on a historical incident, a vendetta performed by Yamamoto Riyo at Gojiin-nibanwara near the outer bridge of Kanda in Edo on the fourteenth of the seventh month of 1835. There are several contemporary accounts, including Takizawa Bakin's *Ibun zakkō*; Ōgai generally based his acount on the *Yamamoto fukushū ki* [Record of the revenge of the Yamamoto].

† For details on the practice of vendetta in Tokugawa Japan, see Sir George Sansom, *A History of Japan, 1615–1867* (vol. 3), pp. 92–93. Sansom states that ". . . there is specific authority for this action in the Code of One Hundred Articles. . . .this document is a kind of Constitution of the warrior society. It says that a man 'must not live under the same sky as one who has injured his lord or his father' (Article 51). It goes on to state that notice must be given to the authorities of the intention to kill an offender, and that permission will be granted so long as there is no delay and so long as no rioting is involved."

1. Sakai Tadamitsu, who became daimyo of the Harima domain in 1814.

2. Referring to the Temmei famine of 1782–1787.

3. Hosokawa Okitake (correctly read Okitoku), who became lord of the domain in 1788.

4. Ogasawara Sadayoshi (correctly read Sadatoshi), the son of Sadayoshi; Sadatoshi inherited the domain in 1822.

5. The fire raged in Edo from the seventh through the twelfth days of the second month of 1834.

6. Matsudaira Muneakira, lord of the castle at Miyazu in Tango since 1805.

7. Ōkubo Tadazane (1781–1837), lord of the castle at Kodawara since 1796; he became Minister of State (*rōjū*) in the Tokugawa shogunate in 1818.

8. The three City Magistrates (*bugyō*): high shogunate officials in Edo administering the offices of City Mayor, Shrines and Temples, and Finance.

9. This was a Shinto deity.

10. Katō Kiyomasa (1559–1611), a warlord of the sixteenth century; he was a retainer of Toyotomi Hideyoshi and later appointed lord of the castle at Kumamoto.

11. Honda Tadataka, lord of the castle at Kobe in Ise province since 1803; his Edo residence was at Kandabashi.

12. Endō Tanenori, lord of the castle in Ōmi.

13. Sakai Tadanori, son of Sakai Tadamichi, the older brother of Lord Tadamitsu (see note 1 above). Tadanori had inherited the Sakai territories in the fourth month of this year (1835).

14. Nishimaru was the Western Enceinte of Edo castle, the residence of the shogun's heir.

15. *Goningumi*: a system of mutual surveillance and insurance, involving neighborhood units of five families, employed by the Tokugawa regime.

16. Tsutsui Masanori (1778-1856), a direct Tokugawa liege vassal; he became Edo City Magistrate in 1821.

17. Mizuno Tadakuni (1794-1851), lord of the castle at Hamamatsu from 1821; he became *rōjū* in 1834, and is well known for the later Tempō Reforms he carried out in 1841.

18. The cousin of the former lord, Sakai Tadamitsu.

19. Yashiro Tarō Hirokata (1758-1841), a contemporary scholar of the National Learning school.

20. Ōta Shichizaburō (1749-1823), a comic writer of the time.

SAKAI JIKEN

1. Tokugawa Yoshinobu (Keiki, 1837-1913), son of Tokugawa Nariaki of Mito. Keiki was the fifteenth and last Tokugawa shogun between 1866 and 1867. In the twelfth month of 1867, Keiki left Nijō castle in Kyoto and took up residence under domiciliary confinement at Osaka castle. Angered by the provocations of the Satsuma *han* in Edo, he mustered an army of twenty thousand men from among old shogunate troops and the soldiers of the Aizu and Kawano domains, and was about to set forth for Edo. His troops were defeated by the combined forces of the Satsuma and Chōshū domains in fierce battles waged at Fushimi and Tosa in the southern part of Kyoto on the third day of the first month of 1868. Keiki left Osaka castle and sailed by an English vessel for Edo castle on the sixth day of the same month. He accepted the emperor's terms of surrender in the fourth month of 1868.

2. Osaka, Hyōgo, and Sakai had been cities directly administered by shogunate officials (*bugyō*, "City Magistrates or Mayors") under the Tokugawa regime.

3. Sugi Kiheita and Ikoma Seiji (dates unknown).

4. Date Munenari (1818-1892).

5. At the time, only the five ports of Yokohama, Hakodate, Nagasaki, Niigata, and Hyōgo were open ports.

6. The flag was given to Tosa as an emblem of the new Imperial forces; the Matsuyama domain was an ally of the Tokugawa cause.

7. Ishikawa Ishinosuke (dates unknown).

8. Ikegami Yasakichi (1831-1868), lieutenant of the Sixth Division.

9. Ōishi Jinkichi (1831-1868), lieutenant of the Eighth Division.

10. Fukao Kanae (1827-1890).

11. Yamanouchi Toyoshige (1827-1872); lord of Tosa from 1848, he retired in 1859.

12. Leon Roche (1809-?).

13. Shinoura Inokichi (1844-1868).

14. Nishimura Saheiji (1845-1868).

15. Yamanouchi Toyonori (1846-1886), lord of Tosa from 1859; he was twenty-three at the time of the story.

16. Hosokawa Yoshiyuki (1835-1876), lord of Higo domain.

17. Asano Shigenaga (1812-1872), lord of the Hiroshima domain.

18. Prince Yamashina (1816-1898), a member of the Imperial family.

19. Higashikuse Michitomi (1833-1912); see note 4 for Date Munenari.

20. A distance of about three hundred and thirty meters.

21. The forty-seven *rōnin* performed a celebrated vendetta on behalf of their former lord, Asano, in 1702.

22. Ii Naosuke (1815–1860), who became *tairō* in 1858, was a political opponent of Tokugawa Nariaki, the lord of Mito. He signed the Japanese-American Commercial Treaty of 1858 without waiting for Imperial approval, and instituted the Ansei purge of his political opposition. His assassination by Mito clansmen was a major event of the decade in which the present story took place.

23. *Go-zannen-sama*: Those who regretfully died for the country.

24. *Ikiun-sama*: Those who were fated not to die.

SANSHŌ DAYŪ

1. Modern editors suggest that Ōgai mentioned the large quantity of religious believers in the area because during the medieval period this part of Japan was a stronghold of the Ikkō sect of Buddhism. The sect later became a strong and often belligerent political force before it was defeated in warfare in the late sixteenth century.

2. The Tōdaiji in Nara is the headquarters of the Kegon sect of Buddhism, one of the first to be imported to Japan from China and Korea. It functioned as the central temple of the provincial temple (*kokubunji*) system instituted in the Nara period.

3. Fujiwara Morozane (1042–1101) was a high court official who held several of the most important ranks. He also earned a certain reputation as a poet.

4. Kudara is the ancient Japanese name for the Korean kingdom of Paekche. In A.D. 552, the king of Paekche sent Buddhist statues and scriptures to Japan. This date is customarily taken to represent the formal introduction of Buddhism into Japan.

5. Prince Takami was a descendant of the Emperor Kammu (ruled 781–806); his son was a founder of the great family of Taira.

6. The Retired Emperor mentioned is Shirakawa (1053–1129), who abdicated the throne in 1086 and continued to supervise the reigns of several successive emperors while retaining the rank of Cloistered Emperor.

REKISHI SONO MAMA TO REKISHIBANARE

1. *Furigana* represent the *kana*, or Japanese phonetic alphabet, written beside the Chinese characters to indicate the pronunciation of a difficult or obscure word the reader might not be expected to know. In Ōgai's time, *furigana* were often added to all the Chinese characters used in works of fiction. Such was evidently the case here.

2. Ōgai gives two examples. The word for head rifleman once was given the pronunciation *teppōgashira* and once *teppō no kami*. Both would be possible pronunciations, but consistency is necessary to avoid confusing the reader. In the second case, the castle at Matera was given the reading of Sora, a possible alternate reading.

3. A play Ōgai wrote in 1904.

4. Nichiren's famous work, *Risshō ankoku ron*. For a description of the text, see

W. T. de Bary, *Sources of Japanese Tradition* (New York: Columbia University Press, 1958), pp. 223-224.

    5. A reference to one of the kabuki troupes of Ichikawa Danjūrō IX (1838-1903), the greatest actor of the Meiji period. His predecessors appear in *"Saiki Kōi,"* a biography Ōgai wrote in 1917.

    6. Present-day Fukushima prefecture.

    7. A reference to the *Wamyō ruijushō*, a compilation completed around 934. Modern linguistics scholars consider it the most accurate source for ancient pronunciations. For a description of the dictionary, see Roy A. Miller, *The Japanese Language* (Chicago: University of Chicago Press, 1967), pp. 120-121.

    8. Fujiwara no Motozane (1143-1166).

    9. See note 3 in *"Sanshō dayū."*

    10. Masakado (?-940) was a famous rebel and general in the Heian period.

GYOGENKI

    1. Yü Hsüan-chi (843[?]-868), also known as Yü-wei and Hui-lan, was a poetess of the late T'ang dynasty in China.

    2. Li was the family name of Lao-tzu, the first Taoist sage and reputed author of the *Tao Te Ching*. Li was the family name of Kao-tsu, the founder of the T'ang. Emperor Kao-tsu himself disliked Taoism and attempted to suppress it. The Taoists only won imperial favor from the time of the third T'ang emperor, Kao-tsung.

    3. I-tsung (833-872), the seventeenth T'ang emperor.

    4. Li Po (701-762) and Tu Fu (712-770), the two most famous names among early T'ang poets.

    5. Po Chü-i (772-846).

    6. Yüan Wei-chih (779-831).

    7. Ling Hu-t'ao (795-872).

    8. Chung-k'uei: a hero of the T'ang dynasty deified as a protector against demons; in sculpture he was represented as a demon queller with a terribly wrathful face.

    9. Wen T'ing-yin (dates uncertain).

    10. Li Shang-yin (813-858).

    11. Tuan Ch'eng-shih (?-863).

    12. Pai-le, a legendary horse expert.

    13. *Chin-shih*, literally "presented scholars," the highest examination in the national examination system.

    14. *Chuang-tzu*, one of the ancient classics of Taoism.

    15. Hsüan-tsung (810-859), the sixteenth T'ang emperor.

    16. The exact nature of this practice is unclear.

    17. The nature of this practice is also unclear. It has been conjectured to have consisted in some form of joint practice between male and female.

    18. Sung Yü, a poet in the kingdom of Ch'ü during the Warring States period. He was a disciple of the famous poet Ch'u Yüan who wrote *Li Sao*. He also wrote *fu* and a work called *Kao-t'ang*. According to the prefaces to these *fu* in the *Wen-hsüan*, the *Kao-t'ang* tells the story of the meeting of King Hsiang of Ch'ü and the goddess of Wu-shan. Once Sung Yü accompanied the king on a trip to the Yun-

meng Lake. When the king asked Sung where the mists and clouds came from, Sung answered that they signified the presence of the goddess who "appeared as the morning clouds at dawn and became the pouring rain at dusk." The king then ordered Sung to write a *fu* about her. The goddess came to the king the same night while he was sleeping. Later, the names Wu-shan and Kao-t'ang were used as symbolic of the places where lovers met, and "the clouds and rain" of the sexual act.

19. Wang Ch'ang (?-375?), a name appearing frequently in T'ang poetry. His real identity is unknown. He was generally regarded as the symbol of an ideal husband.

20. *Tui-shih*, a phrase for the husband and wife relationship between lesbians; it apparently originated in the Han palace where court ladies became attached to each other (cf. *Han shu, wai-chi chüan*).

21. In Chinese, the character *p'in* in Ts'ai-p'in's name means duckweed; the character *hui* in Hui-lan means orchid.

22. For this allusion, see note 18.

23. "Orchid" is Yü Hsüan-chi's reference to herself; see note 21.

JIISAN BAASAN

1. Matsudaira Sashichirō (?-1827).
2. Ienari (1773-1841), the eleventh Tokugawa shogun.
3. Ieyoshi (1793-1853), who became the twelfth Tokugawa shogun in 1837.
4. Rakumiya (1795-1840).
5. Arisugawa Yorihito (correctly read Orihito, 1753-1820).
6. Toda Ujiyuki (1734-1771), daimyo of Mino and Nomura *han*.
7. Matsudaira Munekatsu (?-1761) was the eighth daimyo of the Owari *han*.
8. Matsudaira Munechika (1753-1799), the ninth daimyo of Owari.
9. Arima Masazumi (1747-1772).
10. Matsudaira Haruyuki (1752-1781).
11. Toda Ujiyasu (1758-1793).
12. Harutaka (1754-1782); Naritaka (1777-1795); Narikiyo (1795-1851).

SAIGO NO IKKU

1. Inagaki Tanenobu (1634-1763); he served as the Osaka City Magistrate from 1729-1740.
2. Sasa Narimune (1690-1746), the Osaka City Magistrate from 1737-1744.
3. Ōda Sukenaru (1695-1740), daimyo of Bitchū; appointed Keeper of Osaka castle for the period 1734-1740.
4. Emperor Higashiyama (1675-1706), who ascended the throne in 1687.
5. Emperor Sakuramachi (1720-1750), who ascended the throne in 1735.

TAKASEBUNE

1. Better known as Matsudaira Sadanobu (1758-1829). The Kansei period was from 1789 to 1801.
2. *Gosekku*: the five feasts of 1 January, 3 March, 5 May, 7 July, and 9 September.

3. A special day for children 3, 5, and 7 years old.

4. Suminokura Ryōi (1554-1614).

5. *Okinagusa*: a two-hundred-page volume of stories and anecdotes compiled by Kamizawa Teikan, and revised and published by Ikebe Yoshikata in 1906.

6. Ikebe Yoshikata (1864-1923), scholar and poet.

KANZAN JITTOKU

*Both Gary Snyder and Burton Watson have made translations. In addition, Burton Watson includes in his volume, *Cold Mountain* (Columbia University Press, 1970), a partial translation of the only record of an actual meeting with Han-shan, supposedly written by Lü Ch'iu-yin himself, the chief character in Ōgai's story. Ōgai made use of the same record.

1. 624-649.

2. Yoshida Tōgo (1864-1918) was a historian, professor of Waseda University, and Meiji writer on political subjects. After the Sino-Japanese war, his Japanese geographical dictionary became the standard reference text on this subject.

3. Buddha's attendant on the right, mounted on a white elephant. He is supposed to typify the teaching, meditation, and practice of the Buddha.

4. Buddha's attendant on the left, mounted on a lion. He is the personification of the wisdom of the Buddha.

5. A Chinese *li* was a measure of length reckoned at 360 paces, or about 1,890 feet English measure. *Ri* refers to a Japanese league, equivalent to 2.44 miles.

6. Chih-I (538-597), founder of the T'ien-t'ai school of Buddhism in China.

7. Statue of Piṇḍola-bharadvaja (Japanese: Binzuru Sonja).

8. Miyazaki Toranosuke (dates uncertain) published *Waga fukuin* [My gospel] in 1904 and proclaimed himself the third prophet after Buddha and Christ. He preached his gospel in the Kanda area of Tokyo in Sunday services held in a church he built there in 1907, gaining fame for a while as a self-proclaimed messiah.

SAHASHI JINGORŌ

1. Sōtsushima no kami Yoshitoshi (1568-1615).

2. Ieyasu (1542-1616), the first Tokugawa shogun.

3. Tokugawa Hidetada (1579-1623), Ieyasu's son, who followed him as shogun in 1610.

4. Honda Masazumi (1565-1637), one of Ieyasu's closest retainers since his youth.

5. In 1570, thirty-seven years before the first section of the story.

6. Nobuyasu (1559-1579), son of Ieyasu and elder brother of Hidetada. In 1567 he was married to a daughter of Oda Nobunaga (1534-1582). He later incurred Nobunaga's wrath and was ordered to commit suicide in 1579, as indicated in the story.

7. Takeda Katsuyori (1546-1582) was involved with Ieyasu in several battles over territorial and clan rights. After several defeats he eventually committed suicide and so ended the activities of his important clan.

8. Uesugi Kenshi (1530-1578) and Takeda Shingen (1521-1573), two of the most brilliant warriors in the period prior to the reunification of Japan under Tokugawa

Ieyasu. Accounts of the battles between these two rivals for power are well known in popular Japanese historical literature.

9. Ogimaru (1574–1607).

10. On a false charge that he and his mother, Lady Tsukiyama, were plotting with Takeda Katsuyori against Ieyasu. For a full account of the incident, see A. L. Sadler, *The Maker of Modern Japan* (London: Allen and Unwin, 1937), pp. 92–96.

11. Fukumatsumaru (1580–1607).

12. Akechi Mitsuhide (1528–1582) was a retainer of Oda Nobunaga, the first great general of the Sengoku period. He suddenly revolted and killed Nobunaga, throwing into disaster the whole military campaign mounted by Nobunaga to unify the country. Ieyasu and Hideyoshi, allies of Nobunaga, were forced to change their plans in order to put down Mitsuhide's forces. Hideyoshi quickly made peace with his enemies in southern Japan, the Mōri family, so that he could return north as quickly as possible.

13. Honda Tadakatsu (1528–1610) was a warrior who fought with Ieyasu in more than fifty battles. Ieyasu always praised his valor. Chaya Shirōjirō (1542–1596) was a retainer of Ieyasu who later became a trader and, with permission from Hideyoshi, traded with Annam. He was later purveyor to the Tokugawa family. On this particular incident concerning Ieyasu's attempt to attack Mitsuhide, Sadler writes that ". . . they went on by the country roads, Honda Tadakatsu brandishing his halberd 'Dragon-fly Cutter' in the faces of the rustics with a view to eliciting reliable information about the route, and Chaya Shirōjirō distributing money generously with the same purpose. Both were apparently effective in their fashion." (*The Maker of Modern Japan*, pp. 114–115)

14. Hōjō Ujinao (1562–1591) was the head of his clan in Odawara. Taking advantage of the political confusion brought about by the death of Oda Nobunaga, he tried to extend his power but was put down by Ieyasu, with whom he reached a compromise by marrying one of Ieyasu's daughters. (This incident also figures in the present story.) Ujinao's later schemes against Hideyoshi are of equal historical interest, but are not taken up by Ōgai in the present narrative.

15. Mizuno Katsunari (1563–1651) was the son of Mizuno Tadashige (1541–1600), a warrior who served Hideyoshi in several important capacities. Katsunari himself was much favored by Tokugawa Ieyasu later in life.

16. The book referred to here by Ōgai has not been properly identified by later editors. There are, however, a number of similar accounts in historical records of the period.

17. The Ikkō sect of Jōdo Shinshū Buddhism was involved in a series of armed uprisings at the time of the events taking place in this story. The stronghold of the sect was in Osaka.

18. A collection of historical essays and stories written in 1821.

19. Kakehi Matazō (1526–1560).

20. The *Kanshirai heiki* was a record of diplomatic exchanges between Japan and Korea compiled by Hayashi Shunsai (1618–1680), a distinguished Confucian scholar and the third son of Hayashi Razan (1538–1657), the well-known Confucian advisor to Tokugawa Ieyasu.

YASUI FUJIN

*Kafū quotes this old Tokugawa text in his short novel *A Strange Tale from East of the River,* translated in Edwin Seidensticker's *Kafu the Scribbler* (Stanford: Stanford University Press, 1965).

1. Shinozaki Shōchiku (1781–1851) was a scholar of the school of Ogyū Sorai, the eighteenth-century Confucian philosopher. Shinozaki ran a private school in Osaka in the early nineteenth century that attracted a variety of talented pupils. He was noted also for his Chinese poetry and calligraphy. Chūhei's father Sōshū (1767–1835) had studied in the Sorai school.

2. The Shōheikō was the official Confucian college of the shogunate in Edo.

3. Koga Tōan (1788–1837) was another Confucian scholar in Edo.

4. Matsuzaki Kōdō (1771–1844) was an expert on the Confucian classics and wrote commentaries on the Analects of Confucius. He was a student of Hayashi Jitsuzai (see note 5, below) and later served the lord of Kakegawa as an advisor.

5. Hayashi Jitsuzai (1768–1841) was appointed head of the Confucian college and compiler of the history of the Tokugawa family at the request of the shogun, Tokugawa Ienari (1773–1841).

6. A joking reference to Ono no Komachi, the famous ninth-century beauty and poetess.

7. These dolls represent an old man and old woman who symbolize long life and supposedly the spirits of the pine forest of Takasago. Their story is told in a Noh play of that name.

8. Shionoya Tōin (1809–1867) was a Confucian scholar who studied at the Edo Confucian college and later served the lord of Hamamatsu.

9. The Sankei Juku was Yasui Sokken's private school. The name, literally "Three Plans School," derives from Yasui's dictum that one must plan the day's work in the morning, the year's work during the New Year period, and one's life work when a young man.

10. Kajimaya Seibē was a wealthy sake dealer in the Shinagawa area of Edo; he studied with Nishijima Ran'en, a noted scholar. He was reputed to have amassed a large library.

11. The Master of Ceremonies (*Sōsha*) had as his office the duty to announce the family lineage and the gifts presented by the various feudal lords paying formal homage to the shogun in the Edo castle. He also took charge of the coming-of-age ceremonies and other similar official functions for the shogun.

12. The Recording Secretary (*Oshiaikata*) had as his office the duty to record the visitations of the various feudal lords to Edo castle.

13. The *Chin-wên shang-shu* is a compilation of ancient Chinese documents said to have been revised by Confucius. The collection survived the burning of the books by the first emperor of the Ch'in dynasty about 200 B.C. and was written in the new ideographic characters formalized in the Han dynasty.

14. Fujita Tōko (1806–1855) was a Confucian scholar in charge of compiling the Mito clan history of Japan. He was killed in an earthquake in Edo in 1855. He was an advisor to Tokugawa Nariaki (see note 15, below).

15. A reference to Tokugawa Nariaki (1800–1861), lord of Mito, one of the most

prominent figures in politics at the time of Perry's visit to Japan; he was closely involved in events leading to the Meiji Restoration.

16. Ii Naosuke (1815–1860), the lord of Hikone, supported the shogun against the resurgence of the emperor's forces. He was assassinated at the Sakurada Gate of the shogun's castle in Edo by imperialist samurai from Mito.

17. Nakamura Teitarō (1827–1861) was involved in various plots with the insurrectionist and politician Kiyokawa Hachirō (1830–1863) in a plot to overthrow the government. Both were eventually executed.

18. Kumoi Tatsuo (1844–1870) was a disciple of Yasui Sokken who tried to defend the shogunate against the Imperial Court. At the time of the restoration he plotted to try to separate the imperialist alliance between the clans of Satsuma and Chōshū. He managed to raise troops and fought the government's army at Utsunomiya. He was betrayed by one of his own men in 1869 and was executed in 1870.

19. The *Tso Chuan* [Tso commentary] is a famous Chinese historical classic that purports to explain the Spring and Autumn Annals of Confucius. It was written in the third century B.C.

TSUGE SHIRŌZAEMON

*In his essay "Rekishi sono mama to rekishibanare," in *The Incident at Sakai and Other Stories*, volume 1 of The Historical Literature of Mori Ōgai, edited by David Dilworth and J. Thomas Rimer (Honolulu: The University Press of Hawaii, 1977).

1. Yokoi Heishirō (1809–1869), scholar and statesman of the late Tokugawa period. Shōnan was another of Yokoi's names. Tsuge Shirōzaemon's dates are 1848–1870.

2. "The men of wisdom" refers to such men as Shimazu Hisamatsu (1817–1887), Shimazu Nariakira (1809–1858), Yoshida Shōin (1831–1859), and Arima Shinshichi (1826–1862).

3. Motoda Eifū (1818–1891), a scholar of Chinese classics and Confucianism; later the tutor to the Meiji emperor.

4. Ikebe Keita (1798–1868) and Takashima Shūhan (1798–1866) were arrested on the charge that they criticized the shogunate's closed-door policy and imprisoned in 1842; Ikebe stayed in prison for five years, Takashima eleven years.

5. Euphimi Vasilievich Putiatin (1803–1883).

6. Yoshida Shōin (1831–1859) was later imprisoned in 1854 for attempting to board an American ship in order to sail overseas and learn firsthand the situation abroad.

7. Katsu Yoshikuni (1823–1899) studied naval warfare under Dutch instructors, was commander of the *Kanrin maru* on its trip to America, later was appointed commander-in-chief of the armed forces, in 1872 was Minister of the Navy, and in 1873 became Member of the Senate and Privy Councillor, and was given the title of viscount.

8. Saheita (1845–1875) traveled to America twice; his first trip was from 1866 to 1872. Tahei (1850–1871) curtailed his trip because of tuberculosis and returned to Japan in 1869; he died within two years, while establishing an English school in Kumamoto. Both men changed their names because overseas trips were then still legally forbidden.

9. Inoue Kowashi (1843–1895). Iwakura Tomomi (1825–1883) and Tamamatsu Misao (1810–1872) together plotted restoration of the imperial regime. Inoue and Iwakura were prominent statesmen around the time of the Meiji Restoration. Goin was a pen name of Inoue; *Goin zankō* is a posthumous collection of Inoue's manuscripts, letters, diaries, and so forth.

10. Iwakura-mura, the residence of Iwakura Tomomi in present-day Sakyō-ku in Kyoto. A steady stream of visitors passed through the secret back door.

11. Iki Wakasa (1818–1886), better known as Iki Tadazumi, was so respected for his military expertise that, when Perry landed at Uraga, Iki was entrusted with the defense of strategic points on the land. After the Meiji Restoration he declined a request that he join the Meiji government, preferring to maintain law and order in his own Okayama clan.

12. Ukita Naoie (1529–1581), a warlord of the Sengoku period.

13. The Ikeda were the hereditary daimyo of the Okayama *han* with holdings worth 520,000 *koku* annually. That Chiyo was privileged to ride a palanquin indicates her high status with the Ikeda.

14. The Chinese official Ch'in Kuai of the Southern Sung dynasty, through whom the celebrated patriot Yüan Fei was executed; considered a traitor for having worked for peace with the Tartars, who had invaded Chinese territory.

15. Abe Morie (1846–1907), one of the most renowned swordmasters in his day.

16. The Japanese did not adopt the Western calendar until 1872; in this translation, all dates prior to the change are given as here: "the second month," which does not necessarily correspond to February.

17. Tokugawa Keiki (1837–1913), the fifteenth and last shogun.

18. Kagawa Keizō (1839–1915), Kawada Sakuma (1829–1897), and Katsura Kogorō (1834–1877) were all staunch imperial loyalists. Katsura was later known as Kido Takayoshi (Kōin).

19. Matsumoto Minosuke: dates unknown.

20. Noro Katsunoshin: dates unknown.

21. Itakura Katsukiyo (1822–1889), lord of the Matsuyama *han* and defender of the shogunate cause; eventually defeated by imperial forces, he was imprisoned, later pardoned, and finally allowed to become a priest at the Tōshōgū Shrine in Nikkō.

22. Fujishima Masanoshin: dates unknown.

23. Iki Takumi: dates unknown.

24. Ueda Tatsuo (1830–1870), second son of a rural samurai in Iwami province; an imperial loyalist.

25. *Banki-isshin*, literally "complete renewal of the entire government," a slogan of the imperial restorationists.

26. *Chōshi*: term used to designate those outstanding men who in 1868 were specially selected by the Cabinet (see no. 39 below) to serve as councillors or bureau heads.

27. Bureau of Institutions: an organ set up to study and reorganize government institutions.

28. Matsudaira Yoshinaga (1828–1890), also called Shungaku, lord of Fukui *han* and patron of Yokoi.

29. Ōkubo Kaname (1798-1859), steward of Tsuchiya Tomonao. The incident mentioned here is conjectured to have taken place in the fifth month of 1851.

30. Warden of Osaka castle, Tsuchiya Tomonao; he held this position from late 1850 until late 1858.

31. Fujita Seinoshin (1806-1855), also known by his pen name, Tōko.

32. Mito Nariaki (1800-1860), a member of the Tokugawa family and lord of the Mito domain; he was a staunch imperial loyalist who figured prominently in pre-Restoration politics.

33. Tsuzuki Shirō, Yoshida Heinosuke: retainers of the Hosokawa domain, dates unknown.

34. Yanagida Tokuzō (1845-1869); correct name is Chokuzō.

35. Kashima Matanojō (1846-1870).

36. Maeoka Rikio (1844-1870); Nakai Toneo (dates unknown), conjectured to have been twenty-four or twenty-five at this time.

37. Miyake Tenzen (1818-1882), rabidly antiforeign and pro-emperor, he finally was sentenced to life imprisonment in 1871.

38. The "seven" includes Miyake, at whose house the other six were staying.

39. This translates dajōkan, the highest government organ in the land, set up in 1868 and abolished in 1885.

40. Teramachi, Goryōsha; the former designates a street, the latter a shrine, both of which are still to be found in Kyoto.

41. Yokoyama Sukenojō, Shimotsu Shikanosuke: dates unknown.

42. Ueno Yūjirō, Matsumura Kinzaburō: dates unknown.

43. Miyake Sakon (Sahei): dates unknown. Saga is the northern part of Ukyō-ku, present-day Kyoto.

44. Naka Zuiunsai: dates unknown.

45. Kanamoto Kenzō, etc.: little is known about these men, except for Kanamoto (1829-1871), who was sentenced to strict confinement for three years and died in prison.

46. Kaima Jūrōzaemon (1818-1873), whose zeal for the imperial cause ultimately led to excesses that earned him imprisonment.

47. "The popular lampoons" refer to anonymous satirical poems making the rounds then; for example, one went: "*Massugu ni ikeba ii no ni, Heishirō Yokoi iku kara kubi ga korori to*" ("It would be better to go straight, yet Heishirō goes to the side, so his head bites the dust")—there is a pun on Yokoi and *yoko e* (to the side).

48. Referring to the famous assassination by Mito clansmen of Ii Naosuke at the Sakurada gate of Edo castle in 1860.

49. The Danjodai, established in 1869. It was merged with the Ministry of Justice in 1871.

50. Kondō Jūbē: dates unknown.

51. Tokura Sazen, Saitō Naohiko: dates unknown.

52. Nihoko (1835-1881): more details about her will appear in the material appended by Ōgai to his original story.

53. Niwa Hiroo, Suzuki Muin: dates unknown.

54. Sugi Magoshichirō (1835-1920), Aoki Umesaburō (1873-?), Nakaoka Moku (1848-?), Tokutomi Iichirō (1863-1957), Shimizu Koichirō (1854-1932), Yamabe Takeo (1851-1920).

55. "Imperial Bodyguards Affair" refers to the attempt in 1868 to form a band of men who would protect the emperor's person; Naka Zuiunsai and Totsugawa samurai formed the majority of the band. Yokoi was instrumental in thwarting their efforts.

56. The Negoro family was descended from the Fujiwara clan; their ancestors had served under Tokugawa Ieyasu, and became *hatamoto* of the shogun.

57. Miya Taichū (dates unknown), a Confucian doctor. Kamihira Chikara (1824–1891) was given special pardon in 1878 because of his medical services to the island's inhabitants.

58. Ichinose Tonomo: dates unknown.

59. Kanda Kōhei (1830–1899), scholar of Dutch learning and later politician and baron.

60. Nakai Hiroshi (1838–1894), a learned politician and prolific writer.

61. Koga Jūrō (date unknown), head of the police in the Justice Department.

62. Minami Jun'ichi; both he and the work mentioned here are now unknown.

63. Osatake Takeshi (1880–1946), historian of Meiji times and culture.

64. Arakawa Jinsaku (1840–1901); Wakae Shuridaibu (1812–1872).

65. Tanaka Fujimaro (1846–1909), politician with a long record for distinguished service, for which he was made a viscount.

66. Niwa Juntarō (1846–1922), another high-ranking politician in Meiji times.

67. Matsuyama Yoshine: dates unknown.

68. Yashirō Rokurō (1860–1930).

69. Tsuji Shinji (1842–1915), scholar of Dutch learning and of Buddhism; nothing is known about Gotō Kenkichi.

70. The Kaisei Gakkō was formerly the Bakufu's *Bansho shirabe sho* ("Translation Bureau of Foreign Books"); it later was incorporated as Tokyo Imperial University in 1877.

71. Mimaki Motoyoshi: dates unknown.

72. Empress Shōken (1850–1914), wife of the Meiji emperor.

73. Honda Tatsujirō: dates unknown.

74. This is the Shoryō-ryō, a part of the old Imperial Household Agency. Its function was the maintenance and care of imperial tombs, and the surveying of sites thought to be imperial tombs.

75. Shiba Katsushige (1880–1955), member of the Imperial Household Agency.

76. *Jige-kaden*: a book in thirty-three volumes completed in 1844, it gives the family histories of those of fourth rank and below.

77. Tanimori Tanematsu (1817–1911).

78. Suzuki Katsunori: dates unknown.

79. Toda Tadayoshi (1832–1899).

80. Hashimoto Saneyoshi (dates unknown), a fanatical imperial loyalist.

81. Ueda Keiji's biography of Empress Shōken appeared in 1914.

KURIYAMA DAIZEN

1. Kuroda Tadayuki (1602–1654); he inherited his father Nagamasa's domain evaluated at 520,000 *koku* in 1623.

2. Kuriyama Daizen Toshiaki (1591–1652) was a high retainer of the Kuroda family with a stipend of 23,000 *koku*. He was forty-two at this time.

3. Takenaka Unemenoshō Shigeyoshi (?–1634), daimyo of Bingo.

4. Inoue Yukifusa (1554–1634).

5. Kuroda Mimasaku (1571–1656).

6. Kuroda Nagamasa (1568–1623).

7. Hoshina (1585–1635).

8. Toku (1606–1625).

9. Inuman (1610–1665).

10. Mankichi (1612–1639).

11. Kurimoto Toshiyasu (1549–1631).

12. Kuroda Yoshitaka (1546–1604).

13. Araki Murashige (?–1586), a powerful warrior, was an early ally of Oda Nobunaga and aided him in unifying the country. In 1578, however, he had a falling out with Oda, who attacked his castle at Itami and massacred most of his followers. Araki escaped and lived in retirement as a priest. Later, after Oda's death, he was befriended by Oda's successor, Toyotomi Hideyoshi.

14. Takikawa Kazumasu (1525–1586) was a celebrated military strategist who served Oda Nobunaga in a variety of battles such as the one for the castle of Arioka. Later he served Hideyoshi and upheld his claims against those of the Tokugawa family; when Hideyoshi's family forces were defeated he retired to a temple in Kyoto.

15. Akechi Mitsuhide (1528–1582) killed Oda Nobunaga in the Honnōji temple in Kyoto; fleeing, he was killed himself in an ambush shortly after. Akechi had been a retainer of some importance to Oda, and his deed had profound implications for the history of Japan, since he indirectly brought about the rise of Hideyoshi and Tokugawa Ieyasu.

16. Uesugi Kagekatsu (1555–1622) was one of the major advisors of Hideyoshi. In the battle of Sekigahara (1600) in which Tokugawa Ieyasu emerged victorious, those who supported forces loyal to Hideyoshi's family were defeated and Japan was finally united under the Tokugawa family. Uesugi, who sided with Hideyoshi's family, was defeated by Ieyasu, subsequent to the battle at Aizu, and was sent into retirement with a much-reduced stipend.

17. Ishida Mitsunari (1560–1600) sided with Uesugi Kagekatsu against Tokugawa Ieyasu. He was also defeated at the battle of Sekigahara, then beheaded. Thus the friendly daimyo are those who stood against the Tokugawa family, and supported the forces of the family of Hideyoshi.

18. Kushibashi (1553–1627).

19. Tōjō Nagayori (1577–1631).

20. An ally of Tokugawa Ieyasu.

21. Hosokawa Tadaoki (1563–1645) sided with the Tokugawa forces after the death of Hideyoshi in 1598. Thus the forces fighting for the family of Hideyoshi want to take his wife Gracia (one of the most well-known of the early Christian converts) a prisoner as well. As Ōgai relates, she refused and committed suicide. The incident is a famous one, but Ōgai does not dwell on the details.

22. Akechi Gracia (1564–1600); see note 21.

23. Katō Kiyomasa (1562–1611) was another famous general who, after Hideyoshi's death, sided with the Tokugawa forces.

24. The fall of Osaka castle during the summer campaign marked the end of the power of the family of Hideyoshi. Hideyori, Hideyoshi's son and heir, committed suicide and the family was extinguished. Ieyasu was now undisputed ruler of Japan.

25. Kame (1616–1646).

26. Ukiyo Matabē (1578–1650).

27. Doi Toshikatsu (1573–1644) was a distinguished member of the Tokugawa government, who served Tokugawa Hidetada and Tokugawa Iemitsu. He was considered one of the finest men in the public life of his time.

28. Muroga Masatoshi (1610–1681).

29. Katō Tadahiro (1598–1653) was the son of a celebrated warrior and ally of Toyotomi Hideyoshi, Katō Kiyomasa, who was made lord of Kumano castle in 1600. Tadahiro took over his father's estates while still a young man and allowed a series of quarrels to develop among his retainers. He was officially reprimanded by the shogun, then later called to Edo and exiled. At this point he allegedly tried to take a young son out of Edo illegally, with the results indicated in the story.

30. Abe Shigetsugu (1598–1651).

31. Naruse Masatora (1594–1663).

32. Andō Tatewaki Naotsugu (1554–1635).

33. Takiguchi: dates unknown.

34. Ōgai provides a long list of fortifications and the names of those who planned to man them. The information is impressive in that it shows the extent of the preparations made, but it has not been translated.

35. Ōgai has provided a list of all the high officials in attendance. The names of those who feature in the story are later translated and identified, but the list is not reproduced here.

36. Inoue Awaji no kami Mochina (1593–1642).

37. Sakai Tadakatsu (1587–1662), like Andō, Ii, Doi, and the others, was a principal retainer of the Tokugawa family.

38. Nambu Shigenao was the daimyo of the important northern province of Iwate (Mutsu); his family had served both Hideyoshi and Ieyasu with great distinction. His ancestor Nambu Nobunao (1546–1599) helped secure the northern provinces for Hideyoshi.

39. The famous battle caused by the misrule of the lord of the Shimabara clan, Matsukura Shigemasa. The final results involved the merciless persecution of the Christians all over Japan.

40. At the orders of the Tokugawa shogunate, to prevent any possible fortifications that could be used as rallying points for future rebellions.

41. The so-called Seven Military Classics from ancient China, written by (or attributed to) such important figures in the early dynasties as Sun Tzu, Ch'i Wei-liao, Huang Shih-kung, T'ai Kung, and others.

SUGINOHARA SHINA

*For a fairly complete and accessible account of the main historical events involved, see Sir George Sansom, A History of Japan, (Stanford: Stanford University Press, 1959), vol. 3, pp. 63–67.

1. The ceremony to which Ōgai was invited took place in November 1915. "Suginohara Shina" was published only two months later, in January 1916.
2. Ōtsuki Fumihiko (1847–1928), a scholar of Japanese linguistics. Ōgai based this story on Ōtsuki's *Date sōdō jitsuroku* [Record of the Date disturbances].
3. "Ōshūbanashi" [Tale of Ōshū], date uncertain. An 1832 revision by Takizawa Bakin (1767–1848), the late Tokugawa novelist, was included in his *Onchi gyōsho*, a collection of strange tales and ghost stories of Ōshū, under the title of "Takao ga koto."
4. Ayako (1765–1825) gained a reputation for a time as a student of Japanese literature and a poetess.
5. Date Tsunamune (1640–1711), third lord of the Sendai domain.
6. Date Tadamune (1589–1658), second lord of Sendai.
7. Kamechiyo (1659–1719).
8. Date Munekatsu (1621–1679), the younger brother of Lord Tadamune.
9. Ichi no kami Muneoki (1649–1702).
10. Harada Kai (1617–1671), a high retainer in the Sendai domain, was involved in a plot with Tsunamune's uncle, Date Munekatsu, to have the young Tsunamune put under domiciliary confinement and to have his heir, Kamechiyo, inherit the Sendai domain, with the idea of taking it over. Date Aki pressed a legal suit against Harada Kai with the Tokugawa shogunate in Edo in 1671. When confronted by Aki in the mansion of the shogunate councillor, Sakai Tadakiyo (1623–1681), Kai cut down Aki with his sword, and was himself killed by the Edo City Magistrate, Shimada Tadamasa.
11. Misawa Hatsuko (1640–1689).
12. Shina (1639–1716).
13. Rokusonnō Tsunemoto (917–961), the progenitor of the Seiwa Genji family.
14. Amako Yoshihisa (?–1610), a warlord of the Sengoku period.
15. Mōri Terumoto (1553–1625), a famous warlord of Kyushu who had clashed in battle with Oda Nobunaga and Toyotomi Hideyoshi; he later was reconciled with Hideyoshi and distinguished himself in the Korean campaigns.
16. Gonnosuke Kiyonaga (1598–1651).
17. Hosokawa Tadaoki (1564–1645), general of the Azuchi-Momoyama period; he served both Nobunaga and Hideyoshi, but later joined forces with Tokugawa Ieyasu at the battle of Sekigahara in 1600, and, as a consequence, was enfeoffed with the provinces of Hizen and Higo. He figures in Ōgai's "Abe ichizoku," "Kuriyama Daizen," and "Tokō Tahei."
18. Furihime (1607–1659).
19. Ikeda Terumasa (1564–1613), a warlord of the Azuchi-Momoyama period. He served both Nobunaga and Hideyoshi, later joined with Ieyasu at the battle of Sekigahara, and became the lord of Himeji castle.
20. Kaihime (1612–1642).
21. Kushige Takamune (1582–1613), a court aristocrat of the Shijō line of the northern Fujiwara family. He received the name Kushige when he became the maternal grandfather of Emperor Gosai.
22. Emperor Gosai-in (1637–1685), the one hundred eleventh Japanese emperor, who reigned 1656–1663. His name was formally ruled to be Gosai tennō in 1916. Mikushige no Tsubone (1604–1685) was a Fujiwara.

23. Akamatsu Norifusa (?-1600).

24. *Yukisusuki*, a kind of pampas grass.

25. Date Aki (1615-1671); see note 10 above.

26. See note 10 above.

27. Tachibana Tadashige (1612-1675), lord of the castle at Yanagigawa in Chikugo.

28. Tokugawa Ietsuna (1641-1680), the fourth shogun.

29. Toba (1620-1684); also called Biwako.

30. *Onibanshū*, literally, vassals who protect the lord against the devils (that is, poisoning).

31. Itō Uneme (1650-1669).

32. Itō Shinzaemon (1631-1663).

33. Date Shikibu (1640-1670).

34. Date Kunai Shōyū, who was Date Munesumi, the fourth son of Hidemune, the heir of Date Masamune.

TOKŌ TAHEI

1. The Hosokawa family, a clan prominent in Japan since the Muromachi period, was closely allied with the forces of Tokugawa Ieyasu in the battle of Sekigahara in 1600. Their territories were in Kyushu. Tadatoshi (1586-1641) and his son Mitsuhisa (1619-1649) appear in the opening pages of Ōgai's "Abe ichizoku."

2. The Ōtomo family was another clan located in Kyushu that held great power at the time of Toyotomi Hideyoshi. Ōtomo Yoshimune (1558-1605), mentioned in the text, fought in the Korean campaigns with Hideyoshi but through an act of cowardice was exiled and died in disgrace, in 1605.

3. The Shimabara Rebellion (1637-1638) was a famous insurrection over local misrule in which Japanese Christians were implicated. The Christians in the area of Shimabara in the province of Hizen revolted and were eventually driven into the abandoned Hara castle. Hosokawa Tadatoshi's forces led the attack against the castle. The insurrection was put down, Christianity cruelly suppressed, and Japan's contact with the outside world was sharply cut down.

4. Miyamoto Musashi (1584-1645) was a famous fencing master, student of Zen, and painter. A legend in his own lifetime as well as in the modern Japanese cinema, he traveled throughout Japan engaging in various matches with other well-known swordsmen. A man of extremely independent character, he cared little for public office and devoted himself to the perfection of mental discipline. For the connection between Zen and swordsmanship, see D. T. Suzuki, *Zen and Japanese Culture* (New York: Pantheon Books, 1959).

5. Hosokawa Tadaoki (1563-1645) was a staunch supporter of the Toyotomi family, and, after the death of Hideyoshi, of Tokugawa Ieyasu, for whom he performed a variety of distinguished military exploits. The family rose to its pinnacle of political importance during his lifetime. Tadaoki (Sansai) was the father of Tadatoshi and the grandfather of Mitsuhisa (see note 1 above).

6. Sasaki Kojirō, also known as Sasaki Ganryū (active about 1600), was another famous swordsman who traveled about the country participating in fencing matches.

The match he fought with Musashi, mentioned in the text, was such a celebrated one that the island where it took place was given Sasaki's name, Ganryū. Legend has it that Sasaki was killed by Musashi in another duel fought soon after that time.

7. Shimmen Munisai (active in the late sixteenth century), the father of Musashi, was another famous swordsman around whom many legends have clustered. He remains a prominent figure in modern popular fiction.

8. Ganryū Island is located on the coast of Hizen Province. See note 6 above.

9. The Osaka Winter and Summer Campaigns were waged by Tokugawa Ieyasu in 1614 and 1615 against the followers of the Toyotomi family. With the surrender of Osaka castle after a prolonged siege, Ieyasu emerged the undisputed ruler of Japan.

10. Ogasawara Tadazane (1596–1667), daimyo of Kokura.

11. Bodhidharma (sometimes abbreviated as Daruma) was an Indian mystic who came to China, according to tradition, in A.D. 520 and introduced there what is known as Ch'an Buddhism (Zen in Japan). Pictures of him were often painted by Japanese Zen priests, and Ōgai is doubtless suggesting that Musashi painted the picture shown him by the Tokō family. A picture of Daruma painted by Musashi is reproduced in Suzuki's *Zen and Japanese Culture*.

12. The Yagyū school of swordsmanship, founded by Yagyū Muneyoshi in the late sixteenth century, was adopted by Tokugawa Ieyasu and his successors as the official method to be used in training government officials. Tadatoshi would of course have received training according to Yagyū precepts.

13. Masuda Tokisada (?–1638), also known as Amakusa Shirō, was a young warrior who was one of the leaders of the revolt at Hara castle. He was captured and beheaded by Tadatoshi's forces when the castle fell in 1638.

14. Rokumaru (1643–1714), later Tsunatoshi.

15. Umehara Kuhei (?–1673).

16. Sakai Tadakiyo (1624–1681) held high rank under several Tokugawa shoguns. He was a man of eccentric temperament who wielded tremendous power. Various stories of the difficulty of cajoling him to accept various policies or opinions have been recorded.

SAIKI KŌI

1. Saiki Kōi (1822–1870) gained a reputation as a *daitsūjin*, "a great man of taste," in the late Edo period. He was the intimate of champion sumo wrestlers, famous actors, *haikai* (*haiku* poetry) masters, and *kyōka* (comic verse) poets, and a generous patron in the gay quarters. One of his beneficiaries who appears in the story, Chikusen, published the book *On* [Gratitude] on Kōi in 1900 (in two volumes). Another friend, Eiki, published Kōi's collected poems, *Kōi Koji hokku*.

2. This was the *tsūshō*, or "ordinary name."

3. Ryūchi was a rich merchant who became a master of *kyōka* poetry (see note 15 below), and a patron of literary men and artists. In the popular book *Umegoyomi* [Plum calendar] published by Tamenaga Shunsui in 1832, Ryūchi is depicted in the character Chiba Tobē.

4. *Yomihon* were popular Edo books which emphasized texts for reading rather than pictures. They were generally printed in five- or six-volume sets on cheap paper, with a frontispiece and several illustrations.

5. *Kakihon* were texts in large characters for chanting narrative poems set to music (*jōruri*).

6. *Ninjōbon* were popular romances depicting the love life of the townsmen toward the end of the Edo period. Tamenaga Shunsui (see note 9 below) was a typical author.

7. Kyōden (1761–1816); his original name was Iwase Denzō. He gained a reputation as a writer of popular comic works called *sharebon* and *kibyōshi* until his punishment in 1791 in the course of the Kansei Reform, after which he devoted himself to topics acceptable to the government.

8. Bakin (1767–1848), whose original name was Takizawa Tokuru, got his start as a disciple of Kyōden; he then switched from *kibyōshi* to *yomihon*. His influence, gained through such works as *Satomi hakkenden* and *Chinsetsu yumiharizuki*, continued into the Meiji period.

9. Tamenaga Shunsui (1790–1843) was originally Echizenya Chōjirō. After working at various occupations, he became the disciple of Shikitei Samba. He achieved fame through his *Umegoyomi* [Plum calendar] in Tempō three (1832), and was styled the originator of the *ninjōbon* genre. He was punished in the Tempō Reform on the ground that his writings were contrary to public morality, and the blocks for his books were burned. He died the following year at the age of fifty-four.

10. Kinsui (1795–1862).

11. Ise Teijō (1717–1784) belonged to a house of hereditary experts in court etiquette. He was a scholar of encyclopedic learning and an authority on ancient practices. His pen name was Ansai.

12. Gerhart Hauptmann (1862–1946), the Nobel Prize winner in 1912, was particularly influential in the development of the modern theater, and the German Naturalist movement.

13. Hermann Sudermann (1857–1928), novelist and dramatist, was another leader in the German Naturalist movement.

14. See note 3. Tobē, modeled after Ryūchi, becomes the hero who sets things right at the end of this story of life in the gay quarters.

15. *Kyōka*, literally "mad poems," were verses in *tanka* form, but likely to be comic; in any case, they did not conform to poetic convention in either content or diction.

16. The chopped straw was mixed with plaster or clay for making walls.

17. Hata Seichi (1763–1823), a noted calligrapher; in his prime he was sought out as a pupil of the Chinese calligrapher Hu Chao-hsin in Nagasaki. Ryūchi appears to have received the second character of his pen name from him.

18. There were four generations of the Yayoi'an school. The dates of the founder are unknown; one theory places his death in Tempō one (1830).

19. *Haikai* is a style of linked verse composition that developed from the medieval linked verse (*renga*) tradition and gained its literary stature through the efforts of the great poet Matsuo Bashō (1644–1694). The *haiku* which he made so popular was originally the opening verse for a *haikai* sequence.

20. The "Three Theaters of Edo." The Nakamura-za was founded in 1704 and went out of business in 1893. The Ichimura-za was founded in 1635 and went out of business in 1930. The Morita-za was founded in 1660 and met its end in the Great Earthquake of 1923.

21. Fukagawa, a gay quarter outside the Yoshiwara, is said to have originated from the time teashops were permitted in front of the gate of the Tomigaoka Hachiman shrine in the Kan'ei era (1624-1644). It began to prosper in the late eighteenth century, and later rivaled the Yoshiwara gay quarter.

22. The Shinagawa gay quarter was known as one of the "four lodging places of Edo." In 1718 it was permitted to have two "waitresses" known as *meshimori* in each place of business; by 1764, the number had grown to five hundred. The courtesans here were reputed to be of higher quality than in the other three places.

23. Naitō Shinjuku was originally a posting station on the highway to the province of Kai, and called the Western Entrance to Edo. A mansion of the Naitō daimyo was erected there. Toward the end of the eighteenth century, it was permitted to employ one hundred fifty *meshimori*.

24. The Hisakimanjiya was one of the two highest-class houses (*ōmise*) in the Yoshiwara gay quarter.

25. Sakuragawa Yoshijirō (1809-1874) was a male geisha described in Tamenaga's *Umegoyomi*. He was a pupil of Zenkō, and became Zenkō the Second.

26. Kenkonbō Ryōsai's name was Umezawa Ryōsuke. He first ran a lending library; later he learned *rakugo* (the recitation of comic stories), and became a *gundanshi*, a reciter of warrior tales set to music.

27. Iwakubo Hokkei (1780-1850), an ukiyoe artist. His original work was as a fish dealer, so his artistic name became Totoya, literally "fish house." He is best known as a pupil of Hokusai, and left many prints, particularly with *kyōka*. He also painted pictures of famous places in Japan, and popular prints.

28. *Katōbushi* was a type of Edo *jōruri*. Katō refers to gay quarters east of the Sumida River, that is, Fukagawa; it was an offshoot of *handayūbushi*, which it replaced in popularity. It was originated by Masumi Katō, and is described as restrained in taste (*shibui*) and beautiful.

29. At the time, many male geisha were also doctors.

30. See notes 6 and 9. Sanro was the pen name given him as a disciple of Samba; he later became the second-generation Somabito. Tamenaga took the name of Shunsui in Bunsei eleven (1828).

31. Ōgai moved into this house on 31 January 1902; it was located at 21 Sendagi-chō.

32. The shrine was located in Nezu Suga-chō in Bunkyō-ku until it burned down in World War II. The deity of this shrine was the guardian god of the sixth shogun, Tokugawa Ienobu, and its festival was one of the three great shrine festivals of Edo (with the Kanda and Sannō shrines).

33. Now in Bunkyō-ku. It was so named because it faces across from Ueno Shinobioka.

34. The temple is located in Sendagi-chō, and is of the Tendai sect.

35. Ogura was the "business name" of Takagi Sahei (1814-1879), whose original name was Tōyama. He served as a shopman for Ogura Shōsuke, who was a banker and purveyor for several *han*. He later opened a pawnbroker business in this location under the sign of Oguraya. Ogura had the *haikai* names of Hisako and Sōa.

36. Ogura did not actually have this pen name. See Doi Shigeyoshi, "Saiki Kōi Shūi," *Kokugo to kokubungaku*, 1946, no. 7.

37. The practice of adding the -ami suffix stemmed from such addition to post-

humous "names in the Buddha" used in the Jōdo and Ji sects, identifying the recipient with Amitābha.

38. The principal seat (*honzan*) of the Jishū sect of Buddhism, whose founder Ippen Shōnin was also called Yūgyō Shōnin. Chief priests of this temple have since been designated by this title. *Yūgyō* implies a wandering or traveling by a preacher, as in the case of Ippen, but there may here be a homonymous relationship with *yūkyō*, merry-making.

39. The dramatist Kawatake Kisui was also known as Furukawa Mokuami (1816–1893).

40. The Gangyōji was a temple of the Jōdo sect.

41. Kita Seiro (1766–1848) was a scholar in the Japanese classics and a *kyōka* master.

42. Matsumoto Tōsai (?–1870), a calligrapher of the Bakumatsu period.

43. Tung Ch'i-ch'ang (1555–1636), a master of calligraphy, painting, and Chinese poetry. He painted in the Southern Sung and Ming styles, and was widely studied by Confucian scholars in the Edo period.

44. Katsuta Moromichi (1791–1858) was also known as a *kyōka* master.

45. Chikusa'an Kawaguchi Sōo, (1761–1811), whose ordinary name was Yamanaka Yōsuke, lived in Asakusa and operated a book business, through which he published many *kyōka* collections.

46. The name currently survives in the Suwa shrine in Asakusa.

47. Itchūbushi takes its name from Miyako Itchū. The school was popular in the Osaka-Kyoto area in the late seventeenth century but declined in the late eighteenth century. The fifth-generation Itchū (1760–1822) refurbished the traditional tunes, and the school came to specialize in the so-called *zashiki-jōruri*, which was popular with the rich merchants in the Kuramae area.

48. Uji Shibun founded the Uji branch in 1849.

49. Ikenohata refers to Shinobazuike, a pond in the south part of Ueno Park. In the Edo period there were mercantile houses on the south edge; this was probably on the west side where city dwellers had cottages for retreat.

50. *Funayado*, literally, boat moorings. These were places along the Sumida River where boats could be hired to go to the Yoshiwara, Fukagawa, or Shinagawa gay quarters. In time such places became teashops for assignations.

51. Uesugi Narinori (1820–1889) was the daimyo of the Yonezawa domain.

52. *Jūninshū*, also known as *mikawase jūningumi*, administered the public funds of the Tokugawa shogunate.

53. Vicinity of present-day Ginza Itchōme in Chūō-ku, Tokyo.

54. *Jorō kai'annai* [Guide to harlotry] was published about the time of the Tempō Reforms. It contained names and locations of brothels, prostitutes, geisha, their fees and similar information.

55. *Hikite chaya* were teahouses where arrangements were made for visits to the brothels they served.

56. Umeya Kakuju (1801–1865), whose ordinary name was Murota Matabē, operated a *machiai*, assignation teahouse, named Umenoya in Nagayagawa-chō.

57. *Toba-e*, "Toba pictures," were comic pictures originated by Toba Sōjō, depicting animals and satirical in intent.

58. Kanagaki Robun (1829–1894), the Meiji-period writer. In his youth Robun

studied *kyōka* and playwriting; he was well established as a writer of *kokkeibon* (comic books) by 1867. His ordinary name was Nozaki Bunzō. He is perhaps best remembered as the author of the satirical Meiji work, *Aguranabe* [The Beefeater].

59. The Kawarasaki-za was one of the "eighteen theaters of the Kantō," and functioned as the "stand-by" theater for the Morita-za. It was founded in 1648, lost its license in 1855, and reopened in 1873 under a different name.

60. The eighth-generation Danjūrō (1823–1854), the eldest son of the seventh Ichikawa Danjūrō. He was famous for several roles, such as that of Kirare Yōsa, in addition to those traditional in his house. He died by suicide in Osaka.

61. Katsu Genzō (1816–1893), whose original name was Yoshimura Shinshichi, became the second Kawatake Shinshichi, and used the pen name of Furukawa Mokuami. See note 39. He is credited with instilling new life into the kabuki theater of the late Edo period with his "new historical pieces" and "late *sewamono*."

62. Famous for its connection with a plot to attack foreigners in 1862. It has survived as the Sagami Hotel.

63. Iwai Shigyoku, whose pen name was Hajitsuan.

64. The Shōdenbushi school of *jōruri*, mainly popular in the Osaka-Kyoto area.

65. *Kowatari tōzan*, striped cloth from Sao Thome (San Tome) in India; later, as *wasan*, it was imitated in Kyoto.

66. The seventh Danjūrō (1791–1859) collected the *jūhachiban*, "eighteen best plays" performed by the Ichikawa family since the first Danjūrō. The copyright is in that family, and the plays can only be performed with its permission. Even when performed, the musicians, singers, and stage attendants must wear the Ichikawa *mon* and the brick-red formal costume of the family. Danjūrō VII was banished from Edo in the Tempō Reforms; he was later pardoned in 1849.

67. Tamenaga Shunsui was summoned to the City Commissioner's Office in Edo toward the end of the twelfth month of 1841; he was sentenced on the tenth of the sixth month of the following year. Two literary works place his death on the thirteenth of the seventh month, but the evidence is not clear. The correct date, the twenty-second of the twelfth month of 1843, is recorded on his grave at the Myōzenji temple in Tsukiji Hongwanji.

68. *Tatezakusha*: writing a play in the Edo period involved a cooperative effort. The chief playwright supervised, but he shared the work of writing with two other playwrights. Six or seven apprentices wrote the less important parts. All were employees of the theater, and were paid less than the actors.

69. Sakurada Jisuke (1802–1877) was a leading playwright in the late Edo and Bakumatsu periods. Most of his plays were revisions, but he wrote many original *jōruri*.

70. Juami Donchō (1769–1848) originally operated a cake business in Kanda. He then studied the Confucian classics and became a lay monk. His pen name was Juami, under which he wrote many *jōruri* and *nagauta*. See Mori Ōgai's "*Juami no tegami*," 1916, included in *Mori Ōgai Zenshū* (Tokyo: Chikumi Shōbō, 1971, vol. 4, pp. 194–230.

71. The earthquake occurred on the second of the tenth month of 1855, and affected the entire Kantō area. It is recorded that 16,000 dwellings were demolished, and more than 6,600 persons' obsequies were conducted at temples.

72. Geisha of the town were distinguished from those who operated only within licensed quarters.

73. The bookstore was located in the original Yoshiwara, as distinct from the "New Yoshiwara."

74. The Umenoya was the assignation teahouse operated by Kōi's *kyōka* master, Kakuju. Hasegawa-cho was in the vicinity of the Suitengu in present-day Chūō-ku, Tokyo; Yorozu-chō was near the Shirokiya in Nihonbashi Itchōme.

75. Seki Izan (1804–1879) was originally a plasterer to the shogunate; he became a typical *haiku* poet of his time after studying with Baishitsu. He wrote under the pen names of Tsukinomoto and Umenomoto.

76. Shin Eiki (1823–1904) studied *haikai* poetry under his father, who was the sixth-generation Kikakudō, and succeeded him as Kikakudō VII. He yielded the name to his pupil Ki'ichi in 1887.

77. The ninth Danjūrō (1838–1903) was the fifth son of the seventh Danjūrō. He entered the Ichimura-za in 1857 and became its head in 1869. He succeeded to the name of Danjūrō when he became head of the Kawarasaki-za after it reopened in Shiba.

78. The Araisoren ("Rough Coast League") took its name from the alternate crest of the house of Danjūrō. *Araisogire* is a piece of woven material of dark blue background on which a design of a carp (*koi*) swimming among waves is woven in gold thread. The crest is described as *ryūmon no koi*, where *ryūmon*, literally "dragon gate," usually refers to a type of heavy white silk.

79. Ichikawa Kodanji (1812–1866).

80. The street still exists in Tokyo.

81. A "street" in the Yoshiwara passing through the center in a northeast-southwest direction, extending from the Great Gate to Kyō-machi; many appointment teahouses were lined up along it.

82. Torigoe Tōsai (1803–1896) was a *haiku* poet, originally from Osaka; he was ranked with Izan and Shunko in his day.

83. Harada Bainen (1825–1905), who was the eighth-generation Setchūan.

84. Ransetsu (1654–1707) was known, with Kikaku, as a principal disciple of Bashō. A *haiku* school stemming from him has persisted to the present.

85. Ritō (1681–1755) succeeded the second Setchūan.

86. Ryōta (1718–1787) became a disciple of Ritō about 1738 and later succeeded as the fourth Setchūan. All of these poets show the influence of Zen.

87. Katsuta Fukutarō (1821–1879) was Uji Shibunsai II. See notes 44 and 48 above. He originally had the pen name of Miyako Wajū.

88. Ishibashi Makuni (?–1855) gained a reputation for his erudition in linguistics; he was a master of a teashop in the Edo City Commissioner's Office area.

89. Segawa Jokō (1806–1881), the third of his name; his ordinary name was Kichibē. Along with Sakurada Jisuke III and Kawatake Shinshichi II (Mokuami), he was ranked as one of the "three famous playwrights" of the Bakumatsu period. He is noted for his *sewamono*, of which a representative work was his *Genyadana*.

90. Matsumoto Kōzan (1784–1866), whose family name was Kamijō, was originally a master of a teahouse in the precincts of Fukagawa Hachiman until he turned it over to a younger brother and lived in a separate house. Matsumoto was the business name. He studied under Tani Bunchō, and painted under the artistic names of Shichisōan and Kame Kōzan.

91. Kanō Ansen (1809–1892) was a disciple of Kanō Isen, and artist by appoint-

ment to the shogunate. During the Meiji period, he was active in educational matters for the government.

92. Shibata Zeshin (1807–1891) was a painter and artist in lacquerware.

93. Torii Kiyomitsu (1832–1892) was the eldest son of Kiyomitsu II, and styled Kiyomitsu III; he was a specialist in kabuki pictures (*shibai-e*).

94. Fukushima Chikaharu (1812–1882), whose ordinary name was Iseya Sahei, had the pen names of Kasho and Amenoya. After studying painting under Takashima Senshun and Ukita Ikkei, he specialized in noh and *kyōgen* pictures, and "popular pictures" in the ukiyoe style.

95. Yomo Umehiko (1822–1896) followed Mokuami as a dramatist, and was styled Takeshiba Hyōzō. He wrote for Kanagaki Robun's publication, called *Iroha Shimbun*, under the pen name of Shibagaki Kibun. He produced *yomihon* and *ninjōbon*, and in the Meiji period became associate editor of the *Kabuki Shimpō*.

96. Ashin'an Zebutsu (1816–1874) had the family name of Saitō, and the ordinary name of Gonuemon. His name as a *haiku* writer was Eiho. He became a lay monk, styling himself Zebutsu. He was a pawnbroker and also banker to various noble houses, and earned a reputation as an exponent of the Omote Senke style of tea ceremony and as a painter and calligrapher.

97. Ōtsuya Koboku (1801–1879), whose ordinary name was Ōtsuya Chūemon, operated a brothel first in Fukagawa, later in the Yoshiwara. He studied *haiku* with Eiki, and wrote under the pen name of Koboku.

98. Kanaya Sennosuke (1823–1907), family name Hashimoto. He acquired the name Chikusen (bamboo immortal) because of his dwarfish stature.

99. Gomeirō Tamasuke (dates unknown) was a *rakugo* performer who became very popular during the period from 1830 to 1855.

100. Shumpūtei Ryūshi (?–1868).

101. Miyako Senkoku (1812–1865), family name Yoshida; a master of Itchūbushi, he lived in Genyadana. Uchū, mentioned below, was his disciple.

102. Genyadana was a quiet residential area located at Nihonbashi Ningyō-chō. Its old name was Shin Izumi-chō, Minamigawa, a small street off Sumiyoshi-chō in Edo. It had been formerly land granted to a medical official named Okamoto Genya Hōin by the Tokugawa shogunate.

103. *Kemban*: responsible for the supervision, appointments, and financial matters, including fees and their collection.

104. Daikokuya Shōroku was the operator of a famous *kemban* in the Yoshiwara. His family name was Kataoka; he wrote under the *haiku* names of Shūmin and Sankyūan. He was fond of noh and *kyōgen*, and was officially censured for holding noh performances with costumes forbidden to townsmen.

105. Hanayagi Jusuke (1821–1903) was the founder of the Hanayagi school of dance in 1849. His name was Hanayagi Yoshijirō.

106. According to the widow of Akutagawa, it was not Komurasaki but Wakamurasaki whom he brought into his home at this time.

107. An alternate nuance of the first two lines:

The knot tied
With the purple first hair-paper.

108. Both were in Owari-chō, and were numbered among the twelve famous eel restaurants in Edo.

109. Twenty-five *ryō*, made up of one hundred one *bu* silver pieces wrapped in a square paper parcel, to make *shiruko* ("bean soup") for a nondrinker.

110. *Akuzuri* were relatively small prints, *surimono*, which memorialized the failings of others, and which were first made about the Tempō era (1830–1844).

111. *Shibaraku no tsurane. Shibaraku* [Just a moment!] is one of the *jūhachiban* kabuki dramas of the Ichikawa family; it is considered the finest example of the *aragoto* style, and was first staged by Danjūrō I in 1697. It is performed as a *kaomise*, "face-showing," performance; as such, the hero Gongorō Kagemasa interrupts the action with this speech, full of references to the Ichikawa family, to tell why his role is important. It is revised for each performance, and appears to be a greeting made up on the spot. It always ends with the same line: "I speak with all respect."

112. *Ten*, or "mark." In *haikai* judging, an excellent verse was singled out by writing the sign pronounced *he* at the right.

113. *Sokuten*: making the mark of judgment on a verse as it is composed and set down.

114. *Suao no kaki no heta*: according to Robun, this should be read *kaki no suao no heta*, thus following a passage in the speech as given by Danjūrō IX: *mijuku mo kaeri mimasu no mon, kaki no suao mo heta no tane*, in which *mimasu no mon* is the three-rice-measure crest of the Ichikawa family, and the persimmon-colored robe is also characteristic of the role as they played it.

115. Tamagiku was skilled in the arts of the tea ceremony, flower arrangement, poetry, and as a samisen player in the Katōbushi style. She died of drink on the twenty-ninth of the third month, 1726. In the seventh month of that year at the time of the *Obon*, "Festival of the Dead," teashops hung up lanterns for her soul's repose. Tamagiku Lanterns thereafter became a yearly observance in the Yoshiwara.

116. *Yūgyō shōnin* designates the head priest of the Ji sect, of which the Nichirinji was one temple (also known as Yūgyōji). There is a homophone here with *yūkyō*, referring to amusement at restaurants and the like, and Asakusa was an entertainment center. See also note 38.

117. This was a first performance that took place in the third month of 1858. The play was written by Mokuami; the character Sukeroku is adapted from one of the Ichikawa family's *jūhachiban*—the *Sukeroku Yukari no Edozakura*.

118. *Bantō shinzō*: implies a younger courtesan who handles details and performs services for an "elder sister" courtesan.

119. Sawamura Gennosuke III (1804–1863) was a younger brother of Sōjūrō V, and a pupil of Danjūrō VIII.

120. *Shōaku*: customers were required by the custom of the gay quarters to be faithful to one courtesan.

121. Kikugorō IV (1808–1860); Baikō was his *haiku* name, which he also read in a variant, Baifu. His earlier names were Nakamura Tatsunosuke, Kachō, Kikugi, and Eisaburō.

122. Kōmei (Chinese: K'ung-ming) was a nickname for Chu-ko Liang, a major hero in the Chinese novel.

123. A cholera epidemic broke out from the end of the seventh month to the end of the ninth month of 1858, and reportedly left 28,000 dead.

124. Shibue Chūsai (1805–1858) was a doctor in the Hirosaki *han*, and a learned scholar in the Confucian classics; he was employed in the latter capacity by the Toku-

gawa shogunate. Ōgai had a great personal interest in Chūsai, and wrote a major historical novel-biography about him in 1916.

125. Ichikawa Beian (1779–1858).

126. Rokudaen Arai Gachō (?–1858), whose ordinary name was Tsuchiya Bunshirō, was a brother master in the Shinyoshiwara district. As a *kyōka* master, he was a judge at poetry contests.

127. Enju Taifu (1822–1858).

128. The historical record has it that beginning in the late eighteenth century certain mistresses, known as *shōbengumi* (the urine gang), used such means to secure their dismissal from their patrons without returning the down payments previously made to them.

129. Later the wife of Hanayagi Jusuke (see note 105).

130. Utagawa Toyokuni: it is not clear whether this refers to the third- or fourth-generation Toyokuni. The former, better known as Kunisada I (1786–1865), was the better artist and collaborated with Hiroshige in triptychs (Kunisada doing the landscapes, Hiroshige the figures); Kunisada II's dates are 1833–1880.

131. The idea of form, or shape (Japanese:*sugata*), of spring is that it is *characteristic* of spring—in this case, part of a New Year's door decoration. The second meaning is that its color is characteristic of the Ichikawa kimono color, particularly in *Shibaraku*. So Kōi is looking back with nostalgia at Danjūrō VII in his prime.

132. Miyagi Gengyo, mentioned earlier as a copyist.

133. The Inamoto moved here due to an extensive fire in the Yoshiwara in 1860.

134. Mori Kien (1807–1885), a medical doctor; his name was Yōchiku, his nickname Tatsuo, his ordinary name was Yōshin. He originally served the Fukuyama *han*, but lost his employment in 1837. From 1854, he was a lecturer in the Shogunate Medical Institute; after the Meiji Restoration he was employed in the Ministries of Education and Finance.

135. This was the eldest son by his original wife, Taki, who took the second son home with her where both died before long. Keijirō became a disciple of Yoshitoshi and a block-print artist.

136. Sarudera was the common name of the Kyōzen'in, a branch temple of Asakusadera. It was located on the east side of Asakusa, on Umamichi ("Horse Road"), so named because patrons traveled on horseback to the Yoshiwara on this road. The temple was moved elsewhere in the Meiji period; its old location corresponds to the corner of Kita Umamichi 7-chōme in Tokyo.

137. Ichikawa Shinsha (1821–1878). Monnosuke VII was a famous *onnagata* of the Edo period; Danjūrō VII was his master. Ichizō (1833–1865) was a principal *onnagata* in the Ansei-Bunkyū eras, 1854–1864. Kyūzō (1836–1911) later had the name of Danzō. Bandō Kakitsu (1844–1903) became famous after his performance of Benten Kozō in 1862; he received the name of Kikugorō V in 1868.

138. The Tempō *sen* was an oval copper coin minted from 1835 until just before the Meiji Restoration. Originally equivalent to one hundred *mon*, in the Meiji period it was worth eight *rin* (0.8 *sen*).

139. Literally, *The Red Light Quarters of Kibun, Revisited*; it is included in *Kinsei jitsuroku zensho*, eighteen volumes, under the title *Tsunokuniya Tobē*.

140. Suzuki Shumpō was Ōgai's stenographer.

141. Kubota Beisen (1852–1906) was an artist and man of letters in the Negishi

School. He introduced a new style of news picture in the *Kokumin Shimbun*, but began to lose his sight about 1897, and had to give up illustrating. He was fond of poetry and drama.

142. *On* was published in 1900; see note 1 above.

143. Niihara Motosaburō was Akutagawa Ryūnosuke's uncle; his wife Ei was Kōi's granddaughter.

144. Ōgai's *Hyaku monogatari* was originally published in *Chūō Kōron* magazine in October 1911.

145. Kajimaya Seibē (1866–1924) became a famous photographer. He was born into a sake-brewing family in Hyōgo, then adopted into a branch of the same family in Tokyo. He lived extravagantly in the boom after the Russo-Japanese War, but was finally disowned because of his profligate ways. He went under the name of Ima Kibun, and continued his photographic activities until he was injured by a magnesium explosion; he then became an expert flute performer for the Noh drama.

146. Tomo was actually the wife of Akutagawa's mother's elder brother, in whose house he was raised after his mother, Fuku, became insane.

147. Miyazaki Toranosuke (dates uncertain) was a self-styled messiah who published his gospel in 1904 and built a church for Sunday services in the Kanda area of Tokyo in 1907. Ōgai also refers to him in the closing paragraph of his postscript to "*Kanzan Jittoku*."

148. "Fragrance" (Japanese: *ka*) is an allusion by Kōi to his own name.

149. Ichiyūsai Kuniyoshi (1797–1862) was Utagawa Kuniyoshi. He was a pupil of Toyokuni I, and had the pen name of Ichiyūsai. His work was influenced by foreign pictures, is characterized by realism, and has been compared with the later French Impressionists.

150. Matsui Kanji (1863–1945) was a scholar of Japanese literature. He graduated from Tokyo University and became professor at the Tokyo University of Science and Literature. He edited the dictionary, *Dainihon kokugo jiten*.

151. The *Inri no ki*, in two volumes, by Ishibashi Makuni, was published in 1844.

GLOSSARY

Bakufu.	The government under the Tokugawa.
Bon.	The Festival of the Dead.
Chō.	A linear measurement; about 120 yards.
Daimyo.	The lord of a manor, or a feudal lord, usually the ruler of the area in which he resided.
Furoshiki.	A large cloth in which objects can be wrapped and carried.
Fusuma.	Sliding panel doors in a traditional Japanese room, usually covered with paper.
Go.	A game similar to checkers.
Haiku.	A seventeen-syllable verse.
Hakama.	A man's ceremonial robe, with divided loose trousers, worn on important occasions.
Han.	The feudal domain of a daimyo.
Hanamichi.	A "flower way"; a stage passage through the audience in the kabuki theatre.
Haori.	The traditional cloak or coat worn by men.
Hatamoto.	A retainer of the shogun.
Junshi.	Ritual suicide to follow one's lord to the grave.
Kana.	The Japanese phonetic alphabet that reproduces the forty-seven syllabic sounds. Writing in *kana* requires no use of the more difficult Chinese characters and was often used in the Tokugawa period by women and children who had not learned the more difficult Chinese ideographs.
Kanmon.	An early Japanese coin; its value is difficult to determine. One modern estimate suggests that one *kanmon* was worth about ten American cents, but in the context of Ōgai's stories, the amount seems far too low.
Kimono.	The traditional long-sleeved robe worn by both Japanese men and women.
Koban.	A gold coin of late medieval Japan.
Koku.	About five bushels (English) of rice. The *koku* was used as a measurement of weight and, during the Tokugawa period, as a measurement of currency, since standard yields for fixed acreage could be calculated.

Koto.	A Japanese stringed instrument that can be compared in sound to a Western harp.
Kyōgen.	A type of comic play especially popular in the Tokugawa period.
Kyōka.	A comic poem.
Mai.	A gold coin used during the Tokugawa period; its value fluctuated considerably.
Noh.	The medieval poetic drama.
Obi.	A sash.
Ri.	A linear measure, about 2½ miles.
Rōnin.	A masterless *samurai.*
Ryō.	A gold coin of considerable value. An exact equivalent in modern currency is impossible to provide.
Sake.	Rice wine.
Samisen.	A three-stringed musical instrument often used to accompany singing.
Sarugaku.	In the Tokugawa period, a comic farce with dancing.
Se.	A square measure of land; about a quarter of an acre.
Seppuku.	Ritual suicide by disembowelment, often referred to in the West as *hara-kiri.* After the person committing suicide cuts into his own abdomen, his Second beheads him.
Sewamono.	A style of Kabuki drama dealing with contemporary life.
Shōgi.	The game of chess.
Shogun.	The highest administrative title of the Bakufu, always held by a member of the Tokugawa family.
Shoji.	Sliding screens covered with translucent white paper to let in light.
Sushi.	A popular and delicious food in Japan consisting of rice cakes topped by raw fish or seaweed.
Tan.	A square measure of land; Ten *se*, or about 2½ acres.
Tatami.	Rice straw matting, in units about 6 by 3 feet and two inches thick, used on the floors of traditional Japanese houses.
Tokonoma.	The alcove in a traditional Japanese room where pictures, flowers, or other artistic objects are hung or placed.
Torii.	The gateway to a Shinto shrine.